A Horse of a Different Color

Dandi Daley Mackall

D0683445

SAINT LOUIS

Horsefeathers

Horsefeathers!

Horse Cents

Horse Whispers in the Air

A Horse of a Different Color

All Scripture quotations are taken from the HOLY BIBLE, NEW INTERNATIONAL VERSION®. NIV®. Copyright © 1973, 1978, 1984 by International Bible Society. Used by permission of Zondervan Publishing House. All rights reserved.

Copyright © 2000 Dandi Daley Mackall
Published by Concordia Publishing House
3558 S. Jefferson Avenue, St. Louis, MO 63118-3968
Manufactured in the United States of America

Library of Congress Cataloging-in-Publication Data

Mackall, Dandi Daley.
   A horse of a different color / Dandi Daley Mackall.
     p. cm.
Summary: When faced with the possible loss of Horsefeathers Stables, Scoop gets caught up in a series of white lies which she later regrets.
   ISBN 0-570-07009-0
   [1. Christian life—Fiction. 2. Truthfulness—Fiction. 3. Horsemanship—Fiction.] I. Title.
   PZ7.M1905 Ho 2000
   [Fic]—dc 21   99-050885

1 2 3 4 5 6 7 8 9 10   09 08 07 06 05 04 03 02 01 00

This book is dedicated to my daughter,

Jen, my fellow writer and rider.

Orphan and I raced along the railroad tracks as if our lives depended on it. I could almost feel the giant Burlington Northern chasing us. But it wasn't—not yet.

Faster, Orphan! I might have said it out loud. Or I may have left the words deep inside where only my horse could hear. She surged into a lightning gallop, scaring up the autumn leaves into tiny tornadoes at her hooves. I tried to let my worries swirl away with the leaves.

Horsefeathers Stable was in trouble. Mr. Snyder at the West Salem Bank had laid it all out for me that morning. *"Scoop,"* he'd said, leaning back in his big leather chair, *"you've made your payments on your grandfather's barn—God rest his soul. But taxes are coming due, and that stable of yours hasn't been assessed in five years. You do realize your improvements on your grandad's barn raise the value of the property. Since the bank holds taxes in escrow, no doubt your payments will increase."*

Mr. Snyder went to our church, and I knew he meant well, but he'd lost me way before escrow. *"Jen handles our money, Mr. Snyder,"* I'd said, my voice cracking.

"Taming problem horses is big business. You're a businesswoman now, Scoop. Act like one! Advertise! Publicize! They say everybody gets 15 minutes of fame in this life. You and Horsefeathers could sure use yours now." He slapped his desk and sat up straight. *"I'm glad we had this little talk."*

I'd walked straight out of Mr. Snyder's bank and run all the way to Horsefeathers and Orphan.

In the distance behind me, the train blew a half-hearted whistle that sounded like pain. Orphan kept galloping close to the rusty tracks that hummed and vibrated. The whistle blew louder. My heart raced with my horse's hoofbeats.

Suddenly Orphan stopped. I lurched forward. With no saddle, I had to grab her mane to stay on. My cheek bumped her arched neck. Pain shot through my jaw.

"Horsefeathers, Orphan!" I shouted, pushing myself back to her broad withers. I glanced over my shoulder at the Burlington's snub-nosed engine peeking around the far bend. We'd never get up enough speed to beat the train now.

"Runaway!"

I turned toward the woods to see who was yelling. But Orphan, the most sensible mare in the world, lunged ahead in a half-rear. My knees gripped her sides to keep me from sliding backwards.

"Runaway!" A man, or boy, burst from the

band of trees and came running toward us, his arms waving.

The train snaked closer and closer. Orphan's muscles quivered. I clutched a fistful of black mane a second before she exploded into a dead run. With nothing but her bitless Indian bridle, I couldn't stop her.

Then I saw what Orphan saw. An Appaloosa galloped out of the woods ahead of us. He was running so fast his legs curled under him. About a paddock's length in front of us, he was headed for the tracks.

I leaned into Orphan's stride. She galloped faster—faster than I'd ever ridden. The Appaloosa ignored us, racing madly at the train as if he meant to fight it. We had to head him off.

The train whistle blew louder. I could see the Burlington—dead on a collision course with the Appaloosa. Orphan and I closed in on the wild horse. A few yards farther and he'd be on the tracks—and in the path of the freight train.

"Whoa!" I yelled, praying Orphan would know I wasn't talking to her. "Whoa!"

The Appaloosa slowed just a bit. The train kept coming. Almost here. The whistle screamed.

Orphan surged in a last effort to block the Appaloosa. The horse slid, his legs stiff out in front of him. With a piercing whinny, he crashed into us, bashing Orphan's side and my knee. Orphan stood her ground, and the train whizzed by in a jumble of clanging and clatter.

Thank You, God! I prayed. I grasped the one good rein on the Appaloosa's bridle. He was tacked up Western—Western saddle, bridle, martingale—everything but a cowboy. "Easy now," I said, trying to check Orphan and the gelding for injuries. My knee stung where his bit had rammed me, but I'd live.

The horse didn't try to get away, although from the looks of his broken bridle rein, he had a habit of breaking loose. Now he stood calmly, his sides heaving in and out. But he was okay. And so were we.

I thanked God again as I watched the train pull away. The caboose wiggled and grew smaller down the track before dolphin-diving over the hill and out of sight.

"Great girl, Orphan," I said, patting her black, sweat-foamed neck. Still gripping the Appy's rein tightly, I leaned back on Orphan's soft rump and tried to make my heart stop pounding like galloping hooves.

Footsteps in the leaves made me jerk to attention.

"Man! Stupid—!" The guy stopped a few feet from us, braced his hands on his knees, and panted. "Crazy—horse!"

It gave me a chance to size him up. He was tall and African American, but not as dark as Maggie. He looked older than Maggie and me—

8

maybe even out of high school. But I'm never as good with people age as I am with horse age. Even after running himself clean out of breath, he had the air of an Andalusian horse, also like Maggie—stylish, well-built, born to show.

He let out his breath slowly. Then he grinned up at me and I saw how good-looking he really was. If he'd been a horse, he'd definitely have been an Andalusian, maybe a dressage champion.

"Sorry," he said. "Are *you* okay?" His voice sounded deep, like an actor's.

"Me?" I asked. "Sure."

"But I thought *your* horse was a runaway too. And you don't have a saddle." He scratched his thick, black hair. He wore a navy blue, bulky sweater over faded blue jeans. My jeans were faded from wearing, with a growing hole in each knee. His jeans looked like the kind you buy faded.

"I always ride Orphan bareback," I said, studying his horse instead of him. The gelding was beautiful, a blanket Appaloosa, roan with white hips and large red spots on his back and rump. He was as colorful as the changing leaves.

"Then you—you ran after my horse like that on purpose?" he asked.

I nodded, wishing I could just rescue the horse and not have to try to talk with his owner. Maybe my people skills were one reason Mr. Snyder didn't have much faith in me running Horsefeathers.

The guy reached his hand up to me. "I'm

Ben. Benson Thayer. Thanks, Kid."

Kid? I'm a freshman in high school. I shook his hand anyway. "Scoop," I said. "Sarah Coop, but everybody calls me Scoop."

"How did you do that?" he asked. "I've never seen anyone ride like that—with or without a saddle."

I shrugged and handed him his horse's rein. The gelding still stood as if none of this concerned him. "You shouldn't tie him with his bridle," I said. "Reins break too easy. Now he'll think he can do it whenever he pleases."

"Tell me about it," he said, patting his horse a little too hard for my liking. "This is the fourth time Diablo's broken loose in the last month. But he never ran off like this. I think he heard that train whistle and got spooked. I'd just gotten him to unload too. I drove over from Hamilton for the Saturday training session at Dalton Stables."

Dalton Stables? No wonder the poor horse wanted to take off, I thought. Reaching over, I stroked the gelding's withers below his short, red mane. "Why do you call him Diablo? He seems calm natured." I liked the horse's wide-set eyes, the shape of his ears. I *didn't* like his name.

Ben shook his head. "He used to be calm—when I got him, about two years ago. Talk about your horse of a different color! I don't know why he turned crazy on me. We're putting him back up for auction if he doesn't straighten out."

I slid off Orphan and stood eye-to-eye with the gelding. From behind me, Orphan nuzzled my neck. It tickled. "Why would you auction him?" I don't like auctions. Owners never know what they're getting—and neither do horses.

"He's run away with me on him a couple of times. And I have to fight him to pick up his feet. He won't hold still for me to brush him anymore. And he's started biting. I won't bore you with the rest."

He yanked the rein, but Diablo didn't move. "Well, thanks for the rescue. I owe you big time, Scoop."

"Not really," I said, hugging Orphan's neck. "Orphan's the one who saw your horse and took out after him. I just went along for the ride."

He stopped pulling against Diablo and studied my mare. "Is she a Morgan?"

I shook my head no. "Half quarter horse, half saddle horse." At least that's what I think. We'd never known for sure about the sire. Orphan's mom had been one of Grandad's prized quarter horses. One night the mare jumped the fence and found Orphan's dad. The "half-breed" colt had set my grandfather against my horse his whole life, until the very end.

Ben glanced at his watch. "Great. I missed the whole session at Daltons." He sighed. "I guess they're not doing Diablo much good anyway. Thanks again, Scoop ... and Orphan." He led Diablo away a few steps, the rein taut in an ongoing tug of war.

"It'll take you all day to lead him that way," I called. "Let me rig your bridle so you can ride." Orphan followed me over to them, and I tied an Indian square knot I'd learned from Grandad. "That ought to do it."

He fingered the knot. "How did you do that?" He stared over at the halter-bridle I'd rigged for Orphan. "That's an Indian bridle, isn't it? Are you Indian?"

I shrugged. My dark hair flopped over my shoulder in a single braid, and my skin always looks tan. I like to imagine that I *am* Indian, an Indian princess maybe. But I have no idea what kind of blood runs in my veins. I'm adopted. And if my adopted parents had known more than they'd told me about my heritage, that information died with them when I was 7.

"Look," I said, changing the subject. "I don't mean to butt in, but if you feel your horse bunch, tense up, that's when you need to turn him. Nobody can stop a runaway if he doesn't want to be stopped. Horses are too strong. Try to read him *before* he takes off. Get him interested in something else. And if he does run out with you, don't try to pull him up—not even with two reins. Turn him. Keep him in circles."

"Okay." He reached for his saddle horn and stuck his left foot in the stirrup to mount.

Diablo sidestepped. Ben's foot slid out. "Whoa, Diablo!" he yelled. He turned to me. "This stupid nag never stands still!"

I took hold of the bit shank. "Go ahead and mount." I scratched his horse's cheek. "Turn your foot toward his head more so the toe doesn't poke his ribs."

Ben turned his foot in the stirrup and pulled himself up. His horse didn't move.

"You could slow down your mount too. Balance your weight on the pommel." I didn't want to sound bossy, but I liked this Appaloosa and didn't want him ending up at auction.

Ben stared down from his saddle at me like I had food on my face. "Scoop ...?" he muttered. "You're not ... no way!"

I had no idea what he was getting at. I looked away. He'd been spending time around Stephen Dalton. Maybe Stephen had told him about me—about the time I got caught shoplifting. It had been almost five years ago, before Dotty and I started up at church. But Stephen never lets me forget it. It would have been just like him to gossip about me to a total stranger.

"I've got to go," I said. "I've got chores to do at Horsefeathers, and—"

"You *are* the one!" he cried. "Of course! Why didn't I put it together sooner? I've been looking for you for weeks!"

You're the teenaged horse whisperer!"

I felt my face heat up. He'd heard of me? Nobody's heard of me. Even some of the kids at school, kids I'd had nine years of classes with, didn't know who I was. They all knew Maggie, but not me.

"I can't believe this!" Ben cried. "Do you live around here?"

I pointed south. "I live over that way." Moving my arm to the east, I added, "And Horsefeathers is just over that ridge, about a mile from Dalton's."

"That's weird," he said. "You're next door to Dalton Stables—and they didn't even know about you? I asked Mr. Dalton and his son ... what's his name?"

"Stephen?" I supplied, knowing that even though Stephen and his dad have the richest stable in our part of the state, they would never send me business.

"That's it!" Ben said. "Stephen Dalton said he'd never heard of a teenaged horse whisperer. I'll have to tell them you're practically neighbors."

I'd love to eavesdrop on that conversation.

Ben's Appaloosa leaned down and nuzzled away a few fallen leaves to get to green grass. I wanted to tell Ben not to let his horse get away with grazing while he had his bridle on. Once a horse gets used to that, he'll spoil every ride by fighting to get his head down to graze.

I was dying to know where he'd heard about me—what he'd heard about me. It was the closest I'd ever come to Mr. Snyder's 15 minutes of fame, and I didn't know how to handle it. I wished I'd thought to bring along an empty jar.

My grandfather used to store air from moments in his life he never wanted to forget. I was trying to carry on his tradition, but so far my days hadn't exactly been memorable—until now. Today's air I could label: *My first 15 minutes of fame.*

My best friend Maggie is used to fame. If she'd been there, she would have known exactly what to say. I swallowed something dry in my throat and gave it a try. "Wanna see Horsefeathers?" I asked, hearing how stupid I sounded. Moving to Orphan's shoulder, I swung myself up on her broad back.

Ben jerked up Diablo's head. A long, brown weed stuck out of the Appy's mouth. Dirt-caked roots hung down like giant spider legs. "Let's giddyup!" Ben said.

Diablo took two steps, then jerked to a standstill. Ben gripped the saddle horn. "Now what, you crazy animal?"

I scanned the field, the clearing, the woods. Whatever had caught the Appy's attention enough to make him stop, I couldn't see it. And if Orphan had seen anything, she didn't show it.

"Go!" Ben kicked the gelding with both stirrups. His horse didn't budge. "He *never* used to do this!" Shaking his rein on Diablo's neck, he stuck out his legs, ready for another kick.

"Wait!" I cried too loud. I urged Orphan up to Diablo's head and looked into the horse's deep brown eyes. The white around the eyeballs would have meant wildness in any other breed. But the white eye circles are normal for Appaloosas. He wasn't scared or wild. And the tiny triangular worry wrinkles above his eyes told me he wanted to please. He was just confused—and from the looks of him, he felt confused a lot.

"What's wrong with him?" Ben asked, sounding frustrated. I couldn't help wondering what he might have done to get Diablo going if I hadn't been around.

"Nothing," I said. *Nothing except you.* "For now, we'll just distract him." I scratched the Appy behind the ears. Then I gently folded the tip of one ear forward and stuck it barely under the bridle. "There, you big baby," I told him. "That won't hurt a bit. We'll just give you something to think about."

Diablo tossed his head, shook it once, then fell into step beside Orphan. A couple of paces and the ear popped back up, but we were already on our way to Horsefeathers.

"Not bad," Ben said.

I wondered. Would Ben tell somebody else about me now? Would he talk about me as "that teenaged horse whisperer"? Most of my life I figured nobody bothered talking about me when I wasn't around. If they did, it probably wasn't good. This felt way different. It kind of felt like fame. I couldn't wait to tell Maggie.

Leaves rustled as we trotted in and out of dappled light. "That's Horsefeathers," I said as the old gray barn came into view. From a distance everything looked pretty good—patches of green pastures with a few horses grazing. I knew that up close Horsefeathers wouldn't impress most people. But horses love it. And that's what Horsefeathers is all about—a home for horses, where a horse can be a horse.

"So there's just the one building?" Ben asked as we rode onto Horsefeathers' grounds. He sounded surprised.

"Yeah," I muttered. I could almost picture Mr. Snyder's frown: *You're a businesswoman, Scoop. Act like one!*

Ben heard of *me*, I told myself. The teenaged horse whisperer—that's what he said. That's why we were here at Horsefeathers. But my stomach

17

felt like botflies were buzzing inside.

I led the way to the front of the barn. Orphan exchanged neighs and nickers with Moby and Cheyenne, who trotted into the paddock to meet us. As we rounded the corner, Maggie Brown strolled out of the barn. Model-slim and model-tall, she looked like the actress she plans on becoming. Her powder blue jeans matched her sweater and boots. Blue ribbons weaved through dozens of tiny braids in her hair.

"Maggie!" I cried. I almost couldn't wait to tell her that this guy from Hamilton had heard about me. I hoped he'd come out and say so himself. "Maggie, this is Ben," I said. "Ben, Maggie." I was pretty sure that's all I'd have to say. I could always count on Maggie Brown to take over with clients, to talk their ears off, to charm their socks off so I could get back to the horses.

But she didn't. Maggie didn't say a word.

"Maggie?" I lowered my voice and raised my eyebrows so she'd know this was a potential client, someone she should hook for Horsefeathers.

But Maggie wasn't looking at me. She hadn't taken her eyes off Ben. She stood frozen to the ground, a goofy, googly grin all over her face.

Now what was our potential client going to think? I peeked nervously at Ben. He had the same dumb expression on *his* face. It was as stupid as love at first sight in a sappy movie.

Tell her! I silently urged Ben. *Tell Maggie*

about how you heard of me—the teenaged horse whisperer. But he was as speechless as Maggie.

Orphan broke the silence with a deep whinny that shook her chest and jiggled me on her back. Diablo craned his neck toward Ham and Sugar, two of our horses, when they answered Orphan from the pasture.

But Maggie and Ben paid no attention.

Something plunked in the dirt at Maggie's heels. She didn't blink. I looked up in time to see a bottle cap sail down from the barn roof onto Maggie's head.

"B.C.! Stop it!" I yelled, knowing that where there's a bottle cap, there's my brother. Our dad used to bring home a pocketful of metal bottle caps from the bottling plant at the end of his shift every night. B.C. had kept almost every one of them. *B.C.* doesn't stand for Benjamin Coop, Junior, like some people think. It stands for *Bottle Cap.*

He waved from the roof, then disappeared. B.C.'s bottle cap must have knocked some sense into Maggie. She swung into action, as if the curtain had just risen on one of her plays. "Welcome to Horsefeathers, Ben. I'm Maggie 37 Blue." She slipped into her fake Southern accent. "Thirty-seven is my mother's lucky number. I was born on March 7—third month, seventh day? Thirty-seven? That explains my middle name."

Ben almost glowed at Maggie. "I think I can guess where the *Blue* comes from."

Maggie changes colors, last names, and accents the way leaves change colors. Only she doesn't just do it in autumn.

From the paddock, Moby sneezed. It sounded like a groan.

"And that beautiful mare there is my Moby," Maggie said.

Ben's horse danced in place, refusing to stand still. "And *this*," Ben said, "is Diablo."

"You call that gorgeous Appaloosa *Diablo*?" Maggie squealed.

"That and a few other names not fit for the presence of a lady."

A lady? And what was I? A gelding? I cleared my throat, hoping to remind Ben who he'd heard about and why he'd come with me to Horsefeathers. "Want me to cool your horse for you so you can get a good look at Horsefeathers?" I asked, when nobody looked my way.

Neither one of them seemed to hear me. Neither one seemed to know I was alive.

I sighed. "And then I'll set fire to the barn and call Channel 7 to tell them the Martians have landed and taken over your brains," I added, hopping off Orphan.

Maggie and Ben didn't even turn around.

So much for my 15 minutes of fame.

3

B.C. burst out of the barn in mid-sentence: "—you been for so long, Scoop? Hi, Orphan—can I help? Can I? Can I help with the horses?" He leaned over and picked up his bottle caps from the dirt, without missing a single beat of his chatter. "Moby likes me and so does Dogless Cat but I don't think Carla's horse does but he might just be scared of bottle caps but Sugar isn't but she wouldn't let me pet her—"

My brother has manic depression, and it was pretty easy to see he was leaning toward the manic part. When he gets hyper like that, he can talk the leaves off the trees. His brown hair stuck out like a stack of straw from under a battered black cowboy hat.

"Where did you get that hat, B.C.?" I asked. He's the smallest kid in his fourth-grade class, which is only one of the reasons he hates school. The hat would have been four sizes too big for him if it hadn't been for his bushy hair.

B.C. touched his hat as if he had on a golden crown. "Maggie 37," he said proudly. "*She* gave it to me." B.C. glanced over at Maggie, and he must have finally noticed Ben. "Who's he? Who is that guy, Scoop?"

At least I could tell B.C. about my speck of fame. A little fame is better than no fame at all. "His name is Ben, B.C., and he's here because he heard all about me—that I gentle horses and figure out what's wrong with problem—"

"Why is he staring at Maggie? Why is he looking goofy at her? I don't like him! Can he go away?" B.C.'s voice rose with every question.

The best thing to do with B.C. when he gets like that is to distract him. Our aunt, Dotty, is better at it than I am, even though she's only lived with B.C. since he was 2, and I've had him my whole life.

"You look good in that black hat," I said. "Maggie loves those hats, doesn't she? She's got a couple in every color, I'll bet. That was awful nice of her to give you that."

B.C. swung his whole body my way and melted into a softness that made me think of a newborn foal, sweet and fragile. "Yeah. She's really nice. Do you think she thinks I'm nice?" He didn't wait for my answer. "She's really pretty too. I like the different funny ways she talks sometimes, like she's not from this country. Don't you? Did you know that she likes chocolate pudding? Just like me—and it's her favorite and my favorite too! And she's coming over to our house for supper!"

"Maggie is?" I asked, glancing back at Ben, who was trying to dismount a moving Diablo. He was caught in mid-dismount, flung over his horse like a saddle bag.

"Yeah, because I asked her and she said she'd love to. She said, 'Why, B.C., Honey, I'd love to come to supper at your house.'" He tried to pull off her southern accent, but he's no actor.

I needed to rescue Ben, but I didn't want to set off B.C. again. "Take Orphan in for me, B.C.," I said, handing him the rope rein. "You can walk her in the paddock to cool her off if you want."

B.C. grabbed the lead out of my hand. "Hey! Scoop! Look at me! Look at me! I'm a cowboy!" He tugged Orphan although she didn't put up a struggle.

Orphan has more patience with B.C. than I do. Watching my black beauty put up with my brother's yanking on her made me want to drop everything and hug my horse.

I've had Orphan longer than I've had B.C. The day my folks adopted me they took me to Grandad's barn, which is now Horsefeathers. Orphan's mother had died giving birth and nobody could get the colt to nurse from the bottle. I was 3 years old and had probably never even seen a horse. But I took the bottle and walked over to her and fed her. About a year later, B.C. was born, surprising everybody but God, Dotty says.

"Just walk her, B.C.!" I hollered. "Don't pull so hard!"

I rescued Ben, who maybe didn't even realize I was holding Diablo's bit shank so he could slide down. He brushed himself off and kept glancing sheepishly at Maggie. "Now you know why I call this horse Diablo—*devil* in Spanish," he said. Ben walked over to Maggie as if she were a magnet—and I was the hired stable boy.

Maggie caught my eye. "Scoop? Would you mind taking care of Ben's beautiful Appaloosa while I show him around Horsefeathers?"

I waved her on and wondered if my name might come up during the tour. I'm not sure if it was because of what Mr. Snyder had said about 15 minutes of fame, but I really wanted Ben to tell Maggie he'd heard of me. *You're the teenaged horse whisperer!*

As I led Diablo through the barn, I heard Maggie and Ben laughing about something. The Appy didn't balk or tense up or show any signs of fear at all. Something was wrong with this horse, but it wasn't his disposition or temperament.

Diablo followed me to the paddock. Off in the corner, I heard Maggie's musical voice, still with the southern drawl, "Moby, tell Ben here how old y'all are." Moby began her stomping count. Since the answer was 23, I figured they'd be at it a while.

Diablo and I fell in behind Orphan and B.C.

for cool down laps. B.C. craned his neck to keep an eye on Maggie and Ben, so it ended up with Orphan leading my brother around the paddock. Diablo plodded along so calmly behind them nobody would ever have guessed that less than an hour ago he'd been a runaway.

Cheyenne, Jen's Paint, trotted in from the back pasture to check us out. So did Carla's horse, Ham, and Sugar, the dapple gray we were boarding. They were like aunts and uncles checking out the new kid in the family.

B.C. got bored and took Orphan into the barn to brush her, but I kept Diablo circling the paddock for a good 10 minutes. Every time we passed Moby, I could hear Maggie and Ben deep in conversation, and from the sound of it, they weren't talking about me. As for Maggie's tour of our stable, it wasn't happening either.

"Good boy, Diablo," I said, louder than I needed to, as we passed Ben and Maggie. They didn't even look up. I strained to hear them, hoping they'd gotten around to mentioning me, or at least Horsefeathers.

"I'm a freshman in high school," Maggie said as I came around again within earshot.

"No way!" Ben said. "Are you kidding? I thought you were a senior for sure. So what are you—15?"

"Mm-hmm," Maggie said. But she wasn't—not yet, not for another five months. I'd turn 15 before Maggie 37 would.

"And you ..." said Maggie, eyeing him like a horse trader at a county auction. "I'd say you're ... 17. Probably one of the older kids in your class ... your junior class."

"You're right," Ben said. "I go to Hamilton High."

And I'd pegged him as being out of high school. Maggie knew people like I knew horses. I stopped Diablo right in front of them and lifted his front lip to look at his teeth. At 5 years, a horse will have a full mouth—all 40 teeth for a male. By studying the incisors, I can usually come close to guessing a horse's age. The little cups or holes in the incisors start disappearing as the teeth wear down with grinding. Diablo's cups were gone, but his incisors hadn't changed shape like they do in older horses.

"Your horse is about 9 years old, right?" I yelled over to them.

They both looked up, amazed to find another human being on the earth besides them.

"What?" Ben asked.

"Your horse?" I said. "He's about 9 years old, isn't he?"

"Turned 9 last month," Ben said. "You Horsefeathers guys are good."

Orphan came out of the side barn door at a trot and broke to a canter as soon as she hit the south pasture. B.C. hadn't brushed her long. I hoped he hadn't been rough with her. The other horses fell to attention as Orphan kicked up her heels and playfully tossed her head. Then she galloped off into the pasture, probably heading for the pond or the mud next to it. She'd earned a good roll in the mud after what she'd been through today.

As I led Diablo into the barn, I heard Maggie weave another of her little white lies: "You should give us a month with your horse, Ben. We've had dozens of problem horses come through Horsefeathers and they all leave happier, healthier horses."

Part of me liked the image Maggie was giving Ben of our stable. At least she'd finally gotten around to talking about Horsefeathers. But the other part of me, the part where God whispers to me if I'm listening, felt uneasy about the exaggeration. I couldn't say anything to Maggie while Ben was there, but I would say something after he left.

Diablo didn't flinch when I took him to the cross-ties at the end of the barn's walkway. We'd rigged up two hooks into the lower ceiling and attached thick straps with metal snaps. That way we could tie a horse from two sides (cross-tie) for grooming or saddling up.

My stomach growled. I looked around for B.C. but didn't see him. He'd probably gone home for lunch. That's what I'd planned to do too. Saturday afternoon was Maggie's shift for chores, and I had tons of homework waiting for me. As soon as Ben left, Maggie could take over at the barn. I didn't mind brushing the Appaloosa first though. I was beginning to feel sorry for him. Underneath all that orneriness was a misunderstood sweetheart.

I clipped the leads to Diablo's halter and secured him in the cross-ties just as Maggie and Ben walked into the barn.

"There she is now, brushing your honey of a horse," said Maggie 37. "Didn't I tell you she was amazing with horses?"

I felt my face heat up and hoped I wasn't blushing. I tried to act like I hadn't heard Maggie bragging on me.

"You better watch out, Scoop," Ben warned, coming within a few feet of Diablo and me. "He hates the cross-ties."

"Don't you worry, Ben Thayer," Maggie crooned. "Your horse is safe with Scoop."

Maggie turned to me, so her back was to Ben. She bit her bottom lip and opened her eyes wide. I knew she was signaling me with some secret meaning, but I had no idea what she meant.

"Scoop," she said, "Ben's thinking about letting you work with Diablo. He has to talk with his mother first, of course."

Good for you, Maggie! I thought. Horsefeathers could use the business. We needed the extra money for the tax thing, and maybe this could get word out in Hamilton.

"I'm going to walk with Ben over to Dalton Stables to get his car and his trailer—and make sure those Daltons don't take advantage of the poor boy." Maggie laughed. Only she could say things like that and get away with it.

"And get something to eat," Ben added. "Don't forget that! I'm starving."

"Yes, yes," Maggie said. "And get a bite to eat."

Great. Which means I don't get to eat and I'm stuck with Maggie's chores. But if we got another client for Horsefeathers, I could live with it. I made myself smile. "Okay."

"You're mighty lucky, Ben," Maggie said, smiling at me. "Our Scoop here has worked her magic on dozens of problem horses all over this county. Our phone rings off the hook with people who want to get their horses into Horsefeathers."

"Well—" I knew I should say something. Dozens of problem horses? Hardly. I could count them on one hand and have a thumb left.

But Ben looked so impressed, even more impressed than he had after I'd rescued his horse from the train, more impressed than when he realized who I was.

Maggie and Ben turned to go. "We'll be back soon, Scoop!" Maggie called over her shoulder.

I waved. *Sorry, God,* I prayed, hearing that whispering inside that said I shouldn't tell white lies either.

But I hadn't told a white lie—not really. Maggie 37 did. I could say something to her about it when they got back. And with any luck, we'd have a new boarder at Horsefeathers. Even Mr. Snyder at the bank would be pleased.

Diablo stood still in the cross-ties while I stroked his neck and back with my bare hands. His skin twitched when I touched him. "That's okay, Boy," I said low, pressing lightly in long, smooth strokes across his shoulders and ribs. "Somebody's been brushing you too rough."

On my way to the tack box to get our softest brush, I glanced out the barn door and saw Maggie and Ben strolling down the lane toward Dalton Stables. They were holding hands.

Maggie couldn't help the fact that she'd already had a lot of guys fall for her. But Ben Thayer was different. For one thing, he was 17. Jen's brother Travis was older too, and Maggie had had a crush on him for as long as I could remember. But at least Travis Zucker had the good sense not to crush back.

"Help! Scoop! Hurry!" B.C. screamed from somewhere inside the barn.

"B.C.?" I yelled. "Where are you?"

A stomping and scuffling came from the end of the barn where Diablo was tied. Diablo whinnied in a high-pitched squeal.

"Scoop!" B.C. shouted, terror in his voice.

I raced down the stallway. The first thing I

saw was the Appaloosa rearing in the cross-ties. And the next thing I saw was my brother, his little arms crossed over his head. He crouched, fear-frozen to the floor—inches from Diablo's pawing hooves.

4

Diablo's front hooves pawed the air over my brother's head.

A prayer shot off inside me before I could speak. As calmly as I could, I said, "Move away, B.C. Now."

He didn't move. His whole body shook. Little sobs came out of him.

"B.C.!" I said too loud. "Step back from the horse."

Diablo's hooves came down. B.C. dropped a rubber curry comb from one hand. The Appaloosa reared up again. Without even thinking, I ran to B.C., swooped him off the ground, and threw him away. He fell backwards over a bale of hay.

"Take it easy now," I said, turning back to Diablo, surprised by the lack of fear in his eyes.

He reared up again, one hoof pawing the air, then landed straight-legged on the barn floor, crashing against the dried wooden planks. I held my arms out from my sides and tried talking to him. But the horse backed away from me, straining against the cross-ties.

"Whoa, Boy," I said. His eyes were calm now. He wasn't terrified. He wasn't dangerous. He just didn't want to be tied up. And he didn't think he had to be.

I knew what was coming. I heard the creak on the rafter above him. The hook in the ceiling jerked, then snapped in two. Diablo kept tugging backwards until the second hook pulled clean out of the rafter.

The horse had what he wanted, his freedom. He pivoted and took off trotting out the closest stall door and into the south pasture, trailing the long leads behind him.

I reached over the hay bale and helped B.C. to his feet. "Are you hurt, B.C.?" I asked, brushing off hay and straw, looking for blood.

"I—I was just trying to brush him," B.C. said, his voice shaking as he tried not to cry.

He wasn't hurt. *Thank You, God,* I prayed from deep inside. "You shouldn't have used the hard brush on him, B.C.," I said.

"It wasn't my fault!" he yelled, taking little gasps of air between his words and wiping tears and snot with the back of his hand. "You pushed me!"

"I didn't mean—" I said.

B.C. reached down and picked up his battered cowboy hat. Then he dashed out of the barn.

"B.C.!" I called. I couldn't run after him. He was all right. But if I didn't get to Diablo, who was lugging around several feet of cross-ties, *he* might not be all right.

I ran to the feed bin, scooped up a handful of oats and tore out of the barn to the pasture. Diablo was grazing peacefully between Cheyenne and Sugar. The pulled lead straps from the cross-ties dangled in the short, autumn grass.

Diablo lifted his head as I walked toward him. He kept munching dying grass and didn't make a move to get away.

"Horsefeathers, Diablo!" I said. "You *are* a horse of a different color. You're as moody as B.C."

He let me walk up to him and unsnap the ties. I hoped we could fix the broken hook. This sure wasn't the time to be buying anything new. I scratched the Appy's ears. He stretched out his head and leaned into me, loving every minute of the attention. I gave him my handful of oats.

Two woodpeckers played a duet on a dying poplar tree in the pasture. The breeze brought a dry smell of leaves burning from far off.

"Now don't you go pulling away again, you hear?" I told him. I wasn't sure why Diablo had broken out of the cross-ties like he had. But I had an idea. He'd gotten away with it too often. He'd developed the break-away habit—breaking his bridle rein that morning and our cross-ties now.

I led the Appaloosa back with just the halter.

Inside I tossed the broken lead-ties into an empty stall and took Diablo into Ham's stall because it had a metal ring on one wall. I didn't tie him to it though—not yet. No way was I going to make his bad habit worse.

Instead, I finger-brushed him, rubbing him down gently with nothing but my hands. On his belly, I felt little tufts of balled hair and several tiny bare patches. Somebody had been using spurs—somebody with a temper. An image of Ben and Diablo flashed into my mind—Ben with his legs out straight, ready to kick hard when Diablo balked.

"Don't you worry, Diablo," I muttered, feeling the anger build inside me. "When your owner gets back here, I have a thing or two I'd like to—"

"Scoop?"

I jumped. Diablo didn't—definitely not the high-strung horse Ben made him out to be.

Carla Buckingham grinned at me over the top of the stall. She signed *Hi, Scoop!* to me in American Sign Language. She'd started teaching me how to sign before she left to visit her mom in Kentucky. Her shiny, black hair turned under slightly at her shoulders, perfect as always. Her mother was divorcing her dad, and although Carla didn't talk much about it, the visit with her mom seemed to have grown her up in some ways. She even looked older. If I hadn't known she was 15, I might have guessed she was a senior in high school. I wondered if Ben would have thought so too.

"Carla!" I exclaimed, embarrassed at what I might have been muttering. I knew Carla couldn't have heard me, even with her hearing aids turned up on high, but she can read lips. "I didn't know you'd be here."

"Caroline's coming for her riding lesson, remember?" she said. It sounded more like *Carerine comin' for 'er righ less, memmer?* Carla says she's never been able to hear speech clearly, so she doesn't say words like most people do. But I almost never have a problem understanding her anymore.

I glanced at her tall leather boots and tan jodhpurs. "I forgot all about Caroline and Sugar," I said. "What a day! Wait 'til I tell you."

"Where's Maggie? I thought she was taking the afternoon chores and you were going to finally get going on your history report." Carla came into the stall with Diablo and me. "Nice horse. Whose is it?"

As quickly as I could, I filled her in on Diablo, Ben, and Maggie. I couldn't resist throwing in the part about Ben having heard of me as the teenaged horse whisperer. But Carla didn't pick up on it.

"Thayer. I think I know that name, Scoop," Carla said. She felt the bare spots on Diablo's side. "You're right though. These sure feel like spur scars. What are you going to do?"

"For openers," I said, "I'm going to give Ben

Thayer a piece of my mind. *He's* the problem, not his horse. I'll bet everything Ben thinks is wrong with this horse is really his own fault."

Buckingham's British Pride, Carla's championship bay American Saddle Horse, stuck his head into his stall and didn't seem too pleased to find another horse in it.

Carla kissed the white star on Ham's forehead. "Don't be jealous now," she said, pressing her cheek to his. They looked like they belonged on the cover of *Equitation Magazine*—the model and the model horse. "I can sneak in a ride on you before Caroline comes for her lesson. Okay?"

Carla kept to the paddock with Ham while I tried a couple of moves on Diablo. I tied him to the metal ring, but kept the lead long enough so that when he backed up, the rope went with him. In the stall, he had nowhere to play his tug-of-war, so he gave up. But when I tried to saddle him, he sidestepped and fussed so much that I stopped. It made me mad. Diablo was a good horse going bad because of a bad rider. I couldn't wait to tell Ben Thayer what I thought.

Caroline arrived for her riding lesson, and still no sign of Maggie and Ben. Caroline is in fourth grade like my brother, B.C., but she looks older. When Caroline and her family first brought her horse to Horsefeathers, they thought they'd have to sell her. But Sugar turned out to be one of our biggest successes, thanks to a couple of tricks my grandad passed on to me. In only a few weeks, the dapple gray mare who wouldn't do anything Caroline wanted her to do, had been transformed from a plug into a gentle but spirited mount.

I untied Diablo and left him in the big box stall so I could help Carla saddle Sugar. Carla made Caroline lunge Sugar before riding. Caroline stood in the middle of the paddock arena and held Sugar's 25-foot lunge line, while her horse walked, trotted, and cantered on voice commands.

Saturday was Maggie's shift for cleaning stalls, but I couldn't wait forever. I started in on Sugar's stall, shoveling out manure and sprinkling fresh straw on the floor. By the time I'd finished with every last stall, Caroline's lesson was over, my back ached, and Maggie still wasn't back.

Finally I heard a loud *Honk! Honk!* It was a good thing Caroline's lesson was over and Carla wasn't still riding Ham because those two horses might have been spooked by the blast. Most people have enough sense not to honk their horns at a stable.

The anger had built up in me so much that my stomach hurt. The hollow hunger I'd had there all afternoon had been replaced by a slow burn. I would try to be as polite as I could, but I intended to warn Ben Thayer in no uncertain terms that he was ruining his Appaloosa.

I'd set down the pitchfork, but now I picked it up and leaned against it—just a reminder to

Maggie that *she* should have been the one cleaning stalls today.

Maggie came running up to me, her eyes wide and her smile wider. "Scoop!"

I kept my frown in place.

"I'm sorry, Scoop. I know I was supposed to do the stalls. I'll do them tomorrow, okay? Don't look so mad." She begged with her pitiful, poor puppy look.

It's almost impossible to stay mad at Maggie, and I felt myself softening. "It's not just you, Maggie," I said. "It's Ben and his horse. Maggie, he's ruining that Appaloosa. It makes me so mad when I think about how he must have treated—"

"Oh no, I think you're wrong, Scoop! Ben's not like that." She glanced over her shoulder when another car door slammed outside. Her voice dropped to a whisper. "Don't say anything to make him angry, Scoop. You don't know what's happened!"

"I don't care either, Maggie," I insisted.

Ben strode into the barn. "Maggie, did you tell her yet?"

"Not yet!" she shouted back. Turning back to me, she pleaded with her eyes for cooperation. "Ben, you tell her. It's your news!"

Ben walked up to Maggie and put his arm around her shoulder. Then he flashed his big smile at me. "Sarah Coop, horse whisperer, I'm about to make you famous!"

Famous? I looked to Maggie, but she was making eyes at Ben, who was staring down at her. "What do you mean?" I asked.

"Well!" Maggie began dramatically. "We were halfway through lunch before I realized just who we're dealing with."

"Your friend here was quite a hit with my friends at lunch," Ben said. The way he said it, I knew he was saying it for Maggie's sake—not mine.

"Benson Thayer!" Maggie said in her best British accent. "Blimey, young fellow, will you stop with that smooth tongue of yours?" She turned to me. "Ben drove us to Hamilton and we ate lunch where his friends hang out. They're so cool, Scoop!"

I couldn't have cared less about Ben's friends. And what did all this have to do with making *me* famous—not that I necessarily cared about that either.

"They all thought Maggie was a senior," Ben said. They laughed together, already a secret joke between them. "Maggie, remember the look on Dave's face? He believed us. I mean, he fell for it all."

"Ben told Dave I was a senior at Kennsington High School—" she tried to explain, but kept breaking off to laugh with Ben. "When we first walked in, Ben introduced me as a foreign exchange student from London!"

I tried to smile, but none of it struck me as funny. If it didn't get better fast, I was going to unload on Ben no matter what Maggie said about it.

"Then Maggie started talking with this perfect British accent," Ben said. "And they all believed she was really from England!"

"They really did, Scoop," Maggie said, without even glancing at me.

It was like the two of them couldn't take their eyes off each other. I felt like puking.

"I finally burst out laughing," Maggie continued. "And we told them I wasn't English."

"Then Olson had a great idea," Ben said. "I don't know why I didn't think of it myself!"

Okay. Finally. I didn't care if it was Ben's idea or this Olson character's—just as long as Horsefeathers got something out of it. I leaned the pitchfork against the wall and waited.

Ben turned to me to explain. "Hamilton Community Theater is putting on a performance of *Anything for Love*. It's a British comedy, but with some great, serious moments. And there's one part in the play, one female role, that's perfect for Maggie! It's not a huge role, but it's important to the play—a British airline stewardess."

"Uh huh," I said, already fighting off the surge of disappointment. *This* was how the great Ben Thayer planned to make me famous? By getting Maggie a part in his play?

"But what about Gail, the girl who has the part?" Maggie asked. Maggie glanced so quickly at me I didn't have a chance to give her my secret look to let her know I had just about had it with Ben and his cool friends. "Gail was at lunch too," Maggie explained, as if I needed an entire roster of the luncheon guests.

"Oh, Gail won't mind," Ben assured her. "She knows she's lousy with the accent. She could be the script prompter or the understudy. I'll take you to rehearsal tonight and let our director decide for himself."

Diablo neighed from the stall, reminding me what I'd resolved to tell Ben. "That's great, Maggie," I said without much feeling behind it. "I'm real happy about your fame and all. But I need to talk to Ben about his horse."

Maggie slapped her forehead. "Listen to me rattle on!" she said. "That's not what we meant about making *you* famous, Scoop!"

"It's not?" I asked.

"Of course not!" Maggie laughed. "Ben not

only is an actor himself, but he's the son of an actress! Ben's mother is Della! Can you believe it, Scoop? *THE Della!* Here you were saving a celebrity's horse and didn't even know!"

Della? Della. The name tickled something way back in my brain, but I couldn't come up with the connection. Finally I gave up and shrugged.

"Scoop!" Maggie scolded. She apologized to Ben for me. "The girl spends all her time with horses, Ben. You'll just have to excuse her." Maggie turned back to me and raised her eyebrows. "Della! As in *Della's Folks*, Scoop! You know that show. Your aunt loves *Della's Folks!* Don't you remember when Stephen Dalton and his dad tried to get on the show with Dalton Stables?"

Then it clicked. *Della's Folks.* It was one of the few television programs Dotty ever watched. Della traveled across the state to find interesting people and places. Sometimes she took viewers to a famous restaurant. Other times she covered special events or fairs. I'd never seen the show, but Dotty had told me about a bunch of the episodes.

"Your mother is *that* Della?" I asked.

"Guilty," Ben said, but he looked pretty proud of it.

"Horsefeathers!" I said.

Ben burst out laughing. "That's great! You ought to say that on the air."

"On—on the air?" I asked.

"That's what I've been trying to tell you, Scoop!" Maggie cried. "You're going to be a Della's Folk!"

Me? On TV? Now I knew what they meant by famous. I *would* be famous if I got on that show—at least in our state I would.

"I know what you're thinking," Maggie said. "You don't want to be famous. What would you say with the cameras rolling on you, live on the air with Della?"

That isn't exactly what I was thinking. Actually I was wondering what different people I know would think about it. I knew a guy named Jake who lived in Kennsington. What if he turned on TV one day and saw me? And the kids at my own school? They wouldn't believe it. Me on *Della's Folks*. Now that would be a day's air worth collecting.

"Don't worry about performing for the show," Ben said. "You'll have Maggie, a born actress to help, right? And it only lasts for 15 minutes."

"Think about what that kind of publicity would do for Horsefeathers!" Maggie cried. "We'd have more business than we'd know what to do with!"

It was exactly what Mr. Snyder said we needed. Publicity. And exactly 15 minutes of fame! "When?" I asked.

Ben chuckled. "Well, don't go too fast there.

We didn't get to talk very long to my mother."

"You met her?" I asked Maggie. "You got to meet Della already?"

"Scoop, it was so amazing!" Maggie said. "Ben took me right on the set of Channel 7 News!" Maggie hopped to the same bale of hay I'd thrown B.C. to earlier. She stood on it and acted like she was onstage. "Good afternoon! I'm Della, and this is Channel 7 News. A fire broke out in Ogden County." Maggie broke off her newscaster impersonation. "She was wonderful! The whole thing is wonderful! I never thought I wanted to work on television—just stage and the silver screen. But I've changed my mind."

I picked up a piece of straw just to have something to twist in my hands. "So what did she say?" I asked. "I mean, about me, about Horsefeathers, and all?"

"First, we just told her about how you stopped Diablo this morning," Ben said, holding Maggie's waist and lifting her off the hay bale.

"And then Ben asked his mother if he could leave his horse with us at Horsefeathers." Maggie smiled at Ben as he slowly let go of her waist. "She was all ready to sell Diablo, believe me. But I told her you would work miracles and cure that horse in no time."

"Maggie!" I said. "You shouldn't make those kinds of promises. Diablo—" Somehow this didn't seem like the right time to set Ben straight about his horse. "—Diablo may take time to come around. He's got a lot of things to work through, you know."

"Well, Mom kind of liked the idea of a teenaged horse whisperer, especially doing a show that follows our own horse." He took Maggie's hand, and they both sat down on the hay bale. "Anyway, she went back on the air, and we had to leave. But I'm pretty sure she's hooked."

A thousand questions bumped against each other in my brain. "When—when would we do it?"

"I definitely think it should be soon!" Maggie said. "Horsefeathers is so beautiful in the fall. We don't want them filming us in the winter when everything's all bare and bleak."

"But Maggie," I said. "What if I can't get Diablo to come around that fast?"

"Of course you can!" Maggie said, glancing nervously at Ben. "You'll just have to, Scoop. That's all there is to it. Besides, they don't call you the Teenaged Horse Whisperer for nothing!"

6

Maggie and Ben seemed so sure of the whole setup. "But Maggie," I protested, "getting Diablo to behave might take me weeks or months even."

"Nonsense, Scoop!" Maggie insisted. "Don't worry about fixing Diablo in time. You cured Sugar faster than that! And that horse was much worse than Ben's."

Another white lie. Sugar hadn't been anything like Diablo. She'd been a plug—and only because she was bored with stable life. Diablo had a ton of bad habits. And habits always take a long time to break. I started to say something to Maggie, but Ben was whispering something in her ear. She giggled and tapped his arm lightly. Suddenly I felt as out of place as a Clydesdale in a dressage class.

I couldn't get away from Maggie and Ben fast enough. I felt all mixed up inside. A few minutes earlier, I'd been ready to chew Ben Thayer out for the way he'd handled his horse. And now I was going to be on his mother's TV show. I wanted to have Maggie by herself so I could talk it out with her. But that wasn't possible, not with Ben there.

Without a speck of trouble, I moved the Appaloosa into the corner box stall. It opened to pastures 24 hours a day, like all the stalls at Horsefeathers. But it was the largest stall, in case Diablo wasn't used to the kind of freedom horses get at our stable.

"Scoop!" Maggie called. "Come and listen to this. I was just about to tell Ben my theory about his horse."

I didn't answer. Maggie's theory? Since when did she come up with the horse theories? I knew she was just trying to impress Ben. I pulled down some hay into Diablo's trough.

"Scoop?" Maggie called louder. "Did you hear me?"

"I'm coming!" I yelled. I yanked down another armload of hay to keep Diablo busy. He started right in on it, as if he already felt at home.

Maggie and Ben were still sitting together on the hay bale. Dogless Cat, our tiger-gold barn cat, had curled up on Maggie's lap.

"I was telling Ben that something traumatic probably happened to scare his horse. Doesn't that make sense? Something scared him, and now he doesn't trust people?"

Maggie didn't get the nod of approval she must have been expecting from me. I was almost positive that she was wrong. Trauma wasn't Diablo's problem. Ben was.

She turned to Ben. "Did anything scary happen to your horse?"

I could tell Ben wanted to give her the answer she was looking for. But he shrugged. "I don't know of anything, Maggie. But maybe it did before I got him."

"That could be," Maggie said. "Because you said he started changing right after you brought him home from the auction, right? You called him 'a horse of a different color.'"

Maggie suddenly stood up and ran over to me. "Scoop! Don't you see? It's just like what happened to You-Know-Who!"

I shrugged at her. I had no idea what or who she was talking about. Ben seemed to be staring at my old barn boots. I looked down at them, and saw they were covered with manure. I hoped it wasn't something he'd tell his mother about.

Maggie groaned, frustrated at me for not getting her point. She turned to Ben. "Ben, Scoop and I have this friend who had a major trauma a while back. I mean *major*."

Now I knew where she was going. But why? Why was she doing this? Carla Buckingham didn't have anything to do with Diablo ... or with Ben Thayer.

Maggie kept going. "So this girl found out something terrible about her parents. I mean, really awful. And she changed totally!" Maggie glanced at me. "Remember, Scoop? Ray even said she was like a different person. See what I'm getting at?"

"Who was it?" Ben asked. "Maybe I know her."

"That's not important," Maggie said.

Thank goodness, I thought. At least Maggie hadn't totally lost her senses over this guy.

"Come on, Maggie," he said, so smooth he could have softened new leather. "I won't tell anyone. I'm just trying to understand what you're saying." Ben walked over to Maggie and pressed one arm against the wall Maggie was leaning back on.

"Well," Maggie said. He touched her hand, and her eyelashes fluttered. "It's Carla Buckingham. They just moved here this past summer."

"Buckingham?" Ben repeated. "Her dad's a big shot lawyer, right? I heard my mom talking about him. Her station wanted to hire Buckingham to sue somebody over production rights, but he charged too much. So what was the trauma that changed Carla Buckingham?"

"I don't know if I should say, Ben," Maggie said, pulling at one of her blue hair ribbons.

Of course you shouldn't say, Maggie! I thought.

I walked away to the tack box and put in the broken cross-ties. I didn't like the way things were going.

"Come on, Maggie," Ben coaxed. "Don't you trust me?"

50

"It's not that, Ben," Maggie said. Listening to her, I couldn't tell if Maggie was as gone on this guy as she seemed to be, or if she was being actress Maggie, making sure we kept our spot on *Della's Folks*.

"Come on," Ben coaxed, like he was teasing. "Tell Benson all about it. Our relationship should be built on trust. Trust me."

Relationship? Horsefeathers!

"Oh," Maggie said, and I could tell she was caving in. "All right, but don't you dare tell a single soul, Ben Thayer! Carla Buckingham's parents are getting a divorce. They had this huge blow-up that Carla overheard and—"

I heard a shuffling inside the barn door and looked up to see Carla Buckingham standing in the stallway. "Carla!" I said, loud enough for Maggie to hear me and stop chattering. "I thought you went home already."

Carla shook her head no. Her hair was tucked behind one ear, and I could see she had her hearing aids in. Still, maybe they weren't turned up enough to hear Maggie. I hoped she hadn't been close enough to read Maggie's lips either.

"Carla!" Maggie ran over and gave her a hug. "I've hardly seen you since you got back from Kentucky! Are you catching up on homework?"

Carla shrugged.

"You probably aren't any farther behind than I am," Maggie said, losing her accent. "I have a killer world cultures report due next week!"

"We all do, Maggie," I said.

Nobody said anything for an awkward minute. Then Ben walked up and stood behind Maggie. He cleared his throat.

Maggie put her hand on his arm, as if she were afraid he'd try to leave. Fat chance. "Carla," Maggie said, "this is Ben Thayer. He's going to board his horse at Horsefeathers for a while. Ben, Carla Buckingham. She's our expert in English Equitation around here." Maggie was talking too fast. I knew she was sweating whether Carla had overheard her or not.

"*I—am—pleased—to—meet—you,*" Ben yelled, shooting each syllable into Carla's face. He pointed to himself, like Tarzan. "*Ben.*"

Carla nodded, but her face grew red.

"Carla is an excellent rider ... and teacher too," Maggie babbled. "She wins in horse shows all over the United States. And here at Horsefeathers, she gives all of the English riding lessons to students of all ages."

"All *one* of our students," Carla said softly.

"Allen who?" Ben asked. He frowned and leaned in closer, as if he were the one hard of hearing.

Carla's speech *was* worse than usual, like it gets when she's excited or nervous or angry. I couldn't read which emotion it was though. Her face stayed expressionless. "I need to get home and start studying. Ray's coming over." She nodded slightly and turned to leave.

"What did she say?" Ben asked Maggie. "I couldn't understand anything she said."

I walked Carla out to her bike. "At least we get to board his horse here for a while," I said.

Carla picked her bike up from the pile of leaves at the base of the oak tree. "I guess we can use the business," she said, not sounding too sure.

"Plus, I think he's going to get us some good publicity." I told her all about *Della's Folks*, but she'd never heard of the show.

Carla was looking past me, over my shoulder. I turned to look too. Maggie and Ben were headed toward Ben's car, which was still hooked up to his trailer. Ben opened his driver's side door and Maggie climbed in, waving at us before she slid over.

"That guy, Ben, is he a friend of Maggie's?" Carla asked.

"He is now," I whispered. I waved at them as they drove off, the empty trailer bouncing down the lane.

Carla rode off on her bike, and I finished the evening chores, the chores Maggie should have done. But if she could pull off this publicity thing with Ben's mom, I'd do her chores for a month without complaining.

The sun was setting as I hugged Orphan good-bye. Something inside me felt wrong, but I couldn't quite tell what. Maybe I still felt bad about what Carla might have overheard. But maybe she didn't hear anything. I hadn't had a chance to call Maggie on her white lies, but at least I hadn't spread any of my own.

I kissed Orphan's cheek and took off for home. I could hardly wait to tell Dotty that her niece was about to become famous.

7

In the lane, the tips of maple leaves reached down at me from both sides, like red fingernails. Geese honked deep and musical from the purple sky. Remembering the shock of Ben Thayer's car horn honking, I wondered how the word *honk* could possibly describe both sounds.

I thought I'd be late to supper, but when I got to our lawn, Dotty's old blue Chevy was just pulling up the gravel driveway.

I waved and yelled. "Dotty! Wait 'til you hear!" She was at least one person I could count on to be happy for me in my 15 minutes of fame on *Della's Folks.* Cupping my hands to my mouth, I yelled again, but she didn't turn around. Maybe her car radio had started working again. Dotty loves Christian radio.

The car jerked to a stop. The door opened, and I saw my aunt unfold from the front seat. She still had on her orange Hy-Klas employee apron. With one hand holding her lower back, she reached into the car and came out with an armful of plastic grocery bags.

"Dotty!" I hollered, jogging up to the car.

"Hey, Scoop!" she called, brightening. She's shorter than I am, not much over five feet. I used to think she'd have been a quarter horse if she'd been a horse. But maybe she'd have been a Dartmoor Pony. They only grow to 12 ½ hands high, a little over four feet, but you can count on them to carry you anywhere. They're sensible and sure-footed—like my aunt.

I reached into the backseat and got the rest of the groceries, including a big bottle of grape juice. As I picked it up off the floor, an image of Grandad flashed into my head—Grandad dumping out the pickle jars onto the kitchen floor. Back then, we had no idea what he was doing, besides making a mess for me to clean up after. We thought his obsession with empty glass jars was part of his Alzheimer's disease. But all the time, he had just been making room in those jars for the air of his life—like from the day Pearl Harbor was bombed or the day the war ended. He'd even saved air from the day my folks had adopted me.

Dotty put a hand on my shoulder. "Your grandaddy would have had hisself a time with that purple juice, wouldn't he!" Dotty is so in tune with God that sometimes I think God lets her see into my mind.

I swallowed to keep the lump in the back of my throat. "And I'd have been the one to clean it up," I said, moving toward the door.

"Hey! Where's Maggie?" B.C. hollered down at us from his perch on the roof.

Dotty shielded her eyes from what was left of the sunset. "Well, hey to you too, B.C.! Ain't you coming down for supper?"

My brother disappeared for a few seconds. We heard the thud on the back porch as he jumped down. Then he appeared by the kitchen door in time to open it for Dotty.

Dotty passed through to the kitchen. But when I tried to follow her, B.C. slammed the screen door shut.

"B.C.!" I scolded, juggling to keep hold of the grape juice. "You'll make me drop it. Move!"

"Where is she? Where's Maggie? Why isn't she with you? Did you forget to wait for her? Did you leave her there at Horsefeathers?" He folded his arms and leaned against the door so I couldn't go inside.

"How should I know where Maggie is, B.C.? Get out of my way!"

B.C. leaned forward and peered down the lane. I slid in behind him and dumped the groceries on the kitchen counter.

"Well, lookee here what B.C. done!" Dotty said.

I turned toward the kitchen table. B.C. had set out four plates, as close to matching as we had. In the center of the table were three or four colorful leaves, probably B.C.'s idea of a centerpiece.

B.C. peered in at us through the screen, forcing a face-shaped bubble in it. "Don't sit there, where the big napkin is! That's Maggie's seat! And *I'm* sitting next to her!" He tore off and out of sight.

"You expecting Maggie?" Dotty asked.

"*I'm* not," I said. "But I guess B.C. is." I started putting away groceries. "He asked Maggie to come to supper. She didn't say anything about it to me though." I kept out the cold cuts, hidden in slick, white paper, and the Styrofoam containers marked with black Magic Markers. "Guess what, Dotty?" I kind of wanted to wait until we were sitting down at the table to tell her about the television thing, but it wasn't easy to keep it in.

Dotty's mind must have been somewhere else. "I hope that girl can make it. B.C.'s likely to get hisself all riled if he's counting on it. Besides, I ain't seen Maggie since I don't know when." Dotty's square-toed, black shoes squeaked on the gray linoleum as she set out a loaf of day-old bread. She sighed. "B.C.'s right fond of that little gal."

"Well, join the club," I muttered, stuffing the empty white bag with all the other bags in the crack between the counter and the fridge. Funny thing was, B.C. actually *could* join the club—the Maggie 37 Fan Club. A bunch of fifth- and sixth-grade boys started it when we were in seventh grade. They called themselves *The Maggie-Teers*.

They claimed to have 37 members, but I don't know if they did or not.

"Want me to set out the plastic forks?" I asked. They were in the bottom of the last grocery bag.

"Hmm? Yeah. Thanks, Scoop. Mr. Ford, he was fixing to throw them perfectly good forks away 'cause they been sitting out a spell." She walked toward the refrigerator, changed her mind, ran water in the sink, then opened a cupboard.

She was way too distracted for my news. I'd have to wait until we sat down and she could concentrate on it. "Why are you so late?" I asked, setting out the plasticware.

"Oh that," she said. "New girl. A stocker. I kept getting cans through checkout without prices. I had to run price checks on everything. Only the poor little gal didn't know where nothing was. So it was easier to run check myself."

"I can't believe Mr. Ford hired new help," I said.

"I think she's kin to Mr. Ford's wife or sister-in-law out of Hamilton. Her name's Gail. Gail Gayle."

"Gail Gayle?" I repeated. That was worse than Scoop Coop.

The front door slammed. I walked to the living room to see who it was. Maybe B.C. had been right about Maggie coming to supper after all.

It was darker in the living room. Something there smelled like rust. I turned on the lamp next to what had been Grandad's rocker. In the semi-dark, the gold and brown flecked shag carpet didn't look quite so old. But everything else did—the yellowed window shades, the rain-spotted ceiling, the green vinyl recliner with patches of gray duct tape holding it together.

"She's not here!" B.C. whined. He plopped down in Grandad's old rocking chair and rocked back and forth, a hundred times faster than Grandad had ever rocked. "When will she be here?"

"I don't know, B.C.," I said. But my mind was somewhere else just like Dotty's seemed to be. I wondered if she missed Grandad more than she let on too.

Our house no longer smelled like Grandad. Little by little, his smell had faded away, the way Grandad had faded with his Alzheimer's disease. The day after the funeral, I couldn't smell him when I walked in the front door. For weeks before he died, I'd griped about how our house smelled *old*, old like Grandad. Now I missed that smell.

Even in his old room, Grandad's smell had faded into the same wet, musty smell the rest of the house had in autumn. For days Grandad's robe still hung on the back of the bathroom door. I knew Dotty didn't want to take it down any more than I did, although neither of us mentioned it. Neither of us talked about it when it disappeared one Sunday either. Grandad hadn't owned many personal things—except for his air jars. But Dotty had taken the few things he had out of the room so B.C. could have it back as his own bedroom.

But B.C. still hadn't moved in. I was supposed to help him, but I'd been way too busy.

"Supper!" Dotty hollered from the kitchen.

I headed to the kitchen, but B.C. didn't stop rocking. "Come on, B.C.," I urged.

"We can't start yet!" B.C. said. "We have to wait for Maggie."

"Suit yourself," I said. "But I saw chocolate pudding."

B.C. kept rocking.

Dotty muttered something when I came into the kitchen, and it sounded like *vitamins*.

"Did you say something, Dotty?" I asked. Her trouser stockings bagged down to her ankles. They were the kind that should have stayed up at the knee, but Dotty's calves proved too big a task for them.

"Hmmm?" she said, putting ice water on the table. "Oh, I was just talking to Jesus about the new girl at the Hy-Klas. She gets tuckered out so quick, I wondered if she might need vitamins. And help her get a good night's sleep. Where's B.C.?" Dotty asked, lowering herself to her chair at the table.

I knew she'd asked Jesus about the night's sleep and me about B.C. "Waiting for Maggie," I answered, taking the seat next to Dotty and leaving the stool for B.C.

"Should we wait supper on her?" Dotty asked. "It's late already."

"I'm pretty sure she won't show," I said. "She met this guy at Horsefeathers. That's part of what I have to tell you."

"I hope her mama knows where that girl is at this hour," Dotty said, glancing out the window at the darkness, as if she might find Ben and Maggie in it. "Lord, look after Maggie and that fella." My aunt has such a friendly way of talking to God that it doesn't seem weird when she carries on her three-way conversations with me. "B.C.!" she shouted.

"Anyway, the guy's going to board his horse with us," I said, opening the containers on the table and setting the lids to one side.

"Well, I knew the Lord would look after Horsefeathers," Dotty said. "Thank You, Lord, for bringing Scoop this here new horse." Dotty glanced to heaven and then sneezed. "B.C.!" she yelled again.

"Bless you," I said.

"Thank you, Honey. He sure does!" She shook the ketchup bottle and set it down again. Scooting her chair away from the table, she pushed herself up. The chair groaned. Dotty shut her eyes and shook her head slightly, putting one hand on the table to steady herself.

"Are you okay?" I asked.

"Guess I'm more tuckered out than I reckoned," she said, laughing a little. "I'll fetch B.C."

I'm not sure how she did it, but Dotty came back with my brother in 30 seconds flat. The three of us said grace. B.C. and I peeked at the end of the prayer, when Dotty was talking to God about the new girl at work. I caught him squinting at the back door, like he expected Maggie to burst in with the *Amen*.

B.C. just picked at his food during supper—pork 'n' beans and baloney, with three-bean salad. "Don't eat it all!" he cried when I reached for seconds on the salad. "Maggie won't have anything to eat. And we have to save the pudding too!"

Dotty chattered about the Hy-Klas, where she's worked at checkout ever since she showed up at our house the night our folks were killed. I woke up that morning to find her in the kitchen burning toast. She was there the next morning and the next—although she did switch from toast to cereal. And she's lived with us ever since.

When B.C. and I didn't join in on her conversation or ask any questions about Gail Gayle, Dotty changed the subject. "B.C.," she said, "I love this here pretty table decoration you done for us."

"I did it for Maggie 37," he said.

"Well, I tell you what. Them maple leaves is as red as God's own sunset." Dotty picked up a huge, red maple leaf and a yellow leaf from a gingko tree. She squinted so hard at them, her thick, brown glasses rose higher on her nose. "What do you reckon Adam and Eve thought the first time they seen leaves like this?"

I'd never even thought about it. B.C. dropped his fork and leaned across the table to get a better look at the leaf, as if he'd never seen a leaf before.

Dotty twirled the maple stem between her fingers. "I'll betcha Eve screamed with *de*-light. Maybe her and Adam figured God was giving them a present."

B.C. reached across the table, getting his sleeve in the three-bean salad. He fingered the brown edge of one of the leaf points. My brother usually reminds me of a Shetland pony, feisty and stubborn. But manic depression could switch him into a sensitive Thoroughbred faster than the finish line. I saw it coming in the pupils of his eyes.

"Do you think ..." B.C. swallowed—beans or tears. "Do you think Adam and Eve worried when they saw the leaves turn brown after they left the garden? What would Eve think when the first leaf dried up no matter how much they watered it, and it fell off the tree to the ground?" B.C.'s voice rose louder, with a kind of despair creeping in, as if he were watching it happen and couldn't do anything to help. That's how I felt watching B.C. turn now.

"Adam had taken care of the trees," B.C. cried. "He spent all that time as the gardener. That's what you said, Dotty! I'll bet he tried to make it alive again. Maybe they both tried to stick the leaf back on the tree! And then it started happening everywhere."

"B.C.?" Dotty said softly. "Honey?"

But B.C. was watching his own secret drama in the veins of that maple leaf. "And then all the trees lost all their leaves! They were nothing but bare branches—after looking so pretty. I'll bet Eve cried and cried and cried."

Dotty pried B.C.'s fingers loose from the leaf. The red, paper-thin part ripped away from the stem and she slid the pieces to her lap out of sight.

B.C. left the table without a word, upsetting his glass of grape juice and tipping over his stool. Thick, purple juice dripped like blood down to the linoleum.

Such a dark cloud stayed over the kitchen, even after B.C. left, that somehow I couldn't bring my good news into it. As I soaked up the grape juice with our napkins, I wondered if I'd really ever get my 15 minutes of fame when I couldn't even get 15 seconds of it in my own house.

8

While I put plates and plastic forks in the sink, I heard B.C. on the roof throwing bottle caps around. I would never be the center of attention in my own home. What made me think I could?

I dumped in the Suds dish soap, Hy-Klas' own brand. It took three strong squeezes before any suds appeared in the sink.

Sorry, Lord, I prayed as I watched the suds separate and grow thin. Even the bubbles looked disappointed. *It's just that I want to tell somebody I'm going to be on TV—and I want somebody to think, 'Scoop! Amazing!'*

I wondered if Dotty had gotten over B.C. enough to appreciate my good news yet. I glanced back at the table. "Dotty?"

She looked drained. Even from the sink, I could see puffy bags inside dark circles beneath her eyes. She was rubbing the same spot on the corner of the table, most likely talking B.C. over with Jesus. "Mmm?"

I knew I was probably interrupting her or Jesus. "Nothing."

Then I thought of Jen Zucker, the fourth member of our Horsefeathers team, Cheyenne's owner. Jen had been sick since Wednesday. I could tell her about *Della's Folks*.

"Dotty, I'm going to call Jen while the dishes soak, okay?"

"That's nice," Dotty said. One piece of baloney remained on the little plate in front of her. Without looking at it, Dotty folded the meat and stuck it in her mouth. Then she walked the plate over to the sink.

I was glad B.C. wasn't in the living room. I lifted the receiver and plopped down in the green vinyl chair by the phone. The seat cushion sighed with my weight. The phone rang once.

"Me!" "I get it!" "NO ME!" said somebody, or somebodies, at the Zucker house.

Another phone clicked. "Hello?"

"Mrs. Zucker?" I asked, just as a chorus of *hellos!* burst in my ear.

"Daniel! David! You get off the phone! You hear?"

"Tommy's Pizza Parlor," came another voice. "Anchovies Are Us."

"Tommy Zucker, do you want me to tell your father how un-gentlemanly you're behaving?" Mrs. Zucker's voice was almost lost by a baby's crying. "You're okay, Michelle. There, there," she

67

said. Michelle was one of the triplets, not yet a year old.

It was as if they each took turns at being the center of attention.

"Um ..." I tried again. "Mrs. Zucker? Is Jen home?"

"Scoop!" she screamed. "How *are* you, Dear?" Even with all her kids swirling around her, Mrs. Zucker sounded like she really cared about my answer.

"I'm okay," I said, wondering what it would be like to have a mom and a dad like the Zuckers. I shoved the thought out of my head.

"Is that wild horse behaving herself?" Mrs. Zucker asked. "I was telling Mr. Zucker only this morning I pray every day that God will protect you from that horse. You know Mr. Zucker though. He quoted some old poet or other about how a horse is a girl's best friend."

"Cheyenne's fine, Mrs. Zucker. I had a great ride on her yesterday afternoon."

I could picture Jen's mom on the other end of the phone as clearly as if I could see her through the receiver. She and Mr. Zucker were the only plump Zuckers in that household of 11. Mrs. Zucker reminds me of a Welsh Cob, a compact horse so reliable and comfortable people use them to give rides to kids with special needs. Mr. Zucker might have been a Connemara if he'd been a horse. The Irish native ponies are kind and reliable as Cobs, but they're ready for anything—jumping, hiking, you name it. Jen was lucky.

"Is Jen feeling better?" I asked, raising my voice over Michelle's cries for attention.

"That girl!" said Mrs. Zucker, the concern obvious in her voice. "It's just one illness after another. And I nearly have to sit on her to keep her home from school. Then all she wants to do is study and make up her lessons."

For a minute, I couldn't hear anything except the baby crying, the phone dropping, and shouts in the distance that sounded like somebody being scalped. "Hello?" I said.

The phone clunked and Mrs. Zucker came back on. "I'll get Jen, Scoop."

While I waited for Jen, I glanced around the living room. B.C.'s backpack was still on the couch, where he'd dropped it after school on Friday. I'd thrown my jacket in the corner, where it still lay, covering up a metal magazine rack. I dusted the phone table with my sleeve and wiped the dust on my jeans.

"Hello?" The voice was weak and followed by a cough.

"Jen?" I said. "Are you okay?"

"I'm fine, Scoop," she said, sounding hoarse. "I was just working on that history report, the one on world cultures. I have a lot to do on that one."

"Me too," I said, remembering that I'd forgotten all about it. "Guess what!" I could hardly wait to get it out. This is how it should have gone with B.C. and Dotty—me sharing the news and them getting excited for me. "You'll never guess, Jen!"

"Mmmmm," Jen mumbled through the phone. "Horsefeathers is going to be on *Della's Folks*?"

"You've talked to Maggie?" I asked, unreasonably disappointed that she already knew about it.

"And Carla. What's with this Benson character Maggie's so hung up on?"

We talked for a while about Ben, and I ended up telling Jen about Diablo. "He's not a bad horse, Jen."

"Okay," Jen said, sounding worried, "but are you sure you can get him trained before that TV show?"

Jen's strength, and one of the reasons she makes the perfect treasurer for Horsefeathers, is that she sees ahead and considers everything that might give us a problem. Jen's weakness is that she sees ahead and considers everything that might give us a problem. Already I could feel the added weight of her worry.

"I hope I can get that horse to come around," I said. "But we don't even know for sure the *Della's Folks* thing will happen."

"Maggie 37 sounded sure."

"We don't have a date or anything yet," I insisted, not sure why I was suddenly trying to deflate my own balloon.

"That, I didn't know," Jen said. "Maybe Ben Thayer is just stringing Maggie along with the promise of this publicity."

Jen had a lot of other ideas on how and why the TV show might never happen. By the time I was ready to hang up, I was more depressed than before I called.

"Tommy! Now look what you did!" I didn't know what her brother had done this time, but it must have been bad. It sounded like somebody broke a chair over somebody's head. "I have to go, Scoop!" Jen shouted into the phone. "I'll see you in church tomorrow." And she hung up.

I peeked in the kitchen, but Dotty was finishing up dishes, setting our plates and plastic forks out on her dish towel. I heard B.C. and his bottle caps scampering on the roof.

It was high time to start that world cultures report, but I hadn't checked out any books from the library. I climbed the stairs to my attic room and turned on the horse lamp on my dresser. Yellowed light fell on my horsefeather. It was really a cuckoo feather Carla gave me when we opened Horsefeathers Stable.

The feather stood up between two jars of air—one from the last horse ride Grandad took, sitting behind me on Orphan; and the other from the cemetery the day of his funeral.

Downstairs the door slammed. I could hear B.C. screaming bloody murder.

I ran down and saw B.C., his eyes wide as a frightened colt's. He wiped his nose with the back of his hand. "Told you!" He spit out the words with the force of a BB gun.

"What? What, B.C.?" Dotty asked, wiping her hands on her apron as she strode over to my brother.

B.C. flung open the front door. His face changed expression half a dozen times—surprise, pure joy, let-down, back to excitement. I leaped down the rest of the stairs and crossed to the front door to see for myself.

Maggie 37 Red floated through the door in a red raincoat, red heels, and a red dress I'd never seen before. "There's my B.C.!" Maggie cooed, bending down and cupping his head in her hands. "Don't you go running off from me like you did at the barn, you heartbreaker!"

B.C. could have passed for B.C. Red, his face turned so bright.

"Why aren't you down at Horsefeathers more often?" Maggie asked, as if his absence had offended her personally. "I thought Scoop was going to give you riding lessons after school."

B.C. glared at me. "I thought so too," he said low.

One more little thing I'd forgotten—as if I didn't have my hands full already. Why did I always end up the bad guy? Maggie was the one who stood up B.C. tonight. But somehow I was the one who got blamed.

Maggie swung around and looked outside to the front porch. That's when I saw Ben was there waiting for her. "Well, come on in!" Maggie coaxed. "Nobody's going to bite you."

Ben Thayer stepped in. He did, in fact, look like he was afraid of being bitten ... or maybe just contaminated. His eyebrows rose as he glanced from Dotty to B.C., to the duct-taped chair, to the old sofa. He nodded when I caught him looking in my direction.

"I do not believe you gentlemen have had the honor of making each other's acquaintance," Maggie said in her British accent. "Benjamin Coop, alias B.C., this is Ben Thayer."

"Well, we're sure glad you stopped over," Dotty said, joining them at the door. "Can I get you something to eat?"

"Dotty!" Maggie hugged my aunt. "And *this*," she announced with a wave of her hand in Dotty's direction, "is Dotty!"

"Nice to meet you, Ma'am," Ben said, shaking Dotty's hand. She wiped her hand off first. Ben put his arm around Maggie's waist. "We really can't stay long," he said, as if he spoke for Maggie too.

Maggie's smile didn't fade, but I saw her take one step away from Ben. His hand eased off her waist and dropped at his side.

I still hadn't said anything. Maggie and I hadn't looked each other in the eye either. The minute of silence felt awkward. I wondered if it was just me, or if everybody felt weird.

"We wanted to come by and give you the big news," Ben said. He looked down at Maggie. "Tell them, Maggie."

Maggie looked up at Ben and bit her bottom lip. Then she glanced at me.

"What, Maggie?" I asked.

Ben couldn't wait. "You are all looking at the co-star of *Anything for Love!*"

Maggie giggled. "Oh, I'm not the co-star."

"Well," Ben admitted, "maybe not. But it's a good part." He turned to Dotty. "She knocked the cast and the director off their chairs at rehearsal tonight! It's the role of an English airline stewardess. When they heard Maggie's English accent, ... well, let's just say even Gail knew it was all over!"

"My, my!" Dotty said. "Well, congratulations, Maggie! I'll bet your mama is as pleased as punch!"

For a minute, Maggie looked scared. To Ben she whispered, "See! I told you! You should have taken me home right after play practice!" She looked to me. "Scoop, did my mother call?"

I shook my head no, and Maggie sighed and plopped on our couch, sending up a puff of dust. "We called her from Hamilton. She knows where I was and all. I just didn't tell her when I'd be home. No big deal."

Inside, all I could think about was how this was going to drag Maggie further away from Horsefeathers. Maybe they'd even forgotten all about *Della's Folks*.

"I'll get you all tickets down front for opening night!" Maggie said. "Hamilton Community Theater! Can you believe it?"

Ben took Maggie's hand and sat on the couch beside her. I thought I caught Dotty in a worried frown, but it disappeared. "We'd love to come, wouldn't we, B.C.?" Dotty said.

"You should have seen everybody's faces when you were trying out!" Ben said to Maggie, kind of like the rest of us weren't even there. "I was standing next to Gail. Her mouth hung open so far, her gum fell out!"

Maggie giggled again. She let go of Ben's hand and waved her hands to gesture. "I felt bad for her. Gail did have the role, but she couldn't get the accent. I think she gets to be understudy or something."

"Gail?" Dotty scrunched up her nose, and her glasses rose and fell. "In Hamilton?"

"Yeah," Ben said.

"That ain't Gail Gayle?"

"How did you know, Dotty?" cried Maggie 37. She turned to Ben. "Is that really her real name? I thought maybe it was her stage name."

"Well, ain't that something?" Dotty said. "She's the new girl down at the Hy-Klas."

"Dotty works at the grocery store on Main Street," Maggie whispered to Ben.

Ben glanced at Dotty again, his upper lip curling slightly and his forehead wrinkled. "That's nice."

Maggie got off the couch and walked over to my brother. She squatted down to get eye-level with him. "You're mighty quiet, B.C.," she said. She glanced over at me. "And so is your sister. Aren't you happy for me?"

Dotty flashed me a look too.

"Of course we're happy for you, Maggie," I said, forcing myself to smile, trying to be happy for her. "Congratulations. You're an airline stewardess!"

B.C. glared at me, then gazed at Maggie 37. "She is not, Scoop!" he yelled. "Maggie is a movie star." He said it with awe.

Maggie hugged my brother. "Thank you, B.C." She stood up, next to Ben, whose arm snaked right back around her waist. "But didn't Scoop tell you? We're *all* going to be movie stars! It's all set. Two weeks from today, Horsefeathers will go on TV!"

Ben and Maggie answered all of B.C.'s and Dotty's questions about television and Ben's mother. Finally I broke in. "Maggie, could I show you something in my room for a minute?"

B.C. glared suspiciously at me, probably catching my white lie. I didn't have anything in my room to show Maggie. But I had to talk to her.

As soon as Maggie stepped into my room, I shut the door. "Maggie 37, what's going on?"

"What do you mean?" she asked, going straight for my dresser and the horsefeather. "You and Horsefeathers are going to get a lot of publicity—that's what's going on."

"I mean, between you and Ben? Maggie, in case you forgot, Ben's a junior!"

"A junior whose mother can get us the publicity we need to keep Horsefeathers running." Maggie looked up from the feather and winked at me. Her smile looked genuine enough. "Not to worry, Scoop. Everything's under control."

"But you don't really know Ben, Maggie. He's—"

"You'd be surprised what I know," Maggie said. "I know he's no Travis. He's been around. But we need this publicity, Scoop."

I couldn't believe what I was hearing. "Are you telling me you're playing along with Ben so we can be on his mother's show?"

She raised her eyebrows and winked again. "You handle Ben's horse and I'll handle Ben. Let's get downstairs."

I followed her down the stairs and stood in the front doorway as Maggie and Ben drove off into the black night. *Maggie 37*, I thought, watching them back out the driveway, *I hope you know what you're doing.*

9

Sunday morning, I woke up like a lit firecracker. Sparks of sun shone through my lone, smudged window in the center of the A-frame wall opposite my bed. Sunlight pierced through the jars of air on my dresser. My first thought was *Della's Folks*. I'd even dreamed about fame.

From somewhere inside the house, a wail rose and fell. As the rest of my mind de-fogged, I realized it was just after 7:30 A.M., and the noise was Dotty singing "Amazing Grace" as only Dotty can. She uses a key they haven't invented for musical instruments yet, but she sings with her whole heart.

My next thought was Orphan. *Horsefeathers!* I muttered, picturing my poor horse and all the others waiting on me to bring them breakfast.

Then I remembered—Maggie had claimed Sunday morning chores to make up for Saturday. Dotty had invited her to church with us, although Maggie had only been to our church a couple of times. Maggie had said no thanks, but she'd do Sunday chores for me.

I took in a deep breath of the morning air that seeped through cracks in my wall. Then I dived back under the covers and let myself fall back to sleep. It felt so good, I almost didn't want to waste the time by sleeping.

"You still asleep?" Dotty asked, pulling back the covers. I glanced at the clock and couldn't believe a whole hour had passed.

I downed Frosty Flakes, brushed my teeth, and dressed in record time. I heard an engine outside groan, chug, and click off. Three more tries—groan, chug, click. Then I heard Dotty lumber up to the porch and holler in at us. "It's a glorious day God's given us. I think He'd like us to walk in it."

Dotty was the only one talking on our walk. She rattled on about all the places she'd heard about on *Della's Folks*.

"Has Scoop really cured dozens of horses?" B.C. asked.

I didn't answer. I hadn't realized he'd heard Maggie tell Ben that white lie.

"Well, not dozens, B.C. But a couple anyway, right, Scoop?" Dotty picked up a bright, yellow leaf off the ground, snapped her black purse open and dropped the leaf inside.

"I didn't think so," B.C. said, frowning over at me.

I made a face back. We walked past the car dealership, and I started to take the shortcut to church. Dotty put on her brakes.

"Here now!" Dotty called. "Don't let's go through Mrs. Gurley's property."

I pointed to the brown path so worn it might have been a dirt sidewalk. Directly at the opposite end of the path sat our little white church with the big steeple. "I always go this way, Dotty. Everybody does," I reasoned.

"Don't make it right," she said. "Just look what they done to Mrs. Gurley's nice grass."

"It's twice as far going around the block," B.C. protested.

"B.C.," Dotty said, starting out again on the sidewalk, "you gotta do the right thing even if it takes you the long way around sometimes."

B.C. and I glanced at each other, shrugged, and fell in beside our aunt. The church had just come into sight again when something dropped at our feet. Dotty leaned down and picked up a lime green object the size of a small rubber ball. She held it to her nose and sniffed. "Mmmm, that's the best gift You could have given me, Father," she said—out loud, but to God. "Must be the last green walnut. Just what I needed this morning. Thank You for directing us right here right now."

I knew Dotty wasn't getting in a crack about how we never would have found the walnut if we'd taken that shortcut. My aunt doesn't work like that. She held the walnut up so B.C. and I could take a whiff. It smelled like Indian summer, strong as pines and fresh as just-baked cookies. If *green* had a smell, it would smell like that.

She snapped open her black box purse and dropped in the walnut.

"How come you pray about everything, Dotty?" B.C. asked. "Even walnuts." He looked sad enough to cry.

"I guess I got me a habit of praying. I couldn't leave it off if I wanted," Dotty said.

"Habits are bad," B.C. said.

Dotty reached down and slicked B.C.'s hair to one side. "Well now, there's good habits, and there's bad habits, B.C. Praying is one of the good kind."

"You want to see bad habits, come look at Diablo, B.C.," I said. "That horse has got more bad habits ... than you have." I fake punched him in the arm and ran ahead. We were on the church property. A few stragglers moved toward the sanctuary. Four or five just kept talking out on the front steps.

At the top of the steps stood the Hat Lady (that's what B.C. and I call her because she sits in front of us in church and we've grown up looking over the cool hats she wears every Sunday). "Morning, Scoop," she called. "Congratulations, Honey! I hear you're going to be on the TV with your grandfather's barn."

I started to say something, but Mr. Wilson, who runs the gas station just outside town, motioned me over. "How's it feel to be a celebrity?" he asked. An elderly couple next to him asked him what he meant.

"Thank you," I said, backing away while he told them I was going to be on *Della's Folks*. As I walked into the church, I heard an older woman say, "Ahhh, that *is* something, eh? Put that barn of hers right on the map."

I almost felt dizzy. The idea of people talking about me—saying good stuff about me—seemed too weird. Inside church, I headed to the front for the Zucker pew. Several people pointed at me and said something to whoever was next to them.

"I see you're still talking to the common man then, Scoop?" Travis, Jen's oldest brother, sat down between David and Daniel to keep the peace. If Travis were a horse, he'd be a grand Palomino stallion.

"Hey, Travis," I said. "Guess you heard about *Della's Folks*."

"News travels fast in this town," he said, pulling out another hymnal so each of the twins could hold one.

Jen put down her bulletin and stared up at me. I was surprised at how pale she looked, even though Jen always looks pale. Except for her folks, Jen's whole family is fair-skinned and blond. But she stays paler than all of them, even in the summer. She covered her mouth and coughed. "Hey, Scoop."

"Are you still sick?" I asked.

Jen shrugged. "I'll live. I just can't seem to shake this bug. Can you believe how everybody's talking about Horsefeathers?"

"Hey!" Tommy Zucker leaned across Jen and shouted in my face. "*I* want to be on TV!" Tommy is B.C.'s age, and he can be almost as obnoxious as my brother, when he wants to be.

The organ sounded. "We'll talk after church," Jen whispered. "Horsefeathers meeting tonight?"

"Tomorrow," I whispered, backing up the aisle. "7:00."

I sat in our pew, just behind the Hat Lady, but Dotty and B.C. were nowhere in sight. Dotty wasn't on children's church duty this month, but she'd probably gotten roped into it anyway. B.C. must have tagged along too.

I was hunting up the page for the first hymn when I spotted Carla Buckingham tiptoeing to the back pew. Behind her came her dad, who looked as out of place as a Lipizzaner caught in a herd of wild mustangs. Behind him came Ray Cravens, looking as relaxed as a Tennessee Walking Horse, although he was no regular in church himself.

Carla signed *Good morning!* with her hands, then added something I couldn't make out. I shook my head and she finger-spelled slowly: H-O-R-S-E-F-E-A-T-H-E-R-S M-E-E-T-I-N-G?

I nodded and moved my fist up and down, the sign for *yes*. Then I signed *Monday* and held up seven fingers, hoping she'd know I meant P.M.

I caught Ralph Dalton's critical eye. The Daltons laid claim to the pew directly behind ours. Clearly I was signing too loud for him.

Stephen Dalton leaned forward and whispered, "Ursula wants to know if Maggie Brown is really going out with Benson Thayer." Out of the corner of my eye, I saw the clash of Stephen's bright red hair and Ursula's long blond hair.

I tried to ignore Stephen as we all rose to sing the first hymn. Maggie wasn't *going out* with Ben. She was just being nice to him until we got our interview with his mother. But I couldn't tell Stephen that.

Ursula whispered behind me. "Go on, Stephen! You should tell her!"

I turned back around and started mouthing the words to the first verse. Stephen leaned in. "Scoop, does Maggie know he's been arrested?"

I wheeled around on him. "You're just jealous, Stephen," I said. "Horsefeathers is going to be on TV, and Dalton Stables isn't and you can't stand it! You want to wreck everything."

The Hat Lady turned around to raise her

eyebrows at me. The little bluebird on her hat flopped side to side.

"Are you kidding? I couldn't care less about that little show," Stephen whispered. "I'm just surprised you care about it so much you won't even look out for your best friend. I was just trying to do you a favor. That's all."

The day Stephen Dalton does anybody a favor, horses will meow. Maggie could handle herself—at least for two weeks.

I missed Orphan. I couldn't wait for church to get over so I could see my horse. *Sorry, God*, I prayed, knowing that even if I wasn't paying attention to God, God was paying attention to me. I tried to listen to the sermon, but my mind kept snapping back to *Della's Folks*. I could almost see Orphan on the screen and me riding bareback talking about how I'd cracked Diablo's case and turned him into a perfect riding horse.

"*When we put bits into the mouths of horses to make them obey us, we can turn the whole animal ...*" Pastor Dan got my attention. Bits? Horses?

"Turn with me to James 3:5," he went on. "*Likewise the tongue is a small part of the body, but it makes great boasts. Consider what a great forest is set on fire by a small spark.*"

I knew God was trying to tell me something. He wanted me to get it bad enough that he had Pastor Dan bring in the horse Scripture. But I still couldn't quite figure it out—something about little things people say really counting, changing the direction of stuff like bits do for horses. But as soon as I thought about bits, that made me think about Diablo and all I had to do before *Della's Folks*.

When church finished, I scurried down to the front to tell Jen good-bye. She'd coughed through most of the sermon.

"Hi, Scoop," she said, getting up and brushing something off her green, cotton dress. "Tomorrow at Horsefeathers we'll need to talk about how we're going to handle *Della's Folks*. And—"

"Excuse me, ladies." It was Mr. Snyder from the bank, dressed in a fancy, gray suit. "Could I have just a minute of your time?"

"Mr. Snyder," I said, "did you hear we're going to be getting that publicity you told me we needed?"

"I heard, Scoop," he said. "That's great." But he didn't sound as awed as I thought he should.

"Is something wrong?" Jen asked, obviously picking up the same vibes I was getting.

Mr. Snyder smiled his banker's smile. "Don't worry about it. But I do need to talk to you Monday. Could you drop by the bank right after school?" He looked from one of us to the other.

Jen finally answered. "Sure. I'll come by."

Mr. Snyder shook Jen's hand and then mine. Then he left.

"What do you think that's about?" I asked Jen as soon as Mr. Snyder was out of earshot.

"It could be a lot of things." Jen sighed. "I guess I'll find out on Monday."

10

Dotty had forgotten to turn the oven on before we left for church. She pulled the still-frozen, store-bought lasagna out of the cold oven. "I reckon we'll be eating late," she said, laughing at herself.

I used it as an excuse to get out of the house and off to Horsefeathers. I jogged down our driveway and all the way to the barn. Orphan and Moby were waiting for me in the corner of the pasture closest to the lane. They nickered and whinnied as soon as they saw or smelled me. Sugar trotted up too. Even Ham and Cheyenne and Diablo seemed on the lookout.

Something wasn't right. This kind of a hearty welcome I might expect from Orphan—but not from the other horses. Right away I knew. They were hungry. Starving. Maggie 37 hadn't fed them.

"Horsefeathers, Maggie!" I muttered under my breath, rushing over to Orphan. "I'm sorry, guys!" Rubbing their noses as I passed by, I ran to the barn for feed. They were all standing by their feed buckets when I came back.

"Maggie shouldn't have said she'd feed you if she didn't mean to do it," I told Orphan, brushing him as he and the others ate. "More important things on her mind. That's what she'll say. You wait and see, Orphan."

I brushed every horse in the stable, taking care with Diablo and just rubbing him with a soft cloth. Then I cleaned out their hooves, digging out mud and straw with the metal pick. Only Diablo put up a fuss.

By the time I was finished grooming the last horse, mine was ready to ride. "How about it, Orphan?" I asked.

Bareback, I rode through the pastures, to the woods, where soft pine needles insulated us. We cantered down a country lane and scared up a huge flock of geese, sending them on their way south in a crooked V. It was wonderful. And when we got back, I decided I wasn't ready to quit, although Orphan deserved her freedom. I saddled up Cheyenne, Jen Zucker's Paint. Since Jen liked to ride her Western, that's what I made myself do.

Cheyenne is not at all like Diablo. She's just young and feisty. She'd calmed down a lot since coming to Horsefeathers. Mr. Zucker paid us extra so I could keep her exercised and behaved. I tried to ride her every day if Jen didn't. And Jen hadn't been to the barn for almost a week.

We rode out to the south pasture. Orphan followed us as far as the pond and watched a while before going back to grazing. I walked Cheyenne knee-deep into the pond. We circled the dark water to take her edge off. Water riding slows her down much better than I can. Branches hung over the pond as if weighed down by their own beauty.

The Paint gave me a great ride, and I hated to end it too. I rode her out on County Road 620. One of my goals was to get her so she wouldn't even flinch when a car passed. We were less than a mile from Horsefeathers when behind me I heard a loud *Honk! Honk!*

Cheyenne reared up, something she hadn't done for weeks.

"Horsefeathers!" I muttered. "Take it easy, Girl."

The horn honked again. The driver pulled up beside us, then sped past us in a red blur. He swerved back in front of us, then slowed down just enough to throw something out the window. That's when I saw the driver—Ben Thayer.

He stuck one arm out the window and waved at me. Something rolled behind the car and came toward us in tiny gold sparks. Cheyenne was still fighting me, her back hooves slipping on the side of the road, dangerously close to the ditch. But I saw what Ben had thrown out the window. It was a half-smoked cigarette.

It took circling back and forth along the highway a couple of times, but I finally got Cheyenne calmed down enough to turn into Horsefeathers' lane.

Under the big oak by the barn sat a white pickup truck.

Travis! The first thought that flew to my mind was how handsome Travis is and that maybe he was there to see me. I waved to him from the saddle. He was leaning backwards, his elbows resting on the paddock fence. "I still say you're taking your life in your hands with that beast!" he shouted.

To prove Travis wrong, I urged Cheyenne to canter as close as I could get to him. "Whoa, Cheyenne," I said, inches from Travis. She stopped and stood still while I dismounted. "You were saying, Travis?" I said.

"Well, that Paint doesn't fool me," he said, stroking Cheyenne's neck under her sorrel-and-white mane.

I unsaddled the horse, and Travis took the heavy saddle and set it on top of the paddock fence as if he were lifting a feather. "I'll put that in the tack room for you in a minute, Scoop," he said. Then he turned to me with a steady gaze that wouldn't let me look away. "So how are you handling this sudden fame, Scoop?"

I laughed. "Hasn't exactly happened yet, Travis. You see anybody lining up outside Horsefeathers begging to get in?"

"Not yet. You okay with all this?"

I shrugged. "Is Jen?" I had the feeling Travis wanted to say something, but didn't know how to get to it. "Does Jen think something's wrong?"

"No way!" Travis said, messing up my hair. I'd taken out the ponytail I'd started with. The wind had blown my hair every which way. I probably looked awful. "I'm just asking, Scoop. Being on that show is a pretty big deal. It could change things."

I felt a flutter in my stomach, but didn't know why. "Change what?"

"Well, Horsefeathers for one." His eyes danced with teasing. "You just might be the next Dalton Stables."

"Ooh!" I doubled over as if I'd been punched in the belly. "Now *that* hurt!"

"Or all this fame might change you, Scoop." The smile was gone, and so was the teasing. "And that would be too bad."

I'm not sure what Travis meant by it, but what he said burned its way inside me until I thought I'd break down laughing or crying.

"Travis," I said, when I thought I had a good chance of getting my mouth to work again, "do you know Ben Thayer?"

Travis' forehead formed three wrinkles right

above his nose. "Yeah, I know him, Scoop. At least I know *of* him. He doesn't have the best reputation in Hamilton, if you want to know the truth."

"Why not?" I asked.

"I'm not going to pass along gossip about him. Just trust me. And don't trust *him*, okay? I know Ben's brother, Jackson Thayer. He's a great kid, a year younger than Ben. Jackson and I ran against each other in track. He usually won. Make that—he *always* won. Really nice guy though."

I combed my fingers through Cheyenne's mane. "So what's wrong with Ben?"

Travis pressed his lips together and shrugged. He reached over and scratched Cheyenne's withers. "I ought to go."

I didn't want him to go. "Travis," I pleaded, "just tell me why I shouldn't trust Ben. He's the reason we've got the spot on his mom's show."

Travis placed his large, strong hands on my shoulders. I looked up into his sky blue eyes and felt a lump swelling in my throat. "Take it easy," he said, his voice deep as an ocean. "I can almost hear your brain rattling. What would Dotty tell you to do about all this—the fame, Ben Thayer, his problem horse?"

"Pray?"

"Do that." Travis lifted Cheyenne's saddle off the fence with one arm and ran it to the barn, setting it horn side down the way you should. When he walked back out, Dogless Cat scurried along at his heels.

Travis hopped in his white pickup, and I led Cheyenne over to see him off. "Thanks, Travis," I finally managed to squeak out. If I'd had an empty jar, I would have captured the air, filled with Cheyenne's horse smell and Travis' aftershave, the faint scent of someone burning leaves somewhere, a chipmunk twittering from the oak tree.

"Don't forget—pray." He turned his key in the ignition. The engine grunted but didn't catch. "Oh yeah, and pray for me. I promised the triplets I'd read them a story tonight."

Four more tries, and then the engine kicked over. Travis yelled above the roar of the motor, "I'm getting rid of this truck finally! I'm out of Scotch tape to keep it together!"

I laughed and waved. As I watched the pick-up drive off, with black puffs of smoke coughing out of the tailpipe, I stroked Cheyenne and let her rub her head against me. Then I led her to the paddock and closed her in so I could brush her down.

Still thinking about Travis, I strolled to the barn for brushes. Almost in a dreamlike state, I moved down the stallway and around the corner. But what I saw woke me up like a belly-kick from a wild stallion.

Maggie and Ben Thayer were sitting on a bale of hay—*kissing!*

11

"Maggie?" I asked, stunned. "Maggie!"

Ben didn't look up.

"Scoop!" Maggie exclaimed. "I was just about to—to—to clean Moby's stall. And feed the horses. I forgot to do that this morning. I'm sorry. I meant to. I'll do it right now. You can help, Scoop!" She stood up and walked past me toward the feed bin.

I didn't move. I couldn't.

Maggie came back and grabbed my elbow. "Come along, Scoop," she commanded. "This way."

Dazed, I stumbled along with her. "Maggie, how could you—"

"Shhh-hh!" Maggie whispered. She motioned me into Horsefeathers' office, a small room with one desk table and one chair. Maggie closed the door behind me.

"Maggie!" I said. "What's the big idea?"

"What are you talking about?" she asked, the smile and glow on her face enough to drive me crazy.

"I saw you!" I shouted. I lowered my voice, remembering Ben wasn't far away. "I saw you and Ben out there ... kissing."

"That wasn't kissing," she insisted. "That was rehearsing! Ben has a love scene in the play. He asked me to go over it with him. It was no big deal."

"It didn't look like play acting to me," I said. "Horsefeathers, Maggie! How much do you know about Ben Thayer?"

"Scoop, you sound like my mother!" Maggie scolded. She stopped pacing. "Um, speaking of my mother ... I kind of told her I was stopping by your house this afternoon. I don't think she'd ever call to check up on me. But if she does, we were studying. Okay?"

"Maggie! What is happening to you?"

"What?" Maggie put her hands on her hips like teapot handles. "Now you're making a big deal over *that*? I just don't want her to worry. And I don't want to let Ben down either. Especially now that we may have a date for the show—a week from Saturday! It's not official yet, so one word from him and the whole *Della's Folks* deal is history."

I figured she was right about that. We had nothing in writing—just Ben's word on the deal, and his mother's. I sighed. "Well, will you at least be careful? I don't feel good about this."

"Promise. Scout's honor. And as soon as

we're done with *Della's Folks* ..." Maggie paused, as if thinking hard about it.

"You'll tell Benson Thayer to go play with somebody his own age?" I said.

Footsteps creaked in the stallway outside the office. "Maggie?" Ben called. "You coming? I've got to get going. I can drop you off at your house."

I watched them drive away, with Maggie sitting so close to Ben in the car she might as well have used his seatbelt.

It's no big thing. No big deal. Maggie said so herself. But as I walked home and watched the first stars pop out in the black-purple sky, I couldn't get Maggie 37 out of my mind. How many *little* things would it take to make a *big* deal? How many tiny sparks made a great fire?

~~~~~~~~~~~~~~~~~~~~~~~~~~~~~~~

Monday morning I got up earlier than usual, rushed through Horsefeathers chores, and biked to school. I had to check out a book for my nonexistent world cultures report. I got to West Salem High School at least 10 minutes earlier than normal, but the halls still overflowed with noisy students.

"Hey, good for you!" Brent Lore, a starter on our football team, gave me a pat on the back as he walked by.

It shocked me so much that I stared after him, figuring he must have gotten me mixed up with somebody else. Brent had never even said *hi* to me before.

Allyson White and her friend Katy, both cheerleaders who hang out with the popular group, stopped by my locker. "Scoop! Congratulations!" Allyson said. She wore a maroon sweater and a short maroon-and-white skirt, her cheerleading outfit. "That is *so* cool! How did they find out about you?"

I was starting to feel like I'd walked into the Twilight Zone. "Excuse me?"

"I would *love* to get on television!" Katy said. She and Allyson wore matching uniforms down to the maroon hair ribbons around their ponytails. "I wish I had a horse."

"There she is!" someone shouted from the hall. Two more kids squeezed in so I was blocked from leaving my locker.

Bill and Melissa, West Salem High School's oldest ongoing couple, fell in behind the growing crowd. "When are you going to be on that show, *Del's—*?" Bill asked.

"*Della's Folks*!" Katy finished.

My heart was racing so fast it hurt. "A week from Saturday, I guess."

The first bell rang and the crowd split off. "Call me sometime! I want all the details!" Allyson yelled back. "I can help you with your hair or makeup if you need me!"

I got out the books I needed, then slammed my locker shut. I'd never even imagined kids at school would know about *Della's Folks*. And I sure didn't imagine they'd act like this.

"So, are you signing autographs yet?" Ray Cravens and Carla grinned from across the hall. Ray wore baggy jeans and a flannel shirt, but Carla looked dressed up—a gray straight skirt, dark blouse, and matching jacket. Her hair was pulled back in a French braid.

"Can you believe this?" I said, joining them and heading to class.

"You probably won't want to hang out with us now that you're rich and famous," Carla teased.

"Right," I said. "I'll be shoveling manure like always after school. Some rich and famous!"

But it did feel like fame, the way kids in my morning classes acted toward me. Usually I felt invisible at school. Not today. Twice, kids I hardly knew motioned for me to sit with them.

Just before lunch, I ran into Jen outside her fifth period classroom. "Jen!" I called, threading the halls to get to her.

Jen was carrying a stack of thick library books. It reminded me that I still needed to get a book for world cultures class. "Wait up!"

Jen juggled her load as I walked up. "Hello, Scoop," she said. "Research."

"This has been the wildest day," I said. "Have

kids been asking you about *Della's Folks* and Horsefeathers?"

"And *you*," Jen said. "Do you still need me to go to the bank and talk to Mr. Snyder after school?"

"Yes!" In all the commotion, I'd forgotten about that. "Can you?"

"I'll do it. Travis can run me over for the Horsefeathers meeting after that and I'll tell you what Mr. Snyder wants." A buzzer sounded to change classes. "I don't want to be late." Jen took off down the hall. "Later!" she yelled back.

I didn't run into Maggie all morning, although I caught a good enough glimpse of her before lunch to know that today she was Maggie 37 Maroon, in her cheerleading uniform.

I sat down to wait for her at our usual table as soon as I got to the cafeteria. Before I'd even gotten settled, four kids plopped down around me.

"Hi, Scoop!" said Haley, a girl with curly brown hair and blue glasses. I knew her from church, although we don't have any classes together. "Are these seats saved?"

I shook my head no. I never had to worry about saving Maggie a seat because usually nobody would sit down at my table until Maggie made her entrance.

"See?" said Haley to her friends. "Told you I knew her. We go to the same church."

I didn't know Haley's friends, although I'd

seen them around. I felt like they were waiting for me to say something, to entertain them. "I'm going to get my tray now," I said.

"We'll save your seat!" declared Haley's blond girlfriend. "Hey! Is Della really pretty in person?"

I scooted off the bench and stood up. "Yeah." Actually I'd never seen the woman, not even on television. But she had to be pretty. Besides, I didn't want to disappoint the kid.

"Prettier than on TV?" she asked.

I started for my tray, but turned back to answer her. "Yeah, lots prettier." The answer seemed to make the girl happy. And I'd heard TV made people look 15 pounds heavier than real life, so she probably would look better in person.

I picked up my hot dog and chips and looked around for Maggie.

"Scoop! Over here!" Brent, the football player, was waving his arm in my direction.

He couldn't be waving at me. I glanced over my shoulder, expecting to see somebody waving back at Brent, but nobody was. When I looked his way again, he definitely motioned his head for me to join him at his table.

Allyson was sitting next to Brent, and Greg and Jeff were on the other side of the table.

"Sit down!" Brent said so forcefully my body obeyed even though my mind wasn't working. "Jeff and Allyson and I are the editorial staff of the *Gazette*. We want to do an article on you: 'Teen Horse Whisperer's TV Debut.' What do you think?"

"What do I think?" I repeated stupidly.

"I heard you might get your own TV show out of this deal," Greg said. "What would you do about school? Would you drop out?"

Again, I felt everybody staring at me, waiting for me to say something great. "I don't know if I'll get my own TV show," I said.

Greg looked disappointed, and so did Allyson and Brent.

"I could. I-I guess we'll see how I feel about it later."

"Cool!" Brent exclaimed.

"There you are!" Maggie 37 had come up behind me. "I've been looking all over for you! I've got some people who want to meet you."

I was glad for the chance to get away. I took a quick bite of the hot dog as I followed Maggie to the other end of the cafeteria. I tried to remember what I'd said to Brent and Allyson. I hadn't lied exactly, at least nothing big.

Sorry, God, I prayed, just in case. I returned the waves sent to me by a table full of boys we passed.

Really, it was like Maggie said. No big thing. No big deal.

12

Maggie and I sat down with Rita Martin, the oldest girl in the school, as far as I knew. She'd missed so many classes last year, she had to take most of them over.

"Rita and Ben are old friends," Maggie explained.

Rita and the girl next to her—Sonya something—kind of chuckled. Then Rita said, "Yeah, me and Benson go way back."

"I was getting Rita to fill me in on Mr. Ben Thayer," Maggie said.

Rita filled us in all right. Ben had been arrested for "driving under the influence," which sounded a lot nicer than *drunk driving*. In fact, Rita made every revelation about Ben sound exciting instead of horrible.

"Ask Ben about the time he took Alan's dare and broke into the high school—" Rita burst into laughter that brought tears into the corners of her eyes. "He thought—and then—" But she couldn't go on. Sonya must have known about it too because she seemed to find it just as funny.

"Go on!" Maggie urged, laughing too, even though she couldn't have known why yet.

"I can't!" Rita said, groaning and gasping. "Ask Ben!"

I couldn't eat anymore. Even what I'd already eaten hadn't gone down. Too many galloping horses in my stomach to let a hot dog in. "I need to go to the library before class," I explained, getting up from the table.

Maggie still hadn't given up wheedling the story out of Rita. "Tell me!" she insisted. Then she glanced at me. "Okay. Bye, Scoop. I'll try to come by Horsefeathers after school."

"Cheerleading after school!" yelled a girl from the next table. She had on the same uniform Maggie and Allyson did.

"Oops," Maggie said. "After cheerleading."

"Don't forget we're meeting at 7:00!" I called back to her as I walked my tray to the trash.

Saving the dishes and dumping the food, I felt a shove behind me. I turned to see Stephen Dalton. He pushed in front of me and started scraping his tray into the trash.

"You're making a big mistake hooking up with Ben Thayer, Sarah." He slurped the last drop of milk from his silver milk bag, making a loud yucky sound. Stephen's the only one who calls me Sarah, and he does it to annoy me. It works.

"So nice of you to be concerned," I said. "This couldn't possibly have anything to do with the fact that Horsefeathers is going to be on television and Dalton Stables isn't, could it?"

"Okay. Be that way. But you'll see. That guy is no good. He's nothing but trouble."

I should have ignored him. I should have turned and walked away without saying a word. But I couldn't. "You don't know what you're talking about, Stephen Dalton."

"It's no secret, Scoop. Maggie has no idea what he's really like. He's been in jail. Did you know that?"

Jail? I walked away from Stephen and pretended I hadn't heard him. But if Ben had been in jail, maybe I should warn Maggie again and tell her to break it off with him *now*. On the other hand, maybe Stephen made it all up. And I'd be wrecking my shot at television for nothing.

I asked the teacher on cafeteria duty for permission to go to the school library. At least I could look like I was doing my world cultures report. I was pretty sure Mr. Hatt wouldn't let me do another paper on horses. I'd already done reports on mustang herds and communities, weaning colts, and one on Orphan—I forget what the assignment was.

I browsed the social studies shelves and landed on one book that had two horses pulling a huge wagon loaded with boards. It was a book on Poland. I grabbed it and the book next to it, which was also about Poland, and checked them out just as the bell rang for sixth period.

Mr. Hatt's sixth-period class was the only one I had with Maggie 37—history and world cultures. And I'd only had her in there for a week. She'd switched out of geography as soon as they started making maps.

Still wrestling over what I should tell Maggie, and when, I weaved my way through the crowded halls to the last room at the end of the hall. By the time I walked into class, Maggie was already sitting in the back corner, talking to Rita. I plopped in the chair next to Maggie, but she didn't notice until Mr. Hatt called us to attention.

"Class, class!" he pleaded. "Please pass your outlines to the front."

Maggie finger-waved me and glanced at our teacher. "I forgot all about this," she whispered.

"I regret to say that some of you have not yet cleared your topics with me. We'll take the hour to work on reports. If I haven't given you the okay on your topic, better clear it with me now. Remember—200 points possible on this, so do a good job, people."

I dug into my pack, thankful that I'd at least checked out books. Maggie sat doodling in her notebook. She'd filled two pages with *Mrs. Maggie Thayer. Maggie 37 Thayer. Maggie 37 Red Thayer. Ben + Maggie. Maggie and Ben Blue.*

Maybe she was already in deeper than she let on.

Mr. Hatt called kids up to his desk, one by one, beginning with those of us who hadn't had our topics cleared yet.

I could only find one short paragraph on Polish horses in the first library book I checked out. I'd just gotten it read when Mr. Hatt called on me. "Sarah Coop? Scoop?"

I grabbed both library books and threaded the aisle to Mr. Hatt's little table that he used as a desk. He didn't look up until I took the only empty seat at his table. "What are you writing for me, Scoop?" he asked, folding his hands on the table in front of him. He was the only teacher who wore a suit and tie to school every day. Maggie said he was the best-dressed teacher in our school.

I spread out my two books to make them look like more. He picked up the one without horses on the cover. "Poland?" he said, sounding surprised. "Good choice. Nobody's picked Poland. Good for you, Scoop. How's it coming? How are you narrowing your topic?"

I looked away from his tiny gray eyes and tried not to think how funny it was for a bald man to have a name like Hatt. "Um ..." I wished I'd actually done some work on the report and had something smart-sounding to say. "Well, I thought I could write about how important work horses still are to Poland. You know, like how they still need horses to pull wagons and do other stuff?"

Mr. Hatt sighed. "Horses again?" If *he'd* been a horse, he might have been a Barb, the kind of horse Bedouins ride in North Africa. They're smart horses, but so quick-tempered you don't want to set them off.

"Not just horses, Mr. Barb—I mean, Mr. Hatt," I said quickly. "More like how important horses are to the Polish economy. I'm finding the Polish economy very interesting." Something burned in my stomach. I hoped it wasn't God. I was only stretching the truth a little. It wasn't like Maggie's white lies about how old she was or where she was going after school. Besides, I was pretty sure the Polish economy really was interesting, especially if horses had anything to do with it.

Maybe the burning was just the hot dog from lunch.

"Economy, huh?" I could see Mr. Hatt coming around slowly. One more tug and I'd have him. "But is there enough material to warrant a report on this subject? Have you found ample research books and materials on the Polish horse in Poland's economy?"

"Yes," I said, surprised at how easily I could pull this off. I don't think he had any idea how unprepared I was. "It's amazing, don't you think, how dependent the Polish nation still is on animals and stuff? I mean, their economy is really like an example for all of us." I had no idea what that meant. I pressed my lips together so I wouldn't say something else stupid.

"Good point, Scoop. Go for it!" Mr. Hatt scribbled something down in his grade book and called the next student.

I walked back to my seat, my gaze fixed on the pale gray cement floor, grayer than Mr. Hatt's eyes. I sure hoped Poland's economy ended up being interesting. And I sure hoped the burning that wouldn't stop bubbling in my stomach was nothing more than undigested pig intestines in a bun.

13

After school, three sophomore girls tried to get me to hang out with them. My head buzzed from all the attention. "Bye, Scoop!" seemed to come from every direction. I knew what I needed—who I needed: Orphan. I had to smell the barn, to feel Orphan's fuzzy fall coat. I needed to ride my horse like I needed oxygen.

Orphan pranced to the fence and whinnied for me as I biked up the lane. "Got something for you!" I yelled to her. I dropped my backpack in a pile of leaves under the yellow oak tree and fished out two apples. "Orphan," I said, "we're going on a picnic."

With the apples stuffed into one jacket pocket and a tiny glass jar shoved into my other pocket, I swung up on Orphan and used her lead rope as a single rein. We took off, away from the barn, right through the scattered herd of Horsefeather horses grazing in the pasture. I held on to Orphan's black, flowing mane as she jumped the rocky creek and climbed the gentle slope to the back woods. She knew where I wanted to go—

our secret spot. As far as I knew, Travis was the only other person who knew about the clearing Orphan and I called ours.

As soon as we reached our spot, I could almost feel God's presence. The trees burned with autumn, and I thought about Moses' burning bush. *God*, I prayed, *thank You for making this spot for Orphan and me.*

Orphan stopped and snorted, her eyes fixed on something to our left. I looked and saw what she saw—the perfect spot for our picnic. "Horse-feathers, Orphan," I whispered.

The lone ginkgo tree stood completely bare, its branches like an old man's fingers lifted to heaven. The ginkgo tree, for some reason I never understood, holds on to every leaf until they're the brightest yellow in the world. Then overnight, when no one's around, it drops every last leaf to the ground. Under our ginkgo tree was spread a lush, yellow blanket of tiny leaves, as if waiting for our picnic.

I slid off Orphan and plopped on my back in the yellow blanket, looking up at gray-blue sky. We ate our apples, matching crunch for crunch. I pulled out the small jar from my pocket, whisked it full of the air, filled with Orphan's smell and the crisp, ginkgo breeze. This was definitely air worth saving.

Riding back through fallen leaves made me think of B.C.'s worries about the Garden of Eden.

Then I remembered. I was supposed to go by the elementary school and get my brother for a riding lesson. B.C. would be so mad at me. But it was too late to do anything about it now. I'd have to make it up to him after I got caught up. For now, I had to focus on *Della's Folks*. I had less than two weeks to show amazing improvement in Ben's horse. If I couldn't make some mighty fast progress, there wouldn't even be a *Della's Folks*.

Back at Horsefeathers, I found Carla Buckingham getting ready to ride her horse. Ray held the reins of Ham's English bridle while Carla executed a perfect mount. Her boot found the small, metal stirrup automatically as she positioned the reins in both hands and settled into her saddle.

"Scoop!" She lifted her chin in a wave as I rode up next to her.

Orphan and Ham blew gently into each other's nostrils, and Ham nickered low. It had taken a lot of patience on Orphan's part, but she'd managed to make friends with Carla's high-class American Saddlebred gelding. The bay is one of the most beautiful horses I've ever seen, 17 hands high, with a mane and tail twice as black as Orphan's. Still, I wouldn't trade my horse for a dozen show horses.

"I'll give Ham a good workout, then come help you with the Appaloosa," Carla said. Ham pranced in place and Ray backed out of the way fast. "Is that okay with you?"

"Great," I said. "One less horse to work. And I can use the help with Diablo. Have a good ride." She rode to the paddock rail, her black hair blowing behind her out of her riding helmet.

"You look beat, Scoop," Ray said, staring after Carla.

"Thanks a lot, Ray," I said.

Instead of going out to the pasture, Carla was staying in the arena to practice Ham's gaits. Even though Ham wouldn't be competing in horse shows until late spring, Carla worried about keeping him sharp.

"You know what I mean. Better get rid of those bags under your eyes before you hit the television screen."

Ray was right. And I'd need something cool to wear too. Plus, should I wear my hair down or in a single braid?

Ray was studying me, a hint of a grin on his face.

"What?" I asked, almost afraid to hear his answer. We've been friends for so long, he knows me as well as anybody I know.

"I'm just a little surprised is all. You're really into this TV thing."

"No I'm not," I protested. "I mean, I *am*, but just because we need the publicity. We do, Ray."

"Uh huh," he said slowly. "And if guys like Brent all of a sudden seem to know you're alive, all the better, huh?"

I hopped off Orphan. "I don't know what you're talking about." I had to say it without looking at him. I'd walked Orphan in from the pasture, so she wasn't even warm. Undoing her hackamore bridle, I patted her rump and let her free to roll in the dirt to her heart's content.

"Well," Ray said, watching Carla and Ham as they cantered around the ring in front of us. "I better be off. I haven't done much on that world cultures report. Your class has it too, right?"

I nodded, wondering when I'd get time to work on Polish horses.

He waved at Carla. "I'll phone you tonight!" he called to her. Then he walked off, his long legs carrying him to the barn in half a dozen strides.

Grabbing a handful of oats, I headed to the pasture to catch Diablo. The Appaloosa raised his head when he heard me coming. His coat was caked in mud. I hoped Maggie wouldn't bring Ben by the barn until I got his horse cleaned up.

I led Diablo into the barn by his halter. Sugar, Caroline's gray mare, followed me as far as the paddock. For some reason, her brother Jake's face popped into my mind. It seemed like so long ago when he'd hung out at Horsefeathers. I tried to imagine his expression as he turned on the television and saw Scoop, the Teenaged Horse Whisperer.

I didn't trust Diablo on our make-shift cross-ties yet, so I used the metal ring in Ham's stall and our strongest lead rope, tying a knot that would give if he pulled back on me.

As I walked to the tack box, I kept one eye on Diablo. Sure enough, he tugged backwards. The lead rope lengthened with him until his rump was against the back wall of the stall. With nowhere to go, and no fun breaking loose, he sighed, switched his tail a couple of times, and eased back to the center of the stall.

"See, little Appy," I said when I came back. I scratched him under his mane, and he stretched out his neck for more. "Remember this now. Start a *good* habit, as Dotty would say. If we're going to be a Della's Folk, you better shape up."

I took a clean, tacky cloth and let Diablo sniff it. Then starting at his neck, I rubbed the cloth lightly over the clumps of dried mud. His muscles tightened at even the slightest touch.

"Somebody's been brushing you too hard," I murmured.

"How's he doing?" Carla peeked in from the paddock, her English saddle over one arm.

"This one's not going to be a quick fix, I'm afraid," I said.

"Do you think he'll show progress in time for the TV thing?" Carla asked.

"He has to."

Carla finished cooling Ham, and I kept rubbing down Diablo until I knew he'd had enough.

"What now?" Carla asked, scratching the Appy under his chin. "I can't believe he's given everybody so much trouble. He seems like a real sweetheart." Diablo nuzzled Carla's ear. "Hey! That tickles." Her hearing aid flopped loose and she pushed it back.

I glanced at Diablo just in time to see his ears flatten back. "No you don't!" I shouted, jerking his head away just as his teeth parted. "No biting at Horsefeathers!"

Carla jumped back, covering her ear. "Thanks, Scoop. I never saw it coming." She stroked Diablo's soft muzzle, and the Appy nodded up and down, appreciating it. "Look at you! You didn't even mean it."

"This horse has so many bad habits!" I said. "I hardly know where to start with him."

We tried to think of what would look best on *Della's Folks*, which improvements we should tackle first.

"Ben said Diablo's a nightmare to bridle," I explained, taking down the bridle Ben had been using with his horse. "The bit looks good." I moved the snaffle, a bit broken in two pieces that gives enough control over most horses, without being too rough on the mouth. "Let's see how he does."

I stood in front of the horse, off to one side, and slowly lifted the bridle, cradling the bit in one hand. The Appy jerked his head up and out of reach. I got the feeling he was laughing at me.

"That will look great on TV, Scoop," Carla said sarcastically. "I can see it all now. Want me to hold Diablo down or something?"

"I don't want to force him to do anything," I explained. "And I hate having to hurry him for television. I have a feeling if certain people hadn't forced certain horses to do things they didn't want to do, we wouldn't have such a problem on our hands." I lifted the bridle again and got the same head-jerk reaction.

"You don't like Ben very much, do you?" Carla said.

"I don't know, Carla," I said, trying the bridle again and getting nowhere. "He's the one I've got to thank for giving us all this publicity. But I've heard some pretty bad rumors about him. To tell you the truth, if we didn't need his mother's publicity so much, I'd try to talk Maggie out of having anything to do with him."

"You know," Carla said, taking the bridle from me. "You ought to start thinking about what you want to do during that TV program." She held the bit and tried to coax Diablo to it. Tight-lipped, the horse turned his head to the wall.

"What do you mean, Carla?" I asked.

"You need to take control, Scoop, to make sure Horsefeathers really gets the publicity and not ... not someone else." Carla glanced at me sideways, then back to Diablo.

"Who else would get the publicity?" I hoped she hadn't been talking to Ray about me. I wondered if they'd decided I was just trying to get the fame for myself. "I just want to get more customers for Horsefeathers. That's all." At least that's what I thought I wanted.

"Not you," Carla said. "Maggie."

"Maggie?" I repeated.

"I'm just saying that if you don't decide how you want this show to go, they will."

"*They?* As in Maggie and Ben?"

Carla nodded. "They're pretty thick, in case you haven't noticed."

"Well Maggie told me she's just going along with Ben to make sure we get to do *Della's Folks.* She's going to break it off with him as soon as that's over." But Maggie's notebook flashed to mind, with *Ben + Maggie* scribbled all over it.

"Oh, Scoop," Carla said, "wake up and smell the horses!"

The horse chose that moment to snort and try to pull out of the tie. We backed off and let him fail on his own.

"Anyway," Carla went on. "You should think about what you want to accomplish in that TV time. What kind of a statement do you want to make about Horsefeathers Stable? I know Ben's mother wants to show how you've helped Diablo. But you need to give people a broader picture. I was thinking ..." Carla straightened the reins on the bridle, smoothing them out. "Maybe you want to show people that you can help show horses too—like Ham, for instance. I'd never want to speak on television, but I wouldn't mind riding Ham on TV. You could do the talking and tell everybody how you calmed down Buckingham's British Pride."

Carla tried the bridle again, but Diablo jerked his head up out of reach. "Anyway, it was just an idea."

And one more worry for me to mull over. I hadn't thought about what to do on *Della's Folks*. But if Carla was right, I'd better start thinking pretty soon.

I tried to focus on the Appaloosa. We couldn't let Diablo win this first bridle battle. "I've got an idea," I said. "I think I know how to make him want the bit."

Leaving Carla with Diablo, I ran to the hay loft, where Jen keeps some of the ingredients for her special horse feed recipes. Ferreting through the feed box, I came out with just what I was looking for—a jar of tempting, tantalizing honey.

I ran back to the stall. "Got it," I muttered. "Diablo, you're going to like this."

The Appy turned his head and pricked up his

ears when I unscrewed the lid to the honey. He could smell it, and so could I. I smeared a finger-ful of honey onto the snaffle bit. Before he could pull away again, I slipped the bit into his mouth and tucked the bridle behind his ears.

Diablo couldn't decide whether to fight me or give in to the honey. He did both, throwing his head up and down, while licking and slurping at his bit.

"You think that will do it?" Carla asked, taking the jar so I could hold onto Diablo's lead rope.

"We'll see," I said, slipping the bridle off again. One victory over this horse would take some of the pressure off.

I smeared the bit with honey again. When I lifted the bridle though, he jerked his head up and away. It wasn't going to be that easy—not this time. His habit ran too deep.

"We'll take up where we left off tomorrow," I said, trying not to show how disappointed I was. In the back of my mind I'd imagined a quick fix, amazing Ben and his mother, astounding the television audience.

So far, it wasn't even close.

14

I had just enough time to race home and eat before our Horsefeathers meeting at 7:00. The sky was streaked with dark purple as I plodded up the drive.

B.C. was jerking an old rake through the mass of leaves in front of the porch step. When he saw me, he threw down the rake and yelled, "You didn't come! You were supposed to get me at school! You said I could ride with you at Horsefeathers! Liar!"

"I'm not a liar, B.C.," I said, almost too tired to argue. "I got busy. That's all. I'm sorry. Okay? Don't make such a big deal out of it. We'll do it tomorrow if you want."

He dug a bottle cap out of his pocket and threw it at me, missing me by a mile. "Oh yeah?" he yelled. "If I want? Well, I don't want! I don't want *you*!" He stormed to the front door, a pale light sliding out the door as he opened it. Then he turned and screamed, "I wish I had Maggie as a sister! Not you! I want Maggie!"

I should have stayed at Horsefeathers. Part of me kept telling myself B.C. was overreacting as usual. But the other part of me wanted to run after him and beg him to forgive me. Why couldn't he let me have my 15 minutes of fame without getting in the middle of it and messing it up?

Trudging in the front door, I didn't smell anything cooking, but Dotty was home and at work in the kitchen. "Hi, Dotty," I said, joining her.

"Hi ya, Scoop," she said. She looked tired too, but she turned off the water and set down the plate she was rinsing. Then she walked over to me, wiping her hands on her apron. "How was school today?"

"Okay." I heard B.C. stomping around on the roof. "Sorry I forgot B.C."

"Seemed awful important to him," Dotty said. Sometimes I wish she'd yell at me like other grown-ups. But she can hit harder in a few nice words than most people can with a stern lecture.

I helped her wash enough of our dirty dishes so we could set the table. She'd brought home yesterday's Hy-Klas macaroni, which I love except for the pieces of something red they put in it. (Dotty says nobody knows what the red stuff is.)

We were also having mini hamburgers, the frozen kind people who have a microwave cook in a microwave. Dotty cooked ours in the toaster. One little burger fit into each of the toaster slots if we took the buns off, but they usually still tasted cold in the middle. Plus, I'd have to remember not to eat toast the next day unless I wanted it to taste like hamburger.

B.C. still wasn't talking to me when we sat down at the table. Dotty thanked God for every little thing, right down to the red things in the macaroni.

I wanted to join in praying, at least in my heart. But with all the worries about Diablo and *Della's Folks* and everything else, my heart was too clogged up to keep up with Dotty and God.

~~~~~~~~~~~~~~~~~~~~~~~~~~~~~~~

I had to hurry to get back to Horsefeathers in time for our meeting. It seemed like a year, instead of a week, since we'd all met together in the office. We had a lot of things to talk about.

Soft, yellow light poured from the window of the barn. Somebody had gotten to the office before me. Tiny gnats circled in the beam of light behind the barn in the paddock. I listened for voices inside, but didn't hear anybody.

"Hello!" I called, walking down the stallway. None of the horses had chosen to bed down in the stalls. They'd be out in the back of the pasture, probably taking turns lying down and keeping watch.

Nobody answered, but light came from the office. "Hey! Who's there?" I called out, pushing the half-open door all the way open.

Nobody answered me. Carla sat in the chair behind the desk. Maggie was sitting on the desk. Neither of them spoke.

"What's wrong with you two?" I asked.

Carla motioned with her head for me to turn around. I turned, and my heart felt like it jumped. Behind the door stood Benson Thayer. "You gave me a heart attack!" I cried, holding my hand over my heart and feeling it thumping. "What are you—" I was going to say, *What are you doing here?* But I stopped myself.

"Sorry," Ben answered. He crossed to the desk and leaned on it next to Maggie 37. "Didn't mean to scare you."

I glanced at Carla. She raised her eyebrows at me and nodded, as if she knew all along this would happen.

Maggie 37 Pink, in a silky pink blouse, pink tights, and a pink wool jumper, laughed nervously. "Scoop, can you believe I beat you and Jen here for once?"

"It's a Horsefeathers business meeting, Maggie," I said firmly, meaning, *you have no right to bring him here*.

Carla cleared her throat and leaned back in her chair. "That's what I thought," she muttered.

"What did she say?" Ben asked. Not *what did you say*. Not *sorry, could you say that again*.

Maggie ignored his question and spoke straight to me, saying more with her pleading brown eyes than she did with her pink-lipsticked mouth. "Scoop, I just knew you'd want to find out all you could about *Della's Folks*. We're all set—definitely a week from Saturday. So who knows more about *Della's Folks* than Della's son? Right? That *is* what this meeting is all about, isn't it?" Maggie must not have been as confident as she made out because her accents mixed together so she sounded like a Scottish-German-Spanish-French girl.

"I guess that's the most important thing we have to discuss," I said. "But we—"

"Great! Because Ben and I have done a lot of thinking about the show, and we've come up with some fabulous ideas. I can't wait for you to hear them!" Maggie reached over and squeezed Ben's hand.

I glanced at Carla again. Keeping her hands behind the desk, she signed to me: *Told you so!*

"Go on, Ben!" Maggie begged. "Tell them your idea!"

Ben cleared his throat. "Well, you have to understand that my mother will have ideas of her own, of course. But I think I've watched enough of her tapings to get a feel for what she'll want here."

Maggie flashed a big smile at me. "See?"

See what? I wondered.

Ben continued, "*Della's Folks* has to frame a story, and Diablo provides us with the best story angle here."

Us?

"The way I see it," Ben went on, "we open the slot with some old film footage my mother has of Diablo acting up—running away with me, refusing to stand still. She even caught the horse breaking away once when I had him tied outside our house."

Maggie broke in. "But that should only take a minute or two. And everything else is live, of course. Right, Ben?"

"Right. Then we cut to Horsefeathers. Now, I'm not sure how much we want to shoot of the actual barn. Maybe just the sign above the door, then cut to the paddock."

"Where *I* come in," Maggie interrupted.

Carla was so right. Ben and Maggie must have been planning the whole show on their own.

Maggie continued, talking faster and faster. "Moby and I will make our entrance at a dead gallop, stopping on a dime right in front of the camera. Then I'll go into my routine—a rear, a pivot. We figure there'll be time for me to take Moby around the ring twice—once while I'm standing in the saddle." Maggie finally stopped to catch her breath and look over at me. "What do you think so far, Scoop?"

She didn't want to know what I thought. If Ben hadn't been there—and he shouldn't have been there—I would have told her exactly what I thought. But I couldn't shut him down, not completely. One word from Ben and the whole deal could be history.

"Well," I said. I heard Carla mutter something under her breath, but even I couldn't make it out. "Maggie, you and Moby always put on a great show. That's for sure."

"See Ben?" Maggie cried, as if totally relieved now. "I told you Scoop would agree with me."

"Well, I don't know, Maggie. You didn't let me finish."

Maggie swung back toward me, her forehead in tiny wrinkles and her eyes narrow. "What?"

"I'm just not sure that's the right show for *this* show."

The reaction was dead silence.

I tried again. "I thought the show was about—" I didn't want to say about *me*. Then I'd come off sounding like Maggie. "—about Horsefeathers. Don't we want to tell them about horses getting fixed and cured at Horsefeathers? I didn't have anything to do with training Moby, Maggie. What good will it do to show her off?"

"What good will it do?" Maggie asked, as if she couldn't imagine a more ridiculous question.

Carla leaned forward suddenly. Her chair banged the office floor, making us all turn that way. "Scoop—is—right!" She said it loudly. Her words came out as clearly as she could get them, each one separated from the other. If Ben couldn't understand her this time, it was his own fault.

"Scoop—*did*—work—with—Ham. If I ride Ham on television, people will see she can help show horses. That will bring in more business than entertaining them with horse tricks and stunt riding."

Ben leaned toward Maggie. "What did—"

But Maggie was locked onto Carla. "Moby is not just a trick horse!" she said, her voice rising. "Besides, I don't think the image we want to leave people with is some high-strung show horse. Horsefeathers is supposed to be a home for backyard horses, remember?"

"Like Orphan!" I shouted. "Orphan is the horse who should be on TV! She's exactly what Horsefeathers is all about! And I'm the one who—"

But we were all yelling, and our words bumped into each other, slapping each other down, smothering each idea with a new one. I couldn't even hear myself.

"Stop it!" It was Jen Zucker, standing in the doorway, looking like she might burst into tears. Travis, looking totally confused, stood behind her.

The office grew as silent as if sound had been turned off. I couldn't look at either of them. I wanted to crawl under the desk and hide.

Nobody said anything for a full minute. Then Maggie 37 spoke, her voice thin and frail. "You're late, Jen."

When Jen didn't respond, Travis said, "Sorry.

My fault. My old pickup broke down on the way here."

The room was silent again. It was as if a blanket of shame had been thrown over our angry flames.

Ben turned to Maggie. "I should be going. I'll call you." Then he squeezed between Jen and Travis, without speaking to them, and left.

"What—?" Jen stared from one to the other of us. "What were you arguing about?"

Carla and I didn't answer.

Maggie studied the pink ring on her finger, then said, "We were trying to decide who would get to ride on *Della's Folks* when Horsefeathers is on."

Jen looked disgusted with us. "Well, you may not have to worry about it," she said. "I just finished talking with Mr. Snyder at the bank. By the time *Della's Folks* is on, there may not even be a Horsefeathers."

I f Jen had wanted to punish us for arguing, she
did. Nothing could have struck a bigger blow
than what she said: *There may not even be a Horsefeathers.*

Travis nudged Jen into the office. "Everybody relax a minute," he said. "Jen will tell you
everything."

Jen launched into a detailed account of her
meeting with Mr. Snyder—so detailed, I wanted
to shake her to get to the point. What I got was
that nobody from the county tax office had been
out to the barn since I'd taken it over from
Grandad. In fact, nobody had been out for five
years. And now, the county was sending us a tax
assessor. They needed to assess the value of
Horsefeathers, which would be a lot more than it
was five years ago. But the really bad part was that
our taxes would go way up and so would everything else. We'd have to pay more to the bank
every month to cover the increase in taxes.

"Basically," Jen said, after going through her
conversation with Mr. Snyder blow by blow, "the

bank has been waiting until they knew how much Horsefeathers is worth so they can raise our payments. And now it's going to happen."

Nobody said anything. One of the horses had come into his stall. I heard him sneeze and the floor creak. "So what do we do?" I asked at last. I wondered if Maggie and Carla felt as awful about fighting as I did, but I couldn't look at them.

"Well for starters, we need to pull together," Jen said. "The county tax assessor is coming out a week from Friday for an inspection."

"So soon?" I cried. "Jen, why do they have to come so soon? Can't they wait until after *Della's Folks*?"

"They wanted to come *this* Friday," Jen said. "We're lucky I got them to put it off a week. The question is, do you think we can work together and get things in shape by then?"

I'd been frantic, worrying about getting Horsefeathers in shape for *Della's Folks*. Now we'd have this to worry about first.

"I'm in," Maggie said. Her eyes darted to me, then at Carla.

"I'm in," Carla said.

"Me too," I said, trying to sort out when I could work on the barn, and when I'd have time to work on Diablo.

Travis moved toward the office door. "I'll stop by and help clean stalls and do repairs if you

need me. Ray will too, I bet. It'll all work out."
He winked at me.

"Okay then," Maggie said, hopping off the
desk. "We can do this. No big deal, right? Travis,
could you give me a lift home?"

"If the old pickup cooperates, I can," he said.

Everybody left, and I shut off the office light,
checked on the horses, and walked home. I'd
never yelled at my friends like that. What had gotten into everybody? I wanted to blame Ben for
everything, but knew it wasn't all his fault. Still, as
soon as *Della's Folks* was over, Maggie and I were
going to have a long talk about Benson Thayer.

~~~~~~~~~~~~~~~~~~~~~~~~~~~~~~

That week flew by, and so did the next. At
school, Maggie and I didn't say much to each
other. At lunch, she sat with Rita and her friends.
I got invited to a different table each lunch period. When I saw Maggie in the halls, we'd say hi,
but that was all. Ben took her to play practice
every night, so I couldn't have phoned her even if
I'd known what to say. I missed her.

But every spare minute was taken up at
Horsefeathers. Diablo wasn't about to make my
life any easier. After two days, he took the bridle
without fussing, but he refused to stand still for
the blanket or the saddle. I spent hours doing
nothing but putting the saddle on and taking it
off again day in and day out. By nighttime, my
arms were so sore I could hardly get to sleep.

~~~~~~~~~~~~~~~~~~~~~~~~~~~~~~~

Thursday, the day before the bank assessor's visit, I surprised B.C. and showed up at the elementary building after school. Watching all the little kids stream out as soon as the bell rang, it didn't seem possible that I'd ever been so young.

B.C. may have been the last kid out. His head hung so low, he walked right past me without seeing me.

"Hey, B.C.!" I called.

He looked up like he'd heard a ghost. When he saw me, he broke into a smile that changed the shape of his whole body. "Scoop!"

"You can ride Orphan for just a few minutes. Then I could use your help in the barn."

He pressed his lips together and sucked them in so it looked like he might swallow his own mouth. Then he nodded.

Orphan was waiting for us at Horsefeathers. I felt like a traitor saddling her with one of Grandad's old army saddles. My horse and I have an understanding when it comes to saddles. We don't understand them. But B.C. needed something to hang on to. He didn't say anything as I led him around the paddock, but he smiled and kept reaching up to pet Orphan's neck.

After a couple of times around the arena, I pulled Orphan up. "That's it, B.C.," I said.

"Go again!" B.C. commanded.

"Can't. I have to work with Diablo." I had

only two days left for a miracle with that horse. "Then I need to work on picking up the paddock." I'd spent so much time with Diablo, I'd hardly done anything to the barn. Ray and Travis had pitched in. And on Wednesday, they cleaned all the stalls for me. But I still had a lot to do to get ready for the tax person.

"No!" B.C. grasped the saddle horn with both hands. I had to pry him loose and drag him off my horse. The second his tennis shoes hit the dirt, he took off running, probably headed for the barn roof.

"You're welcome, B.C.!" I yelled after him. At least I'd done my duty, although I knew what he'd be thinking. Marvelous Maggie 37 would have let him ride longer.

Right.

I snapped Diablo to the ring in Ham's stall again. Today I had to work on Diablo's mounting manners. Most of his problems showed up in bad ground manners. I knew the film clips Ben's mother wanted to show of the *before* part of Diablo's *before and after* were problems with saddling and mounting. Riding the horse was the easy part.

It had taken me hours of repetition, but finally Diablo had come around with bridling and saddling. He'd gotten used to the good taste of his bit, and I didn't have to use honey anymore. And he stood still, even when I cinched his saddle tight.

But the minute I lifted my foot to the stirrup to mount, he'd sidestep or walk forward. One more bad habit brought to us by Mr. Benson Thayer. In two days, just two more days, I'd be mounting this moving target in front of the television cameras. The only good part was that as soon as *Della's Folks* was safely taped, I could tell Maggie what I really thought of Ben. She'd probably get mad at me, but if she broke it off with Ben, it would be worth it.

I saddled Diablo, murmuring to him the whole time. Scooting him over in the stall, as close to the corner as I could get him, I placed one foot in the stirrup. He stepped forward, then backwards, leaving me to hop on one foot, with my left boot still in the stirrup.

I tried again, but couldn't get his lead rope tight enough to keep him from walking frontwards or backwards when he felt like it. And he felt like it every time I tried to mount.

"Come on, Diablo!" I begged, bracing myself for another try. "Don't you want to be a TV star?"

This time he let me get as far as standing in one stirrup. I'd just swung my right leg over his back when he lowered his head and bucked.

I grabbed for the saddle horn, but couldn't find it. My foot slipped out of the stirrup and I fell backwards. I shut my eyes and readied myself for landing. But something broke my fall. Then I knocked the *something* over, tumbling backwards. I heard a grunt as I rolled on top of somebody—somebody I still couldn't see as we squished through the straw and fresh manure.

16

Maggie?" I struggled to my feet, as surprised to see her as if she'd been a unicorn. My mouth opened, but I couldn't get any words to come out. I felt like yelling, crying, and hugging her all at the same time.

Maggie tugged on one of her pigtails, making herself look younger than she had been looking lately. "I thought you could use some help," she said.

"No kidding."

Neither of us said anything else for what felt like minutes. For the past few years, Maggie had been the one person I could talk to about anything. And I'd never known her to be at a loss for words. Now the air around us seemed filled with traps, like a pasture full of gopher holes waiting for one false step.

Then Maggie burst into action. "Let's try mounting in the paddock. I could hold Diablo for you. We can use the bridle too."

"Great!" I grabbed Diablo's bridle off the hook outside his stall. "I think this horse is getting too used to the stall anyway. If you hold him, I can use a bale of hay for a mounting block. It won't give him so much time. We can throw him off."

We pushed the nearest bale out to the paddock. I stood on it and had Maggie take the horse. "Lead him up as close as you can get, Maggie. I mean, please? If you don't mind?" It felt so strange to have to watch my words around Maggie, as if the friendship I'd always counted on as rock-solid had turned to glass. I felt like if I said the wrong thing, our whole friendship could break into pieces.

Diablo followed her with no problem, lining up perfectly along the bale of hay. Before he knew what was happening, I jumped up on his back. He didn't budge.

"It worked!" Maggie cried.

"It's just the start," I said, dismounting to the hay bale. Diablo sidestepped and Maggie pulled him back. "I'll have to do this a hundred times before he gets it. That's how he's been with every bad habit. He shouldn't have—" I bit off what was in my mind before it got out of my mouth. I wanted to tell Maggie that Diablo's bad habits were all Ben's fault. That Ben might be the kind of person who leads people into bad habits too. But I couldn't risk it.

"Here we go again," said Maggie. I watched her lead the gelding in a circle before lining him up next to the bale again. She wore blue jeans and a brown sweatshirt. I wondered if she was going by her real name today, Maggie 37 Brown. I didn't care. It just felt so good to have her back, to be working together again.

After each successful mounting, I took a little longer in the air or swinging my leg over.

Finally, after a couple dozen mounts, Maggie said, "He's doing so well, Scoop. Don't you think we could try it from the ground, without the bale?"

We shoved the bale out of the way, then moved Diablo to the center of the paddock. As soon as I stepped in the stirrup though, he immediately walked forward.

Maggie groaned, but she held the Appaloosa for seven more tries until finally, the horse stood still.

"Let's quit while we're ahead," I said, dismounting fast. I knew it would feel like starting over again tomorrow. But we could at least give Diablo something to think about overnight. And with any luck, he'd keep it in his head for Saturday on *Della's Folks*.

"Fine with me," Maggie said.

While I led Diablo to the barn, Maggie whistled for Moby. The big, white mare trotted up to her. I glanced back to see Maggie hugging her horse. It almost felt like old times. It made me think that maybe Carla had been all wrong about

Maggie and Ben. Maggie had said she was just hanging out with Ben until we finished the TV show. Maybe Maggie did know what she was doing and I was making a big deal out of nothing.

When I went back to the paddock, Maggie stood between Moby and Orphan, one hand on each nose. She turned to me. "Scoop, these guys had a good idea. How about a ride?"

It was the best idea any of us had had in a long time. I slipped a hackamore bitless bridle on Orphan and waited while Maggie saddled Moby. Then we took off for the back pasture.

"Race you to the hedge grove!" Maggie cried, bursting to a gallop from a near standstill.

Orphan and I caught them easily. Moby's 23, but she's fast. Orphan and Cheyenne are probably the only horses who could beat her in a real race. I let Moby win, and I knew Maggie knew I did. The pasture burned with autumn, sending up an incense of piney hedge apples, horse's sweat, and friendship. My heart thanked God for every leaf, every breath, everything.

The horses loved it as much as we did and didn't seem to want to pull to the barn like they usually did. Finally, we turned and walked Moby and Orphan together to cool them down. We didn't talk. The only sounds came from the rustling of leaves in regular hoofbeats and the steady squeaking of Maggie's leather saddle.

Finally I broke our silence. "So when *are* you going to saddle soap that saddle, Maggie?"

"Gripe, gripe, gripe," she said, like the old Maggie would have. "And what else are you going to want me to do, Madame Horsefeathers?"

I laughed. "You mean besides cleaning all the tack, scrubbing down the Horsefeathers' meeting room, repairing the paddock fence, fixing Sugar's stall where she gnawed the wood? Oh yeah, and I forgot—the hayloft looks like a tornado went through it."

Maggie sat up straight in her saddle. "Ah, the trials and tribulations of fame. I guess we better get to it then."

I almost felt like I could talk to her about what we both had to be thinking—that the day after tomorrow, Horsefeathers would be on TV. And we hadn't talked about it since the blow-up in our office.

"Scoop," Maggie said, "I keep forgetting to ask you. Can Dotty bring you and B.C. to opening night? I'd ask you to come with us, but the cast party's after the performance."

"And you're going with Ben?" I asked.

"Don't look that way, Scoop! I owe him *something*, don't you think? After all, if it hadn't been for Ben, I'd never even have this role in the play. And we wouldn't be getting this great publicity for Horsefeathers. Right?"

She turned in her saddle to face me. "Don't worry, Scoop. I know Ben's not exactly a choir boy. But I can handle him. Really."

Suddenly Maggie stared ahead, leaned forward, and stood up in her stirrups. It was as if she were electric and someone had just plugged her in.

"What?" I looked where she was looking. Ahead of us in the paddock, Ben Thayer was sitting on our bale of hay.

Maggie took off running on Moby, even though she should have kept cooling her horse. I held Orphan to a walk, although it wasn't easy. She wanted to run after Moby. I could see Maggie dismount inside the paddock and Ben stride over to her, but that's all I could see because Moby's neck was in the way.

When I rode in, Maggie stepped back a couple of paces from Ben and there was an awkward silence.

Ben nodded to me, and I nodded back.

Maggie finally spoke, slipping into her Southern accent. "Ben, play practice isn't for two hours yet. What brings y'all to Horsefeathers?"

"I couldn't stay away," he said.

Maggie giggled. I felt like throwing up.

"Come get something to eat with me, Maggie," Ben said, taking her hand. "I'm starving."

Maggie looked back at me and bit her lip. She turned back to Ben and sighed longingly.

"Scoop and I have *so* much work to do fixing up Horsefeathers."

Good for you, Maggie! I thought. She was right! Maggie could handle herself. Even Benson Thayer was no match for Maggie 37 Brown.

"Come on, Maggie," Ben said. "Some of the gang from the play are meeting to plan the cast party. Besides, can't you do this other stuff tomorrow after school?"

"Mmmm ..." Maggie looked like she was considering it.

No, Maggie! Don't let him talk you into anything. I need you.

"No, I can't, Ben. Scoop needs me. That tax assessor person is coming out tomorrow after school. We have to fix the place up before he gets here."

"What tax assessor?" Ben asked.

Maggie turned to me. "Tell him, Scoop."

I jumped off Orphan and put my arm around her neck. "I don't know who it is. The county tax office is sending somebody to figure out how much Horsefeathers is worth now. Jen knows more about it. I just know that it happens tomorrow after school."

Orphan sneezed twice, and Moby topped her with three sneezes.

"*That's* what you're fixing the place up for? For the tax assessor?" Ben laughed. It felt like he was laughing at me.

"Yeah," I said, not seeing anything funny about it.

"I thought you were doing it for Mom's show."

"Why?" Maggie asked, laughing a little herself, although I didn't think she had any more of an idea than I did about what Ben found so funny.

Ben put his arm around Maggie's shoulder. "You girls have a lot to learn about business," he said. "You've got the wrong idea about this thing. Go ahead and clean up before the Channel 7 crew comes out on Saturday. But for tomorrow, not only shouldn't you lift a finger to make Horsefeathers look better, but if I were you, I'd do all I could to trash the joint."

17

At first, when Ben told us we ought to trash Horsefeathers before the tax assessor came, I was too stunned to respond. Ben kept talking, his voice deep and almost hypnotic. Before I knew it, I was hanging on every word, just like Maggie was doing.

"Mom says at the TV station, whenever they get audited or the tax people come by, they dress down, hide the good equipment, and fire the janitors for a week. It's the way things are done."

"I still don't get it, Ben," Maggie said.

"It's easy, really," Ben went on. "The more the county thinks your property is worth, the higher your taxes will be and the bigger your mortgage payments. All that means *more money* out of your pocket."

"Wow!" Maggie said. She glanced at me. "Aren't you glad Ben stopped by?"

What he said made sense. "Is it legal to make yourself look poorer than you are?" I asked.

Ben laughed again. "Just how *rich* are you?"

He didn't wait for an answer. "The station wouldn't do it if they could get caught. It's just business. It's what they expect. It's all part of the game. So they're coming tomorrow?"

"Yeah," I said. "Jen set it up for Friday after school, at 4:00."

"No problem," Ben said. "You just take them on a poor-man's tour. Walk them by anything that needs repairing. Tell them how hard it's been to drum up business, how most of your horses are just pets—that kind of thing."

"No way I'd be able to think of things to say!" I cried. "Maggie, you have to do it. You have to give them the tour. I can't." She was the master of white lies anyway.

Maggie did a bow. "Like Ben says, no problem."

"This is going to save you a ton of money," Ben said. "Trust me."

"Thanks, Ben!" Maggie exclaimed.

"Don't thank me. Eat with me." Ben took Maggie's hand. Moby pawed the ground, tired of standing around.

Maggie looked wide-eyed back at me. "Do you mind, Scoop? Since we don't have to do all that other stuff now? Ben and I will both help tomorrow before our rehearsal, right Ben?"

"I guess," I said, still mulling over the crash course in business Ben had just given us.

"Thanks, Scoop!" Maggie handed me

Moby's reins and let herself be pulled away by Ben Thayer.

~~~~~~~~~~~~~~~~~~~~~~~~~~~~~~~~~~

That night I tried to get a whole report on the Polish economy out of a few paragraphs in each of my two library books. I'd written one sentence when the phone rang. Dotty had fallen asleep already, and B.C. was messing with his bottle caps, so of course I had to answer it. "Hello," I said, not very friendly.

"Scoop? This is Mrs. Chesley, Maggie's mother. How are you?"

Please, please don't ask for Maggie. "Fine. How are you, Ma'am?"

"Wonderful, thank you," she said. "Could I talk to Maggie, Dear?"

I panicked. "No," I said.

"Excuse me?" She was silent; I was more silent. Then she laughed softly. "Oh, I see. I missed her. Good. You girls have school in the morning. How's that studying coming?"

I swallowed hard. "Okay, I guess," I said. "World cultures class is tough."

"Well, you girls study hard. It's an important class. Sorry to have disturbed you, Scoop. Give my best to your aunt, will you?" She hung up when she figured out I wasn't going to say anything else.

I hung up the phone and replayed our conversation in my head. I hadn't lied to her—not actually. But that whispering voice inside of me made me feel like I had. I'd let her believe Maggie had been here.

God, I prayed, *I'm sorry. Please take care of Maggie and get her home safely.*

~~~~~~~~~~~~~~~~~~~~~~~~~~~~~~~~

I stayed up half the night working on my paper and worrying about Maggie. Twice I fell asleep with my pen in my hand and scribbled all over the page.

I gave up after I'd gutted out two and a half pages. I fell asleep saying my prayers, right after telling God I was sorry I'd let Mr. Hatt think I had lots of material, and right in the middle of the part about being sorry I hadn't worked on my report sooner. I wondered if God was getting as fed up with *sorry* as I was.

~~~~~~~~~~~~~~~~~~~~~~~~~~~~~~~~

Friday morning when I got to school, a mob of kids circled me. "Can I come to the taping?" Allyson asked. "I've never seen a television show being filmed before."

"You just want to try to push your way in front of the camera, Allyson," Brent said, chuckling. "Seriously, Scoop, good luck with that. I'm into horses, but I'll watch anyway."

"Thanks," I said. I'd taken the time to put on my new jeans and my best sweater, the one Maggie told me makes my eyes shine.

"You ought to wear that sweater on the show, Scoop!" Brent said as he walked backwards down the hall. "Looks great on you."

The bell rang. It may have been the first time in my career as a student that I was glad to hear it. I couldn't handle the extra attention, not now. I was too worried about the tax assessor. The farther away from Ben I got, the more questions I had about what he'd said. I was just glad Maggie would be there to do the talking.

In study hall, the librarian helped me find another book to fill in some of the numbers and statistics on Poland's economy. I wrote what I could as fast as I could. I even skipped lunch to copy everything over. But when I was all finished, I knew my report was too much horse and not enough Poland for my teacher. But at least I'd have something to turn in.

Only once during the whole day did I pass Maggie in the halls. She was clearly Maggie 37 Red, in red jeans and a red sweater. We were both running late, so we only stopped for a second.

"Thanks for covering for me!" Maggie whispered. "I got home just after Mom called you."

"I hated that, Maggie!" I whispered back. "I won't cover for you again like that. So don't say you're at my house when you're not. Why are you lying to your mom anyway? Where were you?"

"Play practice. That's all. Mom's afraid it's hurting my grades, so I told her I'd cut out early to study with you. But I just couldn't. No big deal." She smoothed my hair down for me. "So Scoop, are you all set for that tax person this afternoon?"

"Maggie," I pleaded, "don't even kid about this. I'm counting on you. You have to get to Horsefeathers before the tax assessor does. I could never pull this off without you. I wouldn't know what to say."

"No problemo," she said in a new Spanish accent I hadn't heard her use before. "I will most gladly take care of everything. *Adios*!" She twirled off into the stream of kids.

"You lost?" Stephen Dalton stood behind me staring at my report. Instinctively, I hid it from him. "If I were going to *steal* from somebody's report, you don't think it would be yours, do you?"

"How about if *you* get lost, Stephen?" I took off down the hall, but he stuck with me like horseflies in July.

"And I thought you'd need a friend now that Maggie is ... well, *changed*."

I stopped short and he almost tripped over me. "What are you getting at?"

"Don't tell me you haven't noticed what's happening to Maggie *38*. Everybody at school's talking about it. Some kids saw her smoking like a chimney last week. Jeremy swears he saw her drunk last weekend."

"You're making it up, Stephen! You're a lousy gossip and you better stop spreading rumors about my friend!" I stormed away too fast for him to follow.

"No running in the halls!" Mrs. Dorr shouted after me.

Stephen would say anything to hurt Maggie and me. I shouldn't even listen to him for a second. I tried not to think about what he said as I sat through my next class. But my mind kept bringing up changes I'd seen in Maggie too. She'd been letting school slide, letting her Horsefeathers duties slide—all to spend more time with Ben.

Still, it's only part of our plan to keep Ben and his mother around until after the show. Things will go back to normal after that. Like Maggie said, no big deal.

As soon as we got to world cultures, Mr. Hatt split us into small groups to introduce the next chapter. Maggie was in a different group, so I didn't get a chance to talk to her until the end of the hour when we turned in our reports.

I scribbled my name on mine and placed it in the middle of the stack. As I was walking away from the desk, I passed Maggie 37. She was turning in a report three times as long as mine, all typed and perfect-looking. I couldn't believe it.

Good for Maggie! Here I was thinking she'd changed so much she probably hadn't even written a report. And instead, she'd written a much better one than I had—although that wasn't saying much. Why had I let Stephen Dalton get me upset? Why did I let him do it to me again?

"Way to go, Maggie!" I whispered, pointing to her report on top of the pile.

She didn't stop, but brushed by the desk and out the door.

By the time I got to language arts, there were no empty seats except the one next to Stephen Dalton. Stephen stretched his legs out in the aisle and leaned his head back in snooze-position. His red hair smeared gel on the back of his chair. Pimples had declared war on his face, a full frontal attack. Most of them matched his hair color.

Suddenly he sat up and leaned over in the aisle to talk to me. He smelled like week-old pepperoni pizza. "Hey, Scoop, what's the latest with the new Maggie 36?"

"I'm not going to talk about Maggie to you, Stephen. So you can just bother somebody else." I kept my gaze straight ahead and tried to ignore him.

"Oooh," Stephen crooned. "Touchy, touchy. What trouble is she in now?"

"You're way off, Stephen," I said, turning my glare on him. "Way off! Maggie just handed in her report, typed, no less, and at least six or eight pages long."

"That's right," Stephen said. "I heard about that. World cultures, right?" He nodded, like he had some kind of inside information.

"Get off it, Stephen. I'll bet *you* didn't even get your report done!"

"Maybe. But then I don't have a rich boyfriend to buy me one."

18

"What are you saying, Stephen Dalton? What do you mean *buy one?*"

"Maybe that's the wrong word. Maybe he didn't actually have to buy Maggie the report. Ursula said Ben's brother was really good in school. She thought it might be one of his old papers he—"

"Stop it!" Several kids turned back to look at me. Ms. Whitmore frowned.

"Either way," Stephen whispered, "Maggie didn't write any report. *That* you can take to the bank."

~~~~~~~~~~~~~~~~~~~~~~~~~~~~~~~

I biked as hard as I could to get away from school and Stephen. My wheels slipped twice in the mud at the side of the road, stirring up dead leaves. *Stephen's wrong, God,* I prayed. *He's wrong. Maggie would never cheat like that.*

Before I realized where I was headed, I was on Main Street and headed for the Hy-Klas. In an hour the tax assessor would be at Horsefeathers ...

and so would Maggie. I didn't think I could face either one of them.

Although I probably couldn't have put it into words, I needed to see Dotty—maybe not even talk to her, but to see her.

I peeked through the front glass window of the grocery store, but Dotty wasn't at her usual register. Three customers waited in line. An older man thumbed through the *TV Guide*. One woman leaned both elbows on her shopping cart. The third person in line, a teenaged girl with straight, blond hair, craned her neck around, like she was searching for somebody.

By the time I got inside, Dotty was scurrying behind her counter, a box of Hy-Klas Rice in her hand. "There you go. $2.79. Sorry for the wait."

She glanced my way and waved as soon as she saw me. Even in her orange apron and her *Hi! I'm Dottie* (*still* spelled wrong) nametag, she looked like a short, plump angel. When she smiled at me, the warmth of it thawed something inside of me that needed what she had.

Dotty rang up all three customers while I waited off to the side and read cereal boxes. When her customers left, Dotty wiped her forehead with the back of her hand. "Pshew! What a day!" she said, but it didn't sound like a complaint. "Is B.C. with you?"

I hadn't stopped by the elementary school. "I think he's home," I said. Another white lie?

"And Maggie ain't with you?" Dotty stuck a handful of coupons under the tray in her register.

"Maggie?"

"She's been by most every day this week. Tell her I'm right sorry I ain't had time for a good chat. Been extra busy, what with all the extra price checks and all."

"Did Maggie have a boy with her?" I asked.

Dotty sighed and shut her register drawer. "I seen that handsome-looking fella waiting outside for her a couple of times."

I heard a *snap, pop* behind me and turned to see a tall, thin girl with dark purple eye shadow and sparkly mascara weighing down huge brown eyes. She looked like an artist. Her short hair clung to her high cheekbones in sharp points. Everything she had on except the orange apron looked tight and black. She reached long, dark red fingernails to her face and pulled off the remains of the bubble gum bubble she'd popped on her upper lip.

"Gail!" Dotty exclaimed. "*This* is Scoop! I told you about my niece."

Gail lifted plucked-thin eyebrows. "No kidding." She didn't sound thrilled. I wondered if Dotty really talked that much about me.

"Scoop, this is Gail Gayle!" Dotty sounded so excited about getting the two of us together, as if we were long-lost twins finding each other at last. "Why don't you girls get to know each other?"

Dotty reached into her black box purse and took out her billfold. She handed me a bunch of quarters. "Gail, you go on and take a break now. I'll cover bagging for you. We ain't that busy. Have yourselves a soda pop."

The last thing I felt like doing was talking to a stranger. Two baskets pulled into Dotty's lane, and Dotty started the conveyer to move the groceries to her.

"Thanks, Dotty," I said, following Gail, who was already halfway to the door. Outside, we walked to the side of the store where the vending machines sat. I stuck in the quarters, and Gail punched Mountain Dew.

Neither of us spoke until I'd gotten my Coke and popped the top. Gail didn't look any more eager to talk to me than I was to talk to her. She leaned against the machine and crossed her ankles.

There's nothing I hate more than trying to make small talk with somebody I don't even know. I'm horrible at it. But I had to say something. "So ... you're in that play? In Hamilton?"

Gail frowned at me. She stuck her gum on the side of her pop can. "What do *you* know about it?"

"What?" I wondered if Gail was even older than Ben. In some ways she seemed older than Dotty. "Maggie," I said stupidly. "I know Maggie, and she's in the play. Maggie Brown ... or Blue? ... or Pink?"

"Maggie *37*?" When Gail said it, it sounded like a joke. I smiled. "Yeah well, I'm not exactly *in* the play anymore, am I. I'm the script girl, the prompt. I feed them their lines if they forget them. Not that *Miss British Accent* ever forgets hers. So how well do you know *Maggie 37*?" Gail crumpled her can and set it on the ground.

"I don't know." A week ago I would have answered without thinking that I knew Maggie very well, better than I knew anybody. But now, since she'd met Ben, I didn't feel that way. "We've known each other a long time, I guess. Why?"

Gail shook her head and stepped on her Mountain Dew can. "She just doesn't seem like Ben's usual type. That's all."

"What's his usual type?" I hadn't even sipped my drink. I needed to get back to Horsefeathers.

Gail rattled the one long silver earring she wore on her right ear. I counted seven earrings on that ear and none on the other. "*I'm* his usual type. Me and about half of the females in Hamilton. He likes his women wild."

I wondered if Maggie knew.

Gail glanced down Main Street, then peeked around to the front of the Hy-Klas. She leaned against the pop machine and reached into her jacket pocket. She pulled out a lighter and a pack of cigarettes, shook out a cigarette, and lit it.

My throat went dry, and I must have shown how shocked I was.

Gail looked at me like I was a little kid. "Guess you don't smoke." She sucked in, and the tip of the cigarette glowed.

"No." I watched the smoke seep from her nostrils and wondered how anyone could enjoy breathing in smoke. I tried not to cough at the fumes.

"How about your friend Maggie? She smoke?"

"No." I coughed, but with my lips together so the cough bounced around inside me and made my eyes water.

"You sure about that?" Gail blew a steady stream of the gray smoke in my face.

It felt like my eyes were on fire. "I'm sure," I managed.

"Hmmm. That's funny." She flicked ash on the sidewalk. "Does she drink? Beer, I mean?"

"She's only 14," I said.

Gail looked confused. "Maybe she just wanted them for Ben."

"Wanted what?" I asked, watching her flick ashes on the sidewalk.

"Cigarettes on Tuesday. Beer yesterday. That's why she came by the store."

I couldn't believe it. "Maggie can't buy cigarettes. Don't you have to be 21 or something? And she'd *never* buy beer!"

"She wasn't buying them. She was bumming cigarettes off me. And she had me buy the beer for her. No big deal. Half the kids at play practice smoke. The beer was probably for the cast party. She and Ben are supposed to bring it."

Gail threw her half-smoked cigarette down. "I gotta get back, I guess."

When Gail left, I stepped on her still-glowing cigarette, crushing it into the sidewalk. I didn't know what to believe. Gail didn't like Maggie. Maybe she was just making things up about her.

God, I prayed as I biked to Horsefeathers, *I don't know what's true and what's not. Help me sort it out.* I felt as if I were in the middle of a quicksand of lies, sinking deeper, without any idea what I could grab onto.

I wanted the old Maggie back. If I could just hang on, keep my head above the quicksand until *Della's Folks* was over, I'd straighten everything out. Everything would be all right.

19

I expected to see Maggie when I rode up to Horsefeathers. I just hoped Ben wouldn't be with her. I needed to talk to her by herself, to ask her if what Gail said was true. But as I biked up the lane, I didn't see any sign of anybody, except B.C.

B.C.'s backpack sat under the oak tree. I looked up and spotted him on the roof. "B.C.!" I shouted. "You have to go home! Somebody's coming from the tax office! It's business, B.C."

"I know it!" he shouted down. "I've been helping."

He disappeared, and I went over to the fence and said hello to Orphan. From the looks of her, she'd been down by the pond, rolling in the mud. My first thought was I had to hurry and clean her up before the assessor got there. Then I remembered Ben's advice—do whatever we could to make Horsefeathers look like it wasn't worth much.

"I guess you won't mind staying dirty for a while, Orphan," I said. After this tax thing was over, we'd have to give all the horses a bath and maybe keep them in the barn until *Della's Folks* was over. It was hard keeping everything straight in my head—what I'd say to the tax guy, what I'd say to Ben's mother, and what I wanted to say to Maggie.

Maggie. Where could she be?

"I threw all the old branches off the barn roof," B.C. said. He was dirty, and his black T-shirt had a hole in it the size of New Jersey.

"What happened to you?" I asked.

"Nothing. And I cleaned out the water in the paddock. And I tried to sweep the barn floor, but I didn't do too good."

"Thanks, B.C.," I said, hoping he was right about not doing such a good job. "But you don't need to—"

"I need you to help me move things in the hayloft because it looks messy and the bales are so heavy." He stopped and stared down the lane. "Where's Maggie?"

"That's what I'd like to know, B.C." She'd be there. She had to be. Maggie knew how scared I was about this assessment, even with her doing the talking. She'd never leave me to face it on my own. She might have changed, but not *that* much.

B.C. pulled on my sleeve. "Hurry! You left out old saddles too, and we should put them away in the tack room and maybe leave out one of Carla's pretty saddles or Maggie's fancy one with silver all over it."

How was I going to make B.C. understand that I wanted Horsefeathers to look bad? Without letting go of my sleeve, he bent down and picked up a branch and got ready to throw it out of the way.

"Leave it, B.C.," I said.

He squinted back at me as if I'd lost my mind.

"It's okay there. We don't have time to clean up any more now. Leave everything like it is."

"But—" B.C. still held my sleeve. I pried his fingers loose.

"Later, B.C.," I said. "After supper we'll come back and clean everything. I promise. And tomorrow morning we'll work on the loft. Okay?"

I broke away from my brother and climbed the fence into the paddock. Orphan nuzzled my pockets, searching for treats I'd forgotten to bring. "Sorry, Girl," I said. "That's the third time this week I forgot to bring you something."

B.C. wasn't there when I turned back. I hoped he'd walked home. I didn't need him around messing things up.

My watch said 4:00, and still Maggie wasn't there. I couldn't believe it. I would have thought for once in her life she could have shown up on time. She knew how much I'd hate it if I had to make small talk with the tax assessor until she got there.

Orphan followed me into the barn while I got her a handful of oats. A cool wind blew through the stall, making it feel colder inside than outside in the paddock. We walked back outside, and I started in with the pick to clean out Orphan's hooves, when I heard a car door slam.

Please let it be Maggie! Even if Ben's with her— let it be Maggie 37.

"Hello? Is anybody here?"

Horsefeathers! It wasn't Maggie.

"I'm—I'm out here!" I shouted back. Now what was I going to do? How could Maggie do this to me? Didn't she care about Horsefeathers anymore?

I walked into the barn and saw two figures lurking around in the front doorway. I took a deep breath and joined them there, under the Horsefeathers sign.

The woman was tall, African American, with eyes bigger than Maggie's. She wore a dark green business suit, the wool jacket buttoned in the middle. And her high heels must have been three inches high. I wondered if this was her first barn to assess, if maybe she was used to sizing up business offices.

The woman stuck out her hand for me to shake. "I'm Ms. Dane." She nodded at the younger guy in blue jeans and a blue knit shirt that had a Polo pony on it. "And that's Carl."

I shook her hand and nodded at Carl, who

ignored me and wandered off on his own. He walked outside, looking in every direction as he went.

"Scoop," I said. "Sarah Coop."

"Uh huh," she said, looking up at the rafters.

"I—uh—my friend was supposed to be here." I glanced down the lane, but there was no sign of Maggie 37. "Do you—would you mind—uh—if we wait for her?"

Ms. Dane tugged back the sleeve of her jacket to glance at her tiny gold watch. "Well, I'm afraid we can't wait. We're on a tight schedule. We're actually due in Kennsington in an hour. Carl can get a feel for the grounds on his own. Why don't you just show me around and tell me what you do here."

So this was it. No Maggie. I was on my own. It was my stable. Why should *she* care? She and Ben were probably off right now delivering their beer and cigarettes to all their new theater friends.

Ms. Dane shifted her weight and got out a pen and a small notebook from her carrying case. "Could we take a look around now?"

I could do this. I'd watched Maggie in action enough. If she could fake it, then so could I. Motioning around the barn, I said, "You're looking at it, at Horsefeathers. Really, this is about all there is. It used to be fancier when my grandfather ran a horse farm, but I don't have the money to keep it up very well."

Once I'd started talking, it wasn't all that hard. I didn't want to lie. It was all a matter of selecting the right pieces to tell her. That's all.

"Do you board a lot of horses here at Horse-feathers?" she asked, scribbling something on her pad.

"Board? I wouldn't really call it boarding. Several of my friends keep their horses here. We really don't use the stable all that much. We just let the horses eat grass outside."

I led her down the stallway, without turning on the inside lights. When we got in front of Sugar's stall, I said, "Would you like to see the paddock?"

We walked through Sugar's stall, past the stall door the mare had gnawed and chewed until I cured her of cribbing and wind-sucking. "One of these days," I said, "when we have enough money, we'll have to fix that old door."

We passed outside to the paddock. I walked her straight to the broken rung that needed fixing.

"So tell me a little bit about you—Sarah Coop, the Teenaged Horse Whisperer. How do you do what you do?"

I didn't know they'd have so much information about me already. Ben had warned Maggie not to brag about me, to make it seem like our business didn't really have much value. "Oh that," I said, leaning on the broken railing so she'd be sure to see it. "That's really been exaggerated."

Orphan strolled up to me and nudged my arm.

"Sometimes I've helped a friend or two when they couldn't get their horses to behave. It's no big deal. I don't even ride in horse shows."

"But you keep show horses here, don't you?"

"Sometimes," I said. "As for my horse here ..." I pulled a clump of mud out of Orphan's forelock. "Orphan is just a mixed breed. She's not even registered."

As I said it, I glanced up on the barn roof and saw B.C. staring down, listening, his head cocked to the side. He stared at me as if he couldn't believe what he'd heard.

Something inside of me snapped, and all my confidence leaked out. I felt like such a traitor. I'd just put down Orphan, the way Stephen Dalton might have done. And I'd done it to her myself— to my Orphan, the best horse in the whole world.

Footsteps running out of the barn and coming our way made us turn and look. Maggie and Ben were jogging out to us. Maggie's gaze darted back and forth between Ms. Dane and me.

Ben looked just as surprised. Without slowing down, he walked straight to Ms. Dane and kissed her on the cheek. Then before I could grasp what was happening, Ben said, "Mother! What are you doing here?"

20

Mother?" I cried, nearly choking on the word.

I glanced at Maggie. "Did—did he say *mother?"*

Maggie 37 shook the woman's hand. "It's nice to see you again," she said.

"But—but you're not *mother*!" I sputtered. "I mean, you're not *Della's Folks*!"

"Scoop, this is my mother, Della Dane," Ben said, frowning at me.

"But you can't be!" I said. "Why aren't you Della Thayer? Like Ben Thayer?"

Maggie wrinkled her forehead and gave me a secret look to stop babbling. "Scoop, *my* mother's name is different than mine, right? I'm Maggie Brown, and she's Mrs. Chesley since she remarried ... again."

"Mom went back to her maiden name when she and Dad got a divorce," Ben explained.

"Wait a minute," said Della Dane. "Who did you think I was?"

But I couldn't answer her. I couldn't hold back the shame, the embarrassment, the tears another second. I ran past them and to the barn.

I heard Maggie behind me. "It's okay! I'll go after her." Then her footsteps closed in on me. She caught up with me before I could reach the end of the lane.

"Scoop! What is the matter with you?" Maggie bent double and tried to catch her breath.

"Me?" I yelled. "What about *you*? Where were you? You promised you'd be here! You promised you'd take care of the tax people! How could you leave me here alone?" My heart was pounding as loud as a stampede.

"Scoop," Maggie said, glancing toward the paddock. "Keep your voice down." She waved and flashed a fake smile at Ben and his mother.

The younger guy who'd come with Ben's mother climbed the paddock and nodded our way. "Hi, Carl!" Maggie called. To me, she whispered, "He's the cameraman. They're probably just checking out Horsefeathers to get ready for the show tomorrow."

"But what about the tax assessor?" My head hurt and my throat burned with the tears I had to swallow.

"Didn't you see Jen? She said she'd come by right after school to tell you. You ran out so fast, we couldn't catch you. The county office postponed the appointment."

"I didn't come here right after school." I wished I had. I wished I'd never met Gail Gayle, never heard those things about Maggie. Nothing was right anymore.

"So ..." Maggie said slowly, a light coming to her eyes as she put it all together. "You thought Ben's mother was the tax assessor?"

I bit my lip and nodded.

"Oh, Scoop!" Maggie cried. "What did you say? You didn't run down Horsefeathers."

"Of course I did, Maggie. You would have been so proud of me. I white-lied like the best of them. You should have heard me." I felt tears trickle down my cheeks.

Maggie wasn't listening to me anymore. She was miles ahead of me. "Ben can talk to his mother. He can straighten this out. I'll talk to her too and explain everything. It will still be okay. Don't worry."

"I don't care if it never gets straightened out!" I said.

"Scoop," Maggie said, as if she were talking to a little kid. "You don't mean that. Ben can fix everything."

"Ben!" I glanced into the paddock and saw him laughing with his mother. "He's fixed everything, all right! Like you, Maggie!"

"Me? What are you—?"

"You've changed, Maggie!"

"So what? Everybody changes." She didn't look at me. "People mature at different rates. That's what Ben says."

"*Mature?* Is that what you call it? Cheating on your report? Lying to your mother? You think smoking and drinking are mature?" My voice was so loud, Orphan came trotting over to the fence. I didn't care if Ben and his mother *could* hear me.

"Who told you I was smoking and drinking?" Maggie's voice sounded angry, but she avoided my stare. Then she looked up. "It was Dotty, wasn't it! I'll bet Gail told Dotty!"

"It wasn't Dotty," I said. "Dotty never would have believed it or repeated it. Are you saying it's not true, Maggie?"

"It's not true, Scoop!" Maggie took a deep breath and was quiet for a minute. Something came back into her eyes, a softness, like the old Maggie. "It's not *all* true," she said quietly. "Everybody smokes at play practice, Scoop. I tried one puff and I hated it. I gave the rest of the pack to Ben. I guess it was pretty stupid."

"Gail said you bought beer, Maggie."

She didn't answer at first. Then she said, "It was Ben's money and Ben's beer, but he had me sneak the money to Gail and take the beer to his car. He says he doesn't even drink. He was just buying it for the cast party."

"Hey, Good-Lookin'! Did you forget about me?" Ben hollered to Maggie over the paddock fence.

"Just a minute, Ben!" she called back.

"Mom needs to talk to you! I straightened

everything out. They'll still do the shoot tomorrow at 9:00."

"See?" Maggie said, cheering up. "Everything's working out just fine." She whispered to me, "Relax, Scoop. It's no big deal. After everything's over, after *Della's Folks*, and the play, and the cast party, I'll break it off with Ben. You'll see."

But I didn't see. I felt as if all our white lies were falling down and smothering me. All of those *little* things had added up to one very big deal. We'd piled up so many sparks, a fire couldn't be far away.

21

Friday night I couldn't get to sleep. I had let so many *little* things go by without talking them over with God, now they almost seemed too big to carry to Him.

Barefoot, I pulled my blanket off my bed, wrapped it around my shoulders, and tiptoed downstairs. B.C. was asleep on the couch. A pang of guilt struck again. I still hadn't taken the time to move him into Grandad's room. One more *little* thing that had slipped away from me.

The door to Grandad's old room was shut. I pushed it open and stepped in. Moonlight streamed in through the half-opened shade, and tree branches left black claw shapes on the other side of the blind. The floor was cold as winter, so I hopped up on the unmade bed.

"You worried about tomorrow?" Dotty's round shadow appeared in the doorway. She stepped into the room, her blanket dragging from her shoulders like a queen's mantle. She had to stand on her tiptoes to scoot up on the bed beside me. "Is it *Della's Folks* what's got you prowling?"

"Kind of," I said. The beam of light from the full moon outside lit up Dotty's face. She didn't have her glasses on. Her eyes were tiny as peas. "I'm sorry I woke you up, Dotty."

"Nonsense," she said, patting my knee through our blankets. God Hisself sees fit to wake me up at this here hour of His day. Seems like the best time to pray."

"I wish I could be like you, Dotty," I said. Everything always seemed so simple for her. Things were right or they were wrong. Everything that happened or might happen or didn't happen was fair game for her prayers. "You're amazing. You pray about everything."

"Well now," she said, kicking her slippered feet slightly, where they dangled an inch from the floor. "I reckon I always was of a mind to take advantage of a good thing when I seen it. It ain't me that's amazing for praying. I reckon it's God who's amazing for listening, don't you reckon?"

Neither of us said anything. I heard B.C. making weird noises and flopping around on the couch in the next room. I wanted to pray. More than anything I wanted to unload all of it on God. But the pile had grown, like B.C.'s mountain of bottle caps, a bottle cap at a time. I just didn't know where to begin or where to leave off.

"Dotty," I said after a few minutes of just sitting comfortably next to each other. "What do you do when you feel all bottled up inside, like you can't get through to God because you've let little things slide by too long, pretending they weren't really wrong, that they were only white lies, or maybe white lies other people were telling and you were just going along?" I knew I wasn't making sense with my words. I knew nobody else in the world would understand what I was saying, except Dotty.

Dotty reached over and pushed my blanket back over my leg where it had come unwrapped. "I reckon I start by talking on it with God, telling Him I'm right sorry. And thanking Him for sending Jesus to die for me so He can forgive me."

"But what about the really little things?"

"I reckon all that suffering on the cross was good for them little things too. 'Sides, them things ain't all that little if they block you off from God. Father, thank You for caring about them things we think is so little. Show Scoop here the right way to go."

And before I realized it, Dotty had stretched our conversation to include God, thanking Him for rising from the dead and taking us with Him. The three of us talked, or prayed, until I drifted off to sleep. When I woke up Saturday morning, Dotty and I were still in Grandad's bed.

"Aren't you on TV today?" B.C. asked.

Dotty and I rushed around and got dressed. I braided my hair in one long braid, grabbed an apple and ran to the car. Dotty had switched shifts with Gail Gayle at the Hy-Klas so she and B.C. could watch *Della's Folks* on the set.

When we got to Horsefeathers, a dozen people were already pressed up against the fence watching. I recognized Allyson and Brent and several kids from school, the Hat Lady from church, and another of Dotty's friends. Maggie's mom waved to me, and I felt a pang in my heart that meant I was going to have to apologize to her too.

B.C., Dotty, and I piled out of the car and walked toward the barn. Carl the cameraman came trotting up with a big, silver tripod in his hands. "Come with me!" he commanded.

We started to follow him, but he turned around, eyed Dotty and B.C., and said, "Not you two. You can wait over there." He motioned toward the fence and the other spectators.

"Excuse me," I said. "This is my aunt, Dotty Eberhart. And this is my brother, B.C. They're with me." I locked my arms through theirs and pulled them with me.

Carl shrugged and scurried on ahead.

Thank You, God, I prayed. It felt good to do the right thing, even a little right thing. I had no idea what was going to happen next, but I knew in my heart it would be right.

Ben and his mother looked deep in conversation, as two other camera people, one older man and one college-age-looking girl, set up lights and practiced angles. Maggie was in the back of the paddock, practicing standing in her saddle on Moby's back. She looked beautiful in a turquoise cowgirl outfit and matching hat and boots.

Jen and Carla stood off to the side of the paddock, holding Cheyenne and Ham. Both horses looked ship-shape, all tacked up and well groomed. Somebody had brushed Orphan for me. Carla had her on a lead rope. She waved me over as soon as she saw me.

"I'll be right back," I told B.C. Dotty was already at the cameralady's side, plying her with questions.

"How's it going?" I asked Jen and Carla. I took Orphan's lead rope and pressed my cheek against her fuzzy cheek. Inhaling her earthy horse smell, I closed my eyes and thanked God for my black beauty.

"That camera guy told us to wait over here— he didn't know if they'd be needing us or not," Carla said.

"My parents and Tommy and the twins and everybody will be very disappointed if I'm not even on *Della's Folks*," Jen said.

"I'm sorry, guys." I fed Orphan half of my breakfast apple. She licked my palm clean.

"Sorry I missed you after school yesterday," Jen said. "The tax assessor wants to come on Monday if that's okay."

"That's great, Jen. I'm looking forward to it." And he'd get a real Horsefeathers welcome this time, and an honest-to-goodness tour.

"*You* better get over there right now, Scoop," Carla warned, "or Maggie and Ben will edge you out the way they did us."

The crowd was growing. I spotted Ray and Travis and Caroline.

Ben's mother shouted over a microphone. "Testing! Testing! All right, everybody. Five minutes to showtime. To your places. I still need to have a few words with Maggie and Sarah."

I called B.C. to come out and hold Orphan. His grin was as big as a horse's grin. "Does this mean I'll be on TV?" he whispered. "Wait till Tommy sees me!" He waved at Dotty, and she waved back with both hands.

"There you are!" said Della Dane as I walked up. "We've managed to get Diablo cleaned up. We're calling this episode 'A Horse of a Different Color'—playing on the colorful Appaloosa coat and the phrase, meaning a horse that has changed. What we want you to do is show off a little, Sarah."

"Scoop," I said.

She scribbled on her pad. "That's right. Scoop. Okay. So, what can Diablo do now? I have early footage I plan to run on that horse putting up a fight being saddled and bridled and mounted. Ben says the horse will stand still now, right?"

"Most of the time," I said. "It's still going to—"

"Good!" She shouted an order at one of the cameramen, and he moved the tripod closer in. "Maggie? Where's Maggie?"

"Here," she said, dismounting Moby and leading her toward us. Maggie's step didn't have her usual spring. It was one of the few times I'd seen Maggie 37 looking sad.

"Ben says you're the most at ease in front of the camera." Della pulled out a little mirror and put on lipstick right where she was standing. "We'll go to you for commentary on the stables. Is that all right?"

"No problem," Maggie replied.

"Told you, Mom," Ben said, beaming at Maggie. "She's a pro! She can make this place sound like heaven."

"Places, everybody!" Ben's mother checked her mike and got set in front of the camera. "This is live! No re-takes!"

Ben kissed Maggie's cheek. "Knock 'em dead!" he said. One of the cameramen led Diablo out of the barn and handed his lead rope to Ben.

Maggie glanced sheepishly at me. "Don't look at me like that, Scoop," she said after Ben had gone.

"I'm not, Maggie," I said. It was weird. I was about to stand in front of a television camera, to show up in people's living rooms, and instead of feeling frantic, a calm had settled deep inside.

"*Ready in five, four, three, two, one!*" shouted someone from the film crew.

"Look, Scoop," Maggie whispered. "Maybe I am changing. I know you don't want me to. But I'm not like you. You know I don't ... well, think about God that much, not like you and Dotty."

I grinned. "Don't put me in Dotty's league."

"You know what I mean," Maggie said. "I have to be free to change when I feel like it—change personalities, change accents, change colors!"

We kept our voices down, while Ben's mom talked to the TV cameras about how awful Diablo used to be.

"There's nothing wrong with change, Maggie," I said, praying God would give me the right words. "Just don't change your nature—for the wrong reasons." I glanced at Ben, who was fussing with his horse. "God made you colorful as autumn, Maggie. That's what makes you so terrific. That's not what gets you in trouble. It's the little lies. I was telling them too—to everybody, to your mom, even to myself."

Maggie scuffed the toe of her blue boot in the dirt. "The white lies," she said. "I know."

"Now! You!" the camerawoman yelled at Maggie. "The girl on the trick white horse! You're on in five!"

22

Maggie jumped on Moby and took off around the arena in a canter. She was halfway around and standing in the saddle when *Della's Folks* came back on the air. "Here comes Maggie on Moby, just one of the amazing horses here at Horsefeathers Stable." Della sounded like she was everybody's best friend. No wonder her show had been so successful.

Maggie slid down in the saddle and had Moby rear. Then she hopped off and walked straight to the camera, a beautiful, natural grin on her face.

"Maggie," said Della, "tell us a little about Horsefeathers Stable."

"Horsefeathers is really more of a home for horses than it is a stable. We put the horses first here. We leave it up to them whether they want to be outside or inside. We never coop them up in their stalls. We don't just ride horses here, we play with them."

I tiptoed over to B.C. and Orphan. "She's great, isn't she, B.C.?"

"So are you," he said, not looking at me. He fumbled with something in his jacket pocket and came out with an empty pickle jar. I could smell the pickle juice before he took off the lid. "Want me to get the air for you?"

I kissed the top of his wild-man head of hair. "Thank you, B.C.!"

"You should ask her yourself!" Maggie was saying. I'd missed what went on before that.

"That's just what we intend to do," said Della. "Scoop, will you come and show us the new Diablo?"

I walked over to Diablo, but I tugged B.C. with me, and he didn't let go of Orphan. "Sure," I said. "But you have to meet my brother B.C. and my horse, Orphan, first."

You could tell it wasn't what Della had in mind, but the cameras filmed them anyway.

"You're known as the Teenaged Horse Whisperer in these parts," Della said. "Tell us how you earned your reputation."

"That's a good question," I said, putting the saddle blanket on Diablo. He held still for me. "I wouldn't say I'm known as that except to a few people."

Della swallowed hard and looked to Maggie while I got the saddle ready. "Maggie, Scoop's being too modest. Why don't you tell us about all the problem horses she's cured miraculously."

The saddle blanket started to slip, and Maggie must have seen it too. She ran over and straightened it for me, holding it in place so I could hoist the saddle on Diablo.

"I think Scoop is the best handler of horses I've ever seen. She gentles horses, rather than breaking them."

I turned to Maggie. "But I haven't gentled dozens of horses, have I, Maggie?"

Maggie bit her bottom lip and stared at me. I heard Della's foot tapping behind me. Ben mouthed something to her.

Make her understand, God, I prayed.

"To tell the truth," Maggie said looking at me instead of the camera, "and that's something we try to do at Horsefeathers, Scoop hasn't cured *dozens* of horses. She did help Carla over there with Ham. And she's gone a long way toward getting Cheyenne so he's safe to ride."

"Come on over, you guys!" I yelled.

Maggie waved them over too.

Jen and Carla rode their horses over to us and waved into the camera. I heard the entire Zucker clan cheering on the sidelines.

When I finished saddling Diablo, I slipped his bridle on.

Poor Della and Ben looked like we'd ruined everything. But it didn't feel like that to me.

"Well, look at that!" declared Della. "That *is* a miracle! I don't care what you say." She turned to the camera. "Our viewers at home saw for themselves what Diablo was like before you went to work on him. And in only a couple of weeks, you've turned that horse into *a horse of a different color*!"

"Not quite," I said. "Diablo doesn't always stand still like this. He's loaded with bad habits he got from poor handling. And bad habits don't just disappear overnight. I suppose it will take us as long to get rid of the habits as it did for Diablo to pick them up."

"And don't forget that he still tries to bite," Carla threw in.

"You should mount him and show them what he does when nobody holds him!" Jen added.

We laughed. But Ben and his mother didn't.

"And the other day—" Maggie could barely get it out because she was laughing so hard. "—Scoop was in the middle of mounting. And Diablo sidestepped and she flew off!"

"And I landed on Maggie," I said, almost doubled with laughter, "and we both fell down in the stall. And Maggie had manure all over her jeans."

"And what about you?" Maggie cried, tears from her laughter rolling down both cheeks. "*You* smelled like—"

"All right," said Ben's mom, turning away from us to the camera. "I'm afraid we're out of time for this week on *Della's Folks*. Please come back next week. Good day, and good folks."

"That's a wrap!" somebody said.

"I can't believe you did that!" Ben almost screamed at us.

The four of us couldn't stop laughing though, even when Ben marched up to us and yelled.

"You embarrassed my mother. You embarrassed me! And you embarrassed yourselves! You had the chance to put this dump of a stable on the map! And you blew it!"

I held my breath and tried to stop laughing, but I couldn't. "I'm sorry, Ben," I said, but I burst into a laugh, spraying him. That set off Jen and Carla all over again.

"That's it? You're sorry?" Ben asked incredulously. He shook his head in disgust at me. Then he turned to Maggie. "Maggie, I never expected this of you. I thought you knew how show business works. I thought you were a professional. Is this how you're going to act in our play? Because I won't have you embarrass me again—not there."

Jen, Carla, and I grew quiet as we watched Maggie. Her face went blank. I couldn't read what was going on in her mind. I knew how much that play meant to her.

Finally Maggie looked Ben square in the eyes. "Horsefeathers!" she said.

Ben and his mother stormed away as we laughed hysterically until we were all four crying.

Travis Zucker came out of the barn and stopped Ben and his mother. He gave me a nod and the thumbs-up sign. I watched as he spoke with them for a couple of minutes. Then they shook hands, and Ben and Della Dane left.

Travis came over and joined us. "I liked it," he said. "Liked it a lot better than I thought I would."

I couldn't have explained why it felt so good to hear Travis say it, but it did. "So what were you talking to Ben and Ms. Dane about?" I asked.

"I asked them what they planned to do with their Appaloosa now," Travis said, patting Moby's head.

I'd forgotten all about that. "Oh, Travis," I said, suddenly aching for the poor horse, "they're not putting him back out for auction, are they?" On the other hand, going back to Ben wasn't a great option either.

"That was the plan," Travis said. "I knew you were afraid of that, Scoop."

"Did you say *was* the plan?" Jen asked.

"Yep." Travis grinned. "Do you suppose you could find room at Horsefeathers for my new horse? I'm thinking about calling him *Angel*."

"Travis! You bought him?" I threw my arms around him, then realized what I was doing and pulled away. "That's—that's so great! He's a super horse! You couldn't have bought a better horse, once we get rid of the bad habits."

Jen was studying her brother. She leaned forward on Cheyenne's neck. "Where are you getting the money to pay for this horse, big brother?"

"Anybody have any spare Scotch tape?" Travis asked. "Looks like I'll be keeping that old pickup of mine for a while, until I can save up for a new one again."

B.C. was still holding Orphan and laughing and crying right along with us. "Did Tommy see me on TV?" he asked Travis.

"He sure did, B.C.," Travis said. "Everybody did. You were the star!"

Star! I swung around to Maggie. "Maggie," I said, just remembering. "What about your play? Your opening night?"

"I think I'll let the understudy handle it," she said. "You remember Gail Gayle, don't you?"

"Gail Gayle?" Jen asked.

"It's a long story," I said.

"How about you guys come spend the night at my house tonight, and I'll fill you in," said Maggie 37. She put one arm around my shoulder and added, "—the truth, the whole truth, and nothing but the truth."

Glossary of Tack Terms

Tack—horse gear; saddles, bridles, halters, harness equipment, etc.

Bell boots—rubber covering worn over a horse's foot and hoof for protection

Bit—the part of a bridle placed in a horse's mouth and attached to the reins to give the rider more control

Curb bit—bit with a U-shaped bump in the middle, designed to press on the horse's tongue or the roof of the mouth to give greater control

Double bit—two separate bits—a snaffle and a curb—used for English riding; also called a **Pelham bit**

Snaffle bit—a "broken" bit, jointed in the center

Straight bit—a simple, straight bar, with no breaks and no curb

Bridle—horse headgear for riding—usually consists of a headpiece, cheekpiece, throat latch, browband, noseband, with reins attached to a bit

Cantle—the raised back of the saddle seat

Cavesson—noseband, the part of the bridle that goes under the jaw and over the nose

Check-rein—strap that fastens to the bit to keep a horse's head up

Cinch—wide cord girth on a Western saddle

Cooler—a thin blanket to cover a horse while walking him to cool him down; also called a cooling blanket

Cross-tie—a double tie with leads attached to structures on two sides of the horse so the animal may be tied from both sides

English tack—loosely, any tack not Western; two-bit bridle, with two sets of reins; lighter, no-horn saddle with metal stirrups

Girth—a strap or "belt" that goes around a horse's belly, behind the front legs, to hold the saddle on

Hackamore—a bitless bridle, often used for training

Halter—bitless headstall for leading or tying a horse

Lead rope—a rope or lead with a metal snap on one end; used to lead or tie a horse; usually snapped to the halter

Lunge line, or Longe line—a long rein or rope used to exercise a horse by getting him to perform gaits in a large circle around the trainer (called lungeing or longeing)

Martingale—a strap that runs from the bridle, between a horse's front legs, to the girth to help keep a horse from rearing or throwing his head up

Pommel—top front of the saddle; raised as a bump on English saddle; surrounds saddle horn on Western saddle

Rein—strap that runs from the bit to the rider's hands to guide the horse

Surcingle—broad strap that goes over the saddle blanket and around the girth to hold blanket in place

Tapadero—leather hood over some stirrups on Western saddles

Western tack—"cowboy" saddle, or stock saddle and bridle, characterized by a one-bit bridle and a saddle with a high pommel and cantle and a saddle horn

About the Author

Dandi Daley Mackall rode her first horse—
bareback—when she was 3. She's been riding ever
since. She claims some of her best friends have been
horses she and her family have owned: mixed-breeds,
quarter horses, American Saddle Horses, Appaloosas,
Pintos, and Paints.

When she isn't riding, Dandi is writing. She has
published more than 200 books for children and
adults, including *The Cinnamon Lake Mysteries* and
The Puzzle Club Mysteries, both for Concordia. Dandi
has written for *Western Horseman* and other
magazines as well. She lives in rural Ohio, where she
rides the trails with her husband Joe (also a writer),
children Jen, Katy, and Dan, and the real Moby and
Cheyenne (pictured above).

R.

And from beloved authors

JUDITH STACY

"Judith Stacy is a fine writer with
both polished style and heartwarming sensitivity."
—Bestselling author Pamela Morsi

"…lovable characters that grab your heartstrings…
a fun read all the way."
—*Rendezvous* on *The Blushing Bride*

"…a delightful story of the triumph of love."
—*Rendezvous* on *The Dreammaker*

and

MARY BURTON

"This talented writer is a virtuoso,
who strums the hearts of the readers and
composes an emotional tale."
—*Rendezvous*

"Watch for more from this talented author…"
—*Romance Reviews Today*

"Mary Burton is a delightful surprise
for w

DIANA PALMER

has a gift for telling the most sensual tales with charm and humor. With over 40 million copies of her books in print, Diana Palmer is one of North America's most beloved authors and is considered one of the top ten romance authors in America.

Diana's hobbies include gardening, archaeology, anthropology, iguanas, astronomy and music. She has been married to James Kyle for over twenty-five years, and they have one son.

JUDITH STACY

gets many of her story ideas while taking long afternoon naps. She's trying to convince her family she's actually working, but even after more than a dozen novels, they're still not buying it.

Judith is married to her high school sweetheart. They have two daughters and live in Southern California.

MARY BURTON

lives in Richmond, Virginia, with her husband and two children. *Snow Maiden* is her sixth historical romance.

DIANA PALMER

JUDITH STACY · MARY BURTON

A HERO'S
Kiss

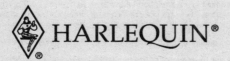

HARLEQUIN®

TORONTO · NEW YORK · LONDON
AMSTERDAM · PARIS · SYDNEY · HAMBURG
STOCKHOLM · ATHENS · TOKYO · MILAN · MADRID
PRAGUE · WARSAW · BUDAPEST · AUCKLAND

ISBN 0-373-83562-0

A HERO'S KISS

Copyright © 2003 by Harlequin Books S.A.

The publisher acknowledges the copyright holders
of the individual works as follows:

THE FOUNDING FATHER
Copyright © 2003 by Diana Palmer

WILD WEST WAGER
Copyright © 2003 by Dorothy Howell

SNOW MAIDEN
Copyright © 2003 by Mary Taylor Burton

This edition published by arrangement with Harlequin Books S.A.

® and TM are trademarks of the publisher. Trademarks indicated with
® are registered in the United States Patent and Trademark Office, the
Canadian Trade Marks Office and in other countries.

Visit us at www.eHarlequin.com

Printed in U.S.A.

CONTENTS

Dear Reader,

I am thrilled to present you with the prequel to my LONG, TALL TEXANS series for Silhouette Books. In "The Founding Father" you will meet Big John Jacobs, the founder of Jacobsville, Texas. He attracted a railroad line to his small ranching property with the help of a gutsy young debutante who preferred John and cold beans to a titled European and caviar. Camellia Ellen is a fiercely independent young woman who flowers when given a chance to escape the rigorous, correct society of her time. She and John begin as enemies but become husband and wife, and spend many happy years together.

I have often wished that I had the opportunity to show how Jacobsville began. It has been fun revisiting the Texas of more than a century ago and dabbling in the subject that I took my degree in—history! I hope you enjoy the characters, and the story.

I am still your biggest fan,

Diana Palmer

THE FOUNDING FATHER

Diana Palmer

For Susan James

CHAPTER ONE

IT TOOK A LOT TO MAKE BIG John Jacobs nervous. He was tall, rawboned, with deep-set green eyes the color of bottle glass, and thick dark brown hair. His lean, rough face had scars left over from the War Between the States. He carried scars both inside and out. He was originally from Georgia, but he'd come to Texas just after the war. Now he lived in one of the wildest parts of southeast Texas on a ranch he'd inherited from his late uncle. He was building up the ranch frugally, heading cattle drives to Kansas and buying livestock with the proceeds. What he had was very little to show for fifteen years of hard work, but he was strong and had a good business head. He'd tripled his uncle's land holdings and bought new bulls from back East to breed with his mangy longhorns. His mother would have been proud.

He noted the deep cut on his left hand, a scar from a knife fight with one of a band of Comanches who'd raided his property for horses. John and his hired help had fought them to a standstill and put them on the run. His ranch was isolated and he had good breeding stock. Over the years he'd had to fight roaming Comanche raiders and renegades from over the Mexican border, as well as carpetbaggers. If it hadn't been for the military presence just after the war ended, courtesy of the Union Army, lawlessness would have been even worse.

John had more reason than most to hate Union officers. But in the part of Texas where his ranch was located, to the southeast of San Antonio, the peace had been kept during Reconstruction by a local commandant who was a gentleman. John had admired the Union officer, who'd caught and prosecuted a thief who stole two horses from the ranch. They were good horses, with excellent bloodlines, which John had purchased from a Kentucky thoroughbred farm. The officer, who rode a Kentucky thoroughbred of his own, understood the attachment a rancher felt to his blood stock. John had rarely been more grateful to another human being. Like John himself, the officer was fearless.

Fearless. John laughed at his own apprehension over what he was about to do. He didn't mind risking his life to save his ranch. But this was no fight with guns or knives. It was a much more civilized sort of warfare. In order to win this battle, John was going to have to venture into a world he'd never seen close up. He wasn't comfortable with high society folk. He hoped he wasn't going to embarrass himself.

He removed his dress hat and ran a big hand through his sweaty brown hair. He'd had Juana cut it before he'd left the 3J Ranch. He hoped it was conservative enough to impress old man Terrance Colby. The railroad magnate was vacationing in Sutherland Springs, not far from the 3J. The popular resort boasted over one hundred separate springs in a small area. John had ridden out there to speak to Colby, without a single idea of how he was going to go about it. He had figured the details would work themselves out if he made the trip.

He was uneasy in company. He'd had to pawn his grandfather's watch to buy the used suit and hat he was wearing. It was a gamble he was taking, a big one. Cattle were no good to anyone if they couldn't be gotten to market. Driving cattle to the railheads in Kansas was becoming ever more dangerous. In some areas, fear of Texas tick fever had caused armed blockades of farmers to deter Texas cattle from entry. If he was going to get his cattle to market, there had to be a more direct route. He needed a railroad spur close by.

Colby owned a railroad. He'd just announced his intentions of expanding it to connect with San Antonio. It would be no great burden to extend a line down through Wilson County to the Jacobs' ranch. There were other ranchers in the area who also wanted the spur.

Old man Colby had a daughter, Camellia Ellen, who was unmarried and apparently unmarriageable. Local gossip said that the old man had no use for his unattractive daughter and would be happy to be rid of her. She got in the way of his mistresses. So Big John Jacobs had come a courting, to get himself a railroad…

It started raining just as he got to town. He cursed his foul luck, his green eyes blazing as he noted the mud his horse's hooves was throwing up and splattering onto his boots and the hem of the one good pair of pants he owned. He'd be untidy, and he couldn't afford to be. Terrance Colby was a New York aristocrat who, from what John had heard, was always impeccably dressed. He was staying at the best hotel the little resort of Sutherland Springs could boast, which was none too luxurious. Rumor was that Colby had come here on a hunting trip and was taking the waters while he was in the area.

John swung down out of the saddle half a block from the hotel Colby was staying at, hoping to have a chance to brush the mud off him-self. Just as he got onto the boardwalk, a carriage drew up nearby. A young woman of no particular note climbed down out of it, caught the hem of her dress under her laced shoe, and fell face-first into a mud puddle.

Unforgivably, John laughed. He couldn't help it. The woman's companion gave him a glare, but the look he gave the woman was much more ex-pressive.

"For God's sake, woman, can't you take two steps without tripping over your own garments?" the man asked in a high-pitched British accented voice. "Do get up. Now that we've dropped you off in town, I must go. I've an engagement for which you've already made me late. I'll call on your father later. Driver, carry on!"

The driver gave the woman and Big John a speaking look, but he did as he was instructed. John took note of the stranger, and hoped to meet him again one day.

He moved to the woman's side, and offered her an arm.

"No, no," she protested, managing to get to her feet alone. "You're much too nicely dressed to let me splatter you. Do go on, sir. I'm simply clumsy, there's no cure to be had for it, I'm afraid." She adjusted her oversized hat atop the dark bun of her hair and looked at him with miserable blue eyes in a pleasant but not very attractive face. She was slight and thin, and not the sort of woman to whom he'd ever been attracted.

"Your companion has no manners," he remarked.

"Thank you for your concern."

He tipped his hat. "It was no trouble. I wouldn't have minded being splattered. As you can see, I've already sampled the local mud."

She laughed and her animated face took on a fey quality, of which she was unaware. "Good day."

"Good day."

She moved away and he started into the barbershop to put himself to rights.

"John!" a man called from nearby. "Thought that was you," a heavyset man with a badge panted as he came up to join him. It was Deputy Marshal James Graham, who often stopped by John's ranch when he was in the area looking for fugitives.

They shook hands. "What are you doing in Sutherland Springs?" John asked him.

"I'm looking for a couple of renegades," he said. "They were hiding in Indian Territory, but I heard from a cousin of one of them that they were headed this way, trying to outrun the army. You watch your back.''

''You watch yours,'' he retorted, opening his jacket to display the Colt .45 he always wore in a holster on a gunbelt slung across his narrow hips.

The marshal chuckled. ''I heard that. Noticed you were trying to help that poor young woman out of a fix.''

''Yes, poor little thing,'' he commented. ''Nothing to look at, and of little interest to a man. Two left feet into the bargain. But it was no trouble to be kind to her. Her companion gave her no more help than the rough edge of his tongue.''

''That was Sir Sydney Blythe, a hunting companion of the railroad magnate, Colby. They say the girl has a crush on him, but he has no use for her.''

''Hardly surprising. He might have ended in the mud puddle,'' he added on a chuckle. ''She's not the sort to inspire passion.''

''You might be surprised. My wife is no looker, but can she cook! Looks wear out. Cooking lasts forever. You remember that. See you around.''

''You, too.'' John went on into the barbershop unaware of a mud-covered female standing behind the corner, trying to deal with wiping some of the mud from her heavy skirt.

She glared at the barbershop with fierce blue eyes. So he was that sort of a man, was he, pitying the poor little scrawny hen with the clumsy feet. She'd thought he was different, but he was just the same as other men. None of them looked twice at a woman unless she had a beautiful face or body.

She walked past the barbershop toward her hotel, seething with fury. She hoped that she might one day have the chance to meet that gentleman again when she was properly dressed and in her own element. It would be a shock for him, she felt certain.

A short while later John walked toward the Sutherland Springs Hotel with a confidence he didn't really feel. He was grateful for the marshal's conversation, which helped calm him. He wondered if Colby's daughter was also enamoured of the atrocious Sir Sydney, as well as that poor scrawny hen who'd been out riding with him? He wasn't certain how he would have to go about wooing such a misfit, although he had it in mind.

At thirty-five, John was more learned than many of his contemporaries, having been brought up by an educated mother who taught him Latin while they worked in the fields. Since then, he'd been educated in other ways while trying to keep himself clothed and fed. His married sister, the only other survivor of his family, had tried to get him to come and work with her husband in North Carolina on their farm, but he hadn't wanted to settle in the East. He was a man with a dream. And if a man could make himself a fortune with nothing more than hard work and self-denial, he was ready to be that man.

It seemed vaguely dishonest to take a bride for monetary reasons, and it cut to the quick to pretend an affection he didn't feel to get a rich bride. If there was an honest way to do this, he was going to find it. His one certainty was that if he married a railroad tycoon's daughter, he had a far better chance of getting a railroad to lay tracks to his ranch than if he simply asked for help. These days, nobody rushed to help a penniless rancher. Least of all a rich Northerner.

John walked into the hotel bristling with assumed self-confidence and the same faint arrogance he'd seen rich men use to get their way.

"My name is John Jacobs," he told the clerk formally. "Mr. Colby is expecting me."

That was a bald lie, but a bold one. If it worked, he could cut through a lot of time-wasting protocol.

"Uh, he is? I mean, of course, sir," the young man faltered. "Mr. Colby is in the presidential suite. It's on the second floor, at the end of the hall. You may go right up. Mr. Colby and his daughter are receiving this morning."

Receiving. Go right up. John nodded, dazed. It was easier than he'd dreamed to see one of the country's richest men!

He nodded politely at the clerk and turned to the staircase.

The suite was easy to find. He knocked on the door confidently, inwardly gritting his teeth to gear himself up for the meeting. He had no idea what he was going to give as an excuse for coming here. He didn't know what Ellen Colby looked like. Could he perhaps say that he'd seen her from afar and had fallen madly in love with her at once? That would certainly ruin his chances with her father, who would be convinced that he only wanted Ellen's money.

While he was thinking up excuses, a maid opened the door and stood back to let him inside. Belatedly he swept off his hat, hoping his forehead wasn't sweating as profusely as it felt.

"Your name, sir?" the middle-aged woman asked politely.

"John Jacobs," he told her. "I'm a local landowner," he added.

She nodded. ''Please wait here.''

She disappeared into another room behind a closed door. Seconds passed, while John looked around him uncomfortably, reminded by the opulence of the suite how far removed he was from the upper class.

The door opened. ''Please go in, sir,'' the maid said respectfully, and even smiled at him.

Elated, he went into the room and stared into a pair of the coldest pale blue eyes he'd ever seen, in a face that seemed unremarkable compared to the very expensive lacy white dress worn by its owner. She had a beautiful figure, regardless of her lack of beauty. Her hair was thick and a rich dark brown, swept up into a high bun that left a roll of it all around her head. She was very poised, very elegant and totally hostile. With a start, John recognized her. She was the mud puddle swimmer from the hotel entrance.

He must not laugh, he must not…! But a faint grin split his chiseled lips and his green eyes danced on her indignant features. Here was his excuse, so unexpected!

''I came to inquire about your health,'' he said, his voice deep and lazy. ''The weather is cold, and the mud puddle was very large….''

''I am…'' She was blushing, now apparently

flattered by his visit. "I am very well. Thank you!"

"What mud puddle?" came a crisp voice from the doorway. A man, shorter than John, with balding hair and dark blue eyes, dressed in an expensive suit, came into the room. "I'm Terrance Colby. Who are you?"

"John Jacobs," he introduced himself. He wasn't certain how to go on. "I own a ranch outside town…" he began.

"Oh, you're here about quail hunting," Colby said immediately. He smiled, to John's astonishment, and went forward to shake hands. "But I'm afraid you're a few minutes too late. I've already procured an invitation to the Four Aces Ranch to hunt antelope and quail. You know it, I expect?"

"Certainly I do, sir," John replied. And he did. That ranch was the sort John wanted desperately to own one day, a huge property with purebred cattle and horses, known all over the country—in fact, all over the world! "I'm sure you'll find the accommodations superior."

The older man eyed him curiously. "Thank you for the offer."

John nodded. "My pleasure, sir. But I had another purpose in coming. A passerby mentioned that the young lady here was staying at this hotel.

She, uh, had a bad fall on her way inside. I assisted her. I only wanted to assure myself that she was uninjured. Her companion was less than helpful,'' he added with honest irritation.

''Sir Sydney drove off and left me there,'' the woman said angrily with flashing eyes.

Colby gave her an unsympathetic glance. ''If you will be clumsy and throw yourself into mud puddles, Ellen, you can expect to be ignored by any normal man.''

Ellen! This unfortunate little hen was the very heiress John had come to town to woo, and he was having more good fortune than he'd dreamed! Lady Luck was tossing offerings into his path with every word he spoke.

He smiled at Ellen Colby with deliberate interest. ''On the contrary, sir, I find her enchanting,'' he murmured.

Colby looked at him as if he expected men with nets to storm the room.

Ellen gave him a harsh glare. She might have been flattered by the visit, but she knew a line when she heard one. Too many men had sought access to her father through her. Here was another, when she'd hoped he might like her for herself. But when had that ever happened? Disappointed, she drew herself up to her full height. ''Please excuse me. I am in the middle of important work.'' She lifted her chin and added deliberately, ''My father's dog is having her bath.''

She turned and stalked toward a door between rooms, while John threw back his head and laughed with genuine glee.

Colby had to chuckle, himself, at his daughter's audacity. She never raised her voice, as a rule, and he'd long since come to think of her as a doormat. But this man pricked her temper and made her eyes flash.

''An interesting reaction,'' he told John. ''She is never rude, and I cannot remember a time when she raised her voice.''

John grinned. ''A gentleman likes to think that he has made an impression, sir,'' he said respectfully. ''Your daughter is far more interesting with a temper than without one. To me, at least.''

''You have a ranch, you said?'' Colby asked.

John nodded. ''A small one, but growing. I have begun to cross breeds to good effect. I have a longhorn seed bull and a small herd of Hereford cattle. I hope to raise a better sort of beef to suit Eastern tastes and ship it to market in Chicago.''

The older man sized up his guest, from the worn, but still useful, shoes and suit and the well-worn gunbelt and pistol worn unobtrusively under the open jacket.

''You have a Southern accent,'' Colby said.

John nodded again. "I am a Georgian, by birth."

Colby actually winced.

John laughed without humor. "You know, then, what Sherman and his men did to my state."

"Slavery is against everything I believe in," Colby said. His face grew hard. "Sherman's conduct was justified."

John had to bite his tongue to keep back a sharp reply. He could feel the heat of the fire, hear his mother and sister screaming as they fell in the maelstrom of crackling flames....

"You owned slaves?" Colby persisted curtly.

John gritted his teeth. "Sir, my mother and sisters and I worked on a farm outside Atlanta," he said, almost choking on memories despite the years between himself and the memory. "Only rich planters could afford slaves. My people were Irish immigrants. You might recall the signs placed at the front gates of estates in the North, which read, No Colored Or Irish Need Apply."

Colby swallowed hard. He had, indeed, seen those signs.

John seemed to grow another inch. "To answer your question, had I been a rich planter, I would have hired my labor, not bought it, for I do not feel that one man of any color has the right to own another." His green eyes flashed. "There were many other small landowners and sharecroppers like my family who paid the price for the greed and luxury of plantation owners. Sherman's army did not discriminate between the two."

"Excuse me," Colby said at once. "One of my laundresses back home had been a slave. Her arms were livid with scars from a mistress who cut her when she burned a dress she was told to iron."

"I have seen similar scars," John replied, without adding that one of the co-owners of his ranch had such unsightly scars, as well as his wife and even their eldest daughter.

"Your mother and sisters live with you?" Colby asked.

John didn't reply for a few seconds. "No, sir. Except for a married sister in North Carolina, my people are all dead."

Colby nodded, his eyes narrow and assessing. "But, then, you have done well for yourself in Texas, have you not?" He smiled.

John forced himself to return the smile and forget the insults. "I will do better, sir," he said with unshakeable confidence. "Far better."

Colby chuckled. "You remind me of myself, when I was a young man. I left home to make my fortune, and had the good sense to look toward trains as the means.''

John twirled his hat in his big hands. He wanted to approach Colby about his spur, which would give him the opportunity to ship his cattle without having to take the risk of driving them north to railheads in Kansas. But that would be pushing his luck. Colby might feel that John was overstepping his place in society and being ''uppity.'' He couldn't risk alienating Colby.

He shifted his weight. ''I should go,'' he said absently. ''I had no intention of taking up so much of your time, sir. I wanted only to offer you the freedom of my ranch for hunting, and to inquire about the health of your daughter after her unfortunate accident.''

''Unfortunate accident.'' Colby shook his head. ''She is the clumsiest woman I have ever known,'' he said coldly, ''and I have found not one single gentleman who lasted more than a day as a suitor.''

''But she is charming,'' John countered gallantly, his eyes dancing. ''She has a sense of humor, the ability to laugh at herself, and despite her companion's rudeness, she behaved with dignity.''

Colby was listening intently. ''You find her... attractive?''

"Sir, she is the most attractive woman I have ever met," John replied without choosing his words.

Colby laughed and shook his head. "You want something," he mused. "But I'm damned if I don't find you a breath of fresh air, sir. You have style and dash."

John grinned at him. "Thank you, sir."

"I may take you up on that invitation at a later date, young man. In the meantime, I have accepted the other offer. But you could do me a favor, if you're inclined."

"Anything within my power, sir," John assured him.

"Since you find my daughter so alluring, I would like you to keep an eye on her during my absence."

"Sir, there would not be adequate chaperones at my ranch," John began quickly, seeing disaster ahead if the old man or his daughter got a glimpse of the true state of affairs at the Jacobs' ranch.

"Oh, for heaven's sake, man, I'm not proposing having her live with you in sin!" Colby burst out. "She will stay here at the hotel, and I have told her not to venture out of town. I meant only that I would like you to check on her from time to time, to make sure that she is safe. She will be on her own, except for the maid we have retained here.''

''I see.'' John let out the breath he'd been holding. ''In that case, I would be delighted. But what of her companion, Sir Sydney?'' he added.

''Sir Sydney will be with me, to my cost,'' Colby groaned. ''The man is an utter pain, but he has a tract of land that I need very badly for a new roundhouse near Chicago,'' he confessed. ''So I must humor him, to some extent. I assure you, my daughter will not mourn his absence. She only went to drive with him at my request. She finds him repulsive.''

So did John, but he didn't want to rock the boat.

''I'm glad you came, young man.'' Colby offered his hand, and John shook it.

''So am I, sir,'' he replied. ''If you don't mind, I would like to take my leave of your daughter.''

''Be my guest.''

''Thank you.''

John walked toward the open door that contained a maid, Miss Ellen Colby and a very mad wet dog of uncertain age and pedigree. It was a shaggy dog, black and white, with very long ears. It was barking pitifully and shaking soapy water everywhere.

''Oh, Miss Colby, this doggy don't want no

bath,'' the maid wailed as she tried to right her cap.

''Never you mind, Lizzie, we're going to bathe her or die in the attempt.'' Ellen blew back a strand of loose hair, holding the dog down with both hands while the maid laved water on it with a cup.

''A watering trough might be a better proposition, Miss Colby,'' John drawled from the doorway.

His voice shocked her. She jerked her head in his direction and loosened the hold she had on the dog. In the few seconds that followed, the animal gave a yelp of pure joy, leaped out of the pan, off the table, and scattered the rugs as it clawed its way to the freedom of the parlor.

''Oh, my goodness!'' Ellen yelled. ''Catch her, Lizzie, before she gets to the bedroom! She'll go right up on Papa's bed, like she usually does!''

''Yes, ma'am!''

The maid ran for all she was worth. Ellen Colby put her soapy hands on her hips and glared daggers at the tall green-eyed man in the doorway.

''Now see what you've done!'' Ellen raged at John.

"Me?" John's eyebrows arched. "I assure you, I meant only to say goodbye."

"You diverted my attention at a critical moment!"

He smiled slowly, liking the way her blue eyes flashed in anger. He liked the thickness of her hair. It looked very long. He wondered if she let it down at bedtime.

That thought disturbed him. He straightened. "If your entire social life consists of bathing the dog, miss, you are missing out."

"I have a social life!"

"Falling into mud puddles?"

She grabbed up the soaking brush they'd used on the dog and considered heaving it.

John threw back his head and laughed uproariously.

"Do be quiet!" she muttered.

"You have hidden fires," he commented with delight. "Your father has asked me to keep an eye on you, Miss Colby, while he's off on his hunting trip. I find the prospect delightful."

"I can think of nothing I would enjoy less!"

"I'm quite a good companion," he assured her. "I know where birds' nests are and where flowers grow, and I can even sing and play the guitar if asked."

She hesitated, wet splotches all over her lacy

dress and soap in her upswept hair. She looked at him with open curiosity. "You are wearing a gun," she pointed out. "Do you shoot people with it?"

"Only the worst sort of people," he told her. "And I have yet to shoot a woman."

"I am reassured."

"I have a cattle ranch not too far a ride from here," he continued. "In the past, I have had infrequently to help defend my cattle from Comanche raiding parties."

"Indians!"

He laughed at her expression. "Yes. Indians. They have long since gone to live in the Indian Territory. But there are still rustlers and raiders from across the Mexican border, as well as deserting soldiers and layabouts from town hoping to steal my cattle and make a quick profit by selling them to the army."

"How do you stop them?"

"With vigilance," he said simply. "I have men who work for me on shares."

"Shares?" She frowned. "Not for wages?"

He could have bitten his tongue. He hadn't meant to let that slip out.

She knew that he'd let his guard down. She found him mysterious and charming and shrewd.

But he had attractions. He was the first man she'd met who made her want to know more about him.

"I might take you for a ride in my buggy," he mused.

"I might go," she replied.

He chuckled, liking her pert response. She wasn't much to look at, truly, but she had qualities he'd yet to find in other women.

He turned to go. "I won't take the dog along," he said.

"Papa's dog goes with me everywhere," she lied, wanting to be contrary.

He glanced at her over his shoulder. "You were alone in the mud puddle, as I recall."

She glared at him.

He gave her a long, curious scrutiny. He smiled slowly. "We can discuss it at a later date. I will see you again in a day or two." He lifted his hat respectfully. "Good day, Miss Colby."

"Good day, Mr....?" It only then occurred to her that she didn't even know his name.

"John," he replied. "John Jackson Jacobs. But most people just call me 'Big John.'"

"You are rather large," she had to agree.

He grinned. "And you are rather small. But I like your spirit, Miss Colby. I like it a lot."

She sighed and her eyes began to glow faintly as they met his green ones.

He winked at her and she blushed scarlet. But before he could say anything, the maid passed him with the struggling wet dog.

"Excuse me, sir, this parcel is quite maddeningly wet," the maid grumbled as she headed toward the bowl on the table.

"So I see. Good day, ladies." He tipped his hat again, and he was gone in a jingle of spurs.

Ellen Colby looked after him with curiosity and an odd feeling of loss. Strange that a man she'd only just met could be so familiar to her, and that she could feel such joy in his presence.

Her life had been a lonely one, a life of service, helping to act as a hostess for her father and care for her grandmother. But with her grandmother off traveling, Ellen was now more of a hindrance than a help to her family, and it was no secret that her father wanted badly to see her married and off his hands.

But chance would be a fine thing, she thought. She turned back to the dog with faint sadness, wishing she were prettier.

CHAPTER TWO

JOHN RODE BACK TO HIS RANCH, past the new-fangled barbed wire which contained his prize longhorn bull, past the second fence that held his Hereford bull and his small herd of Hereford cows with their spring calves, to the cabin where he and his foremen's families lived together. He had hundreds of head of beef steers, but they ranged widely, free of fences, identified only by his 3J brand, burned into their thick coats. The calves had been branded in the spring.

Mary Brown was at the door, watching him approach. It was early June, and hot in south Texas. Her sweaty black hair was contained under a kerchief, and her brown eyes smiled at him. "Me and Juana washed your old clothes, Mister John," she said. "Isaac and Luis went fishing with the boys down to the river for supper, and the girls are making bread."

"Good," he said. "Do I have anything dry and pressed to put on?" he added.

Mary nodded her head. "Such as it is, Mister

John. A few more holes, and no amount of sewing is gonna save you a red face in company.''

"I'm working on that, Mary," he told her, chuckling. He bent to lift her youngest son, Joe, a toddler, up into his arms. "You get to growing fast, young feller, you got to help me herd cattle."

The little boy gurgled at him. John grinned at him and set him back down.

Isaac came in the back door just then, with a string of fish. "You back?" He grinned. "Any luck?"

"A lot, all of it unexpected," he told the tall, lithe black man. He glanced at Luis Rodriguez, his head vaquero, who was short and stout and also carrying a string of fish. He took Isaac's and handed both to the young boys. "You boys go clean these fish for Mary, you hear?"

"Yes, Papa," the taller black boy said. His shorter Latino companion grinned and followed him out the door.

"We have another calf missing, *señor,*" Luis said irritably. "Isaac and I only came to bring the boys and the fish to the house." He pulled out his pistol and checked it. "We will go and track the calf."

"I'll go with you," John said. "Give me a minute to change."

He carried his clothing to the single room that

had a makeshift door and got out of his best clothes, leaving them hanging over a handmade chair he'd provided for Mary. He whipped his gunbelt back around his lean hips and checked his pistol. Rustlers were the bane of any rancher, but in these hard times, when a single calf meant the difference between keeping his land or losing it, he couldn't afford to let it slide.

He went back out to the men, grim-faced. "Let's do some tracking."

THEY FOUND THE CALF, butchered. Signs around it told them it wasn't rustlers, but a couple of Indians—Comanches, in fact, judging from the broken arrow shaft and footprints they found nearby.

"Damn the luck!" John growled. "What are Comanches doing this far south? And if they're hungry, why can't they hunt rabbits or quail?"

"They all prefer buffalo, *señor,* but the herds have long gone, and game is even scarce here. That is why we had to fish for supper."

"They could go the hell back to the Indian Territory, couldn't they, instead of riding around here, harassing us poor people!" John pursed his lips thoughtfully, remembering what he'd heard in Sutherland Springs. "I wonder," he mused aloud, "if these could be the two renegades from Indian Territory being chased by the army?"

"What?" Isaac asked.

"Nothing," John said, clapping him on the shoulder affectionately. "Just thinking to myself. Let's get back to work."

THE NEXT DAY, HE PUT ON his good suit and went back to the Springs to check on Ellen Colby. He expected to find her reclining in her suite, or playing with her father's dog. What he did find was vaguely shocking.

Far from being in her room, Ellen was on the sidewalk with one arm around a frightened young black boy who'd apparently been knocked down by an angry man.

"...he got in my way. He's got no business walking on the sidewalk anyway. He should be in the street. He should be dead. They should all be dead! We lost everything because of them, and then they got protected by the very army that burned down our homes! You get away from him, lady, he's not going anywhere until I teach him a lesson!"

She stuck out her chin. "I have no intention of moving, sir. If you strike him, you must strike me, also!"

John moved up onto the sidewalk. He didn't look at Ellen. His eyes were on the angry man, and they didn't waver. He didn't say a word. He simply flipped back the lapel of his jacket to disclose the holstered pistol he was carrying.

"Another one!" the angry man railed. "You damned Yankees should get the hell out of Texas and go back up north where you belong!"

"I'm from Georgia," John drawled. "But this is where I belong now."

The man was taken aback. He straightened and glared at John, his fists clenched. "You'd draw on a fellow Southerner?" he exclaimed.

"I'm partial to brown skin," John told him with a honeyed drawl. His tall, lithe figure bent just enough to make an older man nearby catch his breath. "But you do what you think you have to," he added deliberately.

"There," Ellen Colby said haughtily, helping the young man to his feet. "See what you get when you act out of ignoble motives?" she lashed at the threatening man. "A child is a child, regardless of his heritage, sir!"

"That is no child," the man said. "It is an abomination…."

"I beg to disagree." The voice came from a newcomer, wearing a star on his shirt, just making his way through the small crowd. It was Deputy Marshal James Graham, well known locally because he was impartially fair. "Is there a problem, madam?" he asked Ellen, tipping his hat to her.

"That man kicked this young man off the sidewalk and attacked him," Ellen said, glaring daggers at the antagonist. "I interfered and Mr. Jacobs came along in time to prevent any further violence."

"Are you all right, son?" the marshal asked the young boy, who was openmouthed at his unexpected defense.

"Uh, yes, sir. I ain't hurt," he stammered.

Ellen Colby took a coin from her purse and placed it in the young man's hand. "You go get yourself a stick of peppermint," she told him.

He looked at the coin and grinned. "Thank you kindly, miss, but I'll buy my mama a sack of flour instead. Thank you, too," he told the marshal and John Jacobs, before he cut his losses and rushed down the sidewalk.

Graham turned to the man who'd started the trouble. "I don't like troublemakers," he said in a voice curt with command. "If I see you again, in a similar situation, I'll lock you up. That's a promise."

The man spat onto the ground and gave all three of the boy's defenders a cold glare before he turned and stomped off in the opposite direction.

"I'm obliged to both of you," Ellen Colby told them.

John shrugged. "It was no bother."

The deputy marshal chuckled. "A Georgian defending a black boy." He shook his head. "I am astonished."

John laughed. "I have a former slave family working with me," he explained. His face tautened. "If you could see the scars they carry, even the children, you might understand my position even better."

The deputy nodded. "I do understand. If you have any further trouble," he told Ellen, "I am at your service." He tipped his hat and went back to his horse.

"You are a man of parts, Mr. Jacobs," Ellen told John, her blue eyes soft and approving. "Thank you for your help."

He shrugged. "I was thinking of Isaac's oldest boy who died in Georgia," he confessed, moving closer as the crowd melted away. "Isaac is my wrangler," he added. "His first son was beaten to death by an overseer just before the end of the war."

She stood staring up into his lean, hard face with utter curiosity. "I understood that all Southerners hated colored people."

"Most of us common Southerners were in the fields working right beside them," John said coldly. "We were little more than slaves ourselves, while the rich lived in luxury and turned a blind eye to the abuse."

"I had no idea," she said hesitantly.

"Very few northern people do," he said flatly. "Yet there was a county in Georgia that flew the Union flag all through the war, and every attempt by the confederacy to press-gang them into the army was met with open resistance. They ran away and the army got tired of going back to get them again and again." He chuckled at her surprise. "I will tell you all about it over tea, if you like."

She blushed. "I would like that very much, Mr. Jacobs."

He offered his arm. She placed her small hand in the crook of his elbow and let him escort her into the hotel's immaculate dining room. He wondered if he should have told Graham about the Comanche tracks he'd found on his place. He made a note to mention it to the man when he next saw him.

ELLEN LIKED THE LITHE, rawboned man who sat across from her sipping tea and eating tea cakes as if he were born to high society. But she knew that he wasn't. He still had rough edges, but even those were endearing. She couldn't forget the image she had of him, standing in front of the frightened boy, daring the attacker to try again. He was brave. She admired courage.

"Did you really come to see my father to inquire about my welfare?'' she asked after they'd discussed the war.

He looked up at her, surprised by her boldness. He put his teacup down. ''No,'' he said honestly.

She laughed self-consciously. ''Forgive me, but I knew that wasn't the real reason. I appreciate your honesty.''

He leaned back in his chair and studied her without pretense. His green gaze slid over her plain face, down to the faint thrust of her breasts under the green and white striped bodice of her dress and up to the wealth of dark hair piled atop her head. ''Lies come hard to me,'' he told her. ''Shall I be completely honest about my motives and risk alienating you?''

She smiled. ''Please do. I have lost count of the men who pretended to admire me only as a means to my father's wealth. I much prefer an open approach.''

''I inherited a very small holding from my uncle, who died some time ago.'' He toyed with the teacup. ''I have worked for wages in the past, to buy more land and cattle. But just recently I've started to experiment with crossing breeds. I am raising a new sort of beef steer with which I hope to tempt the eastern population's hunger for range-fed beef.'' His eyes lifted to hers. ''It's a long, slow process to drive cattle to a railhead up in Kansas, fraught with danger and risk, more now than ever since the fear of Texas fever in cattle has caused so much resistance to be placed in the path of the cattle drives. My finances are so tight now that the loss of a single calf is a major setback to me.''

She was interested. ''You have a plan.''

He smiled. ''I have a plan. I want to bring a railroad to this area of south Texas. More precisely, I want a spur to run to my ranch, so that I can ship cattle to Chicago without having to drive them to Kansas first.''

Her eyes brightened. ''Then you had no real purpose of inviting my father to hunt quail on your ranch.''

''Miss Colby,'' he said heavily, ''my two foremen and their families live with me in a one-room cabin. It looks all right at a distance, but close up, it's very primitive. It is a pretend mansion. As I am a pretend aristocrat.'' He gestured at his suit coat. ''I used the last of my ready cash to disguise myself and I came into town because I had heard that your father was here, and that he had a marriageable daughter.'' His expression became self-mocking when she blinked. ''But I'm not enough of a scoundrel to pretend an affection I do not feel.'' He studied her quietly, toying with a spoon beside his cup and saucer. ''So let me make you a business proposition.

Marry me and let your father give us a railroad spur as a wedding present.''

She gulped, swallowed a mouthful of hot tea, sat back and expelled a shocked breath. ''Sir, you are blunt!''

''Ma'am, I am honest,'' he replied. He leaned forward quickly and fixed her with his green eyes. ''Listen to me. I have little more than land and prospects. But I have a good head for business, and I know cattle. Given the opportunity, I will build an empire such as Texas has never seen. I have good help, and I've learned much about raising cattle from them. Marry me.''

''And…what would I obtain from such a liaison?'' she stammered.

''Freedom.''

''Excuse me?''

''Your father cares for you, I think, but he treats you as a liability. That gentleman,'' he spat the word, ''who was escorting you stood idly by when you fell in a mud puddle and didn't even offer a hand. You are undervalued.''

She laughed nervously. ''And I would not be, if I married a poor stranger and went to live in the wilds where rustlers raid?''

He grinned. ''You could wear pants and learn to ride a horse and herd cattle,'' he said, tempting her. ''I would even teach you to brand cattle and shoot a gun.''

Her whole demeanor changed. She just stared at him for a minute. "I have spent my entire life under the care of my mother's mother, having lost my own mother when I was only a child. My grandmother Greene believes that a lady should never soil her hands in any way. She insists on absolute decorum in all situations. She would not hear of my learning to ride a horse or shoot a gun because such things are only for men. I have lived in a cage all my life." Her blue eyes began to gleam. "I should love to be a tomboy!"

He laughed. "Then marry me."

She hesitated once again. "Sir, I know very little of men. Having been sheltered in all ways, I am uneasy with the thought of...with having a stranger...with being..."

He held up a hand. "I offer you a marriage of friends. In truth, anything more would require a miracle, as there is no privacy where I live. We are all under the single roof. And," he added, "my foremen and their families are black and Mexican, not white." He watched for her reactions. "So, as you can see, there is a further difficulty in regard to public opinion hereabouts."

She clasped her hands before her on the table. "I would like to think about it a little. Not because of any prejudice," she added quickly, and smiled. "But because I would like to know you a little better. I have a friend who married in haste at the age of fifteen. She is now twenty-four, as I am. She has seven living children and her husband treats her like property. It is not a condition which I envy her.''

''I understand,'' he said.

The oddest thing, was that she thought he really did understand. He was a complex man. She had a sudden vision of him years down the road, in an elegant suit, in an elegant setting. He had potential. She'd never met anyone like him.

She sighed. ''But my father must not know the entire truth,'' she cautioned. ''He has prejudices, and he would not willingly let me go to a man he considered a social inferior.''

His thin lips pursed amusedly. ''Then I'll do my utmost to convince him that I am actually the illegitimate grandson of an Irish earl.''

She leaned forward. ''Are there Irish earls?''

He shrugged. ''I have no idea. But, then, he probably has no idea, either.'' His eyes twinkled.

She laughed delightedly. It changed her face, her eyes, her whole look. She was pretty when she laughed.

''There is one more complication,'' he said in a half-serious tone.

''Which is?''

His smile was outrageous. ''We have lots of mud puddles at the ranch.''

"Oh, you!" she exclaimed, reaching for the teapot.

"If you throw it, the morning papers will have a more interesting front page."

"Will it? And what would you do?" she challenged brightly.

"I am uncivilized," he informed her. "I would put you across my knee and paddle your backside, after which I would toss you over my shoulder and carry you home with me."

"How very exciting!" she exclaimed. "I have never done anything especially outrageous. I think I might like being the object of a scandal!"

He beamed. "Tempting," he proclaimed. "But I have great plans and no desire to start tongues wagging. Yet."

"Very well. I'll restrain my less civilized impulses for the time being."

He lifted his teacup and toasted her. "To unholy alliances," he teased.

She lifted hers as well. "And madcap plots!"

They clicked teacups together and drank deeply.

IT WAS UNSEEMLY FOR THEM TO be seen going out of town alone, so Ellen was prevented from visiting John's ranch. But he took her to church on Sunday—a new habit that he felt obliged to acquire—and promenading along the sidewalk after a leisurely lunch in the hotel.

The following week, John was a frequent visitor. He and Ellen became friends with an elegant Scottish gentleman and his wife who were staying at the hotel and taking the waters, while they toured the American West.

"It is a grand country," the Scotsman, Robert Maxwell, told Ellen and John. "Edith and I have been longing to ride out into the country, but we are told that it is dangerous."

"It is," John assured him grimly. "My partners and I have been tracking rustlers all week," he added, to Ellen's surprise, because he hadn't told her. "There are dangerous men in these parts, and we have rustlers from across the border, also."

"Do you have Red Indians?" Maxwell exclaimed. His eyes twinkled. "I would like to meet one."

"They're all in the Indian Territory now, and no, you wouldn't like to meet one," John said. "The Comanches who used to live hereabouts didn't encourage foreign visitors, and they had a well-deserved reputation for opposing any people who tried to invade their land."

"Their land?" the Scotsman queried, curiously.

"Their land," John said firmly. "They roamed

this country long before the first white man set foot here. They intermarried with the Mexican population...."

Maxwell seemed very confused, as he interrupted, "Surely there were no people here at all when you arrived," he said.

"Perhaps they don't know it back East, but Texas was part of Mexico just a few decades back," John informed him. "That's why we went to war with Mexico, because Texas wanted independence from it. Our brave boys died in the Alamo in San Antonio, and at Goliad and San Jacinto, to bring Texas into the union. But the Mexican boys fought to keep from losing their territory, is how they saw it. They considered us invaders."

Ellen was watching John covertly, with quiet admiration.

"Ah, now I understand," the Scot chuckled. "It's like us and England. We've been fighting centuries to govern ourselves, like the Irish. But the British are stubborn folk."

"So are Texans," John chuckled.

"I don't suppose you'd go riding with us, young man?" Maxwell asked him wistfully. "We should love to see a little of the area, and I see that you wear a great pistol at your hip. I assume you can shoot any two-legged threats to our safety."

John glanced at Ellen and saw such appreciation in her blue eyes that he lost his train of thought for a few seconds.

Finally he blinked and darted his green gaze back to the foreigners, hoping his heartbeat wasn't audible.

"I think I'd like that," John replied, "as long as Ellen comes with us."

"Your young lady," the Scotswoman, Nell Maxwell, added with a gentle, indulgent smile.

"Yes," John said, his eyes going back to Ellen's involuntarily. "My young lady."

Ellen blushed red and lowered her eyes, which caused the foreign couple to laugh charmingly. She was so excited that she forgot her father's admonition that she was not to leave the hotel and go out of town. In fact, when she recalled it, she simply ignored it.

THEY RENTED A SURREY and John helped Ellen into the back seat before he climbed up nimbly beside her. He noted that it was the best surrey the stable had, with fringe hanging all the way around, and the horses' livery was silver and black leather.

"I suppose this is nothing special for you," John murmured to her, looking keenly at the horses' adornments, "but it's something of a treat for me."

Ellen smoothed the skirt of her nice blue suit with its black piping. "It's a treat for me, too," she confessed. "I had very much wanted to drive out in the country, but my father only thinks of hunting, not sightseeing, and he dislikes my company."

"I like your company very much," John said in a deep, soft tone.

She looked up at him, surprised by the warmth in his deep voice. She was lost in the sudden intensity of his green eyes under the wide brim of his dress hat. She felt her whole world shift in the slow delight it provoked.

He smiled, feeling as if he could fly all of a sudden. Impulsively his big, lean hand caught hers on the seat between them and curled her small fingers into it.

She caught her breath, entranced.

"Are you two young people comfortable?" Maxwell asked.

"Quite comfortable, thank you, sir," John replied, and he looked at Ellen with possession.

"So am I, thank you," Ellen managed through her tight throat.

"We'll away, then," Maxwell said with a grin at his wife, and he flicked the reins.

The surrey bounded forward, the horses obviously well chosen for their task, because the ride was as smooth as silk.

"Which way shall we go?" Maxwell asked.

"Just follow the road you're on," John told him. "I know this way best. It runs past my own land up to Quail Run, the next little town along the road. I can show you the ruins of a log cabin where a white woman and her Comanche husband held off a company of soldiers a few years back. He was a renegade. She was a widow with a young son, and expecting another when her husband was killed by a robber. Soon after, the Comanche was part of a war party that encountered a company of soldiers trailing them. He was wounded and she found him and nursed him back to health. It was winter. She couldn't hunt or fish, or chop wood, and she had no family at all. He undertook her support. They both ran from the soldiers, up into the Indian Territory. She's there now, people say. Nobody knows where he is."

"What a fascinating story!" Maxwell exclaimed. "Is it true?"

"From what I hear, it is," John replied.

"What a courageous young woman," Ellen murmured.

"To have contact with a Red Indian, she would have to be," Mrs. Maxwell replied. "I have heard many people speak of Indians. None of what they say is good."

"I think all people are good and bad," Ellen

ventured. "I have never thought heritage should decide which is which."

John chuckled and squeezed her hand. "We think alike."

The Maxwells exchanged a complicated look and laughed, too.

THE LOG CABIN WAS POINTED OUT. It was nothing much to look at. There was a well tucked into high grass and briar bushes, and a single tree in what must once have been the front yard.

"What sort of tree is that?" Mrs. Maxwell asked. "What an odd shape."

"It's a chinaberry tree," John recalled. "We have them in Georgia, where I'm from. My sisters and I used to throw the green berries that grow on them back and forth, playing." He became somber.

"You have family back in Georgia?" Ellen asked pointedly, softly.

He sighed. "I have a married sister in North Carolina. No one else."

Ellen knew there was more to it than just that, and she had a feeling the war had cost him more than his home. She stroked the back of his callused hand gently. "Mama died of typhoid when I was just five. So except for Papa and Grandmother, I have no one, either."

He caught his breath. He hadn't thought about

her circumstances, her family, her background. All he'd known was that she was rich. He began to see her with different eyes.

"I'm sorry, about your family," she said quietly.

He sighed. He didn't look at her. Memories tore at his heart. He looked out beyond the horses drawing the surrey at the yellow sand of the dirt road, leading to the slightly rolling land ahead. The familiar *clop-clop* of the horses' hooves and the faint creak of leather and wood and the swishing sound of the rolling wheels seemed very loud in the silence that followed. The dust came up into the carriage, but they were all used to it, since dirt roads were somewhat universal. The boards that made the seats of the surrey were hard on the backside during a long trip, but not less comfortable than the saddle of a horse, John supposed.

"Do you ride at all?" he asked Ellen.

"I was never allowed to," she confessed. "My grandmother thought it wasn't ladylike."

"I ride to the hounds," Mrs. Maxwell said, eavesdropping, and turned to face them with a grin. "My father himself put me on my first horse when I was no more than a girl. I rode sidesaddle, of course, but I could outdistance any man I met on a horse. Well, except for Robert," she conceded, with an affectionate look at her husband. "We raced and I lost. Then and there, I determined that I needed to marry him."

"And she did," he added with a chuckle, darting a look over his broad shoulder. "Her father told me I must keep her occupied to keep her happy, so I turned the stables over to her."

"Quite a revolution of sorts in our part of the country, I must add," Mrs. Maxwell confessed. "But the lads finally learned who had the whip hand, and now they do what I say."

"We have the finest stable around," Maxwell agreed. "We haven't lost a race yet."

"When I have more horses, you must come and teach my partners how to train them," John told Mrs. Maxwell.

"And didn't I tell you that people would not be stuffy and arrogant here in Texas?" she asked her husband.

"I must agree, they are not."

"Well, two of them, at least," John murmured dryly. "There," he said suddenly, pointing out across a grassy pasture. "That is my land."

All three heads turned. In the distance was the big cabin, surrounded by pecan and oak trees and not very visible. But around it were red-and-white-coated cattle, grazing in between barbed wire fences.

"It is fenced!" Maxwell exclaimed.

"Fencing is what keeps the outlaws out and

my cattle in," John said, used to defending his fences. "Many people dislike this new barbed wire, but it is the most economical way to contain my herds. And I don't have a great deal of capital to work with."

"You are an honest man," Maxwell said. "You did not have to admit such a thing to a stranger."

"It is because you are a stranger that I can do it," John said amusedly. "I would never admit to being poor around my own countrymen. A man has his pride. However, I intend to be the richest landowner hereabouts in a few years. So you must plan to come back to Texas. I can promise you will be very welcome as house-guests."

"If I am able, I will," Maxwell agreed. "So we must keep in touch."

"Indeed we must. We will trade addresses before you leave town. But for now," John added, "make a left turn at this next crossroads, and I will show you a mill, where we take our corn to be ground into meal."

"We have mills at home, but I should like to see yours," Mrs. Maxwell enthused.

"And so you shall," John promised.

CHAPTER THREE

TWO HOURS LATER, TIRED AND thirsty, the tourists returned to the livery stable to return the horses and surrey.

"It has been a pleasure," John told the Maxwells, shaking hands.

"And for me, as well," Ellen added.

The older couple smiled indulgently. "We leave for New York in the morning," Maxwell said regretfully, "and then we sail to Scotland. It has been a pleasure to meet you both, although I wish we could have done so sooner."

"Yes," Mrs. Maxwell said solemnly. "How sad to make friends just as we must say goodbye to them."

"We will keep in touch," John said.

"Indeed we will. You must leave your address for us at the desk, and we will leave ours for you," Maxwell told John. "When you have made your fortune, I hope very much to return with my wife to visit you both."

Ellen flushed, because she had a sudden vivid

picture of herself with John and several children on a grand estate. John was seeing the same picture. He grinned broadly. "We will look forward to it," he said to them both.

The Maxwells went up to their rooms and John stopped with Ellen at the foot of the stairs, because it would have been unseemly for a gentleman to accompany a lady all the way to her bedroom.

He took her hand in his and held it firmly. "I enjoyed today," he said. "Even in company, you are unique."

"As you are." She smiled up at him from a radiant face surrounded by wisps of loose dark hair that had escaped her bun and the hatpins that held on her wide-brimmed hat.

"We must make sure that we build a proper empire," he teased, "so that the Maxwells can come back to visit."

"I shall do my utmost to assist you," she replied with teasing eyes.

He chuckled. "I have no doubt of that."

"I will see you tomorrow?" she fished.

"Indeed you will. It will be in the afternoon, though," he added regretfully. "I must help move cattle into a new pasture first. It is very dry and we must shift them closer to water."

"Good evening, then," she said gently.

"Good evening." He lifted her hand to his lips in a gesture he'd learned in polite company during his travels.

It had a giddy effect on Ellen. She blushed and laughed nervously and almost stumbled over her own feet going up the staircase.

"Oh, dear," she said, righting herself.

"Not to worry," John assured her, hat in hand, green eyes brimming with mirth. "See?" He looked around his feet and back up at her. "No mud puddles!"

She gave him an exasperated, but amused, look, and went quickly up the staircase. When she made the landing, he was still there, watching.

JOHN AND ELLEN SAW EACH other daily for a week, during which they grew closer. Ellen waited for John in the hotel dining room late the next Friday afternoon, but to her dismay, it was not John who walked directly to her table. It was her father, home unexpectedly early. Nor was he smiling.

He pulled out a chair and sat down, motioning imperiously to a waiter, from whom he ordered coffee and nothing else.

"You are home early," Ellen stammered.

"I am home to prevent a scandal!" he replied

curtly. "I've had word from an acquaintance of Sir Sydney's that you were seen flagrantly defying my instructions that you should stay in this hotel during my absence! You have been riding, in the country, alone, with Mr. Jacobs! How dare you create a scandal here!"

The Ellen of only a week ago would have bowed her head meekly and agreed never to disobey him again. But her association with John Jacobs had already stiffened her backbone. He had offered her a new life, a free life, away from the endless social conventions and rules of conduct that kept her father so occupied.

She lifted her eyebrows with hauteur. "And what business of Sir Sydney's friend is my behavior?" she wanted to know.

Her father's eyes widened in surprise. "I beg your pardon?"

"I have no intention of being coupled with Sir Sydney in any way whatsoever," she informed him. "In fact, the man is repulsive and ill-mannered."

It was a rare hint of rebellion, one of just a few he had ever seen in Ellen. He just stared at her, confused and amused, all at once.

"It would seem that your acquaintance with Mr. Jacobs is corrupting you."

"I intend to be further corrupted," she replied coolly. "He has asked me to marry him."

"Child, that is out of the question," he said sharply.

She held up a dainty hand. "I am no child," she informed him, blue eyes flashing. "I am a woman grown. Most of my friends are married with families of their own. I am a spinster, an encumbrance to hear you tell it, of a sort whom men do not rush to escort. I am neither pretty nor accomplished..."

"You are quite wealthy," he inserted bluntly. "Which is, no doubt, why Mr. Jacobs finds you so attractive."

In fact, it was a railroad spur, not money, that John wanted, but she wasn't ready to tell her father that. Let him think what he liked. She knew that John Jacobs found her attractive. It gave her confidence to stand up to her parent for the first time in memory.

"You may disinherit me whenever you like," she said easily, sipping coffee with a steady hand. Her eyes twinkled. "I promise you, it will make no difference to him. He is the sort of man who builds empires from nothing more than hard work and determination. In time, his fortune will rival yours, I daresay."

Terrance Colby was listening now, not blustering. "You are considering his proposal."

She nodded, smiling. "He has painted me a delightful picture of muddy roads, kitchen gardens, heavy labor, cooking over open fires and branding cattle." She chuckled. "In fact, he has offered to let me help him brand cattle in the fall when his second crop of calves drop."

Terrance caught his breath. He waited to speak until the waiter brought his coffee. He glowered after the retreating figure. "I should have asked for a teacup of whiskey instead," he muttered to himself. His eyes went back to his daughter's face. "Brand cattle?"

She nodded. "Ride horses, shoot a gun...he offered to teach me no end of disgusting and socially unacceptable forms of recreation."

He sat back with an expulsion of breath. "I could have him arrested."

"For what?" she replied.

He was disconcerted by the question. "I haven't decided yet. Corrupting a minor," he ventured.

"I am far beyond the age of consent, Father," she reminded him. She sipped coffee again. "You may disinherit me at will. I will not even need the elegant wardrobes you have purchased for me. I will wear dungarees and high-heeled boots.''

His look of horror was now all-consuming. ''You will not! Remember your place, Ellen!''

Her eyes narrowed. ''My place is what I say it is. I am not property, to be sold or bartered for material gain!''

He was formulating a reply when the sound of heavy footfalls disturbed him into looking up. John Jacobs was standing just to his side, wearing his working gear, including that sinister revolver slung low in a holster slanted across his lean hips.

''Ah,'' Colby said curtly. ''The villain of the piece!''

''I am no villain,'' John replied tersely. He glanced at Ellen with budding feelings of protectiveness. She looked flushed and angry. ''Certainly, I have never given Ellen such pain as that I see now on her face.'' He looked back at Colby with a cold glare.

Colby began to be impressed. This steely young man was not impressed by either his wealth or position when Ellen was distressed.

''Do you intend to call me out?'' he asked John.

The younger man glanced again at Ellen. ''It would be high folly to kill the father of my prospective bride,'' he said finally. ''Of course, I don't have to kill you,'' he added, pursing his lips and giving Colby's shoulder a quiet scrutiny. ''I could simply wing you.''

Colby's gaze went to that worn pistol butt. ''Do you know how to shoot that hog leg?''

''I could give you references,'' John drawled. ''Or a demonstration, if you prefer.''

Colby actually laughed. ''I imagine you could. Stop bristling like an angry dog and sit down, Mr. Jacobs. I have ridden hard to get here, thinking my daughter was about to be seduced by a bounder. And I find only an honest suitor who would fight even her own father to protect her. I am quite impressed. Do sit down,'' he emphasized. ''That gentleman by the window looks fit to jump through it. He has not taken his eyes off your gun since you approached me!''

John's hard face broke into a sheepish grin. He pulled out a chair and sat down close to Ellen, his green eyes soft now and possessive as they sketched her flushed, happy face. He smiled at her, tenderly.

Colby ordered coffee for John as well and then sat back to study the determined young man.

''She said you wish to teach her to shoot a gun and brand cattle,'' Colby began.

"If she wants to, yes," John replied. "I assume you would object...?"

Colby chuckled. "My grandmother shot a gun and once chased a would-be robber down the streets of a North Carolina town with it. She was a local legend."

"You never told me!" Ellen exclaimed.

He grimaced. "Your mother was very strait-laced, Ellen, like your grandmother Greene," he said. "She wanted no image of my unconventional mother to tempt you into indiscretion." He pursed his lips and chuckled. "Apparently blood will out, as they say." He looked at her with kind eyes. "You have been pampered all your life. Nothing that money could buy has ever been beyond your pocket. It will not be such a life with this man," he indicated John. "Not for a few years, at least," he added with a chuckle. "You remind me of myself, Mr. Jacobs. I did not inherit my wealth. I worked as a farm laborer in my youth," he added, shocking his daughter. "I mucked out stables and slopped hogs for a rich man in our small North Carolina town. There were eight of us children, and no money to be handed down. When I was twelve, I jumped on a freight train and was arrested in New York when I was found in a stock car. I was taken to the manager's office where the owner of the railroad had chanced to venture on a matter of business. I was rude and arrogant, but he must have seen something in me that impressed him. He had a wife, but no children. He took me home with him, had his wife clean me up and dress me properly, and I became his adoptive child. When he died, he left the business to me. By then, I was more than capable of running it.''

''Father!'' Ellen exclaimed. ''You never spoke of your parents. I had no idea…!''

''My parents died of typhoid soon after I left the farm,'' he confessed. ''My brothers and sisters were taken in by cousins. When I made my own fortune, I made sure that they were provided for.''

''You wanted a son,'' she said sorrowfully, ''to inherit what you had. And all you got was me.''

''Your mother died giving birth to a stillborn son,'' he confessed. ''You were told that she died of a fever, which is partially correct. I felt that you were too young for the whole truth. And your maternal grandmother was horrified when I thought to tell you. Grandmother Greene is very correct and formal.'' He sighed. ''When she knows what you have done, I expect she will be here on the next train to save you, along with however many grandsons she can convince to accompany her.''

She nodded slowly, feeling nervous. "She is formidable.''

"I wouldn't mind a son, but I do like little girls,'' John said with a warm smile. "I won't mind if we have daughters.''

She flushed, embarrassed.

"Let us speak first of marriage, if you please,'' Colby said with a wry smile. "What would you like for a wedding present, Mr. Jacobs?''

John was overwhelmed. He hesitated.

"*We* would like a spur line run down to *our* ranch,'' Ellen said for him, with a wicked grin. "So that we don't have to drive our cattle all the way to Kansas to get them shipped to Chicago. We are going to raise extraordinary beef.''

John sighed. "Indeed we are,'' he nodded, watching her with delight.

"That may take some little time,'' Colby mused. "What would you like in the meantime?''

"A sidesaddle rig for Ellen, so that she can be comfortable in the saddle,'' John said surprisingly.

"I do not want a sidesaddle,'' she informed him curtly. "I intend to ride astride, as I have seen other women do since I came here.''

"I have never seen a woman ride in such a manner!" Colby exploded.

"She's thinking of Tess Wallace," John confessed. "She's the wife of old man Tick Wallace, who owns the stagecoach line here. She drives the team and even rides shotgun sometimes. He's twenty years older than she is, but nobody doubts what they feel for each other. She's crazy for him."

"An unconventional woman," Colby muttered.

"As I intend to become. You may give me away at the wedding, and it must be a small, intimate one, and very soon," she added. "I do not wish my husband embarrassed by a gathering of snobby aristocrats."

Her father's jaw dropped. "But the suddenness of the wedding...!"

"I am sorry, Father, but it will be my wedding, and I feel I have a right to ask for what I wish," Ellen said stubbornly. "I have done nothing wrong, so I have nothing to fear. Besides," she added logically, "none of our friends live here, or are in attendance here at the Springs."

Her father sighed. "As you wish, my dear," he said finally, and his real affection for her was evident in the smile he gave her.

John was tremendously impressed, not only by

her show of spirit, but by her consideration for him. He was getting quite a bargain, he thought. Then he stopped to ask himself what she was getting, save for a hard life that would age her prematurely, maybe even kill her. He began to frown.

"It will be a harder life than you realize now," John said abruptly, and with a scowl. "We have no conveniences at all...."

"I am not afraid of hard work," Ellen interrupted.

John and Colby exchanged concerned glances. They both knew deprivation intimately. Ellen had never been without a maid or the most luxurious accommodations in her entire life.

"I'll spare you as much as I can," John said after a minute. "But most empires operate sparsely at first."

"I will learn to cook," Ellen said with a chuckle.

"Can you clean a game hen?" her father wanted to know.

She didn't waver. "I can learn."

"Can you haul water from the river and hoe in a garden?" her father persisted. "Because I have no doubt that you will have to do it."

"There will be men to do the lifting," John

promised him. "And we will take excellent care of her, sir."

Her father hesitated, but Ellen's face was stiff with determination. She wasn't backing down an inch.

"Very well," he said on a heavy breath. "But if it becomes too much for you, I want to know," he added firmly. "You must promise that, or I cannot sanction your wedding."

"I promise," she said at once, knowing that she would never go to him for help.

He relaxed a little. "Then I will give you a wedding present that will not make your prospective bridegroom chafe too much," he continued. "I'll open an account for you both at the mercantile store. You will need dry goods to furnish your home."

"Oh, Father, thank you!" Ellen exclaimed.

John chuckled. "Thank you, indeed. Ellen will be grateful, but I'll consider it a loan."

"Of course, my boy," Colby replied complacently.

John knew the man didn't believe him. But he was capable of building an empire, even if he was the only one at the table who knew it at that moment. He reached over to shake hands with the older man.

"Within ten years," he told Colby, "we will

entertain you in the style to which you are accustomed.''

Colby nodded, but he still had reservations. He only hoped he wasn't doing Ellen a disservice. And he still had to explain this to her maternal grandmother, who was going to have a heart attack when she knew what he'd let Ellen do.

But all he said to the couple was, ''We shall see.''

THEY WERE MARRIED by a justice of the peace, with Terrance Colby and the minister's wife as witnesses. Colby had found a logical reason for the haste of the wedding, pleading his forthcoming trip home and Ellen's refusal to leave Sutherland Springs. The minister, an easygoing, romantic man, was willing to defy convention for a good cause. Colby congratulated John, kissed Ellen, and led them to a buckboard which he'd already had filled with enough provisions to last a month. He'd even included a treadle sewing machine, cloth for dresses and the sewing notions that went with them. Nor had he forgotten Ellen's precious knitting needles and wool yarn, with which she whiled away quiet evenings.

''Father, thank you very much!'' Ellen exclaimed when she saw the rig.

''Thank you very much, indeed,'' John added

with a handshake. "I shall take excellent care of her," he promised.

"I'm sure you'll do your best," Colby replied, but he was worried, and it showed.

Ellen kissed him. "You must not be concerned for me," she said firmly, her blue eyes full of censure. "You think I am a lily, but I mean to prove to you that I am like a cactus flower, able to bloom in the most unlikely places."

He kissed her cheek. "If you ever need me…"

"I do know where to send a telegram," she interrupted, and chuckled. "Have a safe trip home."

"I will have your trunks sent out before I leave town," he added.

John helped Ellen into the buckboard in the lacy white dress and veil she'd worn for her wedding, and he climbed up beside her in the only good suit he owned. They were an odd couple, he thought. And considering the shock she was likely to get when she saw where she must live, it would only get worse. He felt guilty for what he was doing. He prayed that the ends would justify the means. He had promised little, and she had asked for nothing. But many couples had started with even less and made a go of their marriages. He meant to keep Ellen happy, whatever it took.

ELLEN JACOBS'S FIRST glimpse of her future home would have been enough to discourage many a young woman from getting out of the buckboard. The shade trees shaded a large, rough log cabin with only one door and a single window and a chimney. Nearby were cactus plants and brush. But there were tiny pink climbing roses in full bloom, and John confessed that he'd brought the bushes here from Georgia planted in a syrup can. The roses delighted her, and made the wilderness look less wild.

Outside the cabin stood a Mexican couple and a black couple, surrounded by children of all ages. They stared and looked very nervous as John helped Ellen down out of the buckboard.

She had rarely interacted with people of color, except as servants in the homes she had visited most of her life. It was new, and rather exciting, to live among them.

"I am Ellen Colby," she introduced herself, and then colored. "I do beg your pardon! I am Ellen Jacobs!"

She laughed, and then they laughed as well.

"We're pleased to meet you, *señora,*" the Mexican man said, holding his broad sombrero in front of him. He grinned as he introduced himself and his small family. "I am Luis Rodriguez.

This is my family—my wife Juana, my son Alvaro and my daughters Juanita, Elena and Lupita.'' They all nodded and smiled.

''And I am Mary Brown,'' the black woman said gently. ''My husband is Isaac. These are my boys, Ben, the oldest, and Joe, the youngest, and my little girl Libby, who is the middle child. We are glad to have you here.''

''I am glad to be here,'' Ellen said.

''But right now, you need to get into some comfortable clothing, Mrs. Jacobs,'' Mary said. ''Come along in. You men go to work and leave us to our own chores,'' she said, shooing them off.

''Mary, I can't work in these!'' John exclaimed defensively.

She reached into a box and pulled out a freshly ironed shirt and patched pants. ''You go off behind a tree and put those on, and I'll do my best to chase the moths out of this box so's I can put your suit in it. And mind you don't get red mud in this shirt!''

''Yes, ma'am,'' he said with a sheepish grin. ''See you later, Ellen.''

Mary shut the door on him, grinning widely at Ellen. ''He is a good man,'' she told Ellen in all seriousness as she produced the best dress she had and offered it to Ellen.

"No," Ellen said gently, smiling. "I thank you very much for the offer of your dress, but I not only brought a cotton dress of my own—I have brought bolts of fabric and a sewing machine."

There were looks of unadulterated pleasure on all the feminine faces. "New...fabric?" Mary asked haltingly.

"Sewing machine?" her daughter exclaimed.

"In the buckboard," Ellen assured them with a grin.

They vanished like summer mist, out the door. Ellen followed behind them, still laughing at their delight. She'd done the right thing, it seemed— rather, her father had. She might have thought of it first if she'd had the opportunity.

The women and girls went wild over the material, tearing it out of its brown paper wrapping without even bothering to cut the string that held it.

"Alvaro, you and Ben get this sewing machine and Mrs. Jacobs's suitcase into the house right this minute! Girls, bring the notions and the fabric! I'll get the coffee and sugar, but Ben will have to come back for the lard bucket and the flour sack."

"Yes, ma'am," they echoed, and burst out laughing.

THREE HOURS LATER, Ellen was wearing a simple navy skirt with an indigo blouse, fastened high at the neck. She had on lace-up shoes, but she could see that she was going to have to have boots if she was to be any help to John. The cabin was very small, and all of the families would sleep inside, because there were varmints out at night. And not just crawly ones or four-legged ones, she suspected. Mary had told her about the Comanches John and Luis and Isaac had been hunting when a calf was taken. She noted that a loaded shotgun was kept in a corner of the room, and she had no doubt that either of her companions could wield it if necessary. But she would ask John to teach her to shoot it, as well.

"You will have very pretty dresses from this material," Mary sighed as she touched the colored cottons of many prints and designs.

"*We* will have many pretty dresses," Ellen said, busily filling a bobbin for the sewing machine. She looked up at stunned expressions. "Surely you did not think I could use this much fabric by myself? There is enough here for all of us, I should imagine. And it will take less for the girls," she added, with a warm smile at them.

Mary actually turned away, and Ellen was horrified that she'd hurt the other woman's feelings.

She jumped up from the makeshift chair John had cobbled together from tree limbs. "Mary, I'm sorry, I...!"

Mary turned back to her, tears running down her cheeks. "It's just, I haven't had a dress of my own, a new dress, in my whole life. Only hand-me-downs from my mistress, and they had to be torn up or used up first."

Ellen didn't know what to say. Her face was shocked.

Mary wiped away the tears. She looked at the other woman curiously. "You don't know about slaves, do you, Mrs. Ellen?"

"I know enough to be very sorry that some people think they can own other people," she replied carefully. "My family never did."

Mary forced a smile. "Mr. John brought us out here after the war. We been lucky. Two of our kids are lost forever, you know," she added matter-of-factly. "They got sold just before the war. And one of them got beat to death."

Ellen's eyes closed. She shuddered. It was overwhelming. Tears ran down her cheeks.

"Oh, now, Mrs., don't you...don't you do that!" Mary gathered her close and rocked her. "Don't you cry. Wherever my babies gone, they free now, don't you see. Alive or dead, they free."

The tears ran even harder.

"It was just as bad for Juana," Mary said through her own tears. "Two of her little boys got shot. This man got drunk and thought they was Indians. He just killed them right there in the road where they was playing, and he didn't even look back. He rode off laughing. Luis told the *federales,* but they couldn't find the man. That was years ago, before Mr. John's uncle hired Luis to work here, but Juana never forgot them little boys."

Ellen drew back and pulled a handkerchief out of her sleeve. She wiped Mary's eyes and smiled sadly. "We live in a bad world."

Mary smiled. "It's gonna get better," she said. "You wait and see."

"Better," Juana echoed, nodding, smiling. *"Mas bueno."*

"Mas...bueno?" Ellen repeated.

Juana chuckled. *"¡!Vaya! Muy bien!* Very good!"

Mary smiled. "You just spoke your first words of Spanish!"

"Perhaps you can teach me to speak Spanish," Ellen said to Juana.

"Señora, it will be my pleasure!" the woman answered, and smiled beautifully.

"I expect to learn a great deal, and very soon," Ellen replied.

THAT WAS AN UNDERSTATEMENT. During her
first week of residence, she became an integral
part of John's extended family. She learned quite
a few words of Spanish, including some range
language that shocked John when she repeated it
to him with a wicked grin.

"You stop that," he chastised. "Your father
will have me shot if he hears you!"

She only chuckled, helping Mary put bread on
the table. She was learning to make bread that
didn't bounce, but it was early days yet. "My
father thinks I will be begging him to come and
get me within two weeks. He is in for a surprise!"

"I got the surprise," John had to admit, smiling at her. "You fit right in that first day." He
looked from her to the other women, all wearing
new dresses that they'd pieced on Ellen's sewing
machine. He shook his head. "You three ought
to open a dress shop in town."

Ellen glanced at Mary and Juana with pursed
lips and twinkling eyes. "You know, that's not
really such a bad idea, John," she said after a
minute. "It would make us a little extra money.
We could buy more barbed wire and we might
even be able to afford a milk cow!"

John started to speak, but Mary and Juana
jumped right in, and before he ate the first piece
of bread, the women were already making plans.

CHAPTER FOUR

ELLEN HAD JOHN DRIVE HER into town the following Saturday, to the dry goods store. She
spoke with Mr. Alton, the owner.

"I know there must be a market for inexpen-
sive dresses in town, Mr. Alton," she said,
bright-eyed. "You order them and keep them in
stock, but the ones you buy are very expensive,
and most ranch women can't afford them. Suppose I could supply you with simple cotton
dresses, ready-made, at half the price of the ones
you special order for customers?"

He lifted both eyebrows. "But, Mrs. Jacobs,
your father is a wealthy man...!"

"My husband is not," she replied simply. "I
must help him as I can." She smiled. "I have a
knack for sewing, Mr. Alton, and I think I do
quite good work. I also have two helpers who are
learning how to use the machine. Would you let
me try?"

He hesitated, adding up figures in his head.
"All right," he said finally. "You bring me

about six dresses, two each of small, medium and large ones, and we will see how they sell.''

She grinned. ''Done!'' She went to the bolts of fabric he kept. ''You must allow me credit, so that I can buy the material to make them with, and I will pay you back from my first orders.''

He hesitated again. Then he laughed. She was very shrewd. But, he noticed that the dress she was wearing was quite well-made. His women customers had complained about the lack of variety and simplicity in his ready-made dresses, which were mostly for evening and not everyday.

''I will give you credit,'' he said after a minute. He shook his head as he went to cut the cloth she wanted. ''You are a shrewd businesswoman, Mrs. Jacobs,'' he said. ''I'll have to watch myself, or I may end up working for you!''

Which amused her no end.

JOHN WAS DUBIOUS ABOUT HIS wife's enterprise, but Ellen knew what she was doing. Within three weeks, she and the women had earned enough money with their dressmaking to buy not one, but two Jersey milk cows with nursing calves. These John was careful to keep separate from his Hereford bull. But besides the milk, they made butter and buttermilk, which they took into town with their dresses and sold to the local restaurant.

"I told you it would work," Ellen said to John one afternoon when she'd walked out to the makeshift corral where he and the men were branding new calves.

He smiled down at her, wiping sweat from his face with the sleeve of his shirt. "You are a wonder," he murmured with pride. "We're almost finished here. Want to learn to ride?"

"Yes!" she exclaimed. But she looked down at her cotton dress with a sigh. "But not in this, I fear."

John's eyes twinkled. "Come with me."

He led her to the back of the cabin, where he pulled out a sack he'd hidden there. He offered it to her.

She opened it and looked inside. There was a man's cotton shirt, a pair of boots, and a pair of dungarees in it. She unfolded the dungarees and held them up to herself. "They'll just fit!" she exclaimed.

"I had Mr. Alton at the dry goods store measure one of your dresses for the size. He said they should fit even after shrinkage when you wash them."

"Oh, John, thank you!" she exclaimed. She stood on tiptoe and kissed him on the cheek.

He chuckled. "Get them on, then, and I'll

teach you to mount a horse. I've got a nice old one that Luis brought with him. He's gentle.''

''I won't be a minute!'' she promised, darting back into the cabin.

John was at the corral when she came back out. She'd borrowed one of John's old hats and it covered most of her face as well as her bundled-up hair. She looked like a young boy in the rig, and he chuckled.

''Do I look ridiculous?'' she worried.

''You look fine,'' he said diplomatically, his eyes twinkling. ''Come along and meet Jorge.''

He brought forward a gentle-looking old chestnut horse who lowered his head and nudged at her hand when she extended it. She stroked his forehead and smiled.

''Hello, old fellow,'' she said softly. ''We're going to be great friends, aren't we?''

John pulled the horse around by its bridle and taught Ellen how to mount like a cowboy. Then, holding the reins, he led her around the yard, scattering their new flock of chickens along the way.

''They won't lay if we frighten them,'' Ellen worried.

He looked up at her with a grin. ''How did you know that?''

''Mary taught me.''

"She and Juana are teaching you a lot of new skills," he mused. "I liked the biscuits this morning, by the way."

Her heart skipped. "How did you know that I made them?"

"Because you watched every bite I took."

"Oh, dear."

He only laughed. "I am constantly amazed by you," he confessed as they turned away from the cabin and went toward the path that led through the brush to a large oak tree. "Honestly, I never thought you'd be able to live in such deprivation. Especially after...Ellen?"

He'd heard a faint scraping sound, followed by a thud. When he turned around, Ellen was sitting up in the dirt, looking stunned.

He threw the reins over the horse's head and ran to where she was sitting, his heart in his throat. "Ellen, are you hurt?!"

She glared up at him. "Did you not notice the tree limb, John?" she asked with a meaningful glance in its direction.

"Obviously not," he murmured sheepishly. "Did you?" he added.

She burst out laughing. "Only when it hit me."

He chuckled as he reached down and lifted her up into his arms. It was the first time she'd been picked up in her adult life, and she gasped, locking her hands behind his neck so that she didn't fall.

His green eyes met her blue ones at point blank range. The laughter vanished as suddenly as it had come. He studied her pert little nose, her high cheekbones, her pretty bow of a mouth. She was looking, too, her gaze faintly possessive as she noted the hard, strong lines of his face and the faint scars she found there. His eyes were very green at the proximity, and his mouth looked hard and firm. He had high cheekbones, too, and a broad forehead. His hair was thick under the wide-brimmed hat he wore, and black. His ears were, like his nose, of imposing size. The hands supporting her were big, too, like his booted feet.

"I have never been carried since I was a child," she said in a hushed, fascinated tone.

"Well, I don't usually make a practice of carrying women, either," he confessed. His chiseled lips split in a smile. "You don't weigh much."

"I am far too busy becoming an entrepreneur to gain weight," she confessed.

"A what?"

She explained the word.

"You finished school, I reckon," he guessed.

She nodded. "I wanted to go to college, but

Father does not think a woman should be over-educated.''

''Bull,'' John said inelegantly. ''My mother educated herself and even learned Latin, which she taught me. If we have daughters, they'll go to college.''

She beamed, thinking of children. ''I should like to have children.''

He pursed his lips and lifted an eyebrow. His smile was sheer wickedness.

She laughed and buried her face in his throat, embarrassed. But he didn't draw back. His arms contracted around her and she felt his breath catch as he enveloped her soft breasts against the hard wall of his chest.

She felt unsettled. Her arms tightened around his strong neck and she shivered. She had never been held so close to a man's body. It was disconcerting. It was...delightful.

His cheek slid against hers so that he could find her soft lips with his mouth. He kissed her slowly, gently, with aching respect. When he pulled back, her lips followed. With a rough groan, he kissed her again. This time, there was less respect and more blatant hunger in the mouth that ravished hers.

She moaned softly, which brought him to his senses immediately. He drew back, his green eyes glittering with feeling. He wasn't breathing steadily anymore. Neither was she.

"We would have to climb a tree to find much privacy, and even then, the boys would probably be sitting in the branches," he said in a hunted tone.

She understood what he meant and flushed. But she laughed, too, because it was very obvious that he found her as attractive as she found him. She smiled into his eyes.

"One day, we will have a house as big as a barn, with doors that lock!" she assured him.

He chuckled softly. "Yes. But for now, we must be patient." He put her back on her feet with a long sigh. "Not that I feel patient," he added rakishly.

She laughed. "Nor I." She looked up at him demurely. "I suppose you have kissed a great many girls."

"Not so many," he replied. "And none as unique as you." His eyes were intent on her flushed face. "I made the best bargain of my life when I enticed you into marriage, Ellen Colby."

"Thank you," she said, stumbling over the words.

He pushed back a lock of disheveled dark hair that had escaped from under her hat. "It never occurred to me that a city woman, an aristocrat, would be able to survive living like this. I have felt guilty any number of times when I watched you carry water to the house, and wash clothes as the other women do. I know that you had maids to do such hard labor when you lived at home.''

"I am young and very strong,'' she pointed out. "Besides, I have never found a man whom I respected enough to marry, until now. I believe you will make an empire here, in these wilds. But even if I didn't believe it, I would still be proud to take your name. You are unique, also.''

His eyes narrowed. He bent again and kissed her eyelids shut, with breathless tenderness. "I will work hard to be worthy of your trust, Ellen. I will try never to disappoint you.''

She smiled. "And you will promise never to run me under oak limbs again?'' she teased.

"You imp!'' He laughed uproariously, hugging her to him like a big brother. "You scamp! What joy you bring to my days.''

"And you to mine,'' she replied, hugging him back.

"Daddy! Mr. John and Mrs. Ellen are spooning right here in the middle of the road!'' one of Isaac and Mary's boys yelled.

"Scatter, you varmints, I'm kissing my wife!'' John called in mock-rage.

There was amused laughter and the sound of brush rustling.

"So much for the illusion of privacy," Ellen said, pulling back from him with a wistful sigh. "Shall we get back to the business at hand? Where's my horse?"

John spied him in the brush, munching on some small green growth of grass he had found there. "He's found something nice to eat, I'll wager," he said.

"I'll fetch him," Ellen laughed, and started into the brush.

"Ellen, stop!"

John's voice, full of authority and fear, halted her with one foot in the act of rising. She stopped and stood very still. He was cursing, using words Ellen had never heard in her life. "Isaac!" he tacked onto the end, "fetch my shotgun! Hurry!"

Ellen closed her eyes. She didn't have to look down to know why he was so upset. She could hear a rustling sound, like crackling leaves, like softly frying bacon. She had never seen a rattlesnake, but during her visit to Texas with her father, she had heard plenty about them from local people. Apparently they liked to lie in wait and strike out at unsuspecting people who came near them. They could cause death with a bite, or extreme pain and sickness. Ellen was mortally

afraid of snakes, in any event. But John would
save her. She knew he would.

There were running feet. Crashing brush. The
sound of something being thrown and caught,
and then the unmistakable sound of a hammer
being pulled back.

"Stand very still, darling," John told her huskily. "Don't move…a muscle!"

She swallowed, her eyes still closed. She held
her breath. There was a horrifying report, like the
sound of thunder and lightning striking, near her
feet. Flying dirt hit her dungarees. She heard furious thrashing and opened her eyes. For the first
time, she looked down. A huge rattlesnake lay
dismembered nearby, still writhing in the hot sun.

"Ellen, it didn't strike you?" John asked at
once, wrapping her up in the arm that wasn't supporting the shotgun. "You're all right?"

"I am, thanks to you," she whispered, almost
collapsing against him. "What a scare!"

"For both of us," he said curtly. He bent and
kissed the breath out of her, still shaken from the
experience. "Don't ever march into the brush
without looking first!"

She smiled under his lips. "You could have
caught the brush on fire with that language," she
murmured reproachfully. "Indeed, I think the
snake was shocked to death by it!"

He laughed, and kissed her harder. She kissed him back, only belatedly aware of running feet and exclamations when the snake was spotted.

He linked his big hand into her small one. "Luis, bring the horse, if you please. I think we've had enough riding practice for one day!"

"Si, señor," Juan agreed with a chuckle.

THAT EVENING AROUND THE campfire all the talk was of the close call Ellen had with the snake.

"You're on your way to being a living legend," John told her as they roasted the victim of his shotgun over the darting orange and yellow tongues of flame. "Not to mention the provider of this delicious delicacy. Roasted rattler."

Ellen, game as ever, was soon nibbling on her own chunk of it. "It tastes surprisingly like chicken," she remarked.

John glowered at her. "It does not."

She grinned at him, and his heart soared. He grinned back.

"If you want another such treat, you will have to teach me how to shoot a gun," she proposed. "I am never walking into a rattler's mouth again, not even to provide you with supper!"

"Fair deal," he responded, while the others laughed uproariously.

IN THE DAYS THAT FOLLOWED, Ellen learned with hard work and sore muscles the rudiments of staying on a horse through the long days of watching over John's growing herd of cattle.

She also learned how not to shoot a shotgun. Her first acquaintance with the heavy double-barreled gun was a calamity. Having shouldered it too lightly, the report slammed the butt back into her shoulder and gave her a large, uncomfortable bruise. They had to wait until it healed before she could try again. The one good thing was that it made churning butter almost impossible, and she grinned as she watched Mary shoulder that chore.

"You hurt your shoulder on purpose," Mary chided with laughing dark eyes. "So you wouldn't have to push this dasher up and down in the churn."

"You can always get Isaac to teach you how to shoot, and use the same excuse," Ellen pointed out.

Mary grinned. "Not me. I am not going near a shotgun, not even to get out of such chores!"

Juana agreed wholeheartedly. "Too much bang!"

"I'll amen that," Mary agreed.

"I like it," Ellen mused. She liked even more knowing that John was afraid for her, that he cared about her. He'd even called her "darling" when he'd shot the snake. He wasn't a man to use endearments normally, which made the verbal slip even more pleasurable. She'd been walking around in a fog of pleasure ever since the rattler almost bit her. She was in love. She hoped that he was feeling something similar, but he'd been much too busy with work to hang around her, except at night. And then there was a very large audience. She sighed, thinking that privacy must be the most valuable commodity on earth. Although she was growing every day fonder of her companions, she often wished them a hundred miles away, so that she had even an hour alone with her husband. But patience was golden, she reminded herself. She must wait and hope for that to happen. Right now, survival itself was a struggle.

So was the shotgun. Her shoulder was well enough for a second try a week later. Two new complications, unbeknownst to Ellen, had just presented themselves. There were new mud puddles in the front yard, and her father had come to town and rented a buggy to ride out to visit his only child.

Ellen aimed the shotgun at a tree. The resulting kick made the barrel fly up. A wild turkey, which had been sitting on a limb, suddenly fell to the ground in a limp heap. And Ellen went backward right into the deepest mud puddle the saturated yard could boast.

At that particular moment, her father pulled up in front of the cabin.

Her father looked from Ellen to the turkey to the mud puddle to John. ''I see that you are teaching my daughter to bathe and hunt at the same time,'' he remarked.

Ellen scrambled to her feet, wiping her hair back with a muddy hand. She was so disheveled, and so dirty, that it was hard for her immaculate father to find her face at all.

He grimaced. ''Ellen, darling, I think it might not be a bad idea if you came home with me,'' he began uneasily.

She tossed her head, slinging mud onto John, who was standing next to her looking concerned. ''I'm only just learning to shoot, Father,'' she remarked proudly. ''No one is proficient at first. Isn't that so, John?''

''Uh, yes,'' John replied, but without his usual confidence.

Her father looked from one to the other and then to the turkey. ''I suppose buying meat from the market in town is too expensive?'' he asked.

''I like variety. We had rattlesnake last week, in fact,'' Ellen informed him. ''It was delicious.''

Her father shook his head. "Your grandmother is going to have heart failure if I tell her what I've seen here. And young man, this house of yours…!" He spread an expansive hand helplessly.

"The sooner we get *our* spur line," Ellen told her father, "the quicker we will have a real house instead of merely a cabin."

John nodded hopefully.

Terrance Colby sighed heavily. "I'll see what I can do," he promised.

They both smiled. "Will you stay for dinner?" Ellen invited, glancing behind her. She grinned. "We're having turkey!"

Her father declined, unwilling to share the sad surroundings that his daughter seemed to find so exciting. There were three families living in that one cabin, he noted, and he wasn't certain that he was democratic enough to appreciate such close quarters. It didn't take a mind reader to note that Ellen and John had no privacy. That might be an advantage, he mused, if Ellen decided to come home. There would be no complications. But she seemed happy as a lark, and unless he was badly mistaken, that young man John Jacobs was delighted with her company. His wife's mother was not going to be happy when he got up enough nerve to tell her what had happened to Ellen. She was just on her way home from a vacation in Italy. Perhaps the ship would be blown off course and she would not get home for several months, he mused. Otherwise, Ellen was going to have a very unhappy visitor in the near future.

He did make time to see John's growing herd of cattle, and he noticed that the young man had a fine lot of very healthy steers. He'd already seen how enterprising Ellen was with her dressmaking and dairy sales. Now he saw a way to help John become quickly self-sufficient.

WORD CAME THE FOLLOWING WEEK that Ellen's father was busy buying up right of way for the spur that would run to John's ranch. Not only that, he had become a customer for John's yearling steers, which he planned to feed to the laborers who were already hard at work on another stretch of his railroad. The only difficulty was that John was going to have to drive the steers north to San Antonio for Terrance Colby. Colby would be there waiting for him in a week. That wasn't a long cattle drive, certainly not as far as Kansas, but south Texas was still untamed and dangerous country. It would be risky. But John knew it would be worth the risk if he could deliver the beef.

So John and his men left, reluctantly on John's part, to drive the steers north. He and his fellow cowhands went around to all the other ranches, gathering up their steers, making sure they appropriated only the cattle that bore their 3J brand for the drive.

"I don't want to go," John told Ellen as they stood together, briefly alone, at the corral. "But I must protect our investment. There will be six of us to drive the herd, and we are all armed and well able to handle any trouble. Isaac and the older boys are going with me, but Luis will stay here to look after the livestock and all of you."

She sighed, smoothing her arms over the sleeves of his shirt, enjoying the feel of the smooth muscles under it. "I do not like the idea of you going away. But I know that it is necessary, so I'll be brave."

"I don't like leaving you, either," he said bluntly. He bent and kissed her hungrily. "When I return, perhaps we can afford a single night away from here," he whispered roughly. "I am going mad to have you in my arms without a potential audience!"

"As I am," she choked, kissing him back hungrily.

He lifted her clear of the ground in his embrace, flying as they kissed without restraint. Finally, he forced himself to put her back down and he stepped away. There was a ruddy flush on his high cheekbones, and his green eyes were fierce. Her face was equally flushed, but her eyes were soft and dreamy, and her mouth was swollen.

She smiled up at him bravely, despite her concern. "Don't get shot."

He grimaced. "I'll do my best. You stay within sight of the cabin and Luis, even when you're milking those infernal cows. And don't go to town without him."

She didn't mention that it would be suicide to take Luis away from guarding the cattle, even for that long. She and the women would have to work something out, so that they could sell their dresses and butter and milk in town. But she would spare him the worry.

"We'll be very careful," she promised.

He sighed, his hand resting on the worn butt of his .45 caliber pistol. "We'll be back as soon as humanly possible. Your father…"

"If he comes to town, I'll go there to wait for you," she promised, a lie, because she'd never leave Mary and Juana by themselves, even with Luis and a shotgun around.

"Possibly that's what you should do, anyway," he murmured thoughtfully.

"I can't leave here now," she replied. "There's too much at stake. I'll help take care of our ranch. You take care of our profit margin."

He chuckled, surprised out of his worries. "I'll be back before you miss me too much," he said, bending to kiss her again, briefly. "Stay close to the cabin."

"I will. Have a safe trip."

He swung into the saddle, shouting for Isaac and the boys. The women watched them ride away. The cattle had already been pooled in a nearby valley, and the drovers were ready to get underway. As Ellen watched her tall husband ride away, she realized why he'd wanted his railroad spur so badly. Not only was it dangerous to drive cattle a long way to a railhead, but the potential risk to the men and animals was great. Not only was there a constant threat from thieves, there were floods and thunderstorms that could decimate herds. She prayed that John and Isaac and the men going with them would be safe. It was just as well that Luis was staying at the ranch to help safeguard the breeding bulls and cows, and the calves that were too young for market. Not that she was going to shirk her own responsibilities, Ellen thought stubbornly.

Nobody was stealing anything around here while she could get her hands on a gun!

THE THREAT CAME UNEXPECTEDLY just two days after John and the others had left south Texas for San Antonio on the cattle drive.

Ellen had just carried a bucketful of milk to the kitchen when she peered out the open, glassless window at two figures on horseback, watching the cabin. She called softly to Juana and Mary.

Juana crossed herself. "It is Comanches!" she exclaimed. "They come to raid the cattle!"

"Well, they're not raiding them today," Ellen said angrily. "I'll have to ride out and get Luis and the boys," she said. "There's nothing else for it, and I'll have to go bareback. I'll never have time to saddle a horse with them sitting out there."

"It is too dangerous," Juana exclaimed. "You can hardly ride a saddled horse, and those men are Comanches. They are the finest riders of any men, even my Luis. You will never outrun them!"

Ellen muttered under her breath. They had so few cattle that even the loss of one or two could mean the difference between bankruptcy and survival. Well, she decided, there was only one thing to do. She grabbed up the shotgun, loaded it, and started out the back door, still in her dress and apron.

"No!" Mary almost screamed. "Are you crazy? Do you know what they do to white women?!"

Ellen didn't say a word. She kept walking, her steps firm and sure.

She heard frantic calls behind her, but she didn't listen. She and John had a ranch. These were her cattle as much as his. She wasn't about to let any thieves come and carry off her precious livestock!

The two Comanches saw her coming and gaped. They didn't speak. They sat on their horses with their eyes fixed, wide, at the young woman lugging a shotgun toward them.

One of them said something to the other one, who laughed and nodded.

She stopped right in front of them, lifted the shotgun, sighted along it and cocked it.

"This is my ranch," she said in a firm, stubborn tone. "You aren't stealing my cattle!"

There was pure admiration in their eyes. They didn't reach for the rifles lying across their buckskinned laps. They didn't try to ride her down. They simply watched her.

The younger of the two Indians had long pigtails and a lean, handsome face. His eyes, she noted curiously, were light.

"We have not come to steal cattle," the young one said in passable English. "We have come to ask Big John for work."

"Work?" she stammered.

He nodded. "We felt guilty that we butchered one of his calves. We had come far and were very hungry. We will work to pay for the calf. We hear from the Mexican people that he is also fair," he added surprisingly. "We know that he looks only at a man's work. He does not consider himself better than men of other colors. This is very strange. We do not understand it. Your people have just fought a terrible war because you wanted to own other people who had dark skin. Yet Big John lives with these people. Even with the Mexicans. He treats them as family."

"Yes," she said. She slowly uncocked the shotgun and lowered it to her side. "That is true."

The younger one smiled at her. "We know more about horses than even his vaquero, who knows much," he said without conceit. "We will work hard. When we pay back the cost of the calf, he can pay us what he thinks is fair."

She chuckled. "It's not really a big cabin, and it has three families living in it," she began.

They laughed. "We can make a teepee," the older one said, his English only a little less accented than the younger one's.

"I say," she exclaimed, "can you teach me to shoot a bow?!"

The younger one threw back his head and laughed uproariously. "Even his woman is brave," he told the older one. "Now do you believe me? This man is not as others with white skin."

"I believe you."

"Come along, then," Ellen said, turning. "I'll introduce you to...Luis! Put that gun down!" she exclaimed angrily when she saw the smaller man coming toward them with two pistols leveled. "These are our two new horse wranglers," she began. She stopped. "What are your names?" she asked.

"I am called Thunder," the young one said. "He is Red Wing."

"I am Ellen Jacobs," she said, "and that is Luis. Say hello, Luis."

The Mexican lowered his pistols and reholstered them with a blank stare at Ellen.

"Say hello," she repeated.

"Hello," he obliged, and he nodded.

The Comanches nodded back. They rode up to

the cabin and dismounted. The women in the cabin peered out nervously.

"Luis will show you where to put your horses," Ellen told them. "We have a lean-to. Someday, we will have a barn!"

"Need bigger teepee first," Red Wing murmured, eyeing the cabin. "Bad place to live. Can't move house when floor get dirty."

"Yes, well, it's warm," Ellen said helplessly.

The young Comanche, Thunder, turned to look at her. "You are brave," he said with narrow light eyes. "Like my woman."

"She doesn't live with you?" she asked hesitantly.

He smiled gently. "She is stubborn, and wants to live in a cabin far away," he replied. "But I will bring her back here one day." He nodded and followed after Luis with his friend.

Juana and Mary came out of the cabin with worried expressions. "You going to let Indians live with us?" Juana exclaimed. "They kill us all!"

"No, they won't," Ellen assured them. "You'll see. They're going to be an asset!"

CHAPTER FIVE

THE COMANCHES DID KNOW more about horses than even Luis did, and they were handy around the place. They hunted game, taught Luis how to tan hides, and set about building a teepee out behind the cabin.

"Very nice," Ellen remarked when it was finished. "It's much roomier than the cabin."

"Easy to keep clean," Red Wing agreed. "Floor get dirty, move teepee."

She laughed. He smiled, going off to help Thunder with a new corral Juan was building.

JOHN RODE BACK IN WITH ISAAC and stopped short at the sight of a towering teepee next to the cabin he'd left two weeks earlier.

His hand went to his pistol as he thought of terrible possibilities that would explain its presence.

But Ellen came running out of the cabin, followed by Mary and Juana, laughing and waving.

John kicked his foot out of the stirrup of his

new saddle and held his arm down to welcome Ellen as she leaped up into his arms. He kissed her hungrily, feeling as if he'd come home for the first time in his life.

He didn't realize how long that kiss lasted until he felt eyes all around him. He lifted his head to find two tall Comanches standing shoulder to shoulder with Juan and the younger boys and girls of the group, along with Juana and Mary.

"Bad habit," Thunder remarked disapprovingly.

"Bound to upset horse," Red Wing agreed, nodding.

"What the hell...!" John exclaimed.

"They're our new horse wranglers," Ellen said quickly. "That's Thunder, and that's Red Wing."

"They taught us how to make parfleche bags," Juana's eldest daughter exclaimed, showing one with beautiful beadwork.

"And how to make bows and arrows!" the next youngest of Isaac's sons seconded, showing his.

"And quivers," Luis said, resigned to being fired for what John would surely consider bad judgment in letting two Comanches near the women. He stood with his sombrero against his chest. "You may fire me if you wish."

"If you fire me, I'm going with them," Isaac's second son replied, pointing toward the Indians.

John shook his head, laughing uproariously. "I expect there'll be a lynch mob out here any day now," he sighed.

Everybody grinned.

Ellen beamed up at him. "Well, they certainly do know how to train horses, John," she said.

"Your woman meet us with loaded shotgun," Red Wing informed him. "She has strong spirit."

"And great heart," Thunder added. "She says we can work for you. We stay?"

John sighed. "By all means. All we need now is an Eskimo," he murmured to Ellen under his breath.

She looped her arms around his neck and kissed him. "Babies would be nice," she whispered.

He went scarlet, and everyone laughed.

"I GOT ENOUGH FOR THE STEERS to buy a new bull," John told her. "Saddles for the horses we have, and four new horses," he added. "They're coming in with the rest of the drovers. I rode ahead to make sure you were all right."

She cuddled close to him as they stood out behind the cabin in a rare moment alone. "We had no trouble at all. Well, except for the Comanches, but they turned out to be friends anyway.''

''You could have blown me over when I saw that teepee,'' he confessed. ''We've had some hard battles with Comanches in the past, over stolen livestock. And I know for a fact that two Comanches ate one of my calves...''

''They explained that,'' she told him contentedly. ''They were hungry, but they didn't want to steal. They came here to work out the cost of the calf, and then to stay on, if you'll keep them. I think they decided that it's better to join a strong foe than oppose him. That was the reason they gave me, at least.''

''Well, I must admit, these two Comanches are unusual.''

''The younger one has light eyes.''

''I noticed.'' He didn't add what he was certain of—that these two Comanches were the fugitives that the deputy marshal in Sutherland Springs had been looking for. Fortunately for them, James Graham had headed up beyond San Antonio to pursue them, acting on what now seemed to be a very bad tip.

She lifted her head and looked up at him. ''They rode up and just sat there. I loaded my shotgun and went out to see what they wanted.''

"You could have been killed," he pointed out.

"It's what you would have done, in my place," she reminded him, smiling gently. "I'm not afraid of much. And I've learned from you that appearances can be deceptive."

"You take chances."

"So do you."

He sighed. "You're learning bad habits from me."

She smiled and snuggled close. "Red Wing is going to make us a teepee of our own very soon." She kissed him, and was kissed back hungrily.

"Yesterday not be soon enough for that teepee," came a droll accented voice from nearby.

Red Wing was on the receiving end of two pairs of glaring eyes. He shrugged and walked off noiselessly, chuckling to himself.

John laughed. "Amen," he murmured.

"John, there's just one other little thing," Ellen murmured as she stood close to him.

"What now? You hired a gunslinger to feed the chickens?"

"I don't know any gunslingers. Be serious."

"All right. What?"

"My grandmother sent me a telegram. She's coming out here to save me from a life of misery and poverty."

He lifted his head. "Really!"

She drew in a soft breath. "I suppose she'll faint dead away when she sees this place, but I'm not going to be dragged back East by her or an army. I belong here."

"Yes, you do," John replied. "Although you certainly deserve better than this, Ellen," he said softly. He touched her disheveled hair. "I promise you, it's only going to get better."

She smiled. "I know that. We're going to have an empire, all our own."

"You bet we are."

"Built with our own two hands," she murmured, reaching up to kiss him, "and the help of our friends. All we need is each other."

"Need teepee worse," came Red Wing's voice again.

"Listen here," John began.

"Your horse got colic," the elder of the Comanches stood his ground. "What you feed him?"

"He ate corn," John said belligerently. "I gave him a feed bucket full!"

The older man scoffed. "No wonder he got colic. I fix."

"Corn is good for horses, and I know what to do for colic!"

"Sure. Not feed horse corn. Feed him grass. We build teepee tomorrow."

John still had his mouth open when the older man stalked off again.

"Indian ponies only eat grass," Ellen informed him brightly. "They think grain is bad for horses."

"You've learned a lot," he remarked.

"More than you might realize," she said dryly. She reached up to John's ear. "These two Comanches are running from the army. But I don't think they did anything bad, and I told Mr. Alton that I saw two Comanches heading north at a dead run. He told the…"

"…deputy marshal," he finished for her, exasperated.

"When you get to know them, you'll think they're good people, too," she assured him. "Besides, they're teaching me things I can't learn anywhere else. I can track a deer," she counted off her new skills, "weave a mat, make a bed out of pine straw, do beadwork, shoot a bow and arrow, and tan a hide."

"Good Lord, woman!" he exclaimed, impressed.

She grinned. "And I'm going to learn to hunt just as soon as you take me out with my shotgun."

He sighed. This was going to become difficult if any of her people stopped by to check on her. He didn't want to alienate them, but this couldn't continue.

"Ellen, what do you think about schooling?" he asked gently.

She blinked. "Excuse me?"

"Well, do any of the children know how to read and write?"

She hadn't considered that. "I haven't asked, but I don't expect they can. It was not legal for slaves to be taught such things, and I know that Juana can't even read Spanish, although it is her native tongue."

"The world we build will need educated people," he said thoughtfully. "It must start with the children, with this new generation. Don't you agree?"

"Yes," she said, warming quickly to the idea. "Educated people will no longer have to work at menial jobs, where they are at the mercy of others."

"That is exactly what I think. So, why don't you start giving the children a little book learning, in the evenings, after supper?" he suggested.

She smiled brightly. "You know, that's a very good idea. But, I have no experience as a teacher."

"All you will need are some elementary books and determination," he said. "I believe there is a retired schoolteacher in Victoria, living near the blacksmith. Shall I take you to see him?"

She beamed. "Would you?"

"Indeed I would. We'll go up there tomorrow," he replied, watching her consider the idea. If nothing else, it would spare her the astonished surprise of her people if they ever came to visit and found Ellen in dungarees and muddy boots skinning out a deer.

He drove her to Victoria the next morning in the small, dilapidated buggy he'd managed to afford from his cattle sales, hitched to one of the good horses he'd also acquired. Fortunately it took to pulling a buggy right away. Some horses didn't, and people died in accidents when they panicked and ran away.

The schoolteacher was long retired, but he taught Ellen the fundamentals she would need to educate small children. He also had a basic reader, a grammar book and a spelling book, which he gave to Ellen with his blessing. She clutched them like priceless treasure all the way back down the dusty road to the 3J Ranch.

"Do you think the Brown and the Rodriguez families will let me teach the children?" she wondered, a little worried after the fact. "They might not believe in education."

"Luis and Isaac can't even sign a paper," he told her. "They have to make an 'x' on a piece of paper and have me witness it. If they ever leave the ranch, they need to know how to read and write so that nobody will take advantage of them."

She looked at him with even more admiration than usual. He was very handsome to her, very capable and strong. She counted her blessings every single day that he'd thought her marriage-able.

"You really care for them, don't you?" she asked softly.

"When the Union Army came through Atlanta, they burned everything in sight," he recalled, his face hardening. "Not just the big plantations where slaves were kept. They burned poor white people's houses, because they thought we all had slaves down south." He laughed coldly. "Sharecroppers don't own anything. Even the house we lived in belonged to the plantation owner. They set it ablaze and my sister and mother were trapped inside. They burned to death while my other sister and I stood outside and watched." He touched his lean cheek, where the old scars were still noticeable. "I tried to kill the

cavalry officer responsible, but his men saved
him. They gave me these,'' he touched his cheek.
''I never kept slaves. I hid Isaac and Mary in the
root cellar when they ran away from the overseer.
I couldn't save their oldest son, but Mary was
pregnant. She and Isaac saved me from the Union
Army,'' he said with a sigh. ''They pleaded for
my life. Shocked the cavalry into sparing me and
my oldest sister. Isaac helped me bury my mother
and my younger sister.'' He looked down at her
soft, compassionate expression. ''My sister went
to North Carolina to live with a cousin, but I
wanted to go to my uncle in Texas. Isaac and
Mary had no place else to go, so they traveled
with me. They said they wanted to start over, but
they didn't fool me. They came with me to save
me from the Union Army if I got in trouble.
Those two never forget a debt. I owe them everything. My life. That's why they're partners
with me.''

''And how did you meet Luis and Juana?'' she
asked.

''Luis was the only cowboy my uncle had who
wasn't robbing him blind. Luis told me what the
others had done, and I fired the lot. I took care
of my uncle, with their help, and rounded up
stray calves to start my herd.'' He chuckled.
''The cabin was the only structure on the place.

It got real crowded when Isaac and Mary moved in with me. Juana and Luis were going to live in the brush, but I insisted that we could all manage. We have. But it hasn't been easy."

"And now the Comanches are building tee-pees for us," she told him. "They've been hunting constantly to get enough skins. We're going to have privacy for the very first time. I mean..." She flushed at her own forwardness.

He reached for her small hand and held it tight. His eyes burned into hers. "I want nothing more in the world than to be alone with you, Camellia Ellen Jacobs," he said huskily. "The finest thing I ever did in my life was have the good sense to marry you!"

"Do you really think so?" she asked happily. "I am no beauty..."

"You have a heart as big as all outdoors and the courage of a wolf. I wouldn't trade you for a debutante."

She beamed, leaning against his broad shoulder. "And I would not trade you for the grandest gentleman who ever lived. Although I expect you will make a fine gentleman, when we have made our fortune."

He kissed her forehead tenderly. "You are my fortune," he said huskily.

"You mean, because my father is giving us a

railroad spur for a wedding present," she said, confused.

He shook his head. "Because you are my most prized treasure," he whispered, and bent to kiss her mouth tenderly.

She kissed him back, shyly. "I had never kissed anyone until you came along," she whispered.

He chuckled. "You improve with practice!"

"John!" she chided.

He only laughed, letting her go to pay attention to the road. "We must get on down the road. It looks like rain." He gave her a roguish glance. "We would not want you to tumble into a mud puddle, Mrs. Jacobs."

"Are you ever going to forget that?" she moaned.

"In twenty years or so, perhaps," he said. "But I cannot promise. That is one of my most delightful memories. You were so game, and Sir Sydney was such a boor!"

"Indeed he was. I hope he marries for money and discovers that she has none."

"Evil girl," he teased.

She laughed. "Well, you will never be able to accuse ME of marrying you for your money," she said contentedly. "In twenty years or so," she added, repeating his own phrase, "you will be exceedingly rich. I just know it."

"I hope to break even, at least, and be able to pay my debts," he said. "But I would love to have a ranch as big as a state, Ellen, and the money to breed fine cattle, and even fine horses." He glanced at her. "Now that we have two extra horse wranglers, we can start building up our herd."

She only smiled. She was glad that she'd stood up to the Comanches. She wondered if they'd ever have wanted to work for them if she'd run away and hid.

THE TEEPEE THE COMANCHES built for the couple was remarkably warm and clean. No sooner was it up than Ellen built a small cooking fire near its center and put on a black iron pot of stew to cook. Red Wing had already taught her how to turn the pole in the center to work the flap for letting smoke out while she cooked. She also learned that she was born to be a rancher's wife. Every chore came easily to her. She wasn't afraid of hard work, and she fell more in love with her roguish, unconventional husband every day. She did still worry about her grandmother coming down to rescue her. She had no intention of being carted off back East, where she would have to dress and act with decorum.

She sat the children down in the cabin one evening after she and the other women and older girls had cleared away the precious iron cookware and swished the tin plates and few utensils in a basin of soapy water and wiped them with a dishrag.

"What are we going to do?" one of Juana's daughters asked.

Ellen produced the books that the retired Victoria schoolteacher had given her, handling them like treasure.

"I'm going to teach you children to read and write," she told them.

Mary and Juana stood quietly by, so still that Ellen was made uneasy.

"Is it all right?" she asked the adults, concerned, because she'd worried that they might think education superfluous.

"Nobody ever taught me to write my name," Mary said. "Nor Isaac, either. We can only make an x. Could you teach me to write? And read?"

"Me, too!" Juana exclaimed.

Their husbands looked as if they might bite their tongues off trying not to ask if they could learn, too, but they managed.

"You can all gather around and we'll let the

older folk help show the young ones how to do it,'' she said, managing a way to spare the pride of the men in the process of teaching them as well.

"Yes, we can show them, *señora*," Luis said brightly.

"Sure we can," Isaac added with a big grin.

"Gather around, then." She opened the book with a huge smile and began the first lesson.

SHE LOOKED DOWN AT THE dungarees she was wearing with boots that John had bought her. She had on one of his big checked long-sleeved shirts, with the sleeves rolled up, and her hair was caught in a ponytail down her back. She checked the stew in her black cooking pot and wiped sweat from her brow with a weary hand. The Comanches had gathered pine straw from under the short-leafed pines in the thicket to make beds, which Ellen covered with quilts she and the other women had made in their precious free time. It wasn't a mansion, but she and John would have privacy for the first time that night. She thought of the prospect with joy and a certain amount of trepidation. Like most young women of her generation, her upbringing had been very strict and moral. She knew almost nothing of what happened between married people in the dark. What she didn't know made her nervous.

The sudden noise outside penetrated her thoughts. She heard voices, one raised and strident, and she ran out of the teepee and to the cabin to discover a well-dressed, elderly woman with two young men in immaculate suits exchanging heated words with Juana, who couldn't follow a thing they were saying. Mary was out with the others collecting more wood for the fireplace in the small cabin.

"Do you understand me?" the old woman was shouting. "I am looking for Ellen Colby!"

"Grandmother!" Ellen exclaimed when she recognized the woman.

Her grandmother Amelia Greene was standing beside the buggy beside two tall young men whom Ellen recognized as her cousins.

Amelia turned stiffly, her whole expression one of utter disapproval when she saw the way her granddaughter was dressed.

"Camellia Ellen Colby!" she exclaimed. "What has become of you!"

"Now, Grandmother," Ellen said gently, "you can't expect a pioneer wife to dress and act as a lady in a drawing room."

The older woman was not convinced. She was bristling with indignation. "You will get your things together and come home with me right away!'' she demanded. ''I am not leaving you here in the dirt with these peasants!''

Ellen's demeanor changed at once from one of welcome and uneasiness to one of pure outrage. She stuck both hands on her slender hips and glared at her grandmother.

''How dare you call my friends peasants!'' she exclaimed furiously. She went to stand beside Juana. ''Juana's husband Luis, and Mary's husband Isaac, are our partners in this ranching enterprise. They are no one's servants!''

Mary came to stand beside her as well, and the children gathered around them. While the old woman and her companions were getting over that shock, John came striding up, with his gunbelt on, accompanied by Luis and Isaac and the two Comanche men.

Amelia Greene screeched loudly and jumped behind the tallest of her grandchildren.

''How much you want for old woman?'' Red Wing asked deliberately, pointing at Amelia.

Amelia looked near to fainting.

Ellen laughed helplessly. ''He's not serious,'' she assured her grandmother.

''I should hope not!'' the tallest of her cousins muttered, glaring at him. ''The very idea! Why do you allow Indians here?''

"These are our horse wranglers," Ellen said pointedly. "Red Wing and Thunder. And those are our partners, Luis Rodriguez and Isaac Brown. Gentlemen, my grandmother, Amelia Greene of New York City."

Nobody spoke.

John came forward to slide his arm around Ellen's waist. He was furious at the way her relatives were treating the people nearby.

"Hospitality is almost a religion to us out here in Texas," John drawled, although his green eyes were flashing like green diamonds. "But as you may notice, we have no facilities to accommodate visitors yet."

"You cannot expect that we would want to stay?" the shorter cousin asked indignantly. "Come, Grandmother, let us go back to town. Ellen is lost to us. Surely you can see that?"

Ellen glared at him. "Five years from now, cousin, you will not recognize this place. A lot of hard work is going to turn it into a showplace...."

"Of mongrels!" her grandmother said haughtily.

"I'm sorry you feel that way, but I find your company equally taxing," Ellen shot back. "Now will you all please leave? I have chores, as do the others. Unlike you, I do not sit in the parlor waiting for other people to fetch and carry at my instructions.''

The old woman glowered. ''Very well, then, live out here in the wilds with savages! I only came to try and save you from a life of drudgery!''

''Pickles and bread,'' Ellen retorted haughtily. ''You came hoping to entice me back into household slavery. Until I escaped you and came west with my father, I was your unpaid maidservant for most of my life.''

''What else are you fit for?'' her grandmother demanded. ''You have no looks, no talent, no...!''

''She is lovely,'' John interrupted. ''Gentle and kind and brave. She is no one's servant here, and she has freedom of a sort you will never know.''

The old woman's eyes were poisonously intent. ''She will die of hard work here, for certain!''

''On her own land, making her own empire,'' John replied tersely. ''The road is that way,'' he added, pointing.

She tossed her head and sashayed back to the buggy, to be helped in by her grandsons, one of whom gave Ellen a wicked grin before he climbed in and took the reins.

"Drive on," Amelia said curtly. "We have no kinfolk here!"

"Truer words were never spoken," Ellen said sweetly. "Do have a safe trip back to town. Except for cattle thieves from Mexico and the bordering counties of Texas, and bank robbers, there should be nothing dangerous in your path. But I would drive very fast, if I were you!"

There were muttered, excited exchanges of conversation in the buggy before the tallest grandson used the buggy whip and the small vehicle raced forward down the dusty dirt road in the general direction of town.

"You wicked girl!" John exclaimed on a burst of laughter, hugging her close.

"So much for my rescuers," she murmured contentedly, hugging him back. "Now we can get back to work!"

THAT NIGHT, ELLEN AND JOHN spent their first night alone, without prying eyes or ears, in the teepee the Comanches had provided for them.

"I am a little nervous," she confessed when John had put out the small fire and they were together in the darkness.

"That will not last," he promised, drawing her close. "We are both young, and we have all the years ahead to become more accustomed to each other. All you must remember is that I care more for you than for any woman I have ever known. You are my most prized treasure. I love you. I will spend my life trying to make you happy.''

''John!'' She pressed close to him and raised her face. ''I will do the same. I adore you!''

He bent and kissed her softly, and then not so softly. Tender caresses gave way to stormy, devouring kisses. They sank to the makeshift mattress and there, locked tight in each others' arms, they gave way to the smoldering passion that had grown between them for long weeks. At first she was inhibited, but he was skillful and slow and tender. Very soon, her passion rose to meet his. The sharpness of passion was new between them, and as it grew, they became playful together. They laughed, and then the laughing stopped as they tasted the first sweet sting of mutual delight in the soft, enveloping darkness.

When Ellen finally fell asleep in John's arms, she thought that there had never been a happier bride in the history of Texas.

CHAPTER SIX

ELLEN'S GRANDMOTHER AND cousins went back East. Her father came regularly to visit them in their teepee, finding it touching and amusing at once that they were happy with so little. He even offered to loan them enough to build a bigger cabin, but they refused politely. All they wanted, Ellen reminded him, was a spur of the railroad.

That, too, was finally finished. John loaded his beef cattle into the cattle cars bound for the stockyards of the Midwest. The residents of the ranch settled into hard work and camaraderie, and all their efforts eventually resulted in increasing prosperity.

The first thing they did with their newfound funds was to add to the cattle herd. The second was to build individual cabins for the Rodriguez and Brown clans, replacing the teepees the Comanches had built for them. The Comanches, offered a handsome log cabin of their own, declined abruptly, although politely. They could never understand the white man's interest in a stationary house that had to be cleaned constantly, when it was so much easier to move the teepee to a clean spot! However, John and Ellen continued to live in their own teepee for the time being, as well, to save money.

A barn was the next project. As in all young communities, a barbecue and a quilting bee were arranged along with a barnraising. All the strong young men of the area turned out and the resulting barn and corral were quick fruit of their efforts. Other ranches were springing up around the 3J Ranch, although not as large and certainly not with the number of cattle and horses that John's now boasted.

The railroad spur, when it came, brought instant prosperity to the area it served. It grew and prospered even as some smaller towns in the area became ghost towns. Local citizens decided that they needed a name for their small town, which had actually grown up around the ranch itself even before the railroad came. They decided to call it Jacobsville, for John Jacobs, despite his protests. His hard work and lack of prejudice had made him good friends and dangerous enemies in the surrounding area. But when cattle were rustled and houses robbed, his was never among them. Bandits from over the border made a wide route around the ranch.

As the cattle herd grew and its refinement continued, the demand for Jacobs's beef grew as
well. John bought other properties to go along
with his own, along with barbed wire to fence in
his ranges. He hired on new men as well, black
drovers as well as Mexican and white. There was
even a Chinese drover who had heard of the Jacobs ranch far away in Arizona and had come to
it looking for a job. Each new addition to the
ranch workforce was placed under the orders of
either Luis or Isaac, and the number of outbuildings and line camps grew steadily.

Ellen worked right alongside the other women,
adding new women to her dressmaking enterprise, until she had enough workers and enough
stock to open a dress shop in their new town of
Jacobsville. Mary and Juana took turns as pro-
prietors while Ellen confined herself to sewing
chair and sofa covers for the furniture in the new
white clapboard house John had built her. She
and her handsome husband grew closer by the
day, but one thing was still missing from her happiness. Their marriage was entering into its second year with no hope of a child.

John never spoke of it, but Ellen knew he
wanted children. So did she. It was a curious
thing that their passion for each other was ever
growing, but bore no fruit. Still, they had a good

marriage and Ellen was happier than she ever dreamed of being.

In the second year of their marriage, his sister Jeanette came west on the train with her husband and four children to visit. Only then did Ellen learn the extent of the tragedy that had sent John west in the first place. The attack by the Union troops had mistakenly been aimed at the sharecroppers' cabin John and his mother and sisters occupied, instead of the house where the owner's vicious overseer lived. The house had caught fire and John's mother and elder sister had burned to death. John had not been able to save them. The attack had been meant for the overseer who had beaten Isaac and Mary's son to death, along with many other slaves. John was told, afterward, but his grief was so sweeping that he hardly understood what was said to him. His sister made sure that he did know. The cavalry officer had apologized to her, and given her money for the trip to North Carolina, unbeknownst to John. His sister obviously adored him, and he was a doting uncle to her children.

She understood John's dark moods better after that, the times when he wanted to be alone, when he went hunting and never brought any wild game home with him. Ellen and Jeanette became close almost at once, and wrote to each other regularly even when Jeanette and her family went home to North Carolina.

Deputy Marshal James Graham had come by unexpectedly and mentioned to John that he hadn't been able to find the two Comanche fugitives who were supposed to have shot a white man over a horse. It turned out that the white man had cheated the Comanches and had later been accused of cheating several army officers in horse trading deals. He was arrested, tried and sent to prison. So, Graham told John, the Comanches weren't in trouble anymore. Just in case John ever came across them.

Thunder and Red Wing, told of the white man's arrest, worked a few months longer for John and then headed north with their wages. Ellen was sad to see them go, but Thunder had promised that they would meet again one day.

The Maxwells came to visit often from Scotland, staying in the beautiful white Victorian house John later built for his beloved wife. They gave the couple the benefit of their extensive experience of horses, and John branched out into raising thoroughbreds. Eventually a thoroughbred of the lineage from his ranch would win the Triple Crown.

YEARS PASSED WITH EACH YEAR bringing new

prosperity to the 3J Ranch. One May morning, Ellen unexpectedly fainted at a church social. John carried her to the office of their new doctor, who had moved in just down the boardwalk from the new restaurant and hotel.

The doctor examined her and, when John had been invited into the examination room, grinned at him. "You are to be a father, young man," he said. "Congratulations!"

John looked at Ellen as if she'd just solved the great mystery of life. He lifted her clear of the floor and kissed her with aching tenderness. His happiness was complete, now.

Almost immediately, he began to worry about labor. He remembered when Luis's and Isaac's wives had given birth, and he turned pale.

The doctor patted him on the back. "You'll survive the birth of your children, Mr. Jacobs, we all do. Yes, even me. I have had to deliver mine. Something, I daresay, you will be spared!"

John laughed with relief, thanked the doctor for his perception, and kissed Ellen again.

She bore him three sons and two daughters in the years that followed, although only two of their children, their son Bass and their daughter Rose Ellen, lived to adulthood. The family grew and prospered in Jacobsville. Later, the entire county, Jacobs, was named for John as well. He diversified his holdings into mining and real estate and banking. He was the first in south Texas to try new techniques in cattle ranching and to use mechanization to improve his land.

The Brown family produced six children in all. Their youngest, Caleb, would move to Chicago and become a famous trial lawyer. His son would be elected to the United States Senate.

The Rodriguez family produced ten children. One of their sons became a Texas Ranger, beginning a family tradition that lived on through subsequent generations.

John Jacobs founded the first bank in Jacobs County, along with the first dry goods store. He worked hard at breeding good cattle, but he made his fortune in the terrible blizzard of 1885-86 in which so many cattlemen lost their shirts. He endowed a college and an orphanage, and, always active in local politics, he was elected to the U.S. Senate at the age of fifty. He and Ellen never parted for fifty years.

His son, Bass Jacobs, married twice. By his young second wife, he had a son, Bass, Jr., and a daughter, Violet Ellen. Bass Jacobs, Jr., was the last of the Jacobs family to own land in Jacobs County. The 3J Ranch was sold after his death. His son, Ty, born in 1955, eventually moved to Arizona and married and settled there. His daughter, Shelby, born in 1961, stayed in Jacobsville and married a local man, Justin Ballenger. They produced three sons. One of them was named John Jackson Jacobs Ballenger, so that the founding father of Shelby's family name would live on in memory.

A bronze statue of Big John Jacobs, mounted on one of the Arabian stallions his ranch became famous for, was erected in the town square of Jacobsville just after the first world war.

Portraits of the Rodriguez family and the Brown family are prominently displayed in the Jacobs County Museum, alongside a portrait of Camellia Ellen Jacobs, dressed in an elegant blue gown, but with a shotgun in a fringed sheath at her feet and a twinkle in her blue eyes. All three portraits, which had belonged to Bass Jacobs, Jr., were donated to the museum by Shelby Jacobs Ballenger. In a glass case nearby are a bow and arrow in a beaded rawhide quiver, in which also resides a black-and-white photograph of a Comanche warrior with a blond woman and five children, two of whom are also blond. But that is another story...

Dear Reader,

Growing up in rural Virginia, my family was among the first in our community to have a television set. It was a black-and-white Philco—complete with rabbit ears. My dad watched boxing and Mother adored Perry Mason, but the Westerns that dominated the airwaves belonged to me.

What young girl wouldn't lose her heart to the rugged Rowdy Yates, played by Clint Eastwood? Or the brooding Josh Randall that Steve McQueen portrayed in *Wanted: Dead or Alive*? And what about those dashing Maverick brothers?

When I wrote "Wild West Wager" I tried to include many of these same qualities in Jack Delaney, Marlow, Colorado's only saloon owner with a conscience, a man who's presented with a moral dilemma that leaves him speechless. And who puts him in this position but Rebecca Merriweather, the refined beauty from the East? She intends to make Jack live up to their bargain—regardless.

But the troubles in the little town of Marlow don't end with Jack and Rebecca. I hope you'll watch for *Maggie and the Law*, a March 2004 Harlequin Historical release, to find out what becomes of the lonely mountain man Seth Grissom and Lucy Hubbard, a woman who must choose between her marriage vows and the man she loves.

Happy reading!

Judith Stacy

WILD WEST WAGER

Judith Stacy

To David—after thirty years you're still the one.

To Judy and Stacy—you always make me proud.

CHAPTER ONE

Colorado, 1888

SO MANY WOMEN. Which one to pick?

Jack Delaney leaned his elbow atop the batwing doors of the Lucky Streak Saloon and gazed outside at the skirts swishing down Main Street. Midafternoon and the women of Marlow were going about their business, doing whatever it was women did all day.

Jack sighed. Lots of women.

But he needed only one—didn't *want* one, just needed one.

Glancing back over his shoulder he saw Roy Hanover, his bartender, and a couple of cowboys standing at the bar. Not a lot of customers, especially for a warm afternoon.

Jack grumbled under his breath and once more turned his attention outside. For a moment, a vision of New York—his home—swam before his eyes. He'd left there and come west several years ago. Jack's gut twisted into a quick knot at the memory of his decision to leave home—and what he'd left behind.

After rambling around for several years, he'd had a lucky run at a poker table, and two months ago, he'd bought the Lucky Streak Saloon. Jack thought his luck had changed.

He'd been wrong about that, too.

"Something going on?" Roy appeared at Jack's side and rose on his toes to see over the door. Jack had no such trouble. At over six feet tall, he towered over most everything and everybody.

"Looking." Jack pushed his fingers through his black hair, forcing aside the old memories. "Looking for a woman."

Roy's thick mustache bobbed and Jack guessed a grin lurked beneath it. "The girls down at Miss Dora's parlor house can take care of you."

Jack rubbed his chin. He needed a woman, all right. But not just any woman. One with particular...skills.

"I was thinking more along the lines of Rebecca Merriweather," he said.

"Miss Merriweather?" Roy's eyes narrowed. "Are you sure you know who Miss Merriweather is?"

At the mention of her name, Jack's gut tightened again, but for a different reason. He knew exactly who she was. He'd seen her around town. How could he miss her? Dark hair, brown eyes, always dressed in the fashionable gowns of a fine Eastern lady rather than the simple gingham and calico most of the local women wore.

Roy shook his head. ''Miss Merriweather is a respectable woman. Hell, they don't come more respectable than her.''

That was true. The first time Jack had spotted her on the street he'd seen her stiff back, her level chin, her moderate steps. She'd practiced for hours walking with a book balanced on her head, surely, as his sisters had done.

Rebecca Merriweather was a tight little package, all right—that no one had opened.

Jack knew her type. He'd learned the hard way.

''Now, I know you're still kinda new in town, and all,'' Roy said, ''and you already had that run-in with Mrs. Frazier. But Miss Merriweather isn't the kind of woman—''

''Yes, she is.'' Jack fetched his black Stetson from the peg beside the door. ''Miss Merriweather is just the woman I need.''

''You're not going over to her place, are you?'' Roy asked, horror and panic causing his voice to rise.

Jack settled his hat on his head. "That woman has got something I need. And I intend to have it."

He walked outside, leaving his stunned bartender, his two lone customers, the saloon and all its problems behind.

Marlow's main street was a long line of wooden buildings fronted by boardwalks, hitching rails and water troughs. Horses, carriages and wagons filled the dirt street.

The town had pushed outward with the promise of the railroad expected next spring. East Street and West Street bracketed the town, adding more shops, stores and houses to Marlow's already burgeoning economy. Business was increasing in anticipation of the arrival of the railroad. That's why Jack had chosen to invest his money here.

It had seemed like a good idea at the time, anyway.

Jack greeted the men he passed on the boardwalk. He smiled and tipped his hat to the women who crossed his path, but as usual, got little more than a cold stare in return.

Thanks to that ol' battle-ax Mrs. Frazier.

Shortly after he'd arrived in town, the woman had barged into his saloon making demands on how he should run his business. He'd sent her packing, but made himself an enemy. Aside from being the wife of the richest rancher in the area, she also headed up Marlow's social and church functions.

Along with Miss Prim and Proper herself, Rebecca Merriweather.

Jack stopped on the boardwalk and gazed at the unmistakable storefront owned by Rebecca and her aunt. He saw the Marlow Tearoom and Gift Emporium every day from the door of his saloon, just across the street and down the block. Nobody could miss the place.

Pink. She'd painted it pink.

Jack had heard the story many times about Rebecca and the "discussion" she'd had in the middle of the boardwalk with Seth Grissom, the local carpenter—and probably the scariest-looking man Jack had ever laid eyes on—over the choice of color. Rebecca had gotten her way, a fact that hadn't surprised Jack in the least, and Griss was still getting grief over it.

Jack pulled his hat a little lower on his forehead. He didn't think for a minute that Miss Merriweather would eagerly go along with what he wanted. He knew it would take some work on his part to gain her cooperation. And once she agreed, he'd have to proceed cautiously.

A man always had to be careful around a woman like Rebecca Merriweather.

"WHAT ELSE, LADIES?"

Rebecca Merriweather gazed across the table at the two women, ready to add another item to her long list should Doris Tidwell or Nelly Walker come up with anything. Neither, she feared, had noticed the gaping hole in their list of preparations for this Sunday's church social.

Mrs. Tidwell and Mrs. Walker exchanged a troubled look. Rebecca had seen the same expression on the students' faces in Miss Whitney's classroom when she helped at the school.

While the women pondered the social's missing ingredient, Rebecca let her own mind rush on to other matters requiring her attention this afternoon.

The first, of course, was the room in which she and the ladies now sat. Rebecca looked around with pride at what she'd accomplished with the— if at first reluctant—blessing of her aunt Virginia Kent.

When Rebecca had moved here from Maryland to join her aunt six months ago, she'd been stunned by the little restaurant Aunt Virginia had owned. Dismal and unappealing, it drew only a few guests despite her aunt's excellent cooking.

Years spent working at her father's side in his Baltimore department store had sent dozens of ideas exploding in Rebecca's mind. A walk through town and a chat with the mayor confirmed that her initial thoughts were correct.

At first, Aunt Virginia was less than excited about Rebecca's idea to close the restaurant and start over with a new business. She'd opened the little eatery with her husband, now dead, and was getting by well enough.

But Rebecca had sold her on the idea, and within two months the Marlow Tearoom and Gift Emporium had opened. She'd had the interior painted a creamy yellow, put delicate linens and fresh flowers on the tables, and served tea and elegant foods from the china service Rebecca had ordered from her father's store. Everything in the tearoom was meant to appeal to feminine tastes.

At Rebecca's request, her father had also sent some of the unique items he carried in his own establishment, and Rebecca had used a portion of the tearoom's space to sell embroidered hand-kerchiefs, hair accessories and other items the ladies of Marlow couldn't buy elsewhere.

The town's women had warmed up to the tea-room. Now it was a place where mothers brought their daughters for a special afternoon, ladies planned the town's social and civic functions, chatted, shared news and, of course, gossip.

There was always plenty of gossip.

"Oh, I know!" Mrs. Tidwell sat up straighter, her eyes bright with the sure knowledge that she'd figured out the one thing Sunday's church social still needed. "Games!"

Mrs. Walker's lips turned down, disappointed that she hadn't thought of it first.

"Yes, games for the children," Rebecca said and made a note on her tablet. "What sort should we have?"

Mrs. Walker rushed ahead with a half-dozen suggestions before Mrs. Tidwell could respond. Rebecca wrote them all down, nodding in agreement. When she finished, she studied the tablet, then announced, "That's everything. We're sure to have another successful social."

Mrs. Tidwell and Mrs. Walker smiled with pride and helped themselves to their tea and the remaining tiny sandwiches artfully arranged on the pink-flowered platter on the table before them.

"How's the wedding coming?" Mrs. Walker asked.

Mrs. Tidwell, whose niece was getting married soon, proceeded to update them with the details.

Rebecca cringed at the mere mention of a wedding—an old habit, one she'd not completely rid herself of, even after living in Marlow for so long.

Since her mother's death nine years ago, Rebecca had cared for her younger brothers and sisters and helped with her father's business. The years slipped by somehow, and at age twenty-six, staring head-on into the prospect of being labeled a spinster, she was bombarded by her well-intentioned friends and family with "advice" and helpful "suggestions" on how she might improve herself and find a husband.

Rebecca hadn't objected to the idea of being married. In fact, she was all for it. But her age had made her too old to be appealing—except to men whom she found completely unappealing.

Moving to Marlow, Rebecca had made a fresh start. After spurning the advances of the town's older gentlemen—every single one of them, in short order—she'd settled into a comfortable life, one without a constant barrage of suggestions on how to catch a man. The people of Marlow had come to accept her as she was, and that suited Rebecca just fine.

After all, she had everything she could ever want. A pleasant aunt, friends, enough social and civic functions to keep her occupied.

And her business, of course. Rebecca adored

her restaurant and shop. She'd discovered she had a gift for running a business, tackling the problems, making all the decisions—and she loved doing it. So much so that at times she thought that having a husband would be a distraction from the things she truly loved.

Really, the last thing she needed was a man in her life.

"Oh yes, the wedding," Mrs. Tidwell said. "My niece—"

The door burst open, the little bell above it clanging madly.

Mrs. Tidwell gasped. Mrs. Walker's eyes widened to the size of saucers.

Rebecca turned in her chair.

A man. A man had entered her tearoom.

There wasn't a No Men Allowed sign on the door, but there may as well have been. Never in all the months since the place had opened had a man set foot in the Marlow Tearoom and Gift Emporium. Not once.

Heat coiled deep in Rebecca's stomach, then surged outward. Good gracious, this wasn't simply a *man*. It was that awful Jack Delaney.

She'd never been properly introduced, but she knew who he was. Everyone in Marlow knew who he was.

The saloon owner who'd insulted Mrs. Frazier,

and had yet to set foot in church. The man who could ruin a woman's reputation by simply speaking to her on the street.

And he was in her tearoom.

Rebecca got to her feet, her knees quivering, unsure if it was anger, outrage, fear—or something different—that threatened to take her breath away.

"I believe, Mr. Delaney," she said, struggling to keep her voice from shaking, "that you've entered this building by mistake."

He didn't bother to look around. His gaze locked on Rebecca and held there.

"I'm in the right place," he said. "I'm here to see you, Miss Merriweather."

"Me?"

He nodded. "I've got a proposition for you."

CHAPTER TWO

MRS. WALKER'S EYES had yet to blink, and Mrs. Tidwell had recoiled so far that Rebecca feared she might topple out of her chair.

Then, as one, they both turned to Rebecca, their shock at seeing Jack Delaney walk into the tearoom changing from surprise to suspicion. What had Rebecca done to bring on this visit by the town's most notorious saloon owner? their expressions seemed to ask.

Rebecca's stomach knotted. What *had* she done? Her mind whirled, but she came up with nothing—except to worry what would happen to her business when word of this got out.

Jack pulled off his Stetson and glanced toward the door, looking for a peg on which to hang it. There was none, of course, since only ladies visited the tearoom. He pressed his hat to his chest.

"I'd like a few minutes of your time, Miss Merriweather," he said, his voice as smooth as the amber liquid that flowed so freely in his saloon.

Rebecca just looked at him, her mind spinning. What could he possibly want to talk to her about? What could they have to discuss?

And why had she never noticed how handsome he was?

The thought startled her, but she couldn't let it go.

Black hair. Blue eyes with lashes so long he might have been thought pretty, were it not for his crooked nose and square jaw. Tall. Wide, straight shoulders, full chest, lean waist—

Rebecca stifled another gasp, stunned to realize that she was openly staring at the man, and horrified to think that Mrs. Walker and Mrs. Tidwell may have noticed it. But when she dared glance their way, she realized they blatantly ogled him as well.

Curiosity. Rebecca seized upon the notion that they all were simply curious about the man so often the topic of the town's unsavory gossip.

What else could it be?

"Miss Merriweather?" he prompted.

Rebecca blushed, realizing she was still staring and hadn't answered his question.

"I—I can't imagine that we'd have anything to discuss," she said, trying to sound aloof, but managing nothing more than a breathy whisper.

"We do," Jack assured her. Then a little grin

pulled at the corner of his mouth and he leaned toward her ever so slightly. "I'm here to extend you an offer."

A warmth, a strength—something—radiated from him, pulling at Rebecca, urging her to lean toward him. She glanced at the other women. They swayed forward in their chairs, their eyes glazed, answering that same unspoken call.

Rebecca clamped her lips together, catching a whimper before it slipped through. Good gracious, did she have that same expression on *her* face?

She came to her senses, ready to invite Jack Delaney to leave her tearoom before she humiliated herself completely. But he spoke first.

"Ladies, would you excuse us, please?" he asked, favoring Mrs. Tidwell and Mrs. Walker with a full smile.

"Well..." Mrs. Tidwell hesitated, unwilling, it seemed, to give up her front-row seat on the juicy bit of gossip unfolding before her.

"Thank you," Jack said, though the ladies had agreed to nothing. He backed up, opened the door wide and smiled graciously as the two women passed in front of him. Mrs. Walker turned backward as he closed the door, craning her neck for one final glimpse of the goings-on inside.

Rebecca cringed. Those women would make her tearoom the talk of the town before nightfall.

Thanks to Jack Delaney.

"I don't appreciate you barging into my place of business and running off my customers," Rebecca said, unable now to keep the anger from her voice.

"I thought you'd rather discuss my proposition in private." He gestured toward the door. "If you'd like me to ask those ladies back inside, I'm sure they'll be glad—"

"No!" Rebecca forced herself to calm down. "I mean, no. The damage is done now, anyway. What do you want?"

"I have a business proposal for you, Miss Merriweather."

"Forgive me, Mr. Delaney, but I can't imagine what sort of business you and I might have in common."

"I think we have more in common than you realize."

Rebecca couldn't fathom how that might be true, by any stretch of the imagination. He was completely out of place in her tearoom. Big, rugged, masculine. Whiskers shadowed his chin. A sharp contrast to her delicate china service, the lace curtains, the ruffled linens. And she certainly had no interest in anything remotely related to his saloon.

"May I sit down and explain?" Jack asked, waving his hand toward the table the other ladies had just vacated.

Rebecca hesitated. She wished he'd leave. She wished he'd never showed up in her tearoom in the first place. He'd thrown her into a very awkward position.

But he was here now, and if her reputation had to suffer because of it, she should at least hear him out. She was just the tiniest bit curious.

"Very well," she said, trying to sound inhospitable so he wouldn't linger.

Jack pulled out a chair for her. She hadn't expected a modicum of good manners from him, and was surprised.

She almost asked if he cared for a cup of tea, then realized how ridiculous he'd look holding one of her tiny cups in his huge hand.

Rebecca lowered herself into the chair and Jack pushed it beneath her, then he circled the table and sat down opposite her, tossing his hat aside.

He hesitated, as if gathering his thoughts, then looked across the table at her and said, "I need a woman."

Rebecca gasped.

Jack held up his palm, a silent plea for another moment. "What I mean is, I want you." He shifted in his chair. "Actually, what I'm trying to say is that you have some feminine qualities which I'm in need of, and—"

Jack muttered a curse and plowed his fingers through his hair. He looked across the table at her, his cheeks slightly pink.

"This seemed a hell of a lot easier on the walk over here," he said.

Rebecca smiled. She couldn't help it. The infamous Jack Delaney looked sweet and endearing and flustered, a man in need of rescuing if ever she'd seen one.

In a gesture so natural Rebecca thought nothing of it, she reached across the table and patted his hand. Warm. Rough. Hairy. She'd meant it as a gesture of comfort, but a peculiar sensation raced up her arm, making her decidedly *uncomfortable*. She withdrew her hand quickly.

"Perhaps you should just start at the beginning," she suggested.

Jack nodded. "I own the Lucky Streak Saloon."

"Yes, I know," Rebecca said. "You moved here two months ago and you're building yourself a house on West Street."

His brows drew together, wondering, she was

sure, how she knew so much about him. Apparently, he was willing to let it go because he continued without asking her, and that suited Rebecca fine. If Jack didn't already know he was the topic of gossip among the ladies in town, she didn't want to be the one to tell him.

"The house is finished now," Jack said.

"It is?" Rebecca didn't know how that bit of news had escaped the town's rumor mill. Mrs. Tidwell and Mrs. Walker had been here for nearly an hour and hadn't mentioned it. "Are you certain?"

He raised an eyebrow. "Yes, I'm certain. Anyway, I've purchased furnishings for the house from New York—"

"Furniture?" Speculation on what was in the many crates Jack received had run rampant among the ladies in the tearoom for weeks.

He nodded. "Now it's time to fix up the place. Make it liveable. That's what I want you for. I want you to turn the house into a home."

"Me?" Rebecca sat back in her chair. "Mr. Delaney, there are many women in Marlow who could—"

"I want you for the job." Jack waved his hand toward her. "You're a fine, upstanding Eastern woman. You know the way things should be done. I want this house done properly."

"But—"

"I've got company coming from back East," Jack said. "Important company. I want the house to…"

"Be warm and welcoming in the tradition to which your guests are accustomed?" Rebecca asked.

Jack grinned. "I knew I had the right woman for the job."

Flattered by his words, Rebecca smiled along with him. It pleased her to know he thought highly of her, that he'd noticed the way she carried herself. Her mother, God rest her soul, would be infinitely pleased.

Yet she couldn't allow herself to be swept into agreeing to something simply because of flattery.

"I understand your situation, Mr. Delaney," Rebecca said. "But I'm not sure I should accept your offer."

"Why not?"

"I have my own business to run," she said, waving her hands to encompass the tearoom.

"You do," Jack agreed. "But you've got things running smooth. Your aunt is here to help. A few hours a day away from this place won't do it any harm."

Rebecca couldn't disagree. In fact, she often took time away from the tearoom to attend to

charitable causes in Marlow, do a little shopping
or visit friends.

"I'm not sure it would be…decent…for me to
be in your home, among your personal things,"
Rebecca said.

"It's not my home yet. I've got a room over
the saloon. Nothing of mine is in the house."
Jack's expression hardened. "Let's get something straight right now, Miss Merriweather. This
is a business deal I'm talking about. You're being
hired to do a job. That's all."

"But still…"

"I assumed you understood the business
world," Jack said, his tone almost a challenge.
"Was I wrong about that?"

Rebecca sat straighter in her chair, his words
causing her spine to stiffen. Yes, she knew a
great deal about the workings of businesses.
She'd learned it from listening to her father and
working at his side. She'd have taken over his
store, eventually, if she'd been born male.

"I assure you, Mr. Delaney," Rebecca said,
"that I'm well aware of the workings of a business."

"Good," he said. "Then you'll understand
how important this project is to me when I tell
you to name your price for the job."

She stifled a gasp. She'd heard he was wealthy, but never imagined *this*.

"Name it," he told her. "Whatever you want. It's yours."

"Your offer is extremely generous," Rebecca said. "But I'll have to think it over."

"There're some nice things in those crates, Miss Merriweather. I'd like to see them put where they belong by somebody who knows how." Jack rose from the chair. "But if you won't do it, I'll find somebody who will."

He gave her a nod, took his hat and walked to the door. He opened it, then looked back. "You've got until noon tomorrow to give me your answer. After that, I'll offer the work to someone else."

Rebecca watched him walk out, saw the door close, looked at him as he moved past her window and disappeared across the street. But she couldn't force herself out of her chair. Her legs wouldn't hold her up.

She'd been a party to business deals before, when she worked with her father, when she got the tearoom up and running. But no matter what Jack said, the things she felt at the moment had nothing to do with business.

CHAPTER THREE

JACK NEVER LIKED doing the paperwork necessary to run a business. He liked it even less when
the profits went down instead of up.

As he sat at the desk in his room over the
Lucky Streak, golden light from the lantern cast
a dull glow over the ledger before him. Neat columns detailed the saloon's income and each of
its expenses.

Neat columns that told him he was on his way
to losing his shirt over this place.

"Damn..." Jack tossed his pencil aside and
sat back in his chair.

He'd thought long and hard before deciding to
buy the saloon. Opening a new business had its
risks, of course. But he hadn't expected things to
be this bad.

The saloon had been closed for some time before Jack bought it. From the stories he'd heard,
the place had been pretty wild back in those days.
Fistfights and gunplay were routine. The former
owner had caught a bullet during a disagreement

over a card game and sold out to Jack in the midst of a long, slow recovery.

Jack had figured that once he opened the doors and offered a little competition to Marlow's two other saloons, customers would flock in, as they had before. They hadn't.

Of course, Jack didn't allow fights and shoot-outs, though the customers found them entertaining. Even before that old heifer Mrs. Frazier had burst into his place demanding civilized behavior from his clients, he'd decided not to put up with that sort of thing. Not that he particularly cared if two men duked it out or shot each other. He just didn't want his place damaged, or to be stuck with the repair bills.

Rising from the chair, Jack stretched, nearly scraping his knuckles on the low ceiling. He looked around the room, thinking it was simply that: a room. Nothing warm or welcoming about it.

That brought Rebecca Merriweather to mind.

Jack walked to the window that overlooked Main Street and pressed his forehead against the glass, angling for a view of the Marlow Tearoom and Gift Emporium just down the street. The sun had dipped toward the horizon shining its last rays on the pink storefront.

From this distance, he couldn't tell if anyone

was inside, but he suspected there was. Women
always flowed in and out of the place. He'd been
lucky this afternoon to catch only two of them in
there, besides Rebecca.

Jack's stomach twisted a little, thinking of
what a fool he'd made of himself in front of her.
Talking to people—even women—had never
been a problem for him. But, somehow, sitting
across the table from Rebecca had rattled him.

But that was her fault, in a way. She'd caught
him off guard.

He'd expected her to be uppity, which she was.
He'd expected her to be aloof, and she was that,
too.

But he hadn't expected her to be pretty. He'd
seen her on the streets, but like most of the other
women in town, she'd never allowed herself to
come close enough that he could get a good look.

So he had no idea that her brown eyes were
so large and liquid, hadn't suspected she'd have
lips that pink, or that the tip of her nose turned
up ever so slightly.

Yet there she'd sat looking nice, smelling
nicer, done up in dozens of petticoats and carefully coiffed hair. For a moment or two while
he'd sat across from her, she'd actually seemed
warm and a little friendly. Those things he'd
found more surprising than her good looks.

What hadn't surprised him was that she didn't leap at his offer to decorate his house.

Jack looked around the little room he'd been living in for the past few months. He'd never liked it in the first place, and with each day that passed it grew more confining.

He'd been telling himself for weeks now that once the house was finished, once his company arrived from New York, things would be better. He still believed that was true.

All he needed was Miss Rebecca Merriweather's help to make it happen.

Help from Rebecca…a woman. Jack's gut knotted at the realization of what he was opening himself up to by offering her the work. Memories surfaced, stirring his anger.

A woman in his new house. Having the run of the place. Taking over.

Drawing in a slow breath, Jack pushed the idea away, determination hardening in his belly.

He'd accept her help with the house—but he'd make damn sure she remembered her place.

Jack stalked out of the room and down to the saloon.

About a half-dozen men occupied the room, several playing cards, others standing at the bar. Among them was Ian Caldwell, one of Marlow's deputy sheriffs.

Since the saloon opened, Sheriff Harding himself had been by often, but that was to get a bead
on Jack and the saloon, see what was going on,
make sure no trouble was brewing. Harding was
a lawman who brooked no nonsense from anyone, certainly not a drunken cowboy. Ian came
by just to socialize.

"How's it going?" Jack said, easing up next
to Ian at the bar.

He smiled easily. In his thirties, Ian was tall
and slender with neat brown hair, always dressed
in pressed clothes, even though he had no wife
to look after him.

"Just making the rounds," Ian said, and sa-
luted him with his mug of beer before taking another swallow.

"Things quiet?" Jack asked, nodding toward
the street.

"Quiet enough," Ian said. He wore a pistol on
each hip and looked as if he knew how to handle
them. "There's talk around town about you."

Jack grunted. "More talk?"

"Talk that you've got more guts than any
other man in Marlow." Ian shook his head in
disbelief. "Did you really go inside the ladies'
tearoom today?"

"Yeah, I did," Jack admitted. "I had a little
business to discuss with Miss Merriweather."

"Damn…"

Ian finished his beer and headed for the door. Jack walked along with him, and when they reached the boardwalk, both turned toward the tearoom.

"Maybe I'll go over there myself," Ian said. "Have me a cup of that tea the women are all so excited about."

"Just remember to keep your pinkie finger sticking out when you drink," Jack said.

Ian laughed and walked away. Jack stood there for a while, gazing at the tearoom. He considered going back over there, talking to Rebecca again. The notion he'd awakened with this morning to have her decorate his house had gotten stronger as the day went on. Even more so now that he'd gone to her place and talked to her. Having that house fixed up—properly—clawed at his gut. Worth the risk of having a woman like Rebecca involved.

But he decided not to push her. He'd given her until noon tomorrow to make a decision. And if she turned him down…well, maybe it was for the best.

"SO, WHAT DO YOU THINK?" Rebecca asked.

Across the table from her in the tearoom sat her closest friend Lucy Hubbard. A few years younger than Rebecca, Lucy had been married for about four months. She and her husband had moved to Marlow shortly after their wedding. Lucy stopped by the tearoom most every day now that her husband was out of town.

Lucy touched her dark hair. "What does your aunt think?"

She'd told Aunt Virginia about Jack's proposition as soon as she'd composed herself. Virginia hadn't looked up from the dough she was kneading. A simple woman, Virginia wasn't crazy about all the gossip that went on in the tearoom—even where Jack Delaney was concerned.

"She didn't see anything wrong with me working for Mr. Delaney," Rebecca said.

Lucy drew in a sharp breath. "Can you imagine what Mrs. Frazier will say when she finds out?"

"I've thought about it," Rebecca admitted. "But this is a business arrangement. There's nothing personal in it. Mr. Delaney intends to pay me for the work."

"Really?" Lucy leaned closer. "How much?"

Rebecca didn't mind her friend's personal question. Images of Jack's rumored wealth would intrigue Lucy; money was tight for her and her husband.

"We haven't settled on payment yet," Rebecca said, then got back to the more worrisome issue. "But Mrs. Frazier would respect a business arrangement. Don't you think?"

"Your reputation is solid gold in this town. You sing in the church choir, organize all the socials, help at the schoolhouse. No one would dare say anything against you."

When she'd arrived in Marlow, Rebecca had set about contributing her time and energy to the betterment of the town, just as she'd done in Baltimore. That was simply what one *did*.

"And you know what else?" Lucy proposed. "If you got better acquainted with Mr. Delaney, perhaps you could get him to apologize to Mrs. Frazier."

Rebecca's eyes widened. After sitting across the table from Jack this afternoon, seeing the determination on his face, she couldn't imagine anyone talking him into anything.

"It's worth a try," Lucy said. "Wouldn't it be nice not to have to hear Mrs. Frazier complain about him and the Lucky Streak at every meeting?"

"Yes, it would," Rebecca conceded.

A little smile crept over Lucy's face. "Besides, he's awfully handsome."

"Lucy!"

"Well, he is. Don't tell me you hadn't noticed."

"Well, yes. But that has no bearing on my decision."

"Then how about plain old curiosity?" Lucy asked. "Aren't you just dying to know what sort of furniture he had shipped all the way from New York? And just *who* his company is? People so important he'd go to all this trouble?"

"Probably business investors," Rebecca said. "Lots of people are interested in Marlow now that the train is coming through next year."

"Aren't you just the least bit interested in finding out for sure?" Lucy asked.

Rebecca couldn't deny that she was. From the moment Jack had left the tearoom this afternoon—and as soon as she'd composed herself again—the idea of decorating his house had taken root in her mind.

She loved her new home in Marlow, but it was different from the life she'd led in Baltimore. She missed the grand home her family lived in, the extravagant gowns her father treated her to, and the many occasions on which to wear them—even if the conversation at most of those events had turned to speculation on why Rebecca still wasn't married.

"Don't tell me you wouldn't enjoy the challenge," Lucy said, giving her a knowing look.

"That's true," she admitted. Since work on the tearoom had been completed, Rebecca had found herself a little bored with simply running the place. She'd caught herself eyeing the wall connecting her tearoom to Mrs. Wagner's millinery shop next door. Rumor had it that Mrs. Wagner was considering moving to Keaton with her daughter. Rebecca had envisioned purchasing the shop, knocking out the walls, expanding and redecorating her tearoom. On her walks through town she'd often speculated on what other sort of shop or store she might open in Marlow. Since coming here, the business portion of her mind had flourished.

"Mr. Delaney gave me until noon tomorrow to decide."

"So think about it tonight," Lucy said, as she rose from her chair. "Then tomorrow morning tell him you'll accept his offer. After all, it's a business arrangement. Right?"

"Yes, a business arrangement," Rebecca said as they moved toward the door. "Oh, by the way. Several ladies have asked about the scented soaps you made. Can you bring more?"

Lucy looked pleased, and relieved. "Of course."

With her husband out of town for so long now, Lucy had started taking in wash and mending, and baking pies for the Pink Blossom Restaurant to make ends meet. She'd come up with the idea of making scented soaps wrapped in colorful fabric and fancy bows, and asked Rebecca to sell them in her store. They'd gone over well with the ladies.

"Have you heard from Raymond lately?" Rebecca asked, though she wasn't sure if she should since he'd been gone for over a month now.

Lucy's smile faded. "No, not lately. But I'm sure he's terribly busy looking for investments, and things."

"Yes, I'm sure he is," Rebecca agreed.

They stepped out onto the boardwalk as the sun touched the horizon, sending long shadows across the street. "I'll get those soaps over to you as soon—"

Lucy stopped, the words dying on her lips, her attention riveted to Ian Caldwell as he stepped out of the shadows. He stopped as well. But neither spoke. Neither moved. They just stood there face-to-face on the boardwalk.

"Good evening, Deputy," Rebecca finally said.

Ian hurriedly touched the brim of his hat. "Oh,

ah, evening, Miss Merriweather…Mrs. Hubbard.''

"G-good evening," Lucy managed to say.

"Making your rounds?" Rebecca asked when it became apparent that no one else would—or could—speak.

"Yes, ma'am," Ian said, pulling his gaze from Lucy. He shifted. "Well, I'd better get going."

He nodded to both women, then reluctantly stepped off the boardwalk and crossed the street.

"Lucy—" Rebecca began.

"I'm a married woman," she insisted harshly, turning to Rebecca, "and it's sinful to even think about Ian Caldwell."

"I know," she replied softly. "I was only going to thank you for listening to my problem with Mr. Delaney."

"Oh…" Lucy's face softened. "I'm sorry. I shouldn't have snapped at you. It's just that—"

Rebecca touched her friend's arm. "I understand," she said, because really, she did.

"Well, good night," Lucy said, and headed up the boardwalk toward her little house on East Street.

Rebecca watched her for a moment before her gaze drifted to the Lucky Streak Saloon down the block. Images of Jack Delaney floated through her mind. What was he doing inside his saloon?

She couldn't even imagine. She'd never been inside that sort of establishment.

For a moment, Rebecca envied men their lack of concern for their reputation. When faced with a business decision, men only troubled themselves with the merits of the transaction, never how they'd look in the eyes of others should they decide to proceed.

Things were never that simple for women.

In Rebecca's mind she pictured the dozens of crates she'd seen carted down Main Street from the express office to Jack's house these past weeks. Furnishings all the way from New York. Her fingers itched to pry the tops from the wooden boxes in search of the hidden treasures.

And she could name her price for the job. Rebecca eyed the stores on Main Street. Her tearoom generated a nice profit, and she still had most of the money she'd brought from Baltimore. With the cash from Mr. Delaney's job, might she open yet another business in Marlow?

Rebecca paused, suddenly unsure if it was the idea of another business venture that caused her stomach to tingle with delight—or thoughts of Jack.

CHAPTER FOUR

NO SENSE IN WAITING until noon, Rebecca told herself as she slipped out of her bedroom in back of the tearoom. In the adjoining kitchen, past the big cookstove, the worktables and cupboards, she saw that Aunt Virginia's door was still closed, as she'd expected at this early hour.

Rebecca had hardly slept at all last night, tossing and turning, thinking over Jack's proposal.

And Jack.

But while some in Marlow might raise an eyebrow at her decision, Rebecca knew that business was business. This, definitely, was not an opportunity she wanted to let pass her by.

Rebecca quietly opened the kitchen door and glanced up and down the alley. Seeing no one, she stepped outside and closed the door with a soft thud.

She'd decided to go to the saloon early and inform Jack of her decision. She didn't want him in her tearoom again. Rebecca didn't relish the idea of being the topic of gossip for a second day in a row—business deal or not.

With the sun only just now rising above the horizon, Rebecca crossed Main Street and followed the alley to the rear of the Lucky Streak Saloon.

Like most of the other businesses in town, outbuildings, a small barn and paddock and a woodpile were situated across the narrow alley. Yet for all its sameness, Rebecca shivered at the thought of knocking on the rear door of the Lucky Streak. It was, after all, a saloon. Jack's saloon.

Glancing around one final time, Rebecca climbed the wooden steps onto the small porch. She'd chosen a dark green skirt and blouse, thinking the color would make her appear more businesslike. Men always dressed in dark colors, giving them an aura of seriousness. She wondered how much real business would be conducted if men wore pink suits.

Rebecca rapped on the door, waited, and waited. She knocked again, again and again, a little harder each time. Backing up a step, she gazed at the second-floor windows. No movement. She edged closer to the door, but heard nothing. Jack must be up and gone already.

Her heart sank. She'd wanted to get the meeting concluded with as little an audience as possible, but apparently that would not be possible. She raised her arm to give the door a final knock, and it flew open.

Jack glared out at her, his eyes squinted against the sunlight, his hair sticking up on one side. He wore dark trousers, but the top button was unfastened. One suspender crossed his shoulder atop a white shirt that hung open.

Rebecca gasped, horrified at confronting a half-dressed man. She knew she should leave—run, actually. But all she could do was stand there and look at his bare chest.

How could she not? Dark, coarse curls met in the center of his taut belly and arrowed downward among hard, rippling muscles. She'd never seen such a sight in her life. Never.

And now that she had, she couldn't drag her gaze away.

''Oh, Miss Merriweather.''

Hearing her name jolted Rebecca. She broke eye contact with his belly and lifted her gaze to his face. Heat swamped her cheeks and she knew they must be red.

Jack didn't seem to notice, though, as he rubbed the sleep from his eyes and stepped back from the door.

"Come on in," he said and disappeared from the doorway.

Rebecca hesitated a moment, unsure of what to do. How unseemly to be in a saloon, of all places, with Jack, of all people—half-dressed. Yet how silly would she look if she bolted to the safety of her tearoom, only to have him follow later and remind her once again that this was *business?*

Rebecca didn't want to appear silly. Especially not to Jack. She stepped inside the large kitchen.

Sunlight beaming through the grimy windows cast the room in a dim pallor. A layer of dust covered the rickety table, mismatched chairs and cupboards. Spiderwebs clung to high corners. A desolate feel chilled the morning air.

Rebecca shuddered to think of this as someone's home. No wonder Jack had built himself a house. At once she was overwhelmed with the desire to rush to his new house, rip open the crates, turn it into a warm and welcoming home.

"Be right with you," Jack called.

She saw him at the sideboard where he leaned over a bowl of water he'd just pumped, and was splashing his face. He straightened, water sliding down his cheeks, dripping onto the hair of his chest. He groped for a towel nearby and dragged it down his face.

"Didn't expect you this early," Jack said, as he threaded his fingers through his hair, slicking it in place.

Rebecca gulped, trying desperately to keep her gaze on the room and not him. "I shouldn't have come by so early. I…"

"It's okay," Jack said with a shrug.

Indeed, he didn't seem to mind at all that she'd roused him from his bed just after dawn. Nor did he seem to mind that she was standing only feet away as he went through the personal details of dressing.

He closed the buttons on his shirt, shoved the tail into his trousers and fastened the top button, then hiked both suspenders into place.

If they continued to conduct business under these conditions, Rebecca didn't know if she could bear it.

"Can I get you some coffee?" Jack gazed around the kitchen. "I've got some here. Somewhere. Probably."

"No," Rebecca said, anxious to focus on something other than the droplets of water glistening in the dark hair that curled above the top button of his shirt. "I came to discuss your business proposal."

"Sit down," he invited, gesturing to the table and chairs in the corner.

"No, thank you," Rebecca said, not because the furnishings were covered with dust, but because she was suddenly anxious to get this over with and return to the safety of her tearoom.

Jack leaned his hip against the sideboard and crossed his arms over his chest, then nodded for her to proceed.

"Well," she began, "after giving it a good deal of thought, I've decided to accept your proposal."

Caution clouded his expression, as if he'd expected her to reject his offer, and a moment passed before he straightened away from the sideboard.

"Okay, then," he finally said. "The job is yours."

"I can start this afternoon," she told him. Her words sounded hollow in the chilly room. Another awkward moment passed while she waited for him to say something. When he didn't, she went on. "So, I suppose that's that."

"What about your payment?" he asked.

"Oh, yes…" She silently chastised herself for not having thought of that already. How very unbusinesslike of her. Then an idea occurred to her.

"I can't set a price without knowing exactly what the job will entail."

"I'll give you until the work is done to let me

know,'' Jack said. His expression hardened. ''But no longer. I won't have a debt hanging over my head indefinitely.''

''Of course not,'' Rebecca agreed.

His gaze remained harsh and he took a step closer. ''You understand, Miss Merriweather, that I expect you to follow through with our agreement. I can't have you getting halfway into this thing, then losing interest, or quitting.''

''I know how the business world works,'' Rebecca assured him. ''I'll see the project through.''

He watched her for a while, as if judging her words—or maybe just her. His expression grew more stern. ''And you understand you're the hired help. You do what I tell you to do. I have the final say-so.''

''Well, of course,'' Rebecca said, thinking it a little odd he'd even mention those things.

For a few more moments Jack continued to look hard at her, then he nodded briskly, as if satisfied with their deal.

''I've made arrangements for someone to help you with the heavy lifting, moving the furniture and such,'' he told her.

''Fine,'' Rebecca said, then desperate for a diversion, changed the subject. She waved her hand, taking in the room. "I've never actually been in a saloon before."

He grinned, the intensity he'd exhibited a moment ago suddenly gone. "No, I don't suppose you have."

She gave him a small smile in return.

"Would you like to see inside?" He nodded toward the swinging door that led to the saloon.

Such a question. Women—decent women—never went into a saloon. Rebecca couldn't imagine stepping one foot inside the place. Yet, until this morning, she couldn't have imagined standing in the kitchen of a saloon either, entering into a business deal with the most talked-about man in town.

Her gaze bounced from Jack to the door, then back to him again. "There's no one in there, is there?"

"It's a little early for saloon patrons," he said, and she could see he was making an effort not to smile.

"Well, yes, of course it is." She hesitated for another moment. "I—I suppose it would be all right to take a *peek*."

"Peek all you want," Jack said, pushing the door open.

Rebecca squeezed past him, feeling the heat from his body as he held the door for her.

"Or," he said, freezing her in front of him, "get up on the bar and sing, if you're so inclined."

She raised an eyebrow. "How kind of you to offer."

Jack grinned and followed her inside.

The saloon was larger than Rebecca had imagined. A piano and stool sat on the opposite wall. Round tables covered with green baize filled most of the room. A long bar with a brass footrail ran the width of the place, backed by shelves of glasses and dozens of liquor bottles. A large, empty space was centered behind the bar, as if a picture of some sort had once occupied the spot.

"There used to be a painting of a grizzly bear," Jack said, as if reading her thoughts. "I understand it got shot up and the old owner threw it out."

"Are you going to replace it?"

Jack shrugged. "It's one of the items on a long list of things I've got to do."

Rebecca nodded her understanding.

"Disappointed?" Jack asked, and moved a little closer.

She glanced up at him. "I didn't really know what to expect, but is this all men do here? Drink and play cards? No activities? Special events?"

"The men just like to drink and gamble."

"Well, all right," Rebecca said, thinking that surely there must be more to drinking and gambling than she realized, if it kept men entertained for hours. She also wondered if it was worth the fuss Mrs. Frazier made over it.

Thinking of that particular woman spurred Rebecca's conscience. "I'd better go," she said.

To her surprise, Jack followed her outside and walked with her through the alley to the rear corner of the saloon.

At a moment such as this, the conclusion of a business deal, Rebecca had seen her father shake hands with his new associate, clasp his shoulder, offer words of confident praise for their mutual success.

But what of her business arrangement with Jack Delaney? What gesture was appropriate to seal their arrangement?

A handshake? That would be acceptable. But the thought of touching Jack made her stomach quiver, for some reason.

She tried to come up with something to say, but no words formed, just the new, strange feeling that accompanied her quivering stomach. Gazing at Jack, she realized he didn't seem to know what to say either.

Yet words didn't seem to be necessary. Jack leaned down and kissed her.

Stunned, Rebecca froze. Jack didn't seem to notice as he moved his lips smoothly over hers and settled his hands on her shoulders.

Then, without wanting to, Rebecca sighed, giving in to the warmth that spun between them. Delightful. Simply delightful.

Jack lifted his head, ending their kiss. Rebecca hung where she was for a few seconds, raised slightly on her toes, her face tilted up to meet his.

With a slow smile, Jack stepped back. He didn't speak, but really, what was there to say?

Rebecca turned and walked away. When she reached the boardwalk she looked back and saw that Jack still stood in the alley. He waved. She waved back, then turned and ran straight into Mrs. Frazier.

CHAPTER FIVE

WHEN SHE'D ENCOUNTERED Mrs. Frazier on the street outside the Lucky Streak this morning, Rebecca had fought off the guilty look that had crept over her face, greeted the woman, then simply walked away, allowing no time for the questions sure to come. If pressed, how would she explain her business deal with Jack—without blushing red remembering his kiss? Rebecca didn't understand it herself.

Now, as she headed toward West Street, Mrs. Frazier was the furthest thing from her mind, though Jack's kiss still lurked in a cozy corner. Threading her way through the crowd, Rebecca noticed the young married women on the boardwalk, some with babies bundled in their arms, some with a duckline of children following, others with both.

A sense of freedom stirred in her stomach. If burdened with a husband and children, she wouldn't have been available to accept Jack's business proposal. As it was, all she had to do was ask Aunt Virginia to watch over the tearoom this afternoon, and off she went.

Rebecca smiled to herself. Yes, her life was going just the way she wanted it.

Turning the corner onto West Street, she spotted Jack's new house. Everyone in town knew about it. Not the biggest house—Mrs. Frazier held that distinction—but certainly one of the nicest.

A two-story home painted gleaming white with dark-green shutters, it sported a large covered front porch, a picket fence and twin maples in the front yard. A lovely home.

Rebecca opened the gate and walked up the path and onto the porch. The door stood open. The scent of sawdust, fresh paint and wallpaper glue drifted out.

She paused before crossing the threshold, a new sense of pride filling her. After today, would she be known in town for her business sense as well as her charity work? The idea thrilled her. Rebecca squared her shoulders and stepped into the house.

In the large entryway, a staircase rose to the second floor. To the right through an open doorway was a sizeable parlor. On the left was a smaller room, suitable for a bedroom or perhaps Jack intended to use it as an office. She'd have to ask him. Both of the rooms were crammed full of wooden crates.

"Hello?" she called, gazing down the central hallway.

She heard a muffled commotion from the back of the house, but no answer. Apparently, whoever Jack had hired to help her with the heavy work was already on the job. She followed the sound to a room where a large table, chairs, sideboard and cupboard were shoved into one corner. The dining room, of course. Here, too, rows of large and small wooden crates—some of them open already—filled almost all the available space.

Rebecca said a prayer of thanks that Jack had hired someone to help with the crates and move the furnishings. She'd never be able to handle it alone—and what sort of business person would she be if she had to ask for help immediately?

She stepped into the kitchen which adjoined the dining room. Beyond the massive cookstove, she saw the man Jack had hired to build the house. Had she not already known him, she would have run screaming into the street.

Seth Grissom was the most frightening-looking man she had ever laid eyes on. He was huge. If a bear suddenly reared up on its hind legs in front of her, Rebecca was sure it would be *smaller* than Seth Grissom. Not more than thirty years old, he had a full beard and mustache that reached halfway down his chest, and hair that hung to his shoulders, all a golden blond. His clothing was clean, but poorly mended since he had no wife to handle such things.

She'd employed Seth to do the renovations on her tearoom. He'd quietly gone about his work, talking with her rarely. Yet Rebecca had come to realize that beneath his rough exterior lay a gentle, artistic soul. Not only was Seth an excellent carpenter, but also a painter, woodcarver and cabinetmaker. They'd worked well together on the tearoom's renovations until suddenly—she'd never known why—Seth had simply stopped speaking to her.

"Good afternoon, Mr. Grissom," Rebecca said, making an effort to sound friendly. "I understand we'll be working together to finish up the house."

Seth looked up at her from the cabinet door he'd been studying. His eyes narrowed. "Delaney hired *you?*"

"Yes," she said, keeping her smile in place. "He said that you'd help with moving the boxes and—"

"I quit."

"You—what? Mr. Grissom?"

He shouldered his way past her without another word.

"Wait!" Rebecca hurried after him. "Mr.

Grissom, wait! You're supposed to help with—I can't possibly—Mr. Grissom?''

Rebecca stopped at the front door and watched helplessly as he trudged away, taking her business reputation along with him. For an instant, she considered running after him, but sensed it would do no good. Seth Grissom would not easily be swayed once his mind was made up, as it obviously was.

Slowly, she turned and faced the wooden crates. Dozens of them. Many, undoubtedly, filled with heavy pieces of furniture that she couldn't possibly lift—even if she could figure how to get the lids off.

Her shoulders slumped. How would she ever fulfill her end of the business deal now?

JACK PUSHED HIS WAY through the crowded boardwalk outside the Lucky Streak and headed toward his new house, mumbling one curse after another. Just when things were looking up, when everything seemed to finally be falling into place, *this* had to happen.

Five minutes ago, Seth Grissom had walked into the saloon and told Jack that he quit. Quit. Just like that. No explanation, no apology, no nothing.

Turning the corner onto West Street, Jack grumbled another curse, this one at himself. He hadn't bothered to ask Griss the reason; he already knew.

Jack took the front porch steps two at a time and strode down the hallway of his new house. In what was to become his dining room, he jerked to a stop.

Rebecca's bottom was in the air.

He drew in a sharp breath, frozen in midstride, all thoughts of Seth Grissom and the unfinished house flying out of his head.

There it was, right in front of him, draped in the folds of her dark-green skirt, her little bustle perched atop it.

She was bent over the side of a large crate, struggling to reach something in the very bottom, and all he could see was her bottom. And her legs, of course. Long legs. Calves and silk stockings visible where her skirt had hiked up. Leather slippers. Her ankles.

A familiar warmth slammed low in his gut. His mouth went dry. He knew he should say something, make his presence known—he wasn't the kind of man to ogle a woman caught in a compromising situation—but he couldn't seem to form any real words. Nor could he get his feet to move. Only one part of him was working at the moment—and working well.

Just then, one of Rebecca's feet left the floor as she reached deeper inside the crate. She strug-

gled for a moment, then pushed off with the
other foot.

"No...don't..." Jack saw that she'd pushed
too hard, knew what was coming. She teetered
on the edge of the crate for a second, then top-
pled inside headfirst.

Jack rushed to the crate. "Rebecca? Are you
all right?"

Slumped in the bottom of the crate, packing
straw in her hair and stuck to her dress, she gazed
up at him and her eyes widened.

"Mr. Delaney, your organ!" she declared.

"Huh?"

"Your organ," she said again, tugging her
skirt down over her ankles.

Jack shifted uncomfortably. "My...?"

"It's so impressive!"

"Well..."

She struggled to her feet. "I had no idea it was
an Alister Penworthy."

"What?"

"See? Right here." Rebecca pushed the brochure toward him that she'd retrieved from the
floor of the crate. "Alister Penworthy and Sons
is a very old, very well-respected company. Perhaps the most prestigious maker of musical instruments on the East coast."

Jack frowned at the brochure depicting several
models of musical organs on its cover. *"Oh..."*

"It's in one of these crates somewhere," Rebecca said, waving her arm around the room. "I had no idea you played."

"Come on out of there," Jack said, suddenly anxious to change the subject. He looped one arm around her shoulders, the other behind her knees and hefted her out of the crate.

Her breast settled comfortably against his chest and the sweet scent of her hair tickled his nose. The temptation to lean closer and kiss her nearly overcame him. Instead, Jack clamped his lips together to stifle a groan, and set her on her feet.

"I suppose you're here about Mr. Grissom?" Rebecca asked.

"Who?"

"Seth Grissom."

"Oh, yeah. Right," Jack said, forcing his mind from the packing straw clinging to her bodice. "What did you do to him?" he asked, a little more harshly than he'd intended.

"Nothing," she said.

"Then what did you *say?*"

"All I did was greet him—pleasantly, I might add."

"You didn't fire him? Run him off on purpose?" Jack demanded.

Rebecca looked at him as if he'd lost his senses. "No, of course not. Why would I do such a thing?"

Jack ignored her question, unwilling to give her an answer. "You must have done or said *something.*"

Rebecca pressed her lips together, then leaned a little closer looking slightly distressed. "I don't think Mr. Grissom likes me very much."

That was sure as hell true. Jack knew that Griss had taken a ribbing from the men in town about painting Rebecca's tearoom pink, but Jack had thought that was all over with now. Obviously, it wasn't—for Griss, anyway.

"Perhaps if I spoke to Mr. Grissom about the situation?" Rebecca offered.

Jack stifled another curse. One visit from Rebecca and Griss would probably come to the saloon and shoot him in the leg.

"That's not a good idea," Jack told her.

Rebecca drew herself up straighter and announced, "Don't give the situation another thought, Mr. Delaney, I have everything under control."

He raised both brows at her. "You do?"

"Yes," she said briskly. "You needn't worry about a thing. You hired me to do this job and I intend to see it done. So just run along and leave everything to me."

He squared his shoulders. "Look, Miss Merriweather, I've already told you that I'm in charge of the work here. Not you."

Rebecca huffed impatiently. The last thing she wanted was for Jack to think she couldn't handle the job. Yet his interference was irritating—and unnecessary.

"Fine then," she told him and waved her hand toward the front door. "Go out and find a replacement for Mr. Grissom. And hurry up. I have a work schedule and you're slowing things down considerably."

Jack's eyes narrowed as he glared down at her.

For a moment, Rebecca feared he might fire her on the spot. She rushed on. "There. You see how silly that sounds? You have too many important things to concern yourself with. Let me handle the house—you're paying me to do just that."

Jack hesitated. It went against his grain to walk out and leave her in this situation, but she had a point. He had hired her to do the job. He'd made a fuss of insisting it was a business deal.

He'd also told her he wouldn't allow her to run roughshod over him either.

"As soon as I find a replacement for Mr. Grissom," Rebecca promised, "I'll let you know, and if you don't like him, I'll find someone else."

He certainly couldn't argue with that. "Well, all right."

"Good day, Mr. Delaney." With a firm nod she returned to the opened crates.

Jack headed down the hallway. Halfway to the front door, he stopped and looked back.

He'd known all along that Rebecca was independent-minded. Any woman who could come from a big city like Baltimore, make a home in Colorado and build a successful business on tea and funny-looking sandwiches had to be strong. And he should be relieved that Rebecca had taken over preparations at the house, freeing him for other, more important matters.

But he wouldn't stand for a woman—any woman—to jump in and take things over. He'd made that decision years ago.

Still, the idea of Rebecca being alone in the house bothered him on a very different level. The familiar, pleasurable ache presented itself again as he watched her bend over one of the smaller crates. He felt territorial all of a sudden, thinking of some other man in his house. Working. Helping Rebecca.

Watching her bend over.

Damn if he was going anywhere. Jack stalked back into the dining room.

CHAPTER SIX

"I'M HELPING YOU," Jack announced, striding into the room.

Rebecca whirled around. "You blame me for Mr. Grissom's resignation, don't you. That's why you're here."

"I don't blame you."

"Then what is it?" she demanded.

What could he tell her? That he couldn't stand the thought of another man in his house working alongside her? Ogling her fanny when she bent over? Hell no.

"Look, Miss Merriweather," Jack said. "I've got a lot of problems to deal with right now—this place, the saloon—"

"What's wrong with your saloon?" She walked closer.

Jack pulled off his hat and dragged his sleeve across his brow. It wasn't that hot, but he was sweating.

"Business is a little slow. That's all."

"It is? Perhaps if you—" She stopped and

flushed slightly. "Sorry, it's not my place to say anything."

"What were you going to say?"

"Nothing. Never mind." She spared him a quick, apologetic glance. "I tend to be too out-spoken."

"Who told you that?"

"My father. Friends."

Jack shrugged. "I like outspokenness."

"Even in women?"

He grinned. "Especially in women."

She smiled then, the first genuine smile he'd seen. Her face lit up, and for some reason, he lit up, too.

"What were you going to say about the saloon?" he asked.

"Well, when I opened the tearoom, no one really knew what it was about. I had to lure women inside. The men in town are content spending their time at the other saloons. You need to draw them into the Lucky Streak."

Jack sat on one of the low crates. "Got any ideas?"

She thought for a moment. "I provided my customers with all the things ladies find appealing. The table linens, the china. I have framed drawings of current fashions hanging on the walls. Mr. Grissom made them for me."

"Griss drew pictures of ladies' clothing?" Jack asked. Thank God word of that hadn't gotten out. He'd have left town, for sure.

"He copied them from one of my catalogs. He's quite an accomplished artist," she said. "I also schedule special events. We have poetry readings and sing-alongs."

Jack rubbed his chin. "I don't think the men in Marlow are going to take too well to poetry readings in the saloon."

"No, but there are activities men enjoy," she pointed out. "If you provide them, they'll come."

He thought for a minute, then slapped his palms on his thighs and rose. "I'll think about it. Let's get to work."

He headed for the kitchen, found a hammer among the tools Grissom had left behind, returned to the dining room and started prying lids off the crates.

"This is quite lovely," Rebecca said as she lifted a lead crystal pickle server from the packing straw. "Which catalog did you order from?"

"I didn't order anything." Jack paused, hammer in hand. "I sent the floor plan of the house to my sisters. They picked out everything, shipped it here."

"They have excellent taste," Rebecca said.

"Please tell them how much I admire your organ."

"Yeah...I'll do that," he mumbled and went back to work.

"When is your company arriving?" Rebecca asked.

"Can't say for sure, since the train doesn't come all the way to Marlow yet, and the stagecoach line is so unreliable."

"Your family is all back East?" she asked.

"In New York." He tossed the lid into the corner with the others, then glanced back over his shoulder, and there she was again, bent over a crate, her bottom in the air. Once again, he had the same reaction, swift and strong.

Jack pressed his lips together. How the hell was he ever going to get the house finished like this?

"Yes, New York," he said, focusing his thoughts on their conversation. "My family owns a shipyard."

"*Those* Delaneys?" she asked, turning to him with wide eyes. "Why don't you work in the family business?"

For a moment, Jack was tempted to tell her the truth, tell her what had gone on. Something about this woman made him want to confide in her, trust her.

But he couldn't bring himself to do it. "I don't like ships," he said, and went back to work.

AFTER OVER A WEEK of spending his afternoons with Rebecca, Jack found himself looking forward to seeing her each day. The realization surprised him as he climbed onto the porch of the house. He'd finally relented and given her a key; it pleased him knowing that she was already inside, waiting for him.

Today he found her in the kitchen. He stood in the doorway and watched her at the cookstove. Even in her apron with wisps of her hair loose about her face, she looked like an elegant woman.

In his years of rambling around the West, he'd tried hard to forget what it was like to be around a well-bred woman, the type of women he knew in New York. Glimpses of crisp petticoats, graceful movements, attention to detail in dress and appearance. Rebecca displayed all of those things. And suddenly, after all these years, it pleased him to see them.

She must have sensed his presence because she looked up at him. To his pleasure, she smiled.

"Arm wrestling," Jack said.

"Is that how you propose we decide which of

us will move the parlor furniture today?'' She gave him a saucy grin.

Jack hung his hat on the peg beside the door and ambled over to the stove. ''What are you cooking? Smells good.''

''I thought it was time we gave this stove a try.'' She pulled a pan of cookies from the oven. ''Oatmeal.''

''My favorite.'' He breathed in the delicious aroma.

''I made coffee, too. Get some cups down, will you?''

Rebecca had insisted on getting the kitchen in order first. Blue curtains hung on the windows, a matching cloth covered the little table in the corner. A cupboard displayed dishes that Rebecca had said were for everyday; the china set still waited to be arranged in the dining room cabinet.

Jack fetched cups, saucers and a serving plate and put them on the table.

''I've been thinking about what you said the other day about drawing men into the saloon,'' he said. ''It came to me last night—arm wrestling.''

''Hmm…'' Rebecca sank into thought for a moment and, had he not known her so well, it might have irked him that she hadn't immediately pronounced his idea brilliant. One thing he'd learned about her as they'd decorated the house, Rebecca didn't come to any decision without a great deal of deliberate thought.

"I like it," she finally said, filling their coffee cups. "You're intending to stage a tournament?"

"That's what I'm thinking." Jack seated her, then took the chair across from her and helped himself to two cookies.

"Cash prize to the winner?" she asked. When he shook his head, she nodded in agreement. "A bottle of whiskey should suffice—along with bragging rights. Have you thought of having a singer in to perform? You have the piano."

"A singer costs money," he pointed out.

"Pass a hat after the performance. Let the crowd pay."

"What woman in town would sing at a saloon?" he asked, helping himself to another cookie.

She sipped her coffee. "There are some women in Marlow who might appreciate…alternate…employment."

Jack's gaze came up quickly as the meaning of her suggestion dawned on him. Miss Prim and Proper thought he might get some of the girls from Miss Dora's parlor house to sing at his saloon?

Rebecca rushed ahead. "And you might serve

food in the evenings, after the restaurants close. Perhaps some fried chicken, boiled eggs, pickles, that sort of thing. I know someone who might do the cooking, if you're interested.''

''Who's that?'' he asked, anxious to get thoughts of the parlor-house girls out of his head at the same moment he was looking across the table at Rebecca.

''Lucy Hubbard. She's an excellent cook.''

''Is she willing to cook for a saloon?''

''I doubt she'd like the fact advertised, but I'm sure she'd do it.'' Rebecca lowered her voice. ''She needs money.''

Jack grumbled. ''Is that bastard she's married to ever coming back home?''

''He's looking for work, investments,'' Rebecca said.

''Hubbard ought to be shot for going off leaving his wife to fend for herself,'' Jack said. ''Worthless bastard.''

''He tried two different businesses here in Marlow.''

''Damn near impossible to make a go of it when he was spending nearly every night gambling away the day's profits.''

Rebecca gasped. ''He was? Oh, dear. I wonder if Lucy knew?''

"She knew," Jack said sourly. "But she's too good a wife to say so in public."

They finished their coffee and Jack ate the last cookie, then they rose from the table.

"You've got a little something on your lip," Jack said, gesturing toward her.

"Oh." Rebecca reached for a napkin, but Jack stepped closer and tilted her face up.

"It's just a little oatmeal crumb," he said, gazing into her eyes. "Be a shame to let a good bite of cookie go to waste."

She wasn't sure what he meant until he eased closer and kissed her. He blended their mouths together comfortably, yet with an excitement that made Rebecca's heart thud harder in her chest. Jack slid his arms around her and drew her against him. Warmth seeped into her, drawing her closer.

After a long, languid moment, Jack lifted his head. A grin tugged at his lips. "I could have sworn there was a crumb on your mouth."

Rebecca just looked at him, locked in his embrace. Would he kiss her again? She thought—hoped—he would.

But he didn't. Instead, Jack released her and backed up a step.

"You're sure you don't want to arm wrestle

to see which of us is going to move the parlor furniture?'' he asked, grinning.

''I'd hate to embarrass you,'' she said as she cleared the table.

They spent hours working in the parlor, centering the rug, placing the furniture, putting up curtains, hanging pictures. Jack did all of the real work. Rebecca pointed.

He didn't kiss her again.

Darkness settled into the room as he pushed the settee two inches down the wall, then pulled it back another three at Rebecca's request.

''Perfect,'' she declared.

He blew out a heavy breath. ''You're sure? You don't think it needs another half-inch? Quarter-inch, maybe?''

''Well...'' she mused, pretending she hadn't noticed his sarcasm. ''Perhaps we should move everything out into the entryway and start over.''

Jack rounded on her, a playful grin pulling at his lips. ''Maybe I'll just move *you* out into the entryway and fix this room myself.''

He charged toward her. Stunned, Rebecca managed nothing more than a weak squeal as he swept her into his arms.

''Maybe I'll toss you out back with the trash instead,'' he declared, striding out of the room.

''No! Don't!'' Rebecca threw her arms around

his neck, giggling so hard she barely got the words out.

He stopped, but didn't say anything for a moment. They gazed into each other's eyes. A long moment dragged by while some unnamed expectation hung between them. Finally, Jack broke the spell.

"I guess I'll keep you," he said softly, then grinned. "At least until the work is finished."

Jack eased her to the floor. "Get your things. I'll walk you home."

Rebecca got her handbag and hat while Jack fetched his Stetson and made certain the back door was locked. They walked out the front together. She hadn't realized it had gotten so late. Most of the businesses had closed already. Jack hooked her elbow and led her down the alley behind the stores. They stopped at the rear of the tearoom.

Faint light glowed in the kitchen window casting the deserted alley in pale shadows. In the dim light, Rebecca gazed up at Jack.

"I'll finish up the parlor tomorrow and we can…"

Her thoughts evaporated as Jack stepped closer. His gaze seemed to sap her strength. His body gave off a heat, a heat so warming that it caused the same to rise in her. A tingle rushed through her. Never in her life had she been so *aware*. Of another person. Of herself.

He kissed her. Rebecca gasped as his arms circled her, pulled her close. She leaned her head back—unable not to—as his lips covered hers completely. His mouth moved across hers, its warmth somehow chilling her to the bone.

He broke their kiss but his lips hovered near hers. After a long moment, he released her, then reached behind her and opened the kitchen door.

Rebecca's mind reeled with indecision. Should she run inside? Launch herself into his arms again? At once, she wanted to do *both*. Ached to do both.

"Good night," he whispered.

"Good night," she answered, and slipped into the kitchen.

WHEN REBECCA AWOKE the next morning, the world seemed different—even the little room she slept in.

When she'd moved in, she'd taken great pride and pleasure in selecting just the right bed linens. She'd had a friend from church hook the perfect rug. The rocking chair had come from her father's store, selected by him personally. Seth Grissom had built a bookcase for the spot beneath the window, before he'd stopped speaking to her.

The room had been a comfortable retreat. Until this morning.

Rebecca turned away from the mirror, tucking a stray lock of hair into place. The room seemed small. Smaller than she'd noticed before.

The morning passed quickly enough, as it usually did, with she and Aunt Virginia having breakfast, then preparing for their customers. Aunt Virginia barely spoke. But that wasn't unusual, Rebecca realized. Yet, somehow, it bothered her this morning.

She went about serving her customers through the noon hour. Business was brisk. As she moved between the tables serving tea and the delicacies Aunt Virginia had prepared, snippets of gossip reached her ears. Normal gossip. But it held no interest to Rebecca today.

She was almost relieved to leave the tearoom behind and head for Jack's house. Gray clouds gathered overhead, promising rain. But as Rebecca walked along Main Street, it wasn't the potential business investment that drew her attention the way they usually did. It was the women.

Women on the arms of their husbands. Women clutching babies. Women holding tiny hands, shepherding children safely across the street.

She'd seen these things dozens of times. But today, for some reason, everything seemed different.

By the time Rebecca unlocked the front door of Jack's house and let herself inside, the notion occurred to her that perhaps the world hadn't changed. Perhaps *she* had.

Raindrops tapped gently against the windowpanes as she made her way to the kitchen and left her hat and handbag on the table. Jack wasn't there yet.

A heaviness settled around Rebecca's heart as she tied on her apron and strolled slowly to the parlor. Her work here was almost done. In a few days, she'd leave and never return. Jack would have his home and she'd have—

What?

Rebecca stopped, her gaze drifting across the parlor. With pride she admitted that she'd made the most of the lovely furnishings. The house would be a comfortable home.

For Jack.

Her bedroom behind the tearoom seemed suddenly smaller still. Uninviting, compared to this house.

Her spirits lifted as Rebecca realized that she, too, could have a house this nice. Her tearoom was doing well. She had cash. Her father would help her, if needed. The idea grew quickly, causing her stomach to warm at the notion.

A home, a lovely home. She'd have it built, send to Baltimore—New York, perhaps—for the furnishings. She would fix it up, then live in it—

All alone.

A sadness jolted Rebecca and her gaze flew to the window. Jack? Through the drizzling rain, she'd expected to see him, she realized, but he wasn't there.

No one was there.

No one would ever be there.

What had brought on these thoughts? Rebecca wondered. His kiss last night? By far the most delightful. Had it caused her to rethink her entire life?

No, she realized. These feelings had been inside her for a long time—back in Baltimore, even—but she'd refused to acknowledge them.

The lonely ache stabbed her heart. Rebecca eased onto the settee as the vision of her future flashed in her mind.

The large, lovely home she would build.

Who would live in it with her? A husband? A child?

No. Only herself.

Rebecca bounced from the settee and threaded

her way between the marble-topped table and the crates still waiting to be unpacked.

Intolerable. The vision of her future was completely intolerable. This was why she'd refused to accept the thoughts that had lurked in the back of her mind for so long. They were simply intolerable.

But did it have to be that way?

She didn't want to grow old alone. She couldn't—wouldn't—allow that to happen. One hand on her hip, she paced, forcing herself to think.

In order to have a family, one needed a husband. Rebecca cringed at the very thought. She'd already shunned every older gentleman in Marlow who'd expressed the slightest interest in her. She hadn't been able to bear the thought of being courted by any of them.

Should she give them another try?

Mr. Harrison at the bank, with his long nose hairs. Mr. Kessler at the feed store, whose buttons strained across his wobbly belly. And that rancher just outside of town, the one who smelled like cows.

Rebecca shuddered at the thought of marriage to any of them. She couldn't, simply could not, do it. Even if one of the men would actually court her again, which she doubted, after the way she'd already turned them all down. And the younger men in town all had eyes for the younger women, just as they'd had in Baltimore.

So where did that leave her?

She started pacing again. If she couldn't find a husband, she'd never have a child. Unless…

Rebecca gasped in the silent room and stopped still in her tracks. Perhaps she *could* have a child without saddling herself with an unwanted husband.

She looked around at the house she'd spent weeks decorating, the result of the business arrangement she'd entered into with Jack.

He'd given her until the job was done to name her price. He'd never said it had to be *cash*.

Rebecca shivered at the thought racing through her head.

Jack could give her a baby.

CHAPTER SEVEN

GOOD HEAVENS, what was she thinking?

The notion that had come to her in Jack's parlor yesterday had haunted Rebecca all night. She'd left him a note saying she couldn't work on the house—she couldn't possibly look at him, with what was on her mind. Now, with the midday customers expected at the tearoom, Rebecca couldn't face the afternoon at Jack's place.

Not until she decided once and for all what to do.

Rebecca swept the boardwalk in front of the tearoom, absently going about the chore. Over and over her gaze crept down Main Street to the Lucky Streak. No sign of Jack, but that wasn't unusual this time of day. Besides, she had her eye out for a different man. Finally, Deputy Ian Caldwell rounded the corner. Rebecca set the broom aside.

"Morning, Miss Merriweather," he said.

"Good morning." She prattled on with what she hoped was sufficient small talk, then pulled the envelope from her pocket that she'd prepared earlier this morning.

"Would you be kind enough to take this to Mr. Delaney?" she asked, discreetly passing it to the deputy.

He slipped it into his pocket. "Sure," he said.

He hadn't asked for an explanation, but Rebecca felt compelled to provide one; perhaps it was the lawman in him that demanded it.

"I'm sure you know I've been helping Jack with his house," she said. "I wanted him to know I can't be there today."

"I'll take care of it," he promised, then craned his neck for a view through the open door of the tearoom.

"Lucy's not here," Rebecca said.

Disappointment clouded his features. Ian touched his hat brim and moved on.

The ache of loneliness that had crowded Rebecca's heart expanded a bit to include Ian. They were alike, she thought, both wanting something that seemed impossible to acquire.

By noon, the tearoom buzzed with conversation and the clink of bone china and silverware. Since Rebecca had begun working for Jack, it seemed her tearoom was busier than ever. Each day she faced a barrage of questions about Jack and his house. It hardly seemed right to dole out the details of his home that the women craved, so Rebecca kept her comments as vague as possible.

"Lovely furnishings," she reported, "of the utmost quality." She included tidbits of Jack's wealthy family, the shipyard, details that left the ladies in awe. Even Mrs. Frazier hadn't said anything nasty about Jack in days.

She wondered how that would change if word ever got out about what she was contemplating—with Jack's cooperation.

After another day of mulling over the idea, Rebecca still thought that having a child without benefit of a husband seemed like a good idea—it was a business arrangement, after all—but she wanted another opinion. There was only one person with whom she could freely consult.

Rebecca clutched her shawl around her shoulders as she hurried through the alley toward East Street. Rain showers had blown through town for several days bringing a damp and chilly wind, yet Rebecca's belly burned as if on fire.

She rounded the corner onto East Street. A few yards from where the boardwalk ended sat the little house that Lucy and her husband rented. She rapped briskly on the door and Lucy appeared a moment later wearing an apron.

"Rebecca, what a nice surprise. Come in."

The house was one room, the bed partitioned off from the living area with a dark curtain. The meager furnishings attested to the Hubbards' financial difficulties. They also displayed Lucy's determination to overcome those problems.

A basket of other peoples' clothing sat beside the rocker, mending that Lucy had taken in. The sideboard was crowded with baking ingredients for the pies she made and sold to the Pink Blossom Restaurant.

Despite her own problems, Rebecca thought of what Jack had told her about Raymond Hubbard. The man was worthless as a provider. Her overriding thought was that Lucy deserved so much more—in a home and a husband.

Rebecca dropped her shawl and handbag on the table. "I need to talk to you."

Lucy turned, hearing the desperation in Rebecca's voice. "What's wrong?"

"I need some advice."

Lucy pointed to the kitchen chairs and they sat. The house was silent except for the gusts of winds that moaned in around the windows.

"I had a vision of my future," Rebecca said, "and I didn't like what I saw. I don't want to end up alone. I'm wondering if I should marry...even if it's to someone I don't love."

"Oh, Rebecca, no..." Lucy gripped Rebecca's

hand with a strength she hadn't expected. "No, you mustn't do that."

"But isn't it better to be married to someone I don't really love, and have children, than to be alone?"

"There is nothing worse than marriage to a man you don't love," Lucy said, her expression pained.

A quiet moment passed, then Rebecca asked, "You and Raymond...?"

Lucy withdrew her hand. "Raymond came into my life like a godsend. An answer to prayer. Everyone believed everything he said. He insisted we marry quickly. Raymond is...not exactly what he portrayed himself to be."

"Yet you stay with him," Rebecca said.

"I married him before God. It's my duty to make my marriage work, somehow," Lucy said. "But don't put yourself in the position of regretting the biggest decision of your life, Rebecca. Don't do it."

Rebecca nodded. In her heart, she'd known she could never marry a man simply out of desperation. Hearing Lucy say the same thing sealed her decision.

"There's a man out there somewhere who'll be perfect for you," Lucy offered with a hopeful smile. "I just know it."

"I'm sure you're right." Rebecca slipped her shawl around her shoulders and picked up her handbag, her thoughts moving on. "By the way, I told Mr. Delaney you might be willing to cook for his saloon customers. He'll pay you."

"Wonderful." Her smile quickly faded. "But—"

"I know," Rebecca said, understanding her friend's concern. "We'll figure some way for you to deliver the food without ruining your reputation."

Lucy laughed gently and called her thanks as Rebecca left the house.

Storm clouds rumbled overhead as she stepped up onto the boardwalk. Her heart ached a little knowing that Lucy was mired in a loveless marriage. Her own stomach hardened with the determination not to put herself in the same predicament.

So where did that leave her? Rebecca turned the corner onto Main Street, considering her options. Briefly, she thought of adopting a child. Surely, there was an orphans' asylum somewhere eager to find good homes for destitute children. Yet Rebecca was also sure that an unmarried woman didn't constitute a "good home" in anyone's eyes.

That left her once again with the business-

arrangement idea she'd had in Jack's parlor. A
bold step. But no suitors were knocking on her
door—certainly none in Marlow, after the way
she'd treated them all—and she wasn't getting
any younger. If she wanted her future to change,
she'd have to take charge of it herself—just as
she had when she'd left Baltimore, when she'd
opened her tearoom.

Reaching Jack's house, Rebecca went to the
kitchen. Vaguely, the house smelled like him.
She realized she'd missed seeing him these past
few days.

Rebecca returned to the parlor, tying on her
apron. As she dug through the straw, it occurred
to her that since she was going to change her life
so drastically, it was prudent to do it logically.
Selecting the right man to father her child was
of the utmost importance. Jack had been the obvious choice—he owed her, after all—but perhaps she should give the matter further thought.

She wanted an intelligent man, Rebecca decided, standing beside one of the crates. A man
of good breeding. Someone with good looks, and
who understood business. Jack fit all those requirements.

A little smile came to Rebecca's lips. Yes,
Jack met all her requirements. And...

Heat wafted through her at the memory of

Jack's kisses. The touch of his lips had brought her to life in places she'd never imagined. Rebecca's stomach quivered at the thought. He'd lifted her into his arms effortlessly, swept her up, held her against him. His body was strong and hard, all male. Being in his bed—

"Are you all right?"

Jack's voice boomed from behind her. She hadn't heard him come into the house. Rebecca spun around, heat flooding her face. Good gracious, did he have any idea what she'd just been thinking—imagining? Her whole body sprang to life at the sight of him.

"Y-yes," Rebecca stammered. "I'm—I'm fine."

He came closer, scrutinizing her, concern in his expression. "When you didn't come to work on the house these past few days, I thought maybe you were sick."

"Oh, no," she said, giving him a quick smile, hoping it would cover the lie she intended to tell. "I had some things to do at the tearoom. Didn't Ian give you my note?"

"Yes," he told her, still looking closely at her. "I just wanted to be sure."

Kindness. Another wonderful quality he might pass on to her child. Rebecca struggled to keep from smiling.

"Sorry I'm late," Jack said. "I had to oversee the liquor delivery."

Commitment to duty. Excellent.

Rebecca forced her thoughts back to the task at hand.

"I only got here myself," she said. "And I was just—"

What? Imagining herself in bed with him?

She gulped and whirled around.

"Do you need my help in here?" Jack asked.

"No," she answered, making a show of pawing through the packing straw so she wouldn't have to face him.

"Okay. I'll go on up to the bedroom."

"Where?" Rebecca whipped around, her heart banging in her chest. Her gaze swept him from head to toe before she could stop herself. Big, strong. Oh, the babies he could provide...

Jack's brows pulled together. He looked down at his legs. "Have I got something on my pants?"

"No," she croaked. Flames raced up her cheeks. She whirled to the crate and leaned into it. "You run on upstairs. I'll finish here."

She rummaged through the straw until she heard Jack's footsteps on the staircase, then collapsed onto the settee.

Good gracious, she had to get control of herself. This was a business arrangement. She had to remember that.

Rebecca sat up and gave herself a little shake. While Jack—physically—was the perfect man to father her child, she really knew very little about him. Prudence demanded she learn more.

She climbed the stairs and found Jack in the bedroom on the left side of the hallway. Crammed with furniture and crates, it was the largest of the three rooms on the second floor. The window stood open letting in the cool, damp breeze and the dim afternoon light. Outside, the gray sky threatened rain again. Jack busied himself prying the lids from the crates.

Rebecca lingered in the doorway. How intimate the setting. A *bedroom.* Her heart beat a little faster at the thought of stepping into the room with Jack in it.

She pushed her chin higher and drew in a determined breath. She needed information from him to make her final decision about selecting the father of her child, and she was going to get it.

''So,'' she said airily as she came into the room, ''your family all live in New York?''

''Yeah,'' he said, prying another nail from the lid.

''Where are they from, originally?'' She sidled closer.

"England."

"Nobles?" Rebecca asked, trying to make her question sound casual. "Gentry? Country squires?"

Jack uttered a soft laugh. "My mama claimed there was royalty somewhere in the family line, but I don't know for sure."

"*Royalty?*" Rebecca struggled to suppress a smile. "How nice."

Jack just grunted as he set aside the lid of the final crate.

"I couldn't help but notice that your nose is a bit crooked," she said, waving her fingers at her own nose when he looked up. "Is that from a disagreement, or were you...born that way."

"You could say it was a disagreement." Jack smiled faintly at the memory. "By the time we were done, the other fella had come around to my way of thinking."

She laughed politely, then went on.

"You have a large family?" she asked, following him across the room to where the bed frame rested against the wall.

"Pretty big."

"Not a lot of illness? Hereditary diseases?"

Jack shook his head. "No. The family's pretty healthy."

"How many *boys?*"

"My pa's got six brothers. I've got five."

"Do they all still have their hair?"

Jack turned slowly to her. "Are you trying to get at something?"

"Oh, no." Rebecca plastered on a big smile, struggling to look innocent. "Just making conversation."

"Oh. Okay," he said and turned back to his work.

"So do they?" Rebecca asked, leaning closer. "Have all their hair?"

His brows pulled together. "Everybody's still got all their hair—and their teeth, in case you're interested in that, too."

Rebecca struggled to keep her smile in place. "I'm going to unload the crates now."

She busied herself dragging the straw from the boxes, lifting out the items buried beneath it, satisfied that she'd gotten all the information she could about Jack's past. Everything she'd learned so far made him the perfect candidate to father her child.

So why wait?

Rebecca straightened, a quilt clutched in her hands. Why not do it now while she had her nerve up?

She glanced over her shoulder. Jack had assembled the bed frame, fitted the springs and mattress in place.

Jack, her, the bed, all in the same place. A perfect opportunity.

Doubt crossed her mind. What would he think if she hopped onto the bed without warning or explanation and invited him to join her? Would he think ill of her? Think she'd lost her mind? Both were possible. Rebecca couldn't bear the thought that he'd refuse her. Could she lure him into her arms using her feminine wiles? Probably not, since she wasn't sure exactly what feminine wiles were.

No, she decided, better to stick to her original plan. A business agreement. Plain and simple.

She gulped in several deep breaths, readying herself to present her proposal. She thought hard, desperate to come up with the best way to make her presentation. Nothing came to her. Finally, she simply turned to him.

"Jack," she announced, "I've decided what I want for decorating your house."

He didn't bother to glance up from what he was doing. "Yeah? What?"

Rebecca straightened her shoulders. "I want you to give me a baby."

CHAPTER EIGHT

"A BABY?" Jack turned to her, confused. "A *baby?*"

She gave him a brisk nod. "Yes. A baby."

He spread his arms. "Where in the hell am I supposed to find you a baby?"

Rebecca willed herself not to blush. "I don't want you to *find* me a baby. I want you to…give me one."

"*Give* you one? What are you talking about?"

Rebecca didn't answer. She didn't have to. Realization dawned on Jack's face. His jaw sagged. His face paled.

"Are you saying what I think you're saying?" he asked cautiously.

She cringed at having to speak the words aloud. "I want you to…get me…with child."

He narrowed his eyes. "If this is some sort of joke, I don't think it's funny."

"I'm deadly serious." Rebecca took a step closer. "Will you do it? Will you get me…pregnant?"

"Hell no." He drew back looking as prudish as a spinster schoolmarm.

"But Jack—"

He backed away, as if he expected her to attack him and take what she wanted.

"Jack, it's a business—"

"Get the hell away from me." He strode out of the room.

"Wait!" Rebecca clattered down the stairs after him. "Jack, wait. If you'll just listen—"

He grabbed his hat from where he'd left it in the parlor, and pushed past her toward the front door.

"Jack! You *owe* me!"

He froze, his hand on the doorknob.

"You said I could name my price," Rebecca told him. "Is this what your word means? Are you welshing on your debt?"

Slowly, he turned to face her. "Have you taken leave of your senses?"

"No," she told him, standing straighter. "I know exactly what I'm doing."

He stepped closer, crowding her. "You want me to get you pregnant—as part of a business deal?"

"Yes," she said, refusing to back away. "I've given it a great deal of thought. It's what I want."

"And how are you going to explain it to everybody when you turn up pregnant?" he challenged.

"Once I'm…with child…I'll go back to Baltimore, tell everyone I married briefly and that my husband died."

"And you think people are going to believe—"

"You needn't worry about the details beyond your limited role," Rebecca insisted. "This is a business arrangement."

"Like hell it is," he growled.

"You can do it, can't you?" she asked, and looked him up and down. "You can provide me with a child?"

Jack shifted closer, his expression so fierce Rebecca thought she might conceive simply by maintaining eye contact. She backed up a step.

"You're making too much of this," Rebecca said softly.

He leaned down and lowered his voice. "Do you have any idea—any idea—what you're asking?"

She pushed her chin up and met his gaze. "I know exactly what I want. The only question is whether or not you intend to honor your word and live up to our agreement."

He straightened, eyeing her harshly. "So that's

what all those questions were about upstairs. Checking out my pedigree, like I'm some sort of stud service?''

Rebecca blushed. "It's business. The questions were reasonable, under the…circumstances.''

Another long moment dragged by while Jack glared at her. She couldn't read his thoughts, but an odd expression—disgust, hurt, perhaps?—crossed his face, and he latched onto her arm.

"All right,'' he barked. "Fine. Let's go do it.''

Rebecca gasped and pulled against him. *''Now?''*

He held fast to her arm. "Yeah. Now. For starters.''

Her eyes rounded. "For starters?''

"It doesn't always work the first time,'' he told her, none too politely. "So you'd better let your aunt know she'll have to run the tearoom all afternoon.''

"All afternoon?''

"For the next couple of weeks.''

''Weeks?''

"Let's get at it,'' he declared, pulling on her arm.

Rebecca dug in her heels. "Wait—''

"Come on. I don't want this debt hanging over my head any longer,'' he insisted.

"No!'' Rebecca jerked her arm from his grasp.

Her cheeks flamed and her heart pounded wildly. "This is *my* payment and *I'll* decide when I'm ready to collect it."

Jack leaned down until his breath puffed hot against her cheek. She thought he was about to say something more, but didn't. He spun around and bounded up the stairs.

Rebecca braced her arm against the wall, so light-headed she thought she might actually swoon. She gulped in great breaths of air. Good gracious, had her brilliant business plan turned into the worst nightmare of her life?

HE SHOULD HAVE *KNOWN*. Should have known better than to trust a woman—even Rebecca.

Jack stood in the corner of the saloon, ignoring the crowd, his own thoughts holding all his attention.

For years now, since leaving New York, he'd held back his feelings for a woman—any woman. After what he'd been through, the last thing he'd ever intended to do was put his trust in another female.

But with Rebecca he'd done just that. Slowly, she'd won him over. And then she pulls *this* on him? Wanting him to give her a baby?

Anger deepened in his gut. She'd easily agreed to decorate his house—too easily, he'd thought at the time. Did she have this in mind all along? Was Rebecca just another cunning, calculating female?

Visions of her surfaced among his angry thoughts. Baking cookies, helping with his saloon, smiling, making him laugh. Jack didn't want to believe she was truly the type of woman he'd left behind in New York. But still…

The full gamut of thoughts and feelings had plagued him since she'd presented her *business proposal* three days ago. And still, he didn't know what to make of it.

The only constant was that the idea of bedding down with Rebecca had taken over his life.

Jack shifted uncomfortably as he took in the dozens of men at the bar, the packed gaming tables. The crowd was lively in anticipation of tonight's singer. He'd made an agreement with Miss Dora to allow some of her girls to sing at the Lucky Streak, and Jonah Walker, the blacksmith who played the piano in church, was more than anxious to provide accompaniment. This was the third night, and the crowd grew larger each time.

The chalkboard Jack had hung near the swinging doors bore the names of the men who'd signed up for next week's arm wrestling tournament. The flyers he'd hung around town had brought surprising results. Fifteen men, so far, were anxious to take on all comers.

Customers rolled in, bringing money with them. Jack drummed his fingers on the edge of the bar, annoyed to no end that he couldn't enjoy any of it.

All he could think of was Rebecca.

When she'd presented her proposal, he'd been so angry that he insisted they get down to *business* immediately. He'd wanted to shock her, make her realize what she was asking. He'd thought she'd call the whole thing off. She hadn't.

So here he was thinking of her. Thinking of getting into bed with her.

True, the idea had often crept into his mind. Before they'd officially met, when he'd seen her on the street. After she'd agreed to help with his house. The days they'd spent together. When he'd kissed her. Looking at her, being close to her, talking with her, almost always the notion of rolling around under the sheets with her danced in his mind.

But then she'd gone and *asked* him to do just that. Bed down with her. Make love. Insinuate herself into his life. Take over.

And as if that weren't enough, she'd decided to take her own sweet time about when and where, while his body simmered and seethed almost constantly. Plus, he hadn't seen her in days. Since the afternoon when she'd made her so-called business proposal, he'd gone to the house to work, as usual, but he'd never found her there. He could see that she'd been unpacking things, putting them in place. It irked him that she seemed determined to avoid him—which, somehow, just made him want her more…even though he didn't want to.

Jack grumbled under his breath, pushed through the swinging door into the kitchen and went out back into the dark alley. Since Lucy Hubbard had started cooking for his customers he'd made a point to meet her on Main Street and bring the food to the saloon himself. Tonight, when he turned the corner, he spotted Lucy standing in the shadows and, as usual, Ian Caldwell was with her.

Jack watched them for a moment. Nothing untoward was going on, they stood a respectable distance apart, neither touched. Yet something passed between them. Even in the dim moonlight, Jack could see it. Rebecca came into his mind, bringing on a familiar ache.

They exchanged pleasantries and Jack told Lucy once again how much his customers enjoyed her cooking. She blushed modestly when

Jack paid her. He took her basket and headed back to the saloon, waiting in the shadows long enough to see Ian walk with her toward her home on East Street before going into the kitchen again.

A short while later, after Roy had the food and was selling it at the bar, Ian entered the saloon. He got a beer and joined Jack near the kitchen door.

"Good crowd tonight," Ian commented, gesturing with his foamy glass.

"Things are picking up," Jack said, determined to put his problems behind him. "You seen Seth Grissom lately?"

Ian shook his head. "No, can't say that I have."

"I thought maybe he was at one of the other saloons."

"I make the rounds every night," Ian said. "I haven't seen him anywhere, now that you mention it."

"You reckon he's sick?"

"I'll check," Ian said. "More likely he's just tired of getting kidded about Miss Merriweather's pink storefront."

They stood side by side for a while looking out over the barroom. Finally, Jack said, "She's a married woman."

Ian studied the contents of his glass, then sighed heavily. "Yeah, I know."

"Her husband is about as worthless as they come," Jack said. "He ought to be shot."

"I've considered it."

"You'd be better off keeping your distance," Jack said.

"Yeah, I know that, too," Ian agreed. "I can't stop thinking that maybe her husband won't ever come back."

"You intend to step in?"

"I intend to marry her. All she has to do is say the word." Ian finished his beer and left the saloon.

Jack followed him to the door and gazed down Main Street. No lights burned in the windows of the Marlow Tearoom and Gift Emporium. The place had closed hours ago.

But where was Rebecca? Jack wondered. In the kitchen? Reading? Sewing? Working on her plan to take over his life? Plotting how to drive him even crazier by making him continue to wait?

Maybe he'd just go over there tonight and insist they commence their business deal immediately. That would show her who was running things. And he was sure as hell ready——he'd been ready for days now. If he got any more ready he wouldn't be fit to be seen in public.

Jack grumbled under his breath and went back to the bar.

"REBECCA, WHAT'S HAPPENING at Mr. Delaney's house?"

Rebecca, serving tray in hand, paused beside the table where Mrs. Tidwell and two other ladies sat. Midafternoon now, and the other tearoom customers had moved along. Only these three lingered.

"Almost finished," Rebecca reported, as she placed a selection of Aunt Virginia's sandwiches on the table.

"I'd love to see the house," Nelly Walker confided, and the other women nodded in agreement.

"Do you think he'll have a party in the new house?" Mrs. Tidwell asked. The other women looked anxious as well.

"Perhaps when his company arrives," Rebecca speculated. For some reason, it pleased her that the ladies of Marlow had changed their opinion of Jack drastically in only a few short weeks. The last time Mrs. Frazier had said something against him, the other ladies had come to his defense.

"I wonder when that will be?" Mrs. Tidwell mused.

Inez Becker drew herself up. "My Stanley knows," she proclaimed with a triumphant lift of her chin.

Rebecca's interest piqued along with the other ladies'. Stanley Becker ran Marlow's express office. He knew everything that went on in town.

"Well, tell us," Mrs. Walker insisted.

Mrs. Becker took a moment to savor the spotlight, then announced, "My Stanley told me that Mr. Delaney received a telegram this morning. His company will arrive *tomorrow*."

"*Tomorrow?*" Rebecca exclaimed.

"Who was the telegram from?" Mrs. Tidwell asked.

Mrs. Becker let the drama build before answering. "It wasn't signed."

Mrs. Tidwell and Mrs. Walker gasped at the significance. Rebecca gasped at the anxiety that shot though her.

Tomorrow? Jack's company was arriving tomorrow?

Her heart thumped harder in her chest. That meant only one thing: she'd have to get Jack into bed *tonight*.

CHAPTER NINE

MAYBE SHE'D CHANGED her mind.

Jack threaded through the crowd at the Lucky Streak, blocking out the conversation, laughter, the clink of glasses. At the bat-wing door he gazed down the street. Dark. No lights on at the Marlow Tearoom and Gift Emporium.

Not for the first time, he wondered if she'd changed her mind about the business proposal that had turned his life upside down.

Part of him—the part centered in the portion of his brain that still functioned logically—hoped that she had. He hoped, too, that he'd been wrong in thinking the worst of her. He wished that he still didn't feel angry.

Jack turned away from the door. His neck was sore from gazing down the street at the tearoom so many times. He ought to be thinking about tomorrow and the stage from the East he would meet. Things would change for him then. He should have been looking forward to it.

But all he could think of was Rebecca.

A part of him wondered if he should honor his word and give her the payment she wanted for decorating his house—despite the lifelong ramifications? Should he give in to the desire that had driven him to distraction, and go along with what she wanted?

The swinging doors parted and Ian walked into the saloon. Jack greeted him, grateful for the interruption.

"Miss Merriweather stopped me just now," Ian said, and pulled an envelope from his shirt pocket.

Jack hesitated a moment before accepting the pink envelope decorated with Rebecca's curly writing. Would her note state that she'd come to her senses and canceled her business proposal? A flash of unexpected disappointment tightened his gut, along with a thread of anger. She'd kept him tied in knots thinking of sleeping with her, and now she was changing her mind? Just like that?

Logic sifted into Jack's thoughts. Of course, it would be for the best if, in fact, that was what the note said. But still...

Jack ripped open the envelope. On a pink-flowered sheet of stationery was written one word: *Now*.

He grabbed his hat and left the saloon.

WHAT HAD SHE DONE?

Rebecca paced fitfully in the bedroom on the second floor of Jack's house, twisting her fingers together and questioning her own sanity.

Was it too late to change her mind? She hurried to the window and peered out at the dark street. No sign of Jack. Yet. So she could leave, if she wanted. Leave and tell him she'd rethought the whole proposal. And then—

And then what? Turn her back on her only viable chance to have a child, and a rich, full future?

She curled her hands into fists. No. No, she couldn't back away now. The stakes were too high. She had to get through this evening—somehow.

Pacing across the room, Rebecca stopped in front of the large mirror she'd uncrated and Jack had placed in the corner of the room. She eyed her reflection. Pale-yellow nightgown and wrapper covering her from throat to wrist to ankle. Bare feet. Hair caught in a simple ribbon at her nape.

A wave of anxiety crashed over her. The color—was it wrong for her? Would Jack even *care* about the color? Should she have dressed in her nightwear *before* he arrived? And her hair—

should she have left it up? Was taking it down herself too presumptuous? Would Jack prefer to do it himself?

Rebecca's knees shook so severely she had to sit down on the chair beside the fireplace. She waved her hands, fanning her face. Good gracious, she was about to perspire. What would Jack think if he walked in and found her sweating?

And what was taking him so long? Rebecca sprang from the chair, pacing again. She'd given the envelope to Ian before rushing over here, and he'd promised to deliver it to Jack immediately. Did he think she had all evening to wait around? She had to start work early in the morning, for goodness' sake.

Another thought flashed in her mind, Jack's warning that these things didn't always work the first time.

All afternoon.

Weeks.

"Oh…"

She stopped and pressed her palm to her forehead. Her mother had died when Rebecca was young—too young to learn advice crucial to this occasion. What was expected of her? Would Jack think her a harlot if she met his advances with wanton abandonment? Should she simply allow him to proceed as he chose while she contemplated the wallpaper pattern?

Lucy. She should have asked Lucy. Rebecca cringed at realizing she should have thought of her friend sooner.

A noise came from outside. Rebecca rushed to the window and pressed her face to the glass. Her stomach welled with fear, then knotted when she saw no sign of Jack.

An unwanted thought barged into her already churning mind. She'd insisted to Jack that this arrangement was a business deal. She'd told herself over and over that's all it was.

So why, at the moment, did it seem like so much more?

She'd missed Jack, she realized, backing away from the window. These past few days when she'd made a point to come to the house when she knew he wouldn't be there, she'd missed the sound of his heavy footsteps on the floor, his masculine scent, his deep voice echoing through the house. She'd missed talking with him. Jack always seemed to understand her problems—and he wasn't offended when she offered help with his.

Another thought flashed in Rebecca's mind, stilling her pacing. If this weren't simply a business deal, then that must mean—

Rebecca fought off the idea. She wouldn't allow herself to contemplate the notion that Jack meant more to her than an opportunity to have a child.

"Good gracious…" Rebecca mumbled. She had to get a grip on herself. Somehow, she must get through this evening.

With another quick look out the window, Rebecca dashed down the staircase, her wrapper billowing behind her, and raced into the kitchen. Jack had stocked the cupboards already so she went directly to the cabinet beneath the sideboard and withdrew the bottle of whiskey he'd left there.

Without another thought, Rebecca pulled out the stopper and took a swig. Fire ignited in her throat and pooled in her stomach. She coughed, wheezed. Tears blurred her eyes. A moment passed and she was surprised to realize that as dreadful as the stuff tasted, it steadied her nerves. She sipped again and again as she made her way upstairs.

The bedroom seemed warmer as she eased into the chair and tipped up the bottle. The whiskey didn't taste quite so sharp. She drank more, thinking the stuff seemed almost mellow running down her throat.

She settled back in the chair. Why had she

been so upset about this evening? She couldn't quite remember.

The sound of the front door closing and heavy footsteps on the stairs reached her ears, and briefly, she wondered who might be coming to visit at this time of night. A large figure filled the doorway. She squinted in the dim light.

"Jack...how nice of you to...stop by," she said, and giggled.

He was in front of her then, towering over her. Gracious, he was handsome. And so tall, so sturdy. Rebecca couldn't recall just why she'd been afraid of his arrival. All she knew was that some unnamed, unseen force drew her to him— the only place in the world she wanted to be.

Jack took her hands and helped her from the chair. She collapsed into his waiting arms.

REBECCA WOKE with a start. An irrational fear stole though her, then surged nearly uncontrollably as she lay on her side looking at a strange room.

Where was she?

She remained perfectly still on the bed. A lantern burned low on the bureau. Vague recollection filled her head. A mirror, a chair beside the fireplace. Why, they looked exactly like the furnishings she'd placed in—

Jack's room.

Horror whipped through Rebecca. She slapped her hand over her lips to keep from crying out. She was in Jack's room! Jack's bed!

Cautiously, she rolled over.

Jack.

He lay on the mattress next to her, on his side, his back to her. The flesh of his bare shoulder gleamed in the lantern light.

Rebecca nearly cried out. Good gracious, he was *naked.*

Visions of the evening zinged through her mind. Waiting for him in the bedroom, the whiskey, then finally, his arrival. Her heart beat faster remembering how he'd come straight to her, taken her into his arms and—

Cautiously, Rebecca lifted the quilt and peeked under. She wore her yellow nightgown, but it was bunched up around her knees.

Good Lord, what had she done?

Humiliation boiled in her churning stomach. What had she been thinking? How could she have put herself into this compromising position? How could she have imagined *this* could in any way be construed as a business deal?

Rebecca's stomach lurched as she slipped from under the covers, desperate to leave, to get away before Jack woke.

She shoved her arms through the sleeves of her wrapper, grabbed her clothing and dashed for the door.

REBECCA DRAGGED HERSELF from the bed—her own, this time—then fell back onto it. Her head pounded. Her stomach rolled.

Yet those weren't the worst of her problems.

After she'd run though the streets of Marlow in her wrapper, trailing an armload of her clothing in the dead of night, she'd reached the safety of her room. Climbing into bed she'd slept fitfully, then claimed illness when Aunt Virginia had come to check on her sometime after dawn.

Now sunlight streamed in around the edges of the window curtains. The mantel clock told her it was midafternoon.

She rose from the bed but another wave of nausea washed over her, causing her head to pound harder. She felt awful. But worse, she couldn't remember a thing that had happened last night. After Jack's arrival, anyway.

But how could that be? How could she have been deflowered and not recall any of it?

The liquor had wiped out her memory, she realized, sinking onto the bed again. And just because she couldn't remember the details didn't mean it hadn't happened.

Jack had taken her into his arms, she knew that. She'd awakened in his bed. He'd been naked. Her gown was bunched up. Jack certainly was not the type of man to have a woman in his bed and *not* have something happen.

But wouldn't there be some evidence? Sitting on the bed, Rebecca mentally took inventory of her state of wellness. Other than her headache and upset stomach, everything else seemed exactly as it always was. Surely *something* about her ought to be different. Shouldn't it?

Rebecca dragged herself from the bed, washed, slipped into a gray dress and twisted her hair into a simple knot atop her head. In the kitchen cooking odors greeted her. Ordinarily, Aunt Virginia's food caused her mouth to water. Now it turned her stomach.

Carefully, she peeked through the curtain that separated the kitchen from the tearoom and saw about a half-dozen women seated at the tables, and her aunt—an empty serving tray braced against her hip—chatting with them.

The quiet comfort of the tearoom washed over Rebecca and she wanted to go inside, savor the sameness of the day, the food, the conversation. But she hesitated. With one look at her, could the women see what she'd done last night? If, in fact, anything at all had happened?

A feeble flicker of hope rose in Rebecca as she fetched the teapot. Perhaps nothing had happened. Perhaps Jack—

The back door swung open. Jack stood in the doorway. Rebecca dropped the teapot.

A slow, lazy grin spread across his face as he leaned one shoulder against the door. His gaze slid to her feet and rose leisurely—knowingly—to her face.

Rebecca's stomach dropped. Any doubt about what had—or hadn't—happened last night evaporated with one look at Jack's expression.

"Sleep late?" he asked, his voice rich and deep. His brows rose slightly. "After last night, you need your rest."

Rebecca's face flamed.

"You surprised me," he admitted. "I didn't think you'd be so wild in bed."

Her knees weakened. Wild? She'd been wild last night?

His grin widened. "A real hellcat."

Rebecca turned away, her cheeks throbbing with embarrassment. She gripped the sideboard for support.

"I—I'd like you to leave now," she said, straining to keep her voice steady.

Jack's footsteps thudded on the bare floor as he walked closer. "I brought you something."

He'd brought her something? A gift? Her mind raced. Was a gift appropriate after such an occasion? She couldn't imagine how she'd word the thank-you note.

Rebecca turned slowly. Jack stood close. Heat wafted from his body, warming her, threatening to rob what little strength she had left.

"You left these behind," Jack said. He pulled a garment from his pocket and dangled it in front of her.

Her drawers. The pink ones with the lace around the legs and the little bows sewn at the seams. She must have missed them when she'd gathered her clothing and raced from his room. Mortified, Rebecca recoiled at the sight.

Jack shrugged. "If you don't want them, I can hang them behind the bar where that picture used to be, like a flag—"

Rebecca snatched them from his hand. "That's disgusting."

He leaned in and lowered his voice. "Don't worry. I won't tell anybody about your lacy underwear—or that little mole you've got, either."

Rebecca winced and squeezed her eyes shut momentarily, attempting to ward off her embarrassment. It didn't help.

"I figured you'd be ready to go another round this afternoon," Jack said and hitched up his trousers. "We can slip into your room right now and—"

"No!" she told him. "I've—I've changed my mind. I want no part of this arrangement."

Jack shook his head. "Well now, I'm afraid it's too late for you to back out now. You named your price. I'm obligated to pay your debt—no matter how long it takes."

She ducked around him. "I want you to leave."

"It's not that simple."

"Yes, it is," she insisted. Anger pushed its way through her churning emotions, a welcome relief from the embarrassment and humiliation.

He gave her another grin. "Did you know you snore when you sleep on your back?"

"Get out!" Rebecca grabbed a dish from the sideboard and hurled it at him.

He sidestepped the plate, and after one more long, knowing look he gave her a nod and disappeared out the door.

Rebecca burst into tears.

CHAPTER TEN

REBECCA MADE ONLY ONE appearance in the tea-room that afternoon. The women there clucked sympathetically over her supposed illness, which only made her feel worse. They'd also rushed to tell her the latest gossip. The stagecoach expected to bring Jack's company had been delayed.

The last thing she wanted to hear about was Jack Delaney. Rebecca left the tearoom.

The stores in Marlow would close soon but she needed to get out, get some perspective on things. Mostly, she wanted to push last night and this afternoon's confrontation with Jack out of her mind.

That proved impossible.

Crossing Main Street she saw him step through the bat-wing doors of the Lucky Streak, arms folded across his chest as he settled his gaze on her. His look—even from a distance—was so knowing it caused her steps to falter. Quickly, she ducked into Townsend's Dry Goods Store.

She forced her attention onto some newly arrived bolts of fabric, but almost immediately sensed a presence and looked up. At the end of the aisle stood Jack. A small, very private smile spread over his lips.

Rebecca flushed. The gall of that man! Looking at her as if he could still see her naked. She circled the aisle in the opposite direction and left the store.

The Pink Blossom Café, the First Union Bank, the other shops passed in a blur as Rebecca made her way to East Street and turned the corner. Was the man following her? Deliberately taunting her? Tormenting her?

She considered ducking into the odd little museum that had recently opened, but went into Norman's General Store instead. Norman Kirby nodded from behind the counter.

Rebecca wove her way down an aisle studying each item on display. She hoped something on the shelves might spark her interest, take her mind off her situation.

A warm chill slithered up Rebecca's spine. Her senses sprang to life. She looked over her shoulder. Jack stood behind her, so close that she felt his breath on her cheek. She hadn't seen him come in the store or heard his approach.

Rebecca braced herself for yet another pene-

trating look from him, or at least a smug grin.
Instead, he leaned down and snored in her ear.

"Oh!" She pushed past him and out onto the
boardwalk, threading her way through the last of
the day's shoppers. The nerve of that man!

Anger roiled through Rebecca chasing away
most of the embarrassment she'd suffered today.
By the time she reached the tearoom, she'd
calmed down. She went inside and found her
aunt heading for the door.

"You'd better hurry," Virginia said, pulling
her shawl on. "You know Mrs. Frazier doesn't
like to be kept waiting."

"What—oh." Rebecca recalled then that tonight the ladies were meeting at Mrs. Frazier's
house to plan the school's pie social. Rebecca
was expected to be there.

"I can't go," she said, and truly meant it.
"Please give the ladies my regrets."

"Get some rest," Aunt Virginia said and left.

Rebecca collapsed into a chair and braced her
elbows on the table. She covered her face with
her palms.

How could her business proposal have gone so
wrong? It had seemed like a perfectly good idea
at its inception. And why was Jack tormenting
her so?

Time slipped by, the minutes—hours, perhaps—uncounted while she contemplated these weighty issues. No answers came to her, only the prospect of another night in Jack's bed. She'd have to manage it, somehow. She still wanted a child. That hadn't changed.

If only she could remember. Rebecca sat back in the chair. The tearoom had grown dark, lighted only by the two lanterns on the mantel. She scrunched her brow, searched her memory. One of the biggest moments in a woman's life and she couldn't recall any of it. How could that be?

The little bell above the door jangled and Lucy walked in. "What are you doing sitting here all alone?" she asked, easing into the chair next to Rebecca.

"Thinking," she said wistfully. "Why aren't you at Mrs. Frazier's meeting?"

"I had to prepare the food for Mr. Delaney's customers."

Rebecca fought back the urge to grumble under her breath at the mention of Jack's name.

"You know, he's a very nice person. Everyone in town says so—except for Mrs. Frazier, of course." Lucy paused before going on. "I want to talk with you about something."

The tone of Lucy's voice jarred Rebecca's conscience. She'd been so wound up over her own problems she hadn't considered that anyone else might have troubles, too.

"What is it?" Rebecca gave Lucy her full attention.

"It's about Raymond." Lucy folded her hands in her lap.

"Did you hear from him?" Rebecca asked.

She shook her head. "No. That's just it. It's been so long now and I haven't heard from him. No letters, no telegram. Nothing."

"Do you want him to come back?" Rebecca asked gently.

"Part of me wishes he wouldn't," she admitted.

"Is that because of Ian?"

"Ian...he's such a wonderful man—everything that Raymond isn't." Lucy pressed her lips together. "He meets me every night when I take the food to the Lucky Streak, walks me there and back just to make sure I'm all right. He says the kindest things, Rebecca. Nothing out of line, of course. But he makes me feel...special."

"You are special," Rebecca said.

Lucy was quiet for a moment, then drew in a breath. "I've decided to pursue a divorce."

"Raymond has abandoned you, Lucy. It's the only thing you can do," Rebecca agreed.

Long moments stretched in the silent room.

Rebecca didn't envy Lucy her problem. Though she wouldn't admit it, Rebecca was sure she was in love with Ian Caldwell. He was a good man. Lucy deserved a good man.

Drawing in a fresh breath, Lucy said, "So, what have you been up to lately?"

Events of the last twenty-four hours came back to Rebecca, full force. Her stomach twisted into a painful knot at the memory.

But she pushed it away and sat straighter in the chair. Lucy was the only person in the world she could ask such a personal question. If she didn't do it now, she might never do it. And she had to know.

"I need to ask you something," Rebecca said trying desperately not to blush. "But it's terribly personal…"

Lucy looked unconcerned. "Go ahead. I grew up on a farm with seven brothers. Believe me, nothing offends me."

"Is there a way to tell—I mean, are there physical signs if a woman has—" Rebecca stopped, unable to say the words aloud. She leaned closer and whispered into Lucy's ear.

"Oh, certainly." Lucy cupped her hands around Rebecca's ear and whispered back.

Rebecca's brows pulled together. "You're sure?"

"Oh, yes," Lucy assured her.

Rebecca nodded slowly. "Well, thank you. That certainly clears things up. A lot of things, actually."

"You're welcome," Lucy said, rising from her chair. "I'd better run along. I left two pies in the oven."

Rebecca remained in her seat, barely aware that Lucy had left, hardly hearing the door close behind her as her anger grew. All she could do was think. And all she could think of was Jack.

"Oh!" Rebecca sprang from the chair, snatched the fireplace poker from beside the hearth and hit the street. By the time she reached the Lucky Streak, she was boiling.

She blasted into the saloon, throwing open the bat-wing doors so hard they banged against the walls. The place was packed with men sitting at the gaming tables, standing at the bar. Conversation droned. A cloud of cigarette smoke hovered near the ceiling. The men nearest the doors did a double take as Rebecca strode in, the poker clutched in her outstretched hand.

"Where are you?" she screamed, striding forward. Men fell back out of her way. She brandished the poker. "Where are you, you no-good, low-down varmint?"

Rebecca spotted Jack seated with two other

men, their table littered with beer glasses, talking and grinning.

"*You!*"

Jack looked up, saw her. The smile fell from his face.

"You mangy dog!" Rebecca closed the distance between them. He jumped from his chair. She swung the poker, sending glasses and beer crashing to the floor. Every man in the place turned to stare.

Rebecca circled the table, pointing the poker like a sword. "You are lower than a snake!"

Jack held up his palms, backing away. "What the hell's wrong with you?"

"You are *worse* than a snake! You're snake *spit!*" With a two-handed roundhouse swing, Rebecca sliced the poker through the air.

The men scattered. Jack leaped backward. "Put that thing down before somebody gets hurt."

"Yes, Delaney, like you, maybe!" somebody called from the crowd. Laughter broke out.

"I mean it, Rebecca," Jack told her. "Put that down—"

She swung again, this time nearly catching the front of his shirt. "You don't deserve to live, you—you—oh! I don't know a word bad enough for you!"

"How about skunk?" someone suggested.

"Thank you," Rebecca called. She narrowed her eyes at Jack. "You skunk!"

"You tell him, honey!" another man called.

"What the devil's gotten into you?" Jack demanded.

"You filthy *liar!*"

He froze. His face paled. "Oh. I—I can explain, Rebecca. Just put the poker down and—"

She swung again, this time at his head. Jack lurched forward and caught her hands. She held on, but he was too strong. Jack ripped it from her fingers. She lunged for it. He raised it high over his head out of reach.

He caught her arm and leaned down. "Go in the back room," he said quietly.

Rebecca glared at him, her blood still boiling. She didn't intend to do anything he suggested.

"Go on. Nobody here paid for this sort of show," he said, sounding so reasonable she wanted to hit him.

Reality oozed through her anger. He was right, of course, though it didn't suit her in the least. Rebecca glared at him one final time, jerked her arm from his grasp, put her nose in the air and marched through the swinging door into the kitchen. Applause and hoots of laughter erupted behind her.

Jack followed her into the kitchen. They squared off in the middle of the floor. She eyed the poker in his hand. Jack pushed past her to the back door, tossed it out into the night, then slammed the door shut.

"You lied to me!" Rebecca shouted. "You led me to believe you and I had—had—well, you know what I mean. You tormented me over it. And *nothing* happened!"

Jack just looked at her for a moment. "No, nothing happened. When I got there you were drunk. You passed out. I couldn't very well carry you home, so I put you in bed."

"Did—did you…ogle me?" she demanded.

"Hell, no! Do you think I'm the kind of man to go peeping under a woman's skirt when she's passed out drunk?"

"Then how did you know about my mole?"

Jack shifted uncomfortably. "Well, all right, when I was putting you in bed your gown came up a little and I saw it there on your calf."

"You pig."

"What the hell was I supposed to do with you?" Jack demanded.

"You could have put me in one of the *other* bedrooms!"

"Oh. Well, uh…"

"You lied to me, Jack," Rebecca said. "You

lied about everything. You made me think we'd—
we'd—"

"Made love?"

Her cheeks flushed. "Was it all just a game to
you?"

"A game?" Jack's expression tightened.
"*You've* got a hell of a lot of nerve asking *me* if
this is a game!"

"You never intended to go along with our
business arrangement at all, did you," she accused. "You're welshing on your debt. Fine! If
you won't give me what I want, I'll find another
man who will."

He shifted closer, anger drawing his brows together. "Like hell you will."

"It's none of your business. Not anymore."

Jack closed his hand over her arm. "I'm not
going to let you—"

"Just try and stop me." Rebecca jerked away
and stormed out the back door.

CHAPTER ELEVEN

OF ALL THE TALK that had circulated through the tearoom, none of it had been about Rebecca. Thank goodness.

Late afternoon, the tables were empty now. Rebecca had kept to the kitchen today as much as possible, affording her customers the opportunity to talk about her, if they chose. Yet peeking through the curtained doorway, straining for snatches of conversation, she'd picked up nothing to indicate she was today's topic of whispered gossip.

No one had mentioned last night's escapade at the Lucky Streak. So far.

With a sigh, Rebecca loaded dishes onto her tray and headed back to the kitchen. So many emotions churned in her, she wasn't sure she could capture and name any one of them.

"You've been quiet today," Aunt Virginia said, drying a teacup. "I'll bet I know what's on your mind."

Rebecca held her breath.

"Mrs. Wagner's millinery shop next door."

Rebecca heaved a sigh of relief. "What about it?"

"Didn't you hear? She's decided to close the shop and move to Keaton with her daughter."

Rebecca had kept her eye on Mrs. Wagner's shop for months, planning how she could expand the tearoom if the older woman decided to move. Today, she'd been so involved in her own problems, she'd completely missed the news.

"I'll help you with the dishes," Rebecca said, and picked up a dish towel, "then go talk to her."

"You really are distracted today," Aunt Virginia said, shaking her head. "Usually, business is *all* you think of."

Business had been her whole life for months now. It had been her future. It was still her future, she realized.

Business. Not a child.

Sadness gripped Rebecca's heart. After all that had gone on between her and Jack, she knew there was no way they'd continue their business deal now. And, despite the threat she'd made in the kitchen of the saloon last night, she'd never approach another man with the proposal.

So where did that leave her? Exactly where

she'd started. With a tearoom, a head for business, and a lonely future.

The kitchen seemed to close in around Rebecca. She untied her apron. "Do you mind if I talk to Mrs. Wagner now?"

"That's fine, dear. I can manage things here."

Rebecca slipped outside into the alley but didn't go to Mrs. Wagner's shop. She'd been inside dozens of times and knew exactly what renovations she'd make. Instead, she headed toward East Street. If business was to be her future, then she should pursue it. She rounded the corner and ran into Jack.

They both froze, staring into each other's eyes. Rebecca's heart thumped wildly, weakening her knees and causing her hands to tremble.

How could he have this effect on her? Still? After what he'd done, what she'd done? How could she want to throw her arms around his neck, in the middle of the afternoon, on a public street?

"Where are you headed?" Jack asked softly.

"To see Seth Grissom," she said.

Jack's expression hardened. "If you think I'm going to let you ask him to be a party to this ridiculous business proposal of yours, you can—"

"No," she said quickly. "I just want to ask him about doing some renovations for me."

Jack eased off a bit, but didn't look happy. "Keep away from Grissom."

"Why?"

Jack looked at her for a moment, then pushed his hat an inch higher on his head. "The men in town have been giving Griss a hard time about painting your store pink."

"Why on earth would anyone blame him? I'm the one—"

"Because that's the way it is," Jack told her. "Anyway, Griss isn't taking it so well. He keeps to himself now. It would be better if you just left him alone."

She realized then that she almost never saw Seth on the street. She'd assumed he was busy working, but now it seemed he'd become somewhat of a recluse. Thanks to her.

"Maybe I should go apologize," she said.

"No, Rebecca. Stay away."

She looked up at Jack. "I suppose all the men in town are talking about *you* now. After last night."

Jack waved away her words. "It doesn't bother me."

A long, silent moment passed as people hurried by on the boardwalk, horses and carriages rumbled through the street. Rebecca wondered if she'd ever have a moment alone with Jack again. If she'd ever have this opportunity.

"What was the real reason you wouldn't go through with our…arrangement?" Rebecca pulled up her courage. "Did you find me unattractive? Too outspoken? Too…old?"

Jack's frown deepened, his expression changing from confusion to hurt, then to anger.

"I've got a question for you," he said. "When you agreed to fix up my house, did you plan all along to use me to get yourself pregnant?"

Rebecca gasped softly and reeled back. She felt the color drain from her face. Jack's question was so far from her thoughts, it took a full minute for her to understand what he'd said.

"My gracious, Jack, no," she said, almost in a whisper. "I never considered the idea at all until…"

His expression softened marginally. "Until what?"

"Until I saw what a lovely home you had and it made me realize I wanted the same. But not just a house, a baby, too." Rebecca gazed up at him. "Do you really think I'd plotted and schemed against you this whole time?"

Jack didn't answer right away, making Rebecca wonder—for the first time—if maybe that's exactly what he thought of her. Her heart ached. Could he really have such a low opinion of her?

"Jack?" she asked, wanting an answer.

He glanced around, seeming to realize that they were still standing on the crowded boardwalk, then hooked her elbow and led her into the alley. A few minutes passed while he seemed unsure of what he wanted to say—or if he even wanted to say anything.

Finally, he looked down at her. "My mama died."

Rebecca drew in a quick, sharp breath as she saw the hurt in his eyes and remembered the pain of losing her own mother. She wanted to hold him, comfort him, but he went on.

"It was about five years ago," Jack said softly. "That in itself was hard enough to deal with, but then—then other women started showing up at our house."

"Women intent on pursuing your father?" she asked.

"Our family had money, good social standing. My pa was a 'good catch,' as the women liked to say." Jack's expression hardened at the bitter memories. "These women started taking over. Rearranging the furniture, hosting dinners, wearing my mama's clothes and jewelry."

"Oh, Jack, that's terrible."

"No, the terrible part was that my pa didn't do anything to stop them. He wouldn't listen— to me or my brothers and sisters. He was too busy working—or he just didn't care. I never knew which." Jack drew in a breath. "I took it as long as I could, then I left."

"That's how you ended up in Marlow."

Jack nodded. "And I swore I'd never let a woman—any woman—take over my life."

Instinctively, Rebecca latched onto his arm. "That's exactly what you thought I was doing. Oh, Jack, I'm so sorry. I never meant—"

He pulled away, then turned and disappeared around the corner.

Rebecca watched him go, something inside her tearing away with him. Tears welled in her eyes. She wanted to run after him. She wanted to tell him—

Tell him what? Rebecca gulped, forcing down her tears. That she was sorry? That she'd missed him? That the days spent with him had been wonderful? That her heart ached thinking of him?

Rebecca didn't know. Standing on the board-walk, staring at the spot where Jack had disap-peared around the corner, she didn't know what she wanted to tell him.

Not that it mattered. Jack, apparently, wasn't interested in hearing anything she said.

Not even that she loved him.

So, SHE'D RUINED the reputation of two men in Marlow.

Rebecca slipped out the back door into the dark alley, clutching her heavy canvas bag. Hopefully, after tonight, she'd redeem herself—in the eyes of one of them, anyway.

Only a few windows shone with lantern light as Rebecca made her way south on East Street. A cool breeze brought the sound of distant piano music from the saloons, an occasional laugh, and the bay of a dog somewhere in town.

Darting into the alley, she glanced around, then knocked on the back door of Seth Grissom's shop. She heard his heavy footsteps inside. The door creaked as he opened it.

Holding up the lantern, Seth glared out at her. He towered over her. His shoulders nearly touched both sides of the narrow doorway. For a moment Rebecca feared he'd close the door in her face, but he didn't.

She pulled a book from her bag and thrust it at him.

"It's an art book," Rebecca said. "I brought it with me from Baltimore."

Seth glanced at the book, then at her again.

"The Lucky Streak needs a painting behind the bar. You can use the models in the book as a guide," Rebecca said.

Slowly, Seth hung the lantern on a nail beside the door and accepted the book. He flipped it open and his cheeks above his full beard turned bright red.

"These—these women are n-n-naked," he stammered.

Rebecca's face heated, but she pushed on. "It's art."

He turned another page, his eyes bulging. "But—but they don't have on any clothes."

"Yes, I know." She closed the book, brushing her hands over his meatier ones, forcing aside her own embarrassment. "You did those fashion pictures for my tearoom, so I know you can paint something…appropriate…for the saloon."

Seth just looked at her, the red fading from his face.

Rebecca squared her shoulders. "Hopefully, your…donation…to the saloon will give the men in town something to talk about other than you and my pink store."

His expression softened as realization dawned on him.

"Thank you," he whispered.

Rebecca managed a small smile. "Just don't give the model in the painting my face, please."

Seth grinned, his beard and mustache parting to reveal gentle lips and gleaming teeth.

"These are my art supplies." She passed him her bag. "And tell Jack he should have a contest to name your painting. A nickel a vote."

"Yes, ma'am."

Seth stepped inside and closed the door as Rebecca hurried away.

DORIS TIDWELL BROKE THE NEWS. Rebecca nearly dropped her serving tray as she rushed through the tearoom.

"Lucy's husband came home last night," she said to her aunt at the stove.

Aunt Virginia nodded. "You should go to her."

Rebecca hurried down East Street and knocked softly on Lucy's door. After a few minutes it opened. Lucy glanced over her shoulder, then slipped outside and pulled the door closed behind her. She looked pale and drawn, tense.

"Are you all right?" Rebecca kept her voice low.

Lucy gave her a quick nod.

"Did Raymond find work?" she asked. "Or investments?"

"No." Lucy looked away. "I don't know what's going to happen, except…Raymond says he's home to stay."

Rebecca's heart sank. "What are you going to do?"

"Nothing." Tears pooled in her eyes. "Raymond is my husband and…and that's that."

Rebecca touched Lucy's hand. "If you need anything, let me know."

"I will." She swiped at her tears, then ducked into the house and closed the door.

Tears came to Rebecca's eyes as she walked down East Street. Of course, Lucy was doing what she thought was right. Raymond was her husband.

Ian Caldwell came into Rebecca's mind and a new sadness settled around her heart. Ian. He loved Lucy, genuinely loved her. How would he accept this news?

At once, Rebecca wanted to run to Jack. She wanted to lay her head against his broad shoulder. She wanted to hear his voice rumble in his chest as he spoke against her hair. She wanted to feel his big arms around her. She didn't care what they'd been through. She just wanted to be with Jack.

Rebecca turned the corner onto Main Street

heading for the Lucky Streak. Inez Becker fell in step beside her.

"Rebecca, I was just headed over to your tearoom," she said excitedly. "I have news."

"Everyone's already heard," Rebecca said.

"But that's not possible. I saw it myself, just now at the depot." Inez touched Rebecca's arm, stopping her on the boardwalk. "Mr. Delaney's company arrived. And it's not what everyone thought. Not investors at all."

Rebecca braced herself, not sure she wanted to ask another question.

Inez didn't give her the opportunity. "Mr. Delaney's company is a *woman*. I heard him call her by name. Emily. She's young and just lovely. Why, the way he fussed over her, I'd say she's his fiancée. Or maybe even his wife."

CHAPTER TWELVE

IF JACK HADN'T already heard the news, he could have figured it out from the look on Ian's face. Standing at the bar, Jack saw him push through the swinging doors and drop into a chair in a corner table. Jack got a bottle of whiskey and a glass from behind the bar and walked over.

"On the house." Jack put both on the table in front of Ian and sat down beside him. "Do you think Lucy will—"

"She'll stand by her husband." Ian scrubbed his hands over his face and slumped forward, bracing his arms on the table. "But I can't ask her to leave him. All I can do is be here when she decides she's had enough of that bastard."

Jack rose from the chair and clasped Ian on the shoulder. "Let me know if you need anything."

Ian just nodded. He pulled off his badge and dropped it in his pocket, then poured himself a shot of whiskey.

Jack ambled through the crowded tables and

leaned on the bat-wing doors. His gaze drifted to Rebecca's tearoom.

Dark, late, not a light on in the place, but he knew she was inside. A heaviness settled around his heart as he thought of Rebecca, then Ian and Lucy.

What would Ian give to walk to Lucy's house this minute, knock on her door and be invited inside? Jack could do that at Rebecca's place, if he wanted to. Problem was, he wasn't so sure she would invite him in.

He'd done a lot of thinking about Rebecca, about himself, about the two of them. He'd asked her flat out if she'd conspired to deceive him and she'd told him that she hadn't. She'd even apologized. Jack believed her.

But things still weren't settled between them. Now, seeing Ian's misery, Jack knew what he had to do. He pushed through the swinging doors and headed down the street.

Things would never be settled between him and Rebecca until he gave her what she wanted— truly wanted.

REBECCA STOOD at the window of the tearoom staring down the dark street at the Lucky Streak saloon. Light spilled over the top of the door and out the windows, bringing laughter and piano music with it.

Was Jack inside the saloon? Or was he home with Emily?

Rebecca's stomach twisted into a cold knot. All afternoon the tearoom had buzzed with excitement. Who, exactly, was Jack's mysterious guest? Was this Emily really his fiancée? His wife, perhaps?

No one had known the answer, and Rebecca couldn't bring herself to contemplate the question any longer.

With a heavy sigh, she turned away from the window. She'd changed into her nightgown hours ago, but couldn't sleep. With the lantern burning low on the bureau in her bedroom, she'd tried to read but couldn't.

All she could think of was Jack…of what he'd been through after his mother's death…of how he'd suspected her of the same despicable thing. She didn't blame him.

Slowly, she plodded into the kitchen. Food seemed unappealing, but at least cooking was something to do. A soft knock sounded on the back door. Lucy flew into her mind. No one else would come to call at this late hour. She openēd the door.

Jack stood outside.

''We have some unfinished business,'' he said.

Stunned, Rebecca just stared as he moved past her into the kitchen, torn between throwing him out, and throwing herself into his arms. He reached over her head and pushed the door shut.

''Shh.'' Rebecca put her finger to her lips and nodded toward her aunt's closed bedroom door.

''I'm here to give you what you wanted,'' Jack whispered. ''If you still want it.''

Her heart fluttered quickly beneath her breast as she gazed up at him. How handsome he was. How she longed to be in his arms—forever.

Jack pressed his palm to her cheek, caressing it lightly. Rebecca's knees weakened at his touch. Yes, she wanted him, with all her heart she wanted him. But should she allow herself this one moment with him? Because that was all it could ever be. Just tonight.

He eased closer, his warmth robbing her of her strength—and threatening her good judgement.

''What about Emily?'' she asked, managing only a whisper.

Jack frowned. ''What about her?''

''She's home waiting on you, and you're here with me—''

''I don't usually ask my sister along when I visit a woman,'' Jack told her.

She gasped. ''Emily is your—''

"Sister," Jack said.

Rebecca touched her hand to her chest, relieved. "I thought she was your fiancée, or even your wife, and—"

"Rebecca," Jack said softly, easing closer. "Sometimes—not always, but just sometimes—you think too much."

A whisper of laughter bubbled up inside her. "I do?"

"You do," Jack said gently. "And while we're on the subject, let's get something else straight. No, I don't think you're unattractive. No, I don't think you're too outspoken. And hell no, I don't think you're too old."

"Oh, Jack…"

He took her into his arms, pulling her tight against him. With a touch of his finger, he lifted her chin, then settled his lips over hers.

Rebecca melted against him. His warmth, his strength captured her, and she knew there was no place on earth she'd rather be.

He broke their kiss, but still held her close. "About this business deal of ours. I'm willing to hold up my end of our arrangement. But it's up to you. Do I stay? Or go?"

For so long she'd feared an empty, lonely future. That's why she'd proposed the business deal in the first place. Yet now that the opportunity was here, now that Jack had agreed to give her what she wanted, Rebecca didn't know if she could go through with it.

What sort of life would that be? A life without Jack himself? Her heart ached at the thought.

But she didn't know what the future held for her, she had no way of knowing for sure. All she knew was this moment. And at this moment, Jack was what she wanted.

"I don't want you to leave. I don't want to be anywhere but with you, Jack." She looped her arms around his neck. He lifted her into his arms and carried her into her bedroom, pushing the door closed behind him.

Jack laid her on the bed, then sat beside her. He stroked her hair, feeling its silkiness, then lowered his head and kissed her on the mouth. His lips trailed down her cheek and he buried his face against the curve of her throat. She smelled sweet. He claimed her mouth again, deepening their kiss until she parted her lips.

Rebecca gasped and threaded her fingers through his hair. Then she touched his arms, his chest, the heat warming her palms. He pulled off his clothes and tossed them aside, then stretched out beside her.

He kissed her as he unbuttoned her nightgown, then slid his hand inside. Rebecca moaned when he touched her breast, then gasped with pleasure as his lips followed. When he tugged at her nightgown, she raised her arms and he sent it flying.

Jack rose above her and slid between her thighs. He kissed her softly, tenderly as he made a place for himself there. Slowly, cautiously he moved. The rhythm caught Rebecca and she moved with him, unwilling to resist. She wrapped her arms around him and caught a handful of his hair as the pleasure broke within her over and over again. Jack called out her name, and he followed until he was spent.

"WE'VE GOT A PROBLEM," Jack said.

Her arms and legs entwined with his, Rebecca gazed up at his face in the dim light. After their lovemaking, they'd cuddled together, neither speaking until now.

Jack pushed himself up on his elbow. "I've been thinking about you and this business proposal, and I decided that you don't really want a baby."

"I don't?"

"What you really want is a family," Jack said.

A little smile crept over her lips. "How did you know?"

He waited a moment, then said, "Because it's

what I want, too. I just didn't realize it until recently.''

''What happened?''

''I was lonely. I missed my family. Even though my pa hadn't done what I thought was right, I still missed him.''

''So you wrote? Made amends?''

Jack nodded. ''And I convinced Emily to come out here. She'd been through a tough time with a man she thought wanted to marry her, but ended up walking out. She was ready for a change. I asked her to come out here, to start over. But mostly I was being selfish. I wanted some family close to me again.''

Rebecca touched her palm to his cheek. ''Family is important,'' she agreed.

Jack covered her hand with his. ''That's why I think you and I should be a family.''

Rebecca gasped. ''Are you saying—''

''I'm saying that I love you, Rebecca. I want you to marry me—if you love me, that is.''

She threw her arms around his neck. ''Yes, Jack, I do love you.''

He covered her lips with his and smothered her with a hot kiss, then lifted his head. ''And you'll marry me?''

She smiled. ''Yes, Jack, I'll marry you.''

''Good,'' Jack said, and splayed his fingers

across her belly. "Because there's no way in hell I'd ever let you move back to Baltimore with my baby inside you."

"I don't want to move to Baltimore."

"Good." Jack glided his finger along the curve of her jaw. "So, how old *are* you?"

Rebecca smiled. "I'm not getting any younger, that's for sure. In fact, if we want to have a baby, I think we should keep working on it."

Jack buried his lips against the curve of her neck. "Now *that's* the kind of thinking I like."

Dear Reader,

"Snow Maiden" is based on a Russian fairy tale and is inspired by my daughter. Ten years ago this month, my husband and I traveled to Russia to adopt our daughter. At the time she was five months old and living in an orphanage in a small town outside Moscow. To this day, I still remember the cold, the long trip over snowy roads and seeing her for the first time in her brown jumpsuit and red boots. Today she is a bright, healthy young lady who loves music and sports.

Over the years I've developed an interest in all things Russian—from the cuisine to the stories and the rich history. The snow maiden fable is one of my favorite stories. It tells the tale of Grandfather Frost and Mother Spring's daughter, the Snow Maiden, who yearns to leave her enchanted winter forest to live among the humans. The Snow Maiden does go to live in the village of humans and for a time she is happy. But when winter fades into spring and the hot sun shines down on her, she evaporates in the mist, never to be seen again.

I couldn't let a sad ending like that stand, so I took the bones of the tale, gave it an American 1880s twist and added an ending that I hope you will enjoy!

Mary Burton

SNOW MAIDEN

Mary Burton

Dedicated to the Families for Russian and
Ukrainian Adoption, a nonprofit organization
dedicated to increasing public awareness
of Eastern European adoption, offering a network
for adoptive families, preserving the heritage
of adopted children and providing relief
to children who remain in orphanages.

CHAPTER ONE

Denver,
December, 1884

SNOW CONJURED memories of home.

Sophia Petranova stared out St. Martin's stained-glass window at the flurries and let her mind drift to childhood days spent in Russia. She could almost smell her mother's *piroshki* baking in the oven, almost hear the hiss of her grandmother's silver samovar as it brewed black tea and almost feel the sable warming her legs as her father's sledge cut across the icy roads.

Almost.

Sighing, she turned from the window and looked up at the church organ's twenty-foot pipes. Her heart leapt in her chest when she imagined climbing the ladder behind the wind chests to the pipes and tuning the great instrument. Such was the work of an artist, a master, and though she had assisted her stepfather, Ivan

Alexandrovich, with the delicate task before, she
had never done it alone.

The bell in the clock tower chimed three times.
Ivan was over six hours late. Soon another sun
would set and they'd lose another day of work.
Time was running out.

"Sophia!" a familiar voice growled.

Whirling around, Sophia nearly wept with relief. "Ivan!"

"Yes, who else would it be?" Ivan grumbled
in their native Russian. The old man staggered
down the center church aisle uncaring that his
boots tracked mud or that melting snow dampened his long graying beard.

"Where have you been?" Sophia said. She
hurried toward him, and then froze when she
smelled vodka on his breath. "You swore no
drinking. You knew we had to work today."

Bloodshot, weary eyes stared at her. "We
won't be tuning the organ. We are leaving Denver."

Alarm swept through Sophia. She'd been ap-
prenticed to Ivan for six years and recognized the
signs of trouble. "What have you done?"

Ivan's lips flattened into a grim line. "You always think the worst of me."

She struggled to keep her voice calm. Stirring
his anger only gave him more reasons not to

work. "How can I not? You waste so much time when you know Mr. Richmond will not pay us unless we finish the organ by Wednesday. We have only four more days, Ivan. Four days."

"Richmond." The name rumbled in Ivan's throat like an oath. "Peasant."

Richmond had visited the workshop of Charles Anderson where Sophia and Ivan had worked on the organ's construction. He'd been to the church every day during the installation process. Just a glimpse of the businessman's ghost-gray eyes had told Sophia he was sharp, cunning and missed little.

Thoughts of Adam Richmond always left Sophia edgy, restless. "Mr. Richmond is no peasant and this organ is our last chance to prove our worth to Mr. Anderson."

Ivan pulled a bottle from his pocket and uncorked it. "You worry too much."

Numbly, she watched him raise the bottle to his lips and drink. He closed his eyes and savored the vodka burning his throat.

She shoved her hands in her pocket, tugged at the threads unraveling into a hole. "That's what you said when we left Seattle and San Francisco."

The tall, burly man's eyes closed for an instant. "Always like your mother. Nag. Nag. Nag."

Frustration sharpened Sophia's words more than she'd intended. "We *need* this fee to get home!"

He continued as if she hadn't spoken. "Noble bloodlines, distant connections to the Czar." He snorted. "You think you are better than me, yet there's not a ruble to your family name. Worthless. My money put food in our bellies, brought us to America. You are as worthless as your mother."

Sophia's temper snapped. She slapped the bottle from his hand. The glass shattered on the stone floor and vodka trickled into the cracks. "Don't speak about my mother that way!"

Rage reddened his cheeks. "How dare you! If not for me, you'd have gone to an orphanage with all the other unwanted children."

Sophia tilted her chin back. For an instant, she was fourteen years old again, alone and desperate for the mother she'd lost. Old emotions drained her anger and choked off her breath. A moment passed before she regained her balance.

"We are wasting time," she said coolly. "We are staying in Denver. *You* are going to sober up and finish this organ."

He leaned toward her, his dark eyes intent on her face. "Stay if you wish, but *I* am leaving."

His determined tone raised more suspicions. "Ivan, have you been gambling again?"

His face tight with anxiety, he started down the long narrow aisle. "It does not matter."

"You *have* been gambling." Ivan's trail of gambling losses stretched from Denver to St. Petersburg. She hurried past him and blocked his path. He stood a good foot taller than she but she planted her hands against his chest and braced her booted feet. "Who do you owe?"

He hesitated, shrugged. "There are men. They say I owe them money."

Sophia stood rigid in disbelief. A door somewhere in the church opened and the wind outside screeched inside the barren hallways like the lament of an old woman.

Ivan wrung his hands. "It was not my fault," he said more to himself than her. "The cards were marked."

Her body felt numb. "Where did you get the money? We have none to spare."

"I was lucky at cards last week," he said quickly.

Breath hissed through her clenched teeth. "You are never lucky, Ivan."

The spark of indignation in his eyes nearly

made her laugh. "I'm down on my luck now, but I've been up plenty times."

"You had no money! How did you get into another game?"

"I will win it back. You'll see."

The last time he'd gambled he'd sold the chain to her mother's locket. She struggled not to scream. "Where did the money come from?"

He flinched. "The locket."

Sophia sank back as if he'd slapped her. "Mother's locket?"

"Yes."

The gold locket, small but intricately carved, held a miniature of her mother in the oval casing. Since Ivan had stolen the chain, Sophia carried the treasure with her. Two days ago she'd discovered the hole in her pocket and had decided to leave the locket hidden under the floorboards in her room. Somehow he'd known she'd left it behind. "That was mine."

"I needed it."

"It was all I had left of her. You *promised* you'd never touch it."

Sophia could barely think. She wanted to weep for everything she'd lost: her mother, the village she'd not seen in six years, and the home she'd dreamed of making when she returned to Russia.

Pressing her fingertips to her eyelids, she

willed her tears away. If she were ever to return home, she needed the money from this job. And to do that, she needed Ivan. She drew back her shoulders. "You must help me finish the organ."

He shook his head. "*Nyet*. It was your hands that carved the mahogany casing and aligned the bellows. I was but an adviser."

She pushed a strand of blue-black hair off her pale face. "I assembled pieces and parts. Your experience will bring the organ alive. Please Ivan, just another day or two."

"I don't have another day. I must go now."

Sophia dug her calloused fingertips into his arm. "Who will explain your absence to the church committee?"

Bitterness sparked in his eyes like shards of ice. "The committee does not matter. It is Richmond that matters and he does not care about this organ."

"What are you saying? He commissioned it."

"He now only cares about disgracing the minister. He meets with the committee today to destroy the project."

Fresh fears swirled in Sophia's mind. "How do you know this?"

"I hear things."

"But why would he do such a thing?"

He shrugged. "Who knows? Who cares?"

Sophia's mind moved quickly as she re-grouped. If they lost this job, it could be years before she had enough money to return home. "You must talk to the committee. Make them understand that they must build this organ."

"Nyet."

"Ivan, please stay! I'm begging you, please. Just this one last time. If I must I will tune the organ but you must make the committee understand that it has to be finished."

Ivan seemed surprised by her desperation. She'd never begged before. He opened his mouth, ready to summon his deep voice, once so full of pride and life. Instead, he swallowed the unspoken words, then turned away and staggered out of the church.

Sophia's bare fingers curled into fists. Hot tears tumbled over her cheeks and she was aware of only the sounds around her. The sound of children laughing in the chapel. The firm click of shoes down the hallway. A door opening and closing.

She started after Ivan and then stopped.

Adam Richmond stood on the shadow's edge, staring openly, almost rudely at her.

Richmond possessed an earthy, raw quality that belied his fine wool suits and Irish linen shirts. His presence commanded the attention of everyone and he moved with the natural-born grace of a hunter confident of his skill.

She reminded herself that he did not speak Russian and hadn't understood her conversation with Ivan. Still, he stared at her as if he was trying to peer inside her heart. A jolt of electricity shot through her body.

"Mr. Richmond, may I have a word with you?" she asked in English.

"I've seen all I need to see." He abruptly turned and strode out of the room, dismissing her as if she were nothing.

The rejection stung more than it should.

Something inside her hardened, like ice in January. She would not leave as Ivan had. She would stay and make the church committee understand that the organ must be finished.

Adam Richmond be damned.

CHAPTER TWO

WHEN ADAM RICHMOND reached the door that led to the meeting room, he stopped and flexed his right hand, working the stiffness from his joints.

Though he didn't understand Russian, he recognized the anger and desperation in Sophia's hushed tone. Clearly, Ivan had told her he was leaving and she had reached the end of her tether.

Adam should have been happy.

But he wasn't.

Irritated that he was giving Sophia a second thought, Adam reached in his vest pocket and pulled out his gold watch. He glanced at the time then shoved the timepiece back in its place. Soon it would all be over. Ivan's failure would be complete and the troublesome Reverend Nelson would be without a parish.

And Sophia would be gone.

He had never planned on the unexpected pull he'd felt when he'd first heard her singing a melodic Russian folk song. Drawn by the sweet sound of her voice, he'd ventured from the meeting in the craftsman's office to the back workroom. There she'd sat on a stool, bent over a rich mahogany board carving a rose, unmindful of him or the half-dozen other workmen around her. She'd worn brown breeches, a white shirt cinched at her narrow waist and her hair in a thick braid.

Her eyes were as blue as a winter sky and they'd been filled with shining confidence and laughter. When her gaze had shifted to him, the laughter had faded and there'd been a flash of appreciation as her gaze slid over his body. The jolt of desire rocked him and left him hard and wanting.

Many a night, he'd dreamed of peeling the coarse fabric from her skin and making love to her. Many a night he'd wished circumstances were different.

"Sophia." He muttered her name like a curse.

Adam laid his palm flat against the door, needing to touch something tangible, real. Dreams were all fine and good at night, but in the clear light of day practicality reigned. Sophia didn't belong in his world. He had a family to protect and that was that.

Adam shoved open the door and walked into the empty meeting room. He stared down the

length of a long, Spartan table encircled by eight
straight-back chairs as he shrugged off his snow-
dampened coat and laid it on the back of his chair
at the head of the table.

Restless, he moved toward the window and
looked out at a small courtyard. An inch of
snow coated the ground. A row of naked Poplars
dripped with ice.

The snow showed no signs of ending and judging by the heavy, gray clouds, there'd be close
to a foot to contend with by sunrise.

Adam's jaw tightened. He should have been
worried about the snow playing havoc with his
construction schedules and the deliveries to his
brick factory. If it continued at its current pace,
he'd have to shut down operations. Instead, he
worried about Sophia.

Snowflakes would be dampening the knots in
her blue-black braid, coating the shoulders of her
ragged sheepskin coat as she made her way toward her rented rooms on Blake Street. Soon
she'd discover Ivan had fallen behind in his rent
and they'd been evicted. She had no place to
stay.

Adam decided that after this meeting he'd send
a runner to Sophia with money. At least, she'd
have some money in her pocket when she left
Denver.

The idea of Sophia leaving Denver blackened his already foul mood.

This wasn't like him. Contact with women always stayed casual and brief. He'd given as good as he'd gotten, but he'd always been careful not to care too much.

And here he was worrying about a woman he barely knew.

"You look a million miles away, Adam," Claire Richmond said.

Adam turned to see his sister standing in the doorway. Her too-expensive boots clicked against the stone floor and her pencil-thin skirt rustled as she moved, reminding him that her outfit cost more than he'd earned the first months he'd owned the brick factory.

She kissed him on the cheek, then efficiently tugged off her gloves and tucked them in her reticule. Like him, she had a habit of arriving early.

"You looked preoccupied, worried," she said frankly.

For her sake, he smiled. It had been just the two of them for so long, protecting her was automatic. "It's my job to do the worrying. Not yours."

She lifted an eyebrow. "Well, I do worry. You spend so much time alone."

"I like my solitude."

"That may have worked when I was a child, but no more. You need someone in your life, Adam."

When I was a child...

Just eighteen and still so young, Claire knew little of the world or how it worked, yet neither fact tempered her confidence. So young. Adam chose not to remind her of those facts. He wasn't interested in an argument today.

"It's the snow and the holiday," she said unexpectedly. She looked past him to the window. Snowflakes stuck to the glass, clinging only for a moment then melted. "Both always put you in a foul mood."

"They don't," he said.

Her gaze lingered on the snowy view, the brightness in her eyes dimming. "They have the same effect on me. It reminds me of Mama and Rose. You know, I can barely remember what they look like now."

Unconsciously, Adam curled his fingers over the scars on his right palm. Twelve years had passed since the fire that had swept through their wood-framed house, killing their mother and sister. Adam had been trudging through the snow that day, returning from his shift in the factory when he'd seen the flames. He'd run as fast as he could through the white mire to reach them.

He'd clawed his way into the inferno, but the heat had burned his hand and seared his lungs almost immediately. It had been a miracle he'd been able to save six-year-old Claire.

Adam shook off the images. "I prefer to think about the future."

"You never speak of the past," she said quietly. "Have you forgotten them?"

So many times, he'd prayed he could forget. "I haven't forgotten a thing."

"What do you remember?"

Adam shoved out a deep breath. Any other day, he'd have steered the conversation to another topic, but today his emotions were tipped out of balance. "You and Rose had decorated a Christmas tree the day before. Rose strung berries and wrapped them around the tree. She also tore pages out of one of my books and cut them into stars."

Claire smiled, her eyes sparkling. "*I* stole the pages."

If only if it hadn't been so cold that day, his mother would never have banked the fire so high. If only he'd said no to the tree or hadn't stopped to buy toys for the girls. *If only.*

He wrenched his thoughts away from the past and focused on the reason they were here today—Harrison Nelson, the interim church minister.

Bright, young and full of ideas, the young Reverend Nelson had been the one who first suggested constructing the pipe organ. Claire had championed the project and convinced Adam to underwrite it. Nelson's status had risen among the vestry members and there'd been talk about making his job permanent.

Adam had been happy to indulge his sister, until a week ago when his butler had given him a letter intended for Claire. The letter had been from Nelson. It spoke of their love and plans to announce their engagement when the organ was completed and Nelson's position as minister was secure.

Adam's first impulse had been to have Nelson fired on the spot. He'd worked too hard to give his sister a good life to see it ruined by a man who worried more about emotions than practicality.

But Adam had learned long ago to play his cards close to his vest. So he'd kept his temper in check and begun to plot.

Openly withdrawing his support of the organ would ensure the project's failure, but Claire would never forgive him. Instead, Adam focused on Ivan Alexandrovich, who'd already proven he couldn't stay to a schedule. It didn't take much to learn that Alexandrovich, a once-great craftsman, had all but drowned his talent in a sea of vodka and gambling debts. All Adam had to do was call in the Russian's markers to send him running from Denver. With the organ unfinished, Nelson would be fired, leave town, and Claire would get on with her life.

A perfect plan, if not for Sophia.

The sound of voices and footsteps echoed down the long stone hallway. The first to arrive was Mrs. Dalrumple, one of the elite members of Denver society and a founder of the coveted Thirty-Six, a clique of whist-playing society ladies who ran the city's social circles. A tall, slender woman, her pinched features, tight graying chignon and silver-tipped walking stick made her look older than her forty years. She'd been the biggest supporter of the organ, telling anyone who would listen that Denver was finally starting to enjoy real culture.

Mrs. Dalrumple raised an eyebrow when she saw Adam. "You're the last man I'd expected here today. I'd think you had more important details to handle than this humble project of ours."

Humble. The organ had cost well over one thousand dollars of his money. "I want to make sure my investment pays."

Mrs. Dalrumple cleared her throat. "Reverend Nelson has assured me the organ will be finished by this Wednesday. He understands my Dora's hopes are set on playing at the Christmas Day church concert."

Adam was careful to keep all traces of emotion hidden. "Good."

Mrs. Dalrumple allowed Adam to pull back her chair. She sat and took extra time to arrange her skirts before she spoke. "I hope he's not too late. I've an afternoon tea to attend."

"He'll be here," Claire said, glancing at the door again.

Mrs. Dalrumple pulled spectacles from her reticule and put them on. "All here except Reverend Nelson and Mr. Alexandrovich."

Claire met Adam's gaze. "Just a minute or two more."

"I'm sure you're right," Adam said mildly.

The clock struck three before they heard the hurried click of boots echoing down the hallway. A harried and very out-of-breath Nelson appeared in the doorway. He shoved a lock of thick blond hair off his face. "I believe that church clock is fast. It seems I'm always in a race with the thing."

Young Nelson greeted everyone at the table but his gaze lingered a beat too long on Claire.

She dipped her head away from Adam as if to hide the blush in her cheeks.

Adam seethed.

Nelson's unsteady gaze met Adam's. "Mr. Richmond."

Adam shook the young man's hand, surprised Nelson managed a firm handshake despite his fine-boned fingers. "Nelson, good to have you here."

"Good to be here."

Adam sat at the head of the table and Nelson took the chair on his right next to Claire. Mrs. Dalrumple called the meeting to order. She offered a brief welcome then turned the meeting over to Nelson.

Nelson laid his long, slim hands on the table. "We have a bit of a problem."

Mrs. Dalrumple's mood soured. Adam nearly smiled.

"What kind of problem?" Mrs. Dalrumple asked, her voice stiffer.

"It seems Mr. Alexandrovich has disappeared."

Adam leaned forward, his chin resting on his steepled fingers. "What do you mean *disappeared?*"

Nelson's face reddened a fraction. "He and I were supposed to meet this morning. H-He didn't show. Miss Petranova was here most of the day waiting for him, but when I checked the sanctuary moments ago, she was gone too."

The mention of Sophia's name soured Adam's satisfaction. "This isn't good."

Mrs. Dalrumple tapped her cane against the floor. "I was counting on that organ, Reverend Nelson."

"Th-There are other artisans. I've just come from Mr. Anderson's workshop. He will send another craftsman as soon as he can."

"When?" Mrs. Dalrumple said.

Nelson's lips flattened. "January?"

Claire paled. "There is no one that can come earlier?"

Nelson's gaze met Claire's. "No."

Adam kept his voice neutral. "I thought you had this situation under control Reverend Nelson."

"I—I thought I did," Nelson said.

"*Thought* doesn't cut it," Adam said tersely.

"This won't do at all," Mrs. Dalrumple said. "I was counting on that organ being finished on Wednesday. Dora will be humiliated."

Claire leaned forward. "There must be someone in Denver who can finish the organ on time. It's nearly complete."

Nelson looked at her, his pale eyes filled with disappointment.

"*I* will finish it." Sophia's clear, slightly accented voice rang out from the doorway.

CHAPTER THREE

SOPHIA KNEW that her unscheduled arrival would be a shock to the committee. However, when she looked into Adam Richmond's unwavering gaze her breath hitched in her throat. Surprise flickered in his gray eyes, and just for the briefest instant she imagined respect, before his full lips thinned into an icy frown.

Her hastily planned speech to the committee vanished from her mind.

His body was only inches from her and she could feel the energy radiating from him. His bold presence goaded her worries and her first inclination was to beg his forgiveness for her impertinence, as if he were the Czar himself.

But she didn't.

A flicker of annoyance ignited inside her. Sophia's mother had instilled an unwavering pride in her that had sustained her through poverty, the death of her parents and six years with Ivan. She scraped together her bits of courage. "*I* can finish the organ."

Reverend Nelson scrambled to his feet. "Miss Petranova, I've been looking all over for you and Mr. Alexandrovich."

Sophia moistened chapped lips. "Mr. Alexandrovich is not coming."

Nelson pressed his long, slender fingertips to his temple as if his head had started to pound. "When will he be back?"

Guilt tugged at her as she stared at Reverend Nelson. He'd been kind and had given Ivan more chances than he'd deserved. "He has—"

Richmond rose to his feet. "We want the truth this time."

Sophia faced him, stung by his words. "If you will just let me explain."

Richmond's steady regard reminded her that his goal was to derail the project. "As far as I'm concerned, he's fired and we have nothing more to discuss. Miss Petranova, you may go."

Sophia refused to back down when so much depended on this job. "Won't you hear me out?"

Claire Richmond jumped to her feet. "Really, Adam, let Miss Petranova speak."

Mr. Richmond didn't take his eyes off Sophia. "All we've gotten from Miss Petranova is talk.

It's time to face facts, hiring Ivan Alexandrovich was a mistake.''

Reverend Nelson's cheeks burned with color. ''The man came highly recommended and no one can argue with the quality of the work so far. Yes, he's been very slow, but the organ is almost finished, Mr. Richmond.''

Richmond shoved a hand in his pocket and rattled the loose change. He wasn't accustomed to being crossed. ''*Almost* doesn't count.''

Richmond's hostility stoked Sophia's temper. ''*I* can finish the organ by Wednesday. You must give me a chance.''

The lines etched in Richmond's face deepened. ''*A* chance, Miss Petranova? I'd say your stepfather used up any and all his chances. This job should have been completed weeks ago, yet here we stand. Now you want *more* time.''

Despite his quiet voice, his last words reverberated off the walls, making her flinch. ''I'm not asking for my stepfather, but myself. I am giving you *my* word that the organ will be finished by December twenty-fourth.''

Mrs. Dalrumple's icy gaze slid over Sophia, making her very aware suddenly that she still wore her dusty workman's clothes. She'd run all the way from the sanctuary and hadn't taken time to brush her hair or wash the dirt from her face and hands.

The matron tapped the silver tip of her cane on the floor silencing everyone. "Young lady, why on earth should we take your word? You are nothing more than the organ builder's assistant. All you've done is make up excuses for your stepfather's absences."

Trembling, Sophia took a step toward the long table. "I am sorry for my lies and will always regret them." She fisted her fingers. "I do not profess to know as much as Ivan Alexandrovich, but I do know this organ. I built most of it with my own hands and I can finish it."

Mrs. Dalrumple thrummed her fingers on the table. "We would like to believe you, Miss Petranova, but what guarantee do we have that you won't leave like your stepfather?"

Reverend Nelson turned to Mrs. Dalrumple, his body tense with hope. "I can say from first-hand experience, Miss Petranova works hard, sunup to sundown most days. And we have nothing to lose. Anderson Organ Builders have already said they can't send anyone here for several weeks. What would be the harm giving Miss Petranova another try?"

Claire glanced at her brother and then Sophia.

"I for one vote to support Sophia, Mrs. Dalrumple. Dora is so counting on the organ being ready for her musicale."

Mrs. Dalrumple touched the cameo on her collar. "Everyone is coming to hear Dora play."

Mr. Richmond shoved his arms in his coat. "Don't be fooled like my sister, Mrs. Dalrumple. Miss Petranova is better at selling than she is delivering. I don't want her failure to reflect badly on you or Dora."

"I truly admire Dora," Sophia said. "She's been nothing but kind to me and I want her to succeed and be the belle of the holiday season."

Richmond's laugh was low, bitter. He looked at Mrs. Dalrumple. "Be smart. She will make a fool out of you."

Nelson leaned toward Mrs. Dalrumple. "If I could vote, I'd give Sophia a chance, Mrs. Dalrumple. I believe in her."

The older woman stared at Nelson. "I might be willing to give her a try, but I'd want assurances."

Richmond pressed his palms on the table and leaned forward. "And where is Miss Petranova going to live while she does this work? Have you asked her that?"

Mrs. Dalrumple turned to Sophia. "Is there a problem with your room?"

The challenge in Richmond's eyes told her he knew more about her situation than she did. Most likely, Ivan hadn't paid the rent and they'd been evicted. It wouldn't be the first time they'd been thrown out on the streets. "I don't need much. A room at the church perhaps."

Mrs. Dalrumple frowned. "That's not appropriate, my dear."

"It's only for a few days," Sophia countered.

Nelson held up a finger as if an idea occurred to him. "A cot could be found. She could sleep in my office."

Mr. Richmond took Sophia's arm. His grip was gentle but unbreakable. "This is ridiculous. She can't live in Nelson's office. Let's face it, this is over."

"I have an idea!" Claire said, moving toward Sophia.

Richmond's glare would have intimidated the most battle-weary general. "Not now, Claire."

Claire faced her brother and as if he hadn't spoken and said, "Miss Petranova could stay with us!"

Sophia hissed in a sharp breath. Adam's expression looked murderous.

Claire ignored them both and turned to Mrs. Dalrumple. "It really is the perfect solution. We have plenty of room and our house is only four blocks from the church. *And* Adam can personally keep an eye on Miss Petranova."

Mrs. Dalrumple nodded. "It does sound like a good idea."

Mr. Richmond's face darkened. "Claire, you go too far."

Sophia pulled free of Adam's grip. Behind the anger in Adam Richmond's eyes, Sophia saw something else. Lust tangled with worry. "That is kind, but I can manage elsewhere."

Claire placed herself between Sophia and Richmond. "Any rooms you find are likely to be in the roughest part of town. Staying with us is the perfect solution."

She lifted her chin. "Thank you, but I will manage."

Claire placed Sophia's hand in the crook of her own arm. "Miss Petranova, may I call you Sophia?"

Sophia could see the trap being set but didn't know how to free herself. "Of course."

Claire patted Sophia's hand. "Sophia, the church is out of the question, you've no time to find another room and you certainly can't sleep on the streets. Say you will stay with us and put an end to this tedious discussion.''

Mr. Richmond stiffened. ''No!''

''It's only for a few days,'' Nelson said. His cheeks turned crimson but he didn't back down.

Richmond clenched and unclenched his fingers as if they were stiff. ''I don't like strangers in my home.''

Claire's gaze was pointed, direct. ''Adam, do you want this organ finished or not?''

Richmond stared at Claire as if carefully considering what he'd say next. Ivan's words rang in Sophia's head. Richmond didn't want the organ finished. For reasons Sophia could not explain, Ivan was right. And Richmond did not want his sister to know he was behind this debacle.

''Of course I want it finished,'' Richmond said calmly.

Claire arched an eyebrow. ''Then say yes.''

Nelson smiled. ''St. Martin's will be eternally grateful.''

Richmond's jaw tightened, released, tightened again. ''All right, Claire, consider Miss Petranova under my care. But understand this, Claire—I have now done all that I can to see this pet project of yours finished. Don't lay blame at my feet if she fails.''

Claire beamed. ''I wouldn't dream of it.''

Mrs. Dalrumple rose. ''Then the matter is settled. Miss Petranova will finish the organ by Wednesday in time for my Dora's concert.''

Triumph exploded inside of Sophia. She would finish the organ and she would see her dreams of returning home come true.

Then she lifted her eyes to Richmond.

His gaze was as dark as Satan's.

CHAPTER FOUR

SOPHIA GLANCED DOWN at her hands when the meeting room door closed behind her. They were shaking.

If she hadn't wanted to finish this job so badly, she'd have refused Claire's offer outright. Even now, she wondered how she could ever live under Adam Richmond's roof? Just the sound of his deep, raspy voice tugged at her senses and reminded her of unspoken desires she'd never allowed herself to entertain.

Sophia had stayed in her share of seedy rooming houses over the last six years. She'd heard enough bawdy talk to know what happened between when a man and women came together. In truth, she'd never understood what all the fuss was about or why proud women gave themselves to men when in the end their only reward was heartache.

Many men had tried to cajole her into their beds, but she'd turned them all down without a second thought. Yet, these last few weeks, when

Adam Richmond strode into a room her skin tingled, and she'd known true lust.

Sighing, Sophia pushed open the double doors that led to the church sanctuary. The massive stone room was finely constructed as if its builder were daring the heavens to tear it down. Lined in military fashion, pews flanked the left and right sides of the room and faced a wineglass pulpit carved out of cherry.

She paused at a baptismal font located in the back of the church. Running her hand over the white marble, she smiled, comforted. She didn't need to see the font's base to know that engraved into the pristine stone was the simple phrase— *Rose and Eudora, into the hands of the angels.* She'd discovered the words just days into the job. The font always filled her with peace.

She squared her shoulders. Only four days— and three nights—remained until the organ was to be finished. Enough time, even for an apprentice, to tune the organ, and very little time in the grand scheme of life. She would manage living in Richmond House. She'd heard it had seventeen bedrooms and hallways that stretched for miles. Enough space to ensure she never saw Richmond.

"A few days is nothing," she muttered. In a few days the organ would be finished, she'd have enough money to return to Russia and Adam Richmond would be no more than a distant memory.

Oddly irritated, she shifted her focus to the ten-foot-wide organ. Located behind the altar, the organ had been carted across town in five different crates. It should have just taken a week to assemble but with Ivan's absences, the assembly's pace had been slowed to a crawl.

Now as she stared at the magnificent instrument, she forgot all the troubles and gave in to pride. Savoring the scent of linseed oil, she admired her handiwork. Soon, her creation would come to life and sing like no other.

Expelling a breath, Sophia started down the center aisle, nodding reverently to the crucifix hanging behind the altar. She shrugged off her coat, a castoff of Ivan's, and laid it on an empty pew.

A couple of hours of daylight remained. Not so much time, but enough to get started. Sophia headed toward the organ when, outside in the corridor, she heard children's laughter. Smiling, she savored the sound of untrained, enthusiastic voices. She knew most of the children by name and had enjoyed watching them practice for the Christmas Eve pageant.

Their arrival nudged her away from her

gloominess. She looked forward to their afternoon practice. When the great door to the hall opened, she turned with a smile on her face, ready to greet the children.

Mr. Richmond stood in the doorway alone. His presence ate up the threshold and his dark gaze closed the distance between them. Her smile melted.

"You were expecting someone else?" he said.

She smoothed an unsteady hand down her breeches. "The children's choir," she said with a slow shrug.

"I sent them down to the chapel so that we wouldn't be disturbed."

A shivery sensation raced through her body. "We?"

"We've much to discuss." Richmond moved down the long aisle, his pace slow and precise. His gaze lingered on her for what seemed like hours, but of course was but a beat or two. His frown deepened.

She'd been foolish to think he'd allow this small victory of hers. "We have already discussed the organ."

"The committee discussed it. Now it's our turn." He sat in a pew, folded his arms over his chest.

Her hands trembled and she shoved them in her pockets. "What more is there to say?"

His smile was faintly mocking. "This organ is important to you, isn't it?"

"Yes." Richmond wasn't a man prone to small talk. She sensed a trap. "What point do you wish to make?"

Her directness seemed to please him. "How important is the *fee* you'll receive from this job?"

She froze. "Very."

He raised a dark eyebrow. "Is the fee more important than the organ?"

The trap was set. "I see the point of this now. Pride versus money—it's a very old battle, Mr. Richmond."

The smile disappeared from his face. "One that always has a winner."

"Yes." A bitter taste settled in her mouth.

"And if you had to choose between pride and money, Miss Petranova?"

She took a step toward him. "These last few years I lied often to protect Ivan. I hated every bit of it." Her voice was steady but inwardly she wanted to weep. "Today, when I made a promise to your sister, Reverend Nelson and Mrs. Dalrumple, I spoke from the heart, the truth. I will not break my word."

He rose from the pew. The flaps of his black overcoat billowed softly as he moved toward her. Sandalwood mingled with his own masculine scent. "Come now, Miss Petranova, it is just you and me now. No committee to impress. You can be honest with me. You don't care so much about this organ. You care about the fee. You want to return home, do you not?"

He was tightening a noose around her neck and she didn't know how to escape. "I would give almost anything to return home."

Unexpectedly, he took her hand in his and turned it over. Slowly, he traced the lines on her palm and circled her calluses. "I admire you, Sophia."

His touch kindled desire. "You are not here to tell me this."

"It's true nonetheless. I've watched you struggle with this project. Watched you work as hard as any two men to see this organ finished."

The fact that he'd noticed her pleased her. Yet, she wasn't blind. He was manipulating her. "Let us not play games, Mr. Richmond. The day is late and I am tired. What do you want of me?"

"What do I want?" He was silent for so long she thought he might not answer. Then he leaned forward until his lips were but inches from hers.

"It's not the kind of thing a man talks about in church."

His voice had taken on an edginess that sent shivers rippling across her skin. "Tell me."

"Since the day I first saw you in the workshop, I've imagined the scene a hundred times. Your black hair flowing over satin pillows, the candle-light flickering over your naked breasts and hips."

The sound of her own blood pounded in her ears. She'd never experienced such naked long-ing. Madness! "Mr. Richmond..."

He stroked the underside of her chin with his knuckle. "I want to kiss you."

Nyet! Yes. English mingled with Russian, common sense warred with desire. Her mind shouted warnings—run, he plays you like a pup-pet. Still, she couldn't move.

He traced her jawline with his fingertip. Heaven help her, she wanted him to kiss her. Just once. Just once. Without thinking she closed her eyes and tilted her head up in anticipation of tast-ing him.

The next few seconds stretched like hours as she waited. It took an extra beat for her to realize he'd taken a step back. A niggling unease blos-somed in her soul and scraped across her nerves.

Then she opened her eyes and saw the arrogant smile on his face.

Sophia felt as if someone had dumped ice water down her coat. He'd been playing with her as if she were a foolish country girl. She wished with her entire soul that she could melt into the floor.

Mr. Richmond reached in his breast pocket and withdrew a slim wallet. "Don't misunderstand, Sophia. I do want you. But I learned long ago that desire comes second to ambition."

Her cheeks flamed. "Leave this place."

"Not until you hear me out."

"I want nothing from you."

"That wasn't true a moment ago," he said, his voice husky now.

"Get out!" Her voice echoed off the tall stone walls.

"I'll pay you three times your fee if you pack your bags and leave Denver today."

She flinched. "I don't want your money."

He counted out more money. "Five times your fee. You can return home in style."

He offered more money than she'd make in the next two years. If she relented, she could be on the next train to California, buy first-class passage to Russia and a small home near St. Petersburg.

And what of Reverend Nelson, Claire and Mrs. Dalrumple? Ivan had disappointed her so many times with his broken promises, how could she do this to those that had been so kind to her. "Keep your money, Mr. Richmond. I only want what I'm due—when the organ is finished."

His eyes hardened. "Once my offer is off the table, I won't make it again."

The idea of turning down so much money made her dizzy. "Good. You'd be wasting your time and mine if you did."

For an instant, she saw a flicker of respect.

But the moment melted as quickly as snow in August and all that was left was frustration burning in his eyes. He shoved the bills inside his wallet. "You're a fool, Miss Petranova."

She allowed a small smile. "My stepfather has said so often enough."

At the comparison, his expression chilled.

She looked up at him. "Tell me one thing, Mr. Richmond. Why go to the trouble to bribe me? Why not fire me outright?"

"I have my reasons."

The glint in his eyes suggested her words hit a raw nerve. "Ivan told me you wanted Reverend Nelson fired."

"You are on dangerous ground, Sophia."

"Dangerous ground?" She remembered the

way she'd been ready to give herself to him. "Perhaps you are right."

"This isn't over between us." His words were as sharp as steel.

He turned on his heel and started down the long aisle. Drained of all energy, she numbly watched him leave. When he passed through the doors, her knees buckled and she sat down on the bottom step leading to the altar. Her heart hammered in her chest and she cradled her head into her hands. "When did it all spin out of control?"

"By the way, Sophia," Richmond's deep voice had her head snapping up.

Color flooded her cheeks and she rose, ashamed he'd glimpsed her fear.

His gaze locked on her. "We serve dinner at six-thirty in *my* house."

CHAPTER FIVE

FOUR HOURS LATER, Adam stared out the tall windows, streaked with frost into the dark, snowy night. He'd found it impossible to concentrate on business or to wrestle free of the knots tightening his back muscles.

All because Sophia was late.

Cursing, he moved toward a small table where he kept his whiskey decanters. Filling a crystal tumbler, he raised the glass to his lips, and then realizing he had no taste for liquor, set the glass down. He glanced up at the clock on the mantle.

Six fifty-three.

Where the devil was Sophia?

Nelson locked the church every night at sunset so Sophia couldn't still be working on the organ. In good weather, the walk between the church and his house took ten minutes. In this weather, it could take twice that. Even allowing for a stop along the way, she should have been here by now.

Unless she wasn't coming.

He picked up the glass of whiskey, drained the contents, wincing when it burned his throat.

Adam had not intended to speak so frankly to her today. Nor had he expected her response.

But he'd been frustrated that the meeting hadn't gone as he'd planned. When he'd seen her standing alone in the church, an ache burned the pit of his belly. He'd never wanted a woman as he'd wanted her.

So, he'd spoken his mind, half hoping that if he voiced his desires it would loosen their hold over him.

It hadn't worked.

His frankness had stoked a fire in his gut. Whatever slippery grip he'd had on his control nearly vanished when she'd closed her eyes waiting for him to kiss her.

And he'd turned her down.

A decision he'd regret for a very, very long time.

Damn.

He didn't want Sophia finishing the organ, but he wasn't a monster. He didn't want any harm to befall her.

He shoved his fingers through his short-cropped hair and strode back to the window. The temperature had dipped below freezing and the storm had worsened with each passing hour.

Five more minutes.

He'd give her five more minutes and then he'd summon his carriage. He'd retrace the stretch of road connecting his house to the church. If she wasn't there he'd ride down Fourteenth Street past the capital to her boardinghouse.

Double damn.

The grandfather clock in the hallway chimed seven times. He turned, ready to summon his butler to fetch his coat, when a loud knock on the front door echoed through the house.

The instant the butler opened the door the air became suddenly charged. An excitement pulsed through Adam's body. He knew Sophia had arrived.

Adam moved closer to the study door, which stood ajar. He had a clear view of Sophia dressed in her sheepskin coat cinched at her waist. She pulled a wet scarf from her head, revealing wisps of blue-black hair plastered against her forehead. Her cheeks glowed red but her lips had a blue tint.

"Miss Petranova?" said his butler, Fritz. The man's thick accent and blunt manner had many a guest complaining about his harsh and unwelcoming demeanor. The butler's tall, lean build, graying hair and crisp suits added to his standoffish mystique.

But Fritz was loyal. He did his job with un-
failing efficiency and Adam had decided long
ago that he wasn't interested in welcoming
strangers into his house anyway.

"Yes." Her voice was clear, hesitant.

"You are late."

Sophia smiled at Fritz. "You have an accent.
German?"

Fritz looked surprised. "Yes."

Sophia responded in German, asking him a
few questions to which he replied. Adam didn't
miss the hint of surprise in his butler's voice.

Fritz seemed to enjoy conversing in his native
tongue. Sophia asked him several more questions. By the butler's softening tone Adam
guessed that the man had fallen under Sophia's
spell.

A savage jolt of jealousy ripped through
Adam's body. He wondered how many men had
fallen prey to Sophia's sapphire eyes and melodic
voice. Over the years he'd escorted dozens of
bland society misses, but he'd never felt so protective or lustful over a woman.

Adam stepped into the foyer. "Fritz, has our
guest arrived?"

All traces of good humor vanished from Fritz's
face. He efficiently took Sophia's coat and

draped it over his arm. "Miss Sophia Petranova has arrived, sir."

Sophia still wore the breeches and loose shirt tied at her narrow waist. Each time Adam saw the breeches and the way they molded her hips, he grew hard. He tried to imagine what her lips tasted like and the feel of her soft, supple breast in his hand.

Sophia seemed to sense his thoughts. Her cheeks turned crimson but she didn't drop her gaze. "Mr. Richmond."

"Welcome, Miss Petranova. We were beginning to wonder if you were going to arrive."

"I had to return to my rooms and collect my belongings."

He noticed the small bag at her feet. "Won't you come into my study?"

She hesitated. "I don't want to trouble you."

He crossed the foyer and took her elbow. "No trouble at all. I've been wanting to have a word with you."

Sophia reached for her bag, but Fritz brushed her fingers aside. "I can take that."

"I can manage it," Sophia said.

Fritz looked offended. "Don't be absurd. I will put it in your room."

Sophia frowned, as if the idea of staying here still didn't agree with her. "Thank you."

As he followed Sophia into the library, Adam realized he felt off balance again. Even with the cold howling outside, he felt hot. He imagined himself threading his fingers through Sophia's black hair and unbuttoning the row of buttons between her breasts.

Adam gave himself a mental shake. Seducing Sophia was not the point of this meeting, he reminded himself. "Sit by the fire. Warm yourself."

She tensed. "I am fine standing."

It bothered Adam that she looked nervous so he managed a small smile, hoping she'd relax. "I won't bite."

She stared at him as if she were trying to read his mind. "That, I am not so sure of."

Despite himself, he laughed. The woman had spirit, which pleased rather than annoyed him. He poured her a brandy and handed it to her. "You're blue from the cold. It would not be good for anyone if you caught a chill."

She eyed him a second or two longer, then moved to the great hearth where a fire blazed. She set her glass on the mantle and stretched out her long slender fingers toward the flames and rubbed them together. "I did not think Denver got this cold."

"Normally, it doesn't. When we get snow it's

usually no more than a dusting and it doesn't last long.'' He set his untouched glass down. ''Perhaps you brought the snow with you.''

She faced him. ''You did not bring me here to discuss the weather.''

Directness was an uncommon trait in most women. He liked that about Sophia. ''No.''

She possessed a royal bearing. ''Then what?''

''Family.''

Her eyes narrowed suspiciously. ''I don't understand.''

''Behind you, on the mantle,'' he said. ''There is a black lacquer box. Open it.''

She stared to move away. ''If this is about money…''

''No money.''

Slowly she lifted the palm-sized box in her hand. She traced the mother-of-pearl flowers embossed in the top before she opened the lid. Inside the red-velvet-lined box were a handful of melted bits of metal. ''What is this?''

Sadness hammered him. ''They were jacks— the last toy I bought for my sister.''

''Claire?''

''Rose.''

Her confusion was evident as she gingerly touched each piece, then the stiffness drained out of her shoulders. *Rose and Eudora, into the hands of angels.* "You memorialized the font in the church."

It touched him that she'd noticed the font's inscription. Most people overlooked it. "She died twelve years ago in a house fire. What you hold in your hand is my last Christmas gift to her. They fell out of my pocket when I went in to save her. And they are all that I have left of her."

"Why do you tell me this?"

"So that you'll understand." The fire crackled and popped. A log tumbled backward sending a flurry of sparks up the chimney. "I brought my family to Denver after my father died of cholera so that I could build my fortune. There was little left in Virginia after the war and we needed a fresh start. I worked long days in the brick factory. My mother took in wash and cared for Claire and Rose.

"There was a terrible fire." He swallowed, his throat feeling as raw as it did that long ago day when he'd breathed in too much smoke. "Many homes were destroyed. I got Claire out and went back into the burning house. I pulled my mother out, but couldn't find Rose. Mother died within minutes crying out for her children."

Sophia replaced the box on the mantle without speaking. A tear escaped and she savagely wiped it away. "I am truly sorry for your loss."

"Claire is the only family that I have. I'd do anything to protect her."

Her eyes softened. "You love her. This I understand."

He paused, knowing now he took a great risk. He wasn't a man who liked revealing his cards before he had to. "What you don't understand is that Claire wants to marry Nelson."

Her lips tightened. "He is a good, kind man."

Adam swore under his breath. "He is weak. He can't protect her."

Her long pause suggested she didn't agree. "Your sister is a strong woman."

"She deserves better," he said tightly.

She didn't move, but he saw the stiffness return to her shoulders. Without him having to say anything, she understood his train of thought. "And if the organ is not finished, Reverend Nelson will be passed over. He'll have to leave Denver to find another job."

So perceptive, he thought. "This organ has turned into a sort of test laid out by the church vestry for Nelson. They want to know that he is a man who can build this church, make things happen." He leaned toward her. "If the organ is not finished, he will not be hired as the permanent minister."

She stepped back as if needing distance between them. His words had shattered their brief connection. "Why don't you trust your sister to make the right decisions?"

"I know what's best."

She shook her head. "You do not give her enough credit. Claire is not one of these silly girls whose head is turned by flattery."

"How would you know anything about Claire?"

She shrugged. "I am invisible to people when I work. They see the organ, sometimes Ivan, but never me. It gives me a chance to watch people. Claire handles fussy old women, the vestry, even the children's choir with ease. She doesn't need your protection."

He closed the distance between them. "You loved your mother?"

Sophia flinched. "Of course."

He gripped her small-boned wrist, amazed at the strength that radiated from her. "You'd have done anything for her?"

She lifted her chin. "Yes."

He wanted desperately to reach her, to make her understand. "I'm no different than you. All I want is to protect my family. Walk away from the organ, Sophia. You will be well paid for your time. Nelson will leave. Claire will be safe."

"You are wrong in all this, Adam Richmond. You hold on too tight and you need to let go."

No one had spoken to him with such frankness in many, many years. He wasn't sure if he liked it or not. "Are you going to help me or not?"

She was silent for so long he wondered if she'd heard him. "The organ will be finished."

This sparring game they played was getting very old now. "Crossing me is a mistake, Sophia."

"Then you must add it to my list of many."

Before he could fire back a response, she turned and walked out of the room with the grace of a princess.

CHAPTER SIX

SOPHIA'S KNEES TREMBLED slightly as she followed Fritz up the stairs minutes later. Remembering Adam's bright, gray eyes, wild with anger, had her wondering if she'd taken a tiger by the tail. The question was: did she have the strength to fight Adam Richmond or would it not be wiser to simply let go and run?

She wasn't afraid of him. His anger was a part of his passionate nature. He was a man who fought for his own. This, she understood.

No, what worried her now ran much deeper, beyond her own loyalties to Ivan, Claire and the pipe organ. Now, she worried about her heart.

If Adam had remained the cold, ambitious man who'd tried to buy her off earlier today, everything would have remained simple.

But when she'd held Rose's jacks in her hand and felt the heat of Adam's body next to hers, she'd realized that beneath the ice beat the heart of a man who understood family.

Sophia thought of her pipe organ. Her masterpiece. Her pride. Her path home. What had started out as so simple was now tangled and confused.

Her head started to pound. She passed by a Queen Anne chair in the upstairs hallway, upholstered in a rich silk. "Mr. Richmond doesn't strike me as a man who would want such a fussy house," she said in German to Fritz.

"He built this all for Miss Claire," the butler said.

Sophia pictured Claire, small-boned and so lovely. "He worries about her."

Fritz stopped in front of a massive oak door, turned the brass handle and pushed it open. "She is his life."

She envied Claire. It had been a very long time since she'd had family to worry over her. "She is no longer a child."

Fritz nodded. "Mr. Richmond has not quite figured that out yet. But soon I suspect he will no longer be able to deny it."

"She is strong-willed, no?"

Fritz allowed a small smile as he opened her bedroom door. "To say the least."

Sophia's response caught in her throat at the sight of the lavish bedroom. A massive four-poster bed, which was larger than many of the rooms she'd stayed in, took up only a small portion of the room. Covered with an ivory silk bedspread embroidered with hundreds of white roses and lilacs, the bed looked softer than sable.

"This can't be my room," she said. "I thought I'd be staying in the servants' quarters."

Fritz looked a bit offended. "This is your room."

Reverently, she moved into the room. With trembling fingers, she touched the coverlet. Such luxury. Opulence like this had been a part of her world when she was very young but she'd almost forgotten such finery existed.

Tears raised in Sophia's eyes as she thought of her mother's last poverty-ridden years. She would have done anything to prevent her suffering. *Anything.*

Like her, Adam would do anything to protect his sister Claire.

She looked up and caught her reflection in a gilded mirror. She barely recognized the woman who stared back. Where had the carefree young girl of St. Petersburg gone? She swallowed the tightness in her throat.

Fritz moved past her through connecting doors that led to a dressing room. Two lady's maids were already in the room filling a large brass tub with steaming hot water. She ached to soak in the hot water and free her mind of her worries.

Her joy was short-lived, however, when it occurred to her that Adam Richmond did nothing without good reason. Every move was calculated. "Why this room?"

Fritz raised an eyebrow. "It connects to his."

THE IDEA OF STAYING in the room next to Adam's horrified and excited her.

Sophia tossed and turned until well past midnight. Every gust of wind outside, every creak in the house had her tensing and staring at the door connecting her room to Adam's. He wouldn't dare enter her room. Would he?

No matter how much she tried to rid her mind of him, she couldn't stop wondering what it would feel like to have Adam Richmond's long, muscled body next to hers in bed. Or to feel his full lips kissing her neck.

Sophia's blood pulsed. Her breath caught in her throat.

Of course, he never came.

And she woke to bright sunshine and a crashing headache.

"Such a fool," she whispered as she rolled over in the plush bed. To want Adam Richmond, a man who stood between her and her dream, was madness.

A brief knock sounded on her door. Squinting

against the sunlight, she pushed up on her elbow seconds before Claire burst into her room. Her golden hair was twisted into a knot on top of her head and she wore a green wool dress fitted with wide sleeves and trimmed with an ivory cording. "Good morning, Sophia! I hope you slept well."

Self-conscious, Sophia sat straighter. "Excuse my laziness," she said. "I never sleep this late."

Claire waved away her concern. "You're entitled. By the looks of those dark circles under your eyes, I'd say you haven't had a decent night's sleep in years."

Sophia remembered her reflection. "It's been a long time since I slept in such a bed."

"Reverend Nelson told me where you were staying before you came here." She shuddered. "I know that section of town. It's a wonder you slept at all."

She shoved a lock of hair out of her eyes. After her conversation with Adam last night, she wasn't sure what to say to Claire. A part of her wanted to warn her. Another part worried that Adam might be right. "Many a night, I slept with one eye open."

Claire studied the cloudy sky. "Well, you're safe now."

She swung her legs over the side of the bed. "Is it still snowing?"

Claire turned away from the window. "No, and hopefully we won't get any more."

Sophia rose, wrapped a throw blanket over her threadbare nightgown and walked to the window.

She adjusted her focus past the frosted glass to the freshly fallen snow then up to the thick, dark sky. "We will have more snow before nightfall. I can smell it in the air."

Claire groaned. "Wonderful. The Christmas season puts Adam in such a foul mood. Snow makes it worse."

"Why?"

"Because Mother and Rose died on Christmas Eve." Claire shook her head, as if banishing the memory. "I keep telling Reverend Nelson that beneath Adam's rough exterior is the heart of a kind and generous man."

Sophia's heart went out to both Claire and Adam. "You and Reverend Nelson are close?"

Claire hesitated. "We are good friends."

Sophia heard the hitch in the younger woman's voice. "I think more than friends."

Claire blushed. "Yes."

"He is kind, no?"

Claire approached, her face glowing with happiness. "I've never met a finer man."

Love. Sophia could see the love in Claire's eyes. Such affection ran deep. She suspected with

or without the organ or the permanent job at St.
Martin's, Claire would love her Reverend Nelson.

Sophia understood the depths of Adam's concern. This kind of love had the power to bring
exquisite joy and crushing sadness.

Claire held up a petticoat, as if inspecting it.
"I've seen the way you and Adam look at each
other. You are good friends too?"

Sophia didn't mistake the true meaning.
"No."

"There is a spark," Claire said. "I've seen the
way he looks at you."

Sophia drew a deep breath. "I annoy him."

A teasing light danced in Claire's eyes. "You
fascinate him. He's never looked at another
woman like he looks at you."

The flicker of hope irritated Sophia. "Last
night he looked as if he wanted to strangle me."

Claire laughed. "I don't think so." Then just
as suddenly, frown lines appeared between her
eyes. "I am glad there might be something between you two. I've worried that Adam will end
up alone. Then you came along."

Sophia thought of the kiss he'd rejected and
the money he'd offered if she left town. She was
simply an obstacle blocking Adam from his goal.
"I upset his nice neat world, that is all."

Claire laughed. "He's needed that world upset for a long time. Everyone bends to Adam. But you don't."

Needing to change the subject, Sophia turned her attention to the dress. "Who is this for?"

"You, of course."

She captured a piece of the silk between her fingers and savored its softness. "I don't understand. I must go to the church and work today."

"It's Sunday. When I saw Reverend Nelson at the sunrise mass, he told me he would be conducting services all day long. The church is always so much busier before the holidays. You won't be able to get near the organ until tomorrow."

Guilt jabbed Sophia. She had lost all track of time. "You should have woken me. I'd have gone to church with you."

"You needed the sleep so that you'd be bright-eyed for the party."

"Party?" She couldn't help but touch the soft silk of the dress.

"At the Dalrumples'. It's their annual Christmas celebration. You've been invited."

Self-conscious, Sophia released the silk. "It would not be right for me to attend."

Claire started to sort through petticoats and stockings. "You must. You love music and I know you will truly enjoy this outing.'' She tossed the stockings aside and took Sophia's hands in hers. ''Please say you'll come.''

Sophia didn't know how to refuse. ''It has been so long since I had time of my own.''

Claire smiled. ''Then it's settled.''

Beneath the laughter, cunning sparkled in Claire's eyes. So much like her brother. ''I am not accustomed to charity.''

Claire waved away her concern. ''It's not charity. I'm simply lending you a dress for the afternoon.''

''Why did you invite me here to stay?''

All innocence, Claire said, ''So Adam can put his worries to rest about the organ. I want him to know you better and to see you have grit.''

Sophia frowned. ''Grit? What is this?''

''A term my mother used to use. It means you are tough.''

''Ah.'' In truth she didn't feel so strong now. She felt adrift, frightened and more homesick than she'd been in years.

''She would have liked you,'' Claire observed.

''Your *maman?*''

''Yes.''

Sophia felt a kinship with Claire. They had both lost their mothers at young ages. ''It's hard to lose one so close to us.''

Claire's eyes softened and she looked as if she'd say something more. But instead she straightened her shoulders. "Say that you will come."

Sophia did love music. "Yes."

Claire clasped her hands together. "Excellent! Now, we must get you dressed quickly. Adam is not a patient man."

Even the sound of Adam's name had her nerves jumping. "Excuse me?"

Claire moved toward the door, opened it, ready to make a quick escape. "I have persuaded him to join us today. Isn't that wonderful!"

CHAPTER SEVEN

THE NEXT HOUR WAS a whirlwind of activity. Sophia had little time to worry about Adam Richmond as she struggled with silk stockings, corsets and layers of undergarments. She'd been reared as a lady, yes, but six years with Ivan had left her more at home in peasant's clothes.

By the time the clock in the downstairs foyer struck eleven o'clock, Sophia was dressed in a brown velvet skirt with a matching fitted jacket and derby style hat. Her hair was styled in a jet-black crown of curls and pearl drop earrings dangled from her ears.

Her ankles wobbled when she started to walk in the high-heeled shoes. Muttering an oath in Russian, she concentrated on putting one foot in front of the other. Her next step wasn't better than the first, but as she moved down the hallway, her stride became more graceful.

Then she caught sight of Adam at the bottom of the stairs. Magnificent. Dressed in a black tailored suit and overcoat, he moved with straight-back precision, every step conveying confidence and purpose. She tripped.

Hearing her, he glanced up as he shoved his large hand into a leather glove. He froze and simply stared at her.

Sophia felt the distance between them shrink. His intense interest stirred excitement in her stomach.

She tried to will away the tension and descend the stairs with as much grace as she could summon.

To her great relief, she did not stumble again.

When she reached the foyer, Adam continued to stare, silent. Slowly he walked toward her. He circled, taking his time as he inspected every detail of her transformation.

Her nerves bunching, she glanced down at her skirts. "Is something wrong? Have I forgotten something?"

"Shh," he said.

Heat burned Sophia's cheeks as she tugged at her cuff. Unlike last night, his skin was freshly shaven and he smelled of sandalwood, hair tonic and man. "Claire lent me the outfit."

His voice sounded rough, unsteady. "Nicely done indeed. Nicely done."

Desire darkened Adam's gray eyes. Every

muscle in his body radiated with masculine awareness.

Sophia's fingers ached to touch him. So difficult to believe that in the beginning, she'd not seen past the ice to the heat.

All thoughts of the party, Claire and the rest of the world receded. For a heartbeat, there was just Adam.

Fritz entered the foyer, a coat in his hand. He cleared his throat. "Miss Claire insisted that I have you at the party by noon. The snow is slowing traffic, so I suggest you leave now."

Adam didn't move right away. "Where is my sister?" he said, his stare on Sophia.

"Miss Claire had to leave early. Something about refreshments," Fritz said.

Sophia's attention sharpened. "I thought we were all riding together."

Adam took the fur-trimmed coat Fritz was holding and held it out for Sophia. If he was annoyed, he didn't show any signs of it. "My sister is always full of surprises."

Sophia slid her arms into the silken lining of the coat. The coat, soft as down, enveloped her.

Adam leaned close so his ear brushed hers. "I think we can survive a carriage ride alone, don't you, Sophia?" Humor and challenge coated each word.

"That depends. What scheme do you have up your sleeve today?" she answered.

He laughed. "For today, none. I'm calling a truce. Those foppish society people mean something to Claire and she wants to make a good impression, so I am willing to play along for today. Besides, it is Sunday and nothing can be done about the pipe organ."

Adam looked years younger when he laughed.

"I still intend to finish it," Sophia said.

He smiled but there was a glint of steel in his eyes. "One day at a time, Sophia. One day at a time."

Adam guided Sophia out the front door. Cold December wind whirled around them as they moved down the wide marble steps and into his carriage.

Sophia sank into the plush seat. The walls were upholstered in royal-blue velvet and the lap blankets were made of the finest mink. She smoothed her hand over the seat and thought of the six years spent walking nearly everywhere.

The carriage dipped as Adam climbed in and took his seat across from hers. His knees brushed hers as he sat down, then draped the fur over her lap.

The carriage interior felt very small.

Adam pounded on the side of the carriage, signaling the coachman to drive. Within seconds, the carriage jerked, jostling Sophia's knees into Richmond's, and they were off.

Richmond considered her for a long moment, staring until her cheeks started to flush.

Sophia tugged at the lap blanket. "Claire is a matchmaker, I fear."

He folded his arms over his chest. "How so?"

She met his gaze. "She thinks if she wraps me in fancy clothes that somehow you will be more attracted to me."

"She's wrong."

Disappointment tore at her heart. "You don't like the way I look?"

"I learned long ago to look beyond the packaging, no matter how pretty." A grin tugged at his full lips. "I'd want you even if you wore flour sacks."

Sophia couldn't quite breathe.

Adam took her gloved hand in his, traced small circles on her palm. "I heard you pacing last night."

She swallowed. "You put me in the room next to yours. How was I supposed to sleep? You...you could have forced yourself on me."

His face tightened with anger and he dropped her hand. "I've never forced myself on any woman and when you come to my bed you'll come willing and wanting.''

Her mouth felt dry, her lips parched. ''Perhaps *after* the organ is completed we could spend time together.''

''I want to spend time with you *now*. If I had my way, we'd turn this carriage around and head straight back to my house. We'd spend the afternoon in bed and there'd be no talk.''

The idea of lying next to him made Sophia dizzy. Shivery sensations danced down her spine. His rock-hard body radiated a fire that left her breathless.

But as much as Sophia wanted to close her eyes and give in to the sensations, she didn't. This time, she drew back. ''Are you always like this?''

Her words surprised him, but he recovered quickly. Tossing his head back, he laughed. ''No. Thank God. Only you do this to me, Sophia. Only you.''

CHAPTER EIGHT

SOPHIA WAS GRATEFUL when the carriage stopped in front of the Dalrumples' house. She needed distance from Adam so that her reeling senses could clear.

Adam climbed down and held out his hand to Sophia. Accepting it, she looked up at the front doors decorated with twin wreaths entwined with crisp purple ribbons. "How lovely."

Adam didn't spare the house a second glance. "Yes."

She squeezed the folds of her fur-trimmed cape closed. "It's festive."

"The Dalrumples keep a tree in the parlor lit with candles," Adam said, his mood darkening. "If it were to tip over the fire could be devastating."

Sadness filled her. The fire that had killed his mother and sister had scarred more than his hand. "You always think the worst will happen?"

He took her elbow and guided her up the five stone steps to the front door. "Yes."

Her heart went out to him. "So much worry is no good, Adam Richmond. I know this."

He captured her gloved hand. "Give me a life with guarantees, and I'll stop."

"I have learned that you can no more control life than a river's course."

Adam clenched and unclenched his fingers. "You underestimate me."

Her response was cut off when the door opened and a butler welcomed them inside. Mrs. Dalrumple, who'd been speaking to another couple, stopped when she saw Adam and Sophia. Her questioning gaze lingered on Sophia and then her mouth dropped open. "Miss Petranova?"

Sophia thanked the butler as he took her coat. "Yes."

The other couple, hearing Sophia's voice, turned their gazes toward her. She knew them from the church; however, their shocked expressions told her they'd not recognized her at first either.

Mrs. Dalrumple studied her more closely. "I never would have guessed it."

Claire breezed into the foyer with Reverend Nelson behind her. Her smile widened when she saw Adam and Sophia together. She quickly gave her brother a kiss on the cheek then took Sophia by the hand. "You've arrived just in time. My sad little voice is a poor accompaniment to Dora's playing. Say you will sing."

"I don't know the words to your songs," Sophia said.

Claire tugged Sophia toward the parlor. "I will help you with the words."

As Sophia moved down the hallway, she glanced over her shoulder at Adam. He mouthed "good luck" as his sister whisked her into the music parlor.

HOURS LATER, standing by the spinet, with the music and songs swirling around Sophia, it was as if the past six years had never happened. Memories of home came alive and she glimpsed her old self.

Sophia tapped her toe in time to the music, aware that Adam rarely took his gaze off her. His presence left her slightly dizzy and made her question her plans to return to Russia.

When she finished singing "Silent Night" for the second time, the crowd begged for more. But needing a moment's respite, she graciously declined.

She glanced toward the chair Adam had claimed. He wasn't there. Disappointed, she moved up the stairs toward the ladies' sitting room that Claire had told her about.

The Dalrumples' upstairs hallway was papered in a soft cream-and-white striped pattern and decorated with portraits of the Dalrumple children—seven in all. Despite the expensive furnishings, this part of the house exuded an informality that appealed to Sophia. Moving down the hallway, she lingered at each portrait, noting the red highlights in each child's hair.

She hesitated in front of the last portrait, that of a young girl with cherubic features. She raised her hand to the face, but didn't touch. ''To have such a family.''

She'd been so focused on surviving these last few years, she'd dared not entertain dreams of children.

Swallowing a lump in her throat, she lowered her hand. She wanted a house. A husband. Children. Love.

Distressed by the intensity of her feelings, she moved away from the portraits and slipped into the ladies' room. She took a seat in front of a mirrored vanity, grateful to be alone.

Her flushed reflection and watery eyes glared back at her. ''Adam Richmond's not offered you anything other than passion. You'd be wise not to forget that, Sophia,'' she whispered.

Sophia Petranova, she reminded herself, did not worry about what could not be. She concentrated on reality. And a life with Adam Richmond was only a dream.

Determined to distract herself, she uncapped a crystal perfume bottle and savored the lavender scent. She dabbed the stopper behind her ears and the underside of her wrists.

As she rose, ready to return to the party, a child's frustrated cry carried through the door that connected the sitting room to another.

"No nap!" the child shouted. A toy crashed against the floor.

Unable to resist a peek, Sophia cracked open the door and looked into the connecting sitting room.

What she found was a delightful nursery with walls painted robin's-egg blue. A thick braided rug warmed the floor, two low-lying double beds were against one wall and endless blocks and books peppered the floor. In the center of it all were a young boy and girl, about four or five years old, and a very frazzled nursemaid.

The nursemaid, who didn't look to be much older than a child herself, tucked a loose ebony curl back under her white cap. "That's enough out of you two. You'll be taking your nap now."

The girl shook her head, shouted "No," and popped a thumb in her mouth.

Sophia recognized the girl from the portraits as the youngest of the Dalrumple clan.

The boy looked at his sister and like her shouted, "No!"

The nurse started to pick up the blocks. "Ol' Saint Nick don't take kindly to boys and girls who don't listen. He'll be filling your stockings with ashes and coal if you don't mind."

The children's eyes started to fill with tears and Sophia took pity on them. "What's this?" Sophia said, walking into the room. Her skirts swished behind her as she maneuvered through the minefield of toys.

The nursemaid curtsied, her face crimson with embarrassment. "Pardon me, miss. We didn't mean to disturb you."

"You did not disturb me." Sophia chucked each child under the chin. The nursery smelled faintly of milk and sweet cakes and she felt at home, quietly relaxed.

Both children looked up at her, their eyes dancing with curiosity.

Sophia sat in a rocker by a fire crackling in the hearth. She patted her lap. "Would you two like a story?"

The nursemaid wrung her hands. "They're

sticky, miss. They're sure to ruin your fine dress.''

Sophia asked the nursemaid for a towel and beckoned the children closer. As she wiped their small, pudgy hands she said, ''You must promise not to ruin my dress. You see, it is not mine, only borrowed for today.''

The little girl wiggled her clean fingers. ''Like Cinderella?''

Sophia hoisted the child up on her lap. ''And who is this Cinderella?''

''She is a princess.''

Sophia laughed. ''Ah.''

The boy scrambled up on her lap. ''You look like a princess.''

Sophia brushed the bangs from the boy's eyes. ''Maybe for today, but most days, I am just plain and ordinary. Now tell me your names?''

The nursemaid answered for them. ''The girl is Georgia and the boy, Seth. They're Mrs. Dalrumple's youngest.''

''We're not big enough for Dora's party,'' Georgia said.

Seth studied Sophia. ''You talk funny.''

''I'm Russian,'' Sophia said. ''I come from a place very far away.''

Sophia settled the children next to her. ''Would you like to hear a story?''

Georgia gently touched Sophia's earring. "A Russian story?"

Sophia pretended to think. "I will tell you about the Snow Maiden. She was the daughter of woodland spirits and she lived in a winter wonderland far away from people."

"Was she pretty?" Georgia said.

Quick purposeful footsteps echoed in the hallway and before Sophia could answer the door the nursery opened. Adam stood in the doorway, filling the space with his wide shoulders.

Suddenly, Sophia felt foolish and clumsy as she stared into his dark gaze.

The lines of worry, etched at the corners of his eyes, faded. "I thought you'd left."

The nursemaid stood, her shoulders straight and stiff. "We didn't mean to keep her, sir. She was just telling the little ones a story."

"I shall be along in a moment," Sophia said.

"Don't let me interrupt."

"It's a story for children," Sophia said, sitting straighter. "You would not be interested."

"I would," he said easily.

Adam stepped into the room, closing the door behind him. He leaned against the wall and folded his arms over his chest ready to listen.

THE TRUTH WAS wild horses couldn't have dragged Adam away.

Seeing Sophia in the rocker with the children on her lap knocked the wind out of Adam. He'd never seen a more beautiful sight. The children adored her and she'd looked at home and relaxed with them. As he watched her, painful memories of the past faded. In their place, he pictured Sophia surrounded by their children, singing to them as they all stood by the Christmas tree.

"Was she pretty?" Georgia said.

"Who?" Sophia asked. She tore her gaze from him.

The children giggled. "The Snow Maiden."

"Oh yes, very lovely," Sophia said.

Sophia's voice sounded shaky, a little nervous. She was very aware of his presence. And the idea pleased him.

Sophia cleared her throat. "The Snow Maiden had skin as pale as the moon and hair the color of the night. Her gown was made of finely embroidered silk and trimmed with sable."

"What happened to her?" Seth asked.

Sophia lowered her voice. "One day while the Snow Maiden was playing with her friend the bear, she heard flute music coming from the world where people lived."

"People like us?" said Seth.

Sophia touched his nose. "Just like you." She thought a moment. "The Snow Maiden followed the sound of the music to the edge of the winter forest. From there she could see green meadows and the bright sun shining down. She had never seen green grass before and she wanted to run barefoot through it. But she was afraid. Then she saw a handsome shepherd playing his flute. It was his music that she'd heard.''

"What happened?" Georgia asked.

Sophia hesitated. "To know the answer to that, you must get in your beds and under the covers.''

A little coaxing had them both in bed with the covers pulled up to their chins. Sophia tucked the edge of the blankets under the mattress. "The Snow Maiden and the shepherd became good friends and then she returned to the magical woodland. You see, she is the one who tells your St. Nicolas which boys and girls deserve toys.''

Adam suspected the fable had not ended so happily and that Sophia had rewritten the ending for the sake of the children.

"Are you the Snow Maiden?" Seth asked.

Adam laughed when Sophia shrugged. He could almost see the children's minds turning with questions.

"We are *good*," Seth said quickly. "And if you see St. Nick tell him that Seth Dalrumple wants a toy train.''

Georgia sat up. "And Georgia Dalrumple wants a doll with blond hair and a green dress."

Trying not to smile, Sophia kept her tone serious. "If I did happen to see St. Nick, I will pass on your requests. But you must promise to take your nap and not give nanny any more trouble."

Both nodded.

She touched them each on the nose. "Then I will see what I can do."

The children squeezed their eyes tight as if that would make sleep come faster.

Sophia said reluctant goodbyes.

Opening the door, Adam placed his hand in the small of her back and guided her into the hallway. "So what really happened to the Snow Maiden?"

Sophia glanced up at him, a bit surprised. "She fell in love with her shepherd. Love warmed her heart. But the love was too much for her. Like snow on a sunny day, she melted, never to be seen again."

Adam pulled Sophia into a secluded alcove. "Would you vanish if I kissed you?"

CHAPTER NINE

AS SOPHIA STARED into Adam's gray eyes, excitement left her speechless.

He dipped his head and covered her lips with his. At first, his kiss was tentative. But the feel of his lips and the taste of him set her senses on fire and she rose on tiptoes and wrapped her arms around his neck. A moan rumbled in his throat.

Adam wrapped his arm around her waist and pulled her against him. She curled her fingers into his hair and abandoned herself to the moment until the sound of laughter on the staircase reminded her they weren't alone.

Sophia froze.

Adam drew back, muttering an oath. He took her hand in his. "Let's get out of here."

"Where are we going?" she said breathlessly.

"Back to my house."

Adam made hasty goodbyes for both of them to Mrs. Dalrumple and Claire and soon they were in his carriage. Neither spoke or touched one another during the carriage ride to Richmond house.

Both understood that once released, their desire would wash over them like an avalanche.

Sophia tried to let her mind drift—to ignore the *tap, tap, tap* of Adam's long fingers against the leather seat cushion, the scent of his cologne mingling with tobacco, and the way his throat moved when he swallowed. But try as she might, she couldn't let go of the fact that soon he'd be her lover.

Nor did she fool herself. She wanted this. She understood that whatever happened between them might not last beyond tonight. It was a risk, yes, but one she knew she must take.

At Richmond House, Adam escorted her up the front steps and opened the door.

In the foyer, he gave her coat to the butler. "Fritz, Miss Sophia is done for today. When she's ready for dinner, she'll order a cold tray for her room."

Sophia barely registered Fritz's reply before Adam turned to her and mouthed the words, "Five minutes."

Filled with anticipation, and a good case of nerves, Sophia climbed the stairs and entered her room. She unpinned and brushed her long ebony hair until it crackled and glistened, then changed into the pale-pink silk wrapper she found in the armoire.

Seconds later, Adam opened the door connecting their rooms. He'd shed his tie and jacket and rolled up his sleeves to his elbows.

Gas lamps flickered, casting shadows on his angled face. His gaze slid to her neck. A rush of heat flooded her veins and suddenly the air around her felt thick. She could barely breathe.

''You're beautiful,'' he said softly.

''So are you.'' Her voice sounded as if it belonged to someone else.

Adam pulled her to him and kissed her. His scent and heat enveloped her. She slid her fingers through his thick hair, fisting handfuls as he banded his arms around her narrow waist and hauled her against him. His chest and body were firm, taut with wanting.

Then, with a groan, he scooped her up and carried her to her bed. He laid her down and covered her body with his, kissing her lips, her neck as his hands pushed open the lacy folds of her wrapper. When her breasts were exposed, he suckled her pink nipples until she arched her back.

Letting her body fully enjoy Adam's touch heightened her own desires. She spread her legs, allowing him to press his erection against her nakedness. His kisses, the way he cupped her breasts with his calloused hands, left her breathless. Her stomach tightened; her heart pounded.

Adam raised his head. "I've never wanted a woman like I want you, Sophia."

She smiled, trailing her long fingers down his back. Grabbing a handful of his shirt, she pulled it free from his waistband. He rose and pulled the shirt off, then kissed her again, his passion as hot as the summer sun.

In the dim snowy light, she stared at the lines around his eyes, deepened by desire, and marveled at her womanly power. She brushed her fingers over his buttocks, smiling when she felt his muscles tighten.

He tugged at the sash belting her robe. The cool air rippled over her body, triggering elation and a flicker of embarrassment. Her experience with men had been minimal. She sailed into uncharted waters. Suddenly unsure, she tensed.

Confused by her unexpected hesitation, Adam frowned. "What's wrong?"

She met his gaze. "This is new to me."

Understanding dawned in his eyes and he smiled. "I will show you the way."

Adam slid his fingers between her legs. Immediately, her heart raced and the blood in her body pounded with an unknown anticipation. He stroked her until moist heat dampened his fingers. Sophia tottered on a thin line between pleasure and pain. She moaned his name.

He kissed her again and she could feel his erection pressing against her. Instinctively, she opened her legs to him.

Adam shifted his weight, positioned himself over her then came into her with explosive force, pushing through the tightness in one swift move. She gripped his back, sucking in a breath as her body adjusted to him.

Adam stilled after his first invasion. He kissed her and waited until she grew accustomed to him. Finally, pain gave way to a hotter heat and she began to move beneath him.

He matched her tempo in a timeless dance until his thrusts became a frenzied assault. Her own desire climaxed in a blaze of heat and Sophia called out his name. Adam thrust one last time and spilled his seed inside her.

Afterward, he lay back against the pillow, his chest heaving as if he'd just run a mile. Sophia spooned her body against his and touched his cheek, rough now with unshaven beard. The fire he'd aroused in her still warmed her limbs. For the first time in her life, she understood total joy, fulfillment and love.

And she could almost pretend it would last forever.

"I've heard you're a Russian princess? Is that true?" Adam said just after midnight. He tore off a piece of chicken from the cold plate Fritz had left earlier and fed it to her.

Russia felt very far away to Sophia. "Russia has many princesses."

He lay on his side and rested his head on his palm. "So you are a princess?"

She leaned back against the plumped pillows as if she were telling one of her fairy tales to the children. "My mother used to tell me that once our family was second only in power to the Czar. We had chests filled with rubies, we drank out of gold cups, and we wore the finest sables and minks."

He traced her naked thigh with his finger. "What happened?"

"My grandfather wanted more. He wanted not only the wealth of a Czar but he wanted the power as well. And he tried to take it. Of course, he did not win. He was executed and our family was stripped of its power and wealth. I was about eight when this happened. Everyone, including Papa's family, cut us off and we were exiled to the country. Papa tried to make a go of the land, but he knew nothing of farming or hard work. He died when I was ten."

"That explains why you handled yourself so well today. As if you were born to wealth."

She laughed. "You can thank my *maman* for my manners. She refused to let our change in station alter her plans for me. She trained me in the ways of the court, hoping one day I'd make a good marriage."

"Why did she marry Ivan?"

"He was different then—a master craftsman who was respected by all. He had some money and he liked Mama's old connections to the Czar. She was lonely."

"And they married."

"Yes."

"How did you end up in America?"

"Ivan hoped if he and *maman* petitioned the Czar for forgiveness, they could revive some of the old glory. This did not happen and Ivan was bitterly disappointed. He began to drink more." A sigh lifted her shoulders. "When my *maman* died of the cancer, Ivan's debts began to mount. We came to America to escape them."

His jaw tightened as if he didn't like the story. "He will come back for you, won't he?"

"No, not this time."

He traced the line of her jaw with his fingertip. "Does that bother you?"

She shook her head. "I've known for some

time he'd leave me. It's for the best. We both will move on with our lives now.''

Adam kissed her shoulder. ''I have something for you.'' Unmindful that he was naked, he rose and disappeared into his room. When he returned he carried a small black box. ''This is for you.''

Suspicious, she smoothed her hand over the soft exterior. ''What is this?''

''You will be pleased.''

She cracked open the lid. Inside nestled in silk was her mother's locket, polished and cleaned with a new gold chain threaded through the clasp. Tears sprang in her eyes. ''Where did you get this?''

He kept his expression hooded. ''One of my contacts bought it from Ivan.''

Reverently, she clicked open the locket. The portrait of her mother stared back at her. Her heart clenched with joy.

''At first I thought it was a picture of you,'' he said gruffly. ''Then I realized it had to be your mother.''

A tear slid down her cheek. ''This means more to me than I can say.''

''We're very much the same, Sophia. Family is everything.''

''Yes. Family first.'' She kissed him on the lips. ''Thank you.''

He cleared his throat. "I want to take care of you now. I want to build you a fine house and wrap you in silks."

She closed her fingers over the locket. "I don't need these things."

He kissed her hand. "What do you want?"

You. "A simple home, children, laughter."

"I will give you all that if you'll let me. Stay in Denver, Sophia."

He'd not spoken of love, but she knew she had enough for both of them. "I love you," she dared to whisper.

Happiness softened the lines on his face, but he did not answer in kind.

Sophia cupped his face and pressed her lips to him. Soon, their bodies were entwined and they made love. His lovemaking was just as passionate and intense as the first time, but this time he took his time, savoring every inch of her body.

Hours later, Sophia awoke to the morning sun shining in the window. She lay on her side, her body cradled in Adam's arms. As much as she wanted to stay in bed and make love to Adam all day, it was Monday and she had to finish tuning the pipe organ.

It took every ounce of her willpower to rise from the bed and dress. Adam awoke as she laced up her second boot.

Sophia smiled at him, knowing there'd never be another man for her. "Good morning."

He swung his legs over the side of the bed. "Where are you going?"

"To the church. If I leave now, and if I am lucky, I will have the organ finished by sundown."

All traces of good humor vanished from his face. "After last night, everything changed between us. We are on the same side now."

Confused by his shift in mood, she shoved her arms into her sheepskin coat. "We are."

His shoulders stiffened. "Then why are you going to finish the organ?"

Her body stilled. "I gave my word."

He stood, took hold of her arms. "I want to build you a beautiful home, shower you with silks, give you children. But you must not finish the organ, otherwise Nelson won't leave Denver. Do this one thing for me and you will have me forever."

She jerked free. *"This one thing...?"* Her heart contracted as if the life were being squeezed out of it. "These things you will do for me as long as I do as you say."

He jabbed his hands through his hair. "Sophia, you've seen enough of the world to know nothing's free."

Her heart shattered in that moment. "I thought what we had was different."

"It is, but you must be practical."

Sophia felt as if the earth was shattering under her feet. Pride kept her shoulders back. "I must finish the organ."

All the warmth drained from his body. What remained was the cold, chiseled man she'd met just days ago. "Either you are with me or against me," he said tightly.

Shock and a wrenching sadness sliced her heart. Such a fool she'd been.

Through the blur of tears, she summoned the strength to turn and walk out the door.

CHAPTER TEN

ADAM STARED out his bedroom window and watched Sophia walk away. The sun was already turning warm and turning the ice to slush.

Like the snow on a sunny day, she melted never to be seen again.

Sophia's tale of the Snow Maiden had been a grim harbinger of today.

Without her, the house had taken on an eerie silence and for the first time in a very long time, he felt utterly alone in the world.

After what he had said, he knew she wasn't coming back to him. Her pride and sense of honor wouldn't let her. Both were just two reasons why he loved her so much. And why he'd lost her.

The pipe organ, ousting Nelson didn't matter anymore. What mattered was Sophia.

He quickly dressed and thundered into the foyer. "Fritz! Get my coat!"

Almost instantly, the butler appeared with

Adam's coat. Adam slid his arms into the coat with the butler's assistance.

"I'll summon the driver," Fritz said.

Adam accepted his leather gloves from Fritz. "Don't bother, I can move faster on foot."

Adam jerked open the front door. To his surprise he found Claire and Nelson standing there, ready to enter.

Claire glanced up. "Adam, I didn't expect you home this time of day."

Nelson too looked surprised but he recovered first. "Mr. Richmond."

"Nelson, Claire. I don't have time to talk now. I'll be back soon."

Nelson cleared his throat. "Mr. Richmond, we have other news for you."

With great effort, Adam stopped and turned. "It'll have to wait."

Claire tugged off her glove and held out her hand to him. A shiny gold ring banded her ring finger. "We got married last night!"

He mouthed the words, "I'll be damned."

Nelson rushed to say, "We were married in a small chapel on the edge of town." The young man stared him squarely in the eyes and there was no hint of apology or fear. Claire stared up at her new husband, her face beaming with adoration.

Swallowing a lump in his throat, he held out his hand to Nelson. "Take care of her."

Nelson's expression registered his shock but his handshake was firm. "I will."

Adam kissed his sister on the cheek. "Be happy."

She clung to him, choking back tears. "I will." When he released her she stared up at him, worried. She touched his face, then squeezed Adam's hand none too gently. "We just passed Sophia on the street. She was crying."

Adam's gut twisted into knots.

"You've got to set things right with Sophia," Claire said.

"I intend to do just that."

SOPHIA'S MIND WAS muddled with sadness and grief when she stepped into the church sanctuary. She shrugged off her coat as she looked at the pipe organ.

It was stunning. Its polished mahogany and walnut trim and brass pipes glistened in the bright sunlight shining through the stained glass windows. Joy and pride mingled with loss and sadness.

Adam.

Suddenly her legs wobbled and she sank down on the organ's bench. Her eyes filled with unshed tears. "How many tears before the pain eases?" she whispered.

The sanctuary door banged open. "Sophia!" Adam's rich voice reverberated off the walls.

Sophia stood and faced him. The closeness they'd shared had vanished. "I intend to finish the organ."

Desolation deepened the lines on his face as he strode toward her. His gaze didn't waver from her. "I was wrong." His hand under her chin, he tipped her head up. "I'll help you finish the organ."

Confused, she stepped back. "Why are you saying this to me now?"

"I love you."

She stood very still. "I fear your kind of love, Adam. You say you love Claire, yet you've done all you can to keep her from the man she loves. Your love comes with conditions."

"Claire and Nelson were married yesterday."

His news shocked her. She searched his eyes for the anger. There was none. "What are you going to do about it?"

"Nothing."

Warily, she moved a step closer. "You will not try to destroy what they have?"

He shook his head. "No. I'll always be there for Claire if she needs me. But she's made her choice." He took her hand in his. "Marry me Sophia, today."

She wanted to fling herself into his arms, but she held herself back. "I will not change for you. I will be a very willful wife."

"I wouldn't have it any other way." He held her hand tighter. "I'll take you to Russia if that's what you want. I'll track Ivan down and ask his permission. I want to do this right." For the first time, Adam Richmond seemed to struggle for words. "I should have a ring. There should be roses."

She'd never been filled with such joy. "I don't need any of those things." She wrapped her arms around him, savored his scent. "All I want is you."

"You'll marry me?"

"Yes, most definitely yes."

He kissed her until she was breathless. "Then I'm taking you home. Nelson's got a job to do. Let's get that organ finished."

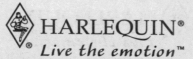

HEAD FOR THE ROCKIES WITH

 Harlequin Historicals®
Historical Romantic Adventure!

AND SEE HOW IT ALL BEGAN!

COLORADO
CONFIDENTIAL

**Check out these three historicals
connected to the bestselling Intrigue series**

CHEYENNE WIFE
by Judith Stacy
January 2004

COLORADO COURTSHIP
by Carolyn Davidson
February 2004

ROCKY MOUNTAIN MARRIAGE
by Debra Lee Brown
March 2004

Available at your favorite retail outlet.

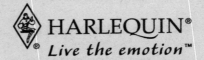 HARLEQUIN®
Live the emotion™

Visit us at www.eHarlequin.com

HHCC

From Regency romps
to mesmerizing Medievals,
savor these stirring tales from
Harlequin Historicals®

On sale January 2004

THE KNAVE AND THE MAIDEN by Blythe Gifford

A cynical knight's life is forever changed when he falls
in love with a naive young woman while journeying
to a holy shrine.

MARRYING THE MAJOR by Joanna Maitland

Can a war hero wounded in body and spirit find
happiness with his childhood sweetheart, now that she
has become the toast of London society?

On sale February 2004

THE CHAPERON BRIDE by Nicola Cornick

When England's most notorious rake is attracted to
a proper ladies' chaperon, could it be true love?

THE WEDDING KNIGHT by Joanne Rock

A dashing knight abducts a young woman to marry his
brother, but soon falls in love with her instead!

Visit us at www.eHarlequin.com

HARLEQUIN HISTORICALS®

HHMED34

If you enjoyed what you just read,
then we've got an offer you can't resist!

Take 2
bestselling novels FREE!
Plus get a FREE surprise gift!

Clip this page and mail it to The Best of the Best™

IN U.S.A.	IN CANADA
3010 Walden Ave.	P.O. Box 609
P.O. Box 1867	Fort Erie, Ontario
Buffalo, N.Y. 14240-1867	L2A 5X3

YES! Please send me 2 free Best of the Best™ novels and my free surprise gift. After receiving them, if I don't wish to receive anymore, I can return the shipping statement marked cancel. If I don't cancel, I will receive 4 brand-new novels every month, before they're available in stores! In the U.S.A., bill me at the bargain price of $4.74 plus 25¢ shipping and handling per book and applicable sales tax, if any*. In Canada, bill me at the bargain price of $5.24 plus 25¢ shipping and handling per book and applicable taxes**. That's the complete price and a savings of over 20% off the cover prices—what a great deal! I understand that accepting the 2 free books and gift places me under no obligation ever to buy any books. I can always return a shipment and cancel at any time. Even if I never buy another The Best of the Best™ book, the 2 free books and gift are mine to keep forever.

185 MDN DNWF
385 MDN DNWG

Name	(PLEASE PRINT)	
Address	Apt.#	
City	State/Prov.	Zip/Postal Code

* Terms and prices subject to change without notice. Sales tax applicable in N.Y.
** Canadian residents will be charged applicable provincial taxes and GST.
  All orders subject to approval. Offer limited to one per household and not valid to
  current The Best of the Best™ subscribers.
  ® are registered trademarks of Harlequin Enterprises Limited.

BOB02-R   ©1998 Harlequin Enterprises Limited

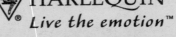

PICK UP THESE HARLEQUIN HISTORICALS AND IMMERSE YOURSELF IN THRILLING AND EMOTIONAL LOVE STORIES SET IN THE AMERICAN FRONTIER

On sale January 2004

CHEYENNE WIFE by Judith Stacy
(Colorado, 1844)

Will opposites attract when a handsome
half-Cheyenne horse trader comes to the rescue
of a proper young lady from back east?

WHIRLWIND BRIDE by Debra Cowan
(Texas, 1883)

A widowed rancher unexpectedly falls in love with
a beautiful and pregnant young woman.

On sale February 2004

COLORADO COURTSHIP by Carolyn Davidson
(Colorado, 1862)

A young widow finds a father for her unborn child—
and a man for her heart—in a loving wagon train scout.

THE LIGHTKEEPER'S WOMAN by Mary Burton
(North Carolina, 1879)

When an heiress reunites with her former fiancée,
will they rekindle their romance or say goodbye
once and for all?

Visit us at www.eHarlequin.com

HARLEQUIN HISTORICALS®

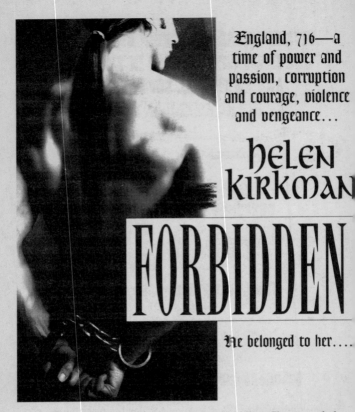
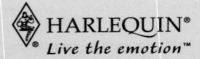

Praise for
Heart of Brass

"Fabulously entertaining—a great romance in an inventive, believable steampunk world!"
—Stephanie Laurens, *New York Times* bestselling author of *The Capture of the Earl of Glencrae*

"*Heart of Brass* is riveting! I couldn't put it down. I can't wait for the next book. Kate Cross is fabulous!"
—Victoria Alexander, #1 *New York Times* bestselling author of *My Wicked Little Lies*

OUT OF THE VAPORS

Five paused in the stairwell of his lodgings and pressed the heel of one palm to his forehead. It felt as though there was something worrying at his brain—like a cat pawing at a closed door.

Luke.

He clung to the rail with one hand, trying to keep himself from falling down the narrow stairs as *her* voice rang in his head. He hadn't been able to get it out. Every time he thought of her, pain followed.

Luke. It was what she had said to him in her bedroom. She had said it like he should recognize it, and just now it had sounded almost plaintive—regretful.

She knew him, and though he knew everything about her he didn't know the connection. She had the upper hand—had him at a disadvantage. That she made him feel that way was simply one more reason to kill her. And he would. . . .

HEART
of BRASS

A NOVEL OF THE CLOCKWORK AGENTS

KATE CROSS

A SIGNET ECLIPSE BOOK

SIGNET ECLIPSE
Published by New American Library, a division of
Penguin Group (USA) Inc., 375 Hudson Street,
New York, New York 10014, USA
Penguin Group (Canada), 90 Eglinton Avenue East, Suite 700, Toronto,
Ontario M4P 2Y3, Canada (a division of Pearson Penguin Canada Inc.)
Penguin Books Ltd., 80 Strand, London WC2R 0RL, England
Penguin Ireland, 25 St. Stephen's Green, Dublin 2,
Ireland (a division of Penguin Books Ltd.)
Penguin Group (Australia), 250 Camberwell Road, Camberwell, Victoria 3124,
Australia (a division of Pearson Australia Group Pty. Ltd.)
Penguin Books India Pvt. Ltd., 11 Community Centre, Panchsheel Park,
New Delhi - 110 017, India
Penguin Group (NZ), 67 Apollo Drive, Rosedale, Auckland 0632,
New Zealand (a division of Pearson New Zealand Ltd.)
Penguin Books (South Africa) (Pty.) Ltd., 24 Sturdee Avenue,
Rosebank, Johannesburg 2196, South Africa

Penguin Books Ltd., Registered Offices:
80 Strand, London WC2R 0RL, England

First published by Signet Eclipse, an imprint of New American Library,
a division of Penguin Group (USA) Inc.

First Printing, May 2012
10 9 8 7 6 5 4 3 2 1

ALWAYS LEARNING   PEARSON

This book is for Joey and Allison, who started out as steampunk acquaintances and quickly became two of my favorite people. I'm so glad my research led me to you!

It is also for my husband, Steve, who will gladly put on a top hat and frock coat and venture to a convention with me. Sweetie, you're the best.

Chapter 1

London, the Age of Steam

"You shouldn't go in there, ma'am. 'Tis no place for a lady."

Arden Grey, known in polite circles as Lady Huntley, and in less polite as "that poor woman," carried a small carpetbag in her gloved hand as she approached the factory door, pewter-colored skirts swishing around her matching pumps. Overhead the lights of a police dirigible swept across the scene, illuminating the night in a wash of glaring silver.

The veil attached to her tiny black top hat did nothing to shield her eyes, and Arden squinted against the intrusive brightness. "You will soon learn, sir, that I am not the usual sort of lady." She'd been born and bred to be one, even married an earl to maintain the illusion, but during her unusual life she'd seen and heard—*and done*—too many dark things to own such a gentle, ignorant title.

The Scotland Yard man tugged the brim of his hat at

her in reply, and stepped back so she might pass. It was obvious from the tight set of his lips that he opposed her presence most vehemently, but knew his place well enough not to voice his disapproval again. In this thoroughly modern world there were still those who believed a woman ought to keep to home, rather than engage in any manner of business.

Tell that to Queen Victoria.

Sagging floorboards creaked under her boots as she entered B. E. Hammond & Sons, the varnish long since worn off this particular section of wood. The foyer was well lit and unassuming, and smelled vaguely of oil and metal. It was quiet now, but during the day this entire building would hum and vibrate with the sounds of working machines. The air would be humid and thick, tasting of steam and the sharp tang of industry.

She fancied she could smell blood, but it was most likely copper. When people used to oppose her father's support of the Automatization Movement, he would reply that it could not be a coincidence that the very life in a man's veins smelled like the same metal used to construct early automatons. He died in the middle of building what would have been his finest work, a piece that now sat hunched, gears gummed up, in the corner of his W.O.R. laboratory. Four years it had sat there, and despite all the brilliant minds the Wardens of the Realm—the mysterious government agency to which Arden herself belonged—set to work in that room, the project had yet to be completed. Arden had even provided them with the schematics of the machine, but to no avail. The automaton remained elusive, an example of her father's genius that would never come to fruition, though the Wardens would continue to try.

Then again, she was a fine one to throw stones, she who clung to a hopeless dream.

Another Scotland Yard man came through a set of double doors and paused there, holding one of them open. "This way, Lady Huntley—if you please."

No, she didn't please, but she walked past the man and through the doorway all the same. She'd rather be at home with a glass—or several—of fine Scotch whiskey, but she'd been summoned here instead. Granted, it had been a welcome rescue from insipid conversation and weak sherry with a group of females who would inevitably take her aside one by one and ask her if she might construct one of her "special devices" for them.

Few people knew the extent of her talents. To most of the world she was simply Lady Huntley, a woman who refused to accept that her husband was most likely dead. She wasn't the mechanical genius that her father was, but she had made a bit of a reputation amongst her sex for an invention she stumbled upon quite by accident. A device very similar—but far superior—to one sold by B. E. Hammond & Sons. It could have been quite scandalous, but since one of the Princesses Royal privately declared it a "miracle of modern medical science" in the field of feminine health, scandal became discreet acclaim. A treatment for "hysteria" that did not require the indiscretion of a trip to a sanitorium, but could be used in the privacy of a lady's boudoir.

The delicate silver chains that hung from the piercing on the side of Arden's nose across her cheek to her right ear quivered under the ceiling fans as she entered the large open room of the factory's assembly department. Recently she'd increased the number of chains from six to seven. One for every year her husband had been missing.

Missing. Not dead.

Two more Scotland Yard men—peelers as they were often called—stood with another man she assumed to be the senior Mr. Hammond, based on the distressed look on his face.

The policemen removed their hats when they spotted her. One of them was Inspector Grant, with whom she'd worked on several prior cases. Mr. Hammond held his fine, but worn, beaver top hat in his shaking hands. His graying hair stuck up in tufts around his head, as though he'd had his hands tugging at it. He had the countenance of a man who had seen—or done—something he should dearly like to forget.

As she approached, Arden withdrew what looked like a small lady's compact from her bag. She pointed the device in the direction of the factory owner and watched the tiny hand beneath the glass swing around like the needle of a compass, finally coming to land on the word REMORSE. The sentimentometer was one of her favorites of all her father's work, even though he'd developed it when she was but a child to determine whether or not she had done something naughty.

She snapped the lid shut and slipped the brass mechanism back into her bag. "Gentlemen."

"Lady Huntley." Inspector Grant greeted her with a curt nod—his only deference to her station. "Thank you for leaving your evening's entertainments to aid us in this grim affair."

"No thanks required, Inspector," Arden replied in her usual crisp tones that often sounded far too severe for her liking. Lucas used to tell her she had the voice of a governess. "What has happened?"

The inspector pointed his pencil at the pale gentleman to his left. "Mr. Hammond was working late this evening in his office above stairs. When he came down to check everything was as it should be for the night, he found the body of a young woman." He gestured for her to follow him and she did. The factory owner stayed behind, working the brim of his hat until it threatened to lose all shape.

"Did you take a reading of Hammond?" Grant asked quietly as they maneuvered through the jammed workspace of wooden tables littered with tools, automaton parts and gears. "Says he was listening to phonographic discs as he worked and didn't hear a peep from down here."

She shook her head, gaze wandering distractedly over the tabletops. "I detected no guilt or malevolence from him. But he does feel remorse. Could be a guilty conscious, or perhaps he is simply mortified that a crime was committed on his property with him being none the wiser." She stopped and picked up a rubber tube that was shaped like . . . a penis. She held it up with her forefinger and thumb, dangling it in all its flaccid splendor in front of the inspector's face. "I didn't know that the Hammonds had begun to incorporate rubber in their designs."

Grant flushed a deep red—the color of a cooked beet. He couldn't quite meet her gaze. "Er . . . yes. You may be aware that Hammond started this factory to make medical instruments to aid in the treatment of hysteria. He was one of the first manufacturers of automatons in England." He cleared his throat, as though he wanted to say more but didn't quite know how to word it, or how to justify it.

He didn't have to. Arden knew all about Hammond and his inventions. A contemporary of her father's, some of his earlier designs were rather ingenious, but it was his work in the field of mechanized human "marital enhancements" that had made him one of the wealthiest businessmen in the kingdom. Any man who dedicated his life's work to the carnal pleasure and emotional well-being of women couldn't be all that bad, could he?

But a murder certainly wouldn't be good for business.

A few steps on she spied a female automaton lying on one of the tables, its realistic limbs splayed, revealing a degree of anatomical correctness that would have made a bawd blush. Arden's lips tucked to one side in a caustic smile. Mr. Hammond obviously had decided to tackle the treatment of gentlemanly vigor as well.

Inspector Grant threw a tarp over the machine, but whether he did so to protect Arden's delicate sensibilities or his own was a mystery that she hadn't the inclination to pursue. Though it did not take even an ounce of emotional sensitivity to ascertain that the inspector was deeply mortified.

When they neared the end of the aisle, Arden detected a familiar, unpleasant odor, one she associated with murder: a mix of what she could only describe as fear, blood, and chamber pot.

Two more peelers and Inspector Grant stood between her and the source of that smell. Well, most of it.

The leg in the torn stocking and expensive silk pump looked like that of a burlesque automaton at first, so white and still was it. Were it not for the blood staining that stocking she might have been able to tell herself that it *was* merely a machine.

"I beg your pardon, Lady Huntley," Grant said in that faint northern accent of his. "But this isn't a pretty sight. You may turn back if you like."

She gave him what she hoped was a grateful smile and not a grim twisting of her lips. She'd often been told her smile could sometimes look a little . . . demented. "Your concern does you credit, Inspector. I assure you I shall endure whatever it is you wish me to see." She could do without seeing a dead body, particularly a bloody one, but if these men could look at it dispassionately then damn it, so could she. It wasn't as though it was her first corpse.

Inspector Grant's face was a resigned shade of pale beneath his muttonchops and heavy mustache. He nodded in acquiescence. "Pull back the sheet please, Mr. Fence."

An ashen-faced youth swallowed hard and bent down to do as he was instructed. Arden's confidence in being able to escape the viewing with the contents of her stomach intact diminished slightly.

The sheet—stained and wet with so much blood it was almost black in spots—pulled back with the resistance of the rind of an orange reluctant to leave the flesh beneath, to reveal the head of a pretty young woman wearing pearl earrings. Her neck was long, decorated with a matching pearl necklace, but beyond that . . . a pile of raw meat. Arden stared for a moment, her eyes not quite able to make her brain see reality. Finally, after a few moments—and a rather inspired bout of gagging from young Mr. Fence—she saw the scene for what it was.

Someone, or something, had torn this precious little girl apart. Her pale blue eyes were wide open, as was her Cupid's bow mouth. Her flawless skin, the pale robin's-egg waxy color of death, was dotted with freckles of blood. She was not a factory worker—a pair of fine silk gloves lay not far from her body. Nor was she a member of the demimonde, for she was far too fresh and sweet looking, and not nearly as fashionable. Her demure, ruined gown cost more than what the retching Mr. Fence probably made in a month.

She was a member of the upper classes, quite possibly of noble birth.

Dear God.

Mindful of her skirts, she lifted them as she moved around the clotted puddle to stand at the girl's head. She squatted down, tugging off her right glove so her fingers could touch the porcelain coolness of a stiff, delicate wrist. The girl had been dead for several hours—long enough for her body to lose all warmth and become fairly rigid.

A thin bruise spread like a stain beneath Arden's fingers. She glanced up at Inspector Grant. The older man was the only one of the three who didn't look ill. He was too experienced, too little shocked by humanity's capacity for violence to be sickened by it anymore. Instead, he looked resigned. And worried. A murdered debutante meant trouble on so many levels for a man in his position.

"She was bound?" she inquired, swallowing against the rolling of her own stomach.

Grant nodded, his shrewd gaze resting on the ravaged girl. "Most likely the bugger—pardon my French, my lady—brought the poor gel here by force."

It was possible, she supposed, but this bruise was purple and slightly yellow, not the usual raw red that one would expect if she had been recently restrained. This bruising was older and could have many causes.

The inspector jerked his head toward the entrance. "Fence, Brown, make use of yourself elsewhere." He watched as the two relieved young men walked away before navigating around the corpse to squat beside her. "Do you think you might . . . be able to use your apparatus on her?"

That was often why she was brought to such scenes. And dear Grant was always so considerate to never take her compliance as a certainty. It was her father who had come up with the general principles of the mechanism prior to his death, and Arden who completed the device. If he hadn't left so many unfinished projects, who knew what might have become of her? Mourning him and missing Huntley, she might have done something rash, especially without her mother to turn to, but instead she turned to cogs and gears and the reassuring hum of steam engines. Loss had given her more purpose than she'd ever wanted before.

"I will try," she told him, as she had every other time he asked. She rested the bottom of her carpetbag on her bent knees and pulled the mouth of it wide open. She didn't have to rummage through a muddle of automata and tools as her father always had, because she had outfitted the case with internal straps and pockets to hold each and every item. She barely had to look in at all to find what she wanted—two pairs of specially augmented goggles, connected by coils of wires.

"Inspector, if you would be so kind?"

Grant's gaze jerked up from the mechanism. "Of course." He took the bag from her lap and placed it to his left, as far from the carnage as his reach allowed. "Explain to me again how these Aetheric Reminiscent Oscillation Goggles work."

Despite the smell and horrific visage before her, Arden smiled slightly as she placed the more ornate pair of goggles over the girl's open eyes. She had begun using the device two years ago and the inspector had yet to refer to it by the correct name. "Aetheric Remnant Oscillatory Transmutative Spectacles," she corrected. "You could use the acronym A.R.O.T.S. if you prefer."

He shook his head. "I'd rather not use the term 'rot' in any capacity given the circumstances, my lady—with all due respect."

Arden glanced at the girl's decimated torso and the decay that had already begun, as she carefully placed the small metal prongs of the headgear on the appropriate spots on the poor thing's skull. "Indeed. You are familiar, of course, with Aether?"

"Of course," he sounded vaguely affronted that she had to ask. "It's the Breath of God."

As a woman whose religion was more science than spirituality, it took considerable restraint for Arden not to argue with the inspector. However, she was not one to besmirch another's beliefs, no matter how ill-informed she believed them to be. "The energy of every living creature, yes," she said. "Some believe it to be the soul, while science argues that it is the result of an electro-chemical process in living tissue that lingers even after we shuck our mortal coil."

Grant sniffed. "Sounds a bit far-fetched to me."

But the "Breath of God" did not? A god who took her husband away from her? Who killed her father and made her mother . . . what she was? If it was the breath of such a creature that gave the engine of her heart fire then she would rather suffocate on a cold hearth. For every religious zealot there was another who decreed the Aether as the playground of the Devil himself.

"Regardless," she continued through a clenched jaw, "there is no dispute that sometimes this energy lingers— around a body, or in a place where the person met their end. These goggles allow me to see the last things this young lady saw by utilizing that very energy." The dark lenses over the sightless eyes of the girl would prevent any light or new images from penetrating once the prongs stimulated the appropriate areas of her brain, es-sentially restoring them to life for a short period. Once engaged, the optical response would parlay those images to Arden's own goggles, where she would view the expe-rience as though it were her own.

"Bloody amazing," Grant allowed. Then, with fresh pink suffusing his cheeks, "Beg your pardon, my lady."

Arden waved his concern away with a flick of her wrist. Then, something caught her eye. She frowned. "In-spector, did Hammond or your men rearrange her cloth-ing?"

"No, ma'am. She's exactly as she was found."

Frowning, she leaned closer, and using the ear wire of the goggles in her hand, lifted the edge of torn gown. A small, bare breast, smeared with crimson, lay beneath. Elsewhere the fabric molded to the gore-soaked area, but not here.

"He took care to cover her," she murmured.

The inspector nodded, seemingly unimpressed by her keen detection. "I reckon the monster knew her."

Arden settled back on her heels. Her knees were beginning to ache from squatting so long. "Let's see if she knew him as well, shall we?" She wiped the ear wire with her handkerchief before placing the second pair of goggles on her own face. With them on she was practically blind, and would remain so until the image transfer began.

Then she would see things she would later regret seeing.

She wound the key protruding from the side of the small control box attached by even more wires to both sets of eye gear. The simple engine inside, attuned as it was to Aetheric energy—a vast resource Arden believed could rival steam and even the new wonder of electricity— whirred to life, sending a charge to the dead girl's mind.

Fuzzy images began to swirl before her eyes, dim and out of focus. She adjusted dials on either side of her goggles, making the images a little clearer. Sometimes, depending on how long the subject had been dead, she had to use all the lenses and settings she had to work with, and even then sometimes she only got a grainy, half-formed image.

She was not to be so fortunate that evening. She had barely slipped the secondary lenses into place when everything came together in razor-sharp clarity.

The girl was running through the aisles of this very factory, the world jostled around her as a man in evening clothes chased her. She saw only his shoulder and part of his side, not his face, but she didn't appear to be running for her life, but with the lazy gait of a girl wishing to be caught. And catch her he did, turning her in his arms. A man's torso came into view—neither too broad nor too thin. His cravat was perfectly tied, decorated with an onyx pin in the shape of a horseshoe.

Arden's heart quickened, as it often did in these macabre situations. Everything was so keen, and sharp. If she could find a way to determine the emotional state and auditory memory as well, it truly would be an immersive experience.

The girl's arms reached for the man, whose face remained maddeningly out of sight. Slowly, her gaze lifted, past the cravat pin, to the throat and jaw of the man wearing it, then the mouth.

"Just a little further," Arden whispered as her heart pounded hard against her ribs. "Come on, dearest. Just a little more."

The world seemed to jump in front of her eyes. Her gaze dropped from the man to the space between their bodies.

Arden cried out.

Her chest was ripped open.

"Lady Huntley!" It was Grant. She could feel his warm hand on her arm. "My lady, are you all right?"

She shook her head, afraid that she would indeed vomit if she opened her mouth. Her hands clutched at the spectacles, and she wanted nothing more than to rip them off her face, but she held on until the images before her faded to blackness, signaling the girl's death. Only when she was certain there was nothing more to see did she remove the apparatus from her own head.

"My dear lady," Grant began, staring at her with wide eyes. "You look . . ."

"Like hell," Arden supplied, smiling at his surprise. Just as quickly her mirth vanished. "He ripped her open while she was alive. She felt it. Saw it."

The inspector turned his gaze toward the dead girl just as Arden did. He reached out and stroked the girl's hair, as a father might. "Poor thing."

"Indeed," Arden muttered, attempting to pull herself together. She raised the back of her hand to her nose and took a deep, calming breath. The bergamot she'd dabbed on her glove lessened the scent of death, reminded her of happier things.

"I didn't see his face, unfortunately. All I can tell you is that he wore expensive clothes and had an onyx cravat pin in the shape of a horseshoe." She sighed. "She knew him. They were lovers. If those marks on her wrists were made by him, they were done so with her consent, and before this rendezvous."

Inspector Grant went pale beneath the dark of his whiskers. "Knew him, you say?"

Arden met his gaze evenly, her typical tight rein over her emotions returning. "Yes. You are not wrong to be alarmed, Inspector. I'm fairly certain your madman is an aristocrat as well."

The inspector swore beneath his breath, and this time he did not apologize for his language. Arden didn't blame him. She'd curse as well, for the inspector's chances of catching this monster just dropped considerably, never mind the odds of actually bringing him to justice.

"If she'd only looked at him I might be able to identify him," she mused ruefully.

Grant shook his head and patted her shoulder one last time before he remembered his station and removed his hand. "Do not fault yourself, my lady. You have been of enormous assistance already."

As Arden removed the spectacles from the girl and

used her palm to close her eyes, she didn't feel as though she'd been of much use at all. She quickly ran through the images in her mind once more. "He was older. Not elderly, but not a boy—perhaps in his late twenties or thirties."

The inspector wrote this down in his little leather-bound notebook.

"And, Inspector Grant?" When he looked up from his writing she said softly, "You should request Dr. Stone examine the body."

A soft flush flooded the lawman's face. The poor thing really had no idea how to handle such situations. He had more modesty than a fourteen-year-old girl. "I see."

Dr. Evelyn Stone was generally employed by Scotland Yard when a female victim had been molested in some way, but her talents were more extensively employed by the Wardens. The brilliant young woman had machines and formulas for making identifications and finding insights into crimes that baffled and impressed the agency to no end.

"She may find something that will aid in our investigation."

Inspector Grant's head snapped up. "*Our* investigation, my lady?"

Arden's lips twisted into a grim smile. "You're going to require my ongoing assistance with this one, sir. I travel in the same circles as our killer, and can therefore go where you cannot."

"Lady Huntley, I cannot allow you to put yourself in harm's way." He was clearly flustered. "To include you so thoroughly in a Yard investigation would be grossly unfair, not to mention ungentlemanly of me."

Not to mention it was terribly gauche of her—a lady—to engage in such horrid pursuits. No doubt that had much to do with her desire to do it.

"*You*, my dear friend, cannot prevent it," she informed him with a touch of warmth to her determined tone. She rose easily to her feet. "Now, do be a good boy and accept that you are powerless in this instance, and escort me back to my carriage."

Being the considerate gentleman he was, Inspector Grant could not refuse a lady's request—especially not the request of such a high-ranking lady as a countess. He also stood and offered her his arm, which she took with a faint smile on her lips.

Arden was all too happy to leave the awful vision of that poor girl behind, but she knew the memory of the sight, as well as what the girl had seen, would linger for at least a fortnight until she managed to put them away with all the other awful things she'd ever seen and buried. Or drowned.

Each peeler she passed tipped his hat and bid her a good evening. The transport team was there to collect the body, and the "cleaners" had arrived to ensure all evidence was collected and every trace of the crime erased. It was standard protocol when the details of a crime were to be kept undisclosed, and since the young woman obviously was of good birth, they had been brought in to save the family from being dragged through more unpleasant scandal than necessary.

Such precautions also kept the jackals of the press from plastering the tragedy all over the pages of the papers and sending the country into a paranoid tizzy that another Jack the Ripper was on the loose. They'd learned their lesson with that particular nasty piece of work.

"You have my gratitude for coming here tonight, my lady," Inspector Grant spoke, as he opened the door of her carriage. Two metal steps flipped down.

Arden turned to him, one foot on the bottom step. "That's very lovely of you to say, Inspector. Thank you."

It wasn't as though she had a choice—it was her duty. Even though she did not answer to Scotland Yard, she reported to the Wardens—an organization higher up the clandestine ladder—and they would expect her to do all she could to aid in the apprehension of this monster.

Grant nodded, and closed the door once she was inside the vehicle. The driver started up the steam engine, and within moments the carriage jerked into motion, the comforting chug filling the interior.

Arden leaned back against the cushioned seat, a wave of weariness washing over her. She was just about to close her eyes when the dirigible made another pass overhead, illuminating the factory yard. Something— someone—on the roof of the factory made her sit bolt upright.

The factory was only two floors, so the distance to the roof wasn't that far, but when she looked up she swore her eyes were wrong, that they were deceiving her.

The man on the roof was dressed in black, so she couldn't tell if he had blood on him or not, and he dove out of sight when the bright light washed over him. However, his clothing wasn't what caught her attention, but his face. A face she knew as well as her own. A face she had once traced every inch of with her fingers, kissed with her lips.

It was the face of her husband.

Chapter 2

His target had escaped him.

The man called Five ran along the roof, keeping to the shadows to avoid the damned dirigible and its glaring light. Below him the carriage carrying his prey rolled through the damp cobblestone street. He kept pace with it as he ran, approaching the edge of the factory roof with an easy speed.

When he reached the edge he jumped and hit the ground in a crouch, the impact reverberating through the heavy soles of his boots as his coat flared out around him. The cobblestones seemed to groan under the impact.

Nimbly, he lunged into his former pace, keeping almost abreast of the vehicle as it traveled through the semideserted street. Not a lot of traffic in this industrial part of the city at this time of night—only the factory workers on the night shift, and they were too busy slaving away or sneaking out for a smoke or a suck of gin to notice an abnormally fast man race by.

Moisture hung in the air, the by-product of so many

steam engines—as though London wasn't damp enough. It permeated his skin and clothes, causing the long leather coat to cling to him uncomfortably. Still, he ran.

An old-fashioned carriage hauled by polished brass automaton horses rolled down the street toward him, metal hooves clomping sharply on the stones, steam billowing from the exhaustion vents disguised as nostrils. It was a hearse, probably on its way to the factory where he had tracked his prey.

"Is it done?"

He was accustomed to the voice in his head now, the intrusive demands familiar instead of distressing. It made the sharing of information particularly simple.

"Not yet," he replied in a low tone.

"What's the delay?"

He turned a corner, following the carriage down another street. "Peelers."

"Avoid apprehension at all costs. Take extra care if you must, but do not fail."

"Failure is not an option." Onward he ran, not the least bit winded. He was rarely ever out of breath anymore— it was the way they'd made him.

He didn't remember what he had been before the Company found him. He was told he had been a criminal of some kind, that he was being offered a new beginning—a chance to repay his debt to society. Now, he was extraordinary, a weapon against evil.

Though the lady in that carriage didn't look evil to him. In fact he'd been rather startled by her face. It wasn't that it was a particularly beautiful face—he'd seen prettier women—but there was something about her auburn hair, peaches-and-cream complexion and shapely mouth that gave him pause.

Nothing gave him pause. Not ever.

He followed the carriage all the way to the exclusive

Mayfair part of London. Despite having no memory of ever being there before, it had seemed strangely familiar when he first happened upon it earlier that evening. When he spied on his target from outside a ballroom window he thought he saw people he knew, but for the life of him he could not remember their names or how he might have come to make their acquaintance.

The only explanation was that he had been so well and efficiently briefed on this Arden Chillingham Grey—Lady Huntley—that she and all her friends seemed recognizable to him. That had to be the reason he felt as though he could find his way through her sandstone mansion with his eyes shut.

The carriage pulled up to the front of the house. A footman readily appeared to assist his mistress from the vehicle as Five watched from his perch atop the high wall that surrounded the house and grounds. When the lady was inside and the carriage on its way round back to the stables, he jumped off the wall and ran across the damp, perfectly manicured grass to the back of the house.

A patrol automaton—man-sized and armed with pistols for hands—came up from a hole that had opened in the ground. Five leaped back into the shadows to avoid detection. The metal had no face save for a pair of irisless eyes that served as scanners, searching for unfamiliar life forms. Slowly, it stepped off its platform onto the grass, the hole grinding closed behind it. It would likely patrol the grounds until dawn and then return to its grave. Fortunately, it strode off in the opposite direction of where Five remained hidden. By the time it made a full rotation, he would be gone.

Then he heard the sound of another hole—rusting metal screeching in his ears—opening behind him.

Bloody hell.

Five slipped around the corner as fast as a blink. Gaslights flickered along a gravel path that led to a lush garden, casting a warm glow that he tried to avoid as he crept closer to a trellis against the side of the house. Private security automatons were sensitive to sound as well as movement. A sneeze or wrong step might very well bring one or both of them down upon him. He could probably destroy each with relative ease, but the noise was bound to raise the alarm inside.

An assassin's best weapon was stealth. Right now he had to be fast as well.

He took a running leap and jumped, pushing himself up with a brief foothold on a ground-floor window casing to grab the edge of the balcony above. He pulled his body up enough so that he could wrap one hand around the balustrade. From there it was easy to maneuver up and over.

The balcony was dark, but the room beyond illuminated with a single lamp. Five peered between the parted gauzy drapes to gauge his location.

It was a bedroom—large and clearly feminine. Could he be so fortunate as to have climbed to the lady's chamber to discover nothing but a layer of fragile glass between them?

Sure enough, she was there, sitting at her dressing table as a young woman removed the pins from her mass of hair glinting with copper in the lamplight. The sight of long, silky locks falling down her back caused a peculiar pinch in his chest. He watched, almost mesmerized as the maid, having removed all pins, ran a silver-backed brush through the thick waves.

The lady looked up, holding her own cinnamon gaze within the mirror. A fraction to the right and she would have seen him, but she was too preoccupied with her thoughts to notice him. She looked sad and shaken as she removed the small gem-set gold studs that secured the chains in her nose and ear. Why did she wear them? he wondered as she placed the jewelry in a carved wooden box. And the ring she removed from her left hand—was it a wedding ring? If so, where was the fortunate groom? Surely he wouldn't allow such an intriguing woman to sleep alone?

Five knew it was wrong, and he didn't care. He stayed where he was, a Peeping Tom as the lady stood and allowed the maid to assist her in undressing. The shimmery gray gown slid down her arms, revealing a fine lawn chemise beneath a corset better suited for a courtesan than a lady: silver satin embroidered with turquoise, magenta and green butterflies. It pushed her breasts together and up as though offering them on a platter. His mouth turned arid as a desert at the sight of them.

He hadn't been with a woman in more than a month, but even if he'd gotten shagged five minutes ago, he would still appreciate this woman's body. Her waist was nipped, her hips flared. He watched brazenly as the maid loosened the lacings on that work of art enough to easily unhook the front, releasing her mistress from its confines.

The chemise was so thin he could see the shadows and blushes of her body beneath. She wasn't yet naked, and he could feel a familiar tightening below his waist—and then she stood there in nothing but her stockings and shoes.

Christ Jesus.

He tore himself away from the door, flattening himself against the side of the house. What the hell was he doing? He was there to kill her, not pant after her like a randy mutt. He had to get control of himself. He had to focus, because it had only taken the sight of her tits for him to think it was a shame she had to die.

His lungs filled with cool night air, exhaled and filled

again. Each cleansing breath eased the arousal inside him, returned his mind to its former cool detachment. When he returned to the door, she was no longer in the room, but in the mirror he could see the adjoining bathing chamber where she soaked in a tub of steaming water, her hair spilling over the side.

She drank from a squat crystal glass as she soaked. Whiskey it looked like. Good, that would make her more relaxed, less likely to fight back.

Five stayed there, outside her door, his breath occasionally fogging the glass, for a long time. Eventually, she pulled the stopper from the tub and let the water drain. She'd consumed another two glasses of whiskey during the bath, and when she wrapped herself in a thin, red silk kimono she swayed on her feet.

No, she would not fight him. She might even welcome him, he thought with his other brain—the one located between his legs. Scowling, he pushed that thought aside.

She extinguished the lamp as she walked past, but his eyesight was keen and the moon bright enough that he could still see her. She dropped the robe across the foot of the sleigh-shaped bed and slipped between the sheets naked, skin glowing from the bath.

He waited a little while longer, until he was certain the whiskey had lulled her into a deeply relaxed state, if not into actual slumber. Then, he turned the door handle. The door was unlocked—people rarely locked outside doors this far from the ground—fortunately for him.

Silent as a cat, Five slipped into the darkened bedroom. The scents of warm water and bergamot welcomed him, closing around him like a favorite robe. He made not a sound as he crept toward the bed where she slept. Even his coat was silent, the butter-soft leather so well-worn and conditioned.

Her breathing was the steady and shallow in and out

of one firmly in the grasp of Hypnos. He eased himself down onto the mattress to sit beside her. She didn't stir.

It was a mistake, but he allowed himself the luxury of studying her now that he was this close. Did he think that a more intimate vantage would allow him to see what it was that made her so unusual to him? Why she was so strangely intriguing? He felt drawn to her, pulled by an invisible force he couldn't identify. He couldn't seem to stop himself from lifting his hand and reaching out to brush her hair back from her temple. She slept on her back, face turned slightly to the left.

Long, thick lashes brushed against her cheeks, several shades darker than the brows arched so strongly over both eyes. Her nose had the barest tilt to it, and her mouth was a perfect bow—lush and bold.

But it wasn't her mouth or her long neck, or even her hair that was her best feature. No, that had to be her skin—perfect unblemished skin the color of fresh cream poured over a bowl of peaches.

Five touched his fingertips against the smooth, pale flesh of her cheek. Such skin looked as though it would feel like cool porcelain, but she was warm to the touch.

He should do it now. All he had to do was snuff her out—like the fragile flame of a candle. It was easy—fingers around her throat and a few minutes of breath-stealing pressure.

It *should* have been easy, but as he withdrew his hand, her eyelids fluttered and opened before he could make his escape.

Perhaps it was a sign of weakness, but he didn't relish the thought of having to look into her eyes as he killed her. Normally there was a sort of honor to meeting his prey's gaze, but not this time.

His hands moved to her throat as she looked up at him. He clenched his jaw, a sour taste in his mouth. His fingers had begun to curl around the warm flesh when her gaze widened and she gasped.

"Luke?"

Five froze at the sound of her voice. His heart—normally calm and steady—jumped against his ribs like a caged animal fighting to get out.

She sat up, blankets falling around her hips. His useless hands fell away, palms skimming down her soft arms. He wanted to pull her close and kiss her. He knew she'd taste of whiskey and cloves. She always used clove tooth powder before bed.

How the hell did he know that?

He stared at her, gaze searching her pale, startled face. She had gained a little weight. It looked good on her, softened her. How could he know that either?

"It's me," she said, as though he should know exactly who "me" was. "Arden."

As if she knew who he was.

He met her gaze, frowning. *Arden.*

A terrible pain lanced through his brain—sharp enough that he cried out, pressing the heel of his hand against his forehead to keep it from cracking and letting his brain ooze out.

"Luke!" Hands touched his shoulders. He could only feel her—the pain blinded him.

"Retreat," a voice in his head commanded, cutting through the pain. Any more of this and his head would explode.

He pushed her away and staggered to his feet, and as soon as he put that small amount of distance between them the pressure in his skull eased. His vision began to clear in time to see his intended victim tossing back the bedclothes. He had to escape. If she caught him he would die. He knew it.

Five tore through the glass doors. Shards exploded

around him, spraying both out and into the room under the force of his body. He grabbed the balcony railing and threw himself over it as though it was no more than a low wall. He landed on his feet on the grass and took off running toward the street. One of the patrol automatons spotted him and fired a shot that whistled past his ear. He didn't slow down—the pain in his head had eased, but a bullet would change that for the worse if it managed to permeate his reinforced skull.

He ran all the way to the hotel where he had lodgings for his time in London. He didn't stop until he was in his room, the door locked behind him. He didn't know what had just happened, other than that he had failed to complete his mission. His superiors would be pissed, but that couldn't be helped.

Did she know him, or had she confused him with someone else? And did he know her once upon a time, or was he confused as well? These were questions he could not answer.

One thing he knew for certain—the woman he was supposed to kill had seen his face, and whether he once knew her or not, there was no way in hell he could let her live.

"Perhaps you only *dreamed* that it was Huntley," Hannah Merritt suggested as she fixed two cups of fragrant tea. Humid jasmine filled the air.

Seated in the delicate rose-hued parlor of Hannah's town house, Arden fixed her friend with a rather sardonic gaze despite the watering of her mouth. Hannah's tea was a particular favorite, as were her cook's biscuits, of which there was a plateful. Arden had already indulged, and what she had eaten sat with a pleasant weight in her belly. Up until now she'd ingested nothing but coffee, one slice of toast and a measure of bourbon. The first had been to clear her confused mind, and the second had been to prepare her stomach for the third once she could think straight.

"Fancy it was a dream that shattered my balcony doors as well?"

"Of course not," Hannah retorted with a *tsk* of her tongue, setting the china pot on a special holder of thin coiled copper tubing that circulated steam. Tea never went cold in this house. "Obviously you had an intruder. Are you certain you won't reconsider my offer of having you come to live here? I have plenty of room since Mama's passing." She offered a cup and saucer with three biscuits arranged on the edge.

"You are a dear friend, and I'd prefer you to remain so." Arden took a sip of hot, fragrant—delicious!—tea. "Why ever would I want to leave my house now that Huntley has returned?" She deliberately mentioned him once more since her friend so pointedly did not believe her.

She did not miss the sympathetic glance Hannah shot her way, nor did she acknowledge it. She bit into a biscuit instead, savoring how the sharp ginger flavor mixed with the more subtle tea. Hannah worried that she didn't know her own mind, but if there was *anything* she, Arden Emmerson Chillingham Grey, knew, it was her own mind.

At least for now.

"I haven't gone mad, Hannah," she announced, dunking what was left of her biscuit into her tea before popping the sodden morsel into her mouth.

Her friend had the grace to look affronted—though it could just as easily have been horror at Arden's manners. "I would never think you had. Not for an instant. Why, you are the most unemotional, dispassionate woman I know." She grimaced when her mind caught up to her tongue. "I mean that you think more than you feel." Another wince.

Arden arched a brow, suppressing the smile that threatened. "Stop it, I beg of you. Such incessant compliments will swell my head." She'd known the other woman too long to truly be offended. They'd been friends since school. Hannah hadn't cared that Arden's father had a lesser title and not much of a fortune—or that he actually *worked*. In turn, Arden hadn't cared that Hannah sometimes spoke before she had a chance to think.

Flushed and flustered, Hannah fluttered a hand in Arden's direction. "You know what I mean. You are not the sort of woman to allow herself to be carried away. You place practicality above passion."

"You're really not making me feel better." She made sure to inject a degree of humor in her tone to soften the bite of the truthful statement. Hannah meant it as a compliment, but Arden hadn't always been emotionless. At one time she'd been quite happy to let passion and feeling rule.

But the source of that passion had disappeared almost seven years ago while on assignment, and ever since she'd found herself at a loss.

Until last night when she'd opened her eyes, certain she was dreaming, and seen her husband's face staring down at her. She had just started to think maybe she would never see his crystalline blue eyes again. Had started to forget just how sharp his nose was, how jet-black his hair. He was older but it *was* him.

He acted like he didn't know her—a vicious insult added to the injury his long absence had already wrought.

One of her hands was seized in Hannah's surprisingly robust grip. "What did Lord Henry say when you told him?"

Arden rolled her eyes at the mention of her brother-in-law. "I haven't told him, and I do not plan to until I know for certain."

"A wise course." Her friend looked so relieved, as though she believed there was a chance Arden would give up the silly notion that her husband still lived. After all, she was the only person in all of England who believed it. Even Luke's own brother had given up hope a long time ago.

Her husband's family hadn't offered much in the way of support after Luke disappeared. His mother had never really liked her, and Arden hadn't known his father. Fortunately, she'd had her own father to lean on for a brief time. And her mother, for an even briefer moment.

Her mother-in-law's coldness hadn't surprised her, but Henry's had. He was always so keen to please Luke, Arden had thought he might actually declare himself her personal protector. That hadn't happened. He'd become more and more distant, and then he began his plans to take over the title. Arden had successfully foiled him for years, but soon the seventh anniversary would roll round and then she would be powerless to stop him. Then she might very well need to take Hannah's offer of a room until she found her own house.

"I must confess I hope Lord Huntley returns just so I don't have to see you in half mourning anymore, or those morbid chains."

Arden raised her fingers to the fine strands of silver. "Queen Victoria herself commended me for my obvious devotion."

Hannah snorted. "Of course she did, but she's an old woman and you, my dear, are not. You still have plenty of life left."

A sharp remark about Hannah's own life rose to Arden's lips, but she bit it back. There was no need to be cruel, especially not when she knew how badly her friend wished her situation was different. Hannah was two years younger than Arden's eight and twenty and had given up almost all hope of ever finding a husband or having children. It wasn't that she was unattractive, and she was certainly rich enough. She simply hadn't found a man she "liked well enough to spend the rest of my life looking at him."

Arden had once suggested she take matters into her control and have a child—she could always go abroad and come back with a child and a conveniently dead husband's name. The suggestion had *not* been well received.

"You are right," she conceded with no little amount of enthusiasm. "It is time I gave up my mourning." No need for it now that Luke had returned. How she wished she could be happier about it, but he hadn't recognized her at all. Hadn't known her. Could he have forgotten her? Or were there darker forces at work?

"Fancy a trip to the dressmaker's?" she inquired, coming to the determined conclusion that she needed to find out what was going on rather than speculate with maudlin thoughts.

"Now?" Hannah's face brightened so vibrantly Arden felt a pinch of guilt beneath her breastbone. The particular dressmaker she had in mind was Madame Cherie, who was also a Warden. She inclined her head toward the parlor door with a curve of her lips. "Fetch your coat."

Hannah leaped to her feet and rushed off to do just that, leaving Arden alone to give in to the chuckle she could no longer contain.

A short time later, footmen handed both of them, and Arden's maid, Annie, into the shiny black steam touring carriage she'd purchased just before the Season began.

Unlike the high, old-fashioned contraptions many of her peers—and Arden herself when occasion called—were often driven about town in, this was lower, with an open top. It looked nothing like a horse-drawn carriage—or even the horseless sort—and she scandalously drove it herself.

Hannah's normally smooth brow furrowed with trepidation as she settled in on the leather bench seat. "Are you quite certain this is at all safe, Arden?"

Arden adjusted a pair of driving goggles over her eyes, positioning them so the leather cups fitted comfortably against her face. "Of course it is! You don't mean to suggest I would ever put you in danger?" She softened her words with a smile.

Her friend didn't look convinced, or very contrite. "Not knowingly, of course not." She peered nervously over the side as she lowered the veil of her hat over her face.

Grinning, Arden glanced over her shoulder at Annie, who was perched on the small seat in the back of the carriage, bonnet tied securely under her pointed chin. "You snug and secure back there, dear?"

"I am, ma'am," the maid replied eagerly. How fortunate Arden was to have an employee with such a spirit of adventure.

"Excellent. We're off!" She released the break, adjusted the accelerator lever and wrapped gloved fingers around the steering wheel. The carriage jerked into motion, eliciting a small squeak from Hannah and a burst of laughter from Arden.

In the country, or late at night when city streets weren't so terribly congested, she would drive fast—the carriage could reach speeds in the vicinity of 35–40 miles per hour. That wasn't possible now, not with the streets thick with carriages and horses. Once they left Mayfair it would be even worse, with omnibuses, bicycles and pedestrians added to the throng.

The new elevated train system would help with congestion and with the unfortunate mess that was the subterranean train system. Who would want to chug through the foul-smelling darkness of belowground when you could zip about above it all? It would be like riding a low-flying dirigible through the city.

Personal flyers—that's what the people of England needed. That would truly be exhilarating. Imagine buzzing around town on an ornothopter! Perhaps she would work on a design for such a contraption.

On the way to Madame Cherie's Oxford Street location, they passed support structures for the elevated rail system. Arden turned her head to glance at Hannah. "Extraordinary, aren't they?" The base was big enough for two carriages to drive through side by side, and at least four stories high. There would be hundreds of these bases all over the city, each supporting a large section of track.

"Yes," her friend agreed, not looking. Her knuckles were white on her bonnet ribbons and the side of the vehicle, hanging on to both as though her life depended upon it. "A tad fast for my liking, however."

Arden smiled and turned her attention back to the street, turning the wheel to avoid a dog that ran toward them barking like mad, tail wagging. Hannah gasped beside her.

By the time they reached the pretty little storefront of Madame Cherie's *Maison de Couture*, Hannah was positively stiff and Arden was having difficulty hiding her annoyance behind amusement. Honestly, did her friend have to be so distrusting as to think she would allow her to come to any harm?

But Hannah had been raised in a sheltered environment, much different from Arden's own upbringing in a house ruled by a man dedicated to creating the impossible and a woman determined to make certain her child was fearless. Hannah had been raised to be a proper lady—afraid of most of the world and its wonders—while Arden had been tossed into that world with all the hope and excitement of a penny dropped into a wishing well. It was no wonder they gravitated toward each other in school—each so fascinating to the other despite their difference in class. Of course, once Arden married Luke, class ceased to matter.

"Come inside, dear," she cajoled, taking one of Hannah's stiff hands in her own. "A little shopping will soothe your nerves."

Hannah obeyed, and by the time they entered the pleasantly warm interior of the shop with its swaths of beautiful fabric and air that smelled faintly of perfume, some of the color had started to return to the dark-haired woman's cheeks.

They were greeted by Madame herself. "Darlings!" she cried, opening her tattooed arms.

Madame Cherie was a little shorter than Arden, putting her somewhere in the vicinity of about five and a half feet. She had thick black hair streaked with white that she wore piled haphazardly on top of her head, dark eyes thickly lined with black kohl and bright red lips. Her skin was the color of cream with just a touch of coffee, and decorated with so many colored pictures Arden often made a game of trying to sort them all out. Today Madame Cherie showed a shocking amount of skin by wearing the latest fashion amongst the artistic crowd—a short violet leather vest that left her midriff bare and a long, gauzy skirt in black and silver.

"Bonjour, Madame," Arden replied. *"Comment ça va?"*

"Tres bien, mon amie." The woman, who was no more

French than Arden was, but far more convincing, fixed her with a direct look. "I had hoped to see you soon, Arden."

"The *countess* is in need of a new wardrobe," Hannah interjected coolly, having found her voice.

Madame—whose given name was Zoe Harper—arched a brow as black as a crow's wing, calling attention to the tiny crosses tattooed along her temple. "*Mais oui.*"

Arden didn't really fancy being caught in the middle of a female equivalent of a pissing contest, so she patted her friend on the shoulder. "There's no need to stand on ceremony here, Hannah dearest. Madame and I have known each other too long to be concerned with titles. Why don't you pick out some fabrics while we discuss designs? Whatever colors you think I should have."

There wasn't a woman in the fashionable world who would turn down the chance to dress a friend however she wanted. Hannah's green eyes brightened considerably before she scurried off to begin hauling bolts of brightly colored silk off the walls.

Both of Zoe's brows jumped at one particularly garish shade of puce. "I believe you might regret that, my friend." There was no hiding the amusement in her voice—not that she would have tried.

Arden smiled. "I still reserve the right to veto any choices. Might we step into the back, dearest? I have something I wish to discuss with you."

The darker woman linked her arm around Arden's. "And I, you."

They left the main room of the shop and passed through a curtained doorway into the sewing room where both humans and automatons—or *androïdes* as the French called them—worked on stitching and constructing gowns for the shop's many clients. The automatons worked much faster and more precisely than the humans, but there were simply some things metal could not do better than human hands.

Zoe's office was located just off this room, so they could sit in relative privacy, their conversation muffled by the sounds of the workroom. Zoe closed the door all the same.

"I believe my husband has returned," Arden said, wasting no time in getting to the point of her visit. She stripped off her gloves with perfunctory tugs on each finger. "He snuck into my room and was hovering over me when I awoke. Do you know anything?" Zoe knew almost everything that happened in London, having contacts in all levels of society. She was one of W.O.R's best intelligence gatherers, though there were some that sought to brand her as a spy-whore—selling secrets to the highest bidder.

Arden knew better. Her friend's moral code might be a tad ambiguous, but once she gave her loyalty to a person she never wavered. Arden was equally loyal to her in return.

"Your . . . husband."

"Yes, only he doesn't seem to know me. It's as though he has some kind of amnesia." Frowning, Arden finished with her gloves and looked up as she slapped them into one palm. Zoe was watching her with an expression that could only be described as a mixture of trepidation and horror. "Good lord, Zoe, what is it?"

Her friend took a bottle of whiskey from a cupboard behind her desk, removed the top and took a deep swallow. Then she passed the bottle to Arden. "It all makes sense now."

Without being given or demanding an explanation, Arden took the bottle and drank, shuddering as the potent liquor hit her stomach in a most comforting manner. If Zoe hadn't bothered with glasses it had to be bad.

She took another drink, then gave the whiskey back. "All right, tell me."

Her friend also tipped the bottle as she leaned against the edge of the desk. Her handsome face wore a ravaged expression, and her dark eyes were bright and rueful.

"Word has it that the Company has sent a ghost after you."

Arden's stomach rolled, threatening to send the whiskey back up. "Ghosts" were Company assassins, called such because they were often able to achieve their bloody goal without being seen or heard. She pressed a shaking hand to her abdomen, but the sick feeling remained. She didn't know how or why, but she knew who the assassin was. "Luke."

Chapter 3

Five paused in the stairwell of his lodgings and pressed the heel of one palm to his forehead. It felt as though there was something worrying at his brain—like a cat pawing at a closed door.

Luke.

He clung to the rail with one hand, trying to keep himself from falling down the narrow stairs as *her* voice rang in his head. He hadn't been able to get it out. Every time he thought of her, pain followed.

Luke. It was what she had said to him in her bedroom. She had said it as if he should recognize it, and it had sounded almost plaintive—regretful.

She knew him, and though he knew everything about her he didn't know the connection. She had the upper hand—had him at a disadvantage.

He despised vulnerability. That she made him feel that way was simply one more reason to kill her. And he would. She had done something that marked her for death—made her deserve it—and as her personal grim reaper it was his duty to deliver her judgment.

He would not fail next time.

The Company knew he hadn't completed the mission and had ordered him to report to an address in Whitechapel this afternoon.

The hem of his leather greatcoat swished against his legs as he continued down the stairs, the pain in his head lessening. As he stepped outside, Five slipped on a pair of tinted spectacles that eased some of the ache in his skull. He swung his leg over the seat of a heavy black-and-copper-colored velocycle parked near the door and slipped on soft, worn leather gloves before starting the machine's engine. It chugged and roared to life, eager to tear through the damp, cobblestone streets.

It didn't feel right to him to stay in this particular part of town. There was somewhere else he should be, but he had no idea where. He had no idea who he was, but his accent was English, so it made sense that he came from London or perhaps nearby. It was a posh accent too, which didn't make sense with what he had been told about his background. It made him think of other things that didn't make sense in his life. But those thoughts hurt too, so he tried not to think them.

He steered the heavy machine into traffic, its ridged wheels gripping the cobblestone street. As he maneuvered the steering bars to guide him around a slow-moving omnibus, an image flashed in his mind—of him, driving a cycle of much higher quality than this one down a dusty country lane. A woman's arms were wrapped around his middle, and her laughter rang with wild delight in his ears.

So clear and sudden was the vision that he almost lost control of the cycle. Swearing, he managed to keep from taking a spill into a rather nasty-looking gutter.

He shook his head as he righted himself. A memory. Could it be that he was regaining his past? The thought plagued him all the way to Whitechapel, where he stopped in front of a nondescript building off Dorset Street, near Miller Court.

He knocked on the door and waited. Within a few moments he heard footsteps approach, and then the heavy portal opened to reveal a tall, thin man he'd seen perhaps two or three times in the past.

"Ah, Number Five. Right on time, I see. Promptness is a virtue, you know. Well, inside with you. I'll take you to the Doctor. He's been waiting for you."

The Doctor. A slight coil of unease wound low around Five's spine as he tucked his spectacles into his coat pocket. He couldn't remember the man ever doing anything awful to him, but wariness filled him regardless. He followed the thinner male down a narrow hall to the last door.

"Here you are. Go right in, lad."

Five thanked him and settled his gloved hand on the latch. It clicked under the pressure of his thumb and the door opened, creaking wide to reveal a small sitting room.

The man he knew as the Doctor stood just inside, on a worn but quality rug of bright crimson and dark blue with traces of gold. He was dressed in crisp trousers, snowy shirt and cravat and a dark brown waistcoat embroidered with hunter-green. His dark hair was heavily pomaded back from his high forehead, revealing the craggy countenance of his face. His moustache had traces of gray in it, but he didn't seem old, yet neither was he young. He was short and lean, but he was the kind of man that made others shift uncomfortably from the coldness of his gaze.

"Five," he said by way of greeting, not looking up from the tray of implements on the table beside him. "Come in."

Five did as he was told. He always did as he was told. Odd, but he suddenly realized he hated being told what to do. He was accustomed to giving the orders. How would this man react if Five told him to go straight to hell and walked out? "What is this place?" he asked.

"Just a building the Company owns," the man replied. "We acquired it after an associate of ours did some work here back in 'eighty-eight. He was one of our best."

"What happened to him?"

"He was killed by the Wardens."

The Wardens. In the business of spying, the rivalry between the Wardens and the Company was the longest and the most volatile. To say that the two were on opposite sides would be an oversimplification. Sometimes they were on the same side, and even then they fought one another. No, it went beyond right and wrong. Their dissension was based on something more complex than morality. They were enemies hell-bent on destroying each other, but wouldn't know what to do without the other there to fight against. The only relationship he could compare it to would be a marriage between two people who despised each other but refused to separate.

Or like that of England and France. "Is that a bloodstain on the wall?"

The man didn't glance at the mark. "Yes. A woman named Mary Kelly was killed in this room."

"Was that the 'work' your 'best' man was up to?" He wasn't certain what made him ask, or what put the sardonic twist in his voice, but he knew he didn't need to hear the other man's answer—the stiffening of his shoulders was enough.

"I hear you've been having some difficulty carrying out your present task." The Doctor finally deigned to look at him—barely a passing glance. "I'm going to remedy that. Have a seat."

The chair was like a barber's chair, only with shackles on the arm and leg rests. Five eyed it warily, not quite ready to give himself over just yet. "Since arriving in London I've been ... remembering things."

The smaller man tilted his head thoughtfully, his gaze focused elsewhere. "Is that so? What sort of things?"

Five shrugged. "Little things—driving in the country, how to get to certain places. I think I might have been someone important, and married."

The Doctor smiled, but there was little humor in it. "We all like to think of ourselves as someone important."

"I'm not imagining things," Five retorted somewhat defensively.

Now the smaller man met his gaze—directly and unflinching. "I didn't say you were, but in a case such as yours, it is perhaps best to do a little investigative work before we tell ourselves you are regaining your memories. Now, in the chair, please."

This time Five did as he was instructed. He sat down in the chair and tried not to drive his knuckles into the doctor's scarred face as the man closed one, then the other shackle. He was now totally at the mercy of another. The realization brought a thin layer of sweat to the back of his neck.

"Any other concerns I should know about? Any idea why you were unable to achieve your objective last evening?"

He leaned his head back against the padded rest. "I had my hands around her throat and she woke up. She said ..." He frowned, not wanting to give the name away. "She spoke as though she knew me. I felt as though I might have known her too."

"But that is impossible," the Doctor argued, piercing the skin of Five's arm with a needle. Five watched as the plunger was depressed, releasing God-only-knew what into his blood. "She is a countess, and there is no way a man such as you would have ever known a woman of her social stature."

That was true, but it didn't change that she had known him. "It threw me off-kilter. I was told to retreat, and so I did." He looked down at his shackled wrists as he spoke, unable to look the other man in the eye as he lied. He had run because she scared the hell out of him, not because he had been told to.

The world tilted slightly. Five blinked as the floor seemed to sway beneath him. Christ, what was in that syringe? He opened his mouth to ask, but his tongue refused to work.

"She won't be able to discombobulate you so easily next time. Close your eyes please. You might feel a slight discomfort—"

The rest of what the Doctor said was lost as white-hot pain lanced through Five's mind. It was as though someone had literally set lightning loose in his head, so bright was the flash. His body arched, limbs straining against the restraints as his brain burned. His own cries echoed in his ears, reverberating throughout the room.

Writhing, Five fought as the pain intensified. It felt like needles of ice piercing his brain, as though his mind was a collection of butterflies being pinned for exhibition.

Again and again the needles stabbed until he couldn't take anymore. The pain and the drug finally took their toll and he faded into sweet, welcoming darkness.

When he woke, the Doctor was sitting on a stool by the table not far away, watching him and sipping a cup of tea.

"How long was I asleep?" he asked.

"Not long."

He tested the shackles. He could snap them if he wanted. "May I leave now?" He didn't like the Doctor. He didn't know why, but the man made his flesh creep.

"In a moment." The Doctor set his cup on a saucer and rose to his feet. "I want to ask you a few questions first, just to make certain you are feeling better."

"Better?" He scowled. "Was I sick?"

"A little," the small man replied, clasping his hands behind his back. "What is your name?"

"Number Five," he replied with a scoff. Did the man really think he wouldn't remember who he was?

"Have you ever been to London before?"

"No."

"Has anything you've seen here seemed familiar to you?"

"No." He'd only been in town for . . . a day? Or was it two? And seeing the sights hadn't been high on his agenda. "Are we finished?"

The Doctor made no move to unlock the shackles. "Almost. What is your mission while here in London?"

"To hunt down the woman who murdered Victor Erlich three years ago."

"Arden Grey, Lady Huntley." The smaller man's eyes narrowed, as though looking for some kind of reaction, and then widened again. "What are your orders when you find her?"

Five looked up, a slow smile of anticipation curving his lips. "To kill her."

The murdered girl was identified as the daughter of Baron Lynbourne. Her name was Angeline, and she had been eighteen years of age. Her parents had held hope of her finding a husband that Season. She was reported to be a spirited girl with a pleasant personality, liked by all who knew her.

The only thing that could have made the tale more tragic would have been if she were an only child. However, Lynbourne and his wife had other children to help them through their terrible grief. Their lives would never be the same, regardless. That was why it was called "loss," after all.

Arden wasn't acquainted with the baron and baroness, at least not closely. Of course they had been introduced once upon a time, and often were invited to the same events, but that was the extent of their familiarity. Still, she ordered an arrangement of white calla lilies to be sent round to them, along with a card expressing her condolences.

That was all she could do. Her loyalty to the Crown prohibited her from approaching them on a more intimate level, but even if it did not, she would hardly open a dialogue with the grieving parents. What would she tell them, that she had seen their daughter's mutilated corpse? That she had seen the moments of her death? These were not the details that comforted the distraught, and they would serve no purpose but to cause them more pain.

But she sent flowers because she was no stranger to loss, or to grief.

Three days had passed since she'd awoken to find Luke in her bedroom, and she was beginning to wonder if he had indeed been a dream, or some grand figment of her imagination.

There was no way she could have imagined his touch—or the ruination of the French doors. No, he was very real.

Was it true what Zoe surmised? Had he been sent by the Company to assassinate her? It seemed too fantastical to believe, but it was just probable enough to tighten her chest. It explained why she'd woken to his hands around her neck, and why he had run. It also explained why he didn't know her.

What in the name of God had those villainous bastards done to her husband?

Tears burned the backs of her eyes, clutched at her throat, but she held them at bay. She would not cry. Tears were the refuge of the hopeless and the helpless, and she was neither.

It was odd that she turned to friends within the Wardens for strength and assistance, when it had been Luke who brought her into that world. Of course, growing up as she had and aiding her father in his work, she had seen some of it, but it wasn't until her marriage that she slowly began to insert herself into that life of intrigue and danger. Becoming a full agent after his disappearance had been just another way to hold on to him—look for him. Who would have thought that it would become such a large, defining part of her? She had purpose. More important, she had a distraction.

Arden knew Luke would be back for her—felt it in her bones. She had neglected to tell Zoe that, however. No doubt her friend suspected it as well. She probably wondered if Luke was a traitor not only to his wife but to his country. Arden had to admit the terrible thought had crossed her mind.

It was time to get out of the house and stop dwelling. This sitting about feeling sorry for herself would not do any more good than feeling helpless would.

Three of the garments she had ordered from Zoe had been delivered the day before—God bless automaton sewing skills! Arden went to her room and summoned Annie to help her dress in a suitable costume for going out.

Opening the armoire, she made her selection of clothing, placed the hanger in the slender compartment to the left, then closed the door and pushed the button on the side of the wardrobe. The heavy oak trembled slightly as the small engine within chugged to life. Soon, she heard the familiar sound of boiling water whooshing through pipes and the gentle hiss of steam—the remnants of which drifted from the copper pipe on top. The entire process lasted perhaps a minute before shutting down. Arden waited another minute before she opened the door once more.

The ensemble she had chosen was a wine-colored gown with a jaggedly ruffled skirt, short sleeves and a bodice made of snug-fitting leather in a matching shade. The front had tightly cinched buckle closures that eliminated the need for a corset beneath. The built-in steam chamber in the armoire had released any wrinkles that might have marred the fabric. She was dressing when Annie arrived to do her hair, which was quickly twisted into a thick knot on the back of her head.

She finished the ensemble with black velvet boots that hugged her calves and a tailored black pelisse which ensured she would be warm in the damp outdoors.

Annie went to call for the carriage with the Huntley crest on it to be brought round. As much as Arden loved to drive her smaller vehicle, in case of threat she was safer inside an enclosed carriage with a driver.

And if that threat happened to be her husband, perhaps he'd see the familiar coat of arms and remember who he was. She sincerely doubted it would happen that way. In fact, she rather hoped that if the sight of her didn't make him remember, then nothing would. It was a selfish hope, but she held it nevertheless.

She pinned a small velvet top hat onto her hair, positioning it with a jaunty tilt toward her left eye. Satisfied that she looked suitable to her social position, she gathered up her gloves and bag and left her room.

Downstairs Arden smelled the clean, lemony scent of a scrubber cleaning the marble floor. The machine stood waist-high, and looked very much like a large, tall cooking pot. A boiler beneath kept the water hot and provided power as the machine propelled itself around the hall, cleaning the floor with long, armlike limbs that had scrub pads instead of hands.

"I'm so sorry about that, my lady," Mrs. Bird, the housekeeper, gushed as she bustled seemingly from out of nowhere to push the little automaton on its way as though it were an errant child. "I meant to have the floor cleaned before you came down."

Arden smiled. "Don't fret so, Mrs. Bird. I shan't expire from seeing housework being tended to. Although you may want to have Ronald look at the scrubber when it's done. It sounds as though it might be having difficulties."

The housekeeper nodded. "Of course, my lady."

She didn't miss the faint blush that filled the widow's smooth cheeks. "You might also want to take one of your apple tarts. I know for a fact that Ronald's very fond of apples."

The woman's eyes widened a fraction. "Is he now? That's very good to know, ma'am."

Still smiling, Arden pulled on her gloves and bid the housekeeper a good morning. Then she ventured out into the gray, drizzly day where her carriage sat waiting. It was a fairly large, impressive vehicle, with puffs of steam drifting from the gleaming brass pipe on the back. Burgundy and black lacquer, it had large black wheels and a padded bench for the driver up front. It was a formal carriage, and could be secured to a team of horses should the occasion—such as a royal invitation—arise. Queen Victoria respected modern advancement, but expected it to respect *her* more. Court fashion was always a decade or two behind the times, no matter if it was for hair or horses.

She glanced up at the driver. "Downing Street, Gibbs."

The burly man tipped his well-worn hat. "As you wish, my lady."

One of her footmen opened the carriage door for her, and the small steps automatically flipped down for her to climb. A large drop of rain landed on her cheek, and she turned to the footman to ask him to run into the house and fetch her umbrella, but Mrs. Bird was already there, object in hand.

"Thought you might be wanting this, my lady."

Gratitude curved Arden's lips. "What would I ever do without you, Mrs. Bird?"

The older woman flushed, but she met Arden's gaze—something servants rarely did. "God willing neither of us will ever have to find out, ma'am."

Arden's throat tightened and she swallowed against it. "Indeed." She climbed into the carriage, not daring to wonder at what might happen should Henry succeed in having Luke declared dead, despite her certainty to the contrary. She certainly had enough money and options to live out the rest of her life as she wished, but for nine years this house had been her home and the people in it her friends, family and employees. Many of them had been with the Grey family their entire careers. She couldn't expect any of them to give up working for an earl to come work for her.

The footman closed the door. Arden tapped her umbrella on the roof to let Gibbs know she was ready to depart. The carriage eased into motion, the familiar sound of the engine a soothing rhythm. It had an almost mesmerizing effect, lulling her into a state of tranquility despite the emotions threatening to rage inside her. It felt very much like when Luke first disappeared. She'd been lost and numb and yet so very, very angry. Yet she'd been unable to give into that rage—not as she wanted anyway. Grief always ruined it, and now she feared if she let it out it simply would never stop.

So she pushed it down, as she did most strong emotions, and forced herself into a state of dispassionate disinterestedness so she could think clearly. However, she wasn't too keen on thinking at the moment either.

The carriage swayed a little as it traveled over cobblestones worn smooth by decades upon decades of carriage wheels, horse hooves and human feet. Arden leaned her weary head against the soft cushions and closed her eyes.

She jerked awake when the carriage stopped, bolting upright and immediately checking her cheek for drool. Thankfully there wasn't any. Weariness clung to her as she blinked and straightened her hat and hair, brushed her hands over her coat and skirt to smooth them.

She peeked around the closed blind. They had reached her destination.

When the door had been opened and the steps lowered, Arden stepped out into the light but steady rain, glad for her umbrella, which she opened and held over herself for shelter.

"Go find yourself someplace warm and dry to wait, Gibbs," she instructed. "In the carriage if you like. I will be ready to depart for home in thirty minutes." He was dressed in the appropriate outerwear for such a day, but she would feel guilty if he came down with a cold.

When he walked away she turned to the row of buildings before her.

Number 13 Downing Street did not technically exist, having been remodeled and partially absorbed by one or two of the other buildings close to the redbrick dwelling that was the official address of the Prime Minister. Of course, Lord Salisbury didn't actually live in the house—he had a much grander estate befitting a man of his rank on Arlington Street in St. James's.

But for her purpose there was still a number 13. It simply wasn't visible on the surface.

Number 13 housed the Wardens of the Realm's London Office. They had smaller locations scattered throughout the Empire, but this was the largest, and home to the Director, who ran the organization. The Wardens were spies, for lack of a better term, dedicated to the protection of Britain and all Her interests. There seemed to be no shortage of intrigue in Europe and the world, much of it involving England, directly or indirectly. Sometimes the job was about keeping someone alive, or making sure someone else disappeared without a trace. And sometimes, it was so political Arden's eyes crossed at the subtleties, backstabbing and dual nature of it all. When those moments got to be too much, she reminded herself that both her father and husband had dedicated themselves to the agency—and to their country. She could do no less.

There was a black door on the building right in front of her to which she had a key. Past that door was a small foyer that housed nothing but an elegant oak and iron-grated lift. The matching gate in front of the lift was locked, but she had a key for it as well and easily walked through to the lift itself. She slid the polished door open, stepped over the slight gap between box and floor, and then shut herself inside, latching the door securely.

She took a punch card from the lining of her bag—the same place where she kept the keys to this mysterious place—and slipped it into the slot provided. There were no buttons to push or levers to pull, for the analytical engine of the machine read the information on her punch card and took her to her desired location. Nor-

mally she used another card that did require a floor selection, but today she was going to see the Director,
which required a special card that only a handful of people were privileged enough to own.

The lift moved slowly at first, grinding and hissing as
the steam engine that powered it came to life. Many
people would be afraid to be in such a seemingly de-
crepit piece of machinery, but Arden wasn't concerned.
There were safety precautions in place in case of emer-
gency, and her father had built the lift, so if there was an
issue she could probably fix it herself—if she survived.

The cage jerked into motion—she placed a palm
briefly against the wall to steady herself. A soft hiss whispered around her as the floor beneath her feet began its
descent.

Down one floor the lift crawled; then it hesitated and
she felt something like a giant hand close around either
side—jostling the cage as it clamped hold. Chains and
cables jangled as they were released. There was a slight
drop, followed by a jar that never ceased to make her
curse like a sailor. Then the lift moved backward, bur-
rowing into the building rather than beneath it. Instead
of relying on cables and pulleys, it now sat upon a track
that ran parallel to the street above. It spent several minutes on this route before it stopped and the door—this
time the one at the back of the box—was cranked open
by an unseen mechanism that sounded as though several
of its parts required lubrication.

Arden remembered to take her punch card before
exiting the lift. The heels of her boots tapped sharply on
the glossy polish of the white and black-veined marble
floor as she strode briskly toward her destination.

Both sides of the large hall were lined with sconces
holding brightly burning lamps, filling the subterranean
hall with blue-tinged light. She'd wager ten pounds that

it wasn't gas in those lamps. Another ten said she'd have better luck sprouting wings than finding out just what the blue substance was.

There was only one door other than that to the lift behind her. It was actually a double door made of carved oak—tall and wide enough for a pair of giants to walk through. A guard stood on either side, dressed in livery of black and gold, the brass buttons on their jackets embossed with the image of a gryphon wearing a crown of roses. It was the symbol of the Wardens—the gryphon symbolizing England and the mythical creature that protected the kingdom, and the roses symbolizing virtue and superior merit.

Spine straight, Arden stood before the guards, fixing them both with a level stare. "Lady Arden Grey, Countess Huntley to see the director."

Neither of the guards' countenances changed, but the smaller of the two—the female—moved to turn the knob on the door nearest her and opened it, bowing as Arden wordlessly swept past.

She stepped over the threshold into what could have been a drawing room or salon in any aristocratic lady's household. The walls were covered in cream-colored, delicately hand-painted paper from the Orient depicting birds in flight. The carpet was pale as well, and just as exquisite in its subtle pattern. All of the furniture was made from dark wood, and upholstered in the darkest crimson velvet.

A young man sat at a desk near the back of the room, not far from yet another door—the entrance to the Director's office. He glanced up, his spectacles glinting in the light. "Good day, Lady Huntley."

"Hello, Mr. Chiler. Is she in?"

"Of course. Allow me to inquire if she is able to accept visitors." The young man rose to his feet and moved to the door. The hand he lifted to knock was almost skeletal-looking—but bones didn't have rivets and bolts. Mr. Chiler's fingers could crush a normal man's hand with very little effort. Arden knew this because she had seen it happen.

A voice called out for him to enter, and he slipped into the office, closing the door softly behind him. All Arden could do was wait for his return. The Director would either have time for her or she wouldn't. There was never any hidden agenda, not here.

Seconds ticked past on the large clocks on the wall. One was set to London time, another to New York, another to Berlin, and one to St. Petersburg. There were others, but before Arden could glance at them, the door to the director's office opened and Mr. Chiler reappeared.

"You may go on in, Lady Huntley," he said in his soothing baritone.

"Thank you." Arden brushed past him to cross the threshold into the inner sanctum.

The room was large, decorated in muted shades of violet, burnt orange, gold and rich fuchsia. Plush sofas and chairs were topped with thick, colorful cushions. Swaths of silk draped the walls, brightened by the light of the lamps. Paintings of India adorned the walls, their bold colors contrasting with the monochromatic photographs of London that hung alongside them.

A large desk sat at the back of the room—a thick slab of ebony atop the backs of four hand-carved elephants, each different in appearance, painted to look as though they should be carrying a rajah through the streets of town.

The woman standing in front of the desk was by far the most exotic part of the room. A little taller than Arden's own above-average height, she was built like an hourglass in black trousers tucked in knee-high black boots, and a fitted dark-purple waistcoat that was boned and laced like a corset. Her thick black hair was coiled into a large, heavy bun at the base of her skull, and large, piercing amber eyes stared out of a face that was just a little too dark and exotic to be wholly English.

Dhanya Withering was rumored to be the illegitimate granddaughter of Queen Victoria, though no one had ever seen any evidence to prove this theory. Her mother was from India and ran a successful bakery in the West End where Arden often went when she had a craving for something delicious and sweet. She had developed quite a taste for cardamom thanks to Dhanya's mama.

"I hear you had some excitement at your home a few nights ago," Dhanya said in lieu of greeting. Her faintly accented English sounded lyrical and exotic to Arden's ears.

"I did," she replied. "Zoe seems to think the Company wants to see me eliminated."

One already incredibly arched brow quirked as the darker woman gestured for her to sit. "I had heard a similar rumor, yes. The price of having the satisfaction of dispatching Victor Erlich to his just reward, no doubt."

Arden wouldn't describe having to kill a man to save herself as satisfying in any degree, but she didn't voice that. It was the only time she'd ever harmed another person. Her talents normally kept her out of harm's way, inventing gadgets and weapons for W.O.R. agents. With God's grace it would be the last time she ever had to take a life. She still dreamed of Erlich on occasion—his wine-soaked breath and grasping fingers.

The director didn't seem to notice her suddenly reflective state—or she chose to ignore it. "I also heard that you believe the man who snuck into your home was none other than your errant husband."

Was she surprised Dhanya had already heard this? No.

"Indeed I do." Arden seated herself in a violet wing-back chair, watching her friend and superior W.O.R. member as she poured them each a cup of chai tea and placed several sweets on a plate. Arden didn't know the names of them all, but there were small golden logs topped with cream, swirls of bright orange batter that had been fried and dipped in sweet syrup, and different-colored squares topped with silver leaf. The sight of them set her mouth to watering.

Dhanya joined her, offering her first tea, then a sweet. "You know that if your husband is working for the Company, the rest of the Wardens will call for an inquiry into your own loyalties."

Arden nodded as she took a bite of a sticky swirl. Bliss! "To be honest, Dhanya, if my husband is truly alive, I don't care if the Wardens want my blood."

The darker woman watched her closely. "Is he a traitor or a victim, then?"

"Victim," she replied immediately. "He looked at me as though I were a stranger."

Licking a drop of syrup from her thumb, the director leaned back in her chair. "You believe his mind has been tampered with."

"I do. When Luke left seven years ago he was determined to bring the Company to an end once and for all. I am convinced they caught him and have somehow altered his mind."

A frown furrowed Dhanya's usually smooth brow. "I have heard of such things happening, but I've never witnessed it for myself. I've always thought it to be the agency equivalent of a monster in the cupboard—something to keep operatives on their toes."

Arden found her tone dubious at best. Why did everyone doubt her judgment? "I *know* my husband. It was Luke."

The director raised her honey-colored gaze. It was like staring into the eyes of a lioness. "Arden . . . my friend. You do realize what will happen to this man, especially if he is your husband?"

Arden's heart staggered against her ribs. "He is one of *us*, Dhanya."

Not a flicker of emotion crossed the other woman's face. "Which is precisely why if you see him again you have to try to reach him. It is because of who he might be and what he might know that we cannot allow him to continue to be used by the Company. If you cannot turn him, or find some way that he might serve our cause, I will have no choice but to give orders that he is to be terminated."

If fear could have fingers, it would have her very soul in those icy digits. "You cannot kill my husband."

The cool façade dropped for a second, and she saw real sympathy—pain even—in her superior's gaze. "If he has been programmed to murder you and is willing to carry out those orders, I will put a bullet in his brain myself."

Arden swallowed hard against the bile churning in her stomach, threatening to rise in her throat. She set her cup and saucer on the desk, unable to countenance the thought of eating or drinking. "I understand."

"I do not think you do." Dhanya leaned forward. "I'm giving you the chance to find him first. I pray to God I don't regret it, but I have faith in your abilities. Find him and fix him and I will rejoice in his return with you, but if you cannot . . ."

There was no need for her to say it again. Arden understood perfectly. "I will find him," she vowed—as much to herself as to Dhanya. Then she rose to her feet—ashamed to find her knees trembling. "I have taken up enough of your time. I will leave you now."

The darker woman also stood, and came around the desk to give her a hug. "You may not believe this, but I very much hope that you succeed."

Arden nodded, not daring to speak for fear she might burst into tears. She had only just found Luke again and now was faced with the very real possibility that she might lose him again—for good this time.

Just as she turned the doorknob to make her exit, Dhanya called after her, "It's good to see you in some color, Lady Huntley."

She managed a smile while inside wishing she'd worn the protection of her blacks and drabs. She wouldn't have felt quite so vulnerable in them.

She said good-day to Mr. Chiler and made her way back to the surface, as far away from the oppressive secrecy of the W.O.R. offices as she could get. The din and dirt of the city was a welcome balm to her troubled soul.

All she had to do was find Luke. He could be anywhere in London, making her task much like attempting to find a hairpin in a pile of automaton scrap. But if that was what she had to do to save his life, to have him return to her, then she would do it, even if it meant putting herself in danger.

The pavement was wet, but the rain had stopped, so she didn't open her umbrella on the way to her carriage. Gibbs stood by the gleaming vehicle, smoking a cigarette. He threw the rolled tobacco to the ground when he spotted her, crushing it beneath his heel.

Normally she would inquire as to how he spent his time, or thank him for being there when she returned, but she couldn't summon the energy to put on a smile and be the good lady.

Gibbs opened the carriage door for her. "Is everything all right, ma'am? If you'll excuse my impertinence, you look a little pale."

Arden smiled wearily as she stepped up. God love the man for being such a pet. "Just tired, Gibbs. Do not fret. 'Tis nothing a strong cup of tea and a nap cannot cure." If only it was truly that simple.

"I'll get you home straightaway, my lady. You just sit back and get some rest." He closed the door as soon as she was inside, and hopped up onto the bench.

Arden was just about to take his advice when she noticed something on the seat across from her. Frowning, she leaned forward to investigate and gasped at what she saw.

Lying on the cushions was a freshly cut, almost bloodred poppy—her favorite flower.

Someone had been in her carriage. Someone had known exactly where to find her and had left this flower so she would know she was being watched. Followed.

And only one person had ever given her poppies before. It was why she had carried a bouquet of them the day she married him. It seemed she might not have to search out her husband after all.

He was going to come to her.

Chapter 4

She was so beautiful it was a shame to have to kill her.

Five watched from the shadows outside the mansion as his prey stood inside, drinking her third glass of champagne served by gleaming automatons that were little more than silver trays on top of moving dustbins. She was surrounded by a small crowd made up of what he assumed were old friends and new admirers, listening intently to what she had to say.

And what man in his proper mind wouldn't admire her? She wasn't a conventional beauty—her features were too strong for that—but she was the kind of woman a body didn't forget, who drew men to her like moths to a lamp. She gave off a wounded air, which attracted the predator within him, but he had been at this intrigue long enough to recognize danger when he saw it. She was no more weak or helpless than he was.

She had gotten his gift, but unlike most women who would have been frightened by such an invasion of privacy, she flaunted it, wearing the bright flower in the upswept mass of her russet hair. It was a bold accessory, made all the more so by her lack of jewelry save for small gold earrings, and pale gold gown. His instinct had been correct—poppies suited her.

"Do you have her?"

For the first time in a long while he was annoyed by the intrusive voice in his head, coming through the tiny mechanism implanted in his ear. "I'm watching her now."

"What is the delay?"

"I can't very well walk into the ballroom and strangle her."

A very pregnant pause followed, and for a moment he thought his employer was gone. *"You will do it tonight."*

His sigh sounded like a growl even in his own ears. "That is my intention."

"Do not make me regret choosing you for this mission."

Five gritted his teeth. How tempting it was to tell the man to go bugger himself. Instead, he said nothing and went back to watching the lady whose life he was expected to take. Pity, that.

"Five?"

"I'll do it." He clenched his jaw to keep from adding "piss off" to the promise.

Silence followed. Then, a soft click. His superior had severed the connection.

Shifting on the balls of his feet, Five adjusted his perch in the tree outside one of the ballroom windows to one of more comfort. Being idle drove him mad, despite such alluring visuals.

He wore a set of spectacles that brought everything closer, allowing him to take in even more detail. His lovely lady lost some of her glow when a new gentleman approached her. She seized another glass of champagne from an automated footman that resembled a strange combination of man and crane—a human torso held aloft by long, spindly legs, with even longer arms that could extend a tray up to six feet into or above a crowd. Its lack of a head made it strangely off-putting. Lady Huntley didn't seem to mind.

This dandy looked to be a gentleman in his mid- to late twenties. He wore impeccable evening dress of black and white, and his dark sideburns were long and neatly trimmed—not quite muttonchops. He looked vaguely familiar. . . .

Five started, frowned and adjusted a knob on the side of the goggles to see if he could bring the man into closer view, sharper focus.

The man looked like *him*. Very much so. How was this possible? Who was he? Was this the mysterious Luke? Had his intended prey mistaken him for someone else in the dark?

For reasons he couldn't fathom, he wanted to kill this man. A sense of deep betrayal had wormed its way up from his gut to twine around his heart. At the moment that feeling didn't matter so much as the fact that the lady did not seem pleased to see the man at all. In fact, they seemed to be having a rather displeasing conversation. So much so that she walked away from him while he was still talking.

Curious. And relieving. If she'd given any hint of intimacy between them he would have snapped the bastard's neck.

Christ, but the resemblance was uncanny. Was it possible that they were related? It was highly possible that Five could be the by-blow of some wealthy nob. That would provide some explanation for his accent and familiarity with Mayfair.

Gliding through the trees, Five watched Arden Grey as she walked almost the entire length of the ballroom. Then she made an abrupt turn toward the French doors that led to the balcony.

She would not be content to stand on that smooth

stone and lean on the balustrade, that much he knew. She was the kind of woman who had to walk off her frustration, release that swirling energy with physical exertion and perhaps a curse or several. No, she would descend the curving stone steps to the gardens below, and perhaps head for the maze.

He would follow her and complete his mission; then he would be free of her and could leave London. Though the image of the man who looked like him would haunt him for some time. *She* would haunt him.

He crouched and waited for her to enter the garden before slipping soundlessly from the tree. The grass didn't even rustle as he stepped upon it. Then, he began to stalk her.

Five moved as he had been trained to—as quietly and gracefully as a cat. He removed the spectacles and secured them in his jacket pocket. Without them he could still see very clearly, and the torches along the path ensured that he was able to keep his eye on her with ease. Her gown caught the moonlight, shining like a beacon to guide his way.

Unaware of being followed, the lady moved at a moderate pace. From where he followed, he could hear her swearing, but she said nothing that gave him any insight as to who the man was or why he upset her so.

In the middle of the maze—which his lady found with surprising ease—she stopped near the pond. A statue of Venus stood in the center of the water like a modest maiden caught bathing in the nude. Smooth stones lined the rim of the pool for a pleasing aesthetic—no doubt there were brightly colored exotic fish in there as well. These wealthy sods had the most ridiculous trophies of their importance.

"Do you often attend parties to which you were not invited and follow unsuspecting ladies into dark places?"

Five's head jerked up. His prey was watching him as though she had known he was there all along, which was, of course, impossible.

Wasn't it?

"I would hardly call you unsuspecting," he replied softly. "In fact, I'd wager you're incredibly suspicious of people in general."

Her eyes narrowed. Even in the darkness he could see the odd expression on her face. "It is a flaw, I know, but it has served me well in the past. But then, this isn't the first time you've followed me."

"Surely you knew I'd come for you again."

She inclined her head and regarded him without an ounce of fear. He respected that, despite being irked by it. "The last time I saw you was almost a week ago. I thought perhaps you'd forgotten about me."

Was she actually flirting? He shrugged. He had lost track of the days as he sometimes did when on assignment. Still, it bothered him that he was missing time. "And now I have you."

She smiled at that—an expression he couldn't quite decipher. "You've had me before, sir. Or do you not remember?"

Again that tickle in the back of his brain. An itch he couldn't scratch. "I'm fairly certain you are a woman any man would loathe to forget."

Her smile saddened. "You don't remember."

"Should I?"

"No, I suppose not. Though I have many memories of you."

He walked toward her, slowly—as he might approach a feral cat. Unease tied a knot deep in his belly. "Then you have me at a disadvantage."

"I sincerely doubt that." She sighed. "You obviously followed me for a reason. What is it?"

Now that he was face-to-face with her, he found his readiness to end her life had waned considerably. There were many things he wanted to do to her, but killing her was not one of them. Still, he had no choice.

"You murdered a man who was very important to my employer." There was no need to lie to her—better she know why her life was about to be terminated.

"I'm afraid you're going to have to be more specific than that."

His eyebrow jumped. Was she sincere or mocking him? "You have that much blood on your hands?"

She crossed her arms over her lovely bosom. "I have no trouble sleeping at night."

"It doesn't bother you that Victor Erlich's widow mourns him still?"

She smirked at him. "Erlich wasn't married. Is he what all this fuss is about?"

"You killed him." He wanted to hear her confess to her crime. Surely she knew there would be retribution?

"And now you're here to avenge him, are you?"

Five gave a curt nod. "I'm here to make certain justice is served." So why hadn't he done it already? Why was he standing here waiting for her to tell him what he already knew to be true?

"Hmm. What was he to you?"

"I beg your pardon?"

"Erlich." She took a step toward him. Inexplicably he wanted to take a step backward. "Was he a friend of yours?"

"I didn't really know him." Now who stalked whom?

She came another step closer, but no more, keeping just out of reach. "You did—a long time ago. You once tried to kill him yourself."

Erlich had been part of the Company just as he was. There was no way he could have tried to kill the man. He might not remember his past, but he knew in his heart that he hadn't been without a sense of right and wrong.

"You're fighting for the wrong side, Luke," she told him. "You think you're doing the right thing, but the Company is using you. You're nothing but a weapon to them."

Five's temper flared. The way she spoke—with that sneer in her cultured tones—made him feel like an idiot, but worse, she made him question the only thing he knew and believed in.

No one else had ever inspired doubt in him like this woman did.

He closed the distance between them in the blink of an eye, startling her. "Forgive me," he said.

She fought him. He wouldn't have respected her quite so much if she hadn't. She struck at his face and chest, not with her nails or open palms, but with her fists. The woman knew how to throw a punch.

He wrapped his arms around her, preventing her from hitting him again as the taste of blood filled his mouth. Then she began kicking at his shins, throwing him off balance.

They fell to the damp grass with her on top. He rolled so their positions were reversed. Her legs tangled in her skirts and he held them with his own. He pinned one of her arms above her head with one hand, leaving him only his right to finish the job. Her other arm was pinned between them. Still she writhed and struggled beneath him. There was nothing seductive about her movements, but Five's body reacted as though she lay beneath him willingly.

He was there to kill her and his cock was hard. Christ Almighty, she drove him to depravity. When this was over he'd no doubt feel the shame of it.

"Stop fighting," he commanded. "This will go much easier for both of us if you just give in."

She stilled, and gazed up at him with eyes that were full of disappointment rather than fear. "You're going to kill me."

"I have to," he explained. He shouldn't have to explain; she knew what she had done. "I'm sorry, but you brought this upon yourself."

Her expression hardened. "I never asked Erlich to try to rape me. I never invited him to put a knife to my throat."

Five went very still. There was so much sincerity in her words that for a moment, he almost believed her. "You'd say anything to save your own life."

"I don't have to say anything at all," she retorted through clenched teeth.

Five wrapped his fingers around her throat and squeezed hard. Releasing her wrist, he came up on his knees and straddled her. It would be quicker—more merciful—if he used both hands. Her breath caught and she gasped for air, struggling against him.

Sudden pain bowed his spine. He gasped as his limbs spasmed, snapping his teeth together as his fingers unclenched. His vision blurred. Blood spread its salty copper on his tongue.

What the hell had she done to him? It felt as though he had lightning in his veins. He twitched, eyes rolling back into his head. She'd better kill him, because if he came back from this he was going to come for her again, and next time he would not be so kind as to simply strangle her.

Then lightning struck him again, and he collapsed on top of her as everything went black.

Chapter 5

Had she killed him?

Arden squirmed out from underneath Luke's incredibly—*incredibly*—heavy form. Once, she'd loved the weight of his body on hers, but not like this—not after sending enough electrical current through his body to bring down an elephant. She'd used the same device to kill Victor Erlich. Of course, she'd used considerably less power on her husband.

He hadn't expected her to simply lie there and allow him to kill her, had he? If so, the Company had truly wiped his memory, because he of all people should know that she was nothing if not resourceful.

Now that she had him, what should she do with him? He was extremely heavy—more than he ought to be, so there was no possible way she could haul him to her carriage, or anywhere else for that matter. Even if she could, it was bound to cause a sensation if they were seen.

What if Henry stumbled upon them? The cretin had already spoken to the family solicitors about having Lucas declared dead in absentia. If he saw his brother as he was now, he'd have him declared insane and hauled off to a private asylum, where they would drug Luke enough to quite possibly contain him, and that was if he were lucky. More than likely they'd declare him a traitor and execute him.

It was foolhardy of her, but she paused for a moment as she knelt over her husband's prone body. He wouldn't be unconscious for long, and she should use this time to physically restrain him, but it had been so long since she had had the pleasure of simply looking at his face.

In the misty light his skin had a gothic novel pallor, his hair an inky black. The lines fanning out from his eyes were more numerous than she remembered, but softened in slumber. Below his long nose his wide mouth was bracketed by faint half-moons so sharp and thin they seemed to have been cut by a wicked blade.

Her well-manicured nails dug into her palms as she curled her hands into fists. Which of the Company's butchers was responsible for this? Who dared abuse Luke's mind so thoroughly that they had obliterated all traces of her and their life together?

She'd make something special to torture them with in case their paths ever crossed.

Rising to her feet, she made her way to the fountain on legs that shook more than she would ever admit. He'd frightened her, her husband. The man who had never once lifted a hand to her, who would never dream of harming her, had come so very close to ending her in a most brutal fashion, and didn't seem the least bit concerned about it.

All right, perhaps he'd worn a touch of remorse in his expression, but not much.

To her shame, scalding tears welled in her eyes as she sat down on the rough stone. How could he have forgotten her? Regardless of what the Company did to him, how could he not look at her and know her? She would never have forgotten him, no matter what they did. Was it because of how they'd parted just before he disappeared?

Her shoulders slumped. Forgetting her was the only excuse for not coming home, and the only way she could redeem him in her own eyes and those of the W.O.R. office. The total obliteration of his past would be the only thing to save him from certain death.

Her fingers trembled as she reached inside the low bodice of her gown and pulled a small device from between her breasts. It resembled a tiny, delicate tuning fork, but was so much more. She tapped the prongs against the side of the fountain and lifted the instrument to her mouth as it vibrated in her hand.

"Alastair, I'm in the maze, by the fountain. I need you. Quickly." Then she wrapped her fingers around the prongs, forcing it to go still. Dear Alastair always came when she called. Tonight he was wearing one of the earpieces that went with this particular invention. The auditory amplification fork vibrated at a particular frequency matched by the earpieces, easily carrying the words of the person holding the fork to the person, or persons, with the proper receptors in their ear.

Arden tucked the device into her bodice once more. Then, something made her go completely still—an extra sense, perhaps, or a disturbance in the Aether. Regardless, she raised her head determined not to reveal that her heart now beat furiously in her throat. Lucas was no longer prone on the ground, but standing a few feet away. He wasn't terribly steady on his feet, but the fact that he was up brought a string of curses falling silent from her lips. *Hurry, Alastair.*

She met her husband's glittering gaze and rose slowly to her feet. Did he want to kill her or kiss her? And why did he just stand there? He had been sent to kill her and could have had the job done twice by now, especially since she hadn't been aware of his return to consciousness. He shouldn't have recovered so quickly. Death was far less disturbing than that damn smile on his face. And people said her smile could look mad.

She arched a brow at him as she folded her arms across her chest. "If you're trying to intimidate me, sir, it won't work."

"No," he replied, the word taking the smirk from his lips but not his eyes—nor his tone—"You don't seem the least bit frightened to find me awake and standing here."

"I'm not." This was why her father made the sentimentometer, because she could lie as naturally as breathing.

"You should be." He took a step closer, shearing the distance between them by more than a full foot. Arden stiffened, but didn't flinch. She refused to retreat from him and held her ground even as some small part inside her shrank back. It was the part of her that realized Luke was no longer the man she knew, but a man who had every intention of killing her.

Still, she would not give up hope. After seven years of having nothing but, she would not forsake it now.

Suddenly, his head whipped to the side, eyes narrowing before turning his attention to her once again. "Did you call in reinforcements, my lady?"

Alastair. She could hear his approach as well, God love him.

"Yes," she replied, amazed at just how firm her voice sounded. "Did you believe I'd simply wait for you to wake up and allow you to take another crack at killing me? You had better have your head examined by your physician as soon as possible if so."

He chuckled. "You sound just like a governess I once had." Then he frowned and blinked.

A memory! Arden's heart leaped in joy, despite the comparison that once annoyed her to no end. "Do I?" Rustling leaves heralded Alastair's imminent arrival. Just a few more moments and then they'd have Luke in custody and could set to work fixing what the Company had done to him.

"Yes," he said, closing the distance between them. "You do."

Before she could speak, or even breathe, Arden was hauled against him by a rough hand on her back. He was solid and warm, more muscled than she remembered. Her heart leaped into her throat, but she refused to let fear or any other emotion get the better of her.

His kiss was exactly as she remembered. All doubt vanished as his lips moved against hers in a manner she could only—gleefully—describe as possessive. She would have wrapped her arms around him and returned the kiss with all the longing she'd locked up inside these long, lonely years if he hadn't released her as abruptly as he had grabbed her.

He grinned. "You don't kiss like her, though. Next time I'd like to explore that a little bit further." And then he took off at a dead run that would have made the most spirited of horses envious and leaped over the hedge, disappearing into the night.

No sooner had he vanished than Alastair ran into the clearing, chest heaving. "What happened? Are you hurt?"

"I'm fine. My attacker fled when he heard your approach."

"Where is he?" he demanded, ginger-brown hair whipping about his face as his gray eyes glanced around.

"Gone," she replied, sinking down onto one of the stone benches. She pointed in the direction he'd run. "Don't worry, though, he'll come for me again."

"How do you know?"

He was her husband, that's how she knew. She knew him better than anyone—or rather she *had*.

Instead of saying just that, she touched her fingers to her lower lip, still warm and slightly moist from the kiss. "We have unfinished business, he and I."

In the waning hours before dawn, Five found himself in a pew in the back of a small church constructed of aged stone in varying—but otherwise unimpressive—shades of beige located within the area of the metropolis known as Square Mile—the original city of London.

It was dark inside the church, but the dark didn't bother him as it did most people. When shadows were so thick he could almost touch and taste them—that was when he felt the most at ease. So he didn't mind sitting there alone, though the church interior smelled of burnt candle wax and furniture polish, and he could hear rats scurrying in the corners.

The rats didn't seem to mind him either—a half-feral creature still a little twitchy from whatever Arden Grey had used to incapacitate him.

He had underestimated her—a mistake he would not make again. He was merely fortunate she hadn't decided to put a bullet in him while he was out. Although a bullet would have a hard time making it through his internal armor to pierce anything vital.

Absently, he rubbed his tingling fingers over the back of his other hand, feeling the metal-plated bones beneath. That was what the Company had done for him. Done *to* him. He frowned.

Familiar static crackled in his head. "*Status Report.*"

Five sighed and pinched the bridge of his nose with his thumb and index finger. Was it too much to ask for a moment's peace? He just needed to think, damn it. "It's not done."

A beat of silence. "*That is unacceptable.*"

Instead of apologizing, or trying to explain, he chose another tactic. "She knows me. How?"

"*She's W.O.R. She's probably seen your file.*"

That could be, but it didn't feel right. "I feel like I know her."

"*Impossible.*"

Inexplicable anger rose within him. "You're lying."

"*You forget yourself.*"

Five laughed humorlessly, slightly mad. Fortunately there was no one else there to witness it. "I have forgotten myself for many years."

"*Do the job.*"

Five didn't reply. He had a mission—one that he had believed in until now. Perhaps the woman was toying with him, using what she knew against him, but that didn't explain the man whose face had been so much like his. There were things going on that the Company didn't know.

Or didn't want him to find out.

"*Five?*"

"She got the best of me with some sort of weapon. Next time I will not fail."

"*See that you don't.*"

The static gave way to the telltale click before he could tell the bastard to go shag himself.

He slumped in the pew, and leaned back against the hard wood, closing his eyes. He would kill Arden Grey, but he was going to get a few questions answered first. She knew who he was, and that put him at a disadvantage.

Her face was so clear in his mind, flawless and sad. Why did she seem so sad when she looked at him? Fear and anger he could understand, but not such sadness. The memory of her tears brought a viselike tightness to his throat.

Tears? His eyes snapped open. She hadn't cried tonight. She hadn't been wearing a peach gown either, but
he could see her so clearly in his mind, tears trickling
down her cheeks as she stood before him in a soft peach
gown. She looked younger as well.

A memory. He did know her, or at least he had at one
time. Turning his mind to trying to figure out how was
pointless. He'd lost the moment, and trying to force it
only made his head hurt.

Still, it was something. He would make the woman
explain it to him the next time he came for her. She
would tell him the truth before he took her life.

"You're certain it was Huntley?"

Arden snatched the tumbler of whiskey from
Alastair's hand. They were at her house, in the library.
"Now that I think about it, no. In fact, I'm quite certain
it was Disraeli."

He grimaced at her sarcasm. "It's been seven years,
Arden."

She downed the contents of her glass in one swallow.
Oh, that lovely burn. It tasted like more. "You think I
don't remember my husband's face? His voice? It was
him, Alastair. Quite frankly I would expect you to be a
bit happier at the news."

It was a low blow and she knew it. She knew how
Alastair felt about her, though neither of them had spoken of it. In truth, she'd been too much of a coward. His
friendship meant too much to her to risk losing it, so she
pretended not to notice how he looked at her, pretended
not to understand the things he sometimes said.

Now he looked at her with so many mixed emotions
in his gray eyes she had to turn her head. "If Huntley is
alive, Arden, there is no one who will be happier than
me, save you." He spoke with such conviction that she

knew he truly meant it. Alastair was one of those rare people who really possessed a noble and honorable heart.

A better woman would have handed him her own heart years ago, but Arden had never quite managed it. He deserved one without prior claim, one free to be given wholly.

"It was him," she said, forcing herself to meet his gaze. Shamefully, tears blurred her vision. "Oh, Alastair. It was Luke, and he tried to kill me." Her voice broke on a sob as she turned away, pressing the back of her hand to her mouth as hot wetness poured down her cheeks.

Damn and blast. She wasn't one of those women who cried all the bloody time. Were the situation reversed she doubted Luke would stand here bawling over her. Yet there was no denying her emotions. She'd dare Queen Victoria herself to remain stoic after facing death at the hands of the man she'd pledged her life and heart to.

Although Prince Albert was more machine than man now, so perhaps her majesty could relate entirely.

Warm fingers took the glass from her other hand. There was a soft thud as it was set aside, and then strong arms encircled her. Like a child she crumpled against the solid wall of his chest, grasping at his lapels as though they were the last vestiges of her pride.

He smelled like bay rum and male, with a sweet hint of pipe tobacco. Inexplicably, the feel of his hands on her back made it seem as though it was going to be all right. If she raised her head she knew he would kiss her. She also knew that kiss would provide ample distraction, give her something to lose herself in, but ultimately would do nothing more than hurt one of her dearest friends and make a mockery of her wedding vows.

And her husband trying to choke her to death hadn't?

Sniffing, Arden pulled away, smoothing her hands

over the marks her fingers had left in the lapels of his jacket. "Forgive me," she murmured, voice a horrid nasal thrum.

A handkerchief appeared before her blurry gaze. She took it gratefully and wiped her eyes. Then, because it could not be ignored, she also blew her nose. Her spaniel, Beauregard, who had been sleeping on a nearby chair, looked up at the noise.

"Please don't give it back," came Alastair's low, gravelly voice.

She laughed—not just because of the expression of mock horror on his face, but because Alastair always made her laugh. "I imagine there are scads of formerly distressed damsels across Europe who have one of these squirreled away in their lingerie drawers."

"They are legion," he replied drily. Then he grabbed the bottle of whiskey from the cabinet and poured her another glass. "Come, sit with me. Tell me everything."

Arden tucked the damp linen into her sleeve and followed him to the sofa.

He did not attempt to hold her, which said more for his character than any daring rescue or dangerous intrigue he'd orchestrated on behalf of the Wardens. He was not one to take advantage of a situation—or put either of them at risk of doing something they'd both regret. He thought too much of her—and too much of himself.

She told him about waking up to find Lucas in her room the night of the murder at Hammond & Sons, and about the poppy in the carriage, and finally how she'd gone out for a bit of air that evening suspecting that he might come for her again. Hoping that he might. The only thing she didn't tell him was about the kiss—not because she didn't wish to hurt him, but because that was private.

When she finished, Arden found Alastair watching

her with a deep frown on his lightly tanned face. "Mind control," he muttered. "Christ Jesus."

"You believe me?" How incredulous she sounded — pathetically so.

He nodded. "I don't want to, but I'd be a fool to do otherwise. I'd rather suspect the Company of doing the impossible than dismiss the notion and end up buggered."

Unlike Inspector Grant, Alastair did not apologize for his choice of words. Then again, he knew Arden could turn a coarse phrase when she wished.

"What do I do?" she asked.

"What do *we* do," he corrected her, pouring a drink for himself as well. "I'm not about to let you go through this alone — Huntley either, for that matter."

Her shoulders slumped with great relief. To have him believe her meant more than she could ever hope to articulate. "All right then, what are we going to do?"

"If he's been sent here to kill you, he's obviously going to try again to complete his mission. We will have to set a trap."

A frown pulled at Arden's brows. "He's strong, Alastair. Unnaturally so. I think he could have snapped my neck with one hand. And he's heavy — more so than a man his size ought to be."

Her friend did not seem surprised by this. "They've undoubtedly augmented him, probably with internal armor and metal plating on some of his bones. We've had success with it recently on some of our own agents as well."

With that statement the pair of them directed their attention at Alastair's right hand. It looked relatively normal except for the scars. His hand had been crushed several years ago. Dr. Evelyn Stone operated, laboriously replacing and reinforcing his bones with metal —

even the joints were delicate and complicated hinges. Arden knew this because she constructed those joints and assisted the smithy in forging the new bones. It had taken hours for Evie to work around the tendons and muscle, but the end result was that Alastair possessed a hand that was incredibly strong and dexterous.

"Isn't the procedure dangerous?" she asked, even though she knew the answer.

He nodded. "If Huntley survived it, no wonder they altered his mind as well. They wouldn't want to risk losing him—he's too powerful a weapon."

A human-automaton hybrid. Arden shuddered at the thought. She was all for the progression of science, but there were some things that seemed wrong—even to her. Saving Alastair's hand was one thing, but filling a man full of metal in order to make him a more efficient warrior was quite another.

Arden raised her glass to her lips and drank. Soon her muscles would become wonderfully languid and she would go to bed, slipping into a dreamless sleep. "We'd better make certain it's a good trap, then. If we fail it could end up costing both our lives."

"Do you own a pistol?" he asked.

"You know I have several."

"Keep one beside your bed—within easy reach. I'll be by in the morning. I believe I know exactly how to capture our boy without harming him."

Hope blossomed in Arden's chest. She reached across the short distance between them and took Alastair's scarred hand in her own. "Thank you."

His fingers curled around hers. She watched as he swallowed, a frown marring his brow. "You do realize that if the Company has tampered with his mind he may not be the man you married. He may never be that man again."

The truth was a hard and bitter lump in her throat. "I know."

He squeezed her fingers, his gray gaze strangely vulnerable. "I want you to know that I'm here if ever you have need of me, no matter what the circumstances. Or the need."

Oh *no*. No, after all these years don't let him do this now. "Alastair—"

She swallowed the rest of her words as his mouth claimed hers. It was a passionate kiss—one that should have weakened her knees and dropped her drawers—but she felt nothing, nothing but the horrid guilt of wondering what she had ever done to win his regard.

He released her, a flush across the top of his high cheekbones, regret dimming his gaze. "I should apologize, but I won't. If Huntley is back I know I'll never have another chance to kiss you again. I couldn't let the opportunity slip away."

Arden opened her mouth, but the words got tangled up in her tongue and refused to come out.

"Not a word," he said, rising to his feet. "We can pretend this never happened if you like, and I will do whatever you ask of me where your husband is concerned. He was my best friend and I will do everything in my power to reunite the two of you."

"Why?" she demanded, finally finding her voice.

The twist of his lips could hardly be called a smile, for it was completely void of humor. "Because I love you, Arden. That's why." Then he turned on his heel and strode from the room, leaving her reaching for the bottle of whiskey.

Chapter 6

Arden had been asleep for a grand total of four hours when someone knocked on her door. Loudly.

"What?" she yelled, stomach and bed rolling as though on the open sea. Most people would swear to never drink again at this point. Arden knew better than to make such empty promises.

The door opened. In the predawn gloom her bleary eyes made out the silhouette of Mrs. Bird. The older woman was in her nightclothes and cap. "I'm terribly sorry, my lady, but there's a gentleman here—"

Arden bolted upright, swallowing hard to keep her stomach where it ought to be. "Is he from the sanitorium?" Had her mother had another apoplexy, or worse?

The housekeeper's expression could only be described as sympathetic—perhaps with a little indulgence tossed in. "No, ma'am. He says Inspector Grant sent him."

Damn and blast. Another murder. "Tell him I will be down directly."

The older woman nodded, then hesitated. "Do you . . . do you require any assistance, Lady Huntley?"

Arden's lips twisted, her expression as unsteady and brittle as her constitution. "You're a love, Mrs. Bird. Take yourself back to bed. I can look after myself."

The housekeeper didn't look as though she believed that last part, but she dipped a curtsy and left the room. Arden crawled out of bed and staggered to the wardrobe. She used her nightgown as a chemise and pulled a gown of thin russet suede over her head. It had a built-in corset that laced in the front. She didn't bother with stockings, just shoved her feet into matching boots. Her head swam as she fumbled with the laces.

She had passed out with her hair up, so she didn't have to tend to that. She was a little steadier on her feet as she walked to the door. She opened it to find Mrs. Bird on the other side holding a glass of cloudy liquid.

"Your tonic, my lady. I thought you might have a need."

"You deserve a raise in wages, Mrs. Bird."

The woman's plump cheeks dimpled. "Indeed, ma'am. Drink up now."

Arden took the glass and downed as much as she could in one swallow. It was foul stuff, but it worked.

Another long swallow. With a grimace, she handed the empty glass back to her housekeeper. "Thank you."

"If I might be so bold, I worry about you, my lady."

Arden stifled an unladylike belch and brought her hand up to clap the other woman's shoulder. "I worry about me too, my dear Mrs. Bird. I will endeavor to alleviate both of our concerns in the future."

Mrs. Bird didn't look as though she believed that any more than Arden did. Arden took her carpetbag from where it sat beside the door and crossed the threshold.

Inspector Grant's man waited for her in the hall at the bottom of the stairs. He removed his cap when he saw her. "Beg your pardon, Lady Huntley. Inspector Grant bade me to tell you he wouldn't have sent for you at such an ungodly hour if he didn't have need of you."

"No need to apologize, sir. Let us not keep the inspector waiting any longer." She took a cape from the closet and allowed the young man to place it around her shoulders before leaving the house.

The police carriage was horse-driven—real horses, not automaton. Good lord, it was going to take forever to get where they were going. At least she would be as sober as she was likely to get by the time they reached the scene.

Thankfully the officer sat up front with the driver, leaving Arden alone in the coach. She rested her head on the hard cushions and closed her eyes, letting the tonic do its work. By the time the ill-sprung, rickety vehicle hobbled to a full stop she was as much herself as she could be.

She didn't wait for someone to open the door for her—it seemed such a silly thing given the circumstances. The steps weren't equipped to automatically drop, so she gave them a nudge with her boot and then descended to the damp pavement.

It had begun to rain since she left the house—and this time Mrs. Bird hadn't thought to make her take her umbrella. At least her cape would save her gown from ruin. She slipped the hood up over her head and trotted after the officer who guided her to where Inspector Grant waited. She had to dodge puddles already forming on the uneven cobblestones.

She didn't know where she was exactly. Given the direction in which they'd traveled and the smell, she guessed they were near the docks. Daylight was a sliver of gray on the horizon, but already there was activity around a few of the warehouses. The workers and middle classes were coming to life just as the upper and lower levels of society were going to bed.

Or being yanked out of them whilst still somewhat inebriated, as the case might be.

"Lady Huntley," the inspector said, doffing his hat. "My apologies for the hour, but we have a situation much like what we had at Hammond's, and I need your expertise."

Arden met his gaze from beneath her hood. "You want to know if it's the same man."

"Yes, ma'am."

She straightened her shoulders as rain pelted her back. Her cloak would be covered with dots of grime when it dried—the air down here was thick and sticky with coal dust, coal being a cheaper method of generating the heat needed to create steam than the gas and oil used in better neighborhoods. "You'd better take me to her then, Inspector Grant." Her stomach recoiled at the thought, but duty took precedence over the fact that she'd felt compelled to drink herself stupid over Alastair's kiss and declaration.

He led her to a narrow alley between two ancient buildings that seemed to have nothing more than spite holding them upright. There, on the worn stones, lay the body of a woman, already wet with her own blood. The rain and filth of the alley only served to spread the crimson stain throughout her clothing and skin.

It was not as bad as the girl at the factory, but bad enough. This woman—and she was just barely one at that—had been slit from belly to throat, her petticoats thrown up around her thighs.

Her stockings had been mended more times than Arden could count, and her petticoats—a dull gray beneath the faded, and too-short blue gown—were patched and frayed. Whatever sorrows and trials life had thrown her, poverty was not one Arden knew except by sight. It was a fact for which she was entirely grateful. How sad to have to sell oneself and still not have enough to purchase tooth powder or a bar of soap.

She crouched beside the body to get a better look, lifted the petticoats with one gloved hand, and saw a glint of thick moisture on the girl's thigh. Men were so free with the stuff. She'd seen it all manner of surprising places and locales. How unfortunate that there wasn't a way to trace the ejaculate to the man. They'd take care where they left it then.

"Did you rearrange her clothing, Inspector?" she asked, darting a quick glance at Grant.

He bobbed his head in a curt nod. "She may have been a dollymop, but she deserves a bit of dignity."

"You dear man." Obviously she was still a little drunk, but the compliment was deserved no matter how much it embarrassed either of them. "He used her then, before he killed her."

"I hope it was before," one of the younger officers commented.

Grant chastised the boy for speaking so in front of Arden, but she called him off. "I hope so, too," she agreed, before turning her attention back to Grant. "Did Dr. Stone deduce that there had been sexual congress with the Lynbourne girl?"

The older man gave a curt nod, his sharp gaze on the young officer. The poor thing was going to get a serious talking-to later, Arden suspected.

"No wonder you asked for me. The murder is very similar to that at Hammond's."

"Except this poor thing was a far cry from a debutante," Grant added.

"Indeed. Well, let's find out, shall we?" She opened her bag and removed her gear.

"Excuse me, Inspector?" One of the officers stood at the entry to the alley. "We have a potential witness, sir. I thought you might like to speak to her."

Grant turned to Arden. "Do you have need of me here, my lady?"

"None at all," she replied, slipping on her spectacles. In fact she preferred to do this sort of thing as privately as possible. She never knew what she was going to see or how it was going to affect her.

Three minutes later she was on her hands and knees retching against the wall of the alley. What had happened to this woman had been awful—some of the most vile images she'd ever had scorched into her mind.

Arden slowly pushed herself up so that she knelt in the alley. Rain dripped from the edge of her hood onto her face, and she welcomed its chill. Her hands shook as she removed the apparatus from the prostitute's head and returned it to her bag. Whoever had killed her was indeed a monster, but not the same monster who'd killed Baron Lynbourne's daughter. This man hadn't worn fancy clothes, and he was missing his front teeth.

And he'd raped her while he killed her—used her in so many awful ways before making the brutal cut. Then he'd delivered his final insult by spending himself on her leg after he was done, as her life flowed across the dirty stones.

A shadow moved across the alley as the lazy fingers of a wet dawn slowly crept in. Arden glanced up, expecting to see Inspector Grant.

Instead she saw a dirty man in need of a shave and a dentist. Her heart stopped at the sight of him. She knew him. She had seen him just a few moments ago through the prostitute's eyes.

Frantically, she groped for the pistol she always carried in her bag. The killer came at her fast. For a second she was too terrified to scream, her mind flashing through the gruesome catalog the woman's eyes had given her. Her normal calm, or facsimile of it, disintegrated like sugar into tea as his filthy hands reached for her. She opened her mouth . . .

There was a snap, and the killer crumpled to the ground beside his victim, his head turned at an impossible angle, sightless eyes bulging and wide.

She might have felt relief if she hadn't looked up and met her husband's bright gaze.

There were few people who could manage to look imposing and dangerous—and altogether too gorgeous—when dripping wet, but Lucas was one of them.

Inky hair fell over his forehead as water trickled down the lean planes of his face. Shadows deepened the lines around his eyes and mouth, made the grim smile on his lips all the more frightening.

Rain poured off the long leather coat that hung from the strong breadth of his shoulders—exaggerated by the leanness of the rest of his frame. He crouched before her, paying no attention to the body of the prostitute or the man he had just killed with the apparent ease of swatting a bug.

"What is it about you that makes people want you dead?" he asked, eyes glinting unnaturally bright in the gray morning.

Arden's fingers closed around the pistol in her bag. Now that the first threat to her safety was gone, she wasn't about to let this one get the better of her. "Part of my charm, I suppose." He chuckled and she added, "Why didn't you let him? He would have done the job for you."

His gaze locked with hers, and what she saw there sent a shiver down her spine. "You're mine," he growled.

"Yours to kill, you mean." It was tempting to let him do it. She didn't want to die, but the thought of him being able to kill her . . . Well, what was the point of going on when so much of her life had been about him and he was lost forever?

She needed a drink, or perhaps a good slap.

His hand came up, and she fought a flinch. Instead of grabbing her already bruised throat, he cupped her cheek. She had the pistol out of the bag.

"Are you going to shoot me?" he asked with a smile, fingers rough against her skin. "Do you think a bullet can stop me?"

Arden placed the end of the barrel against the underside of his chin. "I doubt they thought to armor you here."

He grinned, white teeth flashing in the fading gloom. "That's my girl."

She froze, gaze searching his face for some sign of recognition. "How do you know I'm your girl?"

His grin faded, the light in his eyes turned to ice. He dropped his hand to her neck, but instead of squeezing, he gently stroked the tender and battered skin. "I don't know. But you are, aren't you?"

God, it hurt to swallow; her throat was so tight—a condition that had nothing to do with the strength of his touch, but rather the gentleness of it. "Yes," she whispered, but she did not move the pistol.

His dark brows dipped. "Why can't I kill you? I remember . . . I know I've tried to do this before, but failed. I resolve to do it, but when I'm with you, killing you is the last thing I want to do."

The suggestive timbre of his voice ignited a flame inside her. It had been so long, but intimately she remembered all the times he had spoken to her in that tone—and what generally followed.

She opened her mouth. It was simple. All she had to say was "I'm your wife," but the words refused to come. What if she said it and he couldn't remember?

"Lady Huntley?" came a voice from the mouth of the alley. It was Inspector Grant.

Her husband sprang to his feet, leaving her mourning the warmth of his touch. "I'll come for you again," he promised her.

"I'd be disappointed if you didn't," she retorted coolly. Inside she trembled like a child.

She watched in awe as he scaled the side of one of the buildings using only the structure's windows and ledges for purchase. He climbed like a spider.

Inspector Grant rushed to her side. "Good Lord, what happened?"

Of course he would notice the new body in the alley—and the strange man fleeing the scene.

Arden's shoulders slumped. "The dead man is our murderer. He attacked me."

"The other bloke killed him?"

She nodded, numb.

"Broke the bastard's neck. Can't say that I'm sorry—though I'm going to have the head of one of my good-for-nothing constables for not being here to protect you. I should like to shake your rescuer's hand."

Something snapped inside her and laughter rushed forth like water over a broken dam. She felt like death warmed over; she'd just seen a vicious crime through the eyes of the victim, been attacked by the murderer and then saved by the man she loved who also wanted to kill her. And dear Inspector Grant wanted to shake Luke's hand.

What else could possibly happen next?

Alastair was waiting for her in the parlor, enjoying a cup of coffee, when she arrived home. It was the perfect continuation of the day, and exactly in keeping with Arden's opinion that fate was out to give her a royally good spanking.

He looked perfect, as he generally did. His steely gray frock coat matched his eyes, and his ivory shirt warmed his complexion. He might have at least had the courtesy to look a little worse for wear, but then again he hadn't been the one trying to drown himself in a bottle of whiskey.

His eyes widened at the sight of her. "You look awful."

The insult lessened the guilt she felt over his earlier declaration of love. "How terribly convenient, seeing as that's exactly how I feel."

Others might have flushed at her words, but Alastair merely raised one cinnamon brow as he set his cup on the table in front of him. "Imbibed a bit too much last night, did you?"

"A tad," she replied with forced lightness.

He knew why—it was plain as the knot in his cravat. The bounder didn't even have the decency to apologize for admitting his feelings and ruining what, for Arden, had been a perfectly lovely friendship.

Of course she'd gotten cross-eyed drunk after he left. Her dearest friend loved her, and she was in no way deserving of that love. Lord, she was a proper mess. She loved a man who wanted to kill her. She worked for the government because her husband and father had, not because she particularly enjoyed the work. She hadn't even been a decent enough wife to pop out an heir within the first year of marriage.

And then there was the fact that there was a very good chance she might lose her mind one day, as her mother had done and was still doing.

"Would you care to join me for breakfast, Alastair?" she asked. Self-pity and a good brush with death did wonders for the appetite.

He nodded and rose to his feet. "Mrs. Bird said you were out with Grant. Was there another murder?"

Arden took his arm as he offered it, and shamefully leaned on him a little as they left the room. She stifled a yawn. "Yes, but not by our factory killer."

"You don't have to go every time he whistles, you know. I know Dhanya assigned you to Scotland Yard, but let the fellow solve his own bloody crimes once in a while."

"He wouldn't have sent for me if he hadn't believed the murders might be connected."

"Are you all right?"

Telling him about Luke sat on the tip of her tongue. She wanted very badly to tell him everything about that morning, but if she did he might see Luke as a threat and not be so keen to help her capture him. He would try to protect her, and that was the last thing she wanted right now. He couldn't be her hero anymore—that was her husband's job.

If he didn't kill her first.

"No," she replied honestly. "I'm not all right. But I will be after some coffee and eggs." That was true as well, to an extent. Physically she would feel better, and that would have to do for now.

"Did you bring the device?" she inquired as they ate. Mrs. Bird had set an extra place at the table upon Alastair's arrival, and the two of them sat across from each other at the breakfast nook in the Egyptian drawing room. They had done this before: taken breakfast together. It had never bothered her before, but now she was aware of the intimacy of the act and it shamed her.

How could Alastair have possibly fallen in love with her? It was such a ridiculous notion. Her, of all people. Lord, imagine the freckled little ginger children they'd produce!

He nodded as he smeared peach jam on his toast.

"Yes. I had the footmen take it up to your rooms when I learned you weren't at home."

"Why would you do that?" It came out a bit more suspicious than she intended, but he'd turned her upside down with his declaration, and things that would never have bothered her before suddenly seemed to take on much more meaning. Having something taken to her private rooms was so improper now that Luke was home. Now that Alastair had betrayed her by admitting his feelings aloud.

Nonplussed, Alastair took a bite of toast. He chewed and swallowed, forcing her to sit and wait for his answering, her embarrassment growing with every second. "Because I assume that's where Huntley will come for you, where he believes you to be the most vulnerable."

"Is that where you would choose to attack a woman, in her bed?"

He took a sip of coffee and slowly returned the cup to the table. Then he turned those damned stormy eyes of his to her, seeming to look right to the heart of her. "You're angry with me because of last night. I understand that, but I'm not the man who tried to kill you, Arden. If you expect me to apologize for that you will be sorely disappointed."

Arden massaged her forehead with her fingers, eyes closed in shame. "Forgive me, Alastair. I am a proper wretch this morning."

A slim smile curved his lips. "You are most mornings."

Despite herself and the day she'd already had, though it wasn't yet nine o'clock, a snort of laughter burst out of her. She reached across and wrapped her fingers around his with a gentle squeeze. "You're my dearest friend, Alastair."

Something flickered in the depth of his eyes. Pain— she'd seen enough of the emotion to recognize it. It disappeared as quickly as it had come. He turned his hand palm up so that he could squeeze her fingers in turn. "You've been mine as well. I will miss our friendship."

Arden straightened, heart sputtering. "Are you going somewhere?" Surely he wasn't going to run away just because she couldn't love him in the way he wanted?

"No," he replied with a hint of sadness. "But we won't be able to carry on like this once Huntley returns."

"Why won't we?" she demanded, pulling her hand away. Why did he have to continue bringing up these oh-so-vexing truths?

He fixed her with a stalwart gaze. "Because I have my pride. And because I will not play a part in making one of my oldest friends seem a cuckold." At her outraged scoff he added, "You must know there's been gossip about us, Arden. Even you, with your head filled with books and machines."

She did know, but she had ignored it because she hadn't wanted to lose him. He was her rock, the thing she'd clung to ever since Luke's disappearance. He had given her focus. Given her hope. As Luke's friend it had been as if she still had a piece of her husband with her.

To her great shame, tears sprang to her eyes. They would not have dared appear if she'd been at her best. "I've used you most terribly, Alastair."

He rose from his chair and came down on one knee beside hers. "You haven't done anything I haven't allowed you to do. No need for tears, love. Not for me."

That only made the hot wet pour all the harder down her cheeks. She threw her arms around his neck and buried her face in his shoulder.

"All right," Alastair murmured, planting a kiss on her forehead as he rubbed her back. "Go ahead and cry it all out then. . . . Jesus Christ!"

Arden jumped out of his arms. "What?" she asked. He

was already on his feet, face white as he moved to the window.

"Alastair? What was it?"

He turned his head toward her, steely eyes bright with shock. "Huntley," he rasped. "I swear to God it was Huntley."

Who the hell was he? Five raged as he tore through the streets of Mayfair on his velocycle. Who was the bastard who had the nerve to put his hands on *his* woman? And why had the sight of the two of them embracing—the man consoling her—felt like a blade in his heart?

It had felt like a betrayal, and that stunned him into stupidity. He never should have allowed himself to be seen. Now the man knew he was watching Lady Huntley, and that made him inconvenient. He'd rather not kill any more people than he had to, and instinct told him the man would not be easy to take down—not like the miscreant in the alley that morning.

Five should have let the greasy bastard do his job for him, but the thought of those dirty hands around Arden Grey's throat filled him with a deep, inexplicable rage. He told himself she was destined to die by his hand, but he hadn't allowed that to happen either. The perfect opportunity to snuff out the light in her eyes, and he hadn't been able to do it.

Why? He'd never failed in a task before. It wasn't because he was attracted to her. He had been attracted to other women as well, but if one of them betrayed him he'd snap her like a twig. What made this hungover, auburn-haired wench different?

Why had the sight of her in that man's arms, in that house, made his chest tight? Never in a million years would he have thought Alastair capable of such a betrayal.

Alastair?

The two-wheeled machine beneath him swerved suddenly. He had to jerk on the steering bars to avoid hitting a steam carriage. The driver yelled obscenities at him, but they barely registered in Five's mind. He drove the cycle down the street to his lodgings, parked and took the stairs to his rooms two at a time. His mind raced, a pulse pounding in his temple as he held on to the memory and struggled for more.

The man's name was Alastair. He was the Earl of Wolfred. He was three and thirty, the same as Five. They had been at school together. That's where they became friends. Alastair had stood with him when he married . . .

Pain split his skull, lancing deep into his brain. He stumbled into his room, barely slamming the door before his vision blurred and black swarmed the edge of his mind. He couldn't see his bride's face through the agony.

Her face was what brought the agony — he knew this. He fought to remember her even as his stomach threatened to empty itself and his body trembled. He knew this pain; it was as familiar as an old friend. This was like what the Doctor did to him when he visited, only he hadn't remembered it until now.

He wasn't supposed to remember. Someone had taken his memories away. Taken away his identity, his life.

They had taken away his wife.

Five's knees slammed into the floor, splintering the wood. He crawled across the worn rug, every inch bringing his skull that much closer to exploding. Her laughter rang in his ears, loud and unrestrained. Her skin had felt like a mix of silk and velvet. He remembered once she had tasted of peaches, and she smelled . . . she smelled of bergamot.

Something broke inside his mind. He felt it give like a

string pulled too taut. His temple struck the floor as he collapsed, and he lay there unable to move or make a sound—scarcely able to breathe. His ear felt ticklish and warm. Probably blood.

Darkness took hold and shook him like a dog with a rag doll. His last thought before letting that darkness take him was that Arden Grey smelled of bergamot as well.

Chapter 7

Henry arrived at four—just in time for tea. Arden was in her workshop, thoroughly distracted by a new invention that combined Mr. Tesla's work and her father's research in sending and tracking Aether wave transmissions. She had just attached the small mechanism to Beauregard's collar when Mrs. Bird knocked to tell her of her brother-in-law's arrival.

Arden was tempted to tell Mrs. Bird to turn him away, but they needed to speak. "Put him in the library, Mrs. Bird. We'll take tea there." The library was where she felt the most secure—other than her workshop, and she'd be buggered if she'd let Henry see the inside of her sanctuary. Books bored Henry, whose interests were of a more physical, to the hounds, sort of bent. Luke had been the same to an extent, but he'd never made her feel like an oddity because of her interests.

After wiping them on a small towel, she applied cream to her hands. Then she removed her apron and smoothed her hair. Henry already thought her half mad;

there was no need to strengthen that notion by cultivating the appearance of a harridan.

Beauregard, having none of her insecurities or vanity, ran from the room on his short legs, his entire hindquarters wagging in anticipation of the tummy scratching "Uncle" Henry was certain to perform. For as long as she'd known him, Henry preferred animals to people— or at least he preferred them to her. He hadn't thought much of his older brother marrying the daughter of a practically impoverished baronet. The former Lord Huntley—her father-in-law—had decreed that there were some connections worth more than money, such as Sir Frederick's political and government cronies within the W.O.R. To be honest, there had been moments when she wondered if that was why Luke married her, but she knew it was rubbish. He'd loved her. She was certain of it—even if his brother thought he was "settling."

Before she left the workshop, she couldn't help but check the small viewer on the workbench. A thrill raced through her as she saw the small dot of light moving up the screen. The device worked! Using radio waves she was able to track the dog's movements. While it wasn't sophisticated enough to show her the best path to take, it was better than nothing. She would have to check it to make certain it did indeed have the correct location, and if that worked she could take it to Dhanya. Surely this sort of apparatus would be useful to the Wardens.

And perhaps, in their gratitude, they would go easy on her husband. The idea of what they might do to him if they suspected him of treason . . . Well, there was no point in worrying about that now. It only made her snappy and short of breath, neither trait one she desired to exhibit in front of her brother-in-law.

Her stride was quick as she walked down the stairs. Her boot heels clicked loudly on the polished floor of the open hall, sharp and rapid. Her jaw began to ache, it was clenched so tight. This was what Henry did to her. He did it to her at the party the night Lucas tried to strangle her. In fact, she would rather go up against her physically enhanced, murderous-minded spouse right now than his younger brother.

It wasn't that she didn't like Henry. Once upon a time she quite adored him, but that was before Lucas disappeared, and Henry reverted to thinking ill of her. Before he started talking of having his brother declared legally dead so that he could fully assume the title of Earl Huntley rather than continue on as proxy. He treated her servants as his own, came to call whenever he pleased, and considered allowing her to remain at the house a gesture of his generosity.

It was enough to make her former adoration turn rancid. Never mind that she was probably unfair toward him in her estimation of his motives and assessment of his behavior, he was still *wrong*. She strode into the library with every intention of telling him just that.

Mrs. Bird, invaluable housekeeper as she was, had arranged for extra tea, sandwiches and cake to be delivered to the library. Normally Arden took tea alone, so the extra food must have been taken from what would normally be shared by the servants. Henry had better eat it then, if her household had to go without because of his uninvited arse.

Make that uninvited *arses*, she corrected as she crossed the threshold. Not only was Henry there, but he had brought a guest as well, an average-looking man of just-above-average height whom she recognized as Mr. Kirkpatrick, the family solicitor. How dare Henry ambush her like this! Luckily she hadn't had any liquor to drink — that would have made her relaxed, and she needed to be sharp right now.

Arden smiled, well aware it was probably more a baring of teeth than anything remotely pleasant. "My dear Henry, how lovely to see you. Mr. Kirkpatrick, this is an unexpected surprise; it has been too long."

The solicitor, gentleman that he was, cast an uncomfortable and somewhat tense glance at Henry. "Apologies, Lady Huntley. I thought you expected us this afternoon."

Watching Henry squirm afforded more pleasure than it ought. "Well, it is nice to see you all the same, sir. Will you sit? My cook makes an incomparable tea."

Mr. Kirkpatrick smiled and inclined his head. "How could I refuse? Thank you."

Arden's own smile faded as she turned to her brother-in-law. "Henry. Sit."

He had the good grace to look uncomfortable as he resumed his seat. He might not have much in the way of love for her, but he was intimidated by her all the same. Arden seated herself on the settee where she would be better able to play hostess, but also where she would be the most comfortable.

She poured three cups of tea, added the requested milk and sugar and prepared plates for herself and her callers. It might be petty but she resented having to wait upon them when they were there to make her life difficult. They made small talk as she went through this ritual. Then, when they all had refreshment at hand, she asked, "To what do I owe the pleasure of this visit?"

The solicitor cleared his throat. "Lady Huntley, Lord Henry has asked me to begin proceedings to have Lord Huntley declared dead in absentia."

"Has he?" She shot a dark glance at Henry, who met her gaze with a defiant lift of his chin. "Well, I'm afraid he brought you here for nothing, Mr. Kirkpatrick. You see, my husband isn't dead."

"My dear Arden," Henry began with a sigh, "I know you loved my brother, and your devotion does you credit, but it's been seven years. You can no longer maintain this pathetic obsession."

Pathetic? Oh, he was fortunate she didn't have her discombobulator on her. She'd send enough electricity through him to singe his hair. He'd have a hard time of looking like a dandy then, when all that pomade caught fire.

"It's not 'pathetic,' Henry. It's true. Lucas is in London. I've seen him several times." She hadn't meant to reveal all so soon, nor in this blunt manner, but he gave her no choice. He was going to have Lucas declared legally dead, and she couldn't allow that to happen, no matter whether her husband remembered himself or not.

The color ran from Henry's face. Mr. Kirkpatrick leaned forward, as though a closer inspection of her person might make her words more clear. "You've seen him, my lady?"

"Yes."

"Where?" Henry demanded. Blood had returned to his upper extremities and now his cheeks were positively florid.

"Here," Arden replied. "Outside the party the other night, and elsewhere in London."

"It wasn't him." Henry shook his head most vigorously. "It couldn't have been him. You are mistaken, Arden. Your grief makes you see what your heart wishes were true."

While his heart made him fervently deny it, she realized his own desire to see his brother again. Immediately her animosity toward him eased. Perhaps he found it

easier to insist that Lucas was dead than torture himself
with hope as she had all these years.

She wanted to scream that she'd been right from the
bloody rafters. All of London pitied her, thought her
touched in the head, and she had been *right*!

"It *is* true," she insisted—gently. "Lord Wolfred saw
him as well, earlier today."

The poor thing looked as though she had tossed tea
in his face. She would hug him if she weren't still
miffed.

"This certainly changes things," Mr. Kirkpatrick surmised, clearly thrown off-kilter. He probably didn't have
clients come back from the dead very often. "Do you
suppose Lord Wolfred would be willing to discuss the
encounter with me?"

"I do not see why not." Arden smiled at the man, but
she knew what he was thinking. If Lucas had returned to
England why was he not in this house, with his wife? His
gentlemanly ways kept him from asking in front of
Henry, but the solicitor would have many questions for
her in the near future.

"My brother is not alive," Henry maintained rather
heatedly. "I would know if he was alive."

Arden felt for him, she truly did. "He is, Henry."

"No!" He leaped to his feet, cheeks afire and eyes
blazing. "If Lucas was alive he would be here with you.
With me!"

Slowly, she rose as well, watching him as she would a
growling dog. "I promise you he is alive."

"Then why isn't he here? Why haven't I seen him?"

She stilled, and cast a glance at Mr. Kirkpatrick out of
the corner of her eye. She didn't want to have this conversation in front of the man who held her husband's
fate in his hands. "I'm sure he would be if he could." She

gave him what she hoped was a meaningful look. He knew his brother worked for the W.O.R.—it had been a point of contention between them. Henry didn't think Luke should put himself in harm's way when he had a responsibility to his family.

Henry shook his head. "I don't believe it." A hiccough of laughter escaped him. "I don't *believe* it."

At this point, Arden decided the best course of action was to keep her silence. Mr. Kirkpatrick, however, chose the alternative. "I think perhaps Lord Henry and I should take our leave of you, Lady Huntley."

"No," Henry protested. "She's wrong, or lying. My brother is dead, and I refuse to think otherwise until I've seen him with my own eyes."

"Had you joined me for a walk in the garden so we might continue our conversation the other night, you would have seen him." More than likely Luke wouldn't have shown himself, but there was no need to remark on that.

She might as well have been talking to a door for all the attention her brother-in-law paid her.

The solicitor rose to his feet. "Come along now, Lord Henry. We can continue this meeting at another date." He turned to Arden. "At a time that is convenient for you, of course, my lady."

She nodded. "Of course. Thank you."

The older man then added, "Perhaps his lordship will be able to join us."

Well, at least he hadn't called her a liar as Henry had, but there was an element of disbelief in his voice. She could hardly blame him. She wouldn't believe a word of it either if she wasn't living it.

"I hope so," she replied.

Mr. Kirkpatrick guided Henry to the door and gently

pushed him over the threshold; then he stopped in the doorway and looked over his shoulder at her. "It's not that he wants the title so badly, Lady Huntley, but rather that Lord Henry desperately wants to move forward and stop living in the past."

Arden tried to smile, but simply didn't have the heart for it. "Don't we all, good sir. Don't we all."

Five sat at the rickety table in his room eating the plain but hearty supper his landlady had prepared for him. His head felt like it had been kicked repeatedly by a foul-tempered mule, but at least he had an appetite.

The voice in his ear—in his head—had called to him earlier, after he woke up. He hadn't responded. More than likely he'd catch hell for it later, but for now he felt no remorse. Right now he was trying to sort out whether or not the Company had lied to him, or if his imagination was filling in gaps his memory couldn't.

He didn't like the thought of having been lied to and used. Undoubtedly he wasn't alone in that sentiment, especially when it came to having his trust betrayed. That aside, there was no denying that he had remembered things since being back in England.

Since his first encounter with Arden Grey. She was the key to all of this—his key to the truth. He could not kill her until he discovered just what that truth was.

Seeing her earlier, in such a private moment with that man, had awoken feelings in him that could only be described as jealousy, anger and possessiveness—with a dose of sadness tossed in.

He had killed other women—and men—agents who tried to play both sides, seductresses sent to acquire sensitive secrets. Never had he experienced the sort of trouble Lady Huntley shoved down his throat. Never had it taken him so long to complete this sort of mission; so what was it about her that made him falter?

Was it the fact that she smelled like bergamot, just as this mysterious "wife" of his had? Or was his fractured mind simply substituting her scent for the one his mind had lost?

It was going to drive him mad, this wondering.

He used a chunk of soft bread to mop up the rest of the gravy on his plate and popped it into his mouth. Now that he had eaten, his head didn't hurt quite so much—though the bloodstained handkerchief on the washstand, and the rusty water in the basin, were proof of just how bad it had been.

He was no stranger to his own blood, but knowing it had come from his ears was unsettling, even to him.

A firm rap came upon his door. Assuming it was Mrs. Brown come to collect his dishes, he went to answer without asking who it was. He realized his folly as soon as he pulled the door open and saw his visitor.

The Doctor.

"Hello, Five," the wiry man intoned. "How lovely to find you at home."

Five's eyes narrowed. The Doctor had never visited him before—at least not that he could remember. Truth be told, there were sections of his life even in the years since the Company had brought him in that were about as clear as mud. He used to think it was just the way his mind worked, after forgetting the entirety of his life. Now, noticing the heavy leather satchel in the smaller man's hand, he wasn't so certain.

He knew they had made other people forget things. Maybe they had done that to him as well. This leaden feeling in the pit of his stomach had nothing to do with his dinner and everything to do with his visitor. Instinct warned him to stay out of striking distance of the little man. In his years with the Company he'd seen bigger men than himself brought down by men and women even smaller than the one standing before him.

"Doctor." He kept his tone casual—with just a touch of surprise. "What are you doing here?"

Narrow shoulders shrugged as shrewd, bright blue eyes peered at him from over the wire rim of round spectacles. "Our mutual friend contacted me when you didn't respond. Is everything quite all right?"

A controlled smile curved Five's lips. "Right as rain."

The smaller man inclined his head. "May I come in?"

This was going to get messy, Five realized as he stepped back into the room. "Of course."

The Doctor crossed the threshold with a seemingly relaxed posture, but like all trained killers, there was a tension in him that came from being around another of his ilk. There was a very good chance one of them might not leave this building alive.

Five closed the door. The Doctor surveyed the room with feigned disinterestedness. He was looking for anything that could be used as a weapon or for defense if necessary. Five would do the same thing were the situation reversed. Fortunately, he already knew where all the useful items he owned were stashed.

"So, why didn't you answer when our friend called?"

Five rolled his shoulders, loosening the muscles there. "I was asleep." It was the first time he'd lied to a Company agent, and it rolled off his tongue like a Scot's r's.

"Asleep?" A sandy brow arched. The man had a face like a can of worms, scarred and pockmarked. "You sleep six hours a night, and that's it."

"Unless I'm knocked unconscious."

"Someone knocked you out?" That he sounded so surprised might have been taken as a compliment.

"I remembered something." He shouldn't admit it, but he wanted to see the reaction it got. He watched his companion carefully. "I remembered that I have a wife."

"Did you?" The leather bag was set on the table, the top of it open just wide enough for slim fingers to fit inside. Little bastard thought he wouldn't notice? "Who is she?"

Acting on a hunch, Five shifted his weight to a stance that would allow him to move quickly. "I'm not certain, but I think Arden Grey can tell me."

The Doctor went still, and that was all Five needed. The enigmatic Lady Huntley was right—she knew him, and he should know her. Five pounced. One arm went around the shorter man's neck, and the other came down to seize the wrist of the hand holding the syringe the "doctor" had taken from his case.

"You don't want to do this," the wiry man rasped, fingers of his free hand clawing at Five's forearm.

"You're right," Five growled. "What I want to do is kill you, but I don't want my landlady to find your body. So you're going to take a little nap instead." He squeezed his arm closed, cutting off the man's oxygen. It didn't take long for him to stop struggling and pass out. The man might have been a deadly adversary, but once it came down to sheer size and strength, there was no contest.

Five lowered his burden to the floor and picked up the syringe that had fallen to the rug. He studied it for a moment before taking his coat from the closet and slipping his arms through the sleeves. Then, he grabbed the Doctor's bag from the table and yanked open the door. The pounding in his head threatened to start again as he bounded down the stairs, images dancing in and out of his memory like the flickering of a candle. They teased him; coming just close enough that he could almost recall the exact moment, and then dancing away before he could tell what the hell it was.

His velocycle was parked on the street where he had left it. Frankly, it was a surprise no one had stolen it yet, but anyone who crossed his path in this neighborhood knew a predator when they saw one and knew better than to draw his attention. He set the bag on the back of the cycle and used the straps there to hold it in place. He straddled the machine before flipping the ignition switch, and releasing the kickstand.

He tore off down the street as the sun sank on the horizon, casting a pinkish halo over the city. He had no friends, no idea who he was. He had just rendered one of his brotherhood incapacitated—an act of sedition—and the one person who had any of the answers he wanted was a woman part of him still thought he should kill.

Well, at least he knew what to do next.

Arden retired early. She took a bottle of scotch and a glass with her, and instructed Mrs. Bird that she was only to be disturbed if the house was afire or someone was dead. The housekeeper eyed the bottle in her hand with pursed lips, but she nodded anyway. Dear thing knew to pick her battles.

In the sanctuary of her room, Arden entered the adjoining bath and turned on the water for the tub. After the day she'd had the only thing that could possibly get the knots out of her neck and shoulders—and dull the ache in her heart—was a hot bath and a stiff drink—or six. She undressed as the tub filled.

She drank too much. She knew it. Her servants knew it. Inspector Grant knew it. Hell, perhaps every citizen of London with one working eyeball knew as well. She didn't care. If it weren't for spirits she would have gone mad, or even killed herself, years ago. As she poured a hefty measure of scotch into a glass she recognized her weakness and took comfort in it. She would sleep well tonight.

After adding a few drops of bergamot oil to the water she turned off the taps and stepped in. The water was the perfect temperature and had warmed the back of the copper tub as well. Arden leaned back against the metal with a sigh and took a sip from her glass as she closed her eyes.

Poor Henry. His was the face she saw on the back of her lids. It was almost as if she was seeing him through someone else's eyes, like with the A.R.O.T.S. She'd only ever seen him so discomposed once, and that had been when Dhanya had met with the two of them and told them Lucas was most likely dead.

God, she hoped they could fix Luke. They had to fix him. It didn't seem likely that either she or Henry would survive if they couldn't. Her fingers tightened around her glass. She could kill every agent the Company had at this moment, and it still would give her no peace.

Such thoughts were not conducive to relaxation, so she pushed them as deep into her mind as she could. Soon, thoughts of Luke filled the empty spaces, reminding her of times they'd shared. He'd been gone longer than they had been together, and some of the time they'd shared hadn't been good. They fought a lot, about why he didn't want to have children right away, and when he would cut back on his work for the Wardens. It seemed so foolish now, when she'd give anything to have him back.

She took another sip of scotch. Its warmth slid down her throat to blossom like a flower of heat in her chest. The heat of the bath made its effects all the more potent, and by the time she'd finished the rest a delightful lethargy had taken hold of her limbs.

Her mind turned to more intimate memories. Luke had taught her things she never could have imagined. He was the kind of man whose pleasure was intrinsically tied to the pleasure of his partner. The more aroused he made her, the more aroused he became. These memories woke that familiar tension inside her, caused a delicious thrum between her thighs.

For seven years she'd gone without the touch of any man, not just the one she loved. It was a long time for a woman to go without, especially one who had enjoyed a rather passionate marriage. Arden had learned not only how to look after herself, but how to indulge herself in other ways too.

That was how her delicate little invention was born. Originally the small brass clockwork device that was worn over the fingers like a ring, but rested on the underside of the longer three, was meant to be used as a treatment for aching muscles and knots of tension.

However, curiosity led to experimentation, and suddenly Arden found herself with a discreet way of relieving *all* of her tension. She'd mentioned it to Zoe, who demanded to have one—and refused to take it until Arden agreed to let her pay. Then Hannah of all people had asked for one, and soon she had a surprisingly large clientele of upper-class women who did not want to go to a sanitorium to treat their hysteria, or were unmarried, or quite bluntly, wanted to give themselves what their husbands or lovers could not—at least not on a regular basis.

Best of all was the design. If anyone saw it they might think it an odd piece of jewelry or a trinket, unless they had one of their own. It certainly was more subtle than a brass phallus.

She had yet to perfect a waterproof prototype, so in the bath her plain and nimble fingers had to do the job. She slowly lifted her left leg—it felt as though it weighed five stone—and draped it over the side of the tub. Then she slipped her right hand between her legs, parted the curls there and began to stroke what Luke had called her "sweet spot."

In her mind it was Luke who touched her. In her fantasy he used his fingers and mouth to tighten her nipples to a point just shy of discomfort before sliding down and using his mouth to torture her. In the water she could almost pretend her fingers were his tongue, licking faster and faster as she gasped and cooed, the ache inside her building. She lifted her hips, matching the jerky rhythm of her hand until the protrusion of slick flesh beneath pulsed and spasmed, engulfing her in shuddering ripples of delicious liquid heat. She moaned aloud at the pleasure of it, the release.

Tension drained from her limbs and she sank deeper into the tub. It took a few seconds for her to realize that the leg draped over the side was cold and that her water wasn't much warmer.

She could run more hot water into the bath, but she was beginning to prune, so she pulled the stopper and reluctantly pushed to her feet. Languid from head to toe, her legs trembled slightly with the effort of keeping her upright. Carefully, she blotted her skin with a towel and stepped out of the tub onto the mat where she quickly dried her legs and feet. She hadn't the energy for it, but she hated climbing into bed damp.

Her Japanese silk dressing-gown lay across a brass apparatus that resembled a cross between a radiator and a quilt rack. The rungs of it were actually tubes that circulated hot water, warming whatever was placed over it with a gentle heat. Arden sighed as she slipped her arms into the heated silk, and used her big toe to switch the machine's boiler to the off position.

After cinching the belt of her gown, she retrieved the

scotch and her empty glass and carried both with her into her bedroom. Another little sip before slipping between the sheets, and she wouldn't have to wait for sleep to find her—she'd find it quick enough.

The carpet was soft and plush beneath her bare feet as she padded into the dimly lit room. A small fire crackled in the hearth, warm and inviting as it warded off the evening's spring chill.

"Don't scream."

Arden jumped, a strangled yelp breaking free of her throat. The glass fell from her fingers, thudding heavily on the carpet. It didn't shatter, but a few drops of leftover scotch speckled the top of her foot.

The bottle, however, remained safe in her grip. There was no way she was going to let go of it—not when it was the only weapon she had.

Lucas emerged from the soft shadows in the corner near the fireplace. He was disheveled—hair mussed, shirt open several buttons at the throat. There was a certain tension in his face that concerned her. It was an expression she'd seen before, usually when he was extremely agitated, trying to find the solution for a problem that just would not be solved.

"How about I won't scream, and you won't kill me?" How long had he been there? How had he gotten in without her hearing? She had only been in the next room with the door open.

He nodded. "I'm not here to kill you. I'm not certain I could even if I wanted to." He glanced around the room, as though trying to suss out exactly where he was. What had happened to him? The confident killer was gone, but that did little to console her. He was more dangerous now than he had been with his hands around her throat.

"Why are you here?" she asked softly, holding the bottle of scotch against her stomach.

The corner of his mouth lifted in a self-deprecating smile that seized her heart in her chest. She knew that smile. She *loved* that smile. "It seemed the right idea at the time."

It took every ounce of resolve left in her drink-addled mind not to return that smile and melt into a puddle of feminine goo at his feet. He wasn't the man she married, no matter how much he looked the part. She had to remain smart. Cautious.

He took a step toward her, more sure of himself now. "I heard you in there, fingering yourself. Who were you thinking of, me or the redhead?"

Shame threatened to overwhelm her, but he was the only man she'd ever shared a bed with, and she'd be damned if she'd be embarrassed in front of him. "I'd have to be pretty demented to do that while thinking of a man who wants nothing more than to kill me."

"There are plenty of things I'd rather do to you right now than kill you."

Heat blossomed in her cheeks, but Arden ignored it. She had to stay focused if she wanted to stay alive. "But here you are trying to decide whether or not to kill me."

"Actually, I'm here because I want to know why every instinct I have screams that killing you would be a tragedy. I want to know who I am and how you know me. But most of all I want to know why you smell like bergamot."

Her throat constricted so tight it hurt to breathe. She either seized this opportunity with all her might or let him go. "I smell like bergamot because you gave me a bottle, but I don't think you need me to tell you who you are. You're a smart man; surely you've figured it out by now?" She held her breath.

His gaze slid past her, and when his pale eyes widened she knew he had seen the photograph on her vanity. He brushed past her to get to it, picking it up by its ornate frame. Taken shortly after their engagement, it had started out as one of those awful things where the man sits and the woman stands behind his chair, but Luke hadn't wanted her to stand behind him, so he'd pulled her into his lap instead. The photographer—Henry—took the picture while the two of them were grinning at each other.

When Luke turned his head to look at her, his face was white and grim. The hand that held the frame trembled, but his gaze was sharp and clear. "I'm Lucas Grey, and you're my wife."

Chapter 8

It should be the happiest moment of the past seven years. Her husband was home. He had come back to her.

Arden felt as though she might be ill.

So many nights spent weeping for him, despairing for him, and sometimes cursing him. She'd clung to the dream of having him returned to her, only to have it mocked by the fact that the Company turned him into an assassin. Her assassin. Determined to save him, she could only hope that he would come for her again, because this time she was ready.

And now he stood before her telling her exactly what she wanted to hear, and she didn't know if she could believe him or not. Had he truly remembered, or was this just another cruel act on behalf of an agency that would have her head on a platter?

He set the frame down with a thud. "I have to go."

What the devil? She set the whiskey on her dressing table and hurried after him as he crossed the carpet toward the balcony doors. She hoped he planned to actually open them this time.

"Why?" she asked, hating the whiny edge to her voice. "If you've remembered who you are—"

He whirled on her, bringing her up so short she almost ran right into him. She could feel the heat radiating off him, smell his familiar scent. "They know I'm here." He pointed to his head. "They can hear everything."

"Oh dear," Arden murmured, horror taking hold. "You've gone mad."

Luke scowled at her, pale gaze blazing into her soul. "Don't be daft, Ardy. They put something in my head. They talk to me through it, and they can hear every conversation I have—everything I do."

A smile slipped over her lips—relief despite the tightness in her stomach. "You called me Ardy."

The furrows in his brow eased, giving way to an astonishment that could not be false. "I've always called you that."

A breath of laughter escaped her. She choked the rest of it back, afraid that once she started she wouldn't stop, and from there it would turn to tears. She opened her mouth to ask about the listening device when Luke suddenly turned white.

"Get out of my head, you bastard," he growled.

Arden's blood froze. Had they found him? Or was he, as she had earlier feared, mad as a hatter?

He hit the right side of his skull with the heel of his hand. "I said get the fuck out of my head!"

A high-pitched whine caught her attention. As it increased in volume, the anguish on her husband's face did as well, until he fell to his knees clutching his head, crying out in wordless agony.

Was that blood in his ear?

She pivoted so fast her robe tangled around her ankles, threatening to send her sprawling. She stumbled but didn't fall, her hands finding the standing lever of the contraption Alastair had delivered to her earlier. She pulled.

There was a humming noise followed by a loud thud. She turned to see Luke on his back, limbs splayed. He stared at her with a mixture of trepidation and wonder. She didn't blame him.

"The pain stopped," he said.

She nodded. "I know."

"I can't move."

"I know that too." The Calypso Magnetic Device was a large "floor" generally used to detain automatons, but both she and Alastair figured it would work on a man whose bones had been plated with metal—it worked on Alastair's hand. She had planned to use it only if Luke became violent, but the device proved to be more useful than first intended.

It had been her father who explained to her how magnets interfered with Aetheric transmissive frequencies. Over the years the W.O.R. had used similar instruments to interfere with Company communications and weaponry—and vice versa. Who would have thought she'd employ the same practice to keep her husband's brain from leaking out of his ears.

His gaze seized hers and refused to let go. There was no expression on his angular face. "What now? Turn me over to your friends? Kill me?"

His matter-of-fact tone weighed heavy on her heart. It shouldn't surprise her, and it certainly shouldn't put her on the defensive, but it did a bit. She expected him to trust her, even though she'd ask the same questions of him.

Slowly—more because her head was swimming and less because she thought she ought to be cautious around him—she sank to her knees on the carpet, and stretched out on her side next to him. She needed to be still, or she'd cast up all that glorious whiskey.

The Calypso had no effect on her, though it held him like some sort of exotic specimen on display. She could do whatever she wished with him and he would be powerless to stop her. A heady thought. An arousing one.

Did she want to make love to him or punish him for leaving her alone seven years ago? Both, perhaps. Right now she simply desired to be close to him. It felt so good it hurt, and she could enjoy it without fear that he might try to strangle her at any moment.

"I don't know what I should do," she told him, honestly. "I could alert your brother or the Wardens. I could summon Alastair, or lock you in the cellar. One thing I will not do, however, is let you go." She lifted herself up onto her elbow so she could see him better.

Luke frowned. His face was so close, and turned toward her just enough that she could visually trace the faint lines around his mouth in the firelight. "What did I ever do to deserve such devotion?"

Arden's mouth opened . . . then closed again. For those brief seconds her mind was blank. "You saved me from the man in the alley."

"Only because I planned to kill you myself." His direct gaze made her cringe inside.

"But you couldn't do it."

"No. Something stopped me, every time."

Thank God. "That was you at the factory, wasn't it?"

"I think so."

She frowned. "You don't know?"

He looked as though he wanted to shake his head, but it was held immobile by the Calypso. "A man called the Doctor has tampered with my memory. He's probably the one who took you away from me."

"So, you don't . . . remember everything?" What did he remember? And how much of it included her?

"No. I have images in my mind. Things that I know

without knowing how. The ginger—he's a friend of mine, isn't he?"

Arden inched closer to his warmth. The floor was becoming uncomfortable and a little chilly. She was wearing nothing but a robe, after all. "Your best. Alastair Payne, Earl of Wolfred."

"I had memories of him as well, back at my flat before I passed out."

Dear God, what had they done to him? "Do you lose consciousness often?"

"No. Seeing the two of you together earlier did something—like opening a door in my head. I remembered that both of you . . . meant something to me."

She fought the tears that threatened. "Yes."

"And I loved you?"

Arden ignored the way his voice went up ever so slightly, making the statement a question. Ignored the pain that came with it. "Yes."

Pale eyes met hers. "Of course I did. Intelligent, beautiful and now you're mine."

She went completely still, heart in her throat. He had spoken those exact words to her on their wedding night. Did he remember that night, or just the words?

It didn't matter. It was exactly the right thing to say, and exactly what she needed to hear to give her hope. And it was exactly the sort of sentiment that enabled her to bring her body against his, sliding over until she lay atop him. He looked surprised, but didn't say a word. His gaze warmed, glittering with anticipation. That was all the encouragement she needed. She lowered her head.

His mouth was warm—pliant and oh-so-familiar, yet exciting. Despite all her protests to the contrary, there had been a part of her that worried she might never feel his lips on hers ever again.

What a relief their warm familiarity was.

She slid the tip of her tongue along his bottom lip.
Luke's mouth opened, letting her inside so she could
taste him. Her hands braced on either side of his head,
allowing her better leverage to press her hips against his.
Through her robe she could feel him growing hard in
response to her need. She rubbed against him, lifting her
head just enough to gasp against his lips. He groaned.

"Turn this bloody thing off," he growled.

Arden arched from the waist, reaching for the lever
that would free him to do whatever he wanted to her.
She was so eager for him that she didn't even mind if he
killed her, as long as he made her come first. She couldn't
wait to feel his hands on her skin, inside her. She wanted
to hear his breath, feel it hot on her ear and cheek as he
pounded himself into her.

She froze, remembering the blood she had seen in his
ear and what had caused it.

"I can't," she whispered, meeting his gaze.

His eyes hardened. "You don't trust me."

"I don't want to turn the Calypso off until I can be
certain the Company won't try to hurt you again."

The harsh lines of his features softened, and his gaze
warmed once again. "It's a risk I'm willing to take."

"But I'm not." She slid off him to kneel by his side.
Every inch of her wanted him desperately—to the point
that she was ready to throw caution and caring to the
wind. But after seven years without her husband's
touch, it would not be making love if she took advantage of his immobility without trusting him completely;
it would be what was so crudely referred to as "fucking,"
and that was not how she wanted it to be between them,
not after all they'd been through both together and
apart.

Luke looked at her as if he understood. He obviously
didn't like it, judging from the expression on his angular

face, but he seemed to know her hesitation had to do with more than his present predicament.

They stared at each other for a few seconds. It wasn't uncomfortable, but it left her feeling stripped bare all the same. "You need to send for someone," he told her. "The Company will come for me if they think I'm alone with you."

Arden snorted. "This house would be the wrong place for them to attack."

"I've gotten in here with little difficulty."

She gave him what she knew had to be a slightly condescending smile. "Indeed." That was all the explanation she was prepared to give—just in case he was playing her for a fool. She hated to think it, but she'd be an idiot not to be careful at the very least. It didn't seem wise to remind him that he'd helped her improve security on the grounds and once knew the system as well as she.

"Send for someone," he pressed. "You know you have to, and I can't stay on this thing forever."

He was right. Regardless of what the Wardens might do to him, he would need their help. She couldn't take the transmitter out of his head—she was no surgeon. Only Evelyn could make certain the Company lost their way of spying on him. Only Dhanya would have the power to ensure Luke was treated fairly and protected to the best of W.O.R's ability.

If only they had some way—a humane way—to determine just where his loyalties lay. He seemed sincere, and she wanted to believe he meant what he said. But he had been with an enemy of the Empire for more than half a decade. Realizing that they had used and lied to him did not mean it would be easy for him to betray them. Luke would need the help of all his friends to undo the damage those bastards had wrought.

With a sigh, she rose to her feet and crossed the carpet to the small desk in the corner where she took care of all her personal business. An ebony and brass telephone sat on the polished mahogany top. She removed the portion for listening from the cradle—the metal was cold against her ear. She turned the crank on the side toward her rather than away. She did this three times—one long, one short, one long again.

The connection was made a second or two later. Static crackled. "Jabberwocky."

"Bandersnatch," Arden replied. The code words changed on an irregular basis, and Mr. Carroll's writings were excellent for them, as they weren't really words at all.

"To which number may I connect you, madam?" The operator inquired. There were six of these women who took turns running the Warden switchboard so that there was always an operator no matter the time of day or night.

"Oh-four-two-five-eight-three-nine, please."

"One moment." There was silence, followed by a click and then ringing in the same long-short-long sequence in which she had turned the crank. That would alert Alastair that the incoming call was from a fellow Warden.

The rings repeated once more before he picked up. "This had better be good," he growled, his voice thick with sleep.

She took a deep breath. "It's Arden. Alastair, he's come home."

His silence lasted two thumps of her pounding heart. "I'll be right there."

Five ... er, rather, Luke, almost fell asleep on the magnetic pallet that held him hostage. This room—this house—filled him with a sense of security he couldn't remember ever feeling before. Despite not being able to lift his hand to scratch an itch on the side of his nose, he was content; filled with the naive hope that perhaps his life was not the raging shite storm he suspected it of being.

His wife—he was still trying to wrap his brain around that one—had left him after making her short telephone call. She promised to be back as soon as possible, saying that she was going to her workshop to get something for him.

For all he knew she could come back with a handsaw and a wheelbarrow, but he didn't think so. Not that a handsaw would do her much good against his bones.

His gut told him to trust her, and he had learned several years ago to trust that instinct. In fact, he was fairly certain it was not trusting his instincts that had gotten him into this mess to begin with. If only he could interpret the scant, chaotic images vying for attention in his mind, then he might know how he came to be in this position, but they were only fragments—nothing that made sense.

Trying to make sense of it all made his head hurt, and he'd had enough of that for one day. He closed his eyes and listened to the slight, pleasant buzzing in the back of his mind. It lulled him like the gentle whir of an airship motor, making his eyelids heavy and his muscles as languid as a cat draped over the back of a sofa in front of a sunny window.

There was no one in his mind. No one could eavesdrop on him or shout orders. For the first time in as long as he could remember—which given the grand scheme, wasn't impressively long—he was completely and utterly alone. The whirring was proof of that, caused by the powerful magnet pressed against his head. His eyes closed, and peaceful darkness drew him down regardless of the images swirling behind his lids.

He woke with the sensation of being watched. His eyes reluctantly opened as exhaustion tried to keep them shut.

The ginger man stood over him, watching with a curious expression. Had he not been incapacitated Luke would have leapt to his feet and ruined that pretty face. The pressure holding him to the floor wasn't so lovely anymore, when thoughts of this man holding his wife filled his head.

"Where's Arden?" he demanded.

The ginger arched a brow. "Her workshop. She'll be here in a moment."

Something in that statement ignited Luke's ire like a letter carelessly tossed onto the hearth. This man had been his best friend once. He knew that just as he knew Arden was his wife, but that knowledge aside, he could cheerfully rip the bastard's arms off. "Are you often in her bedroom?"

A groove deepened in Alastair's left cheek as his lips twisted grimly. "Only when her husband, long presumed dead by everyone but her, returns home intent on causing her death."

He didn't share the man's humor. "I have no intention of hurting her."

Alastair gave a slight shake of his head. "You'll understand if I don't take you at your word."

Luke would have shrugged had he been able. "Your opinion doesn't concern me." Actually, it did. And that pissed him off even more.

The other man crouched beside him, a dangerous glint in his gray eyes. "I could kill you right now just to keep her safe."

A cold smile took hold of Luke's mouth. He'd been

right to be jealous of this man who would kill to protect *his* wife. "Best make it look like an accident then. Killing me won't get you into her bed."

His old friend paled a little before his cheeks flushed a dull red. "You're as much a bastard now as you ever were." Then the damnedest thing happened—Alastair grinned. "It really is you. I'll be buggered."

"Not by me you won't," Luke shot back without thinking. The wonder in the other man's eyes told him that this was something that they used to say to each other, years before, when he knew who he was.

This man—Alastair—knew him better than he knew himself at the moment. Or rather, knew more about him. He tried to remember more, but the memories that had come back crowded his brain, crawling over one another, demanding to be recognized. It made him dizzy.

Christ, he hoped he didn't puke. He'd choke to death, pinned to the floor like a bug. Then Alastair could eventually slip into Arden's bed with a clean conscience.

"Are you all right?"

Through narrowed eyes, Luke stared up at the still-hovering ginger. "No."

As his luck—which had been described as being as good or bad as the shithouse rat, depending on how one looked at it—would have it, that was the moment Arden swept into the room. She had some sort of crown in her hand.

She took one look at him and her eyes widened. "Good Lord." Quickly, she crossed the carpet. Had she been wearing shoes he would have described her step as "stamping," but that might have more to do with his head than her stride.

The hem of her dressing gown brushed against his cheek, and he caught the scent of her. Sweet, with a hint of bergamot, and woman. He remembered the noises she had made in the bath, and how he had wanted to climb into the tub with her and give her something to really moan about.

Thankfully he was in enough discomfort that he didn't embarrass himself by getting hard.

There was a thunk as she shoved the lever, and then the humming in his brain stopped, and his body felt lighter—capable of movement. She had turned off the magnet, and any moment the Company would have at him again. This time they might kill him. He wasn't afraid to die—he'd come close so many times he'd begun to think death didn't like him much—but now that he remembered her, he found himself reluctant to give up his wife and her big, worried brown eyes.

"Alastair, help me get him up."

They were intimate enough that she called his old friend by his Christian name. Luke couldn't remember if it had always been that way. Had they become more than friends in his absence? He had no right to be jealous; he'd had lovers of his own. Knowing that he had broken his marriage vows made the sickening in his belly even worse. It didn't matter that he hadn't known he had a wife.

Arden took his left arm, and Alastair the right. Together, they began to pull him upright. The exertion turned both their faces red.

"Heavy son of a bitch," Alastair grunted. Arden did not seem the least bit shocked by his language. Luke couldn't remember if that was new or not.

He pulled free of their hands, sending both of them skidding backward a few feet. Then, head feeling as though it was being beaten by a brick on the inside, he slowly pushed himself to his hands and knees, then his feet.

"I've gained a few pounds," he explained to the three Alastairs wavering before his eyes.

The other man eyed him . . . warily? "So I've noticed."

"Come sit down," Arden commanded, then to Alastair, "Fetch a glass of water, please."

She came to Luke's side to help him as he moved toward a chair on trembling legs. Obviously she wished to help him, but if she couldn't pull him up with help, she certainly wouldn't be able to support him if he fell. He lowered himself slowly onto the chair—too fast and he might break the delicate-looking thing. When she shoved a clean chamber pot into his hands he was thankful. When she pressed a cool, wet face cloth to his forehead he clasped her hand in his and gently squeezed.

"Thank you," he murmured.

He couldn't tell if she smiled or not, because a second later he retched, stomach muscles clenching as the contents of his stomach burned his throat and hit the white porcelain bottom of the pot with a sick splash. He puked twice, holding the pot with trembling hands.

"Are you done?" she asked after a few minutes. She didn't sound disgusted in the least.

"I think so," he replied. He was weak to the point of helplessness. If he was attacked at that moment he doubted his own ability to defend himself, despite his superior strength. She took the chamber pot from him and set it close by.

Alastair returned with the water, which Luke drank greedily. It cleansed his mouth, soothed his throat, made him feel as though living might be a good thing. Arden removed the cloth from his forehead, and replaced it with something cold and hard. Something metal.

"It's not much," she explained. "A lesser version of the one that held you to the floor. It's weak enough that it shouldn't affect the metal in your body unless you touch it, but strong enough to interfere with the Company's device until we can get it out of you."

He glanced up at her—his eyeballs ached. "Can you do that?"

"Not me," she replied with a gentle smile. "But I know of a brilliant surgeon who will know how to go about it."

Luke frowned. A splinter of pain lodged deep in his skull—a hard pinch deep in his brain—but he ignored it. "Stone," he said. "Dr. Stone." Did he know this because he remembered, or because Stone's name had been one of many he had seen listed of known W.O.R. agents and collaborators?

"Yes," she replied with a smile so hopeful it damn near broke his heart. Looking at her was difficult. On one hand he wanted to grab her, throw her on the bed and ride her until they were both sore. He also wanted to hold her, just so he could smell her hair. And then there was part of him—a small part, but it was there—that hadn't accepted that she wasn't the enemy and that still wanted to choke the life out of her.

It was like being awake in a nightmare. He couldn't tell reality from deceit, and he didn't know whom he could trust. He couldn't even trust himself.

"We have to take him to the Director," Alastair said to Arden as he handed Luke a packet of powder. "For the headache."

Luke turned to him. "How did you know?"

The other man frowned. "Please. I've known you since we were eight. By the way, could you show me your right shoulder?"

The powder was bitter as Luke ripped it open with his teeth, but he washed it down with the water he'd been given. He wiped his mouth with the back of his hand before lifting his gaze. "Why?"

Alastair's lips thinned. "Just do it."

"Alastair," Arden admonished, but he ignored her, fixing Luke with a determined stare.

Sighing, Luke unbuttoned his shirt and pulled it down to reveal the tattoo he'd had since long before the Company found him. He had a few, but this was the oldest. The black ink was faded to a teal blue, but the image was clear enough: a gryphon pawing at the air with its talons, beak open in a fierce cry.

"Satisfied?" he asked.

Alastair nodded. "Yes," he rasped. He seemed oddly relieved, happy and yet saddened by the sight. Arden looked as though she was biting her tongue to keep from crying.

It struck Luke then that this was their irrefutable proof. Were it not for the fact that his head felt like it had an axe buried in it whenever he tried to think, he would have realized sooner that they would need to see this for their own peace of mind. And he needed to see their reaction for his own. These people truly knew who he was. After seven years of wondering—of almost reconciling himself to the idea that he might never know—he knew his name.

A name that felt less real to him than the number he had been assigned.

"I'll send for Dhanya in the morning," Arden said, her voice hoarse.

This Dhanya had to be the "Director"—W.O.R.'s commanding officer. She must be new, because he didn't recognize the name. It had been a man running things last he could remember. But these were modern times, and women were employed in many positions once held by men alone.

"You know it cannot be left until morning," Alastair argued as Luke rebuttoned his shirt.

"It can and it will," came her angry, flushed-cheek reply. Her back was as straight as a poker, and Luke couldn't help but notice how her impeccable posture pushed her breasts up and out. Wolfred noticed as well. The only one who didn't seem to notice was Arden. "She'll want to test him and interview him. She'll take him away and I—" Her voice broke, and she turned away from them both, moving to the dressing table where she braced both her hands and bowed her head. In the mirror, Luke could see her squeeze her eyes shut—fighting tears.

And still her back remained straight, her shoulders stiff.

Out of the corner of his eye he saw Alastair start toward her, and he came to his feet in protest. Blood rushed to his head, making him sway, but the nausea had passed and he no longer felt as though his skull was being chipped apart by a dull chisel. His old friend steadied him with a quick hand, which Luke thanked him for but brushed aside.

As though he could read Luke's mind, the earl backed off—not just from him, but from Arden as well.

What the hell did he do now? Comfort her? He hardly knew how. All he knew was that for the last seven years he hadn't known he had a wife, and that for that same seven this beautiful woman had been left wondering if her husband was dead or alive. He'd been out having adventures—granted on behalf of the enemy—and fucking whomever he wanted. Doing other things he hadn't wanted, but had been ordered to do. He'd thought they were the right things. . . .

She had been waiting for him. And he didn't have to be a bloody genius to see that she was afraid of losing him again.

As though he were some sort of prize.

One thing he did know—this was not a woman who took emotions lightly, nor shared them indiscreetly. She was barely holding herself together, and if he coddled her right now, or tried to comfort her, she would break down. She would never forgive him for it.

Instead, he lowered his head so that his mouth was close to her ear. "You know Wolfred is right."

She shot him a glare that made him reconsider the possibility of her dissolving into tears. Her ferocity did something queer inside his chest, deep beneath his ribs. "I know no such thing."

This was not the woman he married—he realized this though he had no solid memory to back it up. This woman was going to make his life very interesting, a thought that he relished despite himself. "You do."

When she straightened and drew back, he did the same. They squared off like opponents about to fire in a duel. She would fight him until she had no more fight in her. He enjoyed a good row as much as the next man, but he'd already made shite of her life. Besides, he didn't trust himself alone with her. Not to shag her and not to kill her. Those two choices made him a danger to her, and made him uncomfortable in his own skin. He had so much blood on his hands, but he couldn't remember a time when he questioned his own honor—at least not in the last seven years. He questioned it now, and she would try to convince him otherwise because she wanted to believe that he was the man she married. He was no more that man than she was that girl.

It was time to take her fight away. He smiled at her, and reached out to touch the silky warmth of her cheek. The sensation brought a rush of emotional memories with it—a million and one touches stored in the dusty cupboard of his mind. With it came a flash of pain that fled as quickly as it came. Arden frowned at him, but she leaned into his palm. So trusting.

Luke dropped his hand and turned to Alastair. The other man's face was void of expression, but his steely eyes betrayed the pain this reunion brought him.

Luke met that gaze unapologetically. "Take me to the Wardens."

Chapter 9

Both men were fortunate that Arden hadn't her Electrical Discombobulation Intensifier at hand, because she would have rendered them both incapacitated and twitching on the floor. And she wouldn't have cared if they soaked their trousers, either.

The nerve of both of them, disregarding her like that. Alastair was supposed to be on her side. And Luke ... was it too much to ask that he spend a few hours with her after seven years apart? Early in their marriage she would get down in the mouth when he'd work long hours without her—what could she do when England was his mistress? But right now she wasn't maudlin. Right now she was incredibly angry.

Of course she was going to accompany them. Luke had tried to persuade her otherwise, but she refused to cave. At least the pair of them were intelligent enough to wait on her rather than leaving her behind. Obviously she couldn't appear before Dhanya in her dressing gown. She needed all the armor she could manage.

She didn't wake her maid or any of the servants.

Beauregard had to be asleep on his bed in front of the kitchen hearth or he'd have been dancing around their ankles barking like mad at them all. This silence felt eerie and tense, not comforting as it normally did.

A little while later, she joined them in the foyer, wearing a teal gown with a corset bodice that laced up the front. Her hair was secured in a black snood and her boots were soft leather, worn to such a degree of comfort that they molded around her feet.

Luke stared at her as she approached. The blatant appreciation in his gaze should have filled her with warmth, should have given her hope. Instead she wanted to slap his handsome face so hard he would have to talk out of the back of his head.

He must have seen the anger and hurt in her eyes—how could he possibly miss it?—because he arched a dark brow. "You didn't look at me with that much venom when I tried to kill you."

"I think perhaps you're still trying," she muttered with a shake of her head. She'd forgotten her chains and her cheek felt oddly bare without the cool metal strands brushing against it.

Luke sighed—the same way he'd always sighed when she said or did something he thought irrational. "If you don't take me to the Director, both you and Alastair risk being accused of treason. I have to turn myself in if I want any hope of getting my life back."

"*Have* to," she repeated bitterly. He had almost won her over with his words, until he used that offensive four-letter one. "That's what you said every time you left this house—and me—to run off and play with the Wardens."

There was no denying his surprise at her vehemence. Arden was angry enough—and her tongue loose from the whiskey she'd had another glass of while she changed—that she felt compelled to remark upon it. "I see the return of your memory is selective at best." Tugging on her gloves, she brushed by him. "Let's get this over with, shall we?"

The men followed after her; Alastair last so he could no doubt keep an eye on Luke. Or perhaps he simply did not wish to be within striking distance of Arden. Once upon a time she would not have reacted with anger. She would have wept, perhaps. Pleaded a little. It was only this unfamiliar, deep-seated rage that kept her from doing both right now.

But she would rather lick one of Mr. Tesla's coil transformers than show just how afraid she was at that moment. For years she had clung to her belief that Luke was alive, that he would come back. Now, she was faced with the possibility of losing him once again to duty, or perhaps to the Executioner General.

Their driver took his perch on the front of the carriage while her husband sat across from her and his best friend took the seat beside her. Perhaps Alastair thought himself better equipped to protect her from that position. Perhaps he was staking a personal claim—she often thought men were like dogs that way. Provided Alastair didn't urinate on her all would be well. What she didn't bother to point out was that with him by her side, it would make killing them both all the easier. Luke could go for both their throats at the same time, and with metal-plated fingers it wouldn't take much pressure to crush both windpipes.

"Why are you being so agreeable?" she asked the man half shrouded by shadow across from her.

He might have arched a dark brow again at the question. Certainly his lips lifted in that lopsided manner that both broke her heart and made her want to strike him. With Luke it was almost impossible to tell if he was laughing with her or at her.

Odd, but while he was gone she had forgiven—

forgotten—most of his faults. Now her irritation with all those peevish behaviors came rushing back.

"How would you have me behave?" His rumble of a voice filled the interior of the carriage despite his quiet tone.

Arden shrugged. If she ignited the lamp she might see him better, but then he would be able to see her as well. She glanced at Alastair, noting how his eyes shone like a cat's in the dark—another augmentation courtesy of the W.O.R. The Wardens and the Company were more alike than she cared to ponder.

"You do not seem the least bit concerned about what might await you at W.O.R. headquarters."

"I'll decide whether or not to be concerned once I'm there." His deep voice filled the darkness. "Are you concerned, Ardy?"

She winced at the pet name, a pinch in her chest. "I'd be a fool not to be, given the circumstances."

Out of the darkness he came, leaning forward so she could see his face in the pale wash of moonlight peeking through the window. Beside her Alastair tensed. "Despite the fact that I don't deserve or require it, you are worried about me. Do you think the Director will execute me on the spot?"

"Or this might all be a ruse and you might not kill only me, but the Director as well."

He didn't seem the least bit put out by her suspicion. In fact he smiled at it. "So much for wifely trust."

"Can I trust you?" she parried. She wanted to, but she'd be a fool to give it so quickly—the Wardens had taught her that.

Luke came closer. He reached out and took the fingers she had fisted in her lap. Out of the corner of her eye she saw Alastair's hand move to the inside of his coat, where he often kept a weapon.

Glacial eyes locked with hers. "If you couldn't, you'd be dead by now."

She glanced down at his hand, wrapped around hers. His fingers were strong. Warm, and slightly rough. She wanted to lift those fingers to her mouth, press her lips against the back of them and let loose the scald of tears that seared the backs of her eyes.

She bit the inside of her mouth so hard she tasted blood.

"The Director will not be half so confident in your assurances," Alastair remarked blandly.

Arden looked up as Luke turned that unnerving gaze on his friend. "I think we both know that the Director's chief concern will be what sort of information I might impart," her husband said. "That should keep me alive long enough to prove myself worthy."

She blinked. He was right, of course. She hadn't thought of it in her irrational state—much to her annoyance— but it was little wonder he was so calm when the Wardens would certainly jump at the chance to know all the Company secrets her husband had stored in his mind.

Secrets that had taken her place.

Bitterness settled on her smarting tongue, and in her heart, sharp and unwanted. She hadn't realized just how angry she was at him for his absence—for so many things. She had been too bogged down in missing him, too smothered by regret to remember that the flaws in her marriage were not hers alone.

The truth was she had often hated the W.O.R. for being such a huge part of their lives. She had despised Luke at times—herself as well. It was only after she'd lost him that she found comfort in the agency, and dedicated herself so thoroughly to it.

She turned her head to find him watching her. His expression was neutral, but her gaze was anything but.

She knew just by the weight of his stare that he knew how she felt, the confusion and torment, and that he understood it as well. But, she supposed, that was the luxury of being the one who left rather than the one left behind.

Would he have waited for her as she had him? Or would she have returned home to find him married to another woman? Perhaps she might have succeeded where he failed and killed him in his sleep, never knowing that he had once been hers.

Luke's lips tilted with just enough of a twist that she knew he could tell what she was thinking. "Shine's already off the penny, isn't it?" His tone was vaguely amused—mocking even—but there was genuine regret in his eyes.

"It could use a little polish," she replied honestly. "But I wouldn't say it's completely tarnished. Perhaps a slight buffing?"

He smiled at that, and so did she. Warmth blossomed in her stomach, spreading outward. All concern and fear were obliterated in that moment. Her head swam pleasantly, and for one hot second she contemplated throwing herself into his arms and shoving her hand down his trousers. But that might distress dear Alastair, who had made his own feelings for her quite clear.

Thank God she had never taken advantage—not fully—of his regard. Alastair was precisely the sort of man a woman fell in love with were she not careful. While Luke . . . Lucas Grey was exactly the sort of man a woman wanted desperately to have fall in love with her. Even now she felt that desire to call him her own, to be the one to hold his heart, pressing down upon her. She wanted to possess a man who remembered even less of her than she had forgotten about him.

Just how much had he remembered? Not all of it, of

that she was certain. She had no way of knowing—short of asking—just how much of the past lived on in his mind. Did he remember the disagreements about duty to their country versus duty to each other, and children?

Perhaps she might have asked, but she didn't wish to do so in front of Alastair, and what was more, their carriage had just chugged to a stop, signaling their arrival at their destination. It was a pretty little street in Chelsea lined with redbrick and white-trim houses that spoke of elegance without pretention, and it was very quiet at this late hour, as any decent neighborhood ought to be. But one of these homes had a thin diamond glazing on all of its ground floor and street-facing windows. It also had special shutters and doors that would snap into place if the right alarm was triggered. And it was equipped with its own arsenal, a safe room, underground tunnels, and housed a series of pipes that could deliver sleeping gas into a specific room or rooms provided you knew the right code to dial on the control panel. One wrong number, and the gas would fill the room you were in instead.

It was the Director's quarters, and very few people in the W.O.R. knew its location. The agency was cautious to the point of paranoia.

"Now what?" Luke asked.

Before Arden could respond, Alastair struck. His fist flew with astonishing vigor into Luke's jaw. She gasped as her husband's head flew back, and the interior of the carriage filled with Alastair's imaginative swearing.

"Bastard's got a jaw like iron," her friend groused, flexing his fingers.

"Not iron," she argued. "He wouldn't be able to move. I suspect it's gregorite that protects his bones—the same metal used to rebuild your hand."

He scowled at her. "What would I do without you to tell me what I already know?"

It was an old argument between them—him saying she talked to him like he was simple, and her saying he treated her as though she was a delicate flower. She was accustomed to such things coming out of his mouth when he was brooding, but that didn't stop her from returning the scowl with one of her own.

"Did you also know that I could have spared your hand and used something less injurious to render him unconscious?"

"Of course you could have. I wonder why you keep me around at all."

Alastair was in fine form tonight. His nerves had to be as sharp and ragged as her own. They would apologize for things said later, but for now they were both open game.

"I keep you around," she said, glancing over her shoulder at him as her man opened the carriage door, "because I can't carry him on my own."

They hadn't tied him up. That was the first thing Luke realized when he regained consciousness. The second was that the "crown" Arden had made for him was no longer on his head. He reached up to touch it and it was gone. Then he spied it sitting on a rough table some seven or eight feet away.

"You don't need it," came a new, slightly exotic voice. "There's not a transmission in the world that can penetrate these walls."

He turned his head toward the voice and noticed that he was in a cellar, sitting in a thronelike chair with a high back and sturdy armrests. No wonder they hadn't restrained him; he was sitting in a Venom Chair. On the outer length of the leg supports ran a line of small needles. Similar needles were poised to snap into place over his neck and arms. If he made any sudden moves those needles would pierce his skin, and the pump attached to the back of the chair would flood the syringe tubes with venom extracted from the blue-whirled kraken off the southern coast of Australia.

It would kill him within a handful of heartbeats.

He'd best not make any sudden moves, then. Slowly, he lifted his gaze to his audience. Arden was there, trying not to look concerned, but he could tell from the way she kept running her fingernails beneath each other that she was nervous—for him. A foolish sentiment, but one that warmed the hollow space in his chest nevertheless.

Wolfred—yes, that was what he used to call the ginger-haired man, not Alastair—stood to Arden's right, square jaw clenched. Bastard packed one hell of a punch. He would have to in order to have knocked him out as he had. Luke couldn't blame them for taking precautions— every good agent did. They didn't trust him any more than he trusted them, and yet something deep inside him had complete confidence in both of them, even though Wolfred was obviously in love with his wife.

The other woman seemed familiar. Her striking features appeared older than he thought they ought— indicating that it had been a long time since he'd last seen her. She wore a long robe of bright orange velvet, and her inky hair hung heavy around her shoulders. She was like some sort of exotic bird—of prey.

"The Director, I presume?" he asked, centering his attention on her.

She took a step forward, expressionless. "You presume correctly. Do you remember me, Lord Huntley?"

He stared at her, picturing her younger, softer. His brain protested with a dull ache, but he ignored it. He could see her, laughing at something Arden . . . no, something that he had said.

"Withering. You're Duncan and Ashwina's daughter. Does she still run the bakery?"

She paled, and he knew he had been right in mentioning her mother. It proved that at least he wasn't pretending to have regained his memory. Unfortunately, it also could be interpreted as vaguely threatening. "Yes, she does."

Luke didn't miss the look the Director—he still hadn't remembered her first name—shot Wolfred. His memory was no longer in question—but his loyalties were. If she asked which side he was on, he would say his own. Perhaps Arden's as well, since he'd only allowed them to bring him here in order to protect her. She brought out the chivalry in him.

"Where have you been these past seven years, Lord Huntley?"

After years of knowing no other identity than the number the Company gave him, being referred to by another name felt wrong. Regardless that he'd had countless aliases during that time, he wasn't playing a part right now, and these people knew things about him that he did not.

"In the employ of an organization called the Company," he replied honestly. "One morning I woke up in Paris with no memory of anything before that day. The Company found me, told me I was one of theirs. I believed them because they seemed to know me."

"I imagine they had completed extensive research," the Director remarked, rather dispassionately, but there was a hard glint in her amber eyes. "Have you any idea how they managed to obliterate your memories?"

He shook his head. "No, though the Doctor often did something that required an injection of some sort. I recall it being painful. And when they first approached me I had a bandage on my scalp. They said I had been injured."

His wife gasped. It was as soft as a whisper, but he

heard it. She was so pale her skin had taken a slight bluish tint.

"You think they did something to my brain."

Arden nodded. "There's been much research into how the mind works recently. I've read papers on doctors performing surgeries that have completely altered criminal behavior. The same practice could be used on the area of the brain that masters memory."

What she didn't say hung heavily in the room. "I might never fully remember my life."

Now she shook her head, her expression a mix of horror and determination. "We'll need to do some tests, but Dr. Stone should be able to ascertain what's been done."

He'd waited so long to remember any detail of his past that he couldn't bring himself to be distraught. He remembered her, or at least enough of her to inspire a visceral reaction. He wanted to hold her, smell the warm skin in the hollow of her neck. He did not, however, want to hurt her in any way. The great joke was that he would probably hurt her very deeply if he couldn't remember their life together.

"Not exactly the homecoming you imagined, is it?" he asked her, forcing a slight smile.

"No." To her credit, her eyes were dry and her shoulders straight. "But it is preferable to the alternative."

Luke grinned. If the Company were the villains they appeared to be, then both he and Arden would be in severe danger, but at that moment he didn't give a rat's arse. Let the Company come. Let Miss Withering do what she would.

"You will be transferred to a W.O.R. facility," the Director told him. "You will be examined and debriefed. Our doctor will see about getting that transmitter out of your head. You will give us everything you have on the Company."

These were nonnegotiable terms, still Luke nodded his consent. "Fine."

"How long are you going to keep him?" Arden asked. The anxiety in her tone inspired an ache in his chest, though the others appeared not to notice that she was the least bit upset.

"For as long as it takes," he answered before Miss Withering could. "Until they are certain I am not a threat to you, or this country."

The Director inclined her head. "Well said."

Luke turned to Wolfred. "You will protect her, won't you? If the Company sends someone else after her?"

His old friend nodded. "I will."

Ignoring his wife's protests, he directed his attention once more to the dark-haired woman. "Then let's get started, shall we?"

Whenever emotions threatened to have the best of her, Arden found peace and control in rationality. That was what she had to do when Lucas handed himself over to the W.O.R. without so much as a blink.

The entire time he was in that infernal chair her heart had been in her throat, her emotions flailing all over the place. And when Dhanya asked Alastair to shackle Luke's hands behind his back in preparation for transport to the W.O.R.'s holding cells, hysteria threatened.

She was not going to be one of those women who came undone in front of witnesses. From a pocket sewn into her skirts she withdrew a delicate silver flask, and opened it with trembling fingers. She took a deep, quick drink before hiding it away once more. As she dragged the back of her hand across her mouth, her gaze locked with her husband's. He was standing now—away from the execution chair—and his hands were behind his back.

Perhaps it was merely the echo of her own conscience, but it seemed disappointment clouded his pale eyes.

Arden lifted her chin. Being that he was the one who had been sent to kill her, she reckoned he had no right to look at her like that. If not for him her nerves wouldn't need a little extra fortification. Alastair gripped Luke's arm and pulled him toward an iron door on the back wall of the cellar. She rather fancied him all restrained and vulnerable. She might slap him if not for the fact that it would hurt her more than him. She might kiss him too—or anything else she wanted. But she would definitely begin with a slap. She smiled at the thought. Her husband responded with a raised eyebrow.

"I apologize for the chains, Lord Huntley," Dhanya said as she unlocked the heavy door and pulled it open. The hinges screeched. "I'm sure you understand the necessity of them, however."

"You'd be a fool not to take precautions, Director." Luke glanced over his shoulder. "You should go home."

Arden shot him a droll look. He hadn't changed that much—still trying to protect his pride under the guise of sparing her seeing him lowered. "I'll forgive you for suggesting that since you don't remember me very well. I believe this is one of those 'for worse' situations I agreed to in front of God and all that."

His lips tilted. "I wouldn't want to stand between you and God. By all means, come along."

He wasn't mocking her, she realized, but teasing her. Odd. He didn't press the matter either. At one time he would have commanded her to go home and she would have listened. Was this a change for the better? Or did he simply not care?

Regardless, she followed behind them, stepping into

the darkened tunnel on the other side of the threshold. There was the sound of a hand crank being turned, a sputtering chug, and then small lamps on either wall flickered to life, filling the damp space with a warm glow.

"Ah, the Director's private rail," Luke remarked as they all gazed upon the small steam engine before them. It was clean and richly appointed, its black lacquer gleaming.

"Yes," Dhanya replied, her expression one of surprise. Arden had to admit to being somewhat curious herself. Luke had never mentioned the private rail before. Very few people knew of it. It was one more secret he'd kept from her that she had been forced to discover on her own.

Just as she'd been forced to discover Rani Ogitani. She hadn't known the woman had once been Luke's lover until the two of them were sent on an assignment together shortly after he and Arden returned from their honeymoon. Luke hadn't said a word. It had been Zoe who commented, saying that Arden was a more confident woman than she to allow her husband to go off with his exotic former mistress. And partner. They had often worked together for the Wardens.

She never admitted it to anyone, but Arden had spent the next fortnight wondering if her husband was sleeping with the gorgeous spy. When he returned home he told her nothing had happened, and she believed him. Two years later he told her he had to go off with Rani again. She tried not to worry about it, but then Rani was found injured and Luke wasn't found at all.

It might be irrational, but Arden had blamed the other woman for Luke's disappearance. She still did.

She turned her attention back to her husband. He glanced at Alastair, who still held his arm. "Not that I would have denied you the pleasure of knocking me out in the carriage, but it wasn't necessary. I have a hazy recollection of this place. I've been here before."

Alastair's gray eyes narrowed. "You're too kind." But Arden thought she saw his lips twitch when Luke grinned. Her shoulders relaxed a little at the sight.

The four of them climbed into the main car. The rail was so secret, even Dhanya's servants knew nothing of it. She drove the engine herself, and thanks to a boiler that kept a constant amount of steam circulating by recycling unvented steam back into water, the engine was prepped for travel at all times. All Dhanya had to do was throw a few switches and levers, and the metal beast roared to life.

Arden and the men sat in plush velvet seats behind Dhanya. To her surprise, Alastair did not sit between Luke and her, but rather put Luke in the middle. Her husband sat with his bound hands behind the seat back.

He turned toward her, effectively obliterating the rest of the world as their conveyance lurched forward, quickly picking up speed. There was nothing but him—sight, smell and warmth. Even her ears seemed deaf to everything but his voice.

"I'm sorry," he murmured.

She nodded, throat suddenly very tight. "You were right, this has to be done." The words tasted like dirt even though they were true. Any other action might very well have led to a conviction of treason for both of them—if he hadn't killed her first. Were these reminders of his mission the rational part of her brain talking, or the part of her that had gotten what it wished for—the return of her husband—and was now terrified by it?

"I would rather be back in your room," he added, his voice dropping to such a degree that it slipped down her spine as a delicious shiver. "I would have liked to join you in the bath and give you something to really moan about."

Oh dear God! Heat flooded her veins, rushed up her

cheeks and tingled between her thighs. Her nipples were so hard her whiskey-addled mind thought they might have petrified after years of neglect. If it weren't for Alastair—who had augmented hearing, she was mortified to remember—and Dhanya, she would ravish him here and now. It would be worth dying for if her trust in him proved misplaced.

Instinct demanded she trust him. Common sense, however, erred on the side of caution. Inebriation wished both would go to hell and let her feel a man inside her for the first time in seven years. *Her* man.

Against her better judgment, she raised her gaze to his. "That ought to give you something to think about later when you're alone in your cell."

His gaze brightened, the blue deepening in the lamplight. "I'm thinking about it now."

"Good," she retorted, cheeks hot. Her lips curved into a smile despite herself. "Perhaps I'll think of it as well, when I take my bath tomorrow evening."

She wasn't certain, but she thought she heard him make a growling noise low in his throat. They stared at each other, wrapped in a blanket of sexual awareness as bittersweet as it was arousing.

"Are we almost there?" Alastair demanded peevishly.

The spell was broken. Arden glanced away, uncertain whom she was more embarrassed for—herself or Alastair. Luke arched a brow, but didn't say a word. Did he wonder if she and Alastair were lovers? He had to suspect there was something between them. She couldn't stand the idea of him thinking she had been unfaithful. She reached over and put her hand on his thigh. When his gaze locked with hers, she shook her head, and squeezed his leg, feeling the hard muscle beneath her fingers. His expression told her he understood, and he gave a slow nod of his head, a smile tilting his mouth.

An ugly thought took hold of her then. He'd been away for years. Had no concept of her existence for all that time. How many women had he been with while she clung to the hope that he was still alive?

While she'd been alone, untouched and unloved, how many lovers had flushed and shivered beneath his strong hands, or worse, evoked the same response in him?

She needed a drink, but another swallow might just as easily send her to a pit of melancholy as keep her from the edge. No, what she needed to do was focus on the present, and everything that was positive about it. The negative would wait—it would always be there.

The remainder of the journey was spent in silence. When they finally came to a stop, Alastair led Luke off the train. The door of this tunnel led into the cellar "dungeon" of the Wardens of the Realm. It wasn't far from W.O.R. headquarters, but like the Director's house, wasn't part of the main compound. Less chance of prisoners escaping and killing agents—or stealing sensitive information.

The guards at the door snapped to attention when they saw Dhanya. Their eyes narrowed when they spied Luke, bound like a criminal.

"This man is a former W.O.R. agent," Dhanya informed them in that no-nonsense tone of hers. "He is to be treated with care and respect until I say otherwise. He will be held in W-one-C-four."

The guards nodded. "Yes, Director," they chorused, and stood back while she inserted the key into the lock.

Arden had never been in this part of W.O.R. properties, but she'd heard the stories of subterranean cells that were medieval in nature. Obviously those stories had been exaggerated somewhat. There were Spartan cells, with large, external-clockwork locking mechanisms, but they were far from cruel.

They walked down a rough stone corridor to a wide set of wooden stairs. Each step was well worn, the middle sagging from years of use, but they were sturdy and barely groaned in protest as the four of them—one with a gregorite-plated skeleton—climbed to the top.

At the top, Dhanya inserted a key into a scarred and dull lock and turned it. She withdrew the key and inserted another, turning it as well. Finally, she slipped a punch card into the slot right above the lock. There followed a sound that was a cross between a slap and a groan as the specially designed keys inside found the proper punch sequence. A heavy thud, and then the punch card was spat out. Dhanya took the card—which looked none worse the wear for having been chewed—and turned the heavy iron handle.

They entered a corridor, the floor of which was covered by a worn red carpet. Here the walls were paneled and papered, both of which appeared to be at least a century old.

"It looks like the home of an impoverished noble," Luke remarked as Alastair marched him along.

"Parliament sees no reason to waste tax monies on renovating what is essentially a prison," Dhanya informed him. "Be glad there's gaslight rather than candles."

Arden thought to remind her that a body didn't generally have to worry about candles exploding and taking the entire building with them, but kept her lips firmly shut. She also resolved not to think of this place as a potential grave for her husband.

They continued on until they were almost at the end of the corridor; then they stopped, and another guard soon joined them to unlock the iron door. It swung open, to reveal the chamber beyond.

Arden's mouth dropped. She'd be jiggered. This was no ordinary cell. This was a bedroom worthy of a gentleman, even if from a previous era. The lamps on the walls filled it with warm light, illuminating the hand-painted wallpaper and four-poster bed. There was an armoire, a dresser with a washbasin, and a desk in the corner. The only thing missing was windows, and the air was slightly stale for their lack.

Luke was surprised as well. "It's nicer than the rooms I let." He stepped inside. "Do I get a valet?"

No one laughed at the joke, but he didn't seem to mind. Alastair stepped in as well. "Turn around. I'll unlock the shackles."

Luke didn't turn. Instead, he extended one arm out in front of him. The shackles hung from his hand. He had snapped them.

Arden's lips twitched. "That's a rather showy manner of making a point," she commented. "We're all aware that you came here of your own volition."

Luke grinned. He could have broken free whenever he wanted. He could have injured any, if not all of them, but he hadn't. The notion nursed the hope that lay tense and heavy in Arden's chest.

Of course, he might be toying with them.

Alastair took the shackles. "Impressive," he remarked before using his augmented hand to squeeze the restraints back into the proper shape. The locks would still need to be fixed, however—if that was at all possible. Arden almost rolled her eyes. The posturing had begun. Any moment one of them would start thumping his chest.

"I'd like a word with my husband," she said, tone crisp. She'd been perfectly agreeable—mostly—with all of their demands and decisions, but this was one upon which she would not concede. "Alone, please."

Alastair looked as though he might protest, but said nothing. Dhanya merely nodded. "Of course. We'll be right outside the door." Then she pulled a pistol from the small of her back—a warning to Luke.

Her husband was still smirking as the door shut, closing them in the clean but slightly stuffy room.

"Aren't you afraid to be alone with me?" he asked.

"Should I be?"

"Yes, but perhaps not for the reason you think."

She raised a brow. "Because you might ravish me rather than kill me? Trust me, my lord, when I say you might do well to be afraid yourself."

He chuckled, a flash of heat brightening his eyes, but it faded to regret as quick as it had flared. "I wish I remembered more of you."

"So do I." She swallowed against the tightness in her throat. "I won't allow them to hurt you."

Luke shrugged shoulders that were so much broader than she remembered. "Pain fades. I don't think your director wants to hurt me. She wants what I know. I'm a genuine piece of Company ingenuity. She'd be a fool not to use me."

It sounded so cold and devoid of caring, but it was practical and true.

"Tomorrow I'll bring you some clothes and toiletries."

He lowered his chin, regarding her with curious eyes. "You kept my things?"

"Of course." Did that seem silly to him? Perhaps she was silly to reveal so much, but after seven years apart, what did she have to lose?

He lifted a hand to trail the back of a finger along her cheek. His touch was so desperately tender, so gentle her chest constricted at it.

"I cannot believe I was such a virtuous man as to deserve so true a wife."

Arden caught at his hand. She pulled it away from her

face but did not let go. "You weren't," she replied honestly. "But I loved you regardless."

"You never gave up hope?" His brows drew together. "All those years and you never let go?"

She forced a smile. This situation was in desperate need of levity. And she was in need of a drink. "I believe tenacity to be a virtue, one which I possess in abundance."

Strong fingers tightened around hers. "You must have wondered if I was dead."

"Of course, but I never gave in to it."

He stared at her—as though she was some queer creature he'd never seen before. The lines between his brows and around his eyes deepened. She wanted to kiss them smooth. In that moment, she knew he was no danger to her—not physically at any rate. "No wonder he's in love with you."

Arden opened her mouth to protest, perhaps defend Alastair, but her words were silenced when he wrapped his other arm around her back and yanked her against him. "Oh!" His chest was so warm and firm.

His head lowered, bringing his mouth to hers. His lips were warm and firm as well, demanding and cajoling. She opened hers to the spicy taste of him, the sweet intrusion of his tongue. Her fingers gripped his biceps, feeling the hardness beneath her fingers. He had always had a lovely physique, but not like this. She didn't know what to make of it. She liked it, but it wasn't the way she remembered him.

He wasn't the way she remembered, and that frightened her. It was also intriguing. The man she married never would have kissed her so roughly, with so little finesse. He would have used his lips to seduce her and slowly build up to tasting her.

She had to admit, she found this new and urgent

method . . . *interesting*. She matched the strokes of his tongue with her own. When he pulled away, she stared up at him with eyes that didn't quite focus.

"Something else to think about when I'm in the bath?" Her voice was thick, slightly slurred.

He didn't smile, but his gaze was hot and bright. "Yes. Think of me. God knows I'll be thinking of you."

Her flush made a fool of her. "You don't really remember me and yet you say such things." But oh, she wanted him to tell her just what he might do to himself while thinking of her. And what he might do to her, in the privacy of his mind.

He pulled her close once more. "I remember enough, but I don't need memories to want you, Arden."

A shiver rippled through her, a little nip of disappointment underneath. She wanted him to remember her, to want her because she was his loyal wife, not just because she was a woman who didn't fear him. "Yesterday you wanted to kill me."

"I wanted to kiss you more."

"That's disturbing on so many levels."

He chuckled and lowered his head in that way he always had the few times she'd seen him flustered or embarrassed. "I suppose it is." A heartbeat passed before he looked up, serious again. "I don't want to hurt you."

She swallowed. His words resonated deep inside her. "I believe you."

"Good. Now, you'd better go. Make certain Wolfred takes you home, and have the Withering woman assign guards to your house. If the Company comes looking for me, you'll be the first place they look."

She would not let him see how much that fact actually scared her. She was not a woman who allowed fear to rule her, and more often than not, bullied the emotion into bowing to her. "I will. Is there anything I can do for you?"

He caught a lock of hair that hung near her cheek and stroked it between his fingers. "Wait for me. Just a little while longer."

This time there was no stopping it. A hot tear slipped down her cheek. God help her if he was a liar, because she'd been sucked in, and believed the words that seemed to drip from his lips as sweet and potent as honeyed cider. She could only nod, and force herself to move away. She needed to leave right now, or she would finally lose her mind. He did not try to stop her.

The door was heavy, but she pulled it open, and stepped out into the corridor where both Dhanya and Alastair waited.

"Are you all right?" Alastair demanded, spying her tears. "Did he do something to hurt you?"

She shook her head, and swiped at her eyes with the back of her hands. She turned to the other woman. "Promise me you'll do whatever's necessary to fix him."

Dhanya nodded. "You have my word."

"Good." But Arden would keep a close eye regardless, just in case Dhanya's duty to the Crown exceeded the boundaries of friendship. With that promise to herself firmly in place, she directed her attention to Alastair.

"Take me home please, Alastair. I'm quite done in."

Dhanya spoke up. "I'll have one of my men drive you both home, and have your carriage returned to you as soon as possible, Wolfred."

"Thank you," Alastair replied, and offered Arden his arm. "Let's get you home."

Arden could have hugged him. "You're a good friend."

It might have been her imagination, but she thought he winced. Regardless, he made good on his promise and saw her safely home. Dhanya sent a couple of guards along behind them to keep watch over her house until late morning when others would take their place. They wore dull metal and black leather armor that blended into the night, but allowed them to move freely. It was quite effective against blade and bullet, and also augmented the wearer's physical strength. Arden warned them about her own security androids so they could avoid an attack.

When she finally crawled into bed, her head was already beginning to ache. She took a powder and some water, and pulled the blankets up around her ears. Sleep came surprisingly quickly despite the excitement of the evening and the fact that she was indeed thinking of Luke.

But her thoughts weren't sexual. All she could think of was how he'd looked at her when he realized she had waited for him in every sense of the word. She wondered if he would still look at her that way when he finally remembered that she was to blame for the Company abducting him in the first place.

Chapter 10

They were going to cut open his skull.

It was the morning of Luke's second day in the luxurious cell, and he had naught to do but sit and wait for the guards to come for him.

Self-preservation told him to run. He even had a plan: When the guards came he would render them both unconscious and slip into the private rail tunnel below. There were all manner of escape routes down there, and other tunnels few people knew about. Somehow—conveniently—he knew about them, and he could use them to get to freedom. The W.O.R doctor had removed the device from his ear the day before, so he could make a run for it without worrying about the Company finding him that easily.

When they did find him, they'd most likely kill him. If he didn't kill them first—and he would certainly try his damnedest to do just that. They had sent him to murder his own wife. They had turned him into what he was with that goal in mind. For years he'd been their ... puppet, for lack of a better term.

That pissed him off. When he got out of this place he was going to make retribution a top priority. If he got out of there, that was. His other priority? His wife.

Christ, she was something. Equal parts wanton and priss. She could play the fine lady, but she didn't mind getting dirty, was frigging brilliant and drank like a man. He found her fascinating, confounding and humbling.

She had remained true to him, if he was to believe her. That must be a thorn in Wolfred's side. He'd seen the two of them together, and found it hard to believe that she hadn't let herself be seduced. Rationally, he knew he'd have no grounds on which to fault her. The world had thought him dead, and he hadn't known she existed. He'd certainly had lovers of his own.

Irrationally, he wanted to make Wolfred—or any other man who might have had her, or even wanted to have her—swallow every one of his bloody teeth. Arden was his. He'd known that the first time he tried to kill her.

Thank God he hadn't succeeded. The very idea of taking her life turned his stomach. And yet, there was a small part of him that continued to insist he do just that, and then go back to the Company where he belonged. It was the cowardly part of him that wanted to do this. It was also the cowardly part of him that wanted to escape.

Because this man, this Earl Huntley, no longer existed inside him. The man Arden had waited for was as dead as the world believed him to be. She was going to be so very disappointed when she discovered that, and yet he couldn't bring himself to run.

It was the possibility of having Arden for his own that kept him in this cell—that made it possible for him to let the W.O.R. literally inside his head.

Dr. Stone had examined him before she removed the communication device from his ear. She was a striking woman of mixed blood. Her accent was vaguely Irish, but she looked as though she might have Spanish and Jamaican ancestry as well. And she didn't seem to find him the least bit intimidating, though he noticed she had two automatonic Pulver rifles pointed toward him from either side of the room. The blast from just one would make a mess of most men. He knew from experience it would hurt like hell, but wouldn't kill him. It would, however, take him down.

Dr. Stone took photographs of the inside of his body using Rontgen's "X-ray" method, and seemed fascinated by the extent of gregorite plating on his skeleton.

"You don't have any of the scarring usually associated with this sort of procedure. I've heard that Company surgeons have developed a way to inject gregorite into the body, along with a catalyst that makes it adhere to bone, but I've never seen it done." She glanced up at him with an expression that looked like a cross between awe and disgust. "Extraordinary."

Then she showed him the photograph of the inside of his head. His skull was covered with plates of metal, each molded to the bone. One plate in the front of his head had a hole in it, revealing the bone beneath.

Dr. Stone tapped the plate in the photograph. "If they altered your brain, this is where they did it. They removed this bit of bone and made a sort of door. Unfortunately I won't be able to get in there and take a good look, but I think I can see enough to determine what procedures might have been done. I would like to do the surgery as soon as possible."

It wasn't a request, so Luke didn't bother with granting consent. "I want to see my wife beforehand."

The handsome woman watched him with doelike eyes. He couldn't tell, nor did he care, what she was thinking. "Of course."

So now he sat in his cell doing the same thing he had

done most of the day before when not being debriefed
by the Director herself—writing down every name, every mission, every fact no matter how minuscule he
could remember about his seven years in the enemy's
employ. It was a lesson in humiliation. Every page of
vellum he filled was another stone of shame laid upon
his shoulders. How could he have allowed himself to be
taken? Surely the Director wondered the same thing.
Wolfred, and especially Arden, must wonder as well. The
Company had buggered him senseless, made him their
whore, and made him fucking oblivious to the fact that
they were the ones responsible for the theft of his life.
Like a green recruit he had believed everything they told
him because he wanted to believe it.

They took everything from him. The best revenge was
to get it back. So shag the humiliation, let them root
around in his head. He would do whatever it took to
personally bring the Company to its knees.

He touched his right ear, and his fingers came away
with tiny specks of dried blood on them. It didn't hurt,
though it probably ought to. If not for the blood, and the
fact that he had seen the device with his own eyes, he
would never know the communicator had been removed.

Not that it mattered in here. The whole place was like
a collection of "cages" similar to the one Mr. Faraday
invented, designed to interfere with transmissions.

He put down his pencil and raised his arms above his
head in a stretch. A loud ripping sound followed as the
seams in the shoulders of the shirt he wore surrendered.

"Bugger," he muttered. The shirt was apparently his,
made of the softest linen he'd ever . . . that he could remember ever touching. Arden had brought it for him
yesterday, along with some trousers that were a bit loose
in the waist and tight in the thigh. The Company obviously had a different training regime for their agents.

Either that, or he had been somewhat lazy seven years ago. Perhaps that was what got him caught.

Wolfred was in good shape. Strong and fit. He was a handsome enough bloke—charming when he wanted to be. He certainly didn't have a nose that looked sharp enough to cut cheese. It said something about Arden that she hadn't fallen into his arms—something that honored her, and scared the shite out of him.

A knock and the sound of keys rattling outside his door took him from his thoughts and scribbling. Slowly, he rose to his feet as the door opened. One of the guards stuck his head in. "A visitor for you, sir."

It was Arden. She swept into the room in skirts the color of paprika under a long violet silk frock coat. Her hair was haphazardly piled on her head with auburn tendrils hanging around her face, and a single gold chain ran from her ear to her nose, rather than the multiple silver strands she'd worn before.

Luke stared. All she was missing was a halo of sunshine. She was a goddess, right down to that smattering of freckles across her nose.

She glanced at the door when it clunked shut, leaving them alone, then back at him. "You wanted to see me?"

Was she even half as impressed by him as he was by her? Doubtful. He hadn't shaved that morning. In fact there were many mornings when he couldn't be bothered to drag a razor over his cheeks. He was rough and crass—a killer. He had consorted with the enemy, and while she was happy to have her husband home, she had to know that he was not that man. Not anymore.

"Yes."

"Was there something you wished to discuss?" Her clipped tone was edged with something so sharp it cut, but didn't hurt. Fear. She was afraid for him, and he could have kissed her for it, even if it was misplaced.

"No."

She frowned. "Then why did you ask for me?"

He chuckled, feeling every inch the ass. But he did not look away. "I wanted you to be the last thing I saw before they cut me open."

Blood drained from her cheeks, leaving them white as chalk. She was a little dark under the eyes—bruised-looking. She'd woken up this morning with a headache, he'd wager. How much did he figure into her reasons for numbing herself with liquor?

"You're going to be fine," she said, teeth clenched. She sounded as though she was trying to convince herself of that as well. "Evelyn is a talented surgeon."

He thought of the Doctor. "So were the people who did this to me. I came out of that not knowing who I was."

"That's different. The Company is evil."

He laughed again, but it was humorless and raw in his throat. "That's what they say about the W.O.R. Good or evil is a point of view, Arden. The Company used me, but don't fool yourself into thinking the Wardens wouldn't do exactly the same thing to a Company agent if they thought it would benefit their cause."

She stared at him as though he was speaking in tongues. Perhaps to her he was. Perhaps he oughtn't challenge her idealism. Sometimes a little black and white was refreshing after a palette of gray.

Her gaze dropped. "You ripped your shirt."

As a change of subject it wasn't exactly subtle, but he'd take it. "Sorry."

The corners of her lips curved delicately upward. Whiskey-colored eyes glittered as they met his. "Did you do it intentionally?"

"No." That would be ridiculous. "It was too tight across the shoulders—" He stopped when her smile became a grin. Damnation, but she was pretty when she smiled.

"That's it," she said. "It's the shirt's fault you have the shoulders of David."

Luke arched a brow, unable to stop his own smile. "The shoulders of David? I'll take that as a compliment."

She flushed—a dark peach filling her cheeks. "It was meant as one. When you come home we'll have your tailor come in."

"When I come home." He was beginning to sound like a damn parrot.

Her eyes were wide, her cheeks flushed as only a redhead's could be. "Why, yes. I assumed you would come home when Dhanya is done with you."

What an interesting choice of words. "Yes. I should come home." With her. Where she slept and pleasured herself in the bath.

She lifted her chin, exposing the delicate, pale flesh of her neck. He watched her throat as she swallowed. He wanted to kiss her there. "I can stay elsewhere, if that is what you wish."

Luke's gaze flew up, brows clamping together in a scowl. "Why the hell would I want that?"

The puffy shoulders of her jacket lifted—absurd balloons trying to pull free from their moorings. She seemed genuinely confused—which either made her totally unaware of her own charms or stupid. His guess was the former. "You didn't know you had a wife until a few days ago."

"I didn't know I had a fucking name until then either. It's your house."

She winced, and he knew he had said the wrong thing. "It's your house. I've just lived there the past nine years."

Nine years. He'd been gone from her longer than they'd been together. "It's *our* house," he amended. That was decidedly gentler than demanding that she remain there or he'd tie her to a bedpost. "And if I survive this procedure with my mind intact—and your Director allows me to live—I want you there when I come home."

Her wide eyes took on a glossy sheen—tears, he realized. "Christ, I didn't mean to make you cry."

Gloved fingers dabbed at her eyes. "You didn't. It's just that I cannot believe you're really here. Your brother will be so happy."

"My brother?" His heart gave a hard thump. A hazy face swam in his mind, slowly coming into focus, a headache hot on its heels. "The man I saw you talking to at the party that night."

She nodded. "Henry. He's missed you too."

"I'm surprised he hasn't had me declared dead."

"Of course not." Her gaze flitted away from his. "He didn't believe you were dead any more than I did."

She was lying, and doing a piss-poor job of it. Usually he'd be angry at it, but it was oddly sweet that she wanted to spare his feelings. "I'm very fortunate to have such a brother. And such a wife."

"Yes, well, there were those who said I was delusional." She smoothed her palms over her hips, still not looking at him.

"Was one of those people Wolfred?"

Arden actually looked affronted. "He looked for you. He went all over Europe searching, paid all manner of bribes. When that turned up nothing he lost hope."

"He's in love with you."

She stiffened, wide-eyed expression narrowing to something just short of a glare. "Don't say that."

"It's true."

"I know, but it makes me feel like I took advantage of his friendship, and there were days he was the only friend I had."

During his years under the Company's control he'd met several women who thought nothing of exploiting a man's affections for their own gain. Hell, he had thought little of turning the tables on a few of those same women. Perhaps that said a lot about the sort of person he was. He hoped, for the sake of this woman, that his old friend hadn't shared his callousness.

"I never should have left you." It was the only apology he could think to make.

Her clear, brown gaze was hard. "But you did."

"Why?" That was the question that had niggled at his dodgy memory ever since it first began to return. "Selective" she had called it. "Was it an assignment?"

Arden tugged on the bottom of her jacket. "That had a great deal to do with it, yes. To be honest, I do not know the whole of it."

Strange. They seemed to have had a good relationship, something of a partnership. Why hadn't he told her what he was up to? Unless, had he been under direct orders not to?

"Withering's predecessor, what happened to him?"

The fair skin between her brows furrowed. The woman frowned so much it was a wonder she didn't have a furrow as deep as a ditch there. "He suffered an apoplexy and died. Why?"

Balls. "I thought he might be able to provide some details of my last mission."

"Oh." Her expression softened. If she gazed at him in pity he just might have to kill her after all. "This all must be damnably frustrating for you."

Luke chuckled. His wife was a master of understatement. "Mildly."

They stared at each other for a moment. Then he said, "You will stay for the procedure?"

She nodded. "I won't be in the operating theater, but

I'll be here when you wake up." She smiled then, and it was damned near impossible not to smile back. She obviously had complete faith in Dr. Stone—or she was a better liar than he thought.

There was a knock on the door, and the guard stuck his head in once more. There was no such thing as privacy in his posh prison. "It's time, your lordship."

It didn't feel the least bit odd to be deferred to by that title. Or rather, it felt oddly *right*. "Thank you." Luke straightened his shoulders. He'd gone up against assassins, been in situations so tenuous it was a wonder he made it through unscathed, yet he was nervous about this. What if it all went wrong? What if he woke up as he had in the Company hospital with no memory whatsoever?

Small, warm fingers entwined with his. He looked down to find Arden standing beside him, holding his hand. She smiled reassuringly. "I'll walk with you, if you don't mind."

"Not at all," he replied. Damn, his voice was hoarse.

The guard put the shackles on him before leading him down the corridor to the lift and up one floor to the operating theater. Arden remained by his side the entire time. She even stood by the operating table as Dr. Stone applied chloroform. His wife's face was the last thing he saw before blackness pulled him under.

He hoped when he woke up he'd remember her.

"Damn it, Dhanya! He's jumped through all your hoops. I want my husband back!" Two days of seeing him as a prisoner had made Arden realize she trusted him more than she thought. And nights of wishing he was there to make good on his promise to give her "something to moan about" only added to her frustration. Perhaps it was incredibly slatternly of her, but she wanted her husband at home, in her bed, and bugger the rest.

Her friend and superior drew her spine straight, her face an imperious mask. "You would do well to remember just who it is you're talking to."

Arden's own shoulders snapped back. "In this place your word may be law, but don't think I won't petition the Queen herself. My husband is a Peer of the Realm."

"And a traitor."

If anyone else had called Luke that, she would have jabbed them with the pronged end of her discombobulator.

"Not a willing one." Arden met the other woman's amber gaze and held it. She was nothing if not willful. Her stubbornness was legendary; without it she would have given up hope for Luke's return years ago. She'd be illegally married to Alastair right now, or at least be his lover. It was only sheer determination that kept her pious, and it had worked out in her favor.

Dhanya folded her arms over her chest. She wore black trousers with a shirt of violet silk and a black waistcoat embroidered in gold. Her long black hair hung down her back in a loose braid. She looked beautiful and impenetrable. Two minutes ago, Arden had found a piece of copper wire in her own hair—left over from a glovewarmer she'd been working on for a client earlier that morning. It wasn't as though she needed the funds such work brought in, but it kept her mind sharp and occupied, and it also gave her access to ladies who knew all the latest gossip. It was in her best interest to know what was going on—especially with a poor girl murdered. There were still no leads, but Arden shamefully had to admit that since finding Luke in her bedroom she hadn't given the murder her full attention. "He's not going anywhere until I am satisfied that you and the rest of Britain is safe from him."

Arden picked up the notepad from the desk and held

it up. The pages were covered with writing in her husband's hand. "He's given you pages of information already. Surely that gives you some degree of confidence."

Elegant shoulders shrugged. "I've yet to confirm any of that. And you shouldn't be reading it."

Arden tossed it back on the desk. "I don't want to read it." She didn't want to know the things he'd done for those monsters. "I want my life back. I want my husband."

Dhanya appeared unmoved, but then she had never been married. She had no idea how it felt to have Luke returned just to lose him again. "I am sorry, Arden, but I will not sanction his release one second before I am ready."

Arden's temper flared into hot pettiness. "Then I'm afraid I won't have that device for you until I'm ready."

The Director flushed. "You said we wouldn't speak of it. And you're being a child."

Her first came down on the desk. "I want my husband!"

A moment passed as silence settled between them, neither prepared to look away first, or even blink. Then Dhanya began to chuckle. Arden followed, much to her own chagrin. Oh, but it felt good to laugh. She sank into one of the chairs in front of the desk and the other woman did the same. Their chuckles faded, leaving both of them wiping at their eyes in silence.

Having regained her composure at last, Arden said, "I need him, Dhanya. I need to have him at home with me. I've waited so long I fear I may go mad if I have to wait much longer."

Resting her elbow on the desk, the Director regarded her with a sympathetic gaze. "You know he's not the man he once was."

Arden nodded, her fingers toying with the bit of wire that had fallen from her hair. "I'm not the same woman.

I'm not sure that's entirely a bad thing." Though that was a lie. If they weren't the same people, would they still love each other? She had been shocked when Luke said there was little difference between the Wardens and the Company. Why, he'd been all about his duty before he disappeared. He believed the W.O.R. to be an instrument of good against Company corruption.

She'd also been surprised at the way he looked at her when she lied to him. She was a very good liar, but she was certain he could sense her deceit. He had never caught her in a lie before—not that she knew of. Of course, she'd never really had anything to lie to him about before.

"A few more days," Dhanya assured her. "Let us monitor his recovery from the procedure, see what he might remember about his last assignment and how he was taken. Then you can take him home—with some provisos, of course. You never know, returning to his home and to you just might trigger memories."

She referred to his spy work. Personally Dhanya would want Arden to be happy, but what mattered to the other woman was uncovering what had happened to Luke, whether or not he had been betrayed. What really gave her pause was Dhanya's mention of his last assignment. No one seemed to know what it was. If Dhanya didn't know, then the former director had taken it to his grave. That meant it involved something extremely sensitive. But what? It had been so secretive that her father had been forbidden to discuss what devices he supplied for the operation. And when Luke disappeared, he'd been taken into headquarters for a private meeting with the former director—a meeting he refused to speak of, but Arden had seen the sadness, and fear in his eyes. He refused to tell her anything, even when she begged him on her knees, sobbing for her husband.

Her heart broke a little at the thought of Papa. Luke had yet to inquire after him, but he would eventually, and she would have to tell him that Papa was gone, and that Mama had fallen to decline.

As soon as her mind turned to her mother she shut it down. That was more heartbreak than she could take at the moment.

"Thank you," she said. "I know you have the Empire to worry about, so I apologize if my wants seem petty in comparison."

Dhanya's full lips curved. "I cannot imagine what you must be going through, so I will apologize if I seem cold in my motives. But threaten me with Her Majesty in the future and you'll never taste Mama's sweets again."

That was a threat that hit home. "I would rather die." It was said with humor, but when Dhanya fixed them tea on the little burner she had in the corner of her office, and brought out a plate of her mother's delicious concoctions, Arden thought perhaps she should keep such threats to herself in the future.

She was on her second cup of tea and fourth sweet when Evelyn arrived. It had only been a little more than two hours since she put Luke under. The sight of the darker woman launched Arden to her feet, dread heavy in her chest, food and tea revolting in her churning stomach. "Is he . . . ?"

Evelyn looked horrified. "Oh, luvvy, no! He's fine. Brilliant, actually. Sleeping now, but you'll be able to see him in a bit."

Choking back a sob, Arden sank into her chair before her knees could give out. "Oh, thank God." When she reached for her empty teacup, Dhanya splashed some whiskey in it from the bottle she kept in her desk drawer. It was the bottle she kept for special or dire occasions. Which of those she considered this, Arden had no idea.

"Evelyn?" Dhanya held up the bottle. When the doctor nodded, she poured some whiskey in a cup for her as well. "Tell us everything."

Evelyn took the whiskey with a tired and grateful smile. Arden couldn't remember ever seeing the woman when she looked as though she was rested. "I made a small incision on Lord Huntley's forehead above the small section of bare bone in his skull. When I inspected the opening I found a small mechanism inside, which I managed to extract intact." She took a sip from her cup.

Arden exchanged glances with Dhanya. "What sort of mechanism?"

"The sort normally used in asylums to release medication into patients in regular intervals."

Dear God. "Did you find anything inside it?" Arden asked, swallowing hard against the horror and disgust twisting inside her.

Evelyn took another drink. "Yes. I need to run a few more tests because I wanted to talk to the both of you first, but I think a chemical compound was being used to inhibit Lord Huntley's long-term memory. Just having the device implanted in his brain would be damaging enough."

The thought turned Arden's stomach. She took another drink regardless. "Will he recover his memory now that it's been removed?" Did she want him to recover?

Her friend shot her a sympathetic look. "I'm not certain, luv. With the gregorite in the way, it's difficult to see just how much damage has been done. Plus, there's so much we don't know about the brain. Add to that the damage that the chemicals have done over years of continued use. . . . I think you should prepare yourself for the possibility that he will never fully regain his memory."

Arden caught her top lip between her teeth. So much of his life—of their life together—lost forever. How

could they ever hope to regain what they once had?
"Thank you, Evie."

"I wish I could have brought you better news."

She cleared her throat. Sympathy was well and good,
but it could quickly become pity, and she would rather
hack off her own hands than be pitied. "Is his mind otherwise sound?"

Evelyn rolled the cup between her palms. "The procedure was completely without incident, so I've no reason
to suspect otherwise."

"That's all I can ask. The rest will be what it will be."

Arched brows from both women met her statement.
"That's very . . . calm of you," Evelyn allowed.

Arden shrugged, careful to keep her inner turmoil to
herself. "It's why God made whiskey." She forced a
chuckle when her friend looked even more shocked.
"I'm just happy he's remembered who I am and stopped
trying to kill me. Honestly, you two. Right now it's
enough just to know I was right."

To her great relief, both of her companions believed
her lies and laughed. Dhanya raised her cup. "To husbands not trying to kill their wives."

"I'll drink to that," Evelyn agreed, lifting her cup in
toast as well. Arden followed suit. She suddenly felt
lighter—a combination of the whiskey and the good
news about Luke. She still had hope. After clinging to it
for the past seven years, she would not abandon it now.
After all, it had served her well.

She sat with the women for a little while longer—
enough to enjoy a second cup of Dhanya's whiskey and
make use of the loo. She was just about to take her leave
when Mr. Chiler's voice came through the orophone on
the desk. "Pardon me, Director?"

Dhanya moved the device—which looked like a miniature gramophone horn—toward her so she could speak

into the flared mouth. She removed a piece of cork from it. "Yes, Chiler?"

"I have Chief Inspector Grant on the telephone. He's looking for Lady Huntley. Would she like to speak to him?"

Dhanya looked to Arden for consent. Arden nodded. "It must be important for him to call me here."

"Ring him through to this station. Thank you, Chiler." A second later the telephone in the office began to ring. Dhanya put the piece of cork back into the orophone before answering the other device. "Certainly, Inspector. Lady Huntley is right here." Dhanya passed the telephone to Arden.

"Inspector Grant?" Arden said into the mouthpiece, holding the listening part to her ear. "What is it?"

"Sorry to trouble you, my lady, but I was of the hope that you might have the time to call upon me at Scotland Yard today."

Arden hesitated. She wanted to see Luke before she left. "Is it important?"

There was a pause on the other end. "My lady, would I call you at this location if it wasn't?"

Whatever it was, Grant obviously didn't want to discuss it over the telephone. No matter that it was a marvel of modern innovation, it was all too easy for operators to listen in on otherwise private conversations—a favorite pastime of many, despite one of W.O.R's telephone exchange operators having been charged with treason for sharing something she'd overheard. "I'll be there as soon as I can, Inspector." She didn't add that it had better be worth forcing her to leave her husband.

He thanked her and she disconnected the conversation by placing the earpiece in its "switch."

"Has there been a break in the investigation of the baron's daughter?" Dhanya asked.

"He didn't say," Arden replied, rising from her chair. "Ladies, I'm afraid I must take my leave of you. Evie, may I check upon Lord Huntley before I depart?"

"Of course." The darker woman made a face that said she hadn't needed to ask. "He's in the infirmary. The nurse will let you in."

She hugged both of the women before leaving, and carried her hat in her hand. She had to ask Mr. Chiler for directions to the infirmary, but found it easily enough. The ward was closed off by a metal door with a slider that opened a few seconds after she knocked. The nurse let her in as soon as she identified herself. Dr. Stone had left her name as a temporary visitor to the locked facility.

Luke was at the far end of the short row of beds, the majority of which were empty. His color was good, and aside from the snowy bandages wrapped around his head, he looked perfectly normal. Peaceful. She couldn't help but smile at the sight of him. Hopefully Evelyn's procedure had severed the last of his ties with the Company.

The armed guard watching over him nodded at her as she approached, and moved a discreet distance away to give her a little privacy, but remained close enough should anyone—herself included—make trouble.

Arden lowered herself to the edge of the narrow cot, sitting on her hip so as not to disturb Luke's slumber.

She reached down and smoothed back the hair that stuck up above the top of the bandage wrapped around his head. It was soft and silky, and brought a lump to her throat. If she had a pound for every time she'd come close to, or had cried since his return, she'd be an extremely wealthy woman. God, someone ought to horsewhip her for this sentimentality.

Dark lashes twitched, then slowly opened. Glassy

pale eyes stared up at her as his lips curved into a lazy smile. "I know you. You're my wife."

Arden grinned like an idiot. It felt as though a huge mass had been lifted from her back. How could she not have been consciously aware of just how afraid she'd been that he would wake up with his memory gone once more? "Yes, I am."

His lids drooped. "Nice wife. You want to crawl in here with me?" One of his hands clumsily patted the side of the bed. "There's plenty of room."

There wasn't enough room for a breath in that bed, let alone her entire girth, but if time had allowed she would indeed attempt to stuff herself in there. "I'd be delighted, but I can't stay. I have an appointment."

Luke frowned, then grimaced when the expression tugged at the stitches on his forehead. It seemed to be a struggle for him to keep his eyes open. "Where?"

"Scotland Yard."

His frown eased, and he lost the battle with his heavy lids. "Duty then. Can't ignore that."

"No," she replied, spine straightening. His words were like a sharp cut to her heart despite being an echo of their past. "I can't."

He didn't speak again—he was sound asleep once more, his chest rising and falling in an easy rhythm. She envied him the escape.

Arden placed the back of her fingers against his warm cheek, feeling the sharp edge of his cheekbone against her knuckles, the scratch of stubble. Quickly, she rose to her feet and walked away, refusing to let the irrational part of her mind wander into all the places it wanted to go. There didn't have to be some foretelling of doom in his words.

Though as she left the infirmary she had to wonder if

it would be Luke's sense of duty that caused friction between them once more, or her own.

The man stepped onto the dirigible docking platform and placed his beaver hat upon his head. Hyde Park smelled of horse shit and airship grease, just as it always did. He'd never understand why so many people insisted on clinging to such antiquated notions as horse-travel, but he didn't care. Let the mindless chattel do as they would. He had more important things to occupy his mind.

It had been almost three days since they lost contact with Five. The Doctor had been unsuccessful in his attempt to subdue the operative and had the injuries to prove it. Five had not returned to his rooms since, and the last information gleaned from the communicator in his ear had placed him at his former London home—with his wife.

Earlier today his contact at the W.O.R. confirmed that Five was in their possession, and orders had been given to detonate the device in Five's brain. As valuable as he had been, he was a liability now and could not be allowed to live. He would be a great loss to the Company, and give the Wardens a glimpse not only into Company technology, but into years of missions and subterfuge.

It was his job to clean up any mess, find out what the W.O.R. knew, and finish Five's original mission. And, in case they were unsuccessful in immediately eliminating Five, he was to do that as well. It was a distasteful business, but he would not rest until Arden Grey, Lady Huntley—and her husband—were dead.

Chapter 11

Chief Inspector Grant was standing outside the Scotland Yard building when Arden arrived. He was smoking a pipe, and judging from the little mounds of ash at his feet, had been doing so quite prodigiously for a while.

"I thought you gave that up because your wife detests the smell," she said, by way of greeting as she stepped out of her touring carriage.

"I did," he replied grimly as she lowered her goggles. A plume of fragrant smoke rose around him in the steam-damp air. "But she'll just have to forgive me for it."

His face was pale, the skin beneath his eyes dark and bruised-looking. She'd seen him look haggard before, but it seemed worse now, as though his position was finally wearing him down.

"There's been another murder, hasn't there?" She didn't wait for him to respond before digging her bag out from behind the driving bench.

"Yes. Another girl with her heart ripped out. We've gotten some of the findings back on the first girl as well. I didn't want to call you, but ..." He took one last haul off the pipe. "Two girls in less than a fortnight. I need your help to find this bastard."

That he didn't mind his language—and didn't apologize for it—proved just how tired and stretched thin the inspector truly was. Arden drew a deep breath, filling her lungs with the smell of pipe tobacco, which she didn't mind in the least. She drew calm around her like a warm blanket. "Where's the latest victim?"

"Here at the morgue." He tapped the bowl of his pipe against the dingy gray stone wall. Scientists might have discovered a fairly clean-burning coal alternative, but there was no undoing the decades of soot ground into every pore of London's buildings and streets. "Didn't want the press to catch wind and put her photograph in the *Times*, soulless vultures."

Arden wasn't surprised by his vehemence. She'd worked with Grant long enough to know that he believed the press to be on par with the lowest of criminals. She didn't quite share his opinion, but she had also worked with him long enough to understand where it came from. They'd almost lost the Ripper because of the press.

She pulled back her shoulders. "You'd better take me to her, Inspector. Perhaps she can give us what her predecessor could not—the identity of her killer."

"I hope so, Lady Huntley." He slipped his pipe into his jacket pocket. "Some of the lads are likening these to the Ripper murders, but I didn't feel half so horrible for those poor souls as I do these dear little girls."

Grant's shoulders were hunched as she followed him to the door exclusively used for Scotland Yard staff. He inserted his punch key in the box on the wall and waited as it finished its sharp clacking before withdrawing the card and turning the heavy, spoked wheel on the iron door. There was a hissing sound, like that of train brakes, only not as loud, followed by a thunk, and then he pushed the door open.

"After you, Lady Huntley."

Arden stepped over the threshold. Given her association with the police force, this wasn't the first time she'd been allowed access to the inner workings of Scotland Yard, and it probably would not be the last. It wasn't a cheery place, though the odd chuckle punctuated the din. The men and women who worked here had that dull-eyed look of people who had seen every possible human evil there was. All of their shock and horror—even sorrow—had been all used up, and there was nothing left.

She inclined her head in greeting to those whose gaze caught hers. No one was surprised to see her. Though Grant took pains to conceal her involvement in Yard business, she was still a known asset to many. The rest simply didn't care.

It wouldn't be that scandalous for society to find out about the work she did for the Yard, only slightly more so if it was discovered she was a W.O.R. agent. The real scandal would be caused by the devices for ladies she made in her workshop. Such was the way—the general populace barely blinked at violence, but sexuality was a different story.

The morgue was in the basement, of course, where bodies were kept cool in the storage area using small amounts of solidified carbon dioxide. It was a dangerous substance, and Arden had seen more than one morgue attendant who had lost a finger or two to frostbite because of it. Still, it was effective.

She pulled her shawl tighter around her shoulders to ward off the chill as they descended the stairs, Inspector Grant carrying her case. She took her flask from her reticule and allowed herself a small sip. She'd always enjoyed a nip now and again, but over the past few years she'd come to depend on spirits more and more. She knew it, and wasn't nearly as bothered by it as she supposed she should be.

It wasn't as though she was a drunkard. It wasn't as though she *needed* it to cope. It just made doing what she had to do so much easier.

The whiskey warmed her from the inside out. She opened her tin of cloves and popped one in her mouth, letting the sharp spiciness roll over her tongue and perfume her breath.

Only the *Curator Mortuorum* was present in the morgue when they entered. She was a tall woman—over six feet—with a sturdy build and thick curly red hair. Arden was thankful for her presence, as Mrs. MacNamara considered herself a caretaker of the dead, and tried to make the viewing experience as pleasant as possible.

"Lady Huntley," the woman said in a deep Scottish brogue. "Good to see you."

Arden slipped her gloved hand into the woman's much larger one. Mrs. MacNamara had an incredibly strong grip. "You as well, though perhaps someday we'll meet in pleasanter circumstances."

The older woman nodded solemnly. "God willing. You're here to see the girl Grant brought in earlier?"

"That's right," the inspector answered. "Would you be so kind as to fetch her? Also, I'd like you to repeat your findings on the Rathbone girl to Lady Huntley."

Rathbone? Ah yes, Arden remembered. That was Baron Lynbourne's family name.

Mrs. MacNamara went into one of the large cooling chambers used to store London's "done in." Newgate had its own morgue for prisoners, so the only bodies that fell into Mrs. Mac's capable hands were those who had suffered a wrongful death. Though on occasion the denizens of Newgate ended up on her table as well. Men with nothing to lose didn't have much respect for human life.

Arden had an awful feeling that one day her own body would end up in the Scottish woman's care. She might have already if Victor Erlich had been a tad bit faster, and she hadn't been able to reach her discombobulator. She hadn't meant to kill him, but she hadn't been about to let him rape her either. Alastair was meant to find the bastard, but she'd been the unlucky one. It was the last time she worked in what they referred to as "the field." She hadn't the love of danger that Alastair and Luke shared, though there were times she'd rather face the wrong end of a pistol than witness the last moments of another person's life.

When the *Curator Mortuorum* returned, she pushed a gurney in front of her. One of the wheels squeaked, and the shroud covering the body had seen better days, but Mrs. Mac took care with her cargo. She brought the gurney to the center of the room, beneath the operating chandelier, before gently peeling back the sheet.

Arden gritted her teeth as her gaze fell on thick chestnut hair—its elaborate coiffure ruined. Next, the deathly pallor of a smooth forehead, a fringe of still lashes, followed by a slack, round cheek. When the entire face had been revealed she gasped, horror sending a rush of tea and whiskey up from her belly. Only sheer fortitude kept her from humiliating herself. Embarrassment burned in the back of her throat, acrid and raw.

Grant whipped his head around to stare at her with those sharp eyes of his. "You know her?"

She nodded, averting her eyes long enough for the nausea to fade and her composure to return. "Cassandra Millingston. Earl Farnsworth's daughter."

The inspector swore—so well and in such detail that Arden could almost see a cloud of blue around the words. She didn't blame him, and she certainly wouldn't ask him to apologize for it. She understood, and agreed with him.

It wasn't just that she knew the girl, or that the victim was an aristocrat, but she knew as Grant did that once word got out that another peer's daughter had been murdered, there would be a panic amongst the upper classes. The Season might very well be called to an early end.

Their killer was undoubtedly of the aristocracy, and if the Season ended prematurely, their chances of finding the bastard would practically disappear with it. If he was indeed of the upper class, he would drift away to the country, and even if he killed again, they might never track him down.

"We have to keep this as quiet as possible," Grant said.

Arden arched a brow. "Rather impossible, don't you think? The moment you tell her parents the rest of the Mayfair set will know within an hour at the most." She didn't point out that a mass exodus would be soon to follow. "The girl's parents are undoubtedly concerned if she went missing last night."

"I shall have to think of something," Grant said in a low voice, gaze flinty. "I'll not let *this* one slip away."

Perhaps the Ripper investigation had affected Grant more than he let on. Arden turned to the *Curator Mortuorum*. "Mrs. Mac, would you be so kind as to show me the rest of the body?"

She was prepared for what lay under the sheet, though her stomach insisted on turning itself inside out at the sight. This young woman had been split open just like Lynbourne's girl, her heart brutally ripped from her chest.

"He's got a sense of anatomy, but I don't think he's a medical man," the Scottish woman informed them.

"Why not?" Arden inquired.

Mrs. Mac gestured with her finger toward a splintered rib, then past to the tattered tissue beneath. "Most with medical training are fastidious, brilliant and arrogant. This monster has no finesse. Even Saucy Jack had to show off his skill with a blade—to an extent. These girls weren't cut; they were torn open."

"I beg your pardon?" Arden frowned. "How is that possible?"

"There's not a knife mark to be found, but look at the bruising." Arden forced herself to look where the coroner pointed. If not for the whiskey her mind might better comprehend what the woman was saying. Oddly enough, the whiskey was the only thing keeping her from casting up her accounts all over Mrs. Mac's boots. "He shoved his hands into their torsos, pulled their ribs apart and tore the hearts from their chests."

Arden swallowed hard. "So the killer had to be uncommonly strong."

Mrs. Mac's expression was full-on incredulous. "Without a doubt, my lady. He had to have gregorite hands to do something like this."

Her first thought was Luke. He was strong enough to do this. And the first night she'd seen him had been at the site of the first murder. But he'd been locked up in his W.O.R. cell last night. He couldn't be the killer. Relief dropped her shoulders just as shame filled her with its dirtiness. How could she think him capable of such madness—even for a second? Never mind that he'd been sent to kill her—that was a mission. This . . . this was just lunacy.

"I found traces of gentleman's hair pomade under her fingernails," Mrs. Mac continued, gesturing toward a small vial on a nearby tray. "I haven't been able to identify the brand yet."

"May I?" Arden asked. At the other woman's nod, she took the vial, removed the stopper and sniffed. A flood of memories rushed at her, tightening her throat and burning her eyes. "Wexell's Best," she murmured, replacing the stopper before tears actually escaped.

Inspector Grant's expression was one of terse hope. "Are you certain?"

Arden smiled sadly. "Yes. My father used it. I'd know the scent anywhere." The thought of her father, on top of everything else, threatened to send her over the edge, but she mentally dug in her heels and forced all of her emotions into a far corner. They'd come for her later, but for now she was safe.

"Surely there can't be that many men of the peerage with augmented arms who use that particular pomade?" Grant scribbled in his notebook.

"I dare say there will be a number more than you hope," Arden advised. "It is a very popular brand—most ladies quite like the scent of it. Plus, it doesn't make a man's hair feel like grease."

The inspector grimaced. "Never understood the stuff myself. If a man wore his hair short as is proper, there'd be no need to slick it all back."

Arden and Mrs. Mac traded amused glances as he scribbled in his book once more.

"Inspector, where did you happen to find the body?" So much easier to refer to the deceased as a thing.

"Hyde Park. We're fortunate the watchman who found her knew better than to make a fuss. Managed to keep all very discreet."

"Hmm. You could narrow your search by concentrating on young or very charming gentlemen." Arden stared at Cassandra Millingston's dead face. Bless Mrs.

MacNamara—she had pulled the sheet up once more so the grisly wound was covered. "He had to be winsome enough for these girls to go off with him. First to the factory and then to Hyde Park."

He didn't look up from his book, but kept writing. "Odd that he would kill so close to where he probably lives, isn't it?"

Arden shrugged. "It might be the only place he could convince her to go. I'll know more once I've seen through her eyes. Would you assist me, Mrs. Mac?"

With the larger woman's assistance, Arden quickly outfitted both herself and the corpse with the Aetheric Remnant Oscillatory Transmutative Spectacles. She took a deep breath as she turned the key, then wished she hadn't. The room reeked of death, and she was soon going to be unable to escape it.

It only took a moment for the device to begin showing her the last few minutes of Cassandra Millingston's life. It was dark, but the moon and a nearby lamp made it possible for her to see the shady outlines of her surroundings. Lover's Walk, that's where she was. She was on the dark path famous for providing the proper concealment for romantic trysts.

From the lazy way she looked around—slowly and slightly unfocused—Arden realized Cassandra had been somewhat intoxicated. She hadn't been fall-down drunk, but tipsy enough that going to the park with a man seemed like a good idea.

Stupid girl. Meeting a man in the dead of night was *never* a good idea, not when reputation was all a girl had to recommend her. Still, Arden couldn't pass judgment. She'd had her own share of kisses—and sometimes a little more—in the dark.

She spun around—Cassandra that was—the world tilting and sliding around her. She had probably laughed out loud. Her hands waved about in the air. She was dancing.

Suddenly, she was pulled into the arms of a man. Her own arms wound around his neck. Arden saw a flash of his jaw—strong, clean shaven—and part of his ear. She couldn't tell the color of his hair in darkness, but it didn't appear to be black.

"Come on," she snarled between clenched teeth, not caring that others could hear. "Show me his bloody face."

But all she saw was the cravat pin—onyx in the shape of a horseshoe. It slipped slightly out of focus. Then, her hands braced against the man's broad chest. She pushed, struggled, turned her head—probably to scream—and then . . . oh, God.

Cassandra Millingston had looked down. She had seen her killer's hand in her chest. She must have felt him break her ribs. Had she felt her heart beat in his grasp just before he . . . ?

It all went black. Arden ripped the spectacles from her head and tossed them at Mrs. Mac. She half ran, half stumbled to the sink in the corner before the sweets, tea and whiskey in her stomach came rushing up. She retched until there was nothing left, and when she was done, she turned the tap to wash it all away, and splashed some water on her cheeks.

She turned to face Mrs. Mac and Grant in humiliation. "Forgive me."

"Here." Grant shoved a brass and leather flask in her face. "Drink."

She had her own, of course, but she didn't feel like whiskey right now—it didn't taste as good when it came back up—so she took the brandy he offered and swallowed a generous amount.

"What did you see?" Grant asked after she'd taken another drink and passed the flask back.

"Not his face," she allowed with a ragged, bitter chuckle. She swiped the back of her hand across her mouth. "His hair isn't black, if that helps. He's clean shaven. Tall, and well built." Most of this they already knew. "And Mrs. Mac is right, he shoved his hand into her chest like she was no more substantial than pudding." Oh, God. She'd never eat pudding again.

She heard the inspector writing it all down as Mrs. Mac patted her softly on the shoulder. When the scratch of pencil on paper stopped she hazarded a glance at Grant and said, "I'm so sorry I couldn't see more."

The gruff Scotland Yard agent looked surprised. "You saw what she did. I don't expect I could ask much more than that from someone who wasn't even there."

Arden shook her head in frustration. "I should be able to build something more helpful. Perhaps if I go through my father's catalog again I will find a solution — something that could prove more efficient and helpful."

A kind and heavy hand came down on her shoulder. Grant stared into her eyes and gave her a firm smile. "My lady, you've already proved your worth to me. Do not diminish it by punishing yourself for things beyond your control. Only God was meant to see everything. To know everything."

Normally she despised when people threw God into the conversation. God was no excuse for her own ineptitude, but this time she let it go. Unless she devised a way to know what a person heard before they were killed, it was doubtful she could have done any more.

She thought of Luke and the listening device the Company had put in his ear. Was it even possible to capture the sounds a person heard before their death? Perhaps if she could access the actual portion of the brain responsible for memory . . . Oh, the things she could do.

Had the Company inventors responsible for the thing

in Luke's head once thought the same thing? Of all they could achieve if only they had the proper bits and pieces? Was she really any better?

"So we're looking for a young, fit gentleman of the upper classes with hair that isn't black, but is pomaded, and hands that have been augmented." Grant looked up from his writing. "That gives us a bit more to go on than just the cravat pin."

Arden wouldn't forget that pin—not even after she was dead would she forget it. She glanced at the dead girl. Her family would be beside themselves. London society would panic. There was very limited time to find this monster.

And as a lady invited to almost every societal function, Arden knew she was the only one who could do it.

She had better find him before he killed again.

Dhanya Withering hadn't become Director of the W.O.R. by being sentimental or by being soft. Contrary to what many believed, it also wasn't because she was supposedly the bastard of a Royal Duke either. She had risen through the ranks by being smart, by putting the welfare of the Empire ahead of her own, and by being a proper bitch when the circumstances demanded it. She had never given priority to her personal feelings.

Until now.

"Are you certain it's wise to let him go?" Alastair asked. They were on the floor above the infirmary, watching Lucas Grey get his bandages changed through the glass.

"No," Dhanya replied, her gaze focused on Grey. "But I'm going to do it regardless."

Beside her, the tall man stiffened. Mentally, Dhanya braced herself. Was this going to turn into one of those unfortunate times when a peer reminded her of her low birth? Would he believe birth made any difference in this place, where she ruled? She was answerable only to the Prime Minister and Her Majesty. Only once had a peer gone over her head to the queen.

Dhanya had won, but it didn't change the fact that most of these titled brats thought themselves above her. She had never gotten that feeling from Lord Wolfred, and she hoped he wouldn't lower himself by doing it now.

"I am worried for Lady Huntley," he informed her.

"Of course you are, as am I." The only difference was, she wasn't in love with Arden. Wolfred thought he concealed his feelings, but one only had to see him look at her once to know the truth.

"We do not know for certain that he will not try again to kill her, as much as I want to believe otherwise."

His words spoke to her own fears, but she reminded herself that a part of the earl hoped that Huntley proved to be a traitor; then he might still have a chance to win the man's widow.

"My instinct tells me he won't hurt Arden, but that's not the sole reason I'm letting him go. The Company's first attempt to assassinate her failed, but that doesn't mean they won't send another." She turned to him. "Lord Huntley is more than equipped to protect his wife."

The slightest wince passed over Wolfred's handsome features—for which Dhanya was sorry—but the man had to reconcile himself with reality and what was right. Arden's life might depend upon it.

"I know you think you can protect her, my lord, but you cannot be with her twenty-four hours a day without drawing notice and causing a scandal. Her husband is our only option, even though he too is bound to be a target."

"He won't be able to protect her at all if he's dead."

"I do not believe Lord Huntley is all that easy to kill, though you are correct. If anyone knows how to kill him it is the Company. That is why I'm putting you in charge of making certain he is as safe as possible. The two of you are old friends; no one will think it odd to see you hovering around him as much as possible."

"You expect me to put all my trust in him?"

Dhanya sighed. "With respect, Wolfred, I don't believe for a moment that it's Lord Huntley whom you do not trust. Tell me honestly, if one of those nurses caring for Grey right now tried to kill him, would you try to save him or let him die?"

A dull flush appeared high on his cheekbones. "I would save him."

"Good." She turned back to the window. "He's given us extensive information about the Company, but I want you to question him as often as possible, see if he's forgotten or seems to be concealing anything. Pay particular attention to anything relating to inventions. The Company seems to have outdone the W.O.R. when it comes to scientific innovation. I want to rectify that. Let Lady Huntley in on that as well. The woman has a brilliant mind for anything machine-related."

"As you wish, Director." There was no denying the coolness of his tone.

Dhanya paused, then lifted her head and turned her body toward his. "Am I asking too much of you, Lord Wolfred? Will it take too much effort for you to pull your head out of your own arse long enough to protect the man who has been your longtime friend, and the woman for whom you have long carried a torch? Because if you're not up to the task of trying to keep both of them alive, I can always find someone else."

Wolfred looked as though he could strangle her with

a smile on his face. "I believe I can pull my head out of my arse long enough to do as you ask, madam."

She sighed. "It's not punishment, for God's sake! I'm asking you to do this because you're the only person I trust to do it besides myself and possibly Zoe. As I've said, you'll raise the least amount of eyebrows, and you probably won't arouse the Company's suspicions. If you want to sulk or despise me for it, go ahead, but remember that I have no compunctions about letting you go if you cease to be of use to me." Perhaps it was a tad bit harsh of her, but she needed to be certain—needed Wolfred to be certain—that personal feelings would not interfere.

He raked a hand through his thick hair. "I appreciate your trust, and I can honestly promise you that I will do everything in my power to protect both Lord and Lady Huntley." There was real conviction in his voice this time, and that eased the weight on her shoulders.

It wasn't fair of her to demand he keep his feelings out of the matter when it was her own friendship with Arden that made it so imperative to let Lucas Grey go home. His presence might bring even more danger down on Arden, but the conviction that he could dispose of any foe that came their way was ample justification. She was forced to trust a man who had spent the last seven years being mesmerized and God-knows-what-else by Britain's greatest enemy.

"Thank you," she murmured.

"How long have you known?"

Dhanya's head whipped up. "What's that?"

He looked indignant. "How long have you known that I . . . have feelings for her?"

Poor thing. This was probably the closest he'd ever come to admitting those "feelings" to anyone, even himself. "A few months," she lied. She'd known ever since she first saw them in the same room years ago. "Don't worry; I'm sure no one else has noticed." Another lie, because she was dead certain that if Lucas Grey was half the man she suspected him of being, he had already figured it out as well.

In fact, he had probably known it before he ever disappeared.

Lord Wolfred nodded. He seemed relieved. Poor bastard. She truly felt for him. He actually thought he could conceal his feelings. He was excellent at playing any part that was necessary in an assignment, but Arden Grey was his Achilles' heel. She was Huntley's as well.

Surely the two of them together could put jealousy aside to protect Arden. If they couldn't, and anything happened to the one friend she had, Dhanya would personally kill them both.

Chapter 12

He was going home.

The thought sat heavy in Luke's stomach, as ominous and unsettling as a disturbed grave.

"You look as though you're going to the gallows," Alastair remarked as they drove through the bustling streets in his touring carriage. It was a slightly boxy vehicle, black lacquered, with brass pipes as big around as a man's wrist coming up each side in sets of two, funneling the steam that made the beast capable of traveling at great speeds. It had a soft top that could fold down like an accordion, but was up today to protect Luke from view—of gossips and potential assassins.

"I'm going to a place where practically everyone knows more about me than I do. And I'm being taken there by a man who knows me better than any of them."

Alastair smiled slightly. "I can see where that might be unsettling for someone accustomed to being in control and prepared for any eventuality."

"Yes," Luke replied drily. "I wager you can see it very clearly."

His companion chuckled and silence fell between them for a few moments as Luke stared out at the city rolling by. It all looked familiar but strange at the same time—like images from a dream he couldn't quite recall. It was annoying.

"Does she even know that I'm coming?"

"Not at all. Arden would have wanted to plan for your arrival, which means she would have alerted the servants. Even if she didn't tell them what was going on, they'd talk. More important, they'd talk with other servants and tradesmen. Someone would have found out when you were expected. This way, there's little chance of someone lying in wait for you."

But of course there were no guarantees. "I'm not sure I like you calling my wife by her Christian name."

Alastair kept his gaze on the street—a good thing given all the traffic. His face was devoid of expression. "She calls me by mine."

"Don't much care for that either." He looked out again at the passing city.

"You had no problem with it seven years ago."

Luke turned his head, maintaining his calm despite the emotions raging inside him. "Did I wonder if you were trying to shag her seven years ago?"

The carriage swerved to avoid hitting a dog barking in the street. Alastair's knuckles were white on the steering bars. "Your wife's fidelity has never been something you've had reason to question."

There was no mistaking the affront in his tone. Luke didn't care. "That wasn't what I asked. Before I disappeared, was I aware of the fact that you, to put it politely, coveted my wife?"

A muscle in the other man's jaw visibly clenched. "It wasn't like that."

Luke didn't give him time to explain—it didn't matter,

did it? "Which begs the question, did you offer me up to the Company so I'd be one less obstacle between you and Arden?"

The vehicle swerved suddenly to the side, careening down a side street before jerking to a halt. Alastair whipped around to face him, and he brought his fist with him.

Luke's head snapped back with the impact, but this time he did not pass out. He came back with a swing of his own. Alastair ducked, and Luke's fist went right through the back wall of the carriage.

Alastair gaped at the hole as Luke pulled his scraped hand free. "You could have killed me, you bloody bastard!"

"If you touch Arden, I *will* kill you." Damn, he was bleeding. He began to untie his cravat with his uninjured hand. He shouldn't have reacted like that. He really could have killed the man, while Wolfred would have knocked him out at worst.

"I have no intention of touching Arden." Alastair shoved him. "And you're paying to have that fixed. You mad bastard."

Luke wrapped his cravat around his bloody hand. "Send me the bill."

"I will." Alastair steered the carriage back into traffic toward Mayfair. "If you were so concerned about someone else making a bid for Arden's affection, perhaps you shouldn't have left her alone for seven years."

"I'm fairly certain I didn't intend to be gone that long," Luke replied drily. He knotted the cravat. "Why did I leave? Was it an important assignment?"

His companion's face tightened. "You never shared all the details with me. You were certain there was a Company spy amongst the Wardens. When you left, you said it was to follow a lead in Paris."

"Did I find the traitor?"

"I don't know. You were pretty closemouthed about the whole thing. Then we lost contact with you." He shot Luke a glance. "That's all I know. You made me promise not to speak of it, not even to Arden. I never have."

That Wolfred didn't break his promise said much about their former friendship—enough that Luke felt like a sack of shite.

"Arden says you looked for me." He refused to feel guilty for trying to hit him regardless.

Alastair shrugged as they made a left turn onto another street. He pulled out to go around a slow-moving cart and slipped back into the lane, narrowly missing being struck by a pair of automaton horses pulling a fancy carriage. Luke raised a brow in admiration.

"You were my friend. Of course I looked. You would have done the same for me."

"Would I?" He couldn't stop the words from falling out of his mouth. When Alastair shot him a questioning glance, he continued. "I remember events, but I don't remember what sort of person I was. Would I have honestly gone after you?"

His companion nodded, eyes on the road. "I'm certain of it."

"Good." Nice to know he hadn't been a right proper bastard. "Child!"

The vehicle swerved again, Alastair cursing the air blue as he missed the boy, who had chased a clockwork doll into the street, by scant inches.

"This is why I prefer velocycles," Luke informed him, grateful for Alastair's quick reflexes. "They're easier to maneuver."

Alastair snorted, his expression dubious. "You like velocycles because they're fast, reckless and entirely too dangerous. You always have."

"Well, it's nice to know I haven't changed completely." And it *was* oddly comforting to know the Company hadn't managed to rob him completely of himself.

"Not completely, no." His friend shot another glance his way. "But enough."

A scowl pinched the skin between Luke's brows. "Enough how?"

The touring carriage turned once more, this time into a long, gravel drive. Luke recognized the house not just as Arden's, but as a place that meant a lot to him. Tiny snippets of memory raced across his mind, few of them making sense, but all of them in this house.

It was home, and he knew it in his bones.

Alastair cut the engine when they reached the house. Angling his body toward Luke, he snatched his hat from the seat between them. "Enough that I don't know if we're friends or enemies."

"Not enemies," Luke replied immediately, certain of the words. "Not sure about friends, but we're not enemies."

White teeth flashed in the other man's tawny face. "Good enough. Now, shall we give your wife a surprise that will make her want to kill us both?"

Mrs. Bird fainted when she saw him. Arden could hardly blame her. She felt rather vaporish herself when Alastair and her husband walked through the front door. Although her reaction might have had a fair bit to do with the fact that he had removed his cravat, leaving much of his throat bare to her gaze. His neck had been a favorite place to bury her face and breathe in the clean, spicy scent of him. She'd kiss him there, dip her tongue in the salt-sweet hollow . . .

She swallowed. Ronald had caught Mrs. Bird before she hit the marble floor, thank God. But who was going to catch her when she fell down the rest of the staircase because her knees were too weak to support her? This was foolishness. He was only a man, after all.

But he was the finest man she'd ever seen—even finer than he'd been before—and a woman shouldn't have to go so long without her man. She might try very hard to be a woman of rational and scientific mind, but she was still a woman, and she'd been raised to indulge all curiosities, to believe that no knowledge was bad knowledge.

Luke had been very happy to educate her when it came to sexual congress—filling in what the books left blank, giving practical experience to what had been simple theory before.

In short, her husband was arousal on legs, and though part of her thought herself silly for it, she wanted him oh-so-badly. And now he was home. Hers.

He couldn't have come at a better time. She'd just returned from the home of Earl and Countess Farnsworth, where she had gone with Inspector Grant to ask the family and staff not to discuss Cassandra's death. They'd done their best to appeal to the household's sense of justice. Everyone seemed heartbroken over the tragedy, so hopefully their desire to see the killer caught would silence even the loosest of tongues. It had been very difficult to witness Farnsworth and his wife's grief. She could only hope that they would behave as the Lynbourne household and keep silent. The less gossip, the less likely it was that the killer would flee.

"What are you doing here?" she demanded, finally finding her voice as she reached the bottom of the stairs. It was as though she couldn't talk and descend at the same time.

"I've come home," he replied, directing a glance at Alastair. "We thought it best not to preannounce the fact."

Yes, she understood. They hadn't wanted to risk an assassin waiting for him. She should have anticipated such a move; then she wouldn't be so off-kilter. She had thought she'd have time to prepare—and that Dhanya would keep him longer than a few days.

Her friend had kept her promise after all. Arden supposed she ought to be ashamed that she had expected otherwise, but she couldn't quite manage it.

The poor servants. They looked as though they had seen a ghost. Dear Mrs. Bird was just beginning to come round. She felt for the poor woman, as she had grown up in this house the same as Luke. They had known each other for most of their lives.

Arden turned to them as a few more servants trickled in. They hadn't expected this, of course, and so when one of the new maids spotted him through a window, she mentioned it to another woman who had been there longer. Word spread fast that Lord Wolfred had arrived with a dark-haired, blue-eyed man. Then, one of the footmen saw him, and chaos ensued.

"Everyone," she said, venturing toward the assembled household, "Lord Huntley has returned." It was overstating the obvious, of course, but some would need to hear it as much as she needed to say it. Saying it aloud, in front of witnesses, somehow made it real.

A loud cheer went up as they fell into line. Arden gestured for Luke to join her and took him through the procession, familiarizing him with old staff, and introducing him to new. They all gazed at him in wonder. Mrs. Bird burst into tears, and Luke actually embraced the slightly older woman, patting her affectionately on the back. "Hush now, Birdy. It's all right."

But the dear soul sobbed with renewed vigor when he referred to her by the pet name he'd used since he'd been a boy. He gazed helplessly over her head at Arden, who couldn't help but smile. She could tell the affectionate name had simply popped into his head. It must be so frustrating to know so much yet not be able to recall it.

He looked fatigued. He had a small bandage on his forehead where Evie had operated, and underneath his eyes was smudged with blue. He was in desperate want of a shave — she'd have to hire a new valet for him. He had a fading bruise where Alastair had hit him, and a red mark over it that looked as if he had been struck again. She glanced down at the cravat wrapped around his hand, and could guess what happened.

"Alastair ducked, did he?" she inquired sweetly after they'd gone through the servants.

Luke glanced down at his hand before grinning sheepishly at her. "He's going to send me the bill."

Rolling her eyes, she shook her head. What was it about men that made them insist on reacting to almost any sort of situation with violence? "I don't understand why the two of you take such pleasure in hitting each other."

"Don't you?" He arched a brow in a manner that told her not to be so obtuse. "I would think it obvious."

Mortification flooded her cheeks. She grabbed his arm and pulled him away from the servants and their sensitive ears. "Not because of me?"

His pale gaze roved over her with predatory interest. She shivered in response — which he acknowledged with a smug grin. *Men.* "History is filled with wars fought over beautiful women."

"I'm not beautiful." She'd spent her entire life being most comfortable and at peace with the fact.

"A woman so intelligent should not be so dim when it comes to her self-worth. Now say good-bye to Alastair so we can talk and I can familiarize myself with my home."

She was halfway across the floor before she remembered how much she despised being ordered about. As much as she wanted some time alone with him, she was nervous about it as well—agitated. This did not mix well with indignation.

"Would you care to stay for tea, Alastair?" she asked sweetly.

Her friend looked over her head, and she didn't have to turn to know whose gaze he sought. Traitor. She could just imagine Luke back there, shaking his head—and none too subtly either.

"Thank you, my dear, but I must be off. I shall leave the two of you to your happy reunion."

Was she being overly sensitive, or did she detect a trace of irony in his tone? Regardless, she walked him to the door, Luke a few steps behind. Alastair kissed her hand and departed. She turned to find her husband watching her closely, a curious expression on his face.

"What?" she demanded. Most of the servants had dispersed now. Mrs. Bird had mentioned making certain Cook prepared "His Lordship's favorite" for supper, as she dabbed at her eyes and smiled like she'd just seen the sun for the first time. Ronald went with her, his arm about her shoulders.

"I just realized that you really aren't attracted to Wolfred."

"I told you he was my friend," she retorted sharply. "Nothing more. Perhaps now the two of you will stop treating me like some bone caught between two hungry dogs."

He actually had the gall to look affronted. "I think both of us would agree we only want what's best for you."

Arden's back straightened. "And I don't think either one of you is the least bit equipped to know what that is.

I have lived without you these past seven years. I have contributed to the Wardens. I have brought in an income of my own. I have assisted Scotland Yard, and *I* killed Victor Erlich—that is why you were sent to assassinate me, remember? So, I am very sorry, my lord, but for years I have lived by no other counsel but my own. I am not about to give my free will over to a man who has forgotten more about me than he knows."

If she thought her bold words would silence or lower him, she was wrong. He stood there, staring down that sharp nose of his at her as his lips lifted in a lopsided smile. "Refresh my memory—have you always been so bossy?"

She folded her arms over her chest. The toe of her right boot tapped in irritation. "I am not bossy."

"Yes you are." He took another step closer, until she could see nothing in front of her but him. "You're acting like a governess again, reprimanding me as though I were an incorrigible child, and I must say . . . I like it."

Arden trembled—literally trembled like a nitwit—as his pale gaze burned a trail from her head to her toes and back again. "Had I known that when we married I would have ordered you about a long time ago."

"So you weren't this bossy back then?"

"No." Perhaps a little, but she'd been a girl then.

"Good." He gave her that lazy, lopsided grin again. "I'd hate to think I'd forgotten that as well. Shall we continue our tour?"

Arden took the arm he offered and set off on legs that wobbled beneath her, damn things. When had he become such a shameless flirt? He had always been charming, but this . . . this made her mouth dry and her heart pound like a debutante at her first ball.

"Where would you like to begin?" she asked as they crossed the great hall.

"Wherever you want to take me," he replied, that amused lilt of his clinging to every word.

The bedroom. That was where she wanted to take him. Then she'd show him just how bossy she could be. Her cheeks heated at the thought.

"The library," she said, ashamed at how hoarse the words came out. "Let's start with the library."

After luncheon—during which the entire staff seemed to appear just to watch Luke eat—Arden suggested they take a walk around the garden before continuing on with the house. She said it was so she could show him improvements to the grounds, but really she wanted to talk to him in private.

He looked tired, but he didn't argue.

"When we return you should rest," she told him as they stepped outside from the back terrace. The breeze carried the scent of lilacs and roses upon it. "You look exhausted."

"Just a headache," he replied a bit too lightly for it to be "just" anything. He touched the bandage on his forehead. "I suppose having someone digging in your brain will do that."

She inclined her head in sympathy. "Dr. Stone says the Company used some sort of chemicals on you."

Luke nodded, squinting against the watery afternoon sun. "She told me."

They walked along the path away from the house. "I'm surprised Dhanya let you go," she admitted. "I thought she'd hold on to you awhile yet."

Hands behind his back, Luke seemed even taller as he walked beside her. Did the metal in him prevent him from slouching? "She might have, were she not so afraid of the Company's retaliation."

Frost breathed along Arden's spine. "You mean they'll come for you."

He shot her a narrow glance, but she didn't fool herself that it was because of the sun. "I believe she's more concerned about them coming for you."

Her heart stopped—just for a second. Just long enough to hurt. Long enough for her to almost give in to the fear. "You failed your mission. They'll want us both now."

"She let me come home so I could protect you."

Arden kept her gaze fastened on him. "Did she tell you that?"

"No." There was a touch of humorless laughter in his tone. "But I'm not stupid."

That was the last thing she would call him—on most days at any rate. "Who's going to protect you?"

Luke turned his head to favor her with a languid grin. "I suppose that would be you."

He said it as though it was a joke, but Arden wasn't stupid either, and she heard what he didn't say—that Dhanya wasn't so concerned about his safety. "I'm sure she believes you can protect yourself. She knows what you're capable of."

"No, she doesn't." He shrugged. "But she knows I'll protect you, so it's a start. They're not going to execute me anytime soon."

"Speaking of death," she began rather lamely, wishing they didn't have to speak of it at all. "We need to discuss your brother."

"Harry?"

"Henry."

"Right." She knew from the set of his jaw that he would not forget his brother's name again. "What of him?"

She sucked in a lungful of breath. There was no easy way to handle this. "I haven't told him you've returned."

"Because he might tell someone, or because you fear it may put him in danger?"

"Because he's going to have you declared dead." She was going to go to hell for being such an awful person, but she simply could not find it within herself to trust Henry, no matter what excuses Mr. Kirkpatrick made for him.

Luke looked confused, and slightly caustic. "Could that not be stopped by telling him I'm back?"

"Without you standing beside me he wouldn't believe it. He's thought you were dead right from the beginning."

"Ah, now I've got it." He actually smiled. "You kept it from him for spite."

"That's not it at all." Perhaps it was, just a little. "He's never believed me when I insisted you were still alive. If I said you had returned without giving proof, he would think I sought to postpone the proceedings."

"Invite him for tea tomorrow." It was a suggestion to her ears rather than an order. "He doesn't deserve to hear it from gossips."

"I'll invite the solicitor as well." When he gave her a questioning look she added, "Just in case Henry thinks you're an actor I've hired, or a hallucination."

"Surely he'll know me when he sees me." Incredulity hung on every word.

"He's mourned you and moved on. That's not easy to come back from."

He regarded her thoughtfully. "Then I suppose it's lucky for me you didn't mourn me."

She smiled, but didn't reply. Perhaps they were both lucky.

They turned around then, and walked back toward the house. The garden was lovely, but not terribly fascinating.

"I'd like to see where the automatons come up."

Arden paused. "You remember them?"

"No," he replied with a shake of his head—a lock of black hair fell over his forehead, stark against the white bandage. "I saw them one night I was here."

It was said casually enough, but it still sent an unpleasant shudder down her spine. She'd almost forgotten how easily he'd gotten past her security and had entered her—their—home with the intent to kill her.

And now he didn't have to sneak in at all.

She pushed the thought from her mind. He was no threat to her—at least not physically. "You see that statue of Pan? It's standing on a movable platform. At night I enter the proper code on the surveillance apparatus control panel and the statue lifts slightly and moves out of the way to allow a patrol automaton to rise out of its holding cylinder. There's another under a specially designed grass lid. The machines then follow their predetermined route, which changes from night to night."

Luke nodded in approval. "So it's impossible to watch the house one night and know the protocol. Smart."

She preened a little under the praise. The randomness of the path had been one of her upgrades to the system. "Thank you, though now that you have shown me the weaknesses in the arrangement, I shall have to make improvements. Despite the system having been implemented while you were here, you were right that it shouldn't have been so simple for you to get into the house." She reached up to touch her chains but found only bare skin. She dropped her hand. "Perhaps steam vents that are triggered when an intruder gets too close to the house."

"That's definitely a deterrent." His brow furrowed— an indicator that he was trying to remember. "Your father installed the automatons, did he not?"

"Yes." She smiled at the memory. "As a wedding present. You asked him if he might not have come up with something a tad more extravagant. It took him a moment to realize you were joking."

Beside her, her husband chuckled—that hadn't changed. "That's the only memory I have of him. How is your father?"

Arden swallowed against the tightness in her throat. She had known he would ask eventually. "He passed three years ago."

The smile melted from his face. "Oh, Ardy. I'm so sorry." When he held out his arms, she stepped into their surprisingly gentle embrace. He could have crumpled her like paper with his strength, and she wouldn't care. Death was a small price to pay for something that felt this good. Her arms went around his waist, and she placed her forehead on his shoulder. So many emotions warred within her—anger that he hadn't been there at the time, and sadness too. But she was also glad he hadn't had to see it. And she was glad to have him here now.

It took a moment, but she managed to fight back the tears. She was already entirely too vulnerable to him, and she had to guard herself against his next question.

He asked it a moment later. "What of your mother?"

Yes, if she had already been crying this would have made it worse. Instead, she drew back, dug her nails into her palms and said, "She's in the country." That's all she was prepared to divulge at that moment. "Let's go inside, shall we?"

If he thought her change of subject odd he didn't mention it.

"I'll show you to your rooms," she said after leading him through the house to the main staircase. "Do you need a powder for your head?"

"No. I generally avoid the things."

"Really?" She paused on the step and turned to face him. "You used to take one whenever you had an ache or pain. And you took one from Alastair the other night."

That seemed to bother him. "The Company used massage and Chinese needle medicine for such things. Meditation as well. It was imperative to keep the mind clear at all times. Opiates are a last resort."

"Fascinating." She started up the stairs again, her brain already turning the information over and over. Could she use one of the small engines in her Personal Hysteria Dissolution Mechanism to create a device to massage the muscles in the neck and shoulders? At least that would be an invention she didn't have to wrap in plain paper and personally deliver under the guise of a social call, like some of her others. Although it might not be as popular. A sanitorium in France had purchased five of the hysteria treatments from her a few months ago, and applauded the effectiveness of the device.

Still, she couldn't shake the thought that her father would have wanted her to use her skill to create something more beneficial to the world. She told herself that women's health was very important indeed. Just because she had a talent for invention didn't mean she had to become the female equivalent of Mr. Tesla, or that Edison fellow.

Personally, after the last few hours she craved a drink more than she wanted to contribute to the scientific community. Or a bath. Perhaps a nap instead. Just a little time to think and be quiet. She had wanted her husband home—for so long—and now she had no idea what to do with him.

Well, that wasn't entirely true. Thoughts of her little machines and paroxysms of pleasure had given her several ideas, but she was too much of a coward to implement any of them. Still, she'd spent so much time thinking about sexual intercourse she was beginning to think she was turning into a fourteen-year-old lad.

When they reached the top of the stairs, she led him down the corridor past her own room to the master suite. It was connected to her own through the shared bath. Her fingers trembled slightly as they curved around the ornate brass doorknob.

"Here you are," she announced so brightly she winced. "I took the liberty of ordering some new toiletries for you, but we'll inquire with the agency about a new valet. Roberts left five years ago to work for a baronet in Kent. Also, as I said before, we'll need to schedule an appointment with your tailor. I presume there's no way of collecting your belongings from that lodging house?"

"It would all be gone now," Luke replied, gazing around the room. Arden had always liked this room. The walls were covered in a rich cream paper that looked as though it would feel like velvet to the touch, and trimmed in ebony. The furniture was simple, but of excellent quality—also made from ebony. Lightweight ivory curtains hung from the windows, but the centerpiece of the room was the large four-poster bed with its stark white pillows and quilt.

"Do you want me to show you where everything is? Or would you like to see how much you remember?"

"I'll do it myself . . . Thank you." His pale gaze held hers. "How did you get the staff to ready my room without telling them I'd returned?"

"I didn't have to tell them anything. The maids just did their regular cleaning of this room yesterday. It's been done once a week, but now that you are back it will be done daily."

He frowned, gaze roving around the room once more, as though taking in the sheer size of it. "You kept it ready for me?"

"Of course," she replied. Why wouldn't she? "I wanted it ready for when you returned."

He wore an unreadable expression when he faced her. His lips were parted, his eyes fierce. When he moved toward her, all grace and strength, she didn't know whether to run to him or *away* from him. Instead, she held her ground.

When he reached her she was caught up in a swift embrace that lacked both finesse and tenderness, but set her heart racing regardless. She fancied she could feel the metal in his grip. His fingers shoved into her hair, pulling at the roots, scattering pins. His other arm was around her back, holding her against him so tightly that, had she remembered how to breathe, she would have been robbed of all breath. Her hands braced against his chest, fingers curving into the fabric of his coat.

His mouth took hers, hard and insistent. She clutched at his lapels. Were there any space between them she would have pulled him closer.

The hooks at the back of her gown let go, one by one, under the nimble attack of his fingers. Arden made no move to stop him. She had no intention of stopping this, even though part of her brain screamed that it was a mistake—that it was too fast, too soon. When the gown gaped around her, she dropped her arms and stepped back from his embrace to let it fall to the floor around her feet. She stood before him in her drawers, chemise and a violet satin corset that pushed up her breasts and nipped her waist in a most flattering fashion.

Luke stared at her, eyes bright as crystal caught by the sun as he shucked off his jacket and waistcoat. The fine linen shirt beneath was another of his old ones, and it pulled tautly across his shoulders. He grabbed two handfuls of it and pulled it over his head.

Moisture leeched from Arden's mouth—and she had a pretty sound idea of where it was going. His chest was as smooth as she remembered, but his abdomen was more muscular, his waist narrower. His shoulders were broader with heavier muscle. She was wrong—he didn't have shoulders like David.

David should be so bloody lucky.

He reached for her and she went willingly, trailing her fingers down the fine line of hair that drifted downward from his navel. Her lips brushed his with the lightest of touches before she turned her back to him. "Unlace me?"

Those agile fingers went to work on her stays. She shivered, gooseflesh covering her arms as his teeth nipped at her bare neck. The corset fell to the floor, but before she could kick it aside, Luke's hands slid up her belly, over her ribs to the ribbons of her chemise. Two tugs and it fell away as well. Those same warm fingers cupped her breasts and gently squeezed her nipples, bringing a tormented moan to her lips.

Too long. It had been far too long.

As the thin fabric slid down her arms she heard him make a low sound in his throat. His hands stilled, still holding her breasts.

"What?" she demanded, annoyed that he had stopped.

"When did you get this tattoo?" His voice was soft, and hoarse.

He must mean the small wing on her right shoulder. It was the only decoration she had other than her chains. "On our honeymoon in India. You wanted me to have something to remember it by forever."

"It seems you were with me even when I didn't know it." He dropped his hands and she turned around as he did, presenting her with his bare back.

Arden made a sound that was somewhere between a gasp and a sob. There, on the back of Luke's left shoulder was a tattoo of a wing. The ink wasn't as faded, and it was larger by design, but there was no denying that it was the mate to hers, right down to the number of feathers.

"I got it four years ago when I was in India on assignment. An old woman in—"

"Calcutta," she finished, tears blurring her vision. The same old woman who had done hers.

He turned. "Yes."

She threw herself at him and he caught her, lifting her. She wrapped her legs around his waist as she kissed him with all the emotion she couldn't possibly put into words burning in her chest, threatening to split her apart.

Part of him had remembered her.

Luke turned and took a few steps. The ivory wallpaper was cool against her bare back, and Arden dug her shoulders into it for support.

His hand came between them, slipping easily through the slit in her drawers so that he could touch her. Arden gasped at the contact. She wanted his fingers inside her—anything that might ease the ache. He slid one inside and she moaned, her head pressing into the wall as she arched her neck. His other arm slid underneath her, holding her so that he could tease her into a tense spiral of wet heat while his mouth sucked hard on one of her nipples.

Arden rode his hand, bringing herself to the brink of orgasm just before his fingers eased away. She opened her mouth to demand that he put them back, but then she felt his forearm against the inside of her thigh and she realized he was unfastening his trousers.

When he returned to her it was with something bigger and smoother than his fingers. The blunt head pressed against her dampness, making her tense with anticipation. Slowly, he pushed forward, and her body opened to him, stretched with such a delicious ache as he filled her.

"Open your eyes." His voice was rough, low.

Her lids were heavy, but she pushed them open to stare into the bright, clear depths of his eyes.

Then he pushed and filled her completely, driving her shoulders farther up the wall.

"Do *not* close your eyes," he commanded. "I want you to look at me."

Arden's belly tingled at his words, the need inside her twisting and churning. She kept her gaze glued to his as they began to move together, instantly matching rhythm. The intensity of his expression, the stark desire in his eyes aroused her far more than anything she'd ever experienced before. It was like making love with a stranger who was somehow so very familiar. Exciting yet comfortable, dangerous yet completely safe. She could do anything with this man, and let him do anything to her, even though it was as if they'd never done this before.

She clung to him as the tension in her mounted, gripping him with her thighs as they thrust and pushed. Faster and faster, harder and harder. She didn't care when she banged the back of her head on the wall. He grunted when she dug her fingernails into his shoulders, but it only made him thrust deeper.

She came with a loud cry of triumphant thanks to whatever gods were in charge of carnal bliss. Luke followed shortly after, pressing her hard against the wall as his entire body stiffened. She held him tightly as the spasms rocked through him, and then draped herself limply over his shoulder as he carried her to the bed.

She smiled at him. "Thank you."

The lines of his face were still a little harsh, but there was humor in his eyes. And heat. So much heat. "Thank me later. I'm not done with you yet."

Chapter 13

Luke woke up alone.

He glanced over his shoulder at the expanse of bed at his back, then propped himself up on his elbow to survey the room, but Arden wasn't there. All that was left of her was a single silk stocking hanging limply from the foot-board.

He'd never had a woman leave him before. "Arden?" No reply. She was well and truly gone then. The realization left a strange hollow feeling in the pit of his belly. If she'd left a few quid on the bedside he didn't think he'd feel much more whorish than he did right then. He'd scratched her itch and now she was off doing whatever it was she did in this mausoleum of a house all day.

Although it was apparently his mausoleum. No wonder it had felt familiar to him. No wonder he'd climbed to her bedroom so easily that first night—instinct had taken over.

Just as some part of him had known to get that tattoo. He could still feel the soft brush of Arden's lips against the ink feathers. He shivered. She had wanted him with a ferocity that matched his own. He'd never wanted to be inside a woman so desperately in all his life—not that he could remember anyway. Perhaps it had always felt like that with her. God help him, but he didn't think he could manage three goes that close together again on a regular basis. Usually he liked to take his time, make the climax as good as possible, then pass out. But with Arden, he felt like a boy again—randy and eager. He came too quick but was ready for business again in a few moments. She hadn't seemed to mind though, her orgasms outnumbering his.

Christ Automaton, but she was a sexual machine. She matched him thrust for thrust, against the wall, on her knees, on top of him. When he'd let sleep claim him he had thought for certain she would do the same, but if she had, she hadn't slept for long.

He glanced at the clock on the mantel. Four o'clock. He'd been asleep for a little over an hour. At least his headache was gone.

Perhaps his wife had taken that with her.

His wife. It was the first time he thought of her that way without immediately feeling a sense of surprise. It was as though shagging her had somehow made it all more real. She was his now, and she would never belong to anyone else so long as he lived.

He had to make certain they both lived. That meant defeating the Company, a task far easier said than done, but if they could survive this immediate threat, there was a good chance they could have a future.

The thought of spending the rest of his days with one woman, in one place, used to scare the shite out of him. Before he had remembered who he was, he couldn't stay in one place longer than a few weeks before the urge to roam came upon him.

Perhaps that urge had simply been homesickness, only he hadn't known it at the time.

Tossing back the covers, he slipped out of bed and walked naked to the wardrobe where he found, in addition to several shirts, a vast collection of waistcoats, a few jackets and a thick velvet robe that he slipped on. At least it fit better than the rest of his old clothing.

He went to the shared bath and turned the faucets for the tub before turning the crank on a strange radiator-like device he deduced was to warm towels or clothing. He placed a heavy towel on it once the tub was full, and slowly sank into the bath. It was a decadent luxury he enjoyed until his skin began to wrinkle.

A little while later, he was dressed in another pair of trousers and a shirt that fit tolerably well. He shoved his feet into a pair of boots that felt like they had been expressly made for him, and realized that they probably had been. Then he went downstairs looking for his missing spouse.

The first maid he stumbled upon stared at him as though he was a ghost—all wide-eyed and pale. She told him that it was most likely Lady Huntley was in her workshop around the back of the house, as that's where she spent much of her time. Then she gave him directions, and when he asked, replied that she would indeed ask Mrs. Bird to send along tea and sandwiches.

When he reached the building he assumed to be the workshop, he knocked and waited for her to grant him entry before walking in. It was a large room and neat as a pin. It had to be, for there were so many bits of machines, strange devices and tools that it would be an indecipherable mess were it less organized.

And in the middle of it was his wife. Arden stood at a long table on the right wall of the room tinkering with something that looked like a Roman centurion helmet made for a Cyclops.

She looked up, her cheeks flushing softly when she

spied him. She looked softer to him—less stern. "I thought you were sleeping."

"I was until I woke up alone." He smiled at the "governess" clip to her words, and closed the distance between them. "What are you working on?"

"Nothing, yet," she replied, glancing down at the helmet. "But when it's done I hope it will be a sort of memory receptacle."

"For me?"

She shrugged. "If you want."

There was something in the way she said it. "Why wouldn't I?"

"Its design is more for storing memories than reviving them, and not all memories are pleasant—as I'm sure you know."

"How could I possibly have unpleasant memories after spending the last seven years under the control of an agency whose sole purpose was to use me as an instrument of death?" He hadn't meant to sound quite so bitter—or amused. Those things he'd done were very real, and yet they seemed to have been the acts of another person. Regaining even just a little of his memory had changed him. He wasn't the Lucas Grey she remembered, but he wasn't Five anymore either. In fact, it was a little overwhelming just to know he had a name.

Arden lifted her head and turned those big brown eyes of hers to his. "Did they make you do many horrible things?"

"I've got blood on my hands, yes. Whether or not the Director will hang me for it remains to be seen." At that moment, looking at her and seeing no judgment in her expression, he realized that he did not want to die. After years of not caring, it felt oddly terrifying to suddenly have a reason to want to live.

"You're not going to hang." She used a wrench to tighten a bolt on the side of the helmet. "I won't allow it."

Luke chuckled. "Break me out, will you? Ferry me away to the far corners of the earth where they'll never find me?"

Her jaw was set as she turned to him. Such a fierce little warrior. "If necessary, yes."

"Why?" He was genuinely confused, and didn't bother to hide it. "Why would you risk so much for a man you barely know anymore?" There, it was out in the open. They were more strangers than anything else. Strangers who were practically obsessed with each other. "Surely not just because you think you owe me anything?"

The helmet fell on the bench with a clatter as the full force of Arden faced him, hands on her hips. "Because you are my husband. Because you could have killed me on several occasions and yet you did not—not because I stopped you, but because you couldn't do it. And because even though the Company tried to obliterate me completely from your mind, you got a tattoo from an old woman in Calcutta that matches that of a woman *you* barely know anymore."

Luke stared at her, a peculiar tightness in his chest. "I don't see how a man could ever entirely forget a woman like you."

She caught her breath. "You say these things and all I want to do is take you inside me and never let you go."

He understood, even as his body reacted to her words. Theirs was such a strange and unique situation that it was difficult to know how either of them felt, let alone understand it. Physical attraction was the one thing they had that needed no explanation or apologies. And maybe if he made her come hard enough, often enough, she'd stop being angry at him.

Because she was angry—even if she didn't know it. He could see it in her eyes, feel it when she had dug her nails into his flesh. She was so very angry, and he couldn't blame her. He was angry too. He'd lost seven years of his life—seven years that had been taken from her as well. The only difference was that she had been aware of it every damn day.

He could take her again now and they'd both like it, but while that might be what they both wanted, it wasn't going to fix anything.

"I'll never say no to shagging you," he replied honestly. "But given that Birdy will come bustling in here any moment with tea, perhaps we should try something less . . . startling instead."

She appeared charmingly indignant. "I didn't mean I wanted to . . . not now!" She scowled at him. "You're not irresistible, you know."

"Only when I say those *things,* then?" He couldn't help but smile at her. He'd smiled more at her in the last few days than he had smiled in the past seven years.

"I should never have told you that," she replied haughtily, but there was a sparkle in her eye that softened her words.

"Is this what we were like before I left?" he asked, toying with a bolt on the workbench.

Arden stilled. Then, she went back to her helmet. "Of course. How else would we have been?"

"I don't know." What he did know was that Arden was lying to him. And he had no idea why.

But he was going to find out.

At what point should she cease to be a coward and stop lying to her husband? This thought plagued Arden long after she left her workshop, into the days that followed. Why did she not simply tell him that she wasn't that same girl he'd married? It wasn't as though he remembered. Wasn't as though he had expectations. Did he? And what of her expectations? How could she articulate that she was afraid to talk of the past because they might never feel that way about each other again?

She had both loved and resented him back then. She'd been angry that she couldn't have her own way, and enraged that the W.O.R. was more important to him than she was. And yet, she cherished every moment they had together before he rushed out to defend his country.

They had been together forty-eight hours, and he was still under the same roof. After seven years of being alone, she wasn't quite sure what to do with him. She wanted to talk to him, spend time with him, but she was afraid of doing just that. What if they had nothing to talk about? Or worse, nothing that the other wanted to hear?

She had sent word to Henry that morning asking him to come visit. Alastair had called upon them earlier, and Luke had given him yet more information he had remembered to write down, but that was it. In fact, Luke seemed far more interested in what she was doing—her inventions, even the naughty ones, enthralled him. He'd never been all that interested before. Usually it annoyed her having someone under her feet while she worked, but he'd been pleasant company.

"You're bloody brilliant," he'd told her, and the awe in his voice humbled her. And last night, he'd come to her room and done things to her he'd never done before. The memory made her knees tremble.

She refused to think about who he might have done them to while she was there alone, wondering if her womanly bits might wither from inattention.

He was a man who could kill her with little effort— and who had killed with little thought—yet he treated her as though she was the extraordinary one. And when she told him about her work with Scotland Yard, she'd been prepared for him to insist that she give it up because he thought it dangerous, or beneath her. Instead he asked about the killings.

"That's why you were in the alley that day," he surmised now as they sat together in the parlor having a glass of whiskey. They were waiting for Henry to arrive. "You thought the whore was another victim."

She nodded. She was becoming accustomed to the fact that his language was sometimes a little rough. So was hers. "But she wasn't. Our bloke kills noble girls." She thought of Cassandra Millingston, and the skill with which Grant—and she—had managed to keep her death quiet. Word had gotten out of the girl's demise, of course, but society believed it to have been an accidental death rather than a murder. That wouldn't last, of course. Eventually, her grief-stricken parents, or the servants, would say something to someone with a big mouth and word would leak out, but for now they had a little bit more time to look for the killer.

"You arranged this meeting with my brother to hasten my reintroduction to society, didn't you? So you can hunt the bastard down."

When he put it like that it sounded rather cold. Unfortunately it was fairly accurate. "And so Henry doesn't find out from gossip, and because you are his brother and he loves you. And because I cannot stand keeping it from him."

He arched a brow, and she scowled in return. "Yes, and because I want to get out into society and find the monster, and if you're with me I know I won't be in any danger."

His gaze brightened. "You trust me with your life?"

"Of course." And she meant it, despite common sense insisting she should not.

Luke's lips curved in a slow smile. "You say these things and I want to bury myself inside you."

How many times was he going to throw that careless remark back at her? She didn't mind—not really. It was just that . . . she was new to this open sexuality. She'd been brought up a lady, and intercourse was something between a husband and wife, hardly discussed, and done only in the dark. Usually in one position. Luke had disabused her of that notion early in their marriage, but he was even more sensual now—demanding, even. And he made a wanton out of her. She wanted him with a ferocity she couldn't remember possessing seven years ago. She was practically shameless with it. Next time he came skulking by her workshop she was going to make certain there was a clear bench.

He wasn't the only one who had changed, but perhaps he didn't feel as though she was quite the familiar stranger she thought him. Instead of clearing the confusion about their marriage cluttering her mind, sex had only thickened the fog. He didn't seem the least bit unsettled at the notion of having a wife, though she was very much aware that she now had someone to answer to after years of independence.

"I admire and appreciate your loyalty," he told her, suddenly serious as he took a sip from his glass. "And just so we're on even ground, I would never allow anything to happen to you. I'd kill anyone who tried to harm you."

His words sent a shiver down her spine. They were so darkly possessive, and yet so incredibly lovely. For that moment she believed she was the most important thing in his world. Perhaps that would change as memories came back and he became more comfortable in what must seem like a new life, but for now, she would simply enjoy it, and not think about how soon it might end.

"I would do the same," she informed him, honestly.

He looked very pleased with himself. "I believe you would. I thought you were going to use that electrical shock device of yours on the tailor this morning."

She shrugged. "He kept poking you with pins."

"He was nervous."

"Nervous?" She snorted. "What's he to be nervous of? He's been doing that job for twenty-five years."

"And I'm the first customer he's ever had come back from the grave."

"Then he should know better than to let it show."

"Perhaps you think he should have had a stiff drink and pretend disinterest?"

Arden froze, like a fox when it first spies the hound. She wasn't a fool, and no one could ever accuse her of not being self-aware. She'd have to be a top-notch idiot not to understand.

"Perhaps. If the stiff drink enabled him to do what had to be done."

His expression was neutral—completely so. He must be one devil of a card player. "If he needs a drink to do his job, perhaps he should find another vocation."

Her smile was brittle. "A valid point, but no one really cares if he drinks, because he is a man." To make her point, or perhaps just for spite, she swallowed the remainder of whiskey in her glass in one go and rose from her chair to stamp toward the liquor cabinet.

"There's no need to be defensive."

"I'm not." She slanted a glance at him as she set her glass on top of the cabinet's polished top. She wanted another drink, but that would only make him right, wouldn't it?

"You drink. A lot."

"Are we really going to have this conversation with your brother due any moment?" she demanded, fingers gripping the cabinet ledge.

Suddenly he was there beside her, looming over her. "It would be better if you didn't imbibe quite so much."

"You know what would be better, Lucas?" Bitterness so thick she could taste it dripped from her tongue. "If you didn't come back here after seven years of not knowing you had a wife and pretend to be someone who knows what's best for me. If you had known that you wouldn't have left in the first place."

Now it was he who went perfectly still. "You've expressed disappointment several times, Arden, but you haven't exactly told me what it was I did that pissed you off so badly you've held a grudge for seven years."

There was a dangerous note in his voice, but she ignored it. He was right. She was pissed off, and there would be no going forward for them until they confronted the past. No matter that he couldn't remember and she would dearly like to forget, it could not be ignored.

"You left me. You went off to do the bidding of your precious Director." That had been Dhanya's predecessor, of course.

"Alastair said I was on the trail of a traitor."

Arden shrugged. "He would know better than I. You rarely discussed the W.O.R. with me."

He frowned. "But you are a Warden."

"Now I am. Back then I was merely the daughter of their chief inventor and the wife of their golden boy. I wasn't one of them. I joined after you went missing. I naively thought I might be able to contribute something, do something that could bring you back."

"You killed Victor Erlich," he said roughly. "That's what made them send me back."

She chuckled—harshly. "I did something right after all."

Warm hands came down heavily on her shoulders—a

little too heavily. All he had to do was squeeze, and her bones would snap like dry tinder. For a second—and only one—she thought he might do just that.

Perhaps she didn't trust him as much as she thought.

His eyes glittered—cold as diamonds with just a hint of blue. "Stop stalling, stop lying and tell me what I did to hurt you so damn badly."

"I don't want to tell you." What a mess she was. Afraid he might not be that same man, and yet just as afraid that he was.

"Why not?"

Her gaze whipped to his. "Because I'm afraid if I tell you, you'll stop looking at me like I'm the most important thing in your life." It came rushing out in one breath, half hysterical, and oh so freeing.

Luke stared at her. He removed his hands from her shoulders, and stood there, arms at his sides. She didn't need her sentimentometer to know that he was frustrated—it rolled off him in waves so thick it was practically tangible.

This was the point when he began to withdraw from her. She knew it. How could he not when she was obviously a bedlamite? Her emotions changed like the weather, as did her behavior. One moment she writhed against him like a snake and the next she pushed him away.

Her father used to do the same thing to her mother at times. She glanced down at the empty glass on the cabinet. Her mother blamed her father's moods on drink. He had liked a whiskey now and again.

If she was honest with herself, he'd liked more than one.

"Luke, I—" Whatever she might have said was cut off by a knock on the door. Mrs. Bird stuck her head in.

"Beg your pardon, my lord and lady, but Lord Henry is here."

Arden smoothed a hand over her skirts. "Have tea sent in, Mrs. Bird. And please see that we are not disturbed while Lord Henry is here."

"Of course, my lady." She directed a small smile at Luke as she closed the door.

"We'll finish this discussion later," he promised once they were alone again, a dangerous note in his voice. Arden knew there would be no avoiding it. Perhaps it would be a relief to get it all out. After all, he was the one who'd pointed out that they were both drastically changed people. If she was really a different woman than the girl he'd married, then she ought to prove it by behaving like the woman she wanted to be rather than a spoiled child stamping her feet because she hasn't gotten her own way.

She met his gaze evenly, chin lifted. "All right."

The door to the parlor opened and in walked Henry. Whatever he'd expected, his brother alive hadn't been it. He turned white as death when he saw Luke, and approached him like a child approaching a large, possibly dangerous dog.

"Luke?"

Luke was the taller of the two, so he had to look down to meet his brother's wide-eyed stare. "Hello, Henry."

Later, all Arden could remember of the moment with any certainty was that Henry Grey threw the first punch.

Chapter 14

Had he known his brother meant to hit him, Luke would have spared the younger man the pain of such action. As it was, Henry's howls were matched by Arden's spaniel Beauregard to form one of the most god-awful rackets he'd ever heard. He'd heard victims of torture who hadn't made such a fuss.

"You broke my damn hand!" his brother cried, cradling the appendage, which did look as though it was badly done in.

Luke tapped his finger against his forehead. "Gregorite plating." Was he a complete arse for finding this situation a little amusing? The runt was lucky he hadn't instinctively hit him back.

Henry stared at him, his face contorted in pain. "You don't have any scars."

"New procedure. Wouldn't recommend it." Out of the corner of his eye he noticed Arden watching him. He didn't want her to know how painful the process had been—he had remembered some of it as well. The last thing he wanted was for her to see him as weak. Though perhaps a better way of making certain that didn't happen would be to step up and resume the role of Lord Huntley.

But he was beginning to think Lord Huntley was a bit of a twat. Or rather, had been, especially if he'd been anything like this younger sibling.

Henry cast a glare at him before slumping into one of the wingback chairs. He had something of a sullen look, but then part of that was undoubtedly pain, and the realization that he had hurt himself far more than he could ever hurt Luke.

"This is rather convenient," his brother commented, turning his petulance toward Arden. "The lord of the manor returning just days before he's to be declared dead."

Luke stiffened, but to her credit Arden showed no reaction to his words. "I couldn't have planned it any better myself."

Henry's chin—so similar to his own—jutted in Luke's direction. "You expect me to believe that this is my brother? That he chose to return now rather than before?"

Arden shrugged. "He had little choice in the matter, I assure you." Then she turned her lovely face to Luke, her expression wry. "Did I not tell you he'd wonder if you were an actor?"

"How much did she pay you?" the younger man demanded of Luke, as though he hadn't heard her—or didn't care. "I'll double it if you renounce her as a liar."

"Watch your mouth, runt," he growled, standing up straight. "I'll break more than your hand." It didn't matter that Arden had lied to *him*. Nobody else was going to accuse her of falsehood, especially this little wanker.

Blue eyes blinked. For a moment, all of Henry's anger was replaced with amazement, but it quickly disappeared under the onslaught of deepening distrust. "Did she tell you to call me that?"

This was ridiculous. Perhaps he'd have more patience if it wasn't for how heated his interrupted conversation with Arden had been.

"I'm Lucas Grey," he informed his brother. "The Earl of Huntley. Either you believe that or you don't, but not believing won't give you the title."

Henry's spine snapped straight, and he jumped to his feet, still cradling his hand. He was pale, but angry red splotches appeared in his cheeks. "You dare accuse me of title-grubbing when you claim to be a man dead these seven years! I should call you out, sir!"

Luke's fists clenched at his sides. He knew he was supposed to love this man as his sibling, but right now he couldn't summon anything more positive than sheer dislike. "Please do. I hope you're a good shot, because you'll have to be."

Arden stepped between them, though there scarcely was need. There was still a good ten feet between the two of them, and though Luke could close that distance very quickly, he wasn't feeling *that* violent at the moment.

"This is not the reunion I had hoped for," she told them both. She turned to the younger. "Henry, what will it take to prove to you that this is indeed Lucas?"

He turned his baleful glare on Luke. "What did you do to the puppy father gave me when I was six?"

Luke had no bloody idea. His memory was weaker the further back he tried to go, and what he had remembered often came to him unbidden. "I sincerely hope I didn't kill it."

Henry's brow lowered in disgust, and his lips curled into a sneer. "I knew you weren't my brother. I'll have Scotland Yard on you. You'll hang for impersonating a Peer of the Realm. Both of you will swing for it."

"Oh, for pity's sake! You're the one who belongs on a stage." Arden fisted her hands on the sweet curves of her hips. "Henry, Lucas has suffered an injury that impedes his memory."

"Again, very convenient."

If he didn't wipe that sneer off his face . . . Luke's head was beginning to ache from trying to remember what had happened with Arden, and now trying to recall something that could prove he was who he was.

Christ, if it wasn't for the fact that he'd remembered the things he had, he would wonder if he was really Huntley as well.

He hadn't killed the puppy. He might be a changed man, but he was never cruel to animals, he knew that. He liked animals, even the foolish, foppish Beauregard who'd tried to make love to his leg just that morning.

"I dressed it up in a pair of your short pants and taught it to sit at your place at the table. Mother didn't find it nearly as amusing as Father and I." He met his brother's gaze. "You cried."

A dull red stain spread across Henry's cheeks. "One of the servants could have told you that."

Luke pinched the bridge of his nose. "Fine. You don't want to believe I'm your brother, then don't. Get the hell out."

"You cannot order me about as though you were master of this house." The younger man's eyes blazed with fury. They looked so very much alike, though Henry was a little heavier. Was the resemblance not enough? Or would his brother rather believe he was dead and gone than accept the truth?

"He is master of this house," Arden informed him. "He hasn't and cannot be declared dead, and once he's out in society, everyone will accept that he is Huntley—alive and well."

"We shall see about that!"

As Henry whirled about, ready to march out, Luke pushed to remember something—anything. If asked, he wouldn't be able to say why it was so important that this man, who looked so much like him but didn't feel like family, believed him. But he needed him to believe.

"When you were ten years old you caught Father with one of the maids. You were so upset you ran and told Mother. I remember that you didn't understand the next day when we found out the maid had been let go. Her replacement was a homely little thing, and Father began spending more time away from home. I told you that you should have kept your mouth shut."

Henry stopped, back rigid. He didn't look over his shoulder. "You said all men of rank had mistresses."

Luke didn't remember that part, and the words made him wince. How jaded had he been at twelve? But that didn't matter so much as the expression on Arden's face. She looked disappointed.

He'd been a top-notch twat indeed.

"I was an idiot," he said, casting his wife a meaningful glance. "And wrong. You never forgave him. Not even when he asked you to while on his deathbed."

Henry gaped at him. It was obvious now that he believed Luke was who he claimed to be. But the wonder in his face quickly gave way to something more disturbed. "Are you quite all right?"

Luke frowned. Then he felt moisture above his lip. He reached up and touched it with his fingers. They came away red. His nose was bleeding. Damnation. He pressed the ball of his hand to his forehead, but it did little to ease the skull-splitting pain—it only made the incision hurt.

"I told you his memory had been impaired," he heard Arden admonish. Slender, but capable hands gripped his shoulders, guiding him.

"Sit down, dearest."

Dearest? How could she use any endearment with him? He was broken, perhaps beyond repair. No, she loved who he used to be, who she thought he was, and he'd do well to remember that, even if the former Lord Huntley didn't deserve it. Still, he did as she commanded.

"Is he dying?" Henry asked. Luke might have laughed if he didn't think to do so might make his head literally split open.

"No, he's not dying!" Arden's sharp tones made him both wince and smile. He opened his eyes so he could see the ferocity in her expression. Henry was suitably cowed.

Such a governess.

She held her hand out to the other man. "Give me your handkerchief." She snapped her fingers. "Now, Henry."

Henry reluctantly obliged, and within seconds the snow-white cotton was shoved under Luke's nose. "Hold this," his wife instructed. "Tilt your head back a little."

He knew what to do for a nosebleed—he was a man, after all, and had been hit in the nose often enough to know the procedure—but he liked having her fuss over him. No one had fussed over him in a very long time, and his chest was tight with it.

"I'm going to send for Dr. Stone," Arden told him, her brown eyes filled with concern. Her fingers combed softly through his hair, and it was all he could do not to close his eyes and lean into her soothing touch.

"I want Dr. Vincent to examine him," Henry announced, in a tone that might have been imperious were it not for a hint of reticence.

Arden paused in the act of pulling the bell for one of the maids, and fixed the other man with a gaze that could freeze Lucifer's bollocks. "Now that you know it's him, you're going to try to have him declared incompetent, are you?"

Henry's shoulders straightened. "If he's my brother I want the family physician to examine him."

"He is your brother, and you want your doctor to claim he isn't mentally or physically fit to be the earl."

She was an astounding woman, Luke realized. At times she seemed almost afraid of him, but back her into a corner or challenge her and she developed a backbone more rigid than the metal covering his bones. Henry was bigger than she, stronger too, and yet she stared him down as if he were no more than a spoiled child. Perhaps that was how she saw him, but Luke saw a man caught up in duty. Henry's apparent callousness wasn't out of a lack of fraternal love—not really—but out of his sense of duty to family, and to the title.

Henry didn't want to believe, because then he'd have to accept that he had buried a ghost, and all the pain that came with that would rear its head.

"It's all right, Ardy," he told her, removing the handkerchief so he didn't sound like a nasal git. The bleeding seemed to have stopped. "If it gives the runt peace of mind, let him have his doctor."

Her face tightened in displeasure, and she hesitated before giving a curt nod. Napoleon couldn't have been so imperious. "Fine." Then to Henry, "You will speak to me beforehand. I won't have you descend upon him whenever you wish."

A flush swept up Henry's neck to fill his face. "You talk to me as though you are my better. This is my family home and I will call on it whenever I please. I let you stay in this house because you were my brother's wife, but you will never be anything more than an impoverished baronet's daughter who got caught fucking an earl and forced him to marry her."

Luke sprang from the chair, lunged toward his brother, and caught the younger man by the throat. He lifted him with one hand, so that his toes dangled just above the ground. Henry sputtered and gasped, clawing at the fingers around his neck.

A chill settled over Luke as he met the other man's bulging gaze, but he knew his anger had to burn in his eyes like a raging blaze. "You may be my brother, but if you insult my wife again, you little twat, I'll crush your windpipe and watch the life drain out of you. I promise you I won't feel the least bit bad about it either."

"Luke. Luke!" It was Arden. He turned his head toward her. "Let him down."

His fingers twitched around the throat in their grasp. It wouldn't take much more than a gentle squeeze — not with his strength. And he knew how to dispose of a body so that no one ever found it.

But that wouldn't win him Arden's trust, and it wouldn't look good to the Wardens, who would probably kill him. He could run. Arden might come with him. He turned his attention back to Henry, whose face was turning a most amazing shade of plum.

The memory came like a flash of light — he was standing in front of this man, but they were both little more than boys. There were four other boys there as well, all of whom had been picking on Henry. They had hit him until he was bruised and bloody. Luke had stopped the fight, and he was prepared to take on all four of those boys to protect his little brother. He did take them all on, and took quite a beating for it himself. This boy had loved him back then. Looked up to him.

He lowered Henry to the ground and released his grip on his throat. His brother gasped for air, wheezing.

"You're an animal," he rasped.

Luke nodded. "But I'm still your brother, and you will

treat my wife with respect. She's the only one who believed I was alive all these years. How long was it before you gave up hope, Henry? How long before you first tried to take what is mine?"

The other man's face was still so purple it was difficult to tell if he was ashamed or not. "I have looked after the accounts, the holdings and everything else associated with the Huntley title."

"Did you look after my countess?" Luke asked in a quiet tone. Henry's averted gaze said more than words ever could. "I'll see your doctor, let him poke and prod me, but now you need to leave, because I don't like you very much, and for the past seven years that's been all the reason I've needed to kill a man."

Henry didn't need more prompting that that. Cradling his injured hand, he tore from the parlor as though the hounds of hell champed at his very heels.

"Well, that went perfectly smashingly, don't you think?"

His mouth curved at Arden's dry tone. "The genuine brotherly love was quite humbling."

She sighed and came toward him, capable and slightly calloused hands cupping his cheeks. She turned his head from side to side, all the while studying his face. It was a little disconcerting knowing she was practically looking up his nose. He was torn between shoving her hands away and kissing her. Instead he asked, "Is it true what he said?"

Her gaze lifted to his as she lowered her hands. "You mean about why we were married, or that I'm a liar?"

"About how we came to be married."

She smiled—an oddly sad expression. "How will you know I'm not lying about it, though?"

"Because a woman who didn't care about her husband wouldn't have waited seven years."

She swallowed, and for a second, her composure cracked. "I suppose not. We were caught together at a lecture my father gave at the Royal Society. You had already asked me to marry you and we were . . . uh, celebrating perhaps a little too enthusiastically."

Luke grinned. "I imagine we were." Damnation, but he wished he could remember it. "How old were you?"

"Oh, nineteen I suppose. You would have been four and twenty. Your mother wasn't impressed that you wanted to marry so young. She thought it was a mistake."

"Obviously I knew what I was doing."

Arden blinked. "Yes, I suppose we both did. Although there were times when I thought you agreed with your mother's sentiments."

Raking a hand through his hair, Luke tried to remember something—anything—that would make him think better of his old self, and couldn't. It hurt too much to push, and he didn't want to risk another nosebleed. "When's my birthday?"

"September twenty-third."

In a few months he would be four and thirty. It might seem a small thing, but this information made him inexplicably happy. Slowly, he was beginning to think of himself as a person, not just Five. And the Earl of Huntley was beginning to feel less like an assumed identity and more like who he really was.

Except for the part about being a complete arse.

"Tell me the rest of it," he commanded. "How did we go from enthusiastic to me deciding the mission was more important than you?"

She sighed. "Fine. Since you're not going to give me a moment's rest. . . ." She turned away, her hands coming up to rub the back of her shoulders. "We had been fighting about whether or not to start a family. I wanted a child, and you thought it was too soon."

A child. He'd never thought of children, not once in all those years with the Company. He'd wondered if he had family, but never if he was a father. What if he had returned here to discover he was a father? Could a child ever understand a father who had tried to kill its mother?

"Was it?"

"Too soon?" At his nod she shrugged. "At the time it felt right, but now . . . Perhaps I was a little young to rush into motherhood. You wanted to distinguish yourself with the W.O.R. You wanted adventure, and you wanted me to join you on those adventures, which I couldn't do if I were confined. You didn't understand how I could possibly want to stay here and raise a family when there were so many injustices in the world that needed right-ing." She smiled ruefully. "And I couldn't understand why you felt compelled to risk your life all the time when you had responsibilities at home—mainly to me."

"So that was it? I walked out because you wanted a child?"

"Not quite. I . . ." She frowned, and he caught the longing glance she directed at the liquor cabinet. "I missed my monthly and was so very excited. I told you I was pregnant and you reacted . . . Well, you were angry. You had already accepted a new assignment—something you wouldn't discuss even with me."

Luke swallowed. "I was on the trail of a traitor." He didn't want to believe he was capable of being such a spoiled tit. He wanted to at least have a seminoble rea-son to leave this woman alone at what must have been such a vulnerable time for her. "At least, that's what Alastair tells me."

"He would know. Anyway, my monthly came and you went off to save the empire with your partner."

The way she avoided his gaze made him uneasy. "Alastair?"

"No. You left with a woman named Rani Ogitani."
Finally her gaze locked with his. "Your mistress."

The Cavendish party was practically a mob when Arden
and Luke first arrived. Word had spread that he had "returned from the grave," and the entire city was like a
hive of bees over it—droning incessantly. It was all anyone could talk about. She'd had literally dozens of callers, most of whom she had to be "not at home" for. And
it was impossible to go anywhere because everyone
wanted to know about her husband and how she felt
about his miraculous return.

This would be the same husband who hadn't spoken
to her more than he had to since the mention of Rani
Ogitani. It had only been two days, but she felt his
withdrawal—and the sting of the last thing he had said
to her. He had muttered something about being a "twat"
that sounded apologetic. Twat was such a foolish-
sounding word, but that wasn't what upset her. What
bothered her was that he obviously withdrew because he
assumed he had slept with the woman—which was exactly what Arden had been scared of when it all initially
happened. It wasn't that she hadn't trusted him—not really. It was because Rani Ogitani was essentially a female
version of him. She lived for danger and adventure. How
could Arden ever compete? She was so petty where the
exotic spy was concerned that she'd harbored a secret
satisfaction when the woman returned from the mission
missing an eye. That satisfaction soured when she learned
Ogitani had suffered the injury while trying to fight the
men who took Luke.

She wished he could have told her that he hadn't slept
with Ogitani, that he didn't find her more satisfying and
desirable than Arden, but he couldn't. Her only consola-
tion was that he didn't remember the woman at all. Or

so he claimed. She didn't think he was lying. He looked too disgusted with himself to lie on top of it.

Then he had looked at her and said, "I wish I wasn't Huntley." He left the room immediately after.

How was she supposed to take that? She told herself she had nothing to do with the proclamation, but she couldn't quite believe it. A little voice that had always popped up whenever she wanted something told her she wasn't good enough to keep him, that all the changes wouldn't be enough to hold his interest, and that the parts of her that were the same no longer attracted him.

She had a glass of whiskey and told the voice to shut the hell up. Still, she felt bruised and stung inside. This was not how she imagined their reunion would be. Lord, had she truly believed everything would just fall into place and they'd go back to how they were before he left? Before she realized she might not be enough for him?

How were they ever going to rebuild on a foundation so shaky? She'd fooled herself into thinking that everything would be perfect if he just came back to her, and now she was faced with just how naive an assumption that had been. In this crowded ballroom, her husband might as well have a target on his back the way the women attacked him. If she hadn't been enough for him when he claimed to love her, why would she ever think she would be now when he barely knew her?

It all made her head hurt, and quite frankly she wasn't at this event to fret and ruminate over her marriage. She was there because it gave her an opportunity to look for the monster who killed those two girls.

Inspector Grant had visited her earlier—after she filled Luke in on everything she knew about his relationship with Rani Ogitani. It hadn't been a long conversation. She didn't tell him how jealous she had been of the woman, or her fears that they had resumed their affair. He didn't remember, and she was surprised to realize it didn't matter anymore. Not as much as it once had. The look of horror on his face at the idea of knowingly breaking his wedding vows had been all she needed.

Perhaps the changes that had overtaken the both of them would have some advantage after all.

Grant had arrived before they could discuss the matter further, and that was just as well. Luke left the room without needing to be asked. As much as it pained her to exclude him, he had not yet been reinstated into the Wardens, and was not privy to W.O.R. information.

"I've compiled a list of suitors that flirted or showed an interest in both girls," Grant informed her, handing her an envelope. "There's half a dozen names on there, all from aristocratic families."

Arden removed the paper and scanned the list of names. In her chest, her heart sank like a stone. There was a lot of breeding and blue blood behind each of these names. "And these are only the ones the parents knew about."

Grant frowned. "You think there may be more?"

A dry chuckled escaped her throat. "I'd wager my left arm there are at least three more. I was once a young girl, Inspector. The secret ones are always the most exciting— the sort you'd recklessly run off with."

"Foolish girls."

"Did you never sweet-talk a girl into sneaking away for a kiss, Inspector?" She couldn't help the edge to her voice. At his flush, she continued. "I doubt any of them thought she was in danger of losing her life with you. Her virtue, perhaps, but not her life. These girls might have chosen the wrong gentleman to sneak away with, but they are not to blame for their deaths."

"A good point, Lady Huntley, and one well taken at that. 'Tis the father in me speaking."

Arden clapped him on the shoulder. "Your girls will grow up all the more world-savvy because of you."

"What sort of man fathers a boy who turns into a killer?" The inspector's face pinched with both pity and disgust. "What sort of tyrant raises such a child?"

"I'm not certain," Arden replied, "but chances are I know him."

Those words haunted her as she stood in the crowded ballroom later that evening. There was very likely a killer in this crush, perhaps that awful father of his as well. So she stopped watching Luke, who stood in the middle of a large group of men and women vying for his attention, and turned her eye to the rest of the gathering. She ignored Henry, who stood on the far side of the room looking sulky and favoring his hand, and his wife, Marianne, who glared at Arden as though she was a monster herself.

Yes, because it was all Arden's fault that Henry was an idiot and punched a man with a gregorite-plated jaw. Obviously she should have seen it coming and thrown herself in front of Henry's fist to spare him the pain.

Every man that passed by her she checked for a horseshoe pin on his cravat. Thus far, she'd counted five—none worn by one of the names on her list. Lord Thomas Fenton was on the list, but he wore a simple diamond stickpin. Lord Elton James was also on the list and wore such an elaborate mess of lace and silk round his neck she couldn't see if he wore a pin at all. She had yet to cross paths with the others.

And even if she were lucky enough to discover one of them wearing the horseshoe, she would then have to discover whether or not he had automatized hands.

"I'm surprised you're not watching your husband," came Alastair's voice as he appeared at her side.

"I could say the same about you," she remarked

lightly, scanning the nearby gentlemen, hoping for a glimpse of a horseshoe cravat pin. "In fact, I'm surprised Dhanya hasn't had you living in a tree outside our house."

He grinned at her. "If you see a very large nest, just ignore it."

Arden smiled back, but it was brief. "Is she concerned that Luke is a traitor, or that the Company may try to kill me again?"

"Both. Have you noticed anyone suspicious skulking about?"

"Nothing. Though I must confess to being a tad distracted."

"How is it?" His tone was low, and soft. Her throat tightened in response.

"Fine."

"You're a lousy liar, Arden."

"No, I'm a tremendous liar, especially to myself. It's telling the truth that gives me trouble." She took a sip from her glass of champagne and grimaced. It was warm. That didn't stop her from downing the remainder in one gulp.

"What has happened?"

"I'd really rather not speak of it, Alastair." She snatched another champagne from a passing footman with a tray, trading it for her empty glass. "If you happen to see a man with a horseshoe-shaped cravat pin would you be so good as to alert me?"

"Of course." He didn't ask why. He rarely did when he assumed a request was work-related. Alastair only worried about her when it came to personal matters.

"Arden, may we talk? Privately?"

She cast a glance at Luke, who hardly seemed to know she was alive. He looked so lovely in his tailored black suit and white shirt. It was amazing what clothes that fit properly could do for a man, even one already as handsome as her husband. It was hardly fair that women had to primp and crimp and stuff themselves into corsets and shoes that often pinched one's toes.

"Of course." She linked her arm through his and allowed him to lead her toward a balcony where they could take a little fresh air and speak without being overheard. They had to walk by the automaton "orchestra," which so many upper-class houses now employed. The musicians were like overgrown dolls in appearance, with pink "skin" and wide eyes. Arden often imagined one of them coming to life and murdering them all in an emotionless rampage. It had never happened, of course, but the creatures unsettled her all the same. They played their programmed music beautifully, and only needed to be wound once during the course of an evening, but they lacked the depth of feeling a human could bring. Though she was scientifically minded, Arden preferred music and art with a human touch.

Outside on the balcony, the evening was cool—a refreshing change after the warmth of the ballroom. The music was softer, the lighting dimmer; everything was altogether more agreeable than the stuffy ballroom. Lanterns illuminated the balcony and the garden below, and made Alastair's hair a rich tobacco.

To Arden's surprise they were completely alone. Obviously everyone was too busy fawning over her husband to make a break for the out-of-doors.

"If you want to talk about Lucas, I don't," she informed him, gripping the stone balustrade in her gloved hands as she stared out into the shadowy garden.

"I think he's already getting enough attention for one night. I want to talk about you. About us."

It was as though an icy hand wrapped around her spine. "What of 'us'?"

Alastair leaned his elbow on the railing next to her. Relaxed as his posture was, he was still much taller than her. He wasn't as tall as Luke, but he was a little broader through the shoulders and chest. She might be intimidated—or perhaps swoon—if she hadn't known him so very long.

"I owe you an apology." He glanced down at his hands. "I let myself believe Luke was dead because that allowed me to think that there might be hope for the two of us. I would get so angry at you for hoping he'd come home, when I was right there, alive and eager."

He looked at her as though he expected her to argue. Oddly enough, she didn't feel the urge. "There were times when I wanted to share your feelings, Alastair, but I simply could not. I never meant to hurt you."

"I know. My behavior has not always been as it ought, nor have my motives always been strictly based in friendship, and for that I apologize."

"Accepted." She smiled at him. "Aren't you glad now that we never did become involved? What a mess we'd be in right now."

His stormy gaze locked with hers. "Yes, because I would have killed him the first night he came for you."

"Oh." There wasn't much else that could be said. "I wouldn't want you to have blood on your hands, Alastair."

"And I don't want him in your bed." The curve of his lips was familiar, but the regret behind it was not. "At least one of us will get what we want. Good night, Lady Huntley." He lowered his head and gave her a chaste kiss on the cheek before straightening and walking away. Arden was left alone on the balcony, face hot.

She truly was an awful person to have let things get so out of hand with Alastair. She'd known he cared for her—fancied himself in love with her—but not to this extent, not to the point that he would have killed the man who was once his best friend for her.

Just what had Alastair meant when he bid her good night and called her by her title? It had sounded so final. There were so many assumptions she might make, but Arden knew in her heart that this was the end of their friendship. He would come if she needed him, but they would never again be as close as they had been these last few years.

Drawing a deep breath of cool night air, she squared her shoulders and headed back inside to the party. She had a killer to find, and she wasn't going to find him moping on the balcony. Plus, there were easily a dozen women inside just dying to ask her about her husband's return, and another half who had expressed interest in one of her devices. The discombobulator was almost as popular as the anti-hysteria machines.

But these thoughts abandoned her as she stepped over the threshold and caught sight of her husband. He was exactly where she had left him, wearing the exact same expression of frustration and amusement, only now the people around him had stepped back to clear a path for the stunning woman in a bloodred gown and matching eye-patch heading straight toward him.

Rani Ogitani, his former partner and mistress.

Chapter 15

He was surrounded like flies on shite, but Luke became aware of two things at once: the crowd around him parting, and his wife.

Being able to finally draw breath without tasting someone's cologne bitter and pungent on his tongue was a blessing, but the look on Arden's face when his gaze found her stole all the air from his lungs. He'd seen predatory women in the past, but the possession in his wife's eyes ignited something very primal deep inside him. He wanted to go to her, take her to a place where they could be alone without some idiot asking him how he was "enjoying being home, har har," and shag till they were both too weak to move.

It would have nothing to do with sexual arousal, love or even attraction. It would be about possession, stark and primal—like a wolf offering his throat to his mate.

After the things she'd told him—that she suspected he was unfaithful, that he went on assignment with a former lover, leaving her alone . . . he couldn't for the life of him figure out why she thought him worth waiting for.

But he had gotten the same tattoo. Having her with him even when he had no idea of it, that had to mean something. Even if it didn't exonerate him, the glint in her eye told him why she had waited.

Because he was hers.

Then he saw her gaze move past him, and her porcelain features turned hard as stone. He turned to see who or what she was staring at, and caught a whiff of perfume that reminded him of incense, danger and sex—and not in what he would call a pleasant manner.

The woman was tiny, but she walked with the grace and confidence of someone whose body was as lethal as any weapon. Her hair was jet-black and fell in a thick, straight curtain to her waist. Her gown was a rich red with a Mandarin collar, tight, corseted bodice and long full skirt. Her ivory arms were bare, and as she walked an occasional flash of leg peeked through a slit in the fabric. He caught a glimpse of garter and red leather boots that came up over her knees. One of her legs was automatonic—he spied a flash of a filigree brass thigh as she moved toward him, her gait purposeful and extraordinarily even, despite the prosthetic.

Over one eye she wore a black leather patch adorned with diamond rivets. Was it actually bolted to her face? A gaze almost as dark as her hair met his, and full lips curved into a seductive smile. He was supposed to be impressed—it was expected of him. Instead, the spot in his head that Dr. Stone had patched up itched as though something had slipped inside and tickled his brain.

"Lucas Grey," she purred, standing right in front of him, so close her jutting breasts brushed his torso. "Lord Huntley returned from the grave. It is *very* good to see you, my lord." Her accent was posh, with just a touch of the Orient.

"I'm sorry," Luke said smoothly, pasting a disarming

smile on his face. "Have we met?" He had a pretty good idea of who she was, given the look Arden had given her, but if he hadn't been told her name it wouldn't have come on its own. She had to be the mistress. He rather liked not remembering her, even though he was certain that made him an even bigger arse.

A few people tittered nervously. Others chuckled at the slight, but most just stood in silence and watched. Her smile drooped. She honestly had expected him to know her, even though she had to have heard about his "amnesia." All of London was talking about it. It had been in the papers for Christ's sake.

"We've done more than meet," she informed him saucily, and a few onlookers sniggered.

"Perhaps if you told me your name," he suggested. It wasn't gentlemanly to embarrass her, but she obviously didn't care about embarrassing him, or Arden. He might deserve it, but Arden didn't.

A slender arm slid through his, and then his wife was at his side. "Huntley, this is Miss Rani Ogitani."

Christ. He'd rather be in the scope of an Aether cannon than caught between these two women. "My apologies for not remembering you, Miss Ogitani. I'm afraid I've had trouble remembering almost every detail of my past, except for Lady Huntley, of course." He must have said the right thing, because Arden squeezed his arm.

The two women stared at each other, but while Ogitani's expression was wary, Arden's was one of patently false pleasantness. Only her eyes betrayed just how angry she was; they glittered like amber under the chandeliers. Truth be told, his wife looked slightly mad, and it was all he could do not to grin at the sight.

"We should get you home soon," his wife said sweetly. "But first, that dance you promised me. Will you excuse us, Miss Ogitani?"

"Of course." The little woman didn't look at all pleased, but short of making some kind of scene—which she'd already done—there was nothing she could do.

The automaton orchestra—which would give a child nightmares—had just started playing a waltz as Luke and Arden joined the other dancers. People watched them curiously, waiting for gossip fodder.

Did he even remember how to waltz? Yes, it appeared so. His body fell easily into the movements, and as they began their dance he pulled her closer. His body remembered what his mind could not. "Shall we smile and pretend all is well?"

The grin she gave him was like a shark about to strike. "Do you really not remember her?"

"Nothing. In fact, I'm not sure what I saw in her to begin with." He didn't mean any insult, but it was true. There was no mystery to such a woman, only a battle of wills and empty sex.

Five would have fucked her, got any information he could and then moved on. It wasn't lost on him that perhaps Five had been a bit of an arse as well. So why hadn't he returned to his former self when his memories began to return? What had changed? He wasn't quite Huntley, but he wasn't Five anymore either.

Who the hell was he then?

Real satisfaction brightened Arden's face. "Good. Because I won't be made a fool of a second time."

He grinned at the promise in her voice. "Have I mentioned that I find bossiness arousing?"

"Have I mentioned that I find being ignored for two days off-putting?"

Luke laughed as he whirled her around. The metal lining his bones increased his strength, and he lifted her off her feet without any thought or effort whatsoever. "I thought perhaps you might not want me in your bed."

"You thought wrong. For what it's worth, I despise having an argument hang over my head. In the future, I would prefer to clear the air rather than to let things fester. I find it most vexing and distracting. I've thought of little else since."

By God, her directness was refreshing. He should have stayed to talk things out, but he had been too fixated on his own shame—and the fact that he wasn't sorry for no longer being the man she married—to think straight. "Forgive me."

Arden nodded, unflinching gaze still locked with his. "It is forgotten." Then a small smile curved her lips. "Next time, however, I use the magnet and force you to talk to me."

On that magnet, he would be helpless, completely at her mercy. The thought should be terrifying, but it was quite the opposite. "Let's go home," he suggested, voice low.

Heat flickered in the cinnamon depths of her eyes. "We finish the dance, otherwise people will talk."

"I don't really care."

She tilted her head, as though his words were unexpected. "All right."

Heart pounding in anticipation, Luke led her from the dance floor. He was only going home with his wife, and yet he felt as though he was about to embark on a dangerous mission, the exhilarating kind.

They didn't say good-bye to anyone. They simply cut through the curious crowd, gazes fixed straight ahead when they weren't looking at each other. Luke instructed one of the footmen to have their carriage brought around, and offered him several pound notes to do it quickly. They collected their outerwear by punching the number they'd been given on the keypad on the wall.

The mechanized belt growled to life and moved at a steady pace of coats and wraps until it stopped at theirs.

They were almost at the bottom of the steps when a voice called out, "Lucas!"

Luke stopped and turned. Rani stood at the top of the incline, an intense expression on her flawless face. She didn't speak; she just stared at him with that one dark eye.

A sense of dread washed over him. In that second he knew that she was no friend, and that she had only called out to delay him—separate him from Arden.

He whirled around just in time to see Arden at the bottom of the steps, and a horseless carriage careening toward her, faster than he'd ever seen one travel before. He raced toward her. If the vehicle hit her it would kill her—that was no doubt the intent.

The machine sped closer. He wasn't going to get there in time.

"Arden, move!" he shouted, his feet a blur over the steps.

She didn't look at him, didn't question him. She must have seen death approaching. He watched out of the corner of his eye as his trusting wife dove out of the way. The vehicle swerved toward her. . . .

Luke pounced, thrusting himself between Arden and the speeding carriage. He barely had time to brace himself for impact, but he turned his head away.

Then the vehicle wrapped around him.

Arden had seen many horrific things since joining the W.O.R., but nothing had prepared her for seeing her husband get hit by a carriage, and vice versa.

It was the quintessential unstoppable force and immovable object—or at least it seemed so in her frozen mind. She could only lie there on the steps—the edge of one digging into the flesh between her corset and underarm—and watch as Luke stretched out his hands a fraction of a second before the vehicle struck.

The front of the carriage caved under the force of his strength, and the velocity at which it hit, with a metallic screech of agony. The carriage drove Luke backward even as he did the same to part of it. Steam billowed around them as the destruction groaned to a halt, melting and moaning.

Luke was bleeding.

Somehow, Arden managed to scamper to her feet. Her ribs ached, but she ran to the twisted mass that held her husband prisoner, and when the man driving the carriage tried to crawl from the vehicle, she pulled her discombobulator from her reticule and shoved it hard against his grimy exposed throat. He spasmed and twitched like a fish flopping on a dock, but he could not escape.

The smell of burnt hair and urine filled the air—an unpleasant side effect of using the device on a higher setting, but at least she knew it was in working order.

She turned toward Luke. A flicker of movement in her peripheral vision made her head snap up in time to see Rani Ogitani hop on the back of a velocycle and roar away.

Arden's jaw clenched. Someday she and Ogitani were going to meet again. But that didn't matter right now. Luke was all that mattered.

He had saved her.

Alastair arrived as she reached Luke. There was a crowd gathered on the steps now—partygoers gawking at her husband's battered form. Alastair looked at the scene in horror.

"Help me," she said.

It took the two of them, despite Alastair's augmented

strength, to help Luke from the wreckage. He was awake, but bloody and unsteady. His hands were a sticky red mess, and there were cuts on his face and neck from flying glass and metal.

They helped him to the steps, where he collapsed on the stone. "Arden . . . are you unharmed?"

She hovered over him, using the handkerchief she'd pulled from inside his coat to dab at the wounds on his face. There were shards of metal and glass embedded in his skin. "I'm sore but unharmed, you great stupid article. What were you thinking?"

Pale eyes met hers. "Of you."

Wonderful, now she was going to start bawling. She sniffed and tried to fend off the blurring burning behind her lashes. "We're taking you to Evie."

"I'm fine. Alastair can stitch me up."

Alastair seemed surprised that Luke would have faith in his abilities. He flashed Arden a guilty glance. Perhaps he was thinking of his earlier claim that he would have killed Luke if she'd been his.

"I've seen Alastair's stitches, and you're going to Evie," she informed him in crisp tones that kept her voice from trembling. "I'm not taking you home until I know for certain you're fine."

"Bossy." His lips curved up on one side. He turned his head toward Alastair. "That one-eyed bitch was involved."

The other man's expression turned grim. "We'll deal with her later. Can you stand?"

As they helped Luke to the carriage that was now waiting for them, Arden turned to Alastair. "Thank you for coming so quickly."

"I heard him scream for you to move. I'm sorry I didn't get here faster."

His eyes flashed like mirrors in the lamplight. Sometimes she forgot that Alastair's hearing had been augmented as well. After Luke disappeared, Alastair had volunteered himself for several W.O.R. experimental "improvements" to make him a better agent.

Is that what the Company called what they did to their agents? What they had done to Luke? Improvements?

Arden settled in with Luke stretched out on the padded bench, his head in her lap. Alastair remained behind. "I'm going to make sure the bastard driving is taken to lockup. I'll meet you at Evie's."

One thing Arden had always admired about the Wardens was that they were like a family, so familiar and intimate, always looking out for one another. In the beginning that devotion had made it difficult for her, because she'd felt outside of it despite her father's lifelong service, and because she felt as though perhaps they pitied her because her husband had gone missing. Now, she was very happy to be a part.

Alastair closed the door and gave her driver directions. Within moments the automaton horses were galloping along the cobblestone streets faster than any real horse could. She cradled Luke's head, her bloodstained fingers gently stroking his face.

"That feels nice," he murmured. His eyelashes tickled the side of her thumb.

Since it seemed that he wasn't in any immediate danger, she allowed herself to think of things other than the moment. "I'm going to go out on a limb and assume that was no accident."

He chuckled, then winced. "The Company trying to tidy up loose ends, I reckon."

She affected a sniff. "Well, they're terribly sloppy at it."

Another chuckle—softer this time. The flesh around his eyes crinkled. God, how she fancied those lines, etched so carefully into his skin by years of smiles and laughter. "I love how you hide your true emotions behind wit."

"Really?" She ran her fingers through his hair, both massaging his scalp and searching for more shrapnel. "My mother always used to say it was highly annoying and very unladylike, and, further, that I would never get a husband if I insisted on saying whatever clever thing was on my mind."

His eyes opened. "And then you got me."

She smiled. "Exactly. You can be sure I made her eat crow then." She hadn't, of course. She just wanted to see him smile again.

He didn't. "I wasn't much of a·catch, I'm afraid."

"You seem to labor under the delusion that I was," she drawled with an arched brow. "Neither of us was or is perfect, although I like to think that we're both a little less self-involved than we once were."

A frown creased Luke's brow and she immediately set to smoothing it with her thumb, carefully avoiding the myriad of tiny cuts there. "This may sound like an excuse, but I don't think I went to that woman just because we fought."

Did it say ill of her that she was thrilled to hear him refer to the gorgeous Rani as "that woman"? "I have to confess, after seeing her on the steps tonight I wondered the same thing. Do you honestly think she tried to kill you?"

"Ardy," he began in a low voice, "I think we both know I wasn't the target, at least not immediately."

Arden swallowed. The carriage had been heading straight toward her. "It seems we were correct in assuming the Company would come for you—for both of us. What makes you so certain Ogitani is involved?"

"I don't know, but Wolfred didn't seem all that surprised when I told him my suspicions." He paused. "Speaking of Wolfred, what did you and he do when you disappeared out onto the balcony earlier?"

She appreciated that he didn't push discussing that she was the initial target. "Saw that, did you? I thought you were too caught up in your admirers to notice if I came or went." She sounded petulant despite the forced lightness of tone.

"Woman, I knew where you were every minute of the evening whether I wanted to or not."

There was just enough humor in his gruff tone that she knew he didn't really mind. The realization made her as giddy as a girl. "Alastair wanted to apologize for making presumptions regarding our friendship."

"That was big of him," he drawled.

"He's a good man."

"I hear sainthood is eminent."

Arden grinned. "Jealous?"

"Deservedly so." Luke sighed. "I suppose I can't blame him for falling in love with you."

Oh. She didn't know how to respond to that. To be frank, the statement raised too many questions she didn't want to ponder, ask or obsess over, such as whether or not he loved her, or she loved him. She knew only that he had put himself in danger for her, and that if she lost him now she might not survive it. She didn't understand the depth of her emotion where he was involved, and at that moment she didn't care. There was just the two of them in this carriage. No one asking questions or watching them. No expectations, just them.

When they reached Evelyn's modest three-story townhome, Luke was able to walk in with just a bit of help from Arden and Gibbs. Arden sent the coachman downstairs to have tea and bread with Evelyn's staff.

The medical rooms were in the back of the house. Evelyn had Luke lie down on a table while she took photographs of his internal workings. It was a process that never ceased to fascinate Arden. To think that it had been an accidental discovery made it all the more amazing.

"I don't see any internal injuries," Evelyn told her as she examined one of the panels detailing Luke's ribs. "Though I'm not certain what it would take to hurt him. A sniper, perhaps. But it would have to be a damn good shot—look, even his heart is encased in metal. Brass, I think."

Arden looked at the ghostly image and saw where her friend pointed. There was indeed a metal casing around her husband's heart—almost like a cage. Knowing what she did about Luke's skeletal plating, she hadn't expected him to be badly injured, though she'd certainly been afraid for him. On one hand it gave her great peace to know how difficult he was to kill. On the other, she didn't want to know all the things that *might* do the job.

"They made him virtually indestructible." The darker woman's awe was obvious. How long before Warden agents started getting the same augmentations? Perhaps Luke hadn't been so wrong when he said there wasn't much difference between the Wardens and the Company. Not much at all, just different views of good and evil.

"But *they* know how to destroy him," Arden said. "I need to keep that from happening."

Evelyn looked away. "You said Rani Ogitani was involved. You know that the W.O.R. has been investigating her?"

"We assumed as much. Why?"

Her friend sighed, and folded her arms over the bodice of her serviceable white blouse and black waistcoat. "I'd be speculating based on gossip if I told you. You

must know there are going to be those who wonder if
Huntley isn't in league with her, especially since they
were seen speaking this evening."

"How the devil did you know they spoke to each
other?" Her jaw tightened. "Alastair." How the devil had
he gotten word here so fast? Did he have a telephone in
his carriage that operated on Aether waves?

"Don't be angry. You know he's acting on the Director's orders. We all want this to have a happy ending,
Arden, but we're not going to risk your life for it, or the
safety of this country."

Arden pointed at the photographs of her husband's
insides. "That man stepped in front of a speeding carriage for me."

Evelyn shrugged, dusky features impassive. "Anyone
with his sort of augments would know he'd be in little
danger if he braced himself the right way, which Huntley
obviously did."

Arden opened her mouth to argue, but was cut off.
"I'm not saying that's what happened; I'm just advising
you to be prepared for people to wonder."

"She's right."

At the sound of Luke's voice, Arden turned. Her husband limped into the room bare-chested and in bare
feet. His arms had been wrapped in temporary bandages
from the elbows down and little red slashes dotted his
face and chest. Without braces, his trousers hung low on
his hips, and she could see a large bruise had begun to
form over his left one.

"Where are your shoes?" Arden demanded crossly,
because it was the only thing she could think of to say
that didn't involve swearing.

He gestured at Evelyn. "She took them."

"Were you afraid he'd run off?" she inquired darkly,
not bothering to temper her tone or her expression.

Evelyn flushed, and retreated a couple of steps. "His left foot was cut." It was a lame excuse and Arden didn't believe it for a second. "If you would take a seat, Lord Huntley, I'll get you stitched up and take care of those fragments."

Luke gingerly hoisted himself up on an examination bed. He looked tired, and in pain, which he had to be despite being so incredibly strong. He was still flesh, after all. His gaze sought hers. "She is right, Ardy. The Wardens will wonder at my loyalty even more now, and no doubt that's exactly what the bitch intended."

"What she didn't intend," said Alastair as he closed the door behind him, "was for you to be the hero and step in front of that carriage. Regardless of your capacity for damage, that will earn you favor with many of the Wardens."

"Such as?" Luke asked drily.

Alastair lifted his chin. "Me."

Heat seeped into Arden's cheeks. Would it be so terribly difficult for Alastair to conceal the depth of his feelings? Maybe just for a little while? He'd done a tolerable job of it before Luke's return. "Did the driver give you any information?"

"He's barely coherent." Alastair turned to her. "What did you do to him?"

"I used my discombobulator on him. He should recover all of his faculties before morning."

"I certainly hope control of his bladder is among them. Good work, though. He might have gotten away if not for you."

"My wife is a most capable woman," Luke remarked, with perhaps a little extra emphasis on "wife." And then to Alastair, "Thank you for your assistance."

The two men stared at each other for what seemed an eternity. Finally, Alastair gave a slight nod and turned his attention elsewhere. "Do you want a hand, Evelyn?"

"You?" The doctor laughed. "You sew like a blind man. Thank you, but no. Lady Huntley can assist me."

Arden stepped forward. Her gown was already ruined from the evening's adventure, so what was a little more blood? Though she was tempted to throw a blanket over her husband's naked shoulders to shield him from Evie's gaze.

"Dr. Stone, I would like for you to examine my wife before we take our leave. She took a nasty fall earlier."

Evelyn shot her a narrow look as she removed one of the temporary bandages from Luke's left arm. "You failed to mention that."

"I didn't think it was important." Arden made a face at her husband. "But I'm in no mind to argue, so I'll submit to an exam when we're done."

The cut on Luke's arm was deep, so deep Arden thought she caught a glimpse of gregorite. She swallowed hard. Mercifully, it wasn't terribly bloody. She washed her hands in the nearby basin and assisted by holding the edges of the wound together while Evelyn used a small stitching apparatus that closed the cut from both sides with two needles that drew the thread back and forth through the skin. Arden made a mental note to discover the name of the inventor and give the man or woman her personal thanks.

Luke barely made a sound as they worked, though she knew from experience the procedure was unpleasant. When they were done, she swabbed the area with Lister's antiseptic liquid, and set to work cleaning the smaller cuts that marked his skin. Using tweezers she assisted in plucking pieces of debris from the wounds as well. She was fine, her hands steady, so long as she didn't look at him. Looking at him—in his eyes—reminded her of what he'd done for her, and the memory of it made her shake.

She wasn't ready to shake. She'd do that later in the privacy of her own room.

"Do you have any idea where Ogitani might be hiding?" Alastair asked, bracing his hands on his lean hips.

Luke shook his head and sucked in a sharp breath when Arden pulled a particularly deep bit of glass from his shoulder. "Sorry," she murmured.

He gave her a brief smile. "I'll survive." Then to Alastair, "I don't remember a damn thing about her, mate. If I do, you'll be the first to know."

"You must admit it's a little convenient that you don't remember."

Arden glanced over her shoulder at the other man, scowling. "This is becoming very tiresome. He's the one who was hurt, remember? Perhaps I think it's convenient that your 'guard' duties lapsed long enough for Luke to be injured."

Anger flashed in Alastair's gray eyes—and hurt. "That's not amusing."

"It wasn't meant to be," she shot back, forcing herself to hold his gaze.

Luke's hand settled over one of hers, blessedly drawing her attention away from Alastair, because she didn't know how much longer she could hold his stare. "I appreciate your faith, but Wolfred's not the one who has to prove himself. I am."

"I wasn't insinuating that Alastair intentionally allowed you to get hurt. I'm merely pointing out that this constant distrust has reached a threshold of foolishness. Do you have to be killed before the W.O.R. will even entertain the notion of your innocence?"

She stared at Luke, but out of the corner of her eyes she saw Alastair and Evelyn exchange a guilty look. Good. She hoped the pair of them felt awful.

"She smelled of incense," Luke said, frowning. "The kind they use in the opium brothels."

"Sandalwood," Alastair replied. "It's a stretch, but it could be she's hiding out in one of them."

"Or it could be that she likes sandalwood," Arden commented, looking between the two of them. "I won't bother to ask how you're both able to identify the incense used in those brothels."

"I'm going to alert the Director," Alastair informed them, cheeks flushed as he avoided making eye contact. "I'll call upon the two of you tomorrow. Evelyn."

When he was gone, Evelyn smiled at her. "I think you embarrassed him. Well done. Lord Huntley, you can get dressed. Arden, come with me so I can examine you. Then I'll give you both something for the pain you're going to have come morning."

A little while later, after confirming that she wasn't seriously hurt, and armed with a bottle of some sort of opiate, Arden found Luke—now fully dressed—and departed. Gibbs was already in his perch when they exited the house.

It was after two a.m. when they arrived home. Arden was in her bedroom, dressed in her nightgown, thanks to help from Annie, when Luke came in. He had stripped down to just his trousers again. She could grow accustomed to having him walk around like that all the time. Even with the cuts and bruises he was still the finest thing she'd ever seen. Modesty was not a virtue Arden could remember ever owning, and it certainly wasn't one she intended to claim anytime soon.

"Did you take some of Evelyn's pain medicine?" she asked, openly admiring the muscles of his abdomen and upper chest.

He shook his head. "No. Makes my head feel like it's stuffed with cotton. You?"

"No. I was just going to crawl into bed." She hesitated. "Would you care to join me?"

"Yes." He walked around to the other side of the bed and removed his trousers. He slipped between the sheets in his small clothes, the thin linen low on his hips.

Arden didn't have any hopes of intimacy as they slid between the sheets, both of them groaning as their battered bodies protested every moment. He pulled her into the warmth of his arms and didn't say a word. Neither of them spoke at all. Their lips found each other, hungry and insistent. Desperation clawed at her from deep inside. She ached all over, but she wanted him.

Needed him.

He lifted the hem of her nightgown, fingers sliding immediately between her thighs. He teased her to the point of aching before draping her knee over the crook of his elbow.

"Put me inside you," he commanded, breath hot against her cheek.

She reached between them and her trembling fingers wrapped around the hard length of his erection. Tilting her hips, she guided him to the entrance of her body and pushed herself forward so that he slowly slid inside.

Even her breath shook it felt so good.

He held her leg away from his injured hip as they rocked together. Their breath mingled, foreheads pressed together. Arden had never needed anything like she needed *this*.

"You feel so good inside me," she whispered, and whimpered when he ground his pelvis harder against hers. Her body ached—inside and out—but even were she dying she wouldn't have stopped.

"So tight," he murmured. "So fucking tight and wet."

She shivered at his words. She'd always liked talking during sex, and so had Luke. "Just for you. I'm wet just for you," she whispered in reply and was rewarded with a shudder, and a deep thrust that made her gasp.

They continued to whisper heated, wanton things to each other, the intensity increasing with their fervent motions. She came hard, a long, shuddering spasm that wrung itself out of her in a low cry. She clutched at Luke's shoulders as he stiffened, groaning as his own orgasm hit.

Afterward, they lay pressed against each other, stroking each other's skin.

"I'm so glad you weren't seriously injured today," she murmured. "I was so scared."

"When I saw that carriage coming at you . . ." He squeezed her, but not tight enough to hurt. "I don't ever want to feel that way again."

Arden wanted to promise him that he wouldn't, and she wanted him to promise her the same, but that wasn't a guarantee either one of them could give. The Company and its agents were out there, and they wouldn't rest until both she and Luke were dead.

Chapter 16

Luke felt as though he'd been hit by a train rather than a horseless carriage. His bones might be unbreakable, but the tissue surrounding them wasn't impervious to injury, and even though he'd stopped the brunt of the vehicle with his hands, his left side had taken a nasty bash, and his forearm had been cut open.

He and Arden had the devil of a time trying to get out of bed the next morning, and each took a bit of Dr. Stone's pain medicine. By the time they were bathed and dressed, Luke didn't feel quite so shite. He even managed to hobble downstairs to the dining room for breakfast. Just what was in that glorious little concoction of the doctor's?

The morning paper was beside his plate. This Lord of the Manor business was odd, yet familiar, and he was more unsettled by the fact that part of his brain accepted the head of the table, the paper and a valet as "usual" than by the things themselves. He'd feel much more comfortable if it were all a surprise.

Then he saw the morning's headline, and that was surprise enough.

**MAN OR MACHINE? LORD HUNTLEY DESTROYS
RUNAWAY CARRIAGE WITH BARE HANDS!
WHISKED AWAY BY VIRTUOUS WIFE**

"Mrs. Bird says they've been turning away callers and press all morning," Arden informed him as she entered the room. She wore a kimono-style gown in rust silk with a teal corset over it.

"I'm not surprised. Are you comfortable in that?"

She nodded. "The corset's tight enough to keep me from moving in ways that might be painful, but not so restricting that it hurts. Still, I'd prefer the pain to death."

"You've obviously never been tortured," he remarked before digging into his eggs.

"Have you?"

Luke glanced up to see her standing beside her chair, knuckles white as her cheeks as she gripped the back. "Yes." As he spoke his mind was filled with a barrage of images of things he'd never realized he'd experienced. The Doctor's face filled almost every one of them. The Company had tortured him to get information, and when that hadn't worked, they'd destroyed his memory and made him their puppet.

If he ever got his hands on that bastard Doctor again, he'd kill him.

Arden must have seen the rage and shame on his face, because she wrapped her fingers around his wrist as she sat down on his right, and squeezed. "I'd do anything to take that away from you."

His gaze locked with hers. "I've lost too much of my life as it is. I appreciate the sentiment, however. We don't need to discuss it any further." He didn't want to talk about it. It felt as though it had happened to someone else—just a snippet from a play he'd seen a long time ago.

She nodded and reached for the pile of correspondence between them. "Invitations to parties, balls, dinners and teas. We've become very popular, it seems."

"Everyone wanting to see for themselves if I'm man or machine." It was ridiculous, really. "They don't seem to realize that inviting us means inviting an assassin into their midst as well."

Her expression of dry amusement was so good he almost believed it—but it didn't quite reach her eyes. That was where he saw the glimmer of fear. "Or perhaps they do. The aristocracy is terribly bored, you know."

This time it was he who reached out to her, wrapping his fingers around her slender, cool ones. "I won't let the Company win."

She nodded—a stilted gesture that didn't say much for her confidence in him. Or perhaps she simply had too much confidence in the Company. "I know you won't."

"Rani Ogitani may have been my lover once, but never after I married you. I need you to know that."

Arden helped herself to the coddled eggs with a frown tucked between her cinnamon brows. "She's gorgeous. What man wouldn't want her?"

"Gorgeous as a cobra," he retorted. "No man who held his bollocks in any sort of esteem would go within ten feet of her."

Astonishment slackened her features as she glanced at him while reaching for the salt cellar. "Really? Every woman I know who has seen her remarks on her beauty."

"I'm not certain what I ever saw in her. There was no emotional attachment, I'm certain."

"You don't sound certain."

"I don't remember much about her."

"Then how do you know you weren't . . . lovers after our marriage?"

"I know. I don't need my full memory to know that I might have been an arse, but I was a faithful one." At least when he knew he had a wife.

She stared at him for a moment, eyes wide, before dropping her gaze to her plate. "I never expected that you would return without the memory of our life. I know it's unfair of me to be angry for things you cannot remember, but I can't seem to help it. You are not the same man, and yet sometimes you are. I don't know how to feel or think."

Luke rubbed his hand over his mouth. If he could take that from her he would, but there was nothing he could do. He wanted her with him for the rest of his days, but was it because of old feelings, or new ones? He had the benefit of seeing all her newness, while she couldn't seem to see beyond their past. "It seems we're both victims of our memories."

Her head turned. "So, what do we do?"

"Damned if I know," he replied with a harsh laugh. "Make some new ones? I really don't want you telling our grandchildren that I betrayed you or tried to kill you." He meant it as a bit of joke, but she looked as though he'd struck her.

"Grandchildren?"

He couldn't say anything right this morning. "Have you changed your mind about having children?"

"I . . . I haven't allowed myself to think about it much at all."

"And don't have to right now." In fact, it was the last thing they should be thinking about while the Company was trying to kill them. Afterward, when he'd sent every one of their agents home in a coffin, then they could discuss children.

They ate in silence. It seemed that he had shocked his normally verbose wife into losing her voice. Whether that was a good thing or bad remained unknown, like much of his life.

The doorbell rang several times during the course of their meal, but it wasn't until Luke was finishing his third cup of coffee that Mrs. Bird entered the room, a rather harried expression on her face, one that made Luke remember a young girl with a similar expression. It took several seconds for him to realize that it was a memory of Birdy in their youth. She'd grown up here, her mother the housekeeper before her. The two of them had played together as children.

She had known him longer than Arden. Longer than Alastair. She seemed to like him well enough, so perhaps he hadn't always been a wanker of the first order.

"Beg your pardon, but Lord Henry is here, my lord."

"We're not at home this morning, Mrs. Bird," Arden replied.

It was obvious that the housekeeper was accustomed to her mistress's clipped way of speaking because she didn't flinch at all, though others might have. "I know, my lady, but he has Dr. Vincent and Mr. Kirkpatrick with him."

Luke had no idea who Mr. Kirkpatrick was, but he remembered Henry mentioning Dr. Vincent during his previous visit. From the way Arden closed her eyes and pressed a hand to her forehead, Kirkpatrick was not a welcome addition.

"Your family solicitor," she murmured, as though reading his mind. "Put them in the blue drawing room, Mrs. Bird. I think we must see them," she said to him.

He agreed. "How do I look?"

"Like a bedlamite," she replied with a slight grin. It seemed they were to find solidarity once more in facing Henry and his companions. "Me?"

"A roughhoused wench." Pushing back his chair he

rose stiffly to his feet. Christ, it hurt. "Think they'll believe I'm not an automaton?"

She groaned as she stood as well. "Automatons are usually made of brass, and wouldn't have survived such a collision with their cogs intact. There would be pieces scattered all the way to Hyde Park."

"So that's a yes?"

"Yes." Together they walked to the door. "Your brother has to have heard what happened last night. He has a lot of nerve showing up with this foolishness this morning."

It was actually noon, but Luke didn't bother to correct her. He suspected that Henry's visit was entirely due to last night's intrigue. It could hardly be seen as proper—or sane—for an earl to cleave a speeding carriage in half.

At a snail's pace, they made their way to the blue drawing room—Luke had no bloody idea where it was, so he let Arden lead. He was still learning his way around the house. Sometimes he knew exactly where to go, and other times he was lost.

It was bloody frustrating, this knowing and not knowing the progress of his life. Bits and snatches came and went, a confusing barrage of images that often made no sense whatsoever. He knew it did him no good to get angry—that made remembering all the more difficult—but sometimes it was impossible. Sometimes things hovered so close, yet just out of his mind's reach, and he had to face the fear that he might never get it all back.

Their journey was peppered with curses, groans and hisses of pain. They shared a glance in the corridor that set them both to laughing, which made the pain both worse and bearable. They were still chuckling when they entered the room.

Two of the gentlemen stood right away, Henry a bit

more slowly. Once again Luke was struck by the resemblance between them. Did they take after their mother or father? Their parents were like ghosts in his mind—half-formed images that told him nothing. Surely there had to be paintings of them somewhere in the vast recesses of this house?

"Gentlemen," he said in greeting, offering his hand to the man closest him. "Please excuse our appearance. I'm sure you heard about the adventure we had last night."

"Adventure?" The man chortled. "I heard it was something much more sinister, Lord Huntley."

At least the man used his title. "Perhaps, Mr. . . . ?"

He looked surprised, jowls jiggling as he jerked back. "Vincent. I delivered your mother of you, my lord."

Luke grinned to ease the doctor's discomfort. "I thank you for that, sir. I'm sure my brother has informed you that I have a sort of amnesia." He shook the other man's hand as well. "Please, sit."

"May we offer you any refreshment?" Arden asked. Luke didn't miss her use of "we." With that one little word she declared them a unit. A matched set. At that moment he didn't care if she meant it. It was enough that she had said it.

The three of them declined, which instantly set the tone for the meeting. It was to be all business, then. They were here for one thing alone—to determine whether or not he should be allowed to own the title that was his by birth.

He wasn't attached to it, but it was one more thing that had been taken from him by the Company. He wasn't about to let his brother take it from him as well. He was going to reclaim his life if it was the last damn thing he did. He'd most certainly regret it later when he had to deal with tenants and rents, but for now it was something he could at least hold a degree of control over.

He waited for Arden to sit before leaning back against the small writing desk. He didn't want these men to see how much pain he was in, and trying to sit would reveal just that. Plus, standing gave him a height advantage, which was a timeless intimidation tactic. He crossed his arms over his chest and caught a glimpse of himself in a mirror on the side wall.

Good lord, he did look like a bedlamite—one that had been lobotomized. His hair was back from his forehead, revealing the healing wound from Dr. Stone's surgery. Little wounds from last night made tiny angry red slashes on his skin, and around his left forearm was a snowy white bandage that he should have pulled his sleeve down to conceal.

"The three of you are here to decide my fate, are you?" he asked gruffly, making eye contact with each one of them. One thing Luke did remember was how to pin a man with his gaze and stare him down. Wasn't that part of being a peer?

"Lord Henry has expressed concern for your health, Lord Huntley," the man he assumed to be Kirkpatrick, the solicitor—no one had introduced them—said convivially. "We are here to offer whatever assistance we can."

"Concern for his inheritance, you mean," Luke corrected. "You needn't speak to me as though I was a child, sir. I assure you that while my memory might be spotty, the rest of my mind is perfectly sound and capable of knowing when I'm being patronized and treated as a half-wit."

The solicitor flushed. Luke cast a glance at Arden and found her practically gaping at him. He fought the urge to grin.

"Why don't you gentlemen just go ahead and line up whatever hurdles I'm to jump over, or ask whatever questions you have so Lady Huntley and I can get back to our life?"

"The life that someone is obviously trying to end," Henry interjected. "Good lord, think of what this scandal does to the family."

"Aren't you a peach." Luke couldn't help but sneer a little. "Your brother is injured, your sister-in-law almost killed, and all you can think of is the scandal. Our mother would be so very proud."

Henry turned crimson but didn't back down. "Our mother would be humiliated by you and your behavior."

"Would she? I've been a prisoner these past seven years, of an enemy of England, and now I've returned, doing everything within my power to bring that enemy to its knees. Do you really believe Mother would be ashamed of her son being one of the few peers in England doing more than arse-warming a bench in Parliament?"

Arden looked as though she was about to applaud. Meanwhile, the men in the room looked heartily ashamed, which had been the point of his impassioned speech. He had no bloody idea if his mum would be proud of him or not. He couldn't even remember her name, and her face was nothing more than a wisp of dream.

But he couldn't think of that now. He had them where he wanted them. He stood up straight even though his battered muscles protested, and used his impressive height to even further advantage. He kept his expression firm, eyes hard. "I am Lucas Harris Stratford Grey, the Earl of Huntley, and if my brother wants the title he can get in line and kill me for it, or wait for someone else to do the job. Meanwhile I have read the correspondence from my stewards, have written to them, and my wife and I plan to visit each of my country estates once the Season is over so that I may resume my responsibilities."

They all stared at him—even Arden. He hadn't told her what he'd been up to those couple of days when he'd been trying to sort out how much of an arse he'd been to her.

"Henry, I thank you for taking care of things in my absence. I only wish you had included my wife in that care, but since she's not part of the earldom I suppose she slipped beneath your notice."

His brother looked as though he might choke—or actually attempt to throttle him. Henry's hand was bandaged from their last encounter, so Luke suspected the younger man wouldn't try anything so rash. "I paid her bills and her staff, which is more than most would have done. I allowed her to live in our family home."

"It is her home—and mine. All you did was oversee the fortune attached to the title. How much of it did you use as your own?"

"Are you accusing me of stealing from my own inheritance?"

"I'm accusing you of being a heartless bastard," Luke shot back. "You couldn't even give her the kindness due your own brother's wife."

Henry didn't respond. He glanced down at his feet, but only for a second before shooting Luke a dark look. Christ, but the runt was angry. Angry at him, and at the entire world.

Luke could relate.

"What say you, Dr. Vincent?" Luke asked, turning a hard gaze to the old physician. "Am I sound? Or am I bound for Bedlam? Before you decide, I think it only fair to inform you that I've received a written thank-you from the prime minister for the sacrifices I've made for this country. Would you care to see it?"

Their horrified expressions revealed that he had won, although he was going to have to answer for it to Arden, whom he hadn't told about the P.M.'s note. First Vincent, then Kirkpatrick took their leave.

"I think you should go as well, Henry," Lucas told his brother. Perhaps he would feel a greater sense of betrayal if his memories were clearer. As it was, he was more annoyed than anything else. "Perhaps we might talk again when you're not so angry."

To his surprise, Henry nodded. "Perhaps. But I shouldn't hold my breath were I you." Even more surprising was the disappointment Luke felt at those words. Surely at one time there had been a measure of brotherly love between them? Some sort of regard or loyalty?

When they were alone once more, he turned to Arden only to find her on her feet, watching him with an oddly amused expression. "Not too many people can say they've gotten personal correspondence from the prime minister."

He shrugged. Even his shoulders ached. "She probably had her secretary write it." That had been one of the biggest surprises of his return—discovering that England had its first female political leader. It shouldn't be that astounding—after all they had a female monarch—but he'd never thought the Tories and Whigs would stand for it, the bunch of old curmudgeons.

"Still, it should go a long way with the Wardens."

"The fact that someone thinks I suffered when really I did it all willingly?" Harsh laughter crawled from his throat. "It doesn't matter that they altered my mind; I thought I was doing the right thing. I believed that I was on the proper side."

She regarded him thoughtfully, yet with an odd sort of impartiality. "You know, it occurs to me that you've punished yourself more than the Wardens ever could. Perhaps you should just admit that you were taken advantage of and start fresh. Or does self-flagellation make you feel more like a man?"

Damn that tongue of hers. She knew just where and how to best strike with it. It stung all the worse because she was right. "The Company made a fool of me."

"And if you're lucky, they'll be the only ones in the span of your life."

"You're so bloody blasé. They robbed me of seven years. Robbed *us*."

"They could have simply killed you," she retorted, "but they decided to use you, and when it came time for you to do what they ultimately wanted of you, you didn't. If anyone should feel foolish, it's the Company. You're alive, we've been given a second chance, and there are worse things in life than losing seven years."

"Such as?" he asked with a scowl. "Have you any idea what it's like to be betrayed by your own mind?"

Arden held out her hand, her lips tight. "Come with me."

The Featherstone Sanitorium was situated in a picturesque location on the western fringes of the city. In the interest of comfort, they took the touring carriage with its superior spring and wider wheels that would hamper the jostling of their aching bodies. Honestly, Arden didn't know how Luke was even able to move, let alone drive, which he had insisted upon doing.

God bless Evie and her magic potions.

She didn't even mind him driving, she was so caught up in her own thoughts and anxieties. Not about Luke, not really. Today with his brother and the other gentlemen she'd gotten her first real glimpse of the man he now was. The old Luke would have tried a bit more charm—smiled and cajoled them into bending to his will. This man simply told them how it was going to be, and dared them to challenge him.

Best of all, he had spoken for her—acknowledged that she had been alone for the past seven years. She hadn't wanted or even needed Henry to look out for her, but neither had her brother-in-law ever offered. Oh, he let her stay in the family house, but without declaring Luke dead he couldn't kick her out. Besides, he and his wife had their own town house. She'd had access to money, and all the bills were paid. She made extra money on the side with her work for the W.O.R. and her inventions, so she never wanted for anything.

Except perhaps the friendship and support of the family she'd married into. The joke of it was that Luke didn't seem to know how much his words had affected her. He hadn't said them to earn her goodwill; he'd said them because he meant them. He might one day forgive his brother for trying to usurp him, but he would never forget that Henry hadn't done right by her.

Luke had never been more beautiful to her than he had in that moment. She loved every little bruise and cut, line and shadow on his gorgeously sharp features. In fact, after all the time and pain, there was part of her that still loved him. There was an even bigger part of her that was in danger of falling in love with the man he was now. There was no artifice to him, no polite veneer. He spoke his mind and offered his emotions freely. He laughed with real delight, raged with raw anger, and when it was impossible to tell where her body began and his ended, he looked at her as though she was the other half of his soul.

Good lord, when had she become so bloody romantic? Where was her rationality now? Laughing at her from some place far away, no doubt, for there was nothing the least bit rational about her feelings for Luke.

She wanted to throw herself over that precipice, but common sense held her back. He remembered little of their life together, so he didn't have those old feelings. What if he couldn't love her now? There was no denying the attraction between them, but that had never been an issue. What if he didn't fall in love with her? Or worse, what if he stayed with her because she was his strongest link to the past he couldn't quite remember?

They passed through the gates at the foot of the sanitorium's drive. When Luke saw the sign with the name of the place on it, he turned his head to give her a questioning look. He was the only man she'd ever seen, with the possible exception of Alastair, who could wear driving goggles and still look good.

Did he wonder if she planned to have him committed?

Judging by the amount of vehicles parked out front, they were not the only visitors who chose to call on this sunny and pleasant day. They parked near the front door, behind a wine-colored carriage pulled by four gleaming brass horses. It was a frivolous display of wealth. An automaton horse could do the work of four, and cost about as much. To have this many was just . . . showing off, though a touring carriage such as her own wasn't cheap either. Her only excuse was that her father had built it.

They removed their goggles, and Arden checked to make certain her broad-brimmed hat was as it should be on her head. She smoothed the front of her peacock-blue driving dress and held out her hand as he came round to her side. Luke took it without a word, offering the comfort of his touch without knowing just how badly she needed it. She'd never brought anyone here—not Hannah, not Alastair.

The sanitorium was an imposing old estate dating back to Henry VIII. Red stone, dark trim and spires that reached toward the sky. Only the bars on the windows betrayed that this was a fortress and not a home.

They climbed the shallow stone steps to the heavy front door. Arden lifted the earpiece from the hook and placed it against her ear. When a voice inquired as to who was calling, she leaned toward the voice amplifier on the wall and said, "Lord and Lady Huntley."

There was a pause and then, "Identification verification, please."

From a small holder inside her glove, Arden extracted a round bit of metal that was notched around the perimeter—resembling a completely unsymmetrical cog—and placed it into the slot of the mechanism on the wall beside the visitor audio phone. The piece fell into place and immediately set the rest of the clockwork device into motion. It rotated clockwise, then clicked back, then forward once more, before it stopped and spit the tiny cog out into a small receptacle, from which Arden retrieved it.

"Come right in." The voice crackled in her ear. "She's in the solarium."

Arden thanked the woman and hung up just as a loud clunk filled the warm air. Slowly, the large doors split apart, sliding open with a low, grating noise. She gripped her husband's fingers tightly now, urging him over the threshold with her.

Luke glanced around at the stately foyer, and the guards all dressed in black, cudgels in their belts. "This is where Henry would have me. Tucked away like a dirty secret."

She stiffened. "Featherstone's not like that. These people need to be here to get the care they need."

He glanced at her, but she ignored it. She'd answer his

questions later. Right now, she just needed to get through this.

"What's in the bag?" he asked.

"A surprise," she replied, hefting the satchel in her right hand.

"What are we doing here, Arden?"

She sighed. His patience was obviously reaching its end. "You asked if I knew what it was like to be betrayed by your own mind. You also asked me why I waited for you. I'm going to answer both."

Silently, he walked alongside her as they continued down a wide, sunny corridor to a large, glassed-in area at the back of the building. There weren't bars on the glass in this area—those were used to keep people from jumping out of windows, and from escaping. All of the furniture in the solarium was bolted to the floor so it couldn't be thrown through a pane.

Here it was warm and bright, and patients sat on padded reclining chairs and enjoyed the day, while staring out at the gardens beyond. Patients walked out there, most with staff escorts, but the people in this section were those for whom actually experiencing the out-of-doors might be more frightening than pleasant, or more dangerous.

Arden spotted her immediately, her graying auburn hair bright in the sun. Her throat tightened as she approached, her fingers slipping free of Luke's. A face the color of cream, freckled across the nose, softly lined and creased, lifted at their arrival. Wide brown eyes crinkled at the corner.

"I know you," the woman said—her words an echo of what Luke had said after Evelyn opened his skull.

Arden smiled. Today was a good day. "Hello, Mama."

"Arden!" The days her mother realized she did indeed know her were often the most difficult. The pleasure in her voice, the bright recognition in her eyes were even more painful than the blank stares that had become more commonplace. The first day her mother asked her name was forever burned into her memory—one she would gladly lose.

A thin hand clutched at hers with surprising strength. "Sit down, my darling. It's so good to see you, dear girl."

Arden blinked away the tears, and braved a glance at Luke. He stood a few feet away, watching them with a startled and heartbroken expression. Oh yes, she was going to love this man whether she wanted to or not. "I've brought you a surprise. Do you remember him?"

Clarinda Chillingham turned her head expectantly. Her brow furrowed as her dark gaze fell on Luke. "Huntley?"

To her surprise, Luke bowed. "Lady Chillingham. You look as lovely as I remember."

Clarinda giggled and switched her attention back to Arden. "Your husband's very handsome, Miranda."

Arden didn't bother to correct her. Miranda was her aunt, her mother's younger sister. "He is, yes. I brought you something else. Do you remember that silly hat you wore last time I visited?"

Her mother smiled. "I love hats. Is it the one you're wearing? I would look good in that one."

Arden chuckled. "You would. Perhaps you can try it on later. I meant this hat." From the satchel she withdrew the helmet she'd been working on—the one designed to store memories much the way the A.R.O.T.S. stored visual moments, only on a lesser scale. The helmet recorded the process of the memory, though not the images of it—data rather than pictures.

Her mother made a moue of dislike. "Why would I want to wear that ugly thing?"

"Please? I brought you sugar biscuits."

Eager hands reached out. "Put it on me."

Arden grinned, and placed the helmet gently on her mother's head before handing her one of the biscuits she'd brought wrapped up inside the satchel. As her mother ate, she asked about various things that had happened in her mother's life. As usual, more recent events were lost to her, but she could recall seemingly mundane things that had happened in her childhood. Arden asked about things that had happened later. Her theory was that her mother's memories were disappearing in reverse chronological order. If she could store the newer memories in the helmet, she might be able to then give them back to her mother at a later date—when the older woman had forgotten them. It wasn't a cure—there would never be a cure—but it might allow her mother to hold on to her life a little longer, and allow Arden to hold on to her.

Soon, her mother would reach the point when Arden no longer existed in her mind, and Arden didn't know what she'd do when that day came.

They visited for a little while. Luke had come forward and sat down with them to listen to Clarinda's stories. He even had a biscuit at her urging.

"My soul, you're handsome," the older woman said, gaze bright as she looked at him. "Did you get into a row?"

Luke touched the healing stitches on his forehead. "Arden hit me," he told her with a grin.

When her mother turned to her—looking like an aging Roman goddess in her bizarre helmet—her gaze was blank for a split second and then exploded into brilliant recognition. "Arden! When did you get here? I'm so happy to see you, dearest girl."

Arden smiled. "I've been here a little while, Mama. I

didn't want to interrupt your visit. I know how much you like to flirt with handsome men."

Clarinda laughed. "I do." She jerked her head toward Luke. "Is he well hung?"

Luke's eyes bulged, and for a moment she thought he might choke, but when he saw her smile, he grinned back. She'd long ago given up being embarrassed by the things her mother said. It was no reflection upon either one of them, merely a common side effect of the dementia. "Now, Mama, you know a lady doesn't speak of such things." Then, in an exaggerated whisper, "I'll tell you later."

Her mother laughed, and things continued on this way for almost another quarter hour, when Clarinda's mood began to wane and she grew increasingly agitated and sharp. It was their cue to leave.

Arden gathered up the helmet that she had removed from her mother's head earlier, and packed it away along with the now-empty square of linen that had held half a dozen biscuits when they arrived. Clarinda wouldn't let Luke go without him giving her a kiss first. He barely managed to kiss her cheek—she turned her head fast and tried to catch him on the mouth.

"Good-bye, Miranda. Give my love to John and the children. And if you see Frederick, tell him I need my blue slippers."

It was the mention of her father that made Arden's eyes burn, not just that her mother was confused again. "I will. Good-bye, Mama." She kissed her mother on top of the head, drew her spine up straight and walked away as an attendant arrived to take her mother back to her room for a nap. Luke fell into step beside her.

"So you do have some idea of what it's like not to remember."

"No. I know what it's like to be someone who isn't remembered, although I suppose I can sympathize more than the average person with your plight. But now you also know why I remained in the station of countess. As much as I believed you would return, I needed to be able to afford the quarterly payments to make sure my mother stayed in Featherstone, where they take such good care of her. Lord knows I wouldn't be able to do it."

He didn't seem the least bit bothered by the fact that her motives had been less than completely pure, that she hadn't "just" been waiting for him. "You were very good with her."

She laughed softly. "A half hour visit isn't the same as day after day of it. I was losing patience before I had to put her in Featherstone, and she was much better then. Does it bother you to know I had other reasons for waiting?" She couldn't help but ask.

Luke shook his head, a reluctant smile shaping his lips. "I feel better, truth be told. It's good to know you're not some kind of saint. It makes me feel less an arse for the things I've done." Then, to her surprise, he reached down and took her hand in his. "That helmet of yours won't help me, will it?"

"No. The best it could do is store the memories you already have. I'm sorry. I'm trying to find something that will help you."

He shrugged. "Maybe it's best if I don't remember it all, though I do wish I could remember more of you. Our first kiss. Our wedding night."

Cheeks flushed, Arden squeezed his hand. "We'll just have to make some new memories."

His gaze locked with hers, bright and clear, as pale blue as spring sky. "We will." His smile grew. "We'll start with the bath."

They laughed together. She felt happy—hopeful. It was the first time she'd experienced either of those emotions whilst leaving this place. Normally when she departed she had to sit in her vehicle for several minutes fighting back tears—or giving in to them. Today, she left smiling, and when they reached the touring carriage, Luke went to the left side and left her to drive.

"I want to look around," he said, but she took it as more than that. She didn't know what, but his "giving of the reins," so to speak, meant something.

It was late afternoon by the time they arrived back in London, and both of them were hungry. They hobbled through the door and were met by the housekeeper.

"Ah, tea please, Mrs. Bird," Arden instructed. "We're famished."

The woman wrung her hands in front of her. "Lord Wolfred is waiting for you in the library, my lady. For you and his lordship. He seems out of sorts, if you don't mind me saying."

Arden rolled her eyes as she stripped off her gloves. "That's his way as of late. Include him in the tea, please." As if to punctuate the need for food, her stomach growled.

Alastair was indeed in the library. He stood near the shelves, a leather-bound book in his hands and a scowl on his face.

"Where the devil have you two been?" he demanded as he looked up.

Arden started, drawing back from the anger in his voice. "None of your business," she retorted hotly. He didn't know the extent of her mother's illness, and she meant to keep it that way. "What's the matter with you?"

He sighed and shoved the book back into its place on the shelf. At the same time, he ran a hand through his thick reddish hair. "Rani Ogitani was fished from the

Thames this morning. She'd been murdered." He couldn't quite look at either of them as he said it.

Indignation swept through Arden's veins. "And you were sent here to see whether or not Luke is responsible." She swore, drawing startled glances from both of them. "There is no way Luke could have done it. For Heaven's sake, Alastair, he can barely move."

"I know. It's not Luke I'm here to see, Arden." His stormy eyes were apologetic but unflinching. "Where were you last night?"

Chapter 17

"Have you gone completely barking mad?" Luke demanded, caught between incredulity and anger. "Arden wouldn't kill anybody."

Alastair did not look convinced. In fact, he looked very much the opposite. "She killed Victor Erlich, and did a good job of it too. Toasted his brain with that discombobulator thing. That's why you were sent to kill her, remember?"

A low scowl cramped Luke's brow. "There's something of a difference between defending oneself and murder."

His old friend turned his back on him to address Arden. "I have to ask, where were you last night?"

"Here," she told him crisply, but she didn't seem the least bit put out that he thought her capable of murdering a woman in cold blood. "We came home from Dr. Stone's and went to bed." Luke watched a soft flush filled her cheeks, and he knew she was thinking about the fact that they hadn't gone immediately to sleep. There was nothing like realizing you were mortal to arouse the libido.

Alastair directed a carefully neutral gaze toward Luke. The bastard was excellent at hiding his emotions when he wanted, Luke would give him that. "Did you take any pain medicine before bed?"

"No. There's no way she could have snuck out without waking me."

"You're certain?" There seemed to be a large amount of challenge in that question. Did he suspect Arden of drugging him? Using some device to keep him asleep while she snuck out of the house to kill a woman she would have to go to a brothel—or worse—to find? Arden was brave, perhaps recklessly so at times—he remembered her facing him alone in the garden when she "discombobulated" him—but she was not stupid.

"When was the last time someone moved without waking you?" Luke asked haughtily. When Alastair didn't immediately concede, he continued. "How was Ogitani killed?"

"Shot to the head."

He chuckled—it was more relief than humor. Perhaps he hadn't been as sure of his wife as he thought. "Well, that proves Arden didn't do it."

"How do you reason that?" Alastair folded his arms across his chest. For a man who was in love with Arden, he certainly seemed hell-bent on finding her guilty. Did he want her to be a killer? Would that make it easier for him to walk away from her? It wouldn't for Luke.

Luke smiled. "Good lord man, have you ever known this woman to use something as straightforward as a gun? She'd use some sort of fantastic gadget." He looked at his wife. "Do you even know how to shoot?"

"Not well," she replied with a slight smile. "You know, for a man without much of a memory, you possess an uncanny ability to predict my behavior and know my mind."

Luke almost grinned back, but then he remembered that Alastair had practically accused her of murder—and was standing there rolling his eyes at them.

"Do you have any evidence implicating Arden?" Luke asked. That was the important question, and one he should have asked before this.

The other man shook his head. "Nothing concrete, of course, but enough that I came here directly. Ogitani had a device implanted in her mind that was similar to the one in yours, only Dr. Stone believes it was used to control the woman rather than affect her memory. She was shot in the exact spot—by someone who knew where to shoot. Also, we confirmed that she was hiding out in an opium brothel in Covent Garden."

"I would never go to an opium brothel," Arden insisted, lips curling with just a hint of disgust. "Do you think me to be a total imbecile, Alastair? I may have rushed headlong into danger on occasion, but really. An opium brothel? You must think I have bollocks the size of Buckingham Palace—or a brain the size of your big toe."

Luke tried not to smile. There was nothing the least bit amusing about this conversation or the circumstances surrounding it. Someone had killed Rani Ogitani—most likely because she had failed in her mission to kill either Arden or him. Or both of them. But his wife had a way of plain speaking that was delightfully blunt, concise and drier than a whore in the middle of a sandstorm.

"The Company would know all of that as well," Luke said, pushing his amusement aside. "In fact, they would know exactly where she was hiding. It seems to me that they shot her where they did to destroy the device as well, and dumped her body so you'd find her immediately. Perhaps they killed her because she failed her mission, or perhaps they did it just to prove a point."

"But you must have already theorized that," Arden commented, frowning. "I would think you would immediately come up with that conclusion, so why are you here? What did you find that made you come to me?"

Alastair reluctantly reached into his coat and pulled out a small wrapped bundle. Luke frowned. So, Wolfred had evidence after all. Why had he not brought it up before this? Whatever it was, Luke knew it meant nothing, because he knew that Arden had slept either in his arms or curled against him all bloody night.

Wolfred peeled back the wrappings to reveal a small brass compact with a poppy engraved in the top. Luke didn't know what the hell it was, but he'd seen Arden with something similar. She loved poppies. He had left one for her in her carriage when he'd been stalking her, though at that time he had no idea why the flower seemed the obvious choice with which to taunt her.

She'd had them in her wedding bouquet. He put one in her hair before making love to her the first time. The memory was like a kick to the chest, it came back so vibrant and real. Along with it came the emotions he'd felt at the time. He might have been an arse at times, but he had adored her.

Quickly, he pulled himself together, shaking off the overwhelming sensations. Arden was looking at the delicate piece in Alastair's hand, her face white. "It's a sentimentometer. May I?"

Alastair nodded and she took it from his palm, opening the top. "It is yours, is it not?"

"What is it?" Luke asked. He couldn't recall—not that it meant anything—ever hearing of such an invention before.

His wife tossed a quick glance at him—she was engrossed in studying the device. "It's an apparatus for determining a person's emotional state. Very useful in an investigation. Alastair, you have to make certain I have access to the body."

"Arden, you know the Director's going to balk at that." He shoved a hand through his hair. "Just tell me if this is yours, and how it came to be with the body. Please. I'll go to Dhanya with you and plead your case. You know she'll show lenience given the circumstances."

"Lenience?" Luke drew back. "There's nothing to be lenient for. Arden didn't do it."

But neither of them paid him any attention, and Arden didn't do as Alastair asked. She scowled at him instead. "You do not agree that Dhanya will have a great interest in Miss Ogitani's last moments?"

Luke's jaw dropped. She could do that? Bloody hell. What had they ever talked about when he courted her, when they married? Perhaps he'd been comfortable being brawn to her brains. Regardless, he was going to have to start reading a lot more if he wanted to keep up with her. And he was going to spend much more time in that workshop of hers.

Wolfred didn't appear nearly as impressed as Luke was, but then he was accustomed to Arden and all her "toys." "You can ask her yourself, but she'll probably want one of the agents who isn't involved to use the spectacles—or do it herself."

Arden made a face. "No one else knows how to use them—nor have they tried. Besides, one wrong adjustment could delete the images altogether. No, Dhanya will want me to do it, and me alone. And we're going to keep it just between the four of us."

Alastair sighed. "You know that appears suspicious, yes?"

Her frustration was palpable—like a child trying to communicate with adults who just smiled and patted it on the head. "Alastair, *this*"—she held up the sentimentometer—"is one of the first I built, and it's been in a W.O.R. vault for four years. A Warden gave this to Ogitani. A Warden with vault clearance."

Realization and horror dawned on Alastair's face. "Damnation."

Even Luke was smart enough to understand what that meant. The traitor. Whoever had given the device to Ogitani was a high-ranking officer in the W.O.R. He wondered if it was the same person who had given him over to the Company seven years ago.

If so, he dearly wanted to meet the son of a bitch.

Rani Ogitani would have been just as beautiful in death as she was in life were it not for the ragged hole in the middle of her forehead. The ghostly pallor of her skin only made her more striking, her hair all the darker. Arden stood over the petite body on the table and stared at it with a surprising lack of feeling. She wasn't sorry for Ogitani, nor did she take any satisfaction in her death. This woman had played a part in trying to kill her, and Luke. Shouldn't she despise Ogitani for that? It was as though any emotions she might have felt toward the woman had died with her.

"This is what's left of the bullet I took from her." Evelyn showed the three of them a distorted piece of metal in a small glass jar.

Luke held out his hand. "May I?"

Evelyn handed it over without hesitation. "Notice the markings that are still visible. They match several bullets we've seen in similar killings over the years. Whoever the assassin was, he makes his own ammunition. I've never seen anything quite like it. It has a fine point that penetrates the flesh and then the bullet spreads, doing even more damage. Small but terribly efficient when it comes to killing."

"The Wasp." Luke peered into the bottle with an intensity that Arden found as unsettling as the flatness of his voice. "He's a Company assassin. This is his calling card. His work. He uses a specially designed rifle inspired by African blowguns that fires with incredible velocity and is accurate from a great distance."

He and Ogitani were the only people in the chilly morgue who weren't surprised. "Until today we didn't have a name," Alastair revealed, regarding him with an expression of cautious wonder. "Are you certain?"

Luke handed the bottle back to Evelyn. "Absolutely. I worked with him on occasion."

"So you'd know him if you saw him." Alastair's excitement was obvious. Arden was still trying to come to terms with the fact that her husband had worked with a Company assassin. He *was* a Company assassin. Dear God. How many W.O.R. agents had he killed?

He didn't know better.... He is no longer that man.... Hell's bells, stop thinking about it!

And then she thought about Victor Erlich, and the expression on the bastard's face as she shoved enough electrical current into his body to kill him. It had had taken more than one go. It hadn't been simple self-defense, or she would have been content to incapacitate him. No, she'd intentionally killed him. At the time she hadn't thought of it as such—she just couldn't seem to stop herself. He had hit her, tried to rape her.

And in return she killed him. On purpose. That made her a killer too. Perhaps Alastair hadn't been so wrong to suspect her of killing Ogitani. Perhaps she and Luke weren't so different after all.

Luke shot the other man a wry glance. "I won't see him. His victims never do. But yes, I would recognize his face." His gaze flicked to Arden, and she saw what he wasn't saying in his eyes.

"The Company sent him to finish the job you didn't. He's here to kill me. Us." Her voice sounded oddly calm in her own ears, despite the icy fear that gripped her heart.

His expression darkened. "Not if I kill him first."

"How do you plan to do that?" Alastair demanded. "You might recognize him, but he'll take extra care to conceal himself from you. Hell, he doesn't even have to get close to kill you both."

"He has a transmission device in his ear, same as I did." He gestured to the corpse. "The same as Ogitani still does. Let Arden look at it. I wager she can come up with something to intercept transmissions—if she hasn't already."

"But they won't be sending her any more messages," Arden interjected, pleased that he thought so much of her intelligence. She had been working with transmissions in making Beauregard's new collar. "They know she's dead. Trying to find them without that originating signal is next to impossible. It would all be guesswork."

Luke's frown eased. "What if they think she's alive? If they think she's not dead, they'll send a signal to drive her out—or at least to listen in to the noise around her."

"They could be listening now," Arden remarked. "In which case, they'll know our plans."

"They're not listening," Luke responded with bitter conviction. "They're too sure of themselves. That's why they didn't have Wasp dig the thing out of her. They don't care if the W.O.R. finds it because they're sure it's inactive. But if they suspect he failed in his mission, they'll not only try to flush Ogitani out, but the Wasp as well."

They were all looking at her now. "Can you do what Lord Huntley suggests?" Evelyn asked.

Arden shrugged. "Yes. It won't be easy, but if the Company does open up the communicative channel I should be able to isolate it. I don't know if I can tell you where it's coming from, but we could eavesdrop on their transmissions."

"I'm married to the most bloody brilliant woman in all of England." Pride shone in Luke's eyes as his lips curved into that lopsided smile that made her knees quiver.

She flushed, but not before she caught the expression on Alastair's face. He was looking at Luke as though he were speaking in tongues. But then, Alastair had always treated her talent for mechanical devices as a given, not as something special. Whereas Luke . . . well, he'd always admired the things she and her father created, but this verbal praise was new.

"Thank you," she said, meeting his gaze. Time stopped for a second, closing in around just the two of them, blotting out everything else.

"Right." Evelyn clapped her hands, breaking the trance. "I'll remove the device as soon as we know what our girl was up to when she died. Arden?"

She started. "Yes. Of course." She hid her embarrassment by turning to the corpse on the table. She took the A.R.O.T.S. from her bag and set each pair into place. As she wound the key she heard Luke ask Alastair what she was doing, but she didn't hear the other man's explanation, as images began to play out in front of her eyes. As the scene unfolded, she reported it to her companions.

"She met him in her room at the brothel. At least I think it's hers—it looks lived in. He's wearing a hat pulled low over his face." She squinted. "I can't see his face. He's wearing a long black greatcoat and carrying a walking stick with a brass ram's head at the top. She's just picked up her coat and they're leaving together." She paused, waiting for them to reach a destination. "They're in an alley behind the building. I think they're arguing, she's gesturing angrily at him, grabbing the front of his coat, and then ... bloody hell."

"What?" Alastair demanded.

Sighing, Arden removed the spectacles. "That's it. She grabbed the front of his coat and then everything went black. I'm assuming that's when she was shot, but she wasn't killed by the man she was with."

"You didn't see his face at all?"

She shook her head. "I'm afraid not. And of course, I have no idea what he sounds like. But ..." She looked at the corpse. "Evie, did you look in her left hand?"

"No." The doctor came forward, the starched white of her apron brushing against her boots. Carefully, she uncurled the fingers of the dead woman's hand. Inside was a shiny brass button. Evie held it up, and Arden's stomach dropped at the sight of it. It had a gryphon wearing a crown of roses on it.

"The Warden crest," she whispered.

Both Evelyn and Alastair looked grim at the discovery. Alastair massaged the back of his neck with one hand while the other balled into a fist. "Since no one's come forward saying they were with Ogitani at the time of her death, we have to suppose her companion was also a traitor."

"Or also dead," Arden added. Perhaps she was naive, but how many traitors could there be within the Wardens' ranks? She thought of how many spies she'd met through her father who had infiltrated the Company and decided she didn't want to know.

"Perhaps it's the same bastard I was onto years ago," Luke remarked, a dark edge to his voice. Arden shivered at the sound of it. He'd been so sweet to her that sometimes she forgot how very dangerous he could be. There was a glint in his eye that told her he yearned for revenge. How many years would it take for him to have it?

Another seven? Would he be lost to her once again as duty and vengeance took over?

She wouldn't wait for him if it happened again. She would not be a fool twice. She would remain his wife, but she would live her own life. Perhaps she'd move to Paris or Greece and have affairs with charming men who spoke languages she didn't understand but liked the sound of.

The thought made her chest hurt, so she pushed it aside for the time being. Getting overly emotional never solved anything.

"You'll want to check the Warden tailors," Luke told Alastair. "Make certain they alert you if anyone brings in a coat to have a new button sewn on." When his friend shot him a startled glance, Luke smiled. "I'm sure you would have thought of it eventually."

Arden almost grinned at the sight of them, so like she remembered. They'd always had a good partnership—one remembering what the other had forgotten, thinking of what the other had missed. Working with Alastair, being friends with him, had allowed her to feel close to Luke during his absence. She thought again that it hadn't been fair of her to use him like that.

"To have gotten away with it for this long, to have vault clearance . . ." Alastair's voice dropped off as he turned his stormy gaze on each of them. "It has to be someone high up."

"And male," Arden reminded him. "That was definitely a man I saw talking to her."

"Were they involved, do you think?" Evie inquired. "I didn't find any evidence of copulation, but I did find a sandy-colored hair in her clothing."

"He was wearing a hat," Arden replied. "I couldn't see his hair clearly, but I don't think it was dark."

"So we're looking for men in higher offices of the

W.O.R. with light hair and a missing button, and a cane with a ram's head on it." Alastair shrugged. "We've worked with less."

Arden packed up her spectacles and snapped the case shut. "If that's everything, I believe I'll take my leave. Evie, if you could get that transmitter out of her ear I would appreciate it. I'll take it with me to analyze. Hopefully someone will try to use it." She turned to Luke as the other woman went to work. She had no desire to watch the potentially bloody procedure. "Will you return home with me, or do you wish to remain?"

He seemed surprised that she would even ask, which didn't paint a pretty picture of her, she supposed. She had been ordering him around a fair bit, but only because she wanted to protect him. That hadn't been good form on her part. He was a man, not a child, and treating him as the latter would only drive him away from her all the faster.

"Why don't you stay for a bit?" Alastair suggested. "I'd like to go over that old investigation and see if anything triggers your memory. There might be useful information in the notes you wrote for the Director. Perhaps we'll unlock a clue."

Luke seemed eager at the prospect, and Arden had no desire to interfere with the rebuilding of an old friendship, no matter how much she wanted him to come home, and to bed, with her. She forced a smile, said goodbye to the three of them and strode quickly to the morgue exit, her boot heels clicking sharply on the tile. The stiff ache in her muscles only made her steps all the more clipped.

"Arden." Luke's voice stopped her at the door.

She paused, made certain nothing of how she felt might show in her face, and turned as he limped toward her. "Yes?"

His reply was to cup the back of her head with one hand and pull her to him in a fierce kiss that more than made up for with passion what it lacked in finesse. When he lifted his head, he stared down at her with an amused tilt to his lips. She must look like a dumbstruck idiot, because that was exactly how she felt.

"What was that for?"

"To give you something to think about until I get home." He released the back of her head, to run his palm down her arm. "I won't be long."

Arden forced a smile. That was what he'd always said, and it had almost always been a lie. "I'll see you then."

"Don't forget this." He pressed a square of linen into her hand. Inside it was the device from Ogitani's ear. That was fast. It wasn't as bloody as she expected, though there were smears of crimson on the cloth. She left him to his excitement and intrigue, and had one of the Warden drivers take her home, where she immediately went to her workshop and set about tinkering with the device, studying it, dismantling it and putting it back together. Work always kept her mind from tiresome, angst-ridden thoughts.

Tonight had felt like old times: Luke and Alastair working together on Warden business, filled with excitement about catching their villain of the day. She had spent so long waiting for the man she had loved to come home, and now it seemed that he might still be that man she . . .

She wasn't certain that was the man she wanted after all.

Neither Luke nor Alastair wanted to remain while Dr. Stone examined the body. It seemed wrong and disrespectful to stay—not that Ogitani deserved their respect, the cold-hearted wretch. Still, it wasn't right, and there was strong evidence to suggest the seductive woman had been under the Company's control rather than operating under her own free will. That made her a pawn, and that was a little too close for comfort for Luke.

It also made it slightly less easy to despise her. What if she had been trying to stop them both when she said his name on the steps that night? But no, he had to be honest. She had tried to save him, but not Arden. She might have retained some sort of sentimentality where he was concerned, but she had been prepared to allow Arden to die, and for that he could never forgive her, no matter how much of a puppet she'd been.

Instead, they took the button with them—Alastair pocketed it, of course—and set out to visit the two tailors who worked exclusively for W.O.R. If the man Ogitani met was smart he'd take his jacket elsewhere to be repaired, if at all. But that would only succeed if he had extra buttons at home. The only places that had those particular buttons were the secretly sanctioned tailors who took care of everything from buttons to braces, drawers to disguises. A Warden's clothes might look fine and ordinary, but there were a myriad of hidden pockets and places to conceal weapons and gadgets—tools of the trade. A "regular" tailor could not be trusted, so there were two men in all of London whom the Wardens relied upon, and they belonged to families who had shared this duty for decades.

The first was a Mr. Gabriel, whose shop was located near Bond Street. As they approached the door, Luke thought it looked vaguely familiar, as though he'd been here before.

"Not quite Poole's and Company," Alastair remarked as they approached, "but no one makes a concealed pocket quite like Gabriel."

Poole was Lucas's tailor. He had a shop on Saville

Row. He knew this because Arden had the man come to the house. "Is this the man who made you that dark blue jacket with the dagger sheaths in the sleeves?"

"The same." The red-haired man glanced at him in surprise. "You're remembering."

"Pieces. Mostly useless stuff." Luke shrugged. It was insignificant. He couldn't even work up much pleasure over the fact. "I wish I could remember more of my marriage."

Alastair paused, his hand reaching for the doorknob. "Perhaps not remembering is a sign to concentrate on now and what's to come rather than the past."

Luke raised a brow. "Meaning I shouldn't want to remember what a prick I was."

"Exactly," came the chuckled reply as the door swung open.

The shop was small but well organized. The worn floorboards were buffed to a high shine and there wasn't a speck of dust on shelves that had seen obvious years of use. The air smelled of chalk and lemon, and vaguely of pipe tobacco.

"Lord Wolfred," greeted the gray-haired man behind the counter. "Good day."

Alastair doffed his hat. "A good day to you as well, Mr. Gabriel. Do you remember my friend Lord Huntley?"

"Of course. A pleasure to see you home once again, my lord. Are you gentlemen here for a fitting?"

"Information," Alastair said with an engaging smile. It was all Luke could do not to show his amusement. The man looked positively friendly. But then, he imagined neither of them would ever be considered jovial by any stretch of the imagination.

They approached the counter. Luke glanced around them, carefully searching the shop for spies or suspicious devices. Unfortunately, it was too easy these days to conceal such apparatus, such as the lens of a small camera in a lapel, the body of the device then being sewn into the lining of the coat.

His hip and arms ached. The cut on his forearm stung and itched. He should have gone home with Arden. He missed her—not that he would admit it aloud. That was why he'd stayed behind. He was coming to depend too much on her. And she was very accustomed to getting what she wanted. It was true that she was bloody brilliant, but he had his own intelligence, and it was time he started using it, else they'd both end up like Rani Ogitani.

Plus, he craved a degree of independence. He couldn't cling to her skirts forever, and it was his own fault that he'd started. He didn't know this world—not as he ought. Not as well as it knew him. That put him at a disadvantage, and he hated that. It was time to start trusting his own judgment.

Wolfred set the button on the counter. "We found this, and came to you in hopes that the owner might have come in to have it replaced."

Mr. Gabriel's dark gaze moved between the two of them. Luke didn't bother trying to be charming. He'd leave that to Alastair. He kept his own expression impassive, his gaze direct.

"You gentlemen know I cannot give out Warden-related information, not even to Wardens, without permission from the Director."

Alastair sighed. "How long have we known each other, Gabriel? This is important. Very important."

"I don't doubt that it is, my lord. But you've known me long enough to know I don't do anything without going through the proper channels. You come back with her permission, or have her contact me, elsewise I'm not going to tell you anything. My apologies."

Luke frowned. "Not even if it means a traitor walks free?"

Gabriel didn't even blink. "In that case, especially not. In those situations, my lord, it is best to do everything by the letter."

"Fine." Alastair took the button from the counter with manicured fingers. "We'll be back with the Director's permission."

When they left the shop, they stood on the street for a moment, in the sunshine.

"Why didn't we get permission in the first place?" Luke inquired, squinting at the gentlemen out shopping.

Alastair tossed him a quick glance as he lit a thin cigar. "I was hoping we'd have something before we involved her. She's going to have her own idea of how this should be handled. Want one?"

Luke shook his head at the offered smoke. "And her way of doing things doesn't always agree with yours, I wager."

The other man grinned around the cigar as he tucked the silver case inside his breast pocket. "Not usually, no."

"Are you going to meet with her?"

"Of course, and you're coming with me. We have to talk to her about getting you reinstated."

They began walking toward the carriage, Luke's hands curled into loose fists at his sides. "I'm not sure I want to be a Warden again."

Alastair came to a dead stop, wisps of smoke curling around his head. He yanked the cigar from his mouth. "What? You can't not be a Warden. You wanted to be a Warden since you were a lad of ten. You told me so."

"Did I?" Luke didn't remember. "Being a Warden led to me losing seven years of my life. I'm not about to repledge my allegiance to an organization which didn't bother looking for me—with the exception of you."

"Fair enough." Alastair crushed the cigar beneath his boot. "You're going to concentrate on your marriage then."

"Wouldn't you?" Luke didn't expect a response—it wasn't necessary. He already knew what Alastair would do.

And that was why Luke didn't trust him—not completely—because Alastair would take Arden over the W.O.R., too.

Chapter 18

"What if Wolfred's the traitor?"

Arden placed her soldering iron in its holder and lifted her goggles so that they sat on top of her head. She felt guilty for not giving more time to Scotland Yard and had been working on a device that was something of a gamble, but might help find the man nicknamed the "Debutante Killer." It was based in chemistry—something she had needed Evie's help with—and was attuned to the scent of Wexell's Best pomade. It was also a metal detector. If she could find a man wearing that pomade, and God help her, a horseshoe cravat pin that would be wonderful, but that wasn't enough. She needed to find a man with those two traits who had also known both victims and had metal-enhanced hands. She was overly warm and grimy, and not in the sort of mood required to play a spy's equivalent of a parlor game. "I don't think I heard you correctly. It sounded as though you just accused your oldest—and only—friend of being a double agent." She glanced up from the device—which she disguised as a fan.

He had the nerve to smile — the bugger — as he leaned
indolently against the door frame of her workshop. He
was wearing a pair of black trousers held up by matching
braces and a white shirt open at the neck. His hair was
damp and fell over his forehead, hiding most of the scars
there. The little marks on his face had already begun to
heal. Unfortunately the both of them were still a little
stiff and sore from their adventure.

"He accused you of murder," he reminded her. "You
have to admit it's a theory worth considering. He was the
one who supposedly went looking for me but never found
me. He was the first to arrive after the incident with the
carriage. He knew where to find Ogitani, and yesterday he
conveniently didn't bother getting the proper permission
to speak to anyone about the button you found."

It *was* a theory worth considering. Were it not for the
fact that she had known Alastair so long she might even
do more than consider it, but the idea that he might have
played a part in Luke's disappearance . . . "No. It's not
him."

Luke's expression hardened. "If he came in here right
now and told you that somehow I was behind it all, you'd
believe that, wouldn't you?"

She scowled at him. "Don't be a jealous idiot. I would
not believe it, and if you are so very concerned about my
affections straying, why don't you give me a good reason
to keep them with you." She hadn't meant to say it aloud,
but his jealousy of Alastair was tiring, and she was still
smarting over the fact that he hadn't come home with
her the day before.

Slowly, he straightened and came toward her. She felt
a little like a gazelle eyeing an approaching lion, and
didn't know whether to run or simply accept her fate and
offer up her throat.

His gaze held hers until he stood mere inches away.

His hand reached out and curled around the back of her neck, pulling her closer. "You're mine," he told her. "I'd kill any man who tried to take you away."

His words both terrified and thrilled her. "What of you?" Her haughty tone was ruined by a slight tremor, but she doggedly held his gaze. "Are you mine?"

"If you'll have me, I am yours alone."

Arden shivered. Her hands came up to press against his chest. The heat of him permeated the fine cotton of his shirt. "I'll have you," she whispered.

His eyes darkened, and his mouth came down on hers with a ferocity that stole her breath. His tongue slid between her eager lips to taste hers, and she devoured him in kind, pouring all the things she couldn't quite say into the kiss.

She was falling in love with him. It wasn't simply that she had never stopped loving him, despite all the heartache. She was coming to love the man he was. It didn't matter that his memory was dodgy. He was good to her mother, and laughed at her jokes. He liked that she was smart and didn't seem the least bit threatened by it. And he made her feel like she was the most desirable woman in all the world.

He turned her so that her back was against the workbench.

"The soldering iron!" she yelped, just as he was about to lift her up.

Luke peered around her at the bench. Their torsos pressed together as he reached over, disconnected the power to the heated device, and moved it out of the way.

"What is this?" he asked, picking up a prototype she'd finished the day before. It was an engine that strapped to the arm and had wires running down to rubberized pads that fit over the tips of the index, middle and ring fingers of the wearer.

Arden flushed a little. They had done such intimate

things together, but talking about her inventions embarrassed her, even with him. "You put the tips on your fingers, and when the engine is engaged, the tips vibrate."

"What's it for?" He was all seductive mock ignorance.

"Massage," she replied—lamely. "It helps cure headaches, stimulates the muscles."

"What else does it stimulate?" He strapped the control box to his forearm and slid his fingers into the tips.

Arden swallowed, the interior of her mouth suddenly bone-dry. "Any part of the anatomy you wish to apply it to."

"Interesting." With his other arm he circled her waist and easily lifted her to the surface of the bench. His gaze held hers as his right hand slipped beneath the rust-colored skirts of her gown. One nudge was all it took to make her thighs fall open.

She should be embarrassed. A lady would be. The kind of woman his mother had wanted him to marry never would have dreamed of inventing such a scandalous device, let alone using one.

The engine hummed to life. Goosebumps slid down Arden's arms. Her nipples tightened. She jumped when he touched her. It was the lightest stroke—a teasing vibration along the cleft of her sex.

"Is it stimulating?" he asked, voice little more than a rumble.

"Yes," she whispered, hoarse. To hell with being a lady. If he'd wanted a lady he would have bloody well married one. She spread her thighs wider to give him better access.

Luke took the hint. Smiling that crooked smile he brought his second finger to her dampness as well, gently rubbing the opening of her body as his first finger eased between the lips to tease the bud of flesh that tightened eagerly. She moaned.

"I love watching your face when you're aroused," he told her, a delicious roughness to his low voice. "Your eyes are like warm whiskey." He wiggled his finger and she gasped in delight.

His other hand braced against the small of her back, holding her in place as she squirmed beneath his ministrations. He didn't kiss her, didn't touch any other part of her body. He just kept his attention locked on her face as his skilled fingers and the magic of the machine built a delicious tension between her legs. It was so incredibly intimate, even though they were fully clothed. She stared into his eyes as her breathing quickened. Her fingers dug into the edge of the bench, allowing her to arch her hips upward to grant him better access.

She matched the rhythm of his touch, pushing against his fingers. The ache grew and spread. She could feel it coiling inside her, urging her to move faster, open wider.

"Come for me," he commanded roughly. "I want to feel you hot and wet on my hand."

That was all she needed to push her over the edge. Her head fell back and she came in a great rippling spasm that tore a long, loud cry from her throat. Luke gave her one more stroke that made her shudder before removing his hand from beneath her skirts.

The low hum of the engine died, and he began unbuckling the straps that held the device to his arm. "That worked well."

She chuckled, sated and limp. "You were right. I am brilliant."

Luke laughed as well. "Was that good enough for me to keep your affections from straying?"

"Almost," she replied, reaching for the buttons of his trousers. He was hard beneath her fingers. "I think I still need a little convincing."

A moment later he slid completely inside her. She felt

her body stretch and wrap around him, instinct demanding that she take him fully.

"Tell me you're mine," he whispered against her lips as he withdrew and slowly filled her again.

"I'm yours," she replied, wrapping her arms around his neck. "Always and forever, I'm yours."

His mouth silenced hers, and his arms wrapped around her, holding her tight as he quickened his thrusts. They came together in a mix of heat and swallowed moans, and as they collapsed against each other, Arden was fully, and happily, convinced.

"Thank you for coming with me." Arden stirred sugar into her cup of coffee. Too bad she hadn't brought any whiskey with her—she could Irish it up a bit.

Odd, that was the first thought of drink she'd had in a while.

"I could hardly allow you to come alone," Luke replied, taking a sip from his cup.

Arden's spine stiffened. They were at the coffeehouse to spy on two suspects in the debutante case; Fredrick Fitzhugh and Maurice Willet. She'd already ruled Willet out, as he was almost as pale as an albino, and the killer was not fair. "If you could not have come, would you have forbidden me to do my job?"

Her husband paused before slowly lowering his cup to its saucer. "I would have asked you to postpone until I could accompany you."

"Why?" Her spoon hit the delicate china sharply. "Because now that you've returned I cannot possibly be equipped to perform the tasks I've successfully done without your assistance these last few years?"

His brows rose ever so slightly, but his expression was carefully blank. "No, because I would worry about you investigating on your own."

"I used to worry about you as well, but you always considered having me along on an assignment more of a hindrance than help. I'm every bit as good at my job as you were." Where was all this anger coming from? It bubbled deep inside her, frothing toward the surface, threatening to spill all over the table.

"I would never suggest otherwise."

"No one's ever captured me and turned me against my country." As the peevish words spilled out of her mouth, she couldn't look at him. She watched Fitzhugh instead. His build fit what she had seen through the dead girls' eyes, and he bore faint scars on his left hand from where it had been crushed in a riding accident. The killer had both hands augmented, didn't he? She'd only seen him use one, and then slide the other into the girl's chest. Had it been his left or right . . . ?

"You're angry at me for being nabbed?"

Her gaze went to her husband, unflinching. Anger made it easy to look him in the eye. "If you hadn't run off after some secret assignment—traitor or not—we could have had these last seven years together."

"I didn't get caught on purpose, Arden."

"You knew the risks."

"As did you. You still do. Did you ask me not to go?"

Her jaw tightened. She was beginning to get a headache. "No. It wouldn't have done any good. You would have patronized me and told me not to worry, that you had a duty to the Crown. And now you'll forbid me from doing the same. You want me to give up my work, don't you?"

Luke watched her as though he thought her a mad woman. "I have no intention—"

"Don't lie to me, Luke," she sneered. "I know you."

His face hardened like stone. Arden found herself staring into the eyes of Five. "You don't know *me* at all, and you've shown no interest in rectifying that."

Arden opened her mouth to defend herself, but nothing came out. He was right. She didn't know him—she only knew the things that weren't as they used to be.

But Luke wasn't done. "You are angry at me for things I have little memory of, that I cannot change. We can't have a future if you can't let go of the past."

"I do not dwell on the past." Lord, she was sputtering like an overly full teapot.

He gave her an exasperated—and slightly amused—look. "You waited seven years for a man who no longer exists. You put your life on hold. I know you think you've done so much, but you haven't. You spend all your time trying to prove yourself to me, to your father, to the W.O.R. You make machines so your mother can hold on to her past, you were jealous of a woman who might have mattered to me almost a decade ago. All your friends are from your past—or mine. Everything you do is linked to something in the past, with the possible exception of your female gadgets. Even your involvement with the Wardens is because you couldn't let go of me."

Arden ground her teeth. Her molars might crack, but she would not give into a fit of girlish tears. "Perhaps I should have let go."

"You should have, but I'm glad you didn't." He reached across the table and offered his hand. "Let the man you married go. The one with you now will never leave you or make you feel second in any way."

She stared at his open hand. He had a tiny scar on the pad of his index finger. He could crush every bone she had with those five digits. Taking it would mean giving him her trust, her heart—perhaps even her soul.

But he offered his in return. He was a lot braver than she was, she realized. Then again, he had little past to cling to. Today and tomorrow were all he had. They could make new memories, a new past, together. It might not work, but what had she spent all those years waiting and hoping for if not this?

Arden placed her hand in his, heart in her throat as their fingers entwined. Their gazes locked over the table. Luke smiled at her—confident, gentle, possessive. He wanted her—not the girl she'd been, but the sharp and prickly woman she'd become. She loved him for it.

She squeezed his fingers tight. And then, she let go.

When Hannah called later that day, Arden was frowning over the newspaper. Someone had told the press that there was a murderer targeting aristocratic young ladies, and the front page was ablaze with the kind of journalism that was certain to cause a panic amongst the upper classes.

She'd known it wouldn't be long. They had been fortunate that it stayed as quiet as it had, but she had foolishly clung to the hope that they would find him before the vultures got their claws into the story. Even when confronted with fearmongering in black and white, she still hoped they might find him before he fled the city along with his potential victims.

There was a party the next night that she and Luke had been invited to. She would make certain she studied all the men in attendance, especially Frederick Fitzhugh. They had to go. Luke wanted to avoid crowds because that would make it easier for their would-be assassin, but he understood the sense of duty and obligation she had where this monster was concerned.

Their rather heated discussion in the coffeehouse the day before had been such an awakening for her.

"Can I say how delightful it is to see you wearing color?"

Arden looked up, and brightened at the sight of her

friend. It seemed an age since they last spoke. "Hannah! What a lovely surprise. Come in. Would you like coffee?"

"I would indeed." The brunette pulled the pin from her wide-brimmed hat and swept it from her head. "How are you, dearest? I tried to call the morning after your horrible accident, but Mrs. Bird was quite adamant that you were not at home. There's no lasting damage, is there? You're not in pain?"

"A little bruised, but that and the stiffness are passing. Come, don't just stand there, sit with me."

Hannah started toward the table. "Where is your husband? If I were you I wouldn't let him out of my sight."

"He's not far," Arden replied with a smile as she poured a cup of coffee for her friend from the silver pot on the warmer. "He's with Wolfred. They're sparring or some other manly pastime."

"Ahh, men and their violence." Hannah plunked down on the chair to her left. "They don't seem to outgrow it, do they?"

"No." And if it made Luke and Alastair friends again, she hoped they never did. Of course, she didn't add that Luke was hoping to take his violence out on this "Wasp" character when he found him.

Perhaps she should be intimidated by the fact that her husband could literally tear a man limb from limb, but she found the knowledge oddly comforting. Now, if he would just forget this foolish distrust of Alastair, she'd be even happier.

"So," Hannah began, cradling her cup in both hands. "How are you enjoying having him home again? Is it all you hoped for?"

"Better, in some ways. In others . . . well, we're still getting to know each other again." Her friend fixed her with an odd stare. "What?"

"This does not sound like marital bliss."

"Hannah, he doesn't even remember most of our marriage, and neither of us are the same people we were seven years ago."

Hannah leaned back in her chair. "I expected to find you over the moon with happiness. At least tell me that he's fulfilling his husbandly duties."

Arden almost choked on her coffee. She had to cough several times before she was at rights again. "I cannot believe you said that."

"This coming from a woman who makes the most scandalous and wondrous toys." Hannah's eyes sparkled. "Surely you're not going miss-ish on me."

"Miss-ish" was not a word Arden ever thought could apply to her. "Of course not. The bedroom is the one place I know exactly where I stand with Huntley."

"I could make a witty remark about 'standing,' but I do not believe you're in the mood for jokes." Hannah set down her cup and covered Arden's hand with her own. "You know it will all work out. You've been given a second chance—your love returned from the dead. Surely if anyone deserves a happy ending it is the two of you."

"I'm as fond of fairy tales as the next person who was ever a little girl, but this is life, Hannah, not a story. I wish it were. But enough of that nonsense. You are positively glowing this morning. You must tell me what has been going on with you."

Hannah actually blushed, a most becoming shade of pink. "I have a beau."

"How could you have not told me that immediately? Here I am droning on while you've been sitting on such a wonderful secret! You must tell me everything." Her enthusiasm was not false. For years she'd wished that Hannah would find someone to make her feel wanted and desirable.

Her friend giggled like a schoolgirl. "It's Lord Thomas Clivington, Viscount Elwood's heir."

Arden raised her brows. "A future Viscount no less. I'm not certain I know Lord Thomas. Is he quite tall with brown hair?"

"Yes. And the most beautiful blue eyes." Some of Hannah's happiness dimmed. "You would probably know him better if I reminded you that he was in that terrible carriage accident four years ago that claimed the life of his fiancée."

"Oh, now I remember. Tragic. Lucky for him that you came along."

"He hasn't been much in society. It took many months for him to recover from his injuries—it required many surgeries, the poor thing. But now he's perfect. Absolutely perfect."

"Thank God for modern medical science. I'm in awe of the things they can do these days." Arden grinned. "I am so happy for you, my friend."

"Oh, thank you." Hannah's smile brightened the room. "He's going to be at the Dawtons' party onboard the *Albion* tomorrow night. Are you planning to attend?"

"Yes. Luke and I both."

"Wonderful!" She clapped her hands. "Then I will be able to introduce you. Oh, Arden, I just know you're going to approve of him."

"I've no doubt."

Her friend's hands were at just the right level that Arden's gaze fell on the delicate ivory scarf tied around Hannah's neck. She felt the blood drain from her face—it seemed to pool in her stomach and curdle there. "That's an interesting piece of jewelry."

Hannah's fingers went to her throat. "Do you like it? Thomas gave it to me. He said it was so I would think of him. I know it was forward of me to accept it, but I couldn't help myself. Arden, I think he might be the *one*."

He certainly was, Arden allowed, valiantly trying to keep the contents of her stomach where they ought to be. She prayed that Thomas Clivington was *not* the one—at least not the one she sought.

The cravat pin Clivington had given Hannah was horribly familiar. It was onyx stones set in gold, and it was shaped like a horseshoe.

She had to be wrong. She could see several such pins at any social event. Her dearest friend's beau was *not* the Debutante Killer.

"You're *certain* this Clivington is the killer?" It wasn't that Luke doubted her, but this was a serious accusation.

"No." Arden pressed her hand to her mouth and then yanked it away. "Luke, it was just the pin. I saw a similar pin through the eyes of those poor murdered girls. I will never forget it. And now I can't help worrying that the killer is courting my dearest friend!"

They were in his bedchamber. She'd come to him the minute he returned from sparring with Wolfred—whom he truly hoped was not their traitor, because he was starting to like the man. Again.

He stripped off his sweat-soiled shirt, wincing as the muscles in his side pulled. He was healing, but not fast enough for his liking. Wolfred had managed to get in a few blows that never should have landed because of it.

"Have you contacted your inspector?"

"No. I wanted to talk to you first."

Like a partner. A husband. He doubted she even realized the significance of what she'd just said.

"Your fear could be irrational, or it might be your instincts telling you something." He tossed the shirt into the laundry-lift in the wall. With the toss of a switch the

steam-powered engine lowered the basket of dirty clothing to the laundry room, and also allowed the maids to
send laundered items up, eliminating the need to carry
heavy baskets up and down stairs. "Did he know the
girls?"

"I don't know."

"Does he have augmented hands or use that awful
hair glue?"

She rubbed the back of her neck. "I don't know that
either, although I have Mrs. Bird inquiring after the former."

"Birdy?" He frowned. "How would she know?"

Arden looked at him as though he was daft. "She's a
servant. Don't you know how servants love to gossip
about their employers? She was going to discreetly ask
Clivington's housekeeper if she saw her at the market
this afternoon."

Servants and spies. Who would have thought they
could be so similar?

"Have Inspector Grant keep an eye on him if Birdy
comes back with confirmation. He's already watching
the Fitzhugh fellow, correct?"

His wife nodded. "Yes." The anxiety and fear in her
countenance wrapped around his chest like a vise. He
would do anything to make her feel safe—to take the
fear away. The depth of his attachment to her made no
sense when there was so much of their past he couldn't
remember, but in his heart he knew he would die for her,
whether he understood it or not.

"It's probably not him. Your friend is hardly a debutante, is she?"

That eased the strain in her features. "No, she's not."

"There, no reason for concern."

She began pacing. "What if we can't prove who the
killer is? What if he kills someone else? What if we find

him but he gets away? It's almost impossible to convict a peer."

"If you find him and he gets away, I'll make certain he doesn't hurt any more girls." He didn't say how, of course; but there could be little doubt.

Arden went completely still—a deer that's heard the cocking of a rifle. Any moment she'd bolt.

Slowly, her face turned toward his. Her wide gaze searched his face—probably to see if he was jesting. "Are you serious?"

He should lie. He should say no, chuckle and pretend he wasn't a madman. "Yes."

She frowned. "You would do . . . *that* for me?"

"If you asked it of me. I would do it without hesitation."

"I . . . I don't know if that knowledge is terrifying or arousing."

"I'm not certain myself," he replied honestly. He shouldn't have said anything at all. He wouldn't blame her if she thought him a complete monster, without any sort of conscience. But it was true. If she asked him to kill, he would do it without an ounce of remorse.

Maybe he was a monster. After all, there was a part of him that was still Five. Had the Company made him a killing machine, or had he always had that potential, just waiting to be unlocked?

"How would you do it exactly?" She glanced away. "Theoretically, of course."

Was she truly considering it? Or did she merely want to gauge the depths to which he would plummet? "I'd sneak into his home, break his neck and toss him down a flight of stairs—make it look like he fell."

"An accident. He'd never be able to hurt any more girls." Arden frowned. "But then no one would ever know what manner of devil he was."

"Is that really that important?"

That frown turned on him. "Of course."

"So you'd ruin his family as well as him. That sounds more like vengeance than justice."

Her cheeks darkened, but she didn't look away. "Who's to say that his family aren't equally evil?"

"That would be like someone thinking you must be as demented as your mother."

She looked as though he'd slapped her. And this time she did look away. "Someday I could be." Then she added, "And you're a bastard for reminding me."

"Yes. It was a cruel way to make my point and I am sorry for it."

"But it was a point well-taken," she replied, no longer angry, it seemed. "It would be wrong of me to punish the killer's family for his sins. And if we find him I would be eternally grateful if you sent the man straight to the devil, but I would not ask you to become like him. I won't allow you to become like him."

Luke was silent for a moment, weighing his next words carefully. "Arden, this man has already ruthlessly killed two girls. I respect the work you do for Scotland Yard, but you should leave the actual apprehension of the bastard to Grant."

She stiffened. "I thought we agreed that you don't get to order me about?"

"I'm not ordering, I'm asking. But since we're on the subject, since I've been home you've done nothing *but* order me about. Unless English law has changed, you're as much my possession as this house. I'm the master here."

Her eyes flashed—russet fire. "Don't you dare compare me to a . . . a chair! I am your wife. I am your equal."

"I would never call you otherwise, but if you expect me to do what you want, you have to be willing to give in to my wishes as well, especially those that involve your safety."

Her jaw was mulish, but there was an air of sheepishness about her. "I'm not accustomed to having to answer to anyone."

He smiled. "I'm not accustomed to any of this. I think we've muddled through fairly well thus far. Or do you have regrets?"

"If I have any regret it's that I didn't ask you to stay with me. I was prideful and foolish, and look what it cost us. We don't even know each other now."

That stung, though he knew it wasn't intentional. A few weeks ago his only goal had been to kill this woman; now he was prepared to kill *for* her. At times he wondered if she'd unmanned him or if he felt all the more a man for having had her devotion.

She drove him to distraction, frustrated him, amazed him and made him want to be better.

Why? What was so special about her that, even when he had no notion of her existence, he got a tattoo that matched hers? The Company had erased his memories, but they hadn't managed to dig deep enough to get rid of her.

They regarded each other in silence for a moment. How did he measure up under her scrutiny? A man who didn't want her bossing him around, but would kill for her if she asked.

"Do you think it's safe to go to the party tomorrow night?"

Luke turned to the armoire and pulled out a clean shirt. "No," he replied, "but we have to. Both Clivington and Fitzhugh are going to be there. If we're going to figure out if one of them is the killer, then we need to go."

She smiled faintly. "We?"

"I'm afraid you're stuck with me." He tucked the shirt into his trousers. "You fine with having a partner?"

Arden walked over to him and adjusted the collar of his shirt, smoothing her hands over it and down his shoulders. Her touch soothed him. "Very. We should keep Alastair close as well. He can look out for a Company threat while we keep our eyes on Clivington and Fitzhugh."

That was a sound plan, provided Wolfred wasn't the one trying to kill them in the first place. Now Luke would not only have to watch his "friend" but two other ponces as well.

It was becoming increasingly difficult to ensure that he could keep himself and Arden alive.

Chapter 19

Evelyn Stone, Arden discovered later that day, was not a woman who took no for an answer.

"I need to see Lord Huntley," the doctor insisted, holding her leather bag in front of her with both hands. They were in the library, where Arden had been researching just how much evidence was needed to try a peer for murder. "Director's orders, Arden. You know I wouldn't insist otherwise."

She did know. Evelyn's vocation elevated her social stature to a degree, as did her reputation for being one of the best doctors in the country, but the fact remained that she was middle class at best. She never seemed to forget that, even when those around her did.

"What's Dhanya doing, sending you here without warning?"

The darker woman smiled. "I reckon that's exactly why she sent me, so the two of you wouldn't have time to prepare."

Arden sighed. God grant her patience. Reaching for the bottle on the desk, she poured a measure of whiskey into a glass. Luke's words about how much and why she drank whispered in the back of her mind, but she ignored them. He should be glad for the whiskey. She'd be a raving lunatic without it.

"Can I pour you one as well?" she asked her colleague.

Evelyn shook her head. "Thank you, no. I've found drink and medical procedures do not mix."

"Are you going to be performing a 'procedure' on my husband?" She fought to keep alarm from her voice. What if Dhanya had her do something that damaged what memory Luke had?

Full rosy lips parted, and dark eyes took on a sympathetic light. "No. I'm going to ask him a few questions, have him perform a few tasks and then go home because I've been wearing these clothes for almost thirty-six hours."

Arden frowned. "What happened?"

She was answered with a grim expression and head shake. "Nothing I'm at liberty to discuss. Let Huntley know I'm here, my friend. Let's get this over with as quickly as possible for both of us."

"Dhanya and I are going to have a little chat about this," Arden muttered as she removed the earpiece from the phone on the desk. She pressed the button for the stables, where Luke was apparently making a few mechanical improvements to her touring carriage.

"Dhanya's on brief leave," Evelyn informed her stiffly. She was always so protective of the other woman.

Arden's gaze lifted to the doctor's as she waited for an answer from the stables. "Is she to whom you've dedicated the past thirty-six hours?"

Evelyn didn't respond, and that was answer enough. Enough to alarm Arden and make her forget she was miffed at Dhanya. "Is she going to be all right?"

The other woman gave a curt nod. "For the most part."

"Is there anything I can do?"

"No." When Arden continued to stare at her, Evelyn sighed. "You did not hear this from me. Dhanya was attacked in her home the night before last."

Arden stifled a gasp. "Was she harmed?"

The doctor gave her a hard look, one that broke Arden's heart. "Oh, poor Dhanya. Was it a random break-in?"

"It wasn't a break-in at all. Her attacker let himself into her house. He had a key. He knew all the security measures."

"The traitor."

Evelyn shrugged. "It would seem so, and rumor has it he's making his move before your husband can turn him over to the authorities. You understand why it's imperative that I speak to Lord Huntley? The Wardens are on me to find out if he's remembered anything else—or if he's still on the Company's side."

Arden's defense of her husband was silenced by a voice in her ear. "'Ello?"

"This is Lady Huntley. Is Lord Huntley still there?"

"Yes, ma'am. Would you like me to fetch him for you?"

"No. Please ask him to return to the house as quickly as possible. Dr. Stone is here to see him. Thank you." She hung up. "Have a seat, Evie. You're hovering."

Her friend eyed the sofa with obvious longing. "I'm afraid if I sit down I won't be able to get back up."

"You're exhausted. I'll have Mrs. Bird bring you some tea. That will invigorate you."

Luke arrived at the same time the tea tray did.

"Who is in charge while Dhanya is on leave?" Arden asked Evelyn after passing her a cup.

Evelyn shot a sharp glance at Luke, as though she expected him to suddenly grow horns. He caught the look and returned it with a sardonic smile. "Wonderful, I can finally put my plan of world domination into motion."

At least the doctor had the grace to look sheepish. "Forgive me. This speculation of a traitor within the W.O.R has us all on edge. Mr. Chiler is taking care of the office as usual, and Lord Wolfred is acting as Director."

Arden didn't miss how Luke's face hardened ever so slightly at the mention of Alastair. Did he still suspect him of being the traitor? Perhaps if she were him she would wonder as well; after all, Alastair had known about Luke's investigation seven years ago, and he had made a grand effort of looking for him when Luke disappeared. But Alastair's grief over the loss of Luke had been real, and Arden was certain his loyalty to his country was incorruptible.

But then she'd also been certain that Luke had gone to Rani Ogitani because he loved her. He'd never breathed a word about the woman being suspected of treason, which he must have known. She had doubted him, believed the worst, and had been wrong.

She did not want to be wrong about Alastair.

Evelyn said she could stay for her examination of Luke, so Arden did. The doctor checked his healing wounds, prodded him where he'd been injured after the incident with the touring carriage, and checked his reflexes and strength. He broke the squeezing device she used to measure his grip.

"Any improvements to your memory?" Evelyn asked with a wry smile as she put the broken apparatus in her bag.

"I've remembered a few new things," he replied.

"Such as?"

"I remember the first time I saw Arden."

Arden gaped at him. "You do?" This was the first she'd heard of it.

Luke smiled slightly. "I don't remember where it was, but you were wearing a yellow gown and had a poppy in your hair."

"Drury Lane," she informed him, voice thick. "It was a production of *A Midsummer Night's Dream*." He remembered her. Tears stung her eyes and she blinked them away.

"Anything pertaining to what you were investigating prior to your disappearance?" Evelyn's impatience cleaved the tender feeling in her chest.

"Not really. There are bits, but they're fuzzy."

"Might I have your permission to attempt mesmerism on you, my lord?"

Luke's gaze rose to the woman hovering over him. "It's that imperative, is it?"

"It is," Evelyn replied, face grim.

"Then go ahead. I'm not certain how well it will work on me."

She held up a syringe. "This will relax you and help overpower any safeguards the Company might have implanted in your mind."

"Evie . . ." Arden's voice trilled upward.

"He'll be fine, luvvy. Don't you worry. I won't hurt him a bit."

Luke turned to her, confidence in his countenance. "It will be all right. And you can stay and watch, right, doctor?"

Evelyn smiled. "Of course. Why don't you set up that contraption of yours to record what he says?"

It soothed her to feel as though she was part of the solution. Arden quickly went to the library where she kept her sound recording equipment. She returned within minutes and set the cylinder machine up on the table near Luke's chair.

The device was of her own design—a modification of that Edison bloke's. While many used wax cylinders, Arden had discovered that a substance called celluloid provided much better quality, though the cylinders could not be shaved and recorded over as wax could. She withdrew one of the sturdy plaster-core cylinders from its protective tube and carefully set it on the mandrel. Then, she wound the large brass key on the machine's carved oak side and positioned the sharp, precise stylus in place for etching Luke's words into the celluloid. All she had to do was flip the switch to engage the gears that powered both the mandrel and stylus.

She tilted the sound amplification horn toward her husband. Evie's drug was working. He flashed her a languid grin. She couldn't help but smile back. If they survived all this intrigue, she was going to make certain she treated him better. She was going to get to know him as well. It was shameful to think that his favorite color might have changed and she wouldn't know.

Evie used her small pocket watch as a pendulum upon which Luke could concentrate as she talked him into a relaxed state. She gave Arden a nod when she was ready to begin questioning him, and Arden flipped the switch on the machine. The soft whirl of the engine and delicate swish of the stylus whispered around them.

"What's your name?" Evelyn asked, pocketing the watch.

"Lucas Harris Stratford Grey, Earl Huntley."

"Are you married?"

"Yes."

"And what is your wife's name?"

Luke smiled. Arden's heart kicked against her ribs. "Arden."

"Lord Huntley, I'd like you to tell me what you remember of the night you disappeared. Before the Company took you."

Luke's brow furrowed. "I was at Rani Ogitani's house."

"Who was Rani Ogitani to you?"

"We worked together at the W.O.R. We had been lovers."

"Were you lovers the night you are at her house?"

Arden shot Evelyn an indignant glance, but the other woman didn't acknowledge it. Arden turned her attention to Luke once more, anxious to hear his answer even though her heart already knew it.

"No. Arden's the only woman I want."

And she had it on recording! Was it foolish to feel so happy for what she'd already known?

Evelyn continued her questions. "What are you and Ogitani doing at her house?"

"I've dropped a few hints that I'm unhappy with the Wardens because I suspect she's a traitor. I'm trying to get her to confess."

"What does she say to you?"

"That she knows how I feel, that she's unhappy as well. She says the Wardens are outdated and foolish to protect an archaic country that still has a monarchy. There's a man she wants me to meet."

"Does she tell you his name?"

"No, but he's on his way there now."

"Do you see him when he arrives?"

Lines creased his scarred brow. "Yes. I can see his face but it's hazy. It's not Wolfred."

She would never in a million years admit it, but Arden secretly sighed in relief. Not Alastair, thank Heaven. How could she have ever doubted him, even slightly?

"Do you recognize the man?" Evelyn was frowning

now as well. If she was surprised by his mention of Alastair she didn't show it.

"No, but I might recognize him if I see him again." Luke's face hardened. "I hope I do see the son of a bitch."

Evelyn patted his shoulder. "I hope so too," she replied, surprising Arden. She'd never known Evelyn to be the least bit bloodthirsty, but this traitor had orchestrated the loss of many Warden lives.

"Do you remember anything else?"

"The man said he'd been looking forward to meeting me and then there was blackness. I don't remember anything else."

Apparently satisfied, Evelyn brought Luke out of the trance. Arden turned off the recording machine and stared at it. Luke had seen the traitor. He knew the man's face. This would all be over soon.

The examination continued for another half hour—until Evelyn was satisfied. "You're healing, regaining your memory, and showing no signs of ill effects—physical or mental—from your years in Company custody. I believe you'll continue to regain memories, though I cannot say for certain that they will all return."

Luke shrugged. "At least I know who I am. For the last seven years I didn't even have a name. Not a proper one."

There was no self-pity in his tone, but Arden's heart broke for him all the same. She cleared her throat. "Evie, can you send a copy of your notes to Dr. Charles Vincent?"

Her friend seemed surprised. "Of course. Has he examined Lord Huntley?"

"He's the family physician," Arden replied. "My husband's brother has some . . . concerns."

"Ah." Understanding dawned in her coffee-colored

eyes. "I believe I understand. I would be happy to send on my findings, though I'm not certain how much weight they'll have if Vincent subscribes to the archaic notion that women shouldn't be doctors."

"He'll accept them, like it or not. We have a female P.M. for Heaven's sake. Everyone knows Victoria herself has sung your praises."

Evelyn's cheeks pinkened as she packed up her satchel. "If you say so. I'll send my notes to Vincent later today. Lord Huntley, perhaps you might write down everything you remember about the man you saw at Miss Ogitani's house. You should also work with one of our artists, see if they can draw an accurate likeness of the man."

"I will."

"I hope you enjoy the party tomorrow night. I understand it's to be a grand affair. An airship, no less."

"I'm looking forward to it," Arden replied. "Were you invited?" Evelyn might not be upper class, but she had treated enough aristocrats to occasionally warrant an invite to such functions.

"No." She had a strange expression on her face. "I have an aversion to airships. You'll have to tell me all about it."

Arden promised to do just that and then walked her friend to the door. "Did you mean it?" she asked once they were alone. "Will he continue to remember?"

Evelyn nodded. "I believe so. Make no mistake, the toxin did its damage, but the mind is an amazing thing. Honestly, I do not believe he'll regain his entire life, but he will remember more of it as time progresses."

"Thank you for helping him."

The other woman turned to her. They stood together in the front hall, the faint drone of a cleaning automaton adding a degree of privacy to their conversation. "For what it's worth, I'm inclined to believe you that he's not a threat. The Wardens will see that he gets justice."

Arden hugged her and they said their good-byes. Then she returned to Luke. He was on his feet, staring out the window at the pleasant day beyond. His arms were folded over his chest and his shoulders were rigid.

She knew that stance. Her blood turned cold at the sight of it. That was how he would always stand before he told her of an assignment he had taken—one that he might not come back from.

"What is it?" she asked when she found her voice and could make it strong.

He half turned, the expression on his face grim. It wasn't an expression she remembered, but it wasn't quite Five either. It was new. "Tomorrow night's soiree is on an airship."

"Yes. I thought I had mentioned that."

"You didn't." There was no censure in his voice, but she flinched at it all the same. "We need to send word to Alastair to make certain there's a strong Warden presence attending. They'll have us—and a large number of Britain's most powerful citizens—cut off from the rest of the world, unable to get to help. Isolated."

"You think the Company will make their play at the party?"

A muscle in his jaw flexed. "I think they're going to try blowing the damn thing right out of the sky."

Of course Luke didn't know exactly how the Company would come for them, but he had a good idea. They would wait until they were in the air, when medical assistance would be next to impossible. If they were lucky the Wasp would have orders just to take out him and Arden. But he knew those bastards, and he knew without a doubt they would take the path of the most carnage. The assassin would be there simply to make sure Luke and Arden didn't somehow escape.

He informed Alastair of this a short time after Dr. Stone took her leave. The three of them—Luke, Alastair and Arden—were in the room that had apparently been his study once upon a time. It was a good room—decorated in rich, comfortable colors. More important, it was soundproof, and built to resemble a Faraday cage, with metal mesh built into the walls, ceiling and floor. It had no windows. Luke didn't want to take any chances of their conversation being overheard.

"Dr. Stone will have to overcome her fear of air travel," Luke commented. "We'll need her to tend to the injured." And there would be people injured, no matter how this played out.

Alastair rubbed his chin. "I will tell her. How many spies do you reckon they'll have onboard?"

"Only as many as they need. Two, perhaps. Three, tops. They'll have another two in a small vessel that will fly alongside our ship to rescue their own if they decide to destroy it. The Wasp will be in one of those. Once he's done his job, they'll fly off in the panic." He didn't have to remind either of them what the Wasp's "job" was.

"We can use the sparrows attached to the ship to give chase."

Luke nodded. The small flying machines were standard on most air vessels now in case of an event that required evacuating the ship. There were larger "airboats," but the sparrows were for crew to aid in the procedure.

"We could just stay home," Arden suggested.

"No longer an option," Luke replied with a sympathetic gaze. "They'll know we're onto them and bring down the ship just to make a point. No, we have to end this."

"I have a gown Zoe—Madame Cherie—made for me during the Erlich affair. The bodice has thin sheets of gregorite sewn into the fabric. I'll wear it."

"Delicate armor." Luke almost smiled. "You're to stay inside the ship at all times."

She stiffened. He knew she would fight him on this. For someone who hated the danger he had put himself in, she certainly seemed to have a knack for diving head-first into it herself. "That won't deter them."

"I won't concede on this, Arden."

Her chin came up at a mulish angle, and her lip came out in a pout that he found surprisingly arousing. She didn't know how difficult it was for him to let her go at all. But she had been a Warden for years, and she knew what she could and could not do. Hadn't she taken him down with one of those contraptions of hers?

"Fine," she agreed. "But if you go off acting like a fool hero, I'll shoot you myself."

He grinned. "Fair enough. Whatever gadgets you have that might help us, now's the time to assemble them. Wolfred, how many Wardens will we have onboard to-night?"

"Seven," the red-haired man replied. "Chiler will be there. He's the son of a viscount, so he was invited. I'll arrange for Dr. Stone—she'll be in demand as the doctor who treated you. Then there will be the three of us and St. John Crane."

"Crane?" That was a name he hadn't heard in a while. "When did he get back?" And why the hell was it that he could remember a man who meant absolutely nothing to him but not his own wedding?

"A year ago," Alastair informed him, seemingly un-surprised that he knew who the man was. "India changed him."

That, Luke reckoned, was an understatement of grandiose proportions. "Is he still as mad as a French-pocked hatter?"

"Without doubt."

"Excellent. He'll be a good addition then."

Alastair smiled, but it didn't quite reach his eyes. "Should I take this to mean you no longer suspect me of being the traitor?"

Luke ignored his wife's gasp. Wolfred was not a stupid man; he had to know Luke would suspect him—just as Wolfred had been suspicious of him. "I suppose so."

"We have another problem," Arden reminded him. "The man who killed those two debutantes may be aboard the ship."

Alastair swore harshly beneath his breath. He raked a hand through his hair. "What in the name of holy hell am I supposed to do about him?"

"Nothing," Luke replied before Alastair could. "He's Arden's to apprehend. I'll watch her back." He'd have to be blind to miss Arden's surprise and obvious pleasure at his words. The thought of her going after a killer scared the piss out of him, but he wouldn't try to stop Wolfred or any other agent from doing their job, and he wasn't going to earn her resentment by stopping her. No matter how much he wanted to do just that.

"I've already contacted Chief Inspector Grant of Scotland Yard," Arden informed the other man. "He's been working the assignment with me, as you probably already know. He has his officers watching both suspects. Which reminds me, I should inquire as to whether or not he can have men on the ship since we cannot keep our own eyes on Fitzhugh and Clivington at all times."

"You do not think the monster will try to harm anyone onboard the ship, do you?" Wolfred asked, incredulous.

"He killed one in a factory with the owner upstairs,

the other in a public park. I'm not going to put anything past him." She rose to her feet. "The two of you will excuse me?"

"Of course." They both stood as well, and did not sit until she had left the room.

"She seems to be handling this very well," Alastair commented once the door had clicked shut.

Luke ran a hand over his jaw and mouth. "She hasn't been drinking as much." The moment he said the words he wanted to take them back, but Alastair merely nodded.

"Good. I'd begun to worry about her. I reckon that decreased dependency on spirits can be attributed to your return."

He snorted. "I would think that would make the habit worse, not better."

Dark gray eyes met his. "I think you underestimate yourself, my friend. And her regard."

"Perhaps, but one thing I don't underestimate is the mess I've wrought."

"You've given us pages of notes on major Company operations, names and addresses. And now we are closer than ever to apprehending a known Company assassin and possibly our traitor."

"Arden told you I remembered his face?"

Alastair nodded. "And that she found the frequency the Company uses to contact all agents. You were right—they did try to contact Ogitani when I let it slip that she was still alive. He's a Warden. All we have to do is find him."

"Before he finds us," Luke amended. "Or rather, before he kills us."

The other man frowned. "Are you worried about that?"

"He's gotten the best of me once—I'd be a fool not to

be concerned," Luke replied. "I have no intention of letting the bastards take me out, but if something should happen . . ." He trailed off. Surely there was no need for him to speak it aloud?

His old friend stared at him in surprise. "Nothing's going to happen."

Luke was touched. Things hadn't exactly been smooth between them since his return, yet Wolfred wanted to keep him around. "Just tell me you'll do it *if* something should go wrong."

"Fine." It was accompanied by a reluctant and somewhat stiff nod. "If we don't all go down in a flaming ball of death, I will look after Arden."

"Thank you. She's lucky to have you as a friend."

Alastair smiled. This time it glinted in his eyes as well. "Huh. That didn't take very long."

"What?" He could make a dozen assumptions, but hadn't a clue as to which might be closest to truth.

Slowly, Alastair rose to his feet. He crossed to the liquor cabinet and refilled his glass. "For you to fall in love with your wife."

Luke started. "That's none of your concern." Good Christ, could it be? "I suppose it could be that I never stopped, but I can't remember."

"She tends to inspire devotion in all who meet her. You're very fortunate in that yours is returned."

He didn't want to have this conversation. They were discussing a woman Luke would kill for and Alastair adored. He didn't want to see just how much the other man cared about his wife, even though he had taken advantage of that emotion when he asked Wolfred to look after her.

"She loves the man I was. She doesn't know the real me yet. Hell, *I* don't know who I really am."

"My God, man. I've seen how she looks at you, and

I've wanted to bash your face in for it. Sort it the hell out, get your head out of your arse and be the man both of you deserve."

Luke stared at his friend's scowling face. "You should be a politician."

Alastair tossed back the rest of the whiskey in his glass. "And you, sir, were right. You shouldn't come back to the W.O.R. — not now anyway. You should take Arden to the country and get started on making fat, brilliant babies."

Had there been even the hint of mockery or bitterness in his tone Luke might have taken offense. Instead, he regarded the other man with remorse. "How can you possibly like me when I've ruined your hopes?"

"Because I wanted you back more than I wanted her, I suppose." He smiled ruefully. "And you can't imagine wanting anything more than her, can you?"

"Nothing," Luke replied honestly. Christ, he meant it. He didn't even want his memory as much as he wanted to spend the rest of his life with Arden.

"And that's why nothing's going to happen to you tomorrow night, because I'm not going to be the one to tell her that the only man who can love her as she deserves is dead. Am I understood?"

Luke nodded. "Completely." And he meant it — because after seven long years of not giving a damn, he finally had something to live for.

Chapter 20

The *Albion* was a beauty of an airship, with a full, pristine balloon hovering above a ship constructed of rich, glossy oak that was the size of any private seafaring vessel.

Arden and Luke were among the last guests to board at the Hyde Park dock. The area was lit with bright lanterns that illuminated the ship in the dark spring night. Specially designed magnets placed on the sides of the ship locked with those on the docking mechanism, keeping the ship in place as the balloon was filled with buoyant gas.

They climbed a portable set of wooden stairs to the door of the ship and crossed the threshold into an interior as grand as most Mayfair homes. Arden glanced around with feigned indifference for familiar—Warden—faces, and immediately spotted Alastair and Mr. Chiler in the crush.

Her "armored" gown was surprisingly light, and fit perfectly. It was a deep moss green with black trimmings. The sleeves were little more than strips of fabric that barely covered her shoulders, and the plunging front showed a shocking amount of décolletage. The bronze satin of her corset peeked out from the low neckline, accentuated by the Huntley yellow sapphires that hung heavily around the base of her throat. Matching earrings dangled from her lobes, and one thin gold chain swung gently between her nose and right ear—if she and Luke survived the night she might add another. Her hair was piled on top of her head in an elaborate style that concealed a small dagger, and her fan was made of sharpened blades that appeared to be nothing more than harmless jet. And in her reticule was her trusted discombobulator.

Beside her Luke was dressed in immaculate evening clothes—black and austere white with an ebony cravat. He looked gorgeous despite the scarring on his forehead. Fortunately a little hair fell over his brow and hid most of it. The little marks from their "accident" had faded thanks to Evelyn's salve, and his face was almost as she remembered it.

He was more handsome to her now than he had been when they first met. She'd always thought a gentleman looked better with a few lines on his face. She'd also always had a bit of a preference for what her mother used to call a "good nose," which Luke possessed.

She had become accustomed to him looking slightly lost, with the odd flicker of wonder as he remembered something, or wearing a flirtatious smile. Tonight he had a predatory expression that took her breath, pale eyes glittering with anticipation. It was the look of a warrior going into battle knowing he would win or die trying.

It was the dying part that terrified her. She had just gotten him back. She could not lose him, not again. Her heart couldn't take it.

She reached down and twined her fingers through his. Gloves separated them, but she felt the warmth of him regardless. He turned his head to look at her and the predator was gone, replaced by a man who looked at her as though she was the most beautiful woman he'd ever seen.

No, he was no longer the man she had married, but she believed perhaps she liked this new version even better—this man who would kill for her, who called her "love" and didn't seem to care if anyone heard.

Now a slow smile played about his lips. He didn't speak, but the fingers wrapped around hers gently squeezed. It was hardly a declaration of love, but by God it felt like one.

Please, she prayed silently. *Don't let anything happen to him.*

A footman passed by with a tray of champagne and she reached for one, then caught herself. She wanted a drink so badly her entire body cried out for it, but she would not give in. Not tonight, when she needed every wit she had as sharp as it could be. Never mind that her knees were trembling. She had killed a man, for Heaven's sake. She was not a stranger to intrigue and danger, and tonight there were more lives at stake than just her own.

Arden dropped her hand and turned away from the temptation, and caught her husband watching her intently.

"I'm very proud of you," he said, his voice so low it was little more than a rumble.

I love you, she replied in her head. Now was not the time to make such revelations, especially not with an audience, but she wanted to—almost as much as she wanted to find a secluded spot and ravish him. Instead, she smiled in pleasure and kept walking.

They didn't get far before they were stopped. Luke's popularity hadn't waned since his first public appearance. In fact, the incident with the touring carriage had only served to make him more in demand. Everyone wanted to fawn over him and tell her how lucky she was, how happy she must be, etc. Arden didn't mind the attention, as the gaggle of well-wishers and busybodies made it virtually impossible for a sniper to take a clear shot.

However, the crush would make it easier for someone to walk right up to them, stab or shoot one of them and then walk away.

Her corset was too tight. She couldn't draw a deep enough breath. Her heart struck hard against her ribs. Blast it all! This was not a time to panic and fall apart like a stupid, vapid waif. She sucked in breath through her nose and out her mouth, silently willing herself to be calm.

It worked.

Alastair nodded to them as they passed—a greeting and also a subtle confirmation that all was in place as they had discussed. Another man nodded and said hello. St. John Crane, she assumed, since he was a tall man, tanned and weathered, with a mad glint in his eye. He didn't stop to chat.

At midnight the pilot's voice crackled over the auditory amplification box to announce that they were about to "set sail." A cheer went up from the crowd. She spotted Fitzhugh among the revelers.

Arden's throat was too dry to cheer.

The ship lurched slightly as the docking mechanism was released, and then slowly began to lift. The motion was delicate, and the ship so large that it was barely noticeable, but Arden felt it in her stomach. For a moment it seemed unavoidable that she would empty her stomach all over her new black boots, but then it eased.

Alastair was to have made arrangements with the pilot to keep the ship on a wide circular pattern rather than a line out and back, so that they wouldn't stray too far from the dock if they needed to land quickly. He also arranged for there to be a small Warden medical crew on the ground. Evelyn was onboard.

They'd been in the air approximately twenty minutes, and Arden was speaking to Lady Waterford, a client of hers who wished to purchase a new anti-hysteria device because she'd worn out the one she purchased last year, when she heard someone cry out, "Arden!"

It was Hannah. She bustled toward her with the glow of a woman in love, and behind her, equally as glowing, was Clivington.

Looking at him, Arden wondered how she could have suspected him of being a killer. He was perhaps in his early thirties, boyish and charming with sparkling eyes. He didn't look as though he could hurt a fly, let alone rip a girl apart.

She didn't have to force a smile onto her face. "Hannah! How delightful to see you. You know Lady Waterford, of course."

Niceties were exchanged, and Hannah introduced Clivington.

"Delighted," Arden said, offering her hand. He wore gloves to cover his scars.

"The pleasure is all mine, Lady Huntley. My dear girl has told me so much about you, I feel I know you already." Even his voice was pleasant.

"And I you," she replied. "I do not recall the last time I saw Hannah quite so happy."

"Would you care to take a walk around the promenade deck with us?" Hannah asked.

"Actually, I promised Huntley I'd reintroduce him to some old friends." She couldn't very well tell them she wasn't allowed to leave the main room, could she?

"Please," Hannah begged. "I should so love to see the

view, and Clivington won't go unless we have a chaperone." She flashed him a grin. "He's entirely too proper."

The man actually blushed. "I would hate to bring scandal upon you, my dear."

She should have had that champagne! The look on Hannah's face was too puppyish to resist. "All right, but only so you can see the view, and then I'm coming back in." As she spoke she saw Fitzhugh heading for the exit as well.

Hannah clapped her hands. "Wonderful!"

As the three of them strode toward the exit to the deck, Arden glanced over her shoulder. Luke was talking to Alastair and another man and didn't so much as glance in her direction. He was going to kill her when he found out she snuck out, but it would only be for a moment, and she'd stay close to the door. She couldn't let the chance to try her invention on Fitzhugh get away.

They stepped out into the cool night air. Arden kept to the shadows as she fumbled in her reticule for the device she'd made specifically to track the killer. Tonight was not a night to take reckless risks and make foolish mistakes. Only the chance to catch a monster could have made her break her word to Luke.

She walked up behind Fitzhugh. The needle on the device whipped toward the section of the viewer attuned to the metal detector, but that was it. Damn. She had used one other component from the crimes to track the murderer—a small sample of the skin taken from beneath Baron Lynbourne's daughter's fingernails. Arden moved to stand beside Fitzhugh as he lit a cigarette and pressed the small, handheld device against the exposed wrist of his hand that rested on the ship's railing.

"Ow!"

"Oh, my apologies, sir," Arden gushed. "I must have caught you with my compact. I am so very sorry."

The gentleman peered down at his wrist where her invention had pinched it. "It's nothing, my lady." But he moved away from her so she couldn't do it again.

Arden checked the device, and her heart fell. No match.

As she turned, she bumped into Hannah, and dropped the device to the deck floor. "Oh! Arden, how clumsy of me." She sounded so much more sincere than Arden had in her apology to Fitzhugh.

"I'm unharmed, dearest. It's nothing." She moved to retrieve the device, but Clivington beat her to it.

"Here you are, Lady Huntley. I think it might be broken. I seem to have pricked my finger on it."

"It's of no concern, Lord Clivington. I feel responsible for your injury. . . ." Her voice trailed off as she took the invention from him. It was open, and the needle swung wildly through the different sections.

It was him.

"It's so beautiful!" Hannah enthused, leaning against the rail. Beneath them, the lights of London glittered like jewels in a polished tiara. "Oh, Clivington, have you ever seen anything so breathtaking before?"

"Only you, my dear."

He meant it. The realization hit Arden like a slap on an already numb cheek. It was then that she knew Clivington was not a man who killed for sport, but rather because he had a compulsion. Not because he wanted to, but because he had to. Something inside of him made him do it, and those two poor girls had "flipped the switch" to his demon. That made him more than terrifying—it made him pathetic. He might kill Hannah, or he might not, but one truth remained—he would kill again.

"Oh no," Hannah said, lifting her left hand. "I forgot my reticule inside. Excuse me while I go and fetch it."

"I'll come with you," Clivington offered, but she brushed him away with a smile.

"I'll be right back. Lady Huntley will keep you entertained in my absence."

Arden opened her mouth to say they could all go inside, but Hannah was already gone, leaving Arden alone with her lovely bedlamite. What the devil was she supposed to say to him? And was it wrong that she now wished she'd had Luke kill him so she wouldn't have to see this . . . *human* side of him?

She drew a deep breath. Right now she had to be calm. Had to be smart. The man had no reason yet to toss her over the side. "My friend certainly seems taken with you, sir." She moved a little closer to the door.

Clivington grinned foolishly. "Do you really think so? I adore the ground she treads upon. She is so without artifice. Her every emotion is plainly written on her face, or truthfully expressed in words. Deceit is not in her repertoire."

"No," Arden agreed. "It is not. Hannah does not believe in hiding her feelings, sometimes to her own detriment."

He shook his head. "Which only shows the mean-spiritedness of the world we live in, the dual nature of it. Do you know, Lady Huntley, that I once offered my affection to a young lady only to find out she was using me to, as she put it, 'form a better acquaintance with the ways of the world'?"

"That's somewhat harsh."

"Indeed." Clivington didn't look quite so boyish now. Arden's stomach fluttered nervously. "Another only wanted to make her lover jealous. I offered the both of them my heart and had it tossed back in my face."

"Is that why you took theirs?" Arden asked, the words tumbling out of her mouth as though she had no control over her mind or tongue. Where was calm? Where the hell was smart?

He staggered back a step as though she had shoved him, the surprise on his face turning to anguish, and then to anger.

Clivington's monster had just shown its face. Blast it all to Hades.

His fists at his sides, he came toward her. Screaming would do no good. Arden shoved her hand into her bag, released the device and reached for her discombobulator. Her trembling fingers closed around the invention just as he reached her. Then there was a soft noise—a sharp bark followed by a cross between a thud and a squish.

Wetness sprayed Arden's face. Had Clivington spat upon her?

Then she saw the hole in his forehead. A rivulet of blood ran down his nose as he crumpled to the ground. He'd been shot.

The door opened, and there was Hannah, who began to scream as soon as she saw Clivington's corpse. Arden flew toward her as another shot whizzed by, embedding itself in the wall where she had just been standing.

"Hannah!" she shouted. "Get back inside!"

But her friend wouldn't budge, and didn't seem to hear. She just kept sobbing and screaming. Suddenly, Luke was there. He hauled Hannah inside and reached for Arden when another shot rang out.

Arden dove to the floor of the deck, where she would be hidden from view by the boards that filled the space between floor and rail. Luke dropped beside her.

"Are you all right?" he demanded.

Arden nodded, trying to ignore Clivington's dead gaze staring at her from down by her feet. She swiped desperately at her face, trying to wipe the man from her skin. He was the killer. "I thought it would feel good—knowing that he was dead. It doesn't."

Her husband's expression was as sympathetic as it was grim. "It never does, love. Now start crawling. We need to find another way back inside. Alastair's gone to the flying machines to take after the shooter."

"How did you know?" she asked as she began to inch forward on her elbows. "Did you hear the shot?"

"Your theory about the frequency of the transmissions was correct. He intercepted a message just before the shot. Alastair's trying to find who sent it. When I didn't see you inside, I knew you were the target." He didn't look at her, but his mouth thinned.

"I'm sorry." It wasn't good enough, but it would have to do for now. "I didn't know how to refuse Hannah." And now her poor friend's world had been torn apart. The practical side of her insisted that it was better to have it done now than for Hannah to find the truth years into their marriage when she did something to inadvertently release the monster inside him, but the more emotional side of her also knew that it didn't matter now.

Hannah would never know what Clivington had been capable of. No one would. He would never stand trial, never be exposed as a monster. No, he would be remembered as a minor hero, struck down by tragedy in his prime. There would be some who might even blame Arden for his death. Hannah would—at least for a while—because the man had simply gotten between Arden and a bullet.

Arden clenched her teeth against that thought to keep it from going any further. Right now she had to concentrate on staying alive, and not on whether she had bits of Clivington's mad brain in her hair.

They continued to crawl farther down the deck. There

was another door, but it seemed to be miles away, and not getting any closer. In the distance, she could hear the whirling of the sparrows as they launched from the ship to chase after the shooters. Not much longer now, and Alastair would have the assassin in custody.

The door ahead of them opened, and they both froze. A man stepped out onto the deck and closed the door behind him. When he turned, they saw it was Mr. Chiler. Arden sighed in relief.

"Mr. Chiler, get down," she urged, coming up onto her hands and knees. Luke tugged at her, but she ignored it. "You might get shot."

"Arden," Luke said sharply. "Get the fuck behind me, now!"

She glanced at him. For a moment—a second really—she thought that this was the moment where he betrayed her and proved her a fool. Then, she looked into his eyes and saw his fear. He recognized Chiler.

As the traitor.

She turned astonished eyes back to the man whom she had grown fond of these last few years. Dhanya's trusted clerk—or perhaps not-so-trusted. Dhanya had made certain he couldn't hear one of their last conversations.

Chiler stood before them, a pistol held in his mechanical hand and a small box with a switch in the other. He wore a victorious smile on his face.

"I'm afraid my last name isn't Chiler, my dear," he told her in a slightly accented voice. "It's Erlich. Not very good with anagrams, are you? Victor was my brother. Now, to take care of you two before I destroy this ship and everyone on it."

Luke yanked her backward just as Erlich pulled the trigger. Arden watched in horror as the bullet struck Luke in the center of the forehead—the one spot he was vulnerable. He collapsed to the deck, blood trickling from the wound.

Arden screamed, but it was cut short by a searing pain exploding in her upper chest. Another shot hit her side. It didn't penetrate her armor, but it hit hard enough to knock her to the floor. She reached for Luke, fingers grasping. She didn't want him to die. She didn't want to die. Not like this.

"I love you," she rasped. She thought she saw his eyelashes flutter.

Then everything went black.

Chapter 21

"I love you."

Luke's eyes opened to see Arden beside him, her pale chest covered in blood. It darkened the already inky fabric of her gown, dripped to the boards beneath her.

"Arden?" He reached for her, his fingers going to her throat. She had a pulse beneath the sticky warmth. It was weak, but it was there.

"How the hell are you still alive?"

Luke froze. Then he turned his head to see Chiler staring at him. "I shot you exactly in the spot that should have killed you."

"Maybe you're just a lousy shot," Luke replied, slowly moving into a crouch. Blood trickled into the inner corner of his eye, but he ignored it. All of his attention was focused on the man he intended to kill.

"They did something to you." Chiler raised the pistol once more and fired. It hit Luke in the stomach — another spot that should have been vulnerable, but was protected by a gregorite-enhanced waistcoat that Alastair had made him wear at the last moment. The shot knocked the wind from him, but his heavy, reinforced bones kept him from falling backward.

Chiler swore, and this time aimed for his throat, but Luke sprang just as the pistol fired. The bullet tore through the fabric of his coat and gouged his shoulder. He barely felt it.

With the sweep of his hand, he managed to knock the gun from the other man's mechanical fingers. His own fingers caught Chiler—Erlich—by the throat and swept him back, into the side of the airship cabin so hard plaster fell around them. The entire ship seemed to tremble. The switchbox fell to the deck. Luke had seen one like it before. It would send a detonation signal via radio waves to a bomb somewhere on the ship. They had to land. Now.

Erlich gasped for breath. "Huntley . . . Five. Do not . . . do . . . this."

The blood froze in Luke's veins. He knew that voice. He had heard it in his head off and on for seven long years.

"You son of a bitch," he snarled. "I ought to rip out your fucking throat."

"You won't," Erlich goaded. "You're one of us, Five. Whether you like it or not. The Wardens don't want you. They don't trust you. If I tell the Director you did all of this, she'll believe me over you."

"She won't believe you over Arden."

The other man's thin lips formed a cold smile. "I think we both know your wife isn't going to live long enough to tell anyone anything."

Luke punched him in the jaw. It gave beneath the force of the blow like a chicken bone, breaking with a satisfying snap. Erlich made a noise like a wounded animal—which Luke supposed he was.

"I don't care if the Wardens hang me," Luke informed

him. "Killing you will be worth it. You destroyed my life."

"You were just another of their lackeys." Erlich's words were deformed by his misaligned jaw. "They never cared if you lived or died."

"I cared," came a voice from behind them. Alastair. How had he gotten back so quickly?

Luke glanced over his shoulder to see his friend approach. "Where'd you come from?"

Alastair gestured to the rail with his thumb. "Crane dropped me off. What's going on, Luke?"

It was the first time since his return that the man had referred to him by his Christian name. "Chiler is Victor Erlich's brother. And your traitor." He used the toe of his boot to nudge the switchbox closer to his friend. "There's an explosive device onboard."

Disappointment, shock and disgust crossed Alastair's face. Then he glanced down and saw Arden. Luke had never seen such horror on anyone's face before.

"Is she . . . ?"

"She's alive," Luke replied. "Get her to Dr. Stone. I'll take care of Erlich."

"I'd love to let you do just that, my friend." Alastair's voice was dark. "But your place is with Arden. I'll take care of our traitor."

Luke glared at Erlich. The smugness on the man's face made him tighten his grip. That made the bastard a little more humble. "Let me kill him."

"You know that's not how it works."

"It's how it should work."

"Luke! Arden needs you. Take care of your wife."

His words cut through the fog of rage surrounding Luke's brain. Slowly, he eased his grip and released Erlich's neck. The man sagged but did not fall. He merely chuckled. "I knew you wouldn't be able to kill me."

Luke did the next best thing—he grabbed Arden's discombobulator from where it had fallen near her hand, and shoved it between Chiler's legs. The man couldn't even scream; he just twitched and pissed himself. He slid to the floor with the sound and grace of a balloon losing its air, spasming like a dying bug.

He tossed the device to Alastair, then left his friend to take care of things while he attended to Arden. He scooped her unconscious and bloodied body into his arms and carried her into the ship where stunned guests gasped in horror. He ignored them and went straight to Dr. Stone, who stood by herself near a door.

"Help her."

He wasn't allowed inside while Dr. Stone performed the surgery.

The ship had a small medical ward that the doctor had been able to turn into a makeshift surgery. The onboard nurse assisted by setting up the equipment for a transfusion, and Luke made himself useful by donating blood. Arden had lost so much already.

The damned dress had saved her life. She would have had a nasty wound in her side had she not being wearing the gown. As it was she was badly bruised. The wound in her shoulder, however, was the bad one. The bullet tore into her just below the collarbone and fragmented. Erlich had been aiming for her heart.

Luke sat in a chair outside the ward, hand curved over his mouth, rubbing his jaw. Waiting. He might have even prayed, though he'd never admit to it.

"I'd like to tend to your wound, Lord Huntley."

He glanced up at the nurse standing before him with a tray of equipment. "Wound?"

She pointed a hesitant finger at his head. "That one, sir."

Luke reached up. It was scabbing over, but he felt the hole in his flesh where the bullet had hit. Was it in there, slowly working its way to his brain? He had a bitch of a headache, but he didn't feel as though he were dying. Might be good to make certain.

"All right."

The girl smiled and set the tray on the table beside him, where his glass of whiskey sat. He hadn't touched it.

He sat perfectly still as she cleaned the area, even though the liquid stung. When she finished wiping at it, she frowned. "You have a metal skull."

"Only on the outside," he replied dumbly.

"The bullet broke the skin but bounced off the plating."

"But there used to be bone there—that's why he shot in that spot."

She shrugged. "It's not there anymore. Good luck for you, I'd say. It looks like it might have been designed to be a vulnerable spot."

Luke didn't respond. He didn't say another word while she worked. Evie Stone had suspected the Company would use that small target as a way to kill him, and had saved his life without knowing whether or not he could be trusted. It would have been one of the few ways the Wardens would have to take him down as well. The nurse tended to his shoulder also—it required stitching. When she left, he got up and began to pace. The ship was safely docked once more and all the passengers had been ushered off, despite their desire to hear firsthand whether Arden lived or not. He'd dismiss them all as vultures if he hadn't seen genuine concern on some faces.

One of the Scotland Yard blokes took Hannah home, and Clivington's body had been carted away. His being killed was a good thing, but there were several people who were going to feel a lot of pain over it. Better that than knowing he was a monster. If there really was a judgment waiting for them all, then Clivington would be answering for his crimes to a power higher than any court in England.

Still, he understood that Arden had wanted to see him pay for his crimes. Luke wanted desperately to make Chiler—Erlich—pay for all that he had done to him, and to Arden and everyone else involved.

Finally, Dr. Stone appeared. She had been sweating a bit around the hairline and her striking face was dewy. Her apron was smeared and stained with blood. Arden's blood.

Luke straightened. "Well?"

"I took the bullet out and stitched her up. It didn't hit any bones or arteries, fortunately, but there was extensive tissue damage from the fragments. She'll heal, but it will take a while."

The air whooshed from his lungs. "So she's going to be all right?"

"I won't lie—I've seen people die from less, but Arden is very strong and she has a lot to live for. I believe that she'll be fine provided infection doesn't set in. I will give you instructions on how to prevent that. Would you like to see her?"

"Is she awake?"

"No, and she won't be for some time. I'll see about making arrangements to take her home. I don't know if any vehicle travels smoothly enough to take the risk."

"What if I carried her?"

She frowned. "You mean in a carriage?"

"No, I mean what if I walked home carrying her?"

She appeared astonished. "I hadn't thought of that. It's a fair bit of a walk."

"I can do it, even with a wounded shoulder. She won't weigh more than a sack of potatoes to me." It was true.

The Company had made him very strong, and his endurance was as high as a man's could be.

"Yes, your strength. My apologies, I had forgotten. All right, then. If you want to take her home I'll make up a list for you and follow behind in a hack."

"Take our carriage," he said. "It has to come home anyway, and it will be safer than a hack."

She smiled, as though amused by the idea that he thought of her safety, or perhaps at the idea of traveling in an earl's private conveyance. "Thank you, my lord. Follow me."

Luke did. She led him into a very clean room that smelled of blood and disinfectant—smells he'd encountered too many times in his years with the W.O.R. and the Company.

On a table in the center of that room was his wife, her skin almost as white as the sheets that covered her. Her face was tinged with dried blood and gore. Dr. Stone had redressed her, and the gown that had looked so beautiful on her just hours before now looked garish and morbid.

He couldn't see her chest move. "She's dead," he whispered, a sudden burning striking the back of his eyes.

A firm hand came down on his arm. "She's only in a deep sleep, my lord. Take her home and I'll follow. I promise I will not leave her side until I know for certain she'll be fine."

Without another word, Luke gently scooped Arden off the table, cradling her against his chest like a child. His battered flesh protested, but his gregorite-plated bones did not. The wound in his shoulder stretched but didn't give, and the bruised area in his stomach ached like a son of a bitch, but he ignored it all. Nothing—absolutely nothing mattered more than Arden at that moment.

Making certain the sheets were tucked around her, he

carried her down the ramp of the ship into the cool spring night. He walked as quickly as he could, with as smooth a stride as he could manage. It was perhaps one half mile to their home, and when he arrived, the entire household was gathered in the hall. Somehow they'd heard about the shooting.

Birdy rushed forward with a horrified look on her face. One of the men had been comforting her—the tall one who worked in the stables. "Is there anything we can do, my lord?"

"Dr. Stone will be here shortly. Have a room made up for her, please. I also expect Lord Wolfred will be by— have some food prepared. Cold meats and bread should do." He hadn't given many commands since moving back into this house, because he hadn't thought it his place, but it felt natural to do so now.

He carried Arden to her room and carefully set her on the bed. He peeled back the sheets and slowly unfastened her gown to slide it off. He unhooked her corset as well, and then removed her blood-stained chemise. He ripped the seams apart on the fragile garment to avoid moving her as much as possible, and tossed it on the floor to be discarded. Then he eased the already turned-down blankets over her naked body. The bruises on her pale skin turned his stomach, and the dried blood made his throat unbearably tight.

What if Erlich had killed her? His eyes burned at the thought, and his chest pinched. He shouldn't think of what-ifs. Erlich hadn't succeeded in his plans, and the man who had stolen so many years of his life was now in the hands of the W.O.R.

Luke sat down on the edge of the bed and watched her sleep. "I heard you," he whispered hoarsely. "When you said you loved me, I heard it. You better wake up soon so I can tell you how much I love you. I don't understand how it happened so fast, but I do love you. You make me give a damn."

He swiped at his eyes with the backs of his hands. "I will not let you leave me. I'm not like you; I couldn't carry on without you. I don't *want* to carry on without you."

"Ahem."

Luke turned. Dr. Stone was in the doorway. "Forgive me, your lordship. Wolfred is here, and I thought you might like to talk to him. I can sit with Arden."

"I can't leave her."

She rubbed the back of her neck with one hand. "What if I told him to meet you in your rooms? You'd only be a few feet away then."

He could do that. "Fine."

The doctor left the room only to return a few minutes later. Reluctantly, Luke rose from the bed. "You'll get me if she wakes?" Now that the rage and shock had worn off he felt . . . lost. Vulnerable. He didn't like it. This was not how his father had told him a man should feel. A man was supposed to be detached at all times.

That was a damn useless memory to recover.

"Of course."

Alastair was waiting for him when he entered his bedroom through the door to the shared bath. He was pacing, but stopped when he saw Luke. "How is she?"

"Good. Asleep, but Dr. Stone thinks she'll be all right."

"Thinks?" The anguish in the other man's face inspired a multitude of emotions in Luke. He wanted to punch him. He also wanted to comfort him. He felt guilty, as though he had stolen Arden from him.

"She's as certain as she can be given the circumstances."

Alastair nodded, as though that sounded more satisfactory than "thinks." "Evie said you carried her home."

"I did." That was all he was going to say. There would

be no sharing of feelings tonight, not when his were so raw. What he needed right now was a good, old-fashioned stiff upper lip. "What of Erlich? And the bomb? Did you catch the Wasp?"

"We did. He was a little surprised to see us board his ship, and tried to take out Crane, but he soon saw the error of his ways. By God that Crane is a madman. After a few moments of Crane's 'persuasive' techniques, the Wasp offered us Company secrets in exchange for his life. We'll put him in the holding cells."

"They will send someone to end him."

"Most likely, but he'll give us everything he knows before then."

"And Erlich?"

Wolfred's reply was interrupted by the arrival of Mrs. Bird, who had a tray laden with various cold meats, cheese, boiled eggs and hearty bread. There were also two pints of ale. A workingman's supper.

Luke thanked her and sent her off to bed with the promise that he'd send for her if they needed anything at all. He turned his attention back to Alastair to find the other man chewing on some bread and cheese.

"The bomb's been found and dismantled, but Erlich's not talking," Alastair informed him. "I don't know if we'll get anything out of him. He'd rather die than be disloyal to the Company. Christ, what a piece of work. All these years he was right under our noses and we were too stupid to see it."

"I take it he was always above reproach?"

"Always." Alastair took another bite, chewed and swallowed. "If I could simply get inside his head I'd make him tell me. When I think of all the secrets he gave those bastards. . . ."

Luke lifted a tankard of ale to his lips and stopped. "Would you settle for his memories?"

His re
course I w

"Wait h
collected th
in the armoi
mother's mem
for refinements
Dr. Stone watch
returned to his ro

"What the hell

"It's something
You don't have to g
only have to make hi

Alastair lifted the h   his two hands,
regarding it with a lopsi   one really is the most
extraordinary woman."

Luke said, "I know."

And he had almost gotten her killed.

It was late the following afternoon when Arden woke up. She felt as though she'd been attacked by a labor automaton—one with hammers instead of hands. It even hurt to draw breath, but in that she had no choice.

She remembered being on the airship, Clivington and then Chiler—Erlich—with a gun ... Luke. How could she have not seen the resemblance between Victor and his brother? How could she have let him get so close to her husband, who could very well be dead right now?

Desperation seized her as she struggled to sit up, but all that did was send a fresh wave of agony through her. She tried to bite back a cry of pain, but only succeeded in strangling it a bit.

"Arden?"

At the sound of his voice, she stilled. Ever so slowly, she lay back against the pillows and turned her head

ew feet away. From
e had slept as well. He
ers from last night, despite
oyed by bullets and blood. He
e and his eyes were bloodshot.
rt, the most beautiful thing she had ever
nd beautiful.
iled. "Are we alive, or is this Heaven?"
is lips tilted. "I'd smell a lot better if this was
Heaven."

Her gaze moved up to his forehead—his poor, battered brow. "I saw Chiler shoot you in the head."

"Turns out Dr. Stone augmented the bone 'door' the
Company left in my skull with gregorite when she did
her initial surgery. I asked her why, and she said she'd
seen enough dead W.O.R. agents to know the Company
always went for the head."

Arden was going to hug Evie the next time she saw
her. She might even kiss her too. "Why would she remove one of the few ways to kill you when the W.O.R.
didn't even know if they could trust you?"

Luke's eyes brightened. "Oh, the Wardens know a
dozen ways to kill me, I'm sure. They'd never be so vul-
gar as to put a bullet in my brain—wouldn't be British."

She chuckled—then wished she hadn't. "Blast, that
hurts. How badly was I injured?"

"Bruised ribs and a bullet to the chest." His face went
gray as he spoke. "He thought he had killed you."

The bandages over her chest felt as thick as a pile of
quilts and almost as heavy. She flexed the fingers of her
left hand. They moved, and it wasn't too painful.

"Did we get them?" she asked around a yawn. Dear
Jesus, that hurt too.

"The Wasp was found dead in his cell this morning.
Turns out the other Company inmates didn't appreciate

that he gave away secrets for his freedom. Erlich is in a private cell, drugged, tied to a chair with the helmet you made on his head."

Her brows drew together. "The one for storing memories?"

"Erlich wasn't going to talk. Now, he doesn't need to."

"Whose idea was it to use the helmet? Yours?"

He nodded, eyes glittering. "I'm smarter than I look."

Arden smiled and held out her hand. His intelligence wasn't something she had ever questioned, and she felt sorry that he had. Her mother had done the same thing often enough, when trying to understand some of the theories and ideas that came out of her father's mouth. They had been very happy together despite that.

"Any news on Dhanya?" she asked.

"She's doing well. Healing. She's coming back to work next week. Alastair's happy to be giving up the post. She came by to see you. Looked like hell, but strong."

"Good." To see something destroy Dhanya would be like watching Buckingham Palace crumble to dust. Chiler would wish for death before Dhanya was done with him. Proper thing.

"Come lie down with me."

"I don't want to hurt you."

"You won't." And even if he did, it would be worth it. She needed him near—as close as he could possibly get. She was cold inside, and only he could bring warmth back to her bones.

Luke left the chair and came around the bed to crawl in the other side. His every movement was carefully controlled so as not to disturb her, and she adored him for it. Still, the bed dipped under his weight. He was a few stones heavier than a man his size should be.

He propped himself up on his elbow. "I'm glad to see you awake."

"I can't guarantee I'll stay that way for long." She yawned again. Having him with her made everything better, made her realize just how exhausted she was.

"If you need to sleep, you sleep."

She stared at him. He stared back. There was nothing uncomfortable about it, yet there was a tension between them that hadn't been there before. She felt as though he was waiting for her to do or say something, and in a way, she was waiting for him to do the same. Had he heard her say that she loved him? Would it be good or bad if he had?

"I thought I'd lost you again," she murmured. In her mind she saw him lying there, bleeding from the shot to his head. The image brought hot tears to her eyes.

He wiped one away as it trickled down her temple. "I thought I'd lost you, too. I almost killed Erlich."

"What stopped you?" She was glad he hadn't killed the traitor—a quick death was too good. But every woman wanted to think her husband would retaliate against someone who hurt her, and she was secretly a little . . . disappointed not to hear that he had to be physically restrained from killing the bastard.

"Alastair reminded me that you were alive, and that you were my first priority."

"Did you need reminding?" She couldn't bring herself to add a smile. She was terribly afraid of the answer.

"No, but I really wanted to kill him for hurting you."

That certainly did away with any disappointment she might feel. His words filled her with a warmth that eased the terrible ache in her shoulder and chest. She smiled.

He kissed her then—softly, tenderly. So sweetly it caused an ache deeper than any bullet ever could. When he pulled back, he gazed down at her with eyes that made her want to stay in this bed forever. To hell with food and bathing.

"I would have gone mad if I lost you," he said softly. "You've become everything to me. I love you."

Arden swallowed hard. Her heart was pounding and her fingers tingled. "I love you, too." It had been so wonderful to hear those words from his mouth after so long.

"I know; I heard you on the ship." He wiped away another tear from her eye. "I don't think I ever stopped loving you. Even when my mind didn't know who you were, that you even existed, my heart did."

He was killing her, did he know that? "I never stopped loving you either."

"Not even when I was an arse?"

She shook her head. "Not even then, though it would have served you right."

They smiled at each other and he kissed her again—a lingering kiss this time that made her wish she wasn't an invalid, that she didn't hurt all over. There was something about almost dying that made one feel very much alive. It filled her with a desperate, anxious feeling. She wanted him naked. Hard. Inside her. But it was impossible, so she settled for simply having him near.

"Do you suppose the Wardens will give us commendations for this?" she asked with a grin. "I think we deserve them. It will certainly look good on our records of service."

Luke's smile faded. "Arden, there's something I need to tell you."

It sounded ominous. "What?"

He looked her straight in the eye. "You're no longer a Warden."

Chapter 22

"They dismissed me?"

Luke winced at the angry shock in her voice. This was not going to be an easy conversation. Perhaps he should have introduced it in a less abrupt manner. "No. You resigned."

Her cinnamon eyes narrowed. "I don't remember resigning."

"I did it for you when I turned in my own resignation." There, it was done. And there was no taking it back. He would not take it back, no matter how angry she was.

Her face went completely blank. "You resigned?"

He nodded. "Yes. As of tomorrow we will no longer have any obligation to the Crown save that of any citizen of the Empire."

She stared at him. The dark circles beneath her beautiful eyes were all the reassurance he needed that he had done the right thing. He was done with being a spy, with putting his life in jeopardy for a country and an agency that would just turn around and demand that he do it again. He refused to be separated from her again. Refused to keep secrets from her, or endanger her because of his actions.

"Why?"

Wasn't it obvious? "Because you almost died last night."

"You can't leave the Wardens just because of me." Her eyes were wide with astonishment.

"I can and I have. And it's not just because of you. It's because of us."

Her expression was incredulous at best—and a tad suspicious. He supposed he couldn't blame her. "But you always loved being a Warden."

"I don't anymore." How could he possibly make her understand? Last night he had faced the idea of life without her, and it nearly drove him mad. How could he have given so much of himself to the Wardens when he had her? Had he been completely selfish and vain? Had he been in such need of a pat on the damn head he risked his life to get it? Or had he simply labored under some misguided sense of honor? He didn't know, and he couldn't remember. It didn't matter anyway.

"This is not something we're going to discuss," he informed her, figuratively putting his foot down. "We're done with the Wardens, and if our marriage means anything to you at all, you'll accept that."

Color filled her cheeks. He didn't care that anger put it there, he was just glad to see it. "You don't speak for me, Lucas Grey."

"In this matter, I do. I don't give a damn if you think it's fair or not. I'm not spending another evening like I did last night, not ever."

"What of all the evenings I spent worrying about you?"

"I'm sorry for them. I'd take them back if I could, but

I can't. I can only do my best to make certain neither of us ever has to worry about the other again."

"Leaving the Wardens won't guarantee the Company won't come after us in the future." A hint of fear shone in her eyes.

"The Company has denied all involvement in Erlich's schemes. They say he acted alone out of a spirit of revenge, and send their apologies to both of us. They assure Her Majesty that nothing like this will ever happen again."

Arden's mouth fell open. "Do you believe them?"

"That he acted alone? No. I know for a fact he didn't, but I do believe you and I will be safe from now on. They've lost the Wasp, Erlich and me because of this operation, and the fact that Victoria has personally spoken out against them means all of Europe will be watching."

"When did the queen speak out?"

"In this morning's paper. Alastair received a telegram from the Company director at W.O.R. offices two hours ago. Basically they're crying for a truce."

"For now."

He nodded. "For now." Of course it would be temporary, but it would last long enough that the two of them wouldn't really matter to anyone once it was over. Erlich had been behind his abduction and the attempts on Arden's life. There was no one in the Company ranks to pick up the grudge. And if they did . . . Luke would kill them. He would die for Arden if necessary, and he would kill anyone who tried to harm her. It was that simple.

Her worried gaze locked with his. "It's over then?"

"Yes."

"And resigning is really what you want?"

He didn't have to think about it. "Yes."

She sighed. "All right. When the Season is over we'll

go to the country. You might change your mind after a few months with only my face for company."

Luke smiled at her. "I doubt it. I rather like your face." Then he kissed her and they didn't speak of it again. He was still smiling when she began to snore softly. A few moments later sleep claimed him as well.

It was the happiest he'd been in his life—he was certain of it.

Over the course of the next few weeks, Arden continued to heal, and at the end of the month she felt good enough to start being social again. There was no shortage of invitations, but two of the people she most wanted to see did not want to see her.

Alastair had left the country shortly after Luke informed him of their resignation from the W.O.R. They didn't speak of it, but Arden reckoned Alastair wasn't yet ready to see her and Luke work on their marriage—and their family. He was supposedly on an assignment in Saint Petersburg that had to do with the royal family there. Maybe one of those exotic Romanov ladies would make him happy for a time.

And Hannah still wouldn't receive her. In time she hoped her friend would forgive her, but for now Hannah blamed her for Clivington's death. She said Arden had no right going outside with them when she'd known there was an assassin after her. Hannah was correct, of course, and Arden was sorry for it, but she would never be sorry Clivington was dead. Since she wasn't about to apologize for that, she supposed it might be a very long time indeed before Hannah came round—if she ever did. So, she visited with Dhanya and Evie instead—Zoe too. It was so nice being able to be friends with them now without the Wardens hanging over them.

She had been right about the commendations. They were both given awards for their service. In fact, Luke was to be granted the Royal Victorian Order by Her Majesty in recognition of the sacrifices he'd made for his country. Arden was very proud of him. It was a nice way to end his career in espionage.

Of course, she and Luke would never truly leave the Wardens. They would indeed consult from time to time, but she looked forward to retiring to the country for a while, where it was peaceful and the most intrigue they ever suffered was a marital scandal on occasion—such as someone taking all the covers, or some other irritating behavior.

She didn't know how long it would last—how much time would pass before Luke began to crave excitement and chafe at the bonds of matrimony. It frightened her thinking he might leave her again one day. As more of his memory returned she began to fear that possibility more and more. She did not want him to feel like a prisoner. On most days, however, she didn't worry about it. She simply enjoyed getting to know him again—the new parts. There was still a lot of him that was the same as the man she married. She liked—loved—both.

He had his own social engagements as well. A few gentlemen from his past had come forward wishing to renew their old acquaintance, and since none of them were spies, or adulterers (that she knew of), she was glad he had the diversion.

They also had his brother, Henry. Once the younger Grey had learned of what had happened on the *Albion,* he'd come to call. There had been no falseness to his concern for Luke—or even Arden. He went so far as to admit that much of his foolishness stemmed from anger and remorse. He'd been angry at Luke for leaving them, angry at Arden for clinging to hope, and then felt terrible for not having more faith when Luke returned. He had tried to have his brother declared dead and everyone knew it. And now everyone knew he'd been wrong. He felt like an arse—to use his own word—and asked their forgiveness.

Well, of course Luke gave it. He was Henry's older brother, after all.

Now Luke was returning from a brief social call with one of his renewed friendships. They'd gone to one of the gentlemen's clubs on St. James's Street. He came home smelling of whiskey and cigar smoke, neither of which were unpleasant, though she had lost some of her taste for the former and had no interest in the latter. She had waited up because she couldn't put off talking to him any longer, and because she was rather hopeful he might come to bed with her after. He hadn't touched her *that way* since the shooting, and she was in desperate need of sexual validation.

She waited for him in his bedroom, wearing his favorite of her peignoir sets—the one with the Chinese embroidery on it.

"Still up?" His rich, melodic voice seemed to rumble down her spine as he removed his coat. "I'd thought you in bed by now."

"It's still early," she replied, twisting her hands in front of her. "I'm feeling almost one hundred percent healed."

"Excellent." His gaze held some of the amusement she'd come to find familiar. He wasn't laughing at her, he was just a little . . . giddy, if one could use such a word to describe a man, when he was around her. She supposed it was a compliment.

"Might we talk?" she asked.

He arched a brow at her tone and began unfastening his waistcoat. The scars on his forehead, she noticed, had begun to fade. He hadn't said any more about growing a fringe—thank the Lord. "Of course. About what?"

"About your decision to leave the Wardens."

He frowned. "Do you wish to continue working for them?" There was an edge to his voice that told her he would fight her on it if she did.

"No," she replied honestly. "Though I do think consulting on occasion was a good suggestion. My concern is for you. You've been a Warden for as long as I've known you. Every Earl of Huntley has been part of the organization as long as it's existed."

Luke shrugged and untied his cravat. "I don't care. It ends with me. We're going to the country."

"But are you certain that's what you want?"

He came toward her and cupped her shoulder with his hands—so gently her healing flesh didn't even pinch. "My duty is to you—as your husband. That's all I want to be. I want to get to know everything about the woman you are now. I want to read to you, rub your feet. I want to have children with you and live to see them grow up and start families of their own." He sighed. "Arden, *you* are my life. I don't want anything else."

"Oh." The word squeaked from her tight throat. Tears flooded her eyes and spilled over her cheeks and she didn't even bother trying to stop them. "Oh, Luke."

He took her into his arms and kissed her. Tenderness soon gave way to hunger, and when he picked her up in his incredibly strong arms her heart began to race. He carried her to his bed and stretched out beside her, his skillful hands caressing her until she writhed beneath his touch.

He undressed them both and joined her again, hard and ready. She accepted him eagerly. He braced himself above her—so careful not to hurt her—as they joined and rocked together, riding the spiral of tension upward until they came together in cries of pleasure.

Afterward they lay together, limbs entwined, simply enjoying the silence. Luke leaned over and kissed her, and Arden smiled happily against his lips. "I love you."

"I love you, too." And then they didn't speak again for a long time. After seven long years of living in the past, Arden knew she could finally look toward the future. Their future.

ACKNOWLEDGMENTS

My foray into steampunk happened quite by accident. In fact, I didn't know there was a name for what I wanted to do; I simply knew I wanted to combine my love of history and science fiction. Once I started doing this, and researching various subjects, I stumbled upon steampunk. And I wondered where it had been all my life. Turns out, steampunk has been around for a long time. I've watched it and read it — I've even worn it — without really knowing what it was. Since discovering there was a name for this wonderful genre I have met so many fabulous, giving people who only want to share their love of steampunk. These folks write books, make fantastic machines, wonderful films and beautiful music. It's not possible for me to list them all, but I need to make mention of these few: Dr. and Mrs. Grymm of Dr. Grymm Laboratories, who are simply the best; Miss Kitty, the Emperor, Bruce and Melanie Rosenbaum, who are so wonderful and sweet my teeth ache; Ay-leen and Lucretia, both of whom are so genuinely lovely and so supportive of the genre; Eli August, whose music could easily be a soundtrack for this book; and Mike Marchand of Ajar Communications, who is quite possibly the nicest person I have ever met.

I have some romance friends to thank as well — Sophie Jordan, Laura Lee Guhrke, Colleen Gleason, Julia Quinn and Caroline Linden, who are always there with a smile or a shoulder whenever I need it.

I also need to thank my agent, Miriam Kriss, for believing in this project, and Laura Cifelli and Claire Zion at Penguin for seeing its potential and buying it. Also, thanks must go to my editor, Danielle Perez, for her support and help in making this book something special, and for discussing TV shows with me. (*Supernatural* for the win!)

And finally, thanks to my amazing husband, who makes the world a better place simply for being the first face I see in the morning and the last one I see at night. I love you bunches.

Don't miss the next book in the
Clockwork Agents series by Kate Cross,

TOUCH OF STEEL

Coming in December 2012 from Signet Eclipse

The only sound louder than the breath panting from her lungs was that of blood dripping onto the toe of her boot.

Claire Danvers crouched behind the grimy chimney stack and pressed her hand to her side. Wet seeped through the boning of her corset and the thin wool of her coat, warming her chilled fingers.

Her lungs burned and her gun hand was cramped, but she refused to set down the pistol. Refused to give up the chase. It would take more than a bullet in her side to stop her now.

Across the roof, she heard Howard scurrying away like the rat he was. He could not escape, not when she had already chased him across five countries. Robert's death could not go unavenged.

Gritting her teeth against the ungodly burning in her side, she braced her shoulder against the sooty brick and leaned hard as she dug her bootheel into the rough stone. She pushed herself to her feet, biting her lip to keep from crying out.

She lifted her gun, blinked the sweat out of her eyes, took aim and fired. The dark figure running toward the edge of the roof ducked as the shot sent bits of brick scattering near his shoulder.

Damn it. A miss. If her vision weren't so blurry she would have gotten him.

Still clutching her side—blood poured over her fingers now—she ran after him, every strike of her heels a new lesson in pain.

You're not going to die just yet, she told herself. *Not until you know for certain you're going to take that bastard with you. He dies first.*

She thought of Robert, of how there hadn't been enough of him left for her to have a proper funeral for him, how he'd been betrayed by the organization to which he had pledged his life. The thought of seeing him again, whether in Heaven or Hell, wasn't what pushed her forward. What kept her running despite the sheer agony was that she had sworn to send Howard to his judgment first.

Moonlight cut through the clouds as Howard leaped from the edge of the roof to the next. Claire didn't hesitate, her stride easily bridging the narrow gap between buildings. A shot whizzed past her ear, and she pitched herself downward. She hit the roof hard, going down on her knees.

"Arrhh!" Lights danced before her eyes as agony ripped through her. Bile rose in her throat as darkness threatened to claim her. She swallowed and staggered to her feet. Howard was putting too much distance between them; he was already at the opposite side.

She raised her pistol and fired again. The sound cracked in the night like the lash of a whip. Howard made a guttural cry. She'd hit the bastard. A grim smile peeled back her lips as she forced herself to move faster.

Her battered knees protested, but her legs did as she willed. Howard had stumbled when she shot him and she was closing the gap between them.

This time, he hesitated at the edge of the roof. He clutched his shoulder as he turned his head to look back at her. His face was different from the last time she had seen him, but then his face was different every time. He was a master of disguise, and Claire doubted that even the higher-ups at the Company knew his true countenance. When she killed him she would peel back the layers of his disguise and see the real him.

He raised his hand—she had winged his gun arm— and waved before dropping over the ledge.

Claire froze, but only for a second. *What the hell?* She ran to the edge. Something closed around her ankle. She looked down.

Stanton Howard grinned up at her from where he hung on a crude rope ladder. She realized it was his hand wrapped around her leg just a split second before he yanked her off-balance. She raised her gun, but it was too late—she was already plummeting toward the alley below.

She twisted her body so that her back was to the ground, raised the gun at the man climbing back to the roof and fired. He staggered, and—

She hit with teeth-jarring force. Pain embraced her entire body, and everything went black.

She woke to the low murmur of nearby voices. Fog swam thick in her brain and her limbs were heavy—almost as heavy as her tongue felt in her mouth.

A dull, faint ache radiated across the back of her skull. Her back was sore and her side burned, but none of these complaints bothered her as much as the fact that she did not know the location of her gun.

Opium. They had given her opium—whoever they were. Drugged her and took her weapon. Her clothes, too. Damn it, that meant she was in a hospital.

Why wasn't she dead? Howard couldn't have allowed her to live out of the kindness of his traitorous heart.

Opening her eyelids took every ounce of strength she possessed. The room was a blur of motion and colors, and her lids felt as though they'd been lined with sand.

"She's waking up." The voice was female, the accent a strange, melodic mix of Irish and some exotic land.

Slowly, her eyes righted themselves and began to focus. Claire blinked. Standing before her was a dusky-skinned woman so strikingly beautiful, she probably had very few female friends, and a tall, stern-looking man with a very British nose. The two of them looked very official, but neither of them had the look of constabulary about them.

"How do you feel?" the woman inquired.

"Like I've been shot and fell off a roof," Claire replied, though her words were slurred—"thot," "rooth."

The woman actually smiled a little. "I imagine so." She came closer to the side of the bed. Claire watched warily as she poured a glass of water from a pitcher on the scarred bedside table. Then she bent at the waist and began turning a crank on the side of the bed. Slowly, as the mechanism ground into use, the upper part of the bed raised, until Claire was almost upright.

The cool lip of the cup pressed against Claire's parched lips. "Drink," the woman instructed.

Claire did not need to be told twice. She gulped the water greedily, closing her eyes in pleasure as the cold water ran over her tongue and down her thick, parched throat. She couldn't remember the last time she'd tasted anything so delicious.

When the cup ran dry the woman refilled it and gave

it back to her. Claire drank again, this time allowing her gaze to roam around the sterile ward.

There was one other patient in the room—a man several beds away. His face was a mask of bandages, and one of his legs was encased in a brass boot that extended above his knee. Rods and knobs attached to the boot kept the leg, and the broken bones within it, in the proper place.

He was obviously not the reason there was a heavily armed guard at the door. Damn. The weapon in his hands—a Baker Scatter rifle—was used to kill rather than simply injure or maim. It was very effective as well, the casings of the bullets designed to fragment and burrow once inside the body like little metal predators.

That gun was meant for her.

"Who are you?" she asked the woman.

"I'm Dr. Evelyn Stone." The doctor took the cup and set it on the table. "You are a very fortunate woman. If that carriage hadn't broken your fall, you might have ended up in far worse shape than you are now."

Yes, such as dead. "Where am I?" And where the hell was her gun?

It was the man who answered. "You're in Warden custody, Miss Danvers."

The Wardens. Hell. God, she wished Howard had killed her. Claire kept her face blank—it wasn't difficult given the heaviness of her muscles. Opiates were the very devil as far as she was concerned. She'd rather have pain than helpless oblivion. "Is that supposed to frighten me?"

The man stared down his imperious nose at her. "If you are not afraid you are clearly less intelligent than most Company agents. I wouldn't aspire to such a claim."

Arrogant British bastard. What did he know of fear? He probably spent his days behind a desk; the most worrisome thing he ever had to face was his undoubtedly bitter wife.

"If you wanted me dead, I'd be dead," she responded, words slurring around her lazy tongue. "That means you've actually deluded yourself into thinking you'll get information out of me. Which one of us is lacking in intelligence now, Mr. Idiot?"

A dull flush flooded his mutton-chopped cheeks. He looked as though he had scrub brushes bolted to the sides of his face, the things were so bushy. "Whether or not you cooperate is entirely up to you, Miss Danvers, just as whether or not you live or die is up to me."

Dr. Stone shot him a dark look, her striking features downright intimidating. "You mean it's up to the Director."

"Yes, well . . ." He sniffed. "She's not here right now, is she? And during her absence I am acting director."

Aw, hell. She had to go and piss on the boots of a man filled to the brim with his own importance. Being locked up or killed was not going to help her find Howard. Time was already against her. He was undoubtedly on his way north by now. Every moment put more distance between them. At least she knew where he was headed.

She had not come this far to lose him now. She could not let Robert's death go unanswered. He was all the family she'd had left, and now she was alone in the world. No one to lean on. No one to tell her when she was wrong or when she had gone too far—when she was too reckless for sense.

"What do you want from me?" she asked, lifting her gaze past that beak of a nose.

Cold eyes brightened with a malicious gleam. If she'd had full control of her limbs she would have stabbed him in the neck with his own cravat pin. "I want to know why you're in London. I want to know whatever Company secrets you have in that pretty little head of yours. I want the name of every enemy agent here on British soil."

And she wanted her brother back. "I can't give you all of that."

"You'll give me something or I'll see you hang."

Dr. Stone grabbed him by the arm. "I'll report you."

He shook her off. "What will it be, Miss Danvers?"

She had to get out of there and soon. This bastard wasn't about to let her go. She needed an ally—someone who knew her, who could provide a little protection until she could figure out how to escape.

"I want something in return."

He made a scoffing noise. "You're not in any position to bargain, girlie."

Claire clenched her jaw. "Then you may as well hang me, *laddie*." She affected a bad British accent on the word. "Then you can explain to your director how the Wardens missed out on capturing Stanton Howard."

What color the man had in his pasty cheeks drained. "Stanton Howard?"

She grinned. "Prepared to bargain now?"

He cleared his throat, glaring at her as though she were a bug he'd dearly like to grind beneath his heel. "What do you want?"

There was only one person she could trust in all of London. "Lucas Grey," she replied. "I want to talk to Lucas Grey."

"You look like shite."

Alastair Payne, Earl of Wolfred, wiped the dirt from his hands with the remains of an old shirt. Smears of oil and dirt stained the once pristine linen. He'd been working on the velocycle for a good three quarters of an hour before his oldest friend, Lucas Grey, showed up, and now the machine was in top condition.

"I've been back in the country for a fortnight and already you're trying to woo me with your considerable charm." A sardonic smile curved his lips. "Really, Luke. People will talk."

Many men would bristle at the affront to their masculinity, but Luke merely chuckled. "What I lack in tact I have in an abundance of sincerity. Arden's worried about you."

It was a cheap shot and they both knew it. Alastair no longer considered himself in love with Arden, but she was still a dear friend. In fact, she and Luke were possibly his only true friends.

"I'm fine."

"No pain?"

As though on cue, his left leg twinged—a bone-deep ache, though there was no longer any bone there to cause discomfort, just metal beneath the flesh. "None. Evie says I simply need to regain a stone or two and I'll be right as rain." He'd been putting his body through its paces in an attempt to regain the strength he'd lost after being left for dead in Spain. He would be strong again. Stronger.

"Good." Luke's pale gaze was sharp as it met his. "And mentally? Are you recovered there as well?"

Anyone else and Alastair would have told them to bugger off, but Luke was no stranger to the affects a life of intrigue and deceit could have on a man's mind. "Better than I ought to be, I'm told."

Luke frowned, dark brows pulling low over pale blue eyes. "According to whom?"

"Evie." He tossed the soiled rag onto a nearby workbench. "She seems to think I'm afraid to admit how deeply the attack affected me."

His friend regarded him for a moment, his sharp face as unreadable as a blank slate. "Are you?"

"No." Alastair settled his hands on his hips. "This concern for my welfare is appreciated, believe me, but I'm getting a little tired of everyone thinking I'm headed for a cell in Bedlam. I've had people try to kill me before."

Luke's expression didn't change. "This is the first time it was someone you fancied yourself in love with."

"I didn't love her," he scoffed.

"Fine. You cared for her, and believed she cared about you, right up until the moment she led you into a trap that resulted in you being stabbed, crushed beneath a carriage and left for dead. I don't understand how you can be all right with that either. I wouldn't be."

"You seemed fine enough when your former mistress tried to kill you," Alastair shot back. It had been little more than a year since Rani Ogitani had revealed herself as a traitor and had almost gotten Luke and his wife, Arden, killed. At the time, Alastair had been in love with Arden, and part of him wouldn't have minded comforting his friend's widow. After all, they'd believed Luke to be dead for seven years before Rani's confession.

Well, Alastair had believed him dead. Arden had never given up hope. Never stopped loving a man who really had no idea how lucky he was to have her. Luke knew now, though. The forced amnesia that had kept him from his wife hadn't completely gone away, but Luke hadn't needed his memories to fall in love with his wife once more.

"I never loved her, and she never pretended to love me."

"I guess that makes you a better judge of character than I am." He sounded like a peevish five-year-old.

Luke's scowl deepened. "This isn't about me. It's about you, you great ginger arse."

"I told you, I'm *fine*. Are you too thick-headed to understand that?"

"You're the one who's mentally impaired if you think

I believe that load of horse shite. You're not fine, Alastair. No one in your situation would be fine."

Alastair paused, on the verge of telling his oldest friend to go straight to hell with hopes of being buggered by the very devil. Luke was only concerned for his well-being, so why was he denying what the other man so clearly understood? What was he trying to prove by lying?

"You're right," he admitted. "I'm not fine, but I will be, and I don't want to talk about it. I don't want to discuss her or what she did—not until I can do so without blaming myself for being such a naive fool. That said, will you please leave it alone?"

Luke's mouth tilted. "Not another word. Show me what you've done to this great hulking beast." He gestured at Alastair's custom-built velocycle, which could travel at great speeds and was equipped with concealed weapons.

Grateful for the change of topic, Alastair showed him the modifications he'd made. "I put a new engine in her. She'll top fifty now."

"Miles?" At his nod, Luke whistled. "I'll have to get you to take a look at my machine. You've always been the more mechanically inclined of the two of us."

Yes, for all the good it had done him. "Bring it over some afternoon. I'll take a look." He pointed out the other improvements he'd made—mostly cosmetic. Tinkering on the velocycle had kept his mind occupied, giving him something to think about other than the fact that he'd been made an arse of by a woman he'd entertained a future with. Though, when he first met Sascha, she'd simply been a substitute for the woman he couldn't have—Arden. That only added salt to a raw wound—that he'd been completely taken in by a woman he'd seen only as a diversion.

A bell rang as Luke studied the velocycle. It was for the handset and mouthpiece that provided communication between the building that stored his engine-based vehicles and the main house. He grabbed the handset on the second bell.

His housekeeper's voice filled his ear. "Begging your pardon, my lord, but there's a young girl here who says she has a message for Lord Huntley's ears alone."

It had to be W.O.R. business. Only the Wardens of the Realm would send a verbal message. Notes were too easily found and read. Verbal messages could be turned into lies if the messenger was set-upon. Verbal messages could be taken to a person's grave.

"Send the girl out, Mrs. Grue."

"Of course, sir. Right away."

Alastair hung up and turned to Luke, who stood beside the velocycle, watching him. "Something wrong?"

"There's a messenger here for you."

Luke frowned. "Warden?"

"I assume so. Are you on assignment?"

His friend shook his dark head. "I haven't done any work for W.O.R. other than consulting on Company operative interrogations."

"It must be important for them to track you down here." They hadn't bothered with him for the last week and a half, but he had no desire to seem petty, so he kept that to himself.

"It had best be." Luke wore a dark expression that would make even Alastair think twice about engaging him.

A few moments later there came a knock upon the door. Alastair opened it to find a young girl of perhaps twelve standing at the threshold. "Lord Wolfred?" she inquired. "I'm Betsey Meekins. I've a message for Lord Huntley."

Her no-nonsense, very adult tone made him smile. "Come in, Miss Meekins." He stepped back so she might enter the building. She crossed the hold as regal as a queen and walked directly up to Luke, who was easily a full foot taller than she.

Betsey offered her hand, which Luke took, a vaguely amused expression replacing his scowl. "Pleased to make your acquaintance, Miss Meekins. What is the message?"

She glanced over her shoulder at Alastair. "They didn't say anything about having an audience, my lord."

"I assure you, Lord Wolfred is trustworthy, and can be privy to anything you wish to tell me."

She shrugged as she turned back to him. "So long as you'll take responsiblity for him. I'm to tell you that a Miss Danvers from America is in the infirmary and will speak only to you."

Color leeched from Luke's lean cheeks. "Danvers. Are you certain?"

The girl nodded. "I'm never uncertain, sir."

Alastair would have chuckled at her youthful arrogance were it not for the expression on his friend's face. He looked as though he'd seen a ghost.

"Tell the acting director I'll be there shortly." Luke took a coin from his pocket and handed it to the girl. "Run along now. There's a good girl."

Betsey curtsied to them both and quickly took her leave. Alastair waited until the door had shut and she would be out of earshot before saying, "Now it's my turn to ask whether you are fine."

Luke chuckled, but there was little humor in it. "I don't think so, my friend. Not at all. I'm off to the Wardens and you are coming with me."

"Good lord, man. What the devil for?" Alastair could not remember Luke ever having asked him to accompany him anywhere.

"So you can plead my case to Arden when my past bites me on the arse."

Understanding dawned. "So Miss Danvers . . . ?" He raised his brow suggestively.

His friend rubbed a hand over his brow. "Is a Company agent. And my former lover."

New York Times bestselling author

KATIE MACALISTER

Steamed
A Steampunk Romance

When one of Jack Fletcher's nanoelectro-
mechanical system experiments is jostled in
his lab, the resulting explosion sends him
into the world of his favorite novel—
a seemingly Victorian-era world of
steampower, aether guns, corsets, and
goggles. A world where the lovely and
intrepid Octavia Pye captains her airship
straight into his heart...

For videos, podcasts, excerpts, and more, visit
katiemacalister.com

Available wherever books are sold or at
penguin.com